THOMAS MANN

Buddenbrooks

THOMAS MANN was born in Germany in 1875. He was awarded the Nobel Prize for Literature in 1929, and left Germany for good in 1933. Among his major novels are *Buddenbrooks* (1901), *The Magic Mountain* (1924), the tetralogy *Joseph and His Brothers* (1933, 1934, 1936, 1943), and *Doctor Faustus* (1948). He is equally well known for his short stories and essays. Thomas Mann died in 1955.

INTERNATIONAL

ALSO BY THOMAS MANN

The Black Swan

Confessions of Felix Krull, Confidence Man

Death in Venice and Seven Other Stories

Doctor Faustus

The Holy Sinner

Joseph and His Brothers

Lotte in Weimar: The Beloved Returns

The Magic Mountain

Royal Highness

Stories of Three Decades

The Transposed Heads

THOMAS MANN

Buddenbrooks

The Decline of a Family

TRANSLATED FROM THE GERMAN BY JOHN E. WOODS

VINTAGE INTERNATIONAL
Vintage Books
A Division of Random House, Inc.
New York

FIRST VINTAGE INTERNATIONAL EDITION, JULY 1994

Library of Congress Cataloging-in-Publication Data
Mann, Thomas, 1875–1955.
[Buddenbrooks. English]
Buddenbrooks : the decline of a family / Thomas Mann ; translated from the German by John E. Woods. — 1st Vintage International ed.
p. cm.
ISBN 0-679-75260-9
I. Woods, John E. (John Edwin) II. Title.
PT2625.A44B82 1994
833'.912—dc20 93-43499
CIP

Book design by Rebecca Aidlin

Manufactured in the United States of America
20 19 18 17 16 15 14 13 12 11

PART ONE

1

WHAT DOES THIS MEAN.—What—does this mean. . . ."

"Well, now, deuce take it, *c'est la question, ma très chère demoiselle!*"

Madame Buddenbrook was sitting beside her mother-in-law on the sofa, its clean lines accented with white enamel and a golden lion's head, its cushions upholstered a pale yellow; she first shot a glance at her husband, the consul, who was seated in an armchair beside her, and then came to the rescue of her young daughter, who was perched on her grandfather's knee near the window.

"Tony!" she said. "I believe that God made me—"

And little Antonie, a petite eight-year-old in a dress of softly shimmering silk, was thinking hard, her pretty blond head turned slightly toward her grandfather, but her gray-blue eyes directed into the room without seeing anything. She first repeated, "What does this mean," then slowly said, "I believe that God made me," and quickly added, her face brightening, "—and all creatures," and, suddenly finding the track smooth—she was unstoppable now and her face beamed with happiness—she rattled off the whole article, as prescribed by her catechism, newly revised and published under the auspices of an august and wise senate in this year of our Lord, 1835. Once you were moving, she thought, it felt just like racing down "Jerusalem Hill" on the sled with her brothers in winter: every thought vanished from your mind, and you couldn't stop if you wanted to.

"Including clothes and shoes," she said, "meat and drink, hearth and home, wife and child, fields and cattle . . ." But at these words, old Monsieur Johann Buddenbrook burst into laughter, a high, pinched giggle that he had secretly kept at the ready. He laughed in delight at being able to mock the catechism, had presumably arranged this little exam for just that purpose. He inquired about Tony's fields and cattle, asked how much she wanted for a sack of wheat, and offered her a contract. His round, pastel pink, good-humored face—try as he would he could not look mean—was framed in snow-white powdered hair, and something like the merest hint of a pigtail brushed the wide collar of his mouse-gray frock coat. He had not, at seventy, proved untrue to the fashion of his youth; he had dispensed with lace between the buttons and the oversize pocket, but never in his life had he worn long trousers. His broad double-chin rested comfortably on the wide lace jabot.

They had all joined in the laughter, mainly out of respect for the head of the family. Madame Antoinette Buddenbrook, née Duchamps, giggled exactly like her husband. She was a stout lady with thick white curls at her ears, her unadorned black dress with pale gray stripes expressed simplicity and modesty, and her beautiful white hands clasped a small velvet reticule on her lap. Over the years, her features had curiously become very like her husband's. Only the shape and lively dark hue of her eyes hinted at her half-Latin origins; her grandfather had been French-Swiss, but she was born in Hamburg.

Her daughter-in-law, Elisabeth Buddenbrook, née Kröger, laughed the Kröger laugh, which began with a splutter as her chin was pressed against the chest. She was, like all Krögers, a person of great elegance, and though perhaps not a beauty, by her clear and cheerful voice, by her easy, sure, and gentle movements, she impressed everyone with her serenity and confidence. Her reddish hair, which swept back high on her head in a little crowning swirl and lay in broad, carefully coiffed waves over her ears, matched well with her extraordinary soft white complexion and the few little freckles. The most characteristic feature of her face, with its rather long nose and small mouth, was the lack of any indentation between lower lip and chin. Her short bodice with high puffed sleeves was fitted to a narrow skirt of filmy silk patterned in bright flowers and open at a neck of perfect beauty, adorned by a satin ribbon glistening with a spray of large diamonds.

The consul fidgeted and bent forward in his armchair. He wore a cinnamon jacket with broad lapels and leg-of-mutton sleeves that closed tight just below the wrist. His fitted trousers were of a white, washable fabric and trimmed with a black stripe down each side. The silk cravat wound around his stiff high-wing collar was fluffed to fill the broad, open neck of his multicolored vest. He had something of his father's deep-set, blue, watchful eyes, though perhaps with a more preoccupied expression; but his features were more earnest and defined, the nose jutted forward in a strong curve, and blond curls ran halfway down his cheeks, which were much less full than the old man's.

Madame Buddenbrook turned to her daughter-in-law, pressing her arm with one hand and giggling as she spoke into her own lap: "Oh, *mon vieux*, always the same, is he not, Bethsy?" She pronounced it "ollweez."

The consul's wife merely waved this aside with her delicate hand, setting her gold bracelet jingling softly; and then the hand performed a gesture peculiarly her own, moving from one corner of her mouth up to her coiffure, as if tucking back a hair that had strayed to her lips.

The consul, however, said with a mixture of indulgent amusement and reproach in his voice, "Now, Father, you are making fun of the most sacred matters again!"

They were sitting in the "landscape room," on the second floor of the spacious old house on Meng Strasse, which the firm of Johann Buddenbrook had recently purchased and in which his family had resided for only a short time. The thick, supple wall coverings, which had been hung so that there was a gap between them and the wall, depicted expansive landscapes in the same pastel colors as the thin carpet on the floor—idyllic scenes in the style of the eighteenth century, with merry vinedressers, diligent farmers, prettily ribboned shepherdesses, who sat beside reflecting pools, holding spotless lambs in their laps or exchanging kisses with tender shepherds. Most of these scenes were suffused with yellowish sunsets that matched the yellow upholstery of the white enameled furniture and the yellow silk of the curtains at both windows.

Given the size of the room, there was not a great deal of furniture.

The round table with its thin, straight legs finely detailed in gold was not placed in front of the sofa, but stood against the far wall, facing the little harmonium—a flute case lay on the lid. Apart from stiff armchairs distributed evenly along the walls, there was only a small sewing table at the window and, opposite the sofa, a fragile and expensive secretary loaded with knickknacks.

Through a glass door, opposite the windows, a columned hallway was visible in the semidarkness, and to the left of someone entering the room were wide folding doors that opened onto the dining room. To the right, however, a crackling fire could be seen through the ornate wrought-iron door of the stove, which was set back in a semicircular niche.

It was cold for so early in the season. Even now—and it was only mid-October—there were yellow leaves on the small linden trees that lined St. Mary's Cemetery across the street, and the wind whistled in the nooks and around its massive Gothic corners. A fine, cold rain was falling. They had already put up the storm windows to oblige the older Madame Buddenbrook.

It was Thursday, the day on which the family regularly gathered every other week; but today, along with relatives who lived in the city, a few good friends of the family had been invited to share a simple dinner, and so they sat in the waning light of evening—the clock was approaching four—awaiting their guests.

Little Antonie had not let her grandfather disturb her sled ride, had merely extended her naturally slightly protruding upper lip in a little pout. Now she was at the foot of "Jerusalem Hill"; unable to bring her swift glide to a sudden halt, she shot on ahead a little beyond her goal.

"Amen," she said. "I know something, Grandfather!"

"*Tiens!* She knows something!" the old man exclaimed and pretended to be itching all over with curiosity. "Did you hear, Mama? She knows something! Is there no one who can tell me . . ."

"If a bolt starts a fire," Tony said, nodding her head with each word, "then lightning has struck. But if there's no fire, then all we got was a thunderbolt!"

And then she folded her arms and gazed at the smiling faces like someone sure of her success. The elder Buddenbrook, however, was annoyed at such wisdom and demanded to know who had taught the child this foolishness, and when it turned out that it had been Ida Jungmann, a young lady from Marienwerder only recently engaged as the girl's governess, it was the consul who had to come to Ida's defense.

"You are too strict, Papa. Why shouldn't the child have her own curious notions about such things at her age?"

"*Excusez, mon cher! Mais c'est une folie!* You know how I detest such darkening of children's minds! Get a thunderbolt, do we? Well, the thunder can just bolt her! You can send that Prussian girl to—"

As a matter of fact, the old gentleman had few good words for Ida Jungmann. He was not a narrow-minded man. He had seen a good piece of the world, had ridden in a coach-and-four to southern Germany to buy grain to supply the Prussian army in '13, had been in Amsterdam and Paris, was a man of enlightened views, who, God knows, did not condemn everything beyond the gates and gables of his hometown. But apart from his business connections, he was more inclined than his son, the consul, to set strict limits to social relationships and to be standoffish with strangers. When, one day, then, his children returned from a trip to West Prussia with this young girl—she was only just twenty—bringing her into the house like some baby Jesus, an orphan, the daughter of an innkeeper who had died just before the Buddenbrooks' arrival, the consul's act of Christian charity had resulted in an outburst, during which the old gentleman spoke almost nothing but French and Plattdeutsch. All the same, Ida Jungmann had proved quite adept at housekeeping and dealing with children, and, given her Prussian sense of hierarchy and loyalty, was admirably suited for her position in the household. She was a woman of aristocratic principles, who differentiated very precisely between the first and second levels of society, between the middle class and the lower-middle class; she was proud to be the devoted servant of the first level, and showed her displeasure if Tony made friends with a schoolmate who, in Mamselle Jungmann's estimation, was merely from a good middle-class family.

At that moment, the Prussian woman appeared out in the columned hall and now entered through the glass door; a rather tall, bony girl in a black dress, with smooth hair and an honest face. She was leading little Klothilde by the hand, an extraordinarily skinny child in a flowered muslin frock, with dull, ashy hair and the face of a silent old maid. She came from a collateral line of the family, one with no property whatever—was the daughter of a nephew of old Herr Buddenbrook, who now served as overseer of an estate near Rostock—and, being the same age as Antonie and a tractable child, she was being raised here in the house.

"Everything is ready," said Mamselle Jungmann and rolled the "r" in her throat—when she first arrived, she had been totally unable to pronounce her "r"s at all. "Klothilde was great help in the kitchen, Trina didn't have to do hardly anything."

At the sound of Ida's odd pronunciations, Monsieur Buddenbrook smirked down into his jabot; but the consul gave his little niece a pat on the cheek and said, "That's the thing, Thilda. Work and pray, every day. Our Tony should follow your example. She tends all too much to idleness and haughtiness."

Tony hung her head and cast her eyes up at her grandfather, because she knew that as usual he would come to her defense.

"No, no," he said. "Chin up, Tony, *courage*! We can't all be the same. To each his own. Thilda is a good girl, but we're not to be despised, either. Am I speaking *raisonable*, Bethsy?"

He turned to his daughter-in-law, who made a habit of concurring in his opinions, whereas Madame Antoinette, more out of tact than conviction, usually took the consul's side. And so the two generations shook hands, *chassé-croisé*, as it were.

"You're very kind, Papa," the consul's wife said. "Tony will try to grow up to be a clever and practical wife. Are the boys home from school?" she asked Ida.

But Tony, who from her grandfather's knee could see the reflection in the "window spy," shouted at almost the same time, "Tom and Christian are coming up Johannis Strasse. And Herr Hoffstede. And Uncle Doctor."

The chimes of St. Mary's began their chorale—dong!-ding-dong!—with so little rhythm that it was not quite clear which hymn it was, though it was full of solemnity, and while the smaller and the larger bells—one merry, the other grave—tolled four o'clock, the bell in the vestibule below rang shrilly through the entrance hall. And indeed Tom and Christian had arrived, along with the first two guests, Jean Jacques Hoffstede, the poet, and Dr. Grabow, the family physician.

2

HERR JEAN JACQUES HOFFSTEDE, the town poet, who was sure to have a few rhymes in his pocket for today as well, was not much younger than Johann Buddenbrook senior, and, apart from the fact that his frock coat was green, their taste in clothing was the same. But he was thinner and more sprightly than his old friend and had small, quick hazel eyes and a long pointed nose.

"Many thanks," he said, after he had shaken the hands of the gentlemen and executed a few of his choicest bows to the ladies, in particular to the consul's wife, whom he especially admired—the kind of bows of which the modern generation was totally incapable, each of them accompanied by a quiet and attentive smile. "Many thanks for your kind invitation, my dear friends. We, the doctor and I, met these two young people," and he pointed to Tom and Christian, who stood beside him in blue tunics with leather belts, "on König Strasse as they were returning from their studies. Splendid fellows—Madame Consul? Thomas—now, there's a serious, steady intellect; he'll have to go into commerce, no doubt of that. Whereas Christian seems to go off in all directions at once, does he not? Something of an *incroyable*, though there's no concealing my *engouement*. He will go on to study, I fancy; he is a lad of wit and brilliant gifts."

Herr Buddenbrook made use of his gold snuffbox. "The boy's a monkey! Be better if he just became a poet, wouldn't it, Hoffstede?"

Mamselle Jungmann pulled the window curtains, tucking one over the other, and the room soon lay in the restless, but discreet and soft candlelight provided by the crystal chandelier and the candlesticks on the secretary.

"Well, Christian," the consul's wife said—her hair had taken on a golden sheen now—"what did you learn this afternoon?" And it turned out that Christian had had lessons in writing, arithmetic, and singing.

He was a lad of seven, who even now looked ridiculously like his father. He had the same rather small, round, deep-set eyes, the same jutting arch to the nose was evident already, and a few lines beneath the cheekbones suggested that the shape of the face would not retain its present childish fullness.

"We laughed ourselves silly"—he was starting to chatter away now, while his eyes wandered from person to person in the room. "I have to tell you what Herr Stengel said to Siegmund Köstermann." He bent forward, shaking his head and addressing the empty air with great emphasis. " 'Externally, my good lad, externally you are sleek and dapper, true, but internally, my good lad, you are black.' " He dropped all his "r"s as he said it, and "black" came out as "bleck"—and his face was so convincingly comic at depicting this "extuhnal" sleekness and dapperness that they all broke into laughter.

"A monkey!" old Buddenbrook repeated with a giggle.

Herr Hoffstede, however, was beside himself with ecstasy. "*Charmant!*" he cried. "Unsurpassable! You have to know Marcellus Stengel! To a tee! No, it's really too precious!"

Thomas, who lacked such talents, stood beside his younger brother laughing heartily, with no trace of envy. His teeth were not very good, were small and yellowish. But his nose was strikingly well chiseled, and both his eyes and the shape of his face greatly resembled those of his grandfather.

Some adults seated themselves on the chairs, some on the sofa, and they chatted now with the children, commented on the unseasonable cold, on the house. Herr Hoffstede was admiring the splendid inkwell—a black-spotted hunting dog of Sèvres porcelain—that graced the secretary. Dr. Grabow, however, a man about the same age as the consul and with a long, kind, and gentle smiling face framed in whiskers, was inspecting the cakes, raisin bread, and various saltcellars set out for display on the table. This was the "salt and bread" sent by relatives and friends to mark the move to a new home. But as evidence that these were gifts from persons of some substance, the bread came in the form of sweet, spicy, heavy pastries and the salt in sturdy gold containers.

"Looks as if I will have some work to do," the doctor said, pointing to the sweets and cautioning the children. And then, rocking his head, he held up a formidable utensil for salt, pepper, and mustard.

"From Lebrecht Kröger," Monsieur Buddenbrook said with a grin. "Always a fair man, my good relative is. I did not present him with anything so fine when he built his summer house out beyond the Burg Gate. But he's always been . . . stylish! generous! a cavalier à la mode."

The bell had set up a clangor through the whole house several times now. Pastor Wunderlich arrived, a portly old gentleman in a long, black coat. His hair was powdered, and he had a merry, fair face in which a pair of gray, alert eyes sparkled. He had been a widower for many years and counted himself among the confirmed bachelors, like Herr Grätjens, the tall broker who had come with him and who was forever rolling up a scrawny hand and holding it to his eye like a telescope, as if examining a painting—he was generally recognized as a connoisseur of fine art.

And Senator Dr. Langhals arrived as well, with his wife, longtime friends of the family; and Köppen the wine merchant—no forgetting him—with his large, ruddy face set between two overstuffed shoulders, and his equally stout wife.

It was after four-thirty when the Krögers arrived at last—both older and younger generations, along with Consul Kröger's sons, Jakob and Jürgen, who were the same ages as Tom and Christian. And, almost simultaneously, here came the parents of the younger Madame Kröger: lumber merchant Herr Oeverdieck and his wife—an elderly, affectionate couple, who made a habit of exchanging the most youthful terms of endearment for everyone to hear.

"Late guests are fine guests," Consul Buddenbrook said, kissing his mother-in-law's hand.

"And arrive en masse!" And after sweeping an arm over the contingent of Kröger in-laws, Johann Buddenbrook shook hands with Herr Kröger, senior.

Lebrecht Kröger, cavalier à la mode, was a large, distinguished man. His hair was lightly powdered, but he wore the latest fashion. Two rows of jeweled buttons sparkled on his velvet vest. His son Justus sported a goatee and a mustache turned up at the ends, but he strongly resembled his father in stature and demeanor and was equally a master of elegant, rounded gestures with his hand.

They did not take seats at once, but stood there in expectation of the main event, engaging in casual, preliminary conversation. And now Johann Buddenbrook, senior, offered his arm to Madame Köppen, and said in a voice audible to all, "Well, if everyone has an appetite, *mesdames et messieurs* . . ."

Mamselle Jungmann and the kitchen maid had opened the white folding doors to the dining room, and the party moved at a confident, leisurely pace in its direction—one could reckon with a nourishing snack at the Buddenbrooks'.

3

As the whole party set in motion, the younger master of the house reached into his left breast pocket, and at the sound of rustling paper his hospitable smile suddenly vanished and was replaced by a tense and worried look, while a few muscles at both temples twitched as if he were clenching his teeth. He feigned a couple of steps in the direction of the dining room, then held back as his eyes searched for his mother, who was bringing up the rear at the side of Pastor Wunderlich and about to cross the threshold.

"Beg your pardon, pastor—a word with you, Mama." And while the pastor gave him an amiable nod, Consul Buddenbrook pressed the old woman to join him at the window in the landscape room.

"To be brief—there's a letter from Gotthold," he said quickly in a low voice and, gazing into her dark, questioning eyes, he pulled the folded and sealed paper from his pocket. "It's his handwriting—this is the third letter now, and Papa only answered the first. What am I to do? It came at two this afternoon, and I would have given it to Father long before now, but how can I spoil the mood for him today? What do you say? There's still time to ask him to leave the room for a moment."

"No, you're right, Jean, it can wait!" Madame Buddenbrook said and with a customary swift motion took hold of her son's arm. "You know what's in it!" she added worriedly. "He simply won't give in, the lad won't. He's taken it into his head that he's due compensation for his share in the house. No, no, Jean, not just yet. This evening, perhaps, right before bed."

"What to do?" the consul repeated, shaking his lowered head. "I've often wanted to ask Papa to give in. It mustn't look as if I have worked my way into Father's bosom and am conspiring against my stepbrother, Gotthold, and I have to avoid even the appearance of such a thing with Father as well. But, in all honesty, I am a joint partner. And for the present Bethsy and I are paying perfectly fair rent for use of the third floor. As far as my sister in Frankfurt goes, it's all arranged. Her husband has received his compensation—with Father still alive—a quarter of the cost of the house, a very favorable settlement that Papa managed quite cleverly, very much to the firm's advantage. But Papa's snubbing Gotthold like this is . . ."

"No, Jean, that's nonsense. His position in the matter is really quite clear. But Gotthold thinks that as his stepmother I care only for my own children's interests and am deliberately estranging his father from him. That is the sad part."

"But it's his fault!" the consul came close to shouting, and then dampened his voice with a glance toward the dining room. "This sorry state of affairs is his fault. Judge for yourself—why couldn't he be reasonable! Why did he have to marry this Demoiselle Stüwing with her . . . shop?" The consul laughed in annoyance and embarrassment at the word. "Father's prejudice against her shop is, to be sure, a weakness of his. But it's a bit of vanity that Gotthold should have respected."

"Oh, Jean, the best thing would be for Papa to give in."

"But can I suggest that to him?" the consul whispered, his hand flying excitedly to his brow. "As regards my personal concerns in the matter, I would have to say: Father, pay up. But I'm joint partner, too, who must represent the firm's interests, and if Papa doesn't think he has any obligation to withdraw moneys from our working capital for a disobedient and rebellious son— We are talking about eleven thousand thalers *courant*. No, no, I can't advise him to do that. But neither can I advise against it. I don't want to have anything to do with it. And the scene with Papa is bound to be so *désagréable*."

"Later this evening, Jean. Come now, they're all waiting."

The consul hid the paper in his breast pocket and offered his mother his arm, and they stepped side by side over the threshold into the brightly lit dining room, where the others had just finished finding their places at the long table.

The wall coverings here displayed white statues of gods standing among slender columns, creating an almost three-dimensional effect against the sky-blue background. The heavy red curtains at the windows had been closed, and in each corner of the room eight candles burned in a tall, gold-plated candelabrum, not to mention those in silver branched candlesticks on the table. Above the massive buffet, which faced the landscape room, hung an enormous painting—a gulf in Italy, its blue misty hue extraordinarily effective in this light. Substantial, stiff-backed sofas upholstered in red damask stood along the walls.

Every trace of worry and care had vanished from Madame Buddenbrook's face as she took her seat between Pastor Wunderlich and Kröger senior, who presided at the window end of the table.

"*Bon appétit!*" she said with a sudden, brief, cordial nod, while her eyes rapidly swept the full length of the table to the children at the far end.

4

As I've said, Herr Buddenbrook, my compliments." Herr Köppen's ponderous voice carried over the general table conversation. The kitchen maid—with her exposed, red arms, a heavy striped skirt, and a little white cap on the back of her head—assisted by Mamselle Jungmann and Elisabeth Buddenbrook's chambermaid from the third floor, had now served the hot herb soup with croutons, and they all began to spoon it cautiously.

"My compliments! Such spaciousness, such *noblesse*. Must say, a man could live well here, must say." Herr Köppen had not been on visiting terms with the previous owners of the house; he had not been a rich man for long, did not come from a patrician family, and unfortunately could not wean himself from the use of several homelier turns of phrase—"must say," for example. Besides which, he said "commliments."

"And not at all expensive," Herr Grätjens remarked dryly—and he should know—and went on inspecting the Italian gulf through his telescoped hand.

As far as possible the ladies and gentlemen were seated in pairs, the long chain of the family broken here and there by friends. But the rule had not been strictly enforced, and the old Oeverdiecks were as usual practically sitting on each other's laps, exchanging loving nods. Kröger senior, however, was enthroned high and erect between the wife of Senator Langhals and Madame Antoinette, dividing his hand gestures and reserved jests equally between those two ladies.

"When was the house built?" Herr Hoffstede addressed his question across the table to the elder Buddenbrook, who was conversing in a jovial and ironical tone with Madame Köppen.

"In—now, wait—around 1680, if I'm not mistaken. My son is much better than I with dates of that sort."

"Eighty-two," the consul confirmed, bowing slightly; he had taken a seat, without a lady companion, beside Senator Langhals, farther down the table. "It was completed in the winter of 1682. At the time Ratenkamp & Co. had started to prosper quite nicely. It's sad—the way the firm fell off in the last twenty years."

Conversation came to a halt, which lasted for a good thirty seconds. They looked into their plates and recalled the once so prosperous family that had built the house, lived here, and then, having sunk into poverty, moved away.

"Ah yes, very sad," Grätjens the broker said, "and when you think what madness led to their ruin— If only Dietrich Ratenkamp hadn't made Geelmaack a partner. God knows, once he started running things, I simply threw up my hands. I knew from very reliable sources, my friends, the awful risks he was taking behind Ratenkamp's back, lending money here and taking out credit there, all in the firm's name. Finally it all came to an end. The banks grew suspicious—nothing left to back him up. You simply have no idea. But, then, who was minding the store? Geelmaack, maybe? They simply ran amok like rats, year in, year out. And Ratenkamp paid no attention whatever."

"He was as good as paralyzed," the consul said. A somber, taciturn look came over his face. Bending forward, he moved his spoon through his soup, letting his little, round, deep-set eyes drift to the head of the table now and then.

"He walked around like a man under enormous pressures, and I think one can understand what they were. And why did he ally himself with Geelmaack? He brought wretched little capital with him and his reputation was not the best. He must have felt he had to shift some part of his dreadful responsibilities to someone else, simply because he sensed that it was all coming to an end. The firm had been badly mismanaged, the old family was *passé*. Wilhelm Geelmaack surely did little more than supply the final push into the abyss."

"Is that your opinion as well, my good consul?" Pastor Wunderlich asked with a circumspect smile while pouring red wine for himself and the lady beside him. "That it would all have turned out just as it did even without Geelmaack and all his extravagant dealings?"

"Possibly not," the consul said, mulling it over and without addressing anyone in particular. "But I do think Dietrich Ratenkamp's alliance with Geelmaack was inevitable—fate simply took its course. He must have acted under the pressure of implacable necessity. Ah, I'm convinced that he halfway knew about his partner's dealings, that he was not totally ignorant of what state his warehouse was in. But he was immobilized."

"Well, *assez*, Jean," the senior Buddenbrook said, laying his spoon aside. "That's merely another one of your *idées*."

With a preoccupied smile, the consul lifted his glass to his father.

But Lebrecht Kröger said, "No, it's time we looked to the happy present." And he carefully and elegantly grasped the neck of his bottle of white wine—a small silver stag decorated the cork—and laid it slightly on its side for a closer examination of the label. "C. F. Köppen," he read and nodded to the wine merchant. "Ah yes, where would we be without you."

Madame Antoinette kept a watchful eye on the movements of her serving girls as the gold-rimmed Meissener plates were changed, and Mamselle Jungmann called orders into the mouthpiece of the speaking tube that connected dining room and kitchen.

The fish course was passed, and as Pastor Wunderlich carefully served himself he said, "A happy present is not something we can always take for granted. These young people who have joined to celebrate with us older folks probably cannot imagine that things were ever any different. I might add that I have played a personal role in the destinies of our Buddenbrooks on a few occasions. And whenever my eye chances to fall upon such items"—and he picked up a heavy silver spoon from the table and turned to Madame Antoinette—"I have to think if it might not be one of the pieces that our friend the philosopher Lenoir, sergeant to His Majesty Emperor Napoleon, held in his hands back in aught six—and then I am reminded of our meeting that day on Alf Strasse, madame."

Madame Buddenbrook gazed at her lap and smiled a half-embarrassed smile full of memories. Tom and Tony, who didn't like fish and had been attentively following the adults' conversation, called up to the head of the table in unison, "Oh yes, tell us about it, Grandmama!" But the pastor, who knew that she did not like to recount what had been a rather upsetting incident for her, began to tell the old story yet once again; the children would have been delighted to hear it even for the hundredth time, and perhaps it was still unfamiliar to one or two of the guests.

"Well, to be brief, picture it: An afternoon in November, and so cold and rainy, Lord have mercy, and I am returning from a pastoral call, walking down Alf Strasse and thinking about the evil times that had befallen us. Prince Blücher was gone, the French were in the town, but one noticed little general excitement. The streets were quiet, people were sitting in their houses, keeping a sharp eye out. Prahl the butcher had stepped in front of his door, his hands in his pockets, and called out in that booming voice of his: 'Well, if this ain't the last straw, if this ain't the last straw—!' And—bang!—a bullet had struck him right in the head. Well, and so then I'm thinking I'd better look in on the Buddenbrooks, that a cheering word might be welcome, what with Madame having to deal with soldiers quartered in her house and her husband down with erysipelas.

"And at that very same moment whom do I see coming toward me? Our revered Madame Buddenbrook. But in what a state? She is hurrying through the rain without a hat, has barely managed to toss a shawl over her shoulders, stumbling more than walking, her coiffure in total dishevelment. No, it's true, madame. One could hardly even call it a coiffure.

" 'What a pleasant surprise,' I say and make bold to catch hold of her sleeve; she has not noticed me at all, and I have my forebodings. 'Where are you off to in such haste, my dear?' She notices me, she looks at me, she exclaims, 'Oh, it's you! Farewell! It's all over! I'm on my way to drown myself in the Trave.'

" 'Heaven forbid!' I say and feel myself turning white. 'That's not the place for you, my dear woman! But what has happened?'

And I hold on to her as tightly as good manners permit. 'What has happened?' she cries and begins to quiver. 'They're into my silver, Wunderlich! That is what has happened. And Jean is down with erysipelas and cannot help me. And he couldn't help if he were on his feet. They're stealing my spoons, my silver spoons, that is what has happened, Wunderlich, and I am on my way to the Trave!'.

"Well, now, I hold our good friend back, I say what one says in such cases: 'Courage, dearest lady,' I say, and 'All will be well,' and 'We shall speak with these people, control yourself, I beg of you, and now let's go!' And I lead her back down the street to her house. We find the militia upstairs in the dining room, just as Madame left them, upwards of twenty men, all occupied with the large chest where the silver is kept.

" 'Gentlemen, with which of you might I discuss this matter?' I ask politely. Well, they begin to laugh and shout, 'With all of us, Papa!' But then one of them steps forward and introduces himself, a man tall as a tree, with a black waxed mustache and large red hands sticking out from his braided cuffs. 'Lenoir,' he says, saluting with his left hand, for he is holding a bundle of five or six silver spoons in his right. 'Sergeant Lenoir. What can I do for the gentleman?'

" 'Sir!' I say, appealing to his *point d'honneur*. 'How do you reconcile your high rank with your preoccupation with such items? The city did not bar its gates to the emperor.'—'What do you want?' he answered. 'War is war. My men need tableware and such.'

" 'They should take into consideration,' I interrupted him, struck by an idea, 'that this lady, the mistress of this house,' I say, for what doesn't one say in such situations, 'is not really a German, but almost a countrywoman of yours, she is French.'—'What, she's French?' he repeats. And what do you suppose this tall dragoon says next?—'An émigrée, you mean?' he says. 'But then she must be an enemy of philosophy!'

"I am dumbfounded, but I managed to choke back my laughter. 'You are,' I say, 'a man of intellect, I see. I repeat that it is unworthy of you to concern yourself with such items.'—He is silent for a moment; but then, suddenly, he turns red, throws his six spoons back in the chest, and shouts, 'But who has told you that I have any other intention than to have a little look at these things? And pretty things they are! And if some one or another of my men should happen to take one along as a souvenir . . .'

"Well, they ended up taking quite enough souvenirs—all appeals to human or divine justice were of no help. They apparently knew no other god than that dreadful little man."

5

DID YOU EVER see him, pastor?"

The plates were changed once more. A colossal smoked ham, brick-red and strewn with bread crumbs, appeared, along with a brown, tart shallot sauce and mounds of vegetables so large that they all could have filled themselves from just one bowl. Lebrecht Kröger took charge of the carving. Casually lifting his elbows, his long index fingers pointed down the backs of knife and fork, he circumspectly cut away one juicy slice after another. Elisabeth Buddenbrook's masterpiece, "Russian preserves," a spicy mixture of fruits conserved in spirits, was passed around.

No, Pastor Wunderlich regretted that he had never met Bonaparte in the flesh. But both the elder Buddenbrook and Jean Jacques Hoffstede had seen him face to face: the former in Paris, right before the Russian campaign, at a reviewing of the troops in the Tuileries gardens, the latter in Danzig.

"No, good Lord, he was not a nice-looking customer," the poet said, lifting his brows and shoving a nicely arranged forkful of ham, brussels sprouts, and potatoes into his mouth. "They say, by the by, that he was quite a merry fellow in Danzig. There was a joke making the rounds at the time. They said he would spend the whole day with Germans at the gaming table, and for no modest stakes, but of an evening he would play with his own generals. '*N'est-ce pas, Rapp,*' he said and grabbed a handful of gold from the table, '*les Allemands aiment beaucoup ces petits Napoléons?*'—And Rapp replied, '*Oui, Sire, plus que le Grand!*' "

Amid the loud general amusement that followed—for Hoffstede had told his anecdote very prettily, even mimicking the emperor's expression a little—Buddenbrook senior said, "Well, all joking aside, I have great respect for his personal greatness. What a personality!"

The consul gravely shook his head. "No, no, we younger people no longer understand why we should admire the man who murdered the Duke of Enghien, who slaughtered eight hundred prisoners in Egypt."

"That is all quite possibly an exaggeration or a fabrication," Pastor Wunderlich said. "The duke may very well have been a licentious and seditious man, and as far as those prisoners go, their execution was surely a duly deliberated and necessary decision made by an official council of war." And he told them about a book that had been published several years before, a book he had read, written by a secretary of the emperor—a work that was well worth the reading.

"All the same," the consul persisted, and trimmed a candle flickering in the branched candlestick before him, "I cannot comprehend it, I cannot comprehend this admiration for the monster! As a Christian, as a man of religious feelings, I cannot find room in my heart for such a sentiment."

His face had taken on a quiet, zealous expression—indeed, he had laid his head a little to one side—and it certainly did look as if his father and Pastor Wunderlich were exchanging very discreet smiles.

"Yes, yes," Johann Buddenbrook chuckled, "but the little *napoléons* weren't so bad, were they? My son is more inclined to go into raptures for Louis Philipp," he added.

"Raptures?" Jean Jacques Hoffstede repeated somewhat sarcastically. "A curious combination! Philipp Egalité and raptures."

"Well, it seems to me that we have a lot to learn from the July Monarchy, by God it does." The consul spoke earnestly and eagerly. "The relationship between French constitutionalism and the new practical ideals and interests of our age is quite congenial and useful—something for which we should be most grateful."

"Practical ideals—well, yes . . ." Buddenbrook senior played with his gold snuffbox and rewarded his jaws with a little rest. "Practical ideals. Nope, set no store by 'em at all!" In his annoyance he had fallen back into Plattdeutsch. "Trade schools and technical schools and commercial schools are popping up like mushrooms, and grammar schools and classical education are suddenly all foolishness, and the whole world has nothing in its head but coal mines and factories and making money. Fine, fine, it's all very fine. But on the other hand a bit *stupide*, over the long term—is it not? I don't know why it offends me so much—though I'm not saying, Jean, that the July Monarchy isn't a fine thing. . . ."

Senator Langhals, as well as Grätjens and Köppen, were on the consul's side. Yes, most definitely, the people of Germany could only respond with its compliments to the French government and similar endeavors. Herr Köppen said "commliments" again. His face had turned quite red in the course of dinner and he was huffing and puffing audibly. Pastor Wunderlich's face, however, remained white as ever, delicate and alert, although he was quite at his ease downing one glass of wine after another.

The candles were burning slowly, slowly lower, and now and then, when their flames flickered to one side, the faint odor of wax drifted over the table.

They sat in high-backed, heavy chairs, dined with heavy silverware on heavy, rich foods, drank heavy, good wine, and said what they thought. The conversation soon turned to business, and as it did they automatically spoke more and more in its jargon—a comfortable, clumsy mode of speech that seemed to embrace both commercial brevity and prosperous indolence, embellished here and there with a touch of sociable self-irony. They did not say "on the exchange," they simply said "on the 'change," with most of the vowels elided and a self-satisfied expression on their faces.

The ladies had not been following the discussion for some time. Madame Kröger was monopolizing things by describing most appetizingly the best method for poaching carp in red wine. "But they must be cut into proper portions, my dears, and laid in the casserole with onions and cloves and zwieback, then placed over the fire with a pinch of sugar and a tablespoon of butter. But never wash them first, dear—the blood has to go in, too, mercy sake."

The senior Herr Kröger kept up a steady stream of the most amiable jokes. Consul Justus, his son, who was sitting beside Dr.

Grabow at the far end of the table with the children, had begun a teasing exchange with Mamselle Jungmann; she squinted her brown eyes and held her knife and fork very erect, while waving them ever so slightly back and forth. Even the Oeverdiecks had become quite loud and lively. The old woman had found a new pet name for her husband: "My sweet honey-ram!" she cried, and her bonnet shook with delight.

The conversation coalesced again when Jean Jacques Hoffstede began to speak on a favorite topic, the trip to Italy he had taken with a rich Hamburg relative some fifteen years before. He talked about Venice, Rome, and Vesuvius; he talked about the Villa Borghese, where the recently deceased Goethe had written part of his *Faust*; he waxed enthusiastic about Renaissance fountains lavishing cool refreshment, about pleasant strolls down tree-lined avenues; and then someone mentioned the large overgrown garden that the Buddenbrooks owned just outside the Burg Gate.

"Yes, egad!" the old man cried. "I am still annoyed that at the time I wasn't able to bring myself to tidy it up a little for more human use. I walked through it the other day—it's a disgrace, what a jungle! What a nice little piece of property it would be if the grass were mown, the trees nicely trimmed in little spheres and cubes."

The consul protested vigorously. "For God's sake, Papa—! I love to roam about there in the shrubbery during summer; but it would all be spoiled if a piece of free and beautiful nature were to be piteously snipped and shorn."

"But if that piece of free nature belongs to me, I'll be hanged if I don't have the right to tidy it up just as I please."

"Oh, Father, when I am lying there in the tall grass under some luxuriant bush, it's more as if I belonged to nature and hadn't any rights at all over it."

"Krischan, don't stuff y'self so much," the older Buddenbrook suddenly shouted. "But as for Thilda—doesn't hurt her none—eats like a thresher, the lass does."

And, indeed, it was amazing what talents this quiet, skinny child with her long, old-woman's face had developed when it came to eating. When asked whether she wanted a second bowl of soup, she had answered humbly, dragging out the words: "Y-e-s, p-l-e-a-s-e!"

She had chosen two of the largest servings of both the fish and the ham, along with ample portions of vegetables, had bent carefully and nearsightedly over her plate, and consumed it all, without any hurry, but in silent and large bites. And her reply to the old man's words came out drawled, amiable, amazed, and simple: "O L-o-r-d, U-n-c-l-e." She was not to be intimidated; she ate—though it might not be quite proper and they might mock her—with the instinctual appetite of a poor relative making the most of a well-laden table; she smiled indifferently and heaped her plate with good things—patient, tough, hungry, and skinny.

6

AND NOW CAME two large crystal bowls of "flat-iron pudding," a layered mixture of macaroons, raspberries, ladyfingers, and custard; meanwhile, at the other end of the table, there was a burst of flame—the children were being served plum pudding, their favorite dessert.

"Thomas, my boy, would you be so good," Johann Buddenbrook said and pulled a large ring of keys from his trouser pocket. "In the second cellar, on the right, the second bin, behind the red Bordeaux, two bottles, you hear?" And Thomas, who was well versed in such tasks, ran off and returned with two very dusty and cobwebbed bottles. And no sooner had the yellow-gold, fruity-sweet vintage Madeira been poured from its humble container into little dessert-wine glasses, than conversation fell away and Pastor Wunderlich stood up, glass in hand, to begin his gracefully phrased toast. His head a little to one side, a subtle and waggish smile playing over his white face, his free hand tracing little delicate gestures, he spoke in the same genial and easy conversational tone he loved to employ in the pulpit. "And now, stalwart friends, be so kind as to join me in emptying a glass of this pleasant nectar with good wishes for the prosperity of our most honored hosts in their new and splendid home—to the Buddenbrook family, both present and absent. Long may they prosper!"

Absent? the consul thought, while returning a bow to the glasses lifted in his honor. Does he just mean those in Frankfurt and perhaps the Duchamps in Hamburg, or does old Wunderlich have something else in mind? He stood up to chink glasses with his father, and their eyes met in a cordial exchange.

Now it was broker Grätjen's turn to rise from his chair, and his speech took some time. He finally came round to a conclusion, and his somewhat shrill voice dedicated a glass to the firm of Johann Buddenbrook, that it might grow, blossom, and flourish to the greater honor of the town.

And Johann Buddenbrook thanked them all for their gracious words, first as the head of the family and second as the senior partner of the commercial enterprise—and sent Thomas back for a third bottle of Madeira, because it had turned out his son had been wrong in assuming that two would suffice.

Lebrecht Kröger spoke as well. He took the liberty of remaining seated, because that created a handsomer effect, and, with the addition of just a few chivalrous gestures of hands and head, he toasted the two ladies of the house, Madame Antoinette and the consul's wife.

He finished his toast, the flat-iron pudding was as good as polished off, and the Madeira was running low—and now, after first clearing his throat, Herr Jean Jacques Hoffstede slowly rose to his feet amid a universal "Ah!" and the joyous applause of the children at the far end of the table.

"Yes, *excusez*! I really could not help but . . ." he said, tapping his long nose with one finger and pulling a paper from his jacket pocket. Profound silence fell over the room.

The page he held in both hands was a thing of pied beauty, in its center an oval framed in red flowers and a mass of gold curlicues, containing the following words:

"On the Occasion of a Joyous Housewarming, Celebrated among Friends Gathered at the Home Newly Acquired by the Buddenbrook Family. October, 1835."

And, turning the page over, he recited in a voice quivering slightly with age:

> Honored friends!—this humble rhyming
> I've prepared must needs be sung
> 'Mid these halls with laughter chiming,
> Blessed by heav'n, with garlands hung.

'Tis to you it's dedicated,
Worthy friend with silver hair,
And your wife so celebrated,
To you both, a noble pair!

Simplest beauty, ablest talent,
Grace your children, and we view
Foam-born Venus and her gallant
Vulcan wed in love anew.

May your future be untarnished,
Nothing mar the joys ahead,
Rather let each day be garnished
By an endless bliss instead.

Ever will I find elation
In your future happiness;
In my smile see confirmation
Of the wishes I profess.

In your splendid home residing,
Always keep that man most dear,
Who in humbler quarters 'biding
Penned these stanzas offered here.

He bowed, and they burst into unanimous, enthusiastic applause.

"*Charmant*, Hoffstede!" Buddenbrook senior cried. "To your health! No, it was very sweet of you."

But when the consul's wife touched glasses with the poet, a very delicate blush came to her fair face, for she had noticed the polite little nod he had directed her way at the words "foam-born Venus."

7

THE GENERAL GOOD CHEER had reached its height, and Herr Köppen clearly felt the need to undo a few vest buttons; but unfortunately that was out of the question, since not even the older gentlemen permitted themselves such license. Lebrecht Kröger was sitting in his chair just as erect as at the beginning of the meal; Pastor Wunderlich was just as white and well mannered as before; the senior Buddenbrook had indeed leaned back a little, but was maintaining the finest decorum; only Justus Kröger was noticeably tipsy.

Where was Dr. Grabow? Elisabeth Buddenbrook unobtrusively got up and withdrew, for she had noticed that at the far end of the table the chairs of Mamselle Jungmann, Dr. Grabow, and Christian were vacant and that from the columned hallway there came the sound of something like suppressed wails. She quickly followed the kitchen maid—who had just served butter, cheese, and fruit—out of the dining room. And, indeed, there in the shadows little Christian lay huddled on the padded bench that encircled the middle column. His soft groans were enough to break her heart.

"O Lord, madame," said Ida, who was standing beside him with the doctor, "Christian, the poor boy, is feeling very ill."

"I'm sick at my stomach, Mama, I'm *damned* sick!" Christian whimpered, while round, deep-set eyes above an oversize nose wandered restlessly from side to side. It was only out of great desperation that he had managed to utter the word "damned."

But the consul's wife said, "When we use such words, Christian, the Lord punishes us with even worse sickness!"

Dr. Grabow felt the boy's pulse; his face seemed to have grown even longer and milder. "A touch of indigestion—nothing significant, Frau Buddenbrook," he consoled her. And then he continued in his slow, pedantic, official voice, "The best thing would be to put him to bed. A little soothing syrup, perhaps a cup of camomile tea to induce perspiration. And a strict diet—madame? I repeat, a strict diet. A little squab, a little French bread . . ."

"I don't want squab!" Christian cried, beside himself. "I never want to eat again! I'm sick at my stomach, *damned* sick!" The potent word appeared to offer him real relief—so great was the fervor with which he uttered it.

Dr. Grabow laughed to himself, but smiled an indulgent, almost melancholy smile. Oh, the young man would eat again soon enough. He would live like the rest of the world. Like his father and grandfather, like his relatives and friends, he would spend his days sitting at a desk and enjoying a fine, rich meal four times a day. But it was in God's hands. He, Friedrich Grabow, was not the sort of fellow to upset the lifelong habits of all these decent, prosperous, and comfortable commercial families. He would come when he was called, and recommend a strict diet for a few days—a little squab, a slice of French bread. Yes, yes—and with a good conscience assure them that it was nothing significant this time. Young as he was, he had held the hand of many a stalwart citizen who had consumed his last joint of meat, his last turkey and dressing, and then—whether death came suddenly and unexpectedly in his office chair or after he had suffered a while in his own solid bed—had commended his soul into God's hands. A stroke, he would say, a paralytic stroke, a sudden and unpredictable death. Yes, yes, and he, Friedrich Grabow, could have tallied up for them all the many times when "it was nothing significant"—when perhaps he hadn't even been called, or when perhaps, upon returning to the office after a good meal, they had experienced a certain brief, peculiar dizzy spell. But it was in God's hands. He, Friedrich Grabow, was himself not averse to turkey and dressing. Today's ham with shallot sauce had been delicious, damn if it hadn't, and then, while you were still huffing and puffing, flat-iron pudding—macaroons, raspberries, and custard, yes, yes. "I repeat, a strict diet—Madame Buddenbrook? A little squab, a little French bread . . ."

8

INSIDE, in the dining room, things were breaking up.

"*Mesdames et messieurs*, I hope you have enjoyed your meal. There is coffee waiting for everyone and, if Madame is feeling generous, a liqueur as well, and of course a cigar for those who want one. I needn't mention that the billiard table is available for anyone who wishes to play. Jean, you can guide our guests out to the back. Madame Köppen—may I have the honor?"

They were in the best of moods as they moved back through the large folding doors into the landscape room, chatting contentedly and telling one another what a fine meal it had been. The consul did not immediately follow, but instead gathered gentlemen interested in billiards around him.

"Would you like to hazard a little game, Father?"

No, Lebrecht Kröger was going to remain with the ladies, but Justus could certainly go on back. Köppen, Grätjens, Senator Langhals, and Dr. Grabow joined the consul, but Jean Jacques Hoffstede told them to go ahead without him. "Later, later. Johann Buddenbrook wants to pipe on his flute, and I simply have to wait for that. *Au revoir, messieurs.*"

As they strode along the columned hall, the six gentlemen heard the flute strike up its first tones in the landscape room, to the accompaniment of Elisabeth Buddenbrook on the harmonium—a small, bright, nimble melody that floated gracefully through the spacious rooms. The consul listened as long as there was music to be heard. He would have liked to remain behind in the landscape room himself, to sit in an armchair and give rein to his dreams and feelings as the tune carried him along. But one had one's duties as a host.

"Bring a few cups of coffee and more cigars to the billiard room," he said to the kitchen maid, who was just crossing the hallway.

"Yes, Lina, coffee, hear? Coffee!" Herr Köppen repeated with a voice as satisfied as his full belly and tried to give the girl's red arm a pinch. He spoke the "c" of "coffee" far back in his throat, as if already tasting and swallowing it.

"I'm certain Madame Köppen was watching through the glass," Consul Kröger remarked.

Senator Langhals asked, "So you live up there, Buddenbrook?"

Stairs led to the third floor, where the consul and his family had their quarters, but there was also another row of rooms along the left side of the hallway. The gentlemen smoked their cigars as they strode down the wide staircase with its openwork railing of white-enameled wood. The consul halted on the landing.

"There are three more rooms on the mezzanine," he explained, "a breakfast room, my parents' bedroom, and another room, open to the garden, though it's not used much. A little hallway serves as a corridor along one side. But—straight ahead!—as you can see, the delivery wagons can drive right through the passageway and on across to Becker Grube, at the rear of the property."

The wide, echoing passageway below was paved with large, square stones. There were offices both to one side of the vestibule door and at the far end of the passage, whereas the doors to the cellar and the kitchen, still fragrant with tart shallot sauce, were to the left of the stairway. On the far side, somewhat higher up, newly painted wooden galleries jutted from the wall: the servants' quarters, the only access a flight of open stairs rising from the passageway. Next to the stairs stood a couple of enormous old cupboards and a carved chest.

They passed through a glass door, then down a few very low steps over which wagons could also pass, and into the courtyard, where the scullery stood off to the left. From here they could look out over the prettily designed garden—at present a damp, autumnal gray, its beds protected by straw mats against the frost. It was closed off at the far end by the "Portal," the summerhouse with its rococo façade. The gentlemen, however, took a path down the left side of the courtyard, which first passed between two walls and then opened onto a second courtyard, in front of the back building.

Here a slippery set of stairs led down into a vaulted cellar with an earthen floor. It served as a warehouse, and a pulley rope for lifting sacks of grain dangled from the highest loft. But they took the dry, clean stairway on the right, which led to the second floor, where the consul opened a white door onto the billiard room.

Herr Köppen flung himself in exhaustion onto one of the hard chairs that lined the walls of the wide, bare, severe-looking room. "I'll watch for now," he exclaimed, brushing the fine drops of rain from his tailcoat. "Damned if that isn't quite a hike through your house, Buddenbrook!"

As in the landscape room, a fire was burning behind the brass grate of the stove. From the three high and narrow windows there was a view out over damp red roofs, gray courtyards, gables.

"A game of carom, senator?" the consul asked, taking cues from the rack. Then he walked around both tables, closing the pockets. "Who wants to play with us? Grätjens? Doctor? All right. Grätjens and Justus. Here, you take the other table—Köppen, you really *must* play."

The wine merchant stood up and, with a mouth still full of cigar smoke, he listened to a strong gust of wind that whistled among the houses, drove pricks of rain against the windowpanes, and howled, caught in the trap of the chimney.

"Damn!" he said, puffing out smoke. "Do you think the *Wullenwewer* will be able to make harbor, Buddenbrook? What wretched weather."

Yes, the news from Travemünde had not been the best, Consul Kröger confirmed, chalking the leather on his cue. Storms all along the coast. Good Lord, it was almost as bad as in '24, when St. Petersburg had the big flood.—Well, here came the coffee.

They helped themselves, took a sip, and began to play. But then the conversation turned to the Customs Union—oh, Consul Buddenbrook was enthusiastic about the Customs Union!

"What an inspiration, gentlemen!" he shouted, taking his shot and turning around eagerly to the other table, where the topic had first been mentioned. "We should join at the first opportunity."

Herr Köppen, however, did not share this opinion—no, he practically snorted his opposition. "And our self-sufficiency? And our independence?" he asked, leaning belligerently on his cue. "What about that? Would it ever occur to Hamburg to go along with this Prussian invention? Why don't we just let ourselves be annexed, Buddenbrook? Heaven forbid, what could a Customs Union do for us, I want to know! Isn't everything going just fine?"

"Yes, for you and your wines, Köppen! And perhaps for Russian products, I'll leave those aside. But we're not importing anything else! And as far as exports go, well, yes, we send a little grain to Holland and England, that's true. But, no, everything's not going fine, unfortunately. Lord knows, we did other business around here in days past. But as part of the Customs Union, the Mecklenburgs and Schleswig-Holstein would be open to us. There's no foreseeing how our own enterprise would pick up."

"Oh, please, Buddenbrook," Grätjens began, bending over the table and taking careful aim, waving the cue back and forth in his bony hand, "a Customs Union—I don't understand. Our system is so simple and practical, is it not? All that's needed is an oath and the ship clears customs."

"A lovely old institution." The consul had to admit that.

"No, really, Herr Buddenbrook, just because you think something is 'lovely'!" Senator Langhals was a little annoyed. "I'm not a commercial man, but if I were to be honest—no, the freeman's oath is fast becoming a farce, I must say. A mere formality, and people pay no regard to it at all. And the state comes out on the losing end. I've heard things that are simply scandalous. I am convinced that, as far as the senate is concerned, our joining the Customs Union would be . . ."

"Then it's going to end in conflict!" Herr Köppen furiously threw his cue to the floor. He said "congflick" and from here on threw caution to the winds in matters of pronunciation. "A congflick, I tell you, 'nd I know something about what that means. No, beggin' your pardon, senator, but there's jist no settin' you to rights, heav'n help you!" And he began to speak heatedly of arbitration committees and the welfare of the state and freemen's oaths and independent states.

Thank God, Jean Jacques Hoffstede arrived! He entered arm in arm with Pastor Wunderlich, two dispassionate and sprightly old gentlemen from the untroubled days of the past.

"Now, my fine friends," he began, "I have something for you: a little joke, a witty epigram taken from the French. Now, listen closely!"

He eased himself onto a chair, facing the billiard players, who leaned on their cues or against the tables. Pulling a piece of paper from his pocket, he laid his long index finger with its signet ring against his pointed nose and merrily read, with naïve epic emphasis:

As Maréchal Saxe took his coach for a ride,
With proud Madame Pompadour right by his side,
Young Frelon remarked as they drove 'cross the heath,
"Behold, the king's sword—and behold, the king's sheath!"

Herr Köppen was taken aback for a moment, then set aside the congflick and the welfare of the state and joined in the laughter, till the room echoed with it. Pastor Wunderlich, however, stepped to the window and, judging from the bounce of his shoulders, chuckled softly to himself.

They stayed a good while back here in the billiard room, because Hoffstede had several more jokes of a similar sort at the ready. Herr Köppen had opened his vest and was in the best of moods, for he was more at home here than in the dining room. He had a droll Plattdeutsch comment to add for every shot, and now and then he cheerily recited to himself: "As Maréchal Saxe . . ."

The little verse sounded more than curious in his rough bass voice. . . .

9

IT WAS RATHER LATER, around eleven o'clock, when the party reassembled in the landscape room and at the same time began to break up. After having her hand kissed by all the men, Elisabeth Buddenbrook immediately went up to see how the ailing Christian was doing, leaving the supervision of the maids and the cleaning up to Mamselle Jungmann, since Madame Antoinette had retired to her room on the mezzanine. The consul, however, accompanied his guests down the stairs to the entrance hall and through the door to the street.

A cutting wind was blowing the rain aslant, and the old Krögers, wrapped in thick fur coats, crept hastily into their majestic equipage, which had been waiting for some time. An unsteady flicker came from the yellow light of the oil lamps burning on poles outside the house—and of those suspended from thick chains across the pavement farther down the street. Here and there the houses, some with bays, some with stoops and benches, protruded into the street as it sloped down toward the Trave. Wet grass sprouted up between the cracked cobblestones. Across the way, St. Mary's Church lay wrapped in shadows, darkness, and rain.

"*Merci*," Lebrecht Kröger said and shook the hand of the consul, who was standing beside the carriage. "*Merci*, Jean, it was very kind of you." Then the door slammed and the equipage rumbled off. Pastor Wunderlich and Grätjens the broker departed as well with thanks. Herr Köppen, in a coat with a fivefold cape and a broad-brimmed gray stovepipe, his stout wife on his arm, said in his most honest bass tones, " 'vnin', Buddenbrook. Now go on back in, don't catch cold. And many thanks, eh? Don't know when I et that well last. And my red at four marks *courant* proved agreeable, it seems? So, g'night, then."

The Köppens walked beside Consul Kröger and his family in the direction of the river, while Senator Langhals, Dr. Grabow, and Jean Jacques Hoffstede moved off in the opposite direction.

Consul Buddenbrook stood a few steps outside the door, shivering a little in his cloth coat, his hands in the pockets of his light-colored trousers, and listened to the footsteps as they faded in the deserted, wet, and badly lit streets. Then he turned and looked up at the gray gabled façade of the house. His eyes lingered on the motto that stood chiseled in antique letters above the entrance: "*Dominus providebit.*" Lowering his head, he entered, and carefully bolted the unwieldy, creaking door. He let the vestibule door fall into its lock with a snap and slowly walked down the dully echoing entrance hall.

The cook was just coming down the steps with a tray full of clinking glasses, and he asked her, "Where's the master, Trina?"

"In the dining room, sir." Her face turned as red as her arms, for she was a country girl and easily disconcerted.

He walked upstairs, and as he moved along the dark columned hall, his hand moved to his breast pocket—there was a rustling of paper. Then he entered the dining room. In one corner a few remnants of candles were still burning on one of the candelabra, illuminating the now cleared table. The tart fragrance of shallot sauce lay stubbornly in the air.

And at the far end of the room, by the windows, Johann Buddenbrook was walking leisurely back and forth, his hands clasped behind his back.

10

WELL, MY SON JOHN! How goes it, lad!" He stopped and extended a hand to his son—a white hand, with short but delicately shaped fingers, the hand of the Buddenbrooks. In the dull and fitful light, his robust body was outlined against the dark red of the curtains, only his powdered wig and lace jabot shining white.

"Not tired yet? I'm just pacing here, listening to the wind—rotten weather! Captain Kloot is sailing back from Riga."

"Oh, Father, all will go well, with God's help."

"Can I depend on it? I admit, you and the Lord are on intimate terms."

Seeing his father's good mood, the consul was feeling a little more at ease.

"Yes, well, to come to the point," he began, "I didn't just want to say good night, Papa, but in fact—now, you won't be angry, will you? I didn't wish to bother you till now, not on such a festive evening—but this letter came this afternoon."

"Monsieur Gotthold—*voilà!*" The old man pretended to remain quite calm as he accepted the bluish paper, still sealed. "Herr Johann Buddenbrook, Sr. Personal. Your good stepbrother is a man of *conduite*, Jean. Did I ever answer that second letter of his that came the other day? And here he's written a third." While his pink face grew more and more somber, he ripped open the seal with one finger, quickly unfolded the thin paper, and leaned over to catch the candlelight, giving the letter a sharp rap with the back of his hand. There seemed to be disloyalty and rebellion even in the handwriting—for whereas the hand of the Buddenbrooks usually hurried lightly across paper in tiny, slanted lines, this large and wildly tilted script had been pressed on the page with eruptive energy. Many words had been underlined with a rapid flourish of the pen.

The consul had withdrawn a little to one side against the wall, where the chairs were; since his father was standing he did not sit down, but instead nervously grasped one of the chairs' high arms, and watched the old man read, scowling, his head bent to one side, his lips moving rapidly.

Father,

I am most likely mistaken to hope that your sense of justice is sufficient for you to gauge my *indignation* upon receiving no answer to my second *urgent* letter, written upon receipt of your reply (which I shall not presume to characterize!) to my initial inquiry regarding the matter at issue. I must, however, assert that I consider the manner in which you have chosen to widen the lamentable rift separating us to be a *sin* for which one day you shall *indeed* be called to answer before the judgment seat of God. It is sad enough that upon a day long past you chose to turn against me so cruelly and completely, merely because in following the inclinations of my heart I wed my present spouse and in so doing took charge of a certain retail establishment, thereby offending your *inordinate* pride. Yet the manner in which you are treating me at present cries out to Heaven, and, should you entertain the idea that in light of your silence I shall be content to remain silent myself, you are *sadly* mistaken. The purchase price of the house you recently acquired on Meng Strasse was some 100,000 marks *courant*, and I am also aware that *Johann*, your joint partner and the son of your second marriage, currently leases lodgings with you and that upon your death will become the sole owner of both your business and your house. You have come to an agreement with my stepsister and her husband in Frankfurt, and I have no intention of interfering in the matter. But as regards me, your eldest son, you have gone so far in your *un-Christian* anger as to refuse me outright any compensation for my share in the house! I kept my peace when you chose to make a payment of 100,000 marks *courant* so that I might set up my own business at the time of my marriage and also promised a single payment of another 100,000 as my share of the inheritance. At the time I was not sufficiently cognizant of the extent of your wealth. Now, however, I see things more clearly, and since I need not regard myself as disinherited on principle, I therefore *lay claim* in this particular instance to a compensation of 33,335 marks *courant*, that is to say, one-third of the purchase price. I do not choose to speculate to what *damnable* influences I owe the treatment I have thus far received and borne so patiently; but I do *protest* said treatment with all the sense of justice I can muster as a *Christian* and a *man of business*, and I assure you for the last time that, should you not choose to respect my just claims, I will no longer be able to respect you either as a *Christian* or as my *father* or as a *man of business*.

Gotthold Buddenbrook

"Forgive me if I take no pleasure in reading this rigmarole aloud to you again.—*Voilà!*" And Johann Buddenbrook grimly tossed the letter to his son.

The consul grabbed the paper just as it fluttered past his knees and with bewildered, sad eyes watched his father start pacing again. The old man was fuming as he reached for a candle-snuffer that lay on the windowsill and strode smartly to the candelabrum at the opposite corner of the table.

"*Assez! N'en parlons plus*, that's what I say. Period. Let's go to bed. *En avant!*" One flame after another vanished, never to rise again, under the little metal cone at the end of the rod. Only two candles were still burning when the old man turned back to his son, barely visible at the far end of the room.

"How do you see it, then? What do you say? You have to say something, you know!"

"What can I say, Father? I'm baffled."

"You're easily baffled!" In his rage Johann Buddenbrook let it fly, although he knew that there was little truth in the remark and that his son and partner often outdid him when it came to seizing the advantage.

"Harmful and damnable influences—" the consul continued. "That's the first bit I can even make out. You have no idea how that torments me, do you, Father? And he calls us un-Christian!"

"You can be bullied by his miserable scribblings—is that it?" Johann Buddenbrook walked over angrily, dragging the candle-snuffer behind him. "Un-Christian! Ha! Very tasteful, I must say—pious and money-hungry. You young people are a pretty lot, aren't you? Your heads full of fancies and Christian humbuggery. What idealism! And we old folks are heartless scoffers. And then there's the July Monarchy and practical ideals. And rather than pass up a few thousand thalers, write your old father a letter chock-full of the rudest insults. And, being a man of business, he deigns to despise me. Well, as a man of business myself, I can count my losses. I know what *faux frais* are—*faux frais!*" he repeated, rolling the "r" like a furious Parisian. "Demeaning myself by yielding won't make a more devoted son of the rascal."

"What can I say, Father! I'm not going to let him be proved right about 'influences.' I have my interests as a partner, and for that reason alone, shouldn't I advise you to stick to your guns? And yet—and I'm as good a Christian as Gotthold—and yet . . ."

"And yet! How right you are to add 'and yet,' Jean. Egad! How do things really stand? Back when he was so infatuated with Mamselle Stüwing, making scene after scene and entering into this *mésalliance* despite my strictest prohibition, I wrote him a letter: *Mon très cher fils*, marry your shop. Fine. I shall not disinherit you, there will be no melodramatics, but our friendship is at an end. Here is 100,000 as a dowry, and I'll leave another 100,000 in my will, and that's all. That takes care of you, there'll not be a penny more. And he didn't say a word. What concern is it of his if we've had success in business? If you and your sister get a sizable amount more? If a house is bought from an inheritance that is yours to begin with?"

"If you only understood, Father, what a dilemma I find myself in. For the sake of peace in the family, I really should advise . . . but . . ." The consul sighed softly and leaned back against the chair. Johann Buddenbrooks propped himself on his candle-snuffer and gazed attentively into the shadows, trying to make out the expression on his son's face. One of the two candles sputtered and died of its own accord. The last flame was flickering behind him. Now and then a tall, white figure emerged from the wallpaper, smiled a gentle smile, and vanished again.

"Father, I find this whole affair with Gotthold so depressing," the consul said softly.

"Nonsense, Jean, no sentimentalities! What depresses you about it?"

"Father—we sat here so cheerful this evening, it was such a lovely celebration, we were so happy and proud of our accomplishments, of having achieved something, of having brought our firm and our family to new heights, to a full measure of recognition and respect. But this acrimony with my brother, your eldest son, Father—let us not have a hidden crack that runs through the edifice we have built with God's gracious help. A family has to be united, to hold together, Father; otherwise evil will come knocking at the door."

"Humbug, Jean! The tomfoolery of an obstinate boy."

There was a pause—the last flame burned lower and lower.

"What are you doing, Jean?" Johann Buddenbrook asked. "I can't see you."

"I'm figuring," the consul said dryly. The candle flared and revealed him standing up straight; he stared into the dancing flame, his eyes colder and more alert than they had been all afternoon. "On the one hand: you give Gotthold 33,335 and Frankfurt 15,000; that comes to a total of 48,335. On the other hand: you simply give Frankfurt 25,000, which means the firm comes out 23,335 to the good. But that is not all. Assuming that you compensate Gotthold for his share in the house, the dam will be broken, meaning that he will *never* be satisfied and that after your death he can claim a portion of the inheritance equal to what my sister and I receive, bringing with it the loss of hundreds of thousands for the firm—lost capital that will no longer be available to me as its sole owner. No, Papa," he concluded with an energetic wave of a hand and stood up taller still, "I must advise against your giving in."

"Well, then, that's that! *N'en parlons plus! En avant!* Let's go to bed."

The metal cone extinguished the final flame. They strode through the thick darkness of the columned hall and shook hands on the landing to the third floor.

"Good night, Jean. *Courage*, do you hear? These are mere annoyances. Until breakfast, then."

The consul climbed the stairs to his living quarters, and the old man groped his way down along the banister to the mezzanine. Then the rambling old house lay tightly wrapped in darkness and silence. Pride, hope, and fear all slept, while rain pelted the deserted streets and an autumn wind whistled around corners and gables.

PART TWO

1

TWO AND A HALF years later, spring arrived earlier than ever—it was only the middle of April—and at the same time an event occurred that set old Johann Buddenbrook humming with delight and gave his son great cause to rejoice.

On a Sunday morning, around nine o'clock, the consul was sitting near the window of the breakfast room at the large brown secretary, whose rounded top he had rolled back by tripping a tiny mechanism. A heavy leather writing case filled with papers lay before him; but he had taken out one gilt-edged notebook with an embossed cover and was now bent over it, writing impatiently in his fine, tiny, hurried hand—so intent that he halted only to dip his quill in the heavy metal inkwell.

Both windows stood open, their curtains gently and soundlessly billowed now and then by a fresh spring breeze laden with the delicate spices of the garden, where the first buds were warmed by a gentle sun and a few birds answered one another in small, pert voices. The sunlight came to dazzling rest behind him on the breakfast table's white linen cloth, sprinkled here and there with crumbs, and its rays gamboled in sparkling little twists and leaps along the gold rims of the bowl-shaped cups.

Both panels of the door to the bedroom were open as well, and through them came the audible voice of Johann Buddenbrook softly singing a comical old song to himself:

> A proper man, a gentleman,
> A man of splendid poses;
> He rocks the baby, cooks the soup,
> And smells of orange and roses.

He was sitting beside a small cradle draped in green silk that stood next to his daughter-in-law's elevated bed, and with one hand he kept it rocking at an even pace. To make things easier for the servants, the consul and his wife had moved down to the mezzanine, and for the time being his father and mother were sleeping in the third room, where Madame Antoinette, an apron over her striped dress and a lace bonnet set atop her thick white curls, now sat busily folding flannels and linens at a table.

Consul Buddenbrook cast hardly a glance into the adjoining room; he was too busy with the task he had set for himself. The look on his face was one of earnest, almost pained piety. His mouth was slightly open, his chin dropped a little, and his eyes misted over now and then. He wrote:

"Today, the 14th of April 1838, at six o'clock in the morning, my dear wife, Elisabeth, née Kröger, was most happily and with God's gracious help delivered of a baby daughter, who shall be christened with the name of Clara. God was indeed gracious, despite Dr. Grabow's pronouncement that the birth was somewhat too early, and even though matters had not stood at the best beforehand and Bethsy endured great pain. Ah, where is there such a God as Thou art, Lord of Sabaoth, Thou who helpest in all dangers and afflictions, and who teachest us to know Thy will aright, that we may fear Thee and be found faithful to Thy will and commandments! Ah Lord, direct and guide us all for as long as we live on this earth. . . ."—The pen hurried along, smooth and agile, here and there executing a commercial curlicue while addressing God in line after line.

Two pages later, it read: "I have had a policy written for my youngest daughter in the amount of 150 *courant*-thalers. Lead her, O Lord, in Thy ways, and give her a pure heart, that she may one day enter the mansions of eternal peace. For we well know how difficult it is to believe with all one's soul that sweet Jesus is ours alone, for how small are our earthly hearts. . . ." Three pages later, the consul added his "amen," but the pen continued to glide, gently rustling across several more pages, describing the precious fount that quenches the thirst of the weary wanderer, the sacred and bloody wounds of the Redeemer, the narrow way and the broad way, and God's great glory. It cannot be denied that after one or another of these statements the consul sensed that enough was enough and he should put his pen aside and go in to his wife, or to his office. But how could he! Was he so quickly weary of communing with his Creator and Redeemer? To break off now would be as good as stealing from the Lord. No, no, as chastisement for such ungodly desires he quoted more long passages from Holy Scripture, prayed for his parents, his wife, his children, and himself, prayed as well for his brother, Gotthold—and finally, after one last Bible verse and a final threefold amen, he dusted the page with gold-sand and leaned back with a sigh of relief.

He now crossed his legs and paged slowly back through the notebook, stopping here and there to read a paragraph of dates and reflections in his own hand, and to take grateful pleasure in how God's hand had always and visibly blessed him in all dangers. He had been so ill with smallpox that everyone had given up all hope for his life, but he had been saved. Once—he had been a mere boy—he was watching the preparations for a wedding and, in the time-honored custom, a great deal of beer was being brewed at home, with a large beer-vat set up on end outside the door. Well, it toppled over, the base striking the boy with such force and making such a racket that neighbors came running to their doors, and it had taken six of them to set it right again. His head had been crushed under it, and blood was streaming down his whole body. He was carried into a shop, and since there was a little life left in him, a doctor and a surgeon were sent for. But his father was told to resign himself to God's will, that the boy couldn't possibly live. But listen to this: God the Almighty had blessed their treatment and brought him back to complete health!—And as he relived this accident, the consul reached again for his quill and wrote a last amen: "Yea, Lord, I shall praise Thee forever!"

Another time, when as a very young man he visited Bergen, God had saved him from drowning. "As it was high tide," it read, "and the ships of the northern line had arrived, we were having considerable difficulty working our way among the other boats to our landing, and it happened that I was standing on the edge of a scout, my feet braced against its oarlocks and my back against our ship, as I tried to bring the scout in closer; unfortunately the oaken oarlocks against which my feet are braced break off and I tumble into the water. I come up the first time, but no one is near enough to grab hold of me; I come up the second time, but the scout passes above my head. There were enough people who would gladly have rescued me, but they were busy shoving in an attempt to keep the scout and the ship from passing over me, and all their shoving would have been to no avail if at just that moment a line from one of the northern-line ships had not broke of its own, allowing the ship to swing out and away, and so by God's Providence I found some room, and although when I came up the third time only my hair was visible, nevertheless, since all those on the scout were lying with their heads out over water, some here, some there, one fellow at the bow managed to grab me by the hair, while I grasped his arm. But as he could not hold on, he screamed and bellowed so loudly that the others heard and came so quickly to grab him by the hips and held so tightly that he did not lose ground. And I, too, held fast, though his teeth were set in my arm, so that eventually he could help me as well. . . ." And then followed a very long prayer of thanksgiving, which the consul skimmed with tears in his eyes.

"Were I of a mind to disclose them," read another passage, "I could provide particulars of my passions. . . ." Well, the consul passed over that, and began instead to read a few lines here and there from the days of his marriage and the birth of his first child. The alliance, if he were honest, had not been exactly what one might call marriage for love. His father had tapped him on the shoulder and pointed out to him that the daughter of wealthy old Kröger would bring a handsome dowry into the firm; and he had concurred with all his heart and ever since had honored his wife as a companion entrusted to him by God.

It had been no different with his father's second marriage.

A proper man, a gentleman,
A man of splendid poses . . .

he was still warbling softly in the bedroom. It was regrettable that he had little use for all these old records and papers. He stood with both feet in the present and worried little about the family's past, although at one time he had contributed a few entries to the heavy gilt-edged notebook in his own somewhat ornate hand, most of them, however, concerning his first marriage.

The consul opened to pages already turning yellow and of stiffer, coarser paper than those he had added. Yes, Johann Buddenbrook's love for his first wife, the daughter of a merchant in Bremen, must have truly been touching, and the one brief year he had been allowed to spend at her side had apparently been the finest of his life. "*L'année la plus heureuse de ma vie*," it said, underscored with a sinuous line, despite the danger that Madame Antoinette might read it.

But then Gotthold had come along, and the child had been Josephine's undoing. The coarse paper revealed some curious remarks on the subject. Johann Buddenbrook appeared to have felt an honest and bitter hatred of this new creature from the moment his first brash movements began to cause his mother such terrible pain—to have hated him when he came into the world, healthy and lively, whereas Josephine had died, her bloodless head buried in her pillows, and never to have forgiven this unscrupulous intruder, growing up so robust and carefree, for the murder of his mother. The consul could not comprehend that. She died, he thought, while fulfilling the higher duty of women, and I would have tenderly transferred my love for her to the child she had paid for with her life, a gift left to me as she departed. His father, however, had seen in his eldest son only the person who had wickedly destroyed his happiness. Later, he had married Antoinette Duchamps, the daughter of a rich and highly respected Hamburg family, and the two had lived side by side, attentive and respectful of one another.

The consul paged back and forth in the notebook. He read, at the very end, the little entries about his own children, when Tom had had the measles and Antonie, jaundice, and how Christian had survived chickenpox; he read about the various trips to Paris, Switzerland, and Marienbad that he and his wife had taken, and then opened to the torn and foxed parchment pages that old Johann Buddenbrook, his father's father, had filled with elaborate curlicues executed in pale gray ink. These entries began with an extensive genealogy, tracing the family's main line—how at the end of the sixteenth century the oldest known Buddenbrook had lived in Parchim and his son had become an alderman in Grabau. How, later, another Buddenbrook, a merchant tailor by trade, had married a woman from Rostock, "had done very well"—this was underlined—and sired a remarkable number of children, some of whom, as fate would have it, lived, others of whom did not. And how another, who called himself Johan, had remained in Rostock as a merchant. And finally how after many years the consul's grandfather had arrived here to found their grain business. Dates were known and recorded for this ancestor: duly entered were the dates when he had a case of boils and when he had genuine pox; there were tidy entries for when he had fallen from the fourth story onto the drying-room floor, and lived to tell of it, although he struck a great many beams on the way down, and for when he had been delirious with a high fever. And he had added many a fine exhortation for his descendants, one sentence of which stood out because it was carefully framed and executed in tall Gothic script: "My son, show zeal for each day's affairs of business, but only for such that make for a peaceful night's sleep." And then came an elaborate proof that the old Wittenberg Bible was indeed his, and that it should be passed on to his firstborn and from him to *his* eldest son.

Consul Buddenbrook pulled the leather writing case to him in order to take out some of the other papers and scan them. There were very old, yellowed, tattered letters that worried mothers had written their sons working in foreign lands, on which those who received them had noted: "Received and taken to heart." There were certificates of citizenship, with the crest and seal of the free Hanseatic city, insurance policies, poems of congratulation, and requests to serve as a godparent. There were business letters, like those a son had written from Stockholm or Amsterdam to his father and partner, containing, along with the reassurance that the wheat was safe and secure, a touching request to extend greetings to his wife and children *at once*. There was a special diary the consul had kept during his trip through England and the Brabant, its cover displaying an etching of Edinburgh's castle and Grassmarket. There was the sad documentation of Gotthold's letters to his father, and finally, cheerfully capping it all, the latest festive poem by Jean Jacques Hoffstede.

He heard the sound of dainty, hasty chimes. Just above the secretary hung a painting in muted colors, a depiction of an old-fashioned marketplace and a church, and in its steeple, a real clock had just struck ten in its distinctive tones. The consul closed the case full of family records and carefully put it away in a back drawer of the secretary. Then he went across to the bedroom.

Here the walls were hung with dark fabric in the same large-flowered pattern used for the long draperies of the new mother's bed. A feeling of peace and convalescence, of triumph over fear and pain, hung in the air, along with the scents of eau de cologne and medicines, their traces blended by the gentle warmth of the stove. Only dim light filtered through the closed curtains.

Both grandparents were standing side by side, bent over the cradle and watching the sleeping child. The consul's wife, however, lay in bed, wearing an elegant lace jacket, her reddish hair perfectly coiffed, a happy smile playing over her rather pallid face. She put out her lovely hand to greet her husband, a gold bracelet tinkling at the wrist, and as was her habit she turned the palm upward as far as possible, which seemed to heighten the warmth of her gesture.

"Well, Bethsy, how are you feeling?"

"Splendid, splendid, my dear Jean!"

Her hand still in his, he turned toward his parents and lowered his face to the baby girl, who was breathing in rapid, noisy gasps, and for a whole minute he took in the warm, benign, touching fragrance she emitted. "God bless you," he said in hushed tones, kissing the brow of this little creature—whose tiny, wrinkled yellow fingers bore an awful resemblance to a chicken's claws.

"She drank and drank something wonderful," Madame Antoinette remarked. "Just look at the stupendous weight she's gained."

"Would you believe me if I say she looks like my Netty?" old Johann Buddenbrook said, his face absolutely radiant with happiness and pride. "Those flashing black eyes, the devil take me if . . ."

The old woman modestly waved this aside. "Ah, how can anyone speak of a resemblance at this point? You're going to church, Jean?"

"Yes, it's ten—high time we left, I'm just waiting for the children."

And the children could be heard now. They were storming noisily down the stairs, to the accompaniment of Klothilde's audible, chastening hisses; but when they entered the room, all dressed in their little fur coats—St. Mary's still bore winter's chill of course—they did so softly and cautiously, first of all because of their little sister, and second, because they had to compose themselves for Sunday worship. Their faces were red and excited. What a holiday! The stork, definitely a very strong, muscular stork, had brought all sorts of marvelous things besides their new sister: for Thomas, a new sealskin school bag; for Antonie, a large doll with real—how extraordinary!—real hair; a colorful picture book for well-behaved Klothilde, who in her quiet, grateful way was occupied almost exclusively with a bag of sweets that the stork had also brought; and for Christian, an entire puppet theater, complete with Sultan, Death, and the Devil.

They kissed their mother and were permitted one cautious peek behind the green silk curtains, and then, together with their father, who had thrown on his cape and picked up his hymnal, they quietly set out for church, the Sunday calm broken only by piercing cries from the newest member of the family, who had suddenly awakened.

2

EACH SUMMER—in June, or maybe even in May—Tony Buddenbrook would join her maternal grandparents in their house beyond the Burg Gate, and for her that was pure joy.

Life was good in the country, in the luxuriously furnished villa with all its barns, servants' quarters, carriage houses—and incredible orchards, vegetable gardens, and flower beds that fell away steeply toward the Trave River. The Krögers lived in grand style, and although this dazzling wealth was of a different sort from the solid if somewhat ponderous prosperity of the Buddenbrooks, it was obvious that everything at her grandparents' was always about two notches more splendid than at home; and that impressed young Miss Buddenbrook.

There could be no thought here of any chore in the house, let alone in the kitchen, whereas on Meng Strasse, although it was of no particular importance to her grandfather—or to her mother, for that matter—her father and grandmother all too frequently reminded her to help with the dusting, always holding up to her the example of humble, devout, and diligent Cousin Klothilde. The aristocratic tendencies of her mother's side of the family stirred within the young lady when she sat in her rocking chair and gave an order to the maid or the butler. In addition to them, the staff of the elder Krögers included two other serving girls and a coachman.

Say what you like, there is something pleasant about waking of a morning in a large bedroom with lovely, cheerful wallpaper and finding that the first thing you touch is a heavy satin quilt; and it is exceptional to have an early breakfast in a room opening onto a terrace, with the fresh morning air drifting in from the front garden through an open glass door, and to be served neither coffee, nor tea, but a cup of chocolate—yes, every morning, a cup of birthday chocolate, with a thick moist piece of pound cake.

True, except on Sundays, Tony had to eat her breakfast all alone, because it was not her grandparents' custom to appear until well after school began. And so, after she had devoured her cake and chocolate, she would pick up her school bag, skip across the terrace, and walk down through the well-tended front garden.

She was really very pretty, little Tony Buddenbrook was. Flowing from beneath her straw hat was a thick head of blond hair, curly of course, and turning darker with each passing year; and the slightly protruding upper lip gave a saucy look to her fresh little face with its lively gray-blue eyes, a sauciness repeated in her small, graceful body. There was self-assurance in the spring of her thin legs in their snow-white stockings. A great many people knew her, and they would greet Consul Buddenbrook's little daughter as she stepped through the garden gate onto the chestnut-lined lane. The vegetable lady, for instance, in her big straw bonnet with bright green ribbons, driving her little cart on the way from the village, would call out a friendly, "And a good mornin' to you, missy!"; and Matthiesen, a tall grain hauler in a black jacket and knee breeches, white stockings, and buckled shoes, would even doff his homely top hat respectfully as he passed.

Tony would stand and wait a while for her neighbor Julie Hagenström, with whom she usually walked to school. Julie, a girl with big bright black eyes and shoulders that she carried a little high, lived in the next villa, which was entirely overgrown with grapevines. Her father, Herr Hagenström, whose family was rather new to town, had married a young woman from Frankfurt—née Semlinger, by the way—a lady who had extraordinarily thick black hair and the largest diamond earrings in the city. Herr Hagenström, partner in the export firm of Strunck & Hagenström, took eager and ambitious interest in the affairs of the town, but his marriage had caused some astonishment among families with stricter traditions—the Möllendorpfs, the Langhalses, the Buddenbrooks. Quite apart from that, however, and despite his active participation on committees, councils, and boards of directors, he was not particularly well liked. He appeared determined to oppose the old established families every chance he got, to dispute their opinions with some wily argument or other, and to push through his own, establishing himself as more competent and indispensable than anyone else. Consul Buddenbrook once said of him: "Hinrich Hagenström is meddlesome and obstructive. He must be out to make me his personal target; he blocks me whenever he can. There was a scene today at the Central Committee for Paupers, and just a few days ago in the Finance Department. . . ." And Johann Buddenbrook added: "A damn troublemaker!" On another occasion both father and son came home to dinner angry and depressed. What had happened? Oh, nothing—they had lost a large consignment of rye to be shipped to Holland. Strunck & Hagenström had snapped it right from under their noses; a sly fox, that Hinrich Hagenström.

Tony had heard such remarks often enough so that she was not inclined to have an especially high opinion of Julie Hagenström. They walked to school together because they were neighbors, but usually they just annoyed each other.

"My father has a thousand thalers," Julie said, assuming she was telling a dreadful lie. "What about yours?"

Tony was struck dumb with envy and humiliation. Then, very calmly and casually, she said, "My chocolate tasted awfully good this morning. What do you drink for breakfast, Julie?"

"Oh, before I forget," Julie replied, "would you like one of my apples? You would? Well, I'm not going to give you one!" And she pursed her lips, and her black eyes grew moist at the sheer delight of it.

Sometimes Julie's brother Hermann, who was a few years older than she, walked with them to school. She had another brother, named Moritz, but he was sickly and was tutored at home. Hermann was blond, but his rather flat nose hung down over his upper lip. And because he breathed only through his mouth, was constantly smacking his lips.

"Nonsense!" he said. "Papa has a lot more than a thousand thalers." The interesting thing about him was that he never took a sandwich to school for his snack, but a lemon bun—a soft, oval milk pastry with raisins—and, to make matters worse, he would top it with tongue sausage or breast of goose. That was the sort of taste he had.

This was something new to Tony Buddenbrook. Lemon buns with breast of goose—that really must taste good, she thought. And whenever he let her peek into his lunch box, she would let it be known that she would like to try it.

One morning Hermann said, "I can't spare any today, Tony, but I'll bring another bun tomorrow, and it'll be yours if you'll give me something in return."

Well, the next morning, Tony walked out onto the lane and waited five minutes, but Julie still hadn't come. She waited one more minute, and then Hermann came out alone; he was smacking his lips softly and swinging his lunch box back and forth on its strap.

"Well," he said, "here's a lemon bun with breast of goose. There's not even any fat on it—nothing but lean meat. What'll you give me for it?"

"Let's see—would a shilling do?" Tony asked. They were standing in the middle of the lane.

"A shilling . . ." Hermann repeated; then he swallowed hard and said, "No, I want something else."

"What?" Tony asked. She was ready to pay anything for this delicacy.

"A kiss!" Hermann Hagenström cried, throwing both arms around Tony and kissing away blindly; but he never so much as touched her face, because she flung her head back with great skill, thrust her book bag against his chest with her left hand, and, summoning all her strength, gave his face three or four slaps with her right. He stumbled backward, but at just that moment his sister Julie dashed out from behind a tree and, like a little black devil hissing with rage, threw herself at Tony, tore off her hat, and scratched her cheeks unmercifully. That event more or less marked the end of their friendship.

Tony had certainly not denied young Hagenström his kiss out of shyness, by the way. She was a fairly cheeky young thing, whose high spirits had caused her parents, in particular the consul, considerable worry, and although she was bright enough and could quickly learn anything demanded of her in school, her behavior was so unsatisfactory that the principal, one Fräulein Agatha Vermehren, finally had to visit Meng Strasse and, though perspiring with embarrassment, politely suggested to the consul's wife that her young daughter be given a serious reprimand—for despite many well-intended warnings she had once again been guilty of a flagrant piece of mischief right out on the street.

There was nothing wrong with the fact that Tony knew everyone on the streets of town, and would chat with almost anyone; the consul was quite agreeable to that, because it revealed a sense of community and love of neighbor, rather than conceit. Together with Thomas, she would scramble about among the piles of oats and wheat spread out in the lofts of the warehouses along the Trave, she would chatter away with the workers and the clerks who sat in their little dim offices on the ground floor, she would even help hoist the sacks on the pulleys. She knew the butchers in white aprons who came walking down Breite Strasse carrying trays of meat; she knew the women who came in from the country with their tin cans of milk, and sometimes she even asked for a ride in their carts; she knew the gray-bearded master goldsmiths who worked in little wooden booths built into the arcades along the market square, knew the women who sold fish, fruit, and vegetables at the market and the porters idling on street corners, chewing tobacco. All fine and good.

But there was a pale, beardless man, of undetermined age and with a wistful smile, whose habit it was to take a morning stroll along Breite Strasse; and it was not his fault that at every sudden sound—if, for instance, someone shouted "ha!" or "ho!"—he would hop about in a kind of dance, and Tony would make him dance the moment she spotted him. And there was nothing nice about the distress that cries of "Madame Brella" or "Miss Mushroom" caused a tiny little woman with a large head, whose habit it was to protect herself in bad weather with a monstrous umbrella full of holes. And it was quite reprehensible for two or three like-minded girlfriends to appear at the door of the elderly lady who sold woolen dolls in the narrow alley off Johannis Strasse—although, admittedly, she did have the most curious red eyes—to tug at her bell as hard as they could, and, when the old woman came out, to ask in a deceptively friendly voice whether this might be the residence of Herr or Madame Spittoon, and then to run away screeching loudly. But Tony had done it all, and, so it seemed, with a perfectly good conscience. Because, if any of these tortured creatures dared to threaten her, it was a sight to behold how she would take a step back, toss her pretty head with its protruding upper lip, and utter a half-shocked, half-contemptuous "Pooh!," as if to say: "Just try and get me in trouble! If you don't happen to know, I am Consul Buddenbrook's daughter."

She walked about the town like a little queen who reserved to herself the right to be gracious or cruel, as the mood or fancy of the moment struck her.

3

JEAN JACQUES HOFFSTEDE had hit the nail on the head in his remarks about Consul Buddenbrook's two sons.

Thomas, who was destined from birth to be a merchant and the future owner of the firm, attended modern, scientific classes beneath the Gothic arches of the Old School. He was a clever, alert, and prudent young man, but he took immense enjoyment in Christian's wonderful gift for imitating the teachers of the humanities classes he attended, where he showed no less talent than his brother, although less seriousness. In particular Thomas enjoyed his imitation of Herr Marcellus Stengel, who worked very hard at instructing his students in singing, drawing, and similar diverting disciplines.

Herr Stengel, who always had a half-dozen marvelously sharpened pencils sticking out of his vest pocket, wore a foxy-red wig, an open buff-colored coat that reached almost to his ankles, and high stiff collars that all but covered his temples; he was a witty man who loved to make philosophical distinctions, such as: "You were asked to draw a line, my good boy, and what have you done? You have made a stroke!"—He said "struck" instead of "stroke." Or, to a lazy boy: "You'll be sitting in the fourth form not for years, but for years on end!"—And he pronounced "years" as "yeahs," and his "fourth form" sounded almost like "fuhth fuhm." His favorite lesson consisted in teaching them "The Woodland Green," during the singing of which several students were sent into the corridor so that they could echo, very softly and carefully, the last word of the chorus's intoned "We wander so merry through field and wood." Once, however, when this task was assigned to Christian Buddenbrook, his cousin Jürgen Kröger, and his friend Andreas

Gieseke, the fire chief's son, instead of executing a gentle echo, they sent the coal box tumbling down the stairs and were told to appear for detention at Herr Stengel's home at four that afternoon—which turned out to be a rather pleasant experience. Herr Stengel had forgotten all about the infraction and asked his housekeeper to bring one cup of tea each for the students Buddenbrook, Kröger, and Gieseke, and soon thereafter he let the young gentlemen go.

Indeed, under the friendly, watchful eye of a humane, snuff-taking old director, the splendid scholars who did their duty beneath the Gothic arches of the Old School—a convent school in bygone years—were harmless and well-intentioned men, united in their view that science and good cheer were not mutually exclusive categories, and they set about their work with benevolence and gusto. In the middle grades there was a certain Pastor Shepherd, a retired cleric who taught Latin, a tall man with brown whiskers and merry eyes, whose greatest joy in life was that his last name and his title were synonymous and who never tired of having his charges translate the Latin word "pastor." His favorite turn of phrase was "Inexhaustibly vacuous!," and no one ever found out if he himself was aware of the joke. And whenever he wanted to flabbergast his students totally, he demonstrated his mastery of the art of sucking his lips into his mouth and releasing them with a sound like a popping champagne cork. He loved to pace about his classroom with long strides and grew astoundingly animated as he laid out for each student the future course of his life, always with the manifest purpose of stimulating his imagination. Then he would return to work in earnest, which is to say, he listened to their recitations of some very clever verses he had composed for explaining difficult constructions and the rules of gender—"What's good for the goose is good for the gender," he would say—and then repeat the verses himself, stressing each rhythm and rhyme with inexpressible triumph.

Tom and Christian's boyhood years—nothing significant to report there. The sun shone in the Buddenbrook house; and down in the offices, business was excellent. Sometimes there was a thunderstorm, an occasional mishap like the following:

Herr Stuht, a tailor on Glockengiesser Strasse, whose wife bought used articles of clothing and so moved in the highest social circles—Herr Stuht, whose woolen shirt followed the contours of his astounding potbelly and fell down over his trousers—Herr Stuht had made two suits of clothes for the young Messrs. Buddenbrook, at a total cost of seventy marks *courant*; except that, at the express wish of the two boys, he promptly agreed to make out a bill for eighty, handing back the difference to them in cash. It was a little business deal—not exactly proper, but certainly not unusual, either. The mishap consisted in the fact that by the hand of some dark fate the entire matter came to light, so that Herr Stuht—having pulled on a black coat over his woolen shirt—had to appear in the consul's private office while Tom and Christian were sternly interrogated in his presence. Herr Stuht stood beside the consul's armchair, his legs spread somewhat but his head respectfully tipped to one side, and gave a speech to smooth things over, the burden of which was that this was "jist one o' them things," and that he would be happy to accept the seventy marks *courant* now that "things'd ended up in a mess." The consul was more than a little upset by their prank. After giving it serious consideration, however, he ended up raising his sons' allowances, for it was written: Lead us not into temptation.

It was obvious that greater hopes were to be placed in Thomas Buddenbrook than in his brother. He conducted himself sensibly, cheerfully, even-temperedly; whereas Christian seemed moody, capable on the one hand of the silliest comedy and on the other of behavior so odd that it would terrify his entire family.

They are sitting at the dinner table; the fruit has been served and is being enjoyed amid genial conversation. Suddenly Christian places a peach he has bitten into back on his plate, his face turns white, and his round, deep-set eyes grow larger and larger above his oversize nose.

"I shall never eat another peach," he says.

"Why not, Christian? What sort of nonsense is that? What's wrong?"

"Just imagine what would happen if . . . just by accident . . . I swallowed this big peach pit and it got stuck in my throat . . . and I couldn't get my breath . . . and I'd jump up and choke and die a horrible death, and then you'd all jump up . . ." And suddenly he adds a short groan, an "Oh!" of total terror, sits up erect in his chair, and turns to one side as if he is about to bolt.

His mother and Mamselle Jungmann do in fact leap to their feet.

"Good heavens—Christian, you haven't swallowed it, have you?!" For it really does look as if that is what has happened.

"No, no," Christian says, gradually calming down, "but what would happen if I *did*?"

The consul, who has also turned pale with fright, begins to scold him, and even his grandfather raps indignantly on the table, forbidding him any such foolish pranks. But for a long time afterward, Christian does not eat a single peach.

4

IT WAS NOT SIMPLY old age that caused Madame Antoinette Buddenbrook to take to her high four-poster in the bedroom on the mezzanine one cold January day, some six years after the family had moved into the house on Meng Strasse. The old woman had been hale and hearty to the end, carrying her head with its thick white curls proud and erect; she had continued to join her husband and children at all the town's principal banquets and had been as gracious a hostess as her elegant daughter-in-law at the parties the Buddenbrooks had themselves given. One day, however, she took ill with something rather undefinable; at first it was only a slight intestinal catarrh, for which Dr. Grabow prescribed a little squab and French bread, but then a colic set in with vomiting spells, which with incredible speed led to a general enervation, a state of gentle, but quite alarming, infirmity.

But after Dr. Grabow's brief but serious conversation with the consul on the stairs, after consultation with a second doctor—a newcomer to town, a stout man with a black beard and a gloomy expression—who now began to arrive and leave with Grabow, the physiognomy of the household changed, so to speak. People walked on tiptoe and whispered in earnest tones, and wagons were not permitted to roll through the passageway. Some new, alien, extraordinary thing seemed to have made an appearance, a secret that they all read in each other's eyes; the thought of death had been admitted into the house and now held silent sway in its spacious rooms.

But that did not mean they were idle, for visitors began to arrive. The dying woman's illness lasted fourteen or fifteen days, and after the first week her brother, old Senator Duchamps, came with his daughter; a few days later the consul's sister and her husband, the Frankfurt banker, made their appearance. These ladies and gentlemen were put up in the house, and Ida Jungmann had her hands full tidying up the various bedrooms and tending to good breakfasts of shrimps and port wine—the kitchen was busy with baking and roasting.

Upstairs Johann Buddenbrook sat beside her sickbed and gazed mutely into space, his brows raised, his lower lip drooping slightly, his Netty's limp hand held in his own. The wall clock emitted its muffled ticks, with long pauses in between, but the pauses between the sick woman's quick, shallow breaths were even longer. A nurse in black was busy at the table making the beef tea that they wanted to try to give her; now and then some member of the family entered soundlessly and then vanished again.

Perhaps the old man was thinking about how he had sat beside the bed of a dying wife that first time, forty-six years before, and perhaps he compared the savage despair that had blazed within him then with the pensive melancholy that showed in his eyes now as he gazed, an old man himself, at the altered, expressionless, and terrifyingly indifferent face of this old woman, who had brought him neither great happiness nor great pain, but who had stood beside him with such clever, good grace over these many long years, and whose life was also now ebbing away.

His thoughts were few; he merely looked back steadily, with a gentle shake of his head, at his life and at life in general, which suddenly seemed so distant and strange—all that unnecessary, noisy hustle and bustle, in whose midst he had stood, and which now was imperceptibly drawing away from him, a distant echo to which he turned an amazed ear. Sometimes he would say to himself in a low voice, "Curious. Curious."

Madame Buddenbrook had sighed her last, very brief, and peaceful sigh, the bearers had lifted her flower-bedecked coffin to carry it awkwardly from the dining room, where the funeral service had been held—but his mood did not change, he never wept once; what remained was that gentle, perplexed shake of the head, and "curious" became his favorite word, repeated with something almost like a smile. No doubt of it, Johann Buddenbrook was also nearing his end.

If he was sitting with the rest of the family, he was mute and seemed distracted, and if he happened to set little Clara on his knee, perhaps to sing her some old funny songs—"Let's ride through town on the omnibus" or "Looka that horsefly on the wall," for instance—he might suddenly fall silent, set his granddaughter back on the floor, and turn away, as if caught up in some long, half-unconscious train of thought, which ended then in "Curious!" and a shake of the head.

One day he said, "Jean—enough, don't you think?"

And at once there began to circulate through the city neatly printed documents, with two signatures affixed, announcing that Johann Buddenbrook, senior, begged leave to declare publicly that his advancing years obliged him to retire from his former business activities, and that as a result the firm Johann Buddenbrook, founded by his late father *anno* 1768, was to be transferred as of this date and under the same name, with all assets and liabilities, to his son and previous partner, Johann Buddenbrook, as its sole proprietor, for whom he begged a continuance of the confidence shown to him from all parties, signed, your obedient servant, Johann Buddenbrook, senior, whose signature would no longer be appended to the firm's correspondence.

From the moment this general announcement had been made, the old man refused to set a foot in the office, and his wistful apathy increased in the most startling fashion, so that by the middle of March, only two months after the death of his wife, it took no more than a case of spring sniffles to send him to his bed. And one night, as his family was gathered about his bed, the time had come for him to say to the consul, "Good luck—you hear, Jean? And chin up, *courage!*"

And to Thomas, he said, "Help your father."

And to Christian, "Make something of yourself!"

And then, gazing at them all, he fell silent and turned his back on them with a final "Curious."

To the very end he did not mention Gotthold, and when the

consul wrote to demand that he appear at the bedside of his dying father, the eldest son's only reply was silence. Very early the next morning, however, before the death announcements had even been sent out and as the consul was on his way downstairs to take care of a few urgent matters in the office, something remarkable happened—Gotthold Buddenbrook, owner of the linen firm Siegmund Stüwing & Co. of Breite Strasse, strode rapidly into the entrance hall. His short legs were clad in baggy trousers of a rough white-checked material. He strode up the stairs toward the consul, somehow managing simultaneously to knit his eyebrows and to raise them up under the brim of his gray hat.

"Johann," he said in a high, pleasant voice, without extending a hand to his brother, "how is he?"

"He passed away last night," the consul said with emotion and grasped the hand in which his brother was holding an umbrella. "He was the best of fathers."

Gotthold's brows sank so low that his eyelids closed. After a brief silence, he said with emphasis, "And nothing changed, Johann, even at the end?"

And the consul immediately pulled his hand away—indeed, he backed up a step—and his round, deep-set eyes flashed as he said, "Nothing."

Gotthold's eyebrows wandered back up under the brim of his hat, and with some exertion he focused his eyes on his brother. "And may I expect any justice from *you*?" he asked in a low voice.

The consul's gaze fell now; but then, without lifting his eyes, he lowered his hand in a decisive gesture and softly replied, "In this sad and solemn moment I gave you my hand as a brother. As for business matters, I have no choice but to respond as the director of a respected firm, whose owner, sole owner, I have become today. You can expect nothing from me that would contradict the duties incumbent upon me in *that* position. Any other feelings I may have must be left unstated."

Gotthold departed. But when it came time for the funeral—when the whole crowd of relatives, acquaintances, business friends, delegations of grain haulers, office personnel, and warehouse workers filled the rooms, stairwells, and corridors, and every hired carriage in the city stood below on Meng Strasse—he reappeared, to the genuine delight of the consul, even bringing along his wife and his three grown daughters: Friederike and Henriette, both very tall and very lanky, and Pfiffi, the youngest at eighteen, who was very short and very plump.

And after they had arrived at the grave, the Buddenbrook family plot at the edge of a little wood in the cemetery beyond the Burg Gate, and after the Reverend Kölling, pastor of St. Mary's, a robust man with a bulldog head and a rough manner of speaking, had praised the temperate life led by the deceased, a life pleasing to God, unlike that of "debauchers, gluttons, and drunkards"—an expression that caused many heads to shake among those who recalled the discretion displayed by old Pastor Wunderlich, only recently deceased—after all the solemnities and formalities had been completed and the seventy or eighty hired carriages began to roll back into town, Gotthold Buddenbrook offered to accompany the consul, because there was something he would like to say to him, man to man. And what do you know: sitting there next to his stepbrother in the back seat of the high, wide, overstuffed carriage, he crossed one short leg over the other, and proved quite conciliatory and cordial. He had come more and more to the realization, he said, that the consul had to proceed in this fashion, and that he did not wish to have hateful memories of his father. He would renounce his claims, all the more so since it was his intention to retire from business and live out his life quietly on his inheritance and whatever profits he might realize from the sale of his linen business, which no longer provided him any pleasure and was indeed not doing well enough for him to bring himself to invest in it any further.

And, with a pious inward glance to heaven, the consul thought, "His rebuke of his father hath brought him no blessing"; and Gotthold probably thought much the same thing.

On arriving at Meng Strasse, Gotthold went upstairs with his brother to the breakfast room, where both gentlemen, chilled from standing out in the spring air so long in only their dress coats, drank a cognac together. And, having exchanged a few polite and sober words with his sister-in-law and having given the children a pat on the head, Gotthold departed and was not seen again until the next "children's day" at the Krögers' country villa. He was already busy settling his affairs.

5

THERE WAS ONE THING that the consul regretted: that his father had not lived to see his eldest grandson join the firm, an event that occurred at Easter that same year.

Thomas was sixteen years old when he left school. He had grown a great deal in the last few years, and ever since his confirmation by Pastor Kölling, who had strongly urged him to be "temperate in all things," he had worn men's clothes, which made him look even taller. Around his neck hung the long gold watch chain that his grandfather had promised him, its fob a medallion that displayed the rather mournful family coat-of-arms: an irregularly hatched background, a bleak moor landscape, and a solitary, leafless willow beside a marsh. The signet ring with a green gemstone was even older, had presumably been worn by the very well-situated merchant tailor from Rostock, and the consul had inherited it along with the large Bible.

Thomas's resemblance to his grandfather had grown quite strong with time, as had Christian's to his father; most noticeably, he had the old man's round, firm chin and straight, well-chiseled nose. His light brown hair was parted on one side and fell back in two waves from his narrow, finely veined temples; in contrast, his long eyelashes and brows, one of which he liked to raise just the least bit, were unusually fair and colorless. He was composed and prudent in his gestures, in his manner of speech, even in his laugh, which revealed his rather bad teeth. He felt both excited and serious about his future profession.

Right after breakfast, the consul took him down to the offices. The day's solemn ceremonies began with a formal introduction to

Herr Marcus, the chief clerk, to Herr Havermann, the cashier, and to the other personnel as well, although he had long been friends with them all. For the first time, he sat in his swivel chair, diligently stamping, copying, and filing, and that afternoon his father also took him down to the Trave for a tour of the warehouses—the "Linden," the "Oak," the "Lion," and the "Whale"—and although Thomas had long been perfectly at home here, too, he was now presented as a co-worker.

He set to work with total devotion, imitating the quiet style and dogged industry of his father, who would often grind his teeth as he worked—and enter prayers for help in his diary. The task before them was to recover the considerable losses that the old man's death had meant for the "firm"—the very word was cloaked in a certain divinity. Late one evening, in the landscape room, the consul laid out a rather detailed account of their finances for his wife.

It was indeed very late, half past eleven, and the children, even Mamselle Jungmann, were asleep in their rooms down the hall; the third floor stood empty now and was used only occasionally for guests. The consul's wife was sitting on the yellow sofa, next to her husband, who was smoking a cigar and scanning the market quotations in the *Advertiser*. She was bent down over her silk embroidery, her lips moving slightly as she counted a row of stitches with her needle. Six candles were burning in the candelabrum on the dainty, gold-detailed sewing table beside her; the chandelier was not in use.

Johann Buddenbrook, now fast approaching his mid-forties, had visibly aged in the last few years. His little, round eyes seemed to lie deeper than ever; his large, aquiline nose stood out more sharply; and although the part in his hair was as precise as ever, it looked as if the ashy blond at his temples had been lightly dusted with a powder puff. His wife, however, was still in her late thirties, and, though never beautiful, she had preserved her radiant presence most admirably, and her soft white complexion with its scattered freckles had lost nothing of its delicacy. Her reddish, fashionably coiffed hair shone in the candlelight.

With just a hint of a sidelong glance from her pale blue eyes, she said, "I wanted to suggest something for you to consider, my dear

Jean. Would it not be a good idea to hire a butler? I've become quite convinced of it. When I think of my parents . . ."

The consul let his newspaper slip to his knees, and as he took the cigar from his mouth a certain vigilance came into his eyes—this meant spending money.

"Yes, my dear, my darling Bethsy," he began, stretching out these first words as long as possible to give himself time to put his objections in order. "A butler? Since the death of my beloved parents, we've kept all three girls working for us in the house, quite apart from Mamselle Jungmann, and it seems to me . . ."

"Oh, but the house is so large, Jean, it's simply dreadful. I'm always saying, 'Lina, my child, no one's dusted in the back building for such a long time,' and yet I don't want to demand too much of the girls, it keeps them huffing and puffing just to maintain everything nice and tidy up front here. A butler would be so nice for running errands and such. We could find some honest, unassuming country fellow. Oh, and I almost forgot Jean—Louise Möllendorpf is going to let her Anton go. I've seen him serve at dinner, he's very reliable."

"I must admit," the consul said, shifting somewhat uneasily back and forth, "that the whole idea comes as a surprise. We'll not be going out in society for a while, and we're not giving any dinners ourselves."

"No, no; but we do have guests quite often, and that's not my fault, dear Jean, though you know how much I do enjoy it. A business friend of yours visits in town, you ask him to dinner, he's not yet taken a room at an inn, and so of course he spends the night here with us. Or some missionary may spend a week with us. The week after next, we're expecting Pastor Mathias from Cannstatt. Well, in a nutshell, the salaries are so insignificant. . . ."

"But they add up, Bethsy! We have four people on the household payroll, and don't forget all the men employed by the firm."

"Can it be we really cannot afford a butler?" Elisabeth asked with a little smile, tilting her head slightly in her husband's direction. "When I think of the servants my parents have . . ."

"Your parents, dear Bethsy! Well, now, I really must ask if you have any clear idea of the state of our finances?"

"No, Jean, it's true I have no real detailed understanding . . . ."

"Well, that's easily taken care of," the consul said. He sat up erect on the sofa, crossed his legs, took a puff on his cigar, and, squinching his eyes a little, began marshaling the figures with exceptional proficiency.

"To be brief: At one time, before my sister's marriage, my dear departed father had a nice round sum of 900,000 marks *courant*, that is, as I need not say, apart from real estate and the intangible value of the firm. Eighty thousand went to Frankfurt as a dowry, and 100,000 was spent setting up Gotthold in business: which leaves 720,000. Then came the purchase of this house, which, despite what we got for the old place on Alf Strasse, cost us, including improvements and new furnishings, 100,000: leaving 620,000. Then 25,000 was sent to Frankfurt in compensation: leaving 595,000. And that would have been the state of affairs at Father's death had not all these expenses been offset over the years by earnings of around 200,000 marks *courant*. His total estate, therefore, came to 795,000. At which point another 100,000 was sent Gotthold's way, and 267,000 to Frankfurt: leaving, if one discounts the few thousand marks *courant* Father left in his will to the Holy Ghost Hospital, the Businessmen's Widows Fund, and so forth, approximately 420,000, plus another 100,000 from your dowry. That more or less describes, in round figures, apart from all sorts of minor fluctuations, the state of our finances. We are not so uncommonly rich, my dear Bethsy, and one must keep in mind that, even as business of late has dropped off, our business expenses have remained the same and cannot be reduced, given the scale on which the firm operates. Were you able to follow me?"

His wife nodded with some hesitation; her embroidery still lay in her lap. "Quite well, my dear Jean," she said, although she had not understood everything and certainly did not see why all these huge sums should prevent her from hiring a butler.

The consul drew on his cigar till it glowed, leaned his head back, and let out the smoke. Then he continued: "You're thinking, in fact, that, come the day your dear parents are called to their heavenly reward, we can expect a handsome sum, and you're quite right. All the same—we cannot be so imprudent as to depend too much on that. I know that your father has had some rather painful losses—due, as we all are aware, to your brother, Justus. Now, Justus is a very charming fellow, but not exactly a good businessman, and he has also had some setbacks that were not his fault. He has met with very costly losses from some of his customers, and as a result of his weakened capital position, he had to borrow money at very high interest from the banks, and your father has had to spring into the breach several times with significant sums to prevent even greater misfortune. That sort of thing cannot be repeated, and yet I fear it will be, because—forgive me, Bethsy, for speaking so candidly—that certain *savoir faire* that we all find so agreeable about your father, who no longer has anything to do with the business, does not stand your brother in good stead as a businessman. You know what I mean—he is *not* exactly prudent, is he? A little flighty, a little given to putting on airs. Certainly your parents lack for nothing, and no one could be more delighted by that than I. They live life in splendid style—as their circumstances permit. . . ."

His wife smiled indulgently; she knew her husband's prejudices against the elegant tastes of her family.

"That's all," he added, laying what remained of his cigar in the ashtray. "For my part, I shall place my ultimate trust in the Lord, that He will keep me healthy and strong, so that by His grace I can restore the firm's fortunes to their previous solid position. I hope that you clearly understand the matter now, dear Bethsy?"

"Perfectly, Jean, perfectly," Elisabeth was quick to reply, for she had given up entirely on a butler for this evening. "But let's go to bed, shall we? It has grown quite late."

In any case, a few days later the consul came in from the office in a good mood, and it was decided over dinner that they would hire the Möllendorpfs' Anton.

6

WE'LL PUT TONY in a boarding school. Fräulein Weichbrodt's would be best," said Consul Buddenbrook, and he was so definite that that was what was done.

Thomas was proving his talents in the office, Clara was growing up quite nicely, and poor Klothilde had an appetite that would please most anyone—but they were less satisfied, as has been hinted, with Tony and Christian. As far as the latter was concerned, the least of the problems was that he was required to drink coffee with Herr Stengel almost every afternoon—although one day Frau Buddenbrook had finally had enough and sent an ornate note to that gentleman requesting his presence on Meng Strasse for the purpose of a conference. Herr Stengel appeared in his Sunday wig, wearing his highest stiff collar, his vest studded with pencils sharpened to darts, and sat with the consul's wife in the landscape room, while Christian eavesdropped on the conversation from the dining room. The excellent pedagogue expanded eloquently, though somewhat nervously, on his opinions, spoke of the important difference between a "line" and a "stroke," mentioned the lovely woodland green as well as the coal box, making frequent use during the course of his visit of the word "consequently," which seemed to him aptly suited to his elegant surroundings. After fifteen minutes, the consul appeared, chased Christian away, and expressed to Herr Stengel his keen regret that his son had given him cause for dissatisfaction.

"Oh, by no means, Herr Consul, heaven forbid! Young Mr. Buddenbrook has a sharp mind, is an exuberant lad. And consequently . . . a little high-spirited, if I may be permitted to say so, hmm . . . and consequently . . ."

The consul politely gave him a tour of the house, at which point Herr Stengel took his leave. But, no, that was not the worst of it.

The worst of it was an incident that had only recently come to their ears. One evening Christian Buddenbrook and one of his good friends were permitted to attend a performance of Schiller's *William Tell* at the municipal theater. The role of Tell's son Walter, however, was being played by a young woman, a certain Demoiselle Meyer–de la Grange, and she was the cause of the incident. Whether it was appropriate to her role or not, she was in the habit of wearing a diamond brooch on stage—the jewels were notoriously genuine and generally known to have been the gift of Consul Peter Döhlmann, the son of Döhlmann the lumber merchant on Erste Wall Strasse, just outside the Holsten Gate. Consul Peter was one of the gentlemen known around town as *suitiers*—so, too, for example, was Justus Kröger—which implied that his style of life was rather loose. He was married and even had a little daughter, but for some time now he had been separated from his wife and lived quite the bachelor life. The fortune his father had left him, apart from the business which he still ran after a fashion, had been quite considerable. But it was rumored that he was already living off the capital. He spent most of his time and took his breakfast at the Club or the Rathskeller, but he could often be seen wandering the streets at four in the morning and took frequent business trips to Hamburg. But, above all, he was such a passionate lover of the theater that he never missed a performance and took a personal interest in the players. Demoiselle Meyer–de la Grange was the latest in this year's series of actresses whom he had favored with diamonds.

The point is that the young lady—who was wearing her diamond brooch on this occasion as well—looked so charming and was so touching in the role of Walter Tell that Christian Buddenbrook was moved to tears; indeed, he was quite swept away, resulting in the kind of gesture that can arise only out of strong emotion. During intermission he paid one mark and eight and a half shillings for a bouquet from the flower shop across the street, and with it in hand, this fourteen-year-old whippersnapper with a big nose and small, deep-set eyes marched backstage and, since no one was there to stop him, discovered Fräulein Meyer–de la Grange engaged in conversation with Consul Peter Döhlmann outside the door to her dressing room. At the sight of Christian waltzing up with his bouquet, the consul almost stumbled into the wall, he laughed so hard.

This newest *suitier*, however, presented his compliments to Walter Tell with a very serious face, handed him or her the flowers, rocked his head slowly back and forth, and said in a voice so sincere that it sounded as if he were in great pain, "Your acting is simply beautiful, Fräulein."

"Damned if it ain't Krischan Buddenbrook!" Consul Döhlmann exclaimed in his thick Plattdeutsch.

Fräulein Meyer–de la Grange, however, raised her pretty eyebrows and asked, "The son of Consul Buddenbrook?" Then she sympathetically patted her newest admirer's cheek.

Such were the facts that Peter Döhlmann shared with his fellows at the Club that same evening and that spread like wildfire all over town, even reaching the ear of the school director, who in turn asked to speak with Consul Buddenbrook about the matter. And how did he take it? He was less angry than simply overwhelmed in his distress. He was an almost broken man as he sat down in the landscape room to tell his wife about it.

"He's our son, and look how he's turning out."

"Good heavens, Jean, your father would have laughed about it. And if you tell my parents about it this Thursday, Papa will find it terribly amusing."

The consul flared up. "Ha! Right! I have no doubt it will amuse him, Bethsy! He will enjoy hearing how his frivolity and irreverent notions have been passed on not only to Justus, that *suitier*, but quite obviously to one of his grandsons as well. Damnation, you simply force me to say such things! He goes to see this—person! Spends his allowance on this harlot! No, he doesn't know what he's doing; but the tendency is there! The tendency is there!"

Yes, it was a serious matter; and the consul was all the more outraged when it turned out that Tony, as noted, was not behaving all too well, either. True, with time she had ceased making the pale man dance or visiting the doll lady; but she had a way of tossing her head that was getting saucier and saucier, and she exhibited, especially after spending a summer in the country with her grandparents, a serious proclivity to be vain and haughty.

One day the consul surprised her, much to her annoyance, reading Clauren's *Mimili* with Mamselle Jungmann; he thumbed through the book—and it was closed for good. A short time later it came out that Tony—Antonie Buddenbrook—had gone for a walk beyond the town gates with a young high-school friend of her brother's, just the two of them. Frau Stuht, the same woman who moved in the highest social circles, had seen them and happened to mention to the Möllendorpfs, from whom she was buying some used clothing, that Mamselle Buddenbrook was getting to be quite grown up. And the wife of Senator Möllendorpf had merrily repeated the story to the consul. The walks were forbidden. But then it was learned that Mademoiselle Tony was retrieving notes from a poorly plastered-over hollow in the old tree just outside the Burg Gate, and was leaving a few notes there herself, all of them either from or addressed to that same high-school student. Once this came to light, it seemed imperative that she be placed under the strict supervision of a boarding school, the one run by Fäulein Weichbrodt, Mühlenbrink 7.

7

Therese Weichbrodt was hunchbacked, so hunchbacked that she was not much taller than a table. She was forty-one years old, but, having never set much store by external appearances, she dressed like a woman in her sixties. Little cushions of gray curls at her ears were topped by a bonnet, its green ribbons dangling over her childlike shoulders; and she had never been known to spruce up her homely black dress—except for a large oval brooch with a fancy porcelain miniature of her mother.

Little Fräulein Weichbrodt had clever and piercing brown eyes, a gently arching nose, and thin lips that she could press together with great determination. Her small body and all its movements were certainly droll enough, and yet the general impression she left commanded respect. This was primarily due to her use of language. When she spoke, it was with spirited thrusts of her lower jaw and rapid, insistent shakes of her head, each consonant carefully stressed, each word exact, clear, definite, and free of every dialect. But she exaggerated her vowels to such an extent that, for example, she did not say "butter," but "botter," sometimes even "booter," and called her obstreperous yapping dog "Booby" instead of "Bobby." When she told one of her students, "Doon't bee seelly, chawld!," while rapping the table with the knuckle of her index finger—that left an impression, no doubt of it. And when Mademoiselle Popinet, the French girl, would take much too much sugar for her coffee, Fräulein Weichbrodt had a way of eyeing the ceiling, playing an imaginary piano on the tablecloth, and remarking, "Take the whool sugarbool, I soorly woold!"—and Mademoiselle Popinet would turn bright red.

As a child—my God, how tiny she must have been as a child—Therese Weichbrodt had called herself "Sesame," and had retained this mutation of her name, allowing the better and more studious of her charges, both boarders and day students alike, to call her that. "Call me 'Sesame,' child," she said to Tony Buddenbrook on the very first day, giving her a little kiss on the forehead that made a soft popping sound. "I prefer it." Her older sister, Madame Kethelsen, however, was called Nelly.

Madame Kethelsen, who was somewhere in the vicinity of forty-eight, had been left penniless by her late husband, and now lived in a little room on the top floor of her sister's house and took her meals with the students. She dressed in much the same fashion as Sesame, but unlike her was extremely tall. She wore woolen warmers at her gaunt wrists. She was not a teacher, had not the least notion of how to be strict—she was harmless and quietly cheerful by nature. If one of Fräulein Weichbrodt's charges played a joke on someone, she would laugh aloud in her amiable way, so heartily that it almost sounded like a wail, until Sesame would rap insistently on the table and cry, "Nelly!"—though it sounded more like "Nally!"—intimidating her into silence.

Madame Kethelsen obeyed her younger sister, let herself be scolded like a child, and the fact was that Sesame felt true disdain for her. Therese Weichbrodt was a well-read—indeed, almost learned—spinster, whose life was a series of small, earnest battles to maintain the faith of her childhood, her optimistic piety, and the conviction that she would one day be recompensed in the great beyond for her hard and lackluster life. Madame Kethelsen, however, was uneducated, a woman of innocent and simple temperament. "Sweet Nelly," Sesame would say, "my God, what a child she is, has never had a doubt in her life, has never known the struggle of faith—she's so happy." Such words betrayed equal portions of contempt and envy—a definite, though forgivable, weakness in Sesame's character.

The brick-red suburban house was surrounded by a prettily tended garden, and its main floor, set well above the foundation, was taken up by classrooms and the dining room; bedrooms were located on the second floor and even in the attic. Fräulein Weichbrodt did not have many charges, for she took only older girls and provided just three years of instruction, even for her day students; Sesame was also very strict about admitting only the daughters of the very best families. Tony Buddenbrook was, as noted, received with a display of affection; indeed, for that evening's dinner Therese made her "bishop's punch," a red, sweet libation that was drunk cold and in whose preparation she was a master. "A leetle moore beeshop?" she asked with an amiable shake of her head—and it sounded so tempting that no one turned her down.

Fräulein Weichbrodt sat atop two sofa cushions at the head of the table and reigned over the meal with vigor and discretion; she held her deformed little body rigidly erect, rapped vigilantly on the table, cried "Nally!" and "Booby!," and with a single glance managed to shame Mademoiselle Popinet, who was about to misappropriate all the aspic served with the cold veal roast. Tony had been assigned a place between two other boarding students: Armgard von Schilling, a blond, sturdy girl, the daughter of a Mecklenburg country squire; and Gerda Arnoldsen from Amsterdam, an elegant and exotic presence with heavy chestnut hair, close-set brown eyes, and a pale, beautiful, and slightly haughty face. Chattering away across from her was the French girl, who looked like a Negress with her monstrous gold earrings. At the foot of the table sat another boarding student, Miss Brown, a haggard English girl with a sour expression.

With the aid of Sesame's "bishop's punch," Tony quickly became acquainted with them all. Mademoiselle Popinet had had another nightmare last night—*ah, quelle horreur!* She usually screamed, " 'elp! 'elp! Thiefs, thiefs!," sending them all leaping from their beds. It also came out that Gerda Arnoldsen did not play the piano like the other girls, but the violin, and that her papa—her mother was no longer alive—had promised her a genuine Stradivarius. Tony had no talent for music—like most Buddenbrooks and all Krögers. She could not even identify the chorales they played at St. Mary's.—Oh, the organ in the Nieuwe Kerk in Amsterdam had a *vox humana*, a human voice, that sounded simply marvelous! Armgard von Schilling talked about the cows at home.

From the first moment, it was Armgard who made the greatest

impression on Tony, and that was because Armgard was the first girl she had ever actually known from a noble family. To be called *von* Schilling, how wonderful that must be! Her parents had the most beautiful old house in town, and her grandparents were prominent people; but their names were simply "Buddenbrook" and "Kröger," and that was a dreadful shame. Armgard's noble status made the granddaughter of the stylish Lebrecht Kröger flush with admiration; but secretly she sometimes thought that that splendid syllable *von* would actually suit her far better—because, good heavens, Armgard hadn't the vaguest how lucky she was. She walked around with those good-natured blue eyes, that heavy braid, that broad Mecklenburg accent—and never gave it a thought. She wasn't at all elegant, didn't make the slightest claim to be, hadn't any notion what elegance was. But the word "elegant" was firmly fixed in Tony's little head, and she was most emphatic about applying it to Gerda Arnoldsen.

Gerda was a little superior and there was something intriguing and foreign about her; despite Sesame's objections, she liked to do up her splendid reddish tresses in striking ways, and a lot of the girls found her violin playing *silly*, a word that implied very severe condemnation. And yet they had to agree with Tony that Gerda Arnoldsen was an elegant young lady—the impression she made, so advanced for her age, her little habits, the things she owned, all very elegant. For example, the ivory toilet set from Paris, which Tony knew enough to admire in particular, since her home was filled with all sorts of grand treasures that her parents or grandparents had brought back from Paris.

The three young girls quickly became fast friends, they attended the same classes and lived together in the largest bedroom on the second floor. They were sent to bed at ten, and what amusing and cozy times they had chatting as they undressed—in low voices, of course, since next door Mademoiselle Popinet was already dreaming of burglars. Her roommate was little Eva Ewers, a native of Hamburg, whose father was a collector and connoisseur of the arts who had moved to Munich.

The striped brown blinds were pulled, the low lamp was burning under its red shade on the table, the faint scent of violets and freshly laundered clothes filled the room—the mood was languid and hushed, one of dreamy, carefree weariness.

"Good heavens," Armgard said, sitting on the edge of her bed, half undressed, "Dr. Neumann is such a fine lecturer. He just walks into the classroom, stands beside the desk, and starts rattling away about Racine."

"He has a fine high forehead," Gerda remarked as she combed her hair by candlelight in front of the mirror between the two windows.

"Yes, he does!" Armgard quickly responded.

"And you only mentioned him, Armgard, because that's just what you wanted to hear. You're always gazing at him with your big blue eyes as if . . ."

"Are you in love with him?" Tony asked. "I simply can't get this shoelace untied. Gerda, *please*. That does it! Now. Are you in love with him, Armgard? Marry him, then; it would be a very good match, he'll be a professor someday."

"Aren't you horrid! I'm not in love with him at all. I'm certainly not going to marry some teacher. It has to be a country gentleman."

"A nobleman?" Tony was holding a stocking in one hand; she let the hand fall and gazed thoughtfully and directly at Armgard.

"I don't know yet. But he'll have to have a large estate. Oh, you don't know how I look forward to that, girls. I'll be up at five, and I'll oversee everything." She pulled her blanket up and gazed dreamily at the ceiling.

"In her mind's eye she can see five hundred cows," Gerda said, staring at her friend's reflection in the mirror.

Tony was not talked out yet; but she let her head fall back onto her pillow, laced her hands behind her neck, and pensively stared at the ceiling as well.

"I'll marry a merchant, of course," she said. "He'll have to have lots of money, so that we can furnish the house elegantly. I owe that much to my family and the firm," she added very soberly. "You'll see, that's exactly what I'll do."

Gerda had finished with her hair and was now brushing her broad, white teeth, holding her small ivory mirror in the other hand.

"In all *likelihood*, I shall never get married," she said with some effort, because of the peppermint powder in her mouth. "I can't see why I should. The idea doesn't appeal to me at all. I'll go back to Amsterdam and play duets with Papa, and then later I'll live with my married sister."

"What a shame!" Tony cried impulsively. "Really, what a shame, Gerda! You should marry someone from here and stay on forever. Why, you could marry one of my brothers, for example."

"The one with the big nose?" Gerda asked, and yawned, releasing a dainty, casual sigh, but covering her mouth with her hand mirror.

"Or the other one, it doesn't matter. Lord, you could decorate your house so splendidly. But you have to use Jakobs, the upholster on Fisch Strasse. He has very elegant taste. And I would visit you every day."

But then they heard Mademoiselle Popinet's voice: "*Ah! voyons, mesdames.* To bed, *s'il vous plaît*. It's too late to get married tonight."

Tony spent her Sundays and holidays on Meng Strasse or out at her grandparents' villa. What fun it was on a lovely Easter morning to search for eggs and marzipan rabbits in the Krögers' vast gardens. And then there were the summer vacations at the shore, staying at a resort hotel, eating at the table d'hôte, swimming, and riding donkeys. And some years, when the consul had business to attend to, they made longer journeys. But, above all, there was Christmas, with three exchanges of gifts: at home, at her grandparents', and in the evening at Sesame's, when the "bishop's punch" flowed freely. The most splendid time, however, was always on Christmas Eve at home, for the consul insisted that the Holy Feast of the Christ Child be celebrated in an atmosphere of stately radiance. Once they had all solemnly gathered in the landscape room, while the servants and all sorts of poor and old people had crowded into the entrance hall downstairs to have their blue and ruddy hands shaken by the consul, the choirboys of St. Mary's would strike up a carol in four-part harmony—it was so festive that it simply made her heart pound. Then, with the scent of fir drifting through the cracks of the closed high white doors, her mother would read the Christmas story from the old family Bible with its huge funny letters; and once the last echoes of a second carol had died away outside, they would begin singing "O, Tannenbaum" as they moved in solemn procession through the columned hallway and into the dining room, where the wallpaper had white statues and the radiant, fragrant tree reached to the ceiling and was decorated with white lilies and flickering candles and the table, laden with gifts, reached from the windows to the door. Meanwhile Italians were playing barrel organs outside in the snow-covered streets, and from far off you could hear the hubbub from the Christmas market in the town square. Except for little Clara, all the children joined the adults in the columned hall for a late supper at a table heaped with carp and turkey with dressing.

It should also be mentioned that Tony Buddenbrook visited two estates in Mecklenburg during these years. She spent a couple of weeks one summer at the estate of Armgard's father, Herr von Schilling, which lay on the coast just across the bay from Travemünde. And, on a second occasion, she joined her cousin Thilda at the estate that Herr Bernhardt Buddenbrook was in charge of. The estate was called "Grudging," and didn't bring in a penny; but it was not to be despised as a vacation spot.

And so the years meandered along, and, all in all, Tony's adolescence was a happy time.

PART THREE

*(Dedicated to my sister Julia,
in memory of our bay on the Baltic)*

1

One June afternoon, shortly after five o'clock, the family was sitting in the garden in front of the "Portal," where they had taken their coffee. They had set the light, rustic, stained-wood furniture on the lawn, because it was too warm and close inside the summerhouse, a single white room whose only decoration was a tall mirror framed by fluttering birds and two enameled French doors at the rear—which weren't real; if you looked closely you could see that the handles were just painted on.

The sparkling coffee service was still on the table, around which they sat in a semicircle: the consul, his wife, Tony, Tom, and Klothilde—sour-faced Christian was a little off to one side, memorizing Cicero's second oration against Catiline. The consul was busy with his cigar and the *Advertiser*. His wife had laid her embroidery in her lap and smiled now as she watched little Clara search the lawn for violets with Ida Jungmann, because now and then you could find them there. Her chin propped in both hands, Tony was reading Hoffmann's *Serapion Brethren*, while Tom tickled the back of her neck very circumspectly with a blade of grass, which she wisely chose not to notice. And Klothilde, looking skinny and old-maidish in her flowery cotton frock, was reading a story entitled "Blind, Deaf, and Dumb—and Happy Nonetheless," all the while scraping up cookie crumbs into little piles on the tablecloth, then transferring them carefully in a five-fingered grip to her mouth.

The sky and its few white stagnant clouds began to pale. The late-afternoon sun enhanced the color of the garden's tidy symmetry of paths and flower beds. The fragrance of mignonettes lining the beds ebbed and flowed on the breeze.

"Well, Tom," the consul said, taking his cigar from his mouth, "it looks as if that sale of rye to van Henkdom & Co. that I told you about is going to go through." The consul was in a good mood.

"What's his offer?" Thomas asked with interest and stopped teasing Tony.

"Sixty thalers a thousand kilos. Not bad, is it?"

"That's excellent!" Tom knew that was a very good price.

"Tony, your pose is not exactly *comme il faut*," Elisabeth remarked, and Tony took one elbow from the table, without raising her eyes from her book.

"It doesn't matter," Tom said. "She can sit however she likes, she'll always be Tony Buddenbrook. It's no contest—she and Thilda are the fairest in the family."

Klothilde was embarrassed to death. "O Lord, Tom—?" she said, and it was unbelievable how she could draw out those three brief syllables. Tony endured the remark in silence—it was no use, Tom was quicker than she. He would be sure to have a comeback that would make them all laugh. She merely took a deep breath through her flared nostrils and shrugged. But when her mother began to talk about the ball coming up at Consul Huneus's and mentioned something about new patent-leather shoes, Tony took her other elbow off the table and joined eagerly in the conversation.

"Talk, talk, talk," Christian wailed pitifully. "I'm having a terrible time with this. I wish I were a businessman, too."

"Right, you want to be something different every day," Tom said. At this point Anton came across the yard; they all watched his approach expectantly—there was a calling card on the tea tray.

"Grünlich, Commercial Agent," the consul read. "From Hamburg. A pleasant man, pastor's son, people speak well of him. There's some business I have with him at the moment. . . . Anton, ask the gentleman—is it all right with you, Bethsy?—if he would like to join us."

A thirty-two-year-old man of medium height came across the garden, hat and cane in the same hand, his stride rather short, his head thrust forward; he wore worsted gloves and a yellow-green wool coat of long cut. Under a shock of very blond but thinning hair was a rosy, smiling face, with a conspicuous wart at one side of the nose. His chin and upper lip were clean-shaven, but, following the English fashion, he had long side-whiskers—of a striking tawny, golden color. While still at some distance, he made a sweeping gesture of courtesy with his large pale gray hat. And now, approaching with one last, long stride, he bowed to them all by executing a semicircle with his upper body.

"I am disturbing you by breaking into your family circle like this," he said in a soft voice, both refined and reserved. "One reads good books, one converses the afternoon away pleasantly. I really must beg your pardon."

"You're quite welcome here, my good Herr Grünlich," replied the consul, who along with his sons had stood up to shake their guest's hand. "It's a pleasure to greet you outside the office, surrounded here by my family. Bethsy, this is Herr Grünlich, a man I'm proud to do business with. My daughter, Antonie. My niece, Klothilde. You already know Thomas. This is my other son, Christian, who's still in school."

At each name, Herr Grünlich responded with a bow. "As I said," he went on, "I really don't want to intrude. I've a business matter to discuss, and if I might ask the good consul to join me for a walk in the garden . . ."

Elisabeth replied, "We would take it as a favor if you would not rush off with my husband on business and would put up with our society for a while. Please, have a seat."

"A thousand thanks," Herr Grünlich said, visibly touched. Tom had brought a chair over to him, and he perched himself erect on its edge, hat and cane on his knees, one hand stroking his whiskers, and he coughed a little cough that sounded like "Huh-uh-hmm!"—all of which seemed to say, "So, that's the introduction. Now what?"

The consul's wife began the main conversation. "You're from Hamburg?" she asked, tilting her head to one side, her handiwork resting in her lap.

"Indeed I am, Madame Buddenbrook," Herr Grünlich replied with another bow. "My residence is in Hamburg, but I am on the road a great deal. There's simply so much to be done, my business is going so extremely well . . . ahem, very well, I must say."

Elisabeth raised her eyebrows and shaped her mouth as if it were about to emit a respectful, "Is that right?"

"My very existence is one of unceasing activity," Herr Grünlich added, turning halfway toward the consul and coughing another little cough, when he noticed Fräulein Antonie's gaze resting on him, her eyes cold and measuring—the kind of look with which young ladies size up young men, but which threatens at any moment to resolve itself into disdain.

"We have relatives in Hamburg," Tony remarked, for something to say.

"The Duchamps," the consul explained, "my late mother's family."

"Oh, I'm perfectly aware of the connection," Herr Grünlich hastened to say. "I have the honor of a slight acquaintance with the family. Excellent people, one and all, such heart, such intellect. Ahem. Indeed, it would be a better world if all families had such qualities. One finds in that family such faith, such charity, such sincere piety, in short, the very ideal of true Christianity; and yet all of it united with a cosmopolitan refinement and brilliant elegance that I personally find quite charming, Madame Buddenbrook."

Tony thought: How does he know my parents so well? He tells each of them exactly what they want to hear.

But the consul responded with approval: "A combination of qualities quite becoming to any gentleman."

And his wife could not resist extending their guest her hand, her gold bracelet tinkling as she turned the palm upward as far as possible to heighten the gesture's warmth. "You speak my deepest sentiments, Herr Grünlich," she said.

Herr Grünlich now made another bow, settled himself in place again, stroked his whiskers, and coughed as if to say, "Let us continue."

The consul's wife mentioned the dreadful days Herr Grünlich's hometown had experienced in May of '42. "Dreadful indeed," Herr Grünlich responded, "the fire was a terrible calamity, a heartbreaking ordeal. Damages of 135 million, and the figures are a rather precise calculation. Though, for my part, I can only express my deepest gratitude to Providence that I was not inconvenienced in the least. The principal conflagration was in the parishes of St. Peter and St. Nicholas. . . . What an enchanting garden," he said, interrupting himself, while thanking the consul for an offered cigar, "and so uncommonly large for a garden in town. And what a burst of floral color. Oh, gracious, I must admit my weakness for flowers and nature in general. Those poppies there add a rare, ornamental touch."

Herr Grünlich praised the house's elegant grounds, praised the town in general, praised the consul's cigar as well, had a kind word for everyone.

"Might I be so bold as to inquire what you are reading, Mademoiselle Antonie?" he asked with a smile.

For some reason Tony suddenly scowled and replied, without looking at Herr Grünlich, "Hoffmann's *Serapion Brethren*."

"You don't say! An author who achieved the most extraordinary things," he remarked. "But I beg your pardon—I've forgotten the name of your second son, Madame Buddenbrook."

"Christian."

"A beautiful name. I do love, if I may say so"—and Herr Grünlich turned again now to the head of the household—"those names that betray in and of themselves the faith of those who bear them. The name Johann is, I am aware, handed down in your family from generation to generation . . . and who would not be immediately reminded of our Lord's beloved disciple. If I may be permitted to mention it," he continued eloquently, "like most of my forebears, I am named Bendix—which may be regarded as a colloquial abbreviation of 'Benedict.' And what are you reading, Master Buddenbrook? Ah, Cicero! A difficult text, the work of a great Roman orator. *Quousque tandem, Catilina*. Huh-uh-hmm, yes, I've not entirely forgotten my Latin, either."

The consul said, "Unlike my dear departed father, I have always had some reservations about this everlasting preoccupation of young minds with Greek and Latin. So many serious and important matters are necessary to prepare a man for the practical side of life."

"My opinion entirely, Herr Buddenbrook," Herr Grünlich hastened to reply. "You took the words out of my mouth. A difficult text, and as I failed to add, a *not unexceptionable* one. Quite apart from everything else, I can recall several passages in those speeches that are blatantly offensive."

There was a pause. Tony thought, "Now it's my turn." Because Herr Grünlich's gaze was resting on her again. And how right she was—it was her turn. Herr Grünlich suddenly bounced up off his chair a little, his hand formed in a brief, cramped, and yet elegant gesture toward the consul's wife, and whispered vehemently, "Please, just look at that, Madame Buddenbrook!" Then, interrupting himself loudly, as if Tony should hear only this part, he added, "I beg you, hold that position!" And now he went on again in a whisper, "Do you not see it? How the sun plays in your daughter's hair? I have never seen more beautiful hair!" He blurted this out in solemn rapture to no one in particular, as if speaking to God or his own heart.

Elisabeth smiled agreeably, and the consul said, "Don't put notions in the girl's head." Tony scowled again.

A few minutes later, Herr Grünlich stood up. "I shall not cause you any further inconvenience, no, by heaven, no further inconvenience, Madame Buddenbrook. I came on business . . . but who could resist. Yet, duty calls now. Might I request of you, Consul Buddenbrook . . ."

"I need not tell you," Elisabeth said, "how very happy it would make us if you could stay in our home during your visit in town."

Herr Grünlich stood there for a moment, struck dumb with gratitude. "I am deeply obliged to you, Madame Buddenbrook," he said, his expression underscoring how touched he was. "But I dare not further abuse your kindness. I have taken a couple of rooms at the City of Hamburg Inn. . . ."

A *couple* of rooms, Elisabeth thought to herself—which was precisely what Herr Grünlich had intended for her to think.

"In any case," she said in conclusion, offering her hand again with her customary heartfelt motion, "I hope that we have not seen you for the last time."

Herr Grünlich kissed Madame Buddenbrook's hand, waited a moment for Antonie to offer hers, which did not happen, described a semicircle with his upper body, took one large step backward, bowed yet again, and then, tossing his head back, donned his hat with a flourish and strode off with the consul.

"A pleasant gentleman," the latter repeated when he had rejoined his family and taken his seat again.

"I think he's *silly*," Antonie dared to say, stressing the last word.

"Tony! Good heavens, what a thing to say!" Elisabeth cried, somewhat shocked. "Such a Christian young man."

"And so well bred and urbane," the consul added. "You don't know what you're talking about." It was not unusual for her parents to change roles like this out of courtesy—it only reinforced the unanimity of their opinions.

Christian wrinkled his nose and said, "He certainly talks big! One converses away! We weren't conversing at all. And poppies add a rare, ornamental touch. Sometimes he acts as if he's only speaking aloud to himself. I am disturbing you, I really must beg your pardon. I have never seen more beautiful hair." And Christian's imitation of Herr Grünlich was so perfect that even the consul had to laugh.

"Yes, and puts on big airs!" Tony started up again. "He talked about nothing but himself. *His* business is doing extremely well, *he* loves nature, *he* prefers this name or that, *his* name is Bendix. What do we care, I'd like to know. He was just tooting his own horn," she suddenly shouted angrily. "He's only telling you, Mama, and you, Papa, what you want to hear, just to ingratiate himself."

"That's no reproach, Tony," the consul said sternly. "One finds oneself among strangers, shows oneself from one's best side, chooses one's words, and tries to please—that's quite normal."

"I think he is a good man," Klothilde said softly, drawing out the words, although she was the only person in whom Herr Grünlich had shown not the least interest. Thomas withheld his judgment.

"Enough," the consul concluded. "He is a hardworking Christian and a well-educated man. And you, Tony, are a grown young lady of eighteen, soon to be nineteen, whom he treated very politely and gallantly—you should curb your fault-finding. We all have our weaknesses, and you are, beg your pardon, the last person to cast stones. Tom, let's get back to work."

Tony muttered "Gold whiskers!" and scowled, as she had done several times already.

2

A FEW DAYS LATER, at the corner of Breite and Meng Strasse, as she was returning from a walk, Tony ran into Herr Grünlich. "How genuinely distressed I was, Fräulein, to discover I had missed you," he said. "I took the liberty of paying my respects to your good mother and was grieved to find you weren't at home. But how delighted I am now to meet you after all."

Fräulein Buddenbrook came to a halt—Herr Grünlich was speaking to her. But she kept her eyes lowered, directing them no higher than his chest; and playing at the corners of her mouth was the mocking and totally merciless smile with which a young lady measures a man and finds him wanting. Her lips moved—how should she reply? Ah, it had to be something that would cast this Bendix Grünlich off for good and all, annihilate him—but it also had to be a deft, witty phrase that would both impress him and cut like a knife.

"The feeling is not mutual," she said, her eyes still fixed on Herr Grünlich's chest; and, having shot her poisoned dart, she left him standing there, simply walked on, her head set back and flushed with pride at her sarcastic rhetorical powers; but upon returning home, she learned that Herr Grünlich had been invited to share a veal roast the next Sunday.

And he came. He came in a bell-shaped pleated coat, not in the latest fashion but of the best quality, lending him an air of solidity and dignity—and smiling and pink-faced as always, his thinning hair carefully combed, his whiskers curled and scented. He ate mussel ragout, julienne soup, baked sole, roast veal with mashed potatoes and brussels sprouts, maraschino pudding, and pumpernickel with Roquefort cheese—and at each course he offered a new tribute appropriate to the delicacy. For example, raising his dessert spoon, he gazed at a statue woven into the wallpaper and said aloud to himself, "God forgive me, I can do no other; I've eaten a large serving, but this pudding is just too splendid. I simply *must* implore my hostess for a second helping." And then he flashed Madame Buddenbrook a roguish look. He spoke with the consul about business and politics, propounding some very serious and germane principles; he chatted with the consul's wife about fashions, balls, and the theater; he had kind words for Tom, Christian, and poor Klothilde, even for little Clara and Mamselle Jungmann. Tony kept her silence. He made no attempt to engage her attention, either, except that now and then he tilted his head to gaze at her with a look filled with both distress and encouragement.

When Herr Grünlich departed that evening, he had only strengthened the impression left behind on his first visit. "A man of perfect manners," Elisabeth Buddenbrook said. "A respectable, Christian gentleman," her husband said. Christian was even better at imitating his gestures and speech. And Tony scowled as she said good night; she was filled with a vague foreboding that she had not seen the last of this gentleman, who had conquered her parents' hearts with such unusual dispatch.

And, indeed, returning home one afternoon from a visit with other young ladies, she found Herr Grünlich ensconced in the landscape room, reading Walter Scott's *Waverley* aloud to her mother—in impeccable English, because, as he explained, his flourishing business had meant many trips to England. Tony picked up a book and took a seat at the far end of the room.

Herr Grünlich asked in a gentle voice, "Apparently what I am reading is not to your taste, Fräulein?"

She tossed her head back and, in a pointed, sarcastic tone, replied something like, "Not in the least."

But he was not to be thrown off. He began to speak of his parents, who had died much too soon, and talked about his father, who was a preacher, a pastor, a man whose Christian principles and urbanity were on the same high plane.

But then, although Tony was not present at his farewell visit,

Herr Grünlich left for Hamburg. "Ida," she said to her trusted friend Mamselle Jungmann, "that man is gone!" But Ida Jungmann replied, "Wait and see, child. . . ."

Eight days later, there was a scene in the breakfast room. Tony came down at nine and was amazed to find both her father and mother at the table. With eyes red from sleep, but hungry and ready for the day, she took her seat, after first offering her forehead to be kissed; she helped herself to sugar, butter, and some of the green herb cheese.

"It's so nice to find you still here for once, Papa," she said, wrapping her hot egg in a napkin and cracking it open with her teaspoon.

"I've been waiting for our sleepyhead to appear," said the consul, who was smoking a cigarette and drumming softly on the table with his folded newspaper. With her usual slow and graceful gestures, his wife finished her breakfast and leaned back in the sofa.

"Thilda is already busy in the kitchen," the consul continued, giving weight to each word, "and I would be at work myself if it weren't for an important matter that your mother and I would like to discuss with our daughter."

Tony, her mouth full of bread and butter, looked at her father, then at her mother, with a mixture of curiosity and alarm.

"Go ahead and finish your breakfast, my child," Elisabeth said. But Tony laid her knife down and cried, "Just tell me straight out, Papa, please!" To which the consul, still drumming with this newspaper, replied, "Just eat."

Without any real hunger now, Tony silently drank her coffee and ate her egg and the bread she had smeared with green cheese, and as she did she began to suspect what this was all about. Her face turned a little pale and lost its morning glow; she said "No thanks," when offered honey and soon afterward declared in a subdued voice that she was finished.

"My dear child," the consul said after a moment of silence, "the matter about which we want to speak with you is contained in this letter." And now he tapped the table with a large, bluish envelope instead of with his paper. "To be brief: Herr Bendix Grünlich, whom we have all come to know as an honest and warmhearted man, has written me that during his recent stay he conceived a deep affection for our daughter and now asks formally for her hand. What does our good child think of that?"

Tony was sitting back in her chair, her head lowered, her right hand slowly twirling her napkin ring. Suddenly her eyes opened wide—dark with sadness and filled with tears. And in a beleaguered voice she blurted, "What does that man want from me! What have I ever done to him?" And then broke into tears.

The consul glanced at his wife and gazed with some embarrassment into his empty cup.

"Dear Tony," her mother said gently, "there's no need for such vehemence. Surely you know that your parents want only the best for you, and they cannot advise you to refuse to take this path in life. You see, I am assuming that you have no special feelings for Herr Grünlich, but I assure you that will come in time. A young girl like you never knows what she really wants. Your head and your heart are both all in a muddle. One must give the heart time and keep one's mind open for the good advice of more experienced people, who care and plan for your happiness."

"I don't know anything about him," Tony managed to say plaintively, pressing her little white, egg-stained batiste napkin to her eyes. "I only know that his whiskers are a funny gold color and his business is flourishing." Her upper lip always quivered when she cried, and the effect was unutterably touching.

In a sudden display of gentleness, the consul pulled his chair nearer to her and smiled as he stroked her hair. "My little Tony," he said, "what could you possibly know about him? You're a child, don't you see, and you wouldn't have known any more about him if he had been here for fifty-two weeks rather than four. You're a little girl who's seen nothing of the world and has to depend on the eyes of other people, who only want the best for you."

"I don't understand. . . . I don't understand. . . ." Tony sobbed in bewilderment, rubbing her head like a kitten against his caressing hand. "He comes in here . . . says nice things to everyone . . . goes away . . . and writes that he wants to . . . I don't understand. . . . What gave him the idea . . . What have I ever done to him?"

The consul smiled again. "You've said that once already, Tony, and it only shows just what a helpless child you are. Surely my daughter doesn't believe I would want to push her into anything, to torment her. All this can be weighed quite calmly—indeed, must be weighed calmly, because it is a serious matter. And that is how I will respond to Herr Grünlich for now, neither rejecting nor accepting his proposal. There are so many things to consider. So, then . . . we shall see—agreed? Now your papa has to go to work. Adieu, Bethsy."

"*Au revoir*, my dear Jean."

"You really should eat just a little honey, Tony," Elisabeth said, now that she was alone with her daughter, who sat motionless in her chair, head hung low. "One must eat properly."

Tony's tears gradually dried. Her head was hot and crowded with thoughts. Lord, what a predicament! She had always known, of course, that someday she would be the wife of a businessman, would make a good, advantageous match worthy of her family and the firm. But now suddenly, for the first time, someone was serious about actually wanting to marry her. How was she supposed to act? Suddenly she, Tony Buddenbrook, was dealing with all those terribly momentous phrases that she had only read about: "consent to a proposal," "hand in marriage," "for as long as ye both shall live." . . . Lord! All at once it was a totally new situation.

"And you, Mama?" she asked. "Your advice, then, is that I . . . consent to his proposal?" She hesitated for a moment at the words "consent to his proposal"—it all sounded so stilted and forced; but she managed to speak them with dignity for the first time in her life. She began to be just a little ashamed of her initial bewilderment. It seemed no less absurd that she should marry Herr Grünlich than it had ten minutes before, but she was beginning to find considerable satisfaction in the importance of her position.

Her mother said, "Advise you to consent, my child? Did Papa advise that? No, he told you not to reject it, that's all. Because it would be irresponsible of either of us to do that. The alliance that has been proposed is most definitely what is called a good match, my dear Tony. You would be introduced to the finest circles in Hamburg and would live in grand style."

Tony sat there, frozen in place. Suddenly she saw what looked like silk curtains parting, like the ones in her grandparents' salon. Would she, as Madame Grünlich, drink chocolate every morning? It probably wasn't appropriate to ask.

"As your father said—you have time to consider it," her mother continued. "But we want you to bear in mind that such an opportunity for future happiness does not present itself every day, and that this marriage is precisely the sort to which duty and destiny call you. Yes, my child, you must keep that in mind as well. The path opening before you today is the one to which destiny has called you, as you well know."

"Yes," Tony said, thinking all this over. "Certainly." She was quite aware of her obligations to her family and the firm, was proud of those obligations. She was Antonie Buddenbrook—Consul Buddenbrook's daughter, who walked about town like a young princess, to whom Matthiesen the grain hauler doffed his homely top hat. Her family's history was in her bones. Even the merchant tailor in Rostock had done *very* well, and the family had continued to prosper spectacularly ever since. Just as it was Tom's job to work in the office, her calling in life was to add to the luster of her family and the firm of Johann Buddenbrook by marrying a wealthy and prominent man. . . . Yes, this was certainly the right kind of match; but Herr Grünlich, of all people. She pictured him and his tawny whiskers, his pink, smiling face, that wart beside his nose, his mincing steps; she thought she could feel his wool suit, hear his bland voice.

"I was quite sure," her mother said, "that we would be open to quiet words of reason. Have we perhaps reached a decision?"

"Oh, heaven forbid," Tony cried, and there was sudden outrage even in the "oh." "Marry Herr Grünlich, what nonsense! I was constantly making fun of him with sarcastic comments. I can't imagine how he can even stand me. He must have *some* pride."

And with that, she began dripping honey on her slice of country bread.

3

THAT YEAR the Buddenbrooks took no holiday trip during Christian and Clara's school vacation. The consul explained that he was much too busy—but the unresolved issue of Antonie was likewise a reason for them to wait out the summer on Meng Strasse. The consul had sent a diplomatic letter to Herr Grünlich; but progress in the matter was hindered by Tony's stubbornness, which took the most childish forms. "Heaven forbid, Mama!" she would say, "I can't stand him"—with as much stress as possible on the penultimate word. Or she would declare solemnly: "Father"—usually Tony called him "Papa"—"I will never consent to his proposal."

And the whole affair would probably have remained stuck right there for some time, if it had not been for an event that occurred in the middle of July, some ten days after the conversation in the breakfast room.

It was afternoon, a warm afternoon with a blue sky. Madame Buddenbrook had gone out, and Tony was sitting alone, reading, at the window in the landscape room, when Anton presented her with a calling card. Before she even had time to read the name, a gentleman appeared in the room—wearing a bell-shaped coat and pea-colored trousers. It was, obviously, Herr Grünlich, and his face bore an expression of tender supplication.

Tony sat up on her bench in horror, then started forward as if intending to flee from the room. How could she possibly speak to a man who had asked for her hand in marriage? Her heart was pounding clear up in her throat, and she had turned ashen. As long as she had been sure that Herr Grünlich was at a safe distance, she had actually enjoyed the earnest exchanges with her parents and the sudden importance attached to herself and her decision. But here he was again now! Standing right in front of her! What would happen? She felt as if she was going to burst into tears again.

Herr Grünlich approached her now, with tripping steps, his arms widespread, his head tilted to one side in the pose of a man who wishes to say, "Here I am! Slay me if you will!" Instead he cried, "What a stroke of Providence! To find *you* here, Antonie!" He called her "Antonie."

Tony was standing in front of the window seat, her book still in her right hand, and, pouting her lips and raising her head a little more with each word to emphasize her outrage, she said, "What—do—you—think—you're—doing!"

But tears were welling up within her all the same.

Herr Grünlich, however, was at too great an emotional pitch to notice her protest.

"How could I wait any longer? Had I any choice but to return?" he asked fervently. "A week ago I received the letter from your *dear* father, and that letter filled me with hope. How could I remain any longer in this uncertainty, Fräulein Antonie? I could bear it no more. I threw myself into the next coach. Hastened here as fast as I could. I have taken a couple of rooms at the City of Hamburg Inn . . . and here I am, Antonie, to hear from your own lips that last, decisive word that will make me happier than I can possibly express."

Tony went rigid; she was so stunned that her tears vanished. So this had been the effect of her father's discreet letter, which was meant to postpone any decision indefinitely. She stammered the same sentence three or four times: "You've made a mistake. You've made a mistake."

Herr Grünlich had pulled an armchair over near her window seat; he sat down now, forcing her to take her seat again as well; bending forward, he took her hand, limp with helplessness, in his own and continued in an impassioned voice, "Fräulein Antonie, since that first moment, that first afternoon—you recall that afternoon, do you not?—when there in the circle of your family I first saw you, an elegant, unimaginable vision of loveliness, your name has been written"—he corrected himself—"engraved on my heart in indelible letters. Since that day, Fräulein Antonie, my sole, my ardent wish had been to gain your beautiful hand until death do us part. And your *dear* father's letter awakened within me a hope, which you will now make a happy certainty, will you not? Surely I may count upon the fact that you share such feelings, that you do return them." And here his free hand grasped her other hand and he gazed deeply into her eyes, wide with fright. He was not wearing worsted gloves today; his long hands were threaded with strong blue veins.

Tony stared at his pink face, first at the wart beside his nose and then into his eyes, which were as blue as a goose's.

"No, no!" she erupted in dismay. Then she added, "I will not give my consent to your proposal!" She was trying to speak firmly, but she was crying now.

"What have I done to deserve such doubt and hesitation?" he asked, his voice sinking deeper until it was almost a reproach. "You are a young lady who has been pampered and watched over with loving care, but I swear to you, pledge you my word as a gentleman, that I would cater to your every whim, that you would lack nothing as my wife, that in Hamburg you would lead the life you truly deserve."

Tony leapt up, pulling her hands away, and, amid a flood of tears, she shouted in total desperation, "No! No! I told you *no*! I've turned you down. Good God in heaven, don't you understand?"

And now Herr Grünlich stood up, too. He took a step back, spread his arms wide, displaying both palms to her, and spoke with all the seriousness a man of honor and determination can muster: "You realize, Mademoiselle Buddenbrook, do you not, that I cannot allow myself to be insulted in this fashion?"

"But I am not insulting you, Herr Grünlich," Tony said, now regretting that she had lost her temper. Good God, why was this happening to her! She had not imagined courtship quite this way. She had thought you had only to say, "I am honored by your offer, but I cannot accept it," and that would be that.

"I am honored by your offer," she said, as calmly as she could, "but I cannot accept it. There, and now I must go. Please excuse me, I am very busy."

But Herr Grünlich blocked her exit. "You are rejecting me?" he asked in a flat, unemotional voice.

"Yes," Tony said; and by way of precaution she added, "unfortunately."

And Herr Grünlich heaved a huge sigh, stepped back two more giant steps, bent his torso to one side, and, leaning askew from the waist up, pointed toward the carpet and cried in a dreadful voice, "Antonie!"

They both stood like this for a moment, facing one another—he in a pose of honest and imperious rage; Tony pale, trembling, tearful, a moist handkerchief pressed to her mouth. Finally he turned around, put his hands behind his back, and paced the length of the room twice, as if he were quite at home here. Then he stopped at the window and gazed out into the early dusk.

Tony walked slowly and rather gingerly toward the glass door. She got only as far as the middle of the room—and there was Herr Grünlich beside her.

"Tony," he said in a low voice, gently grasping her hand. And then he sank—sank!—slowly to the floor on one knee. Both tawny, golden muttonchops fell across her hand. "Tony," he repeated, "behold me here. You have brought me to this. Do you have a heart, a feeling heart? Hear me out. You see before you a devastated man, a man who will perish, if"—he hastily interrupted himself—"indeed, a man who will surely die of grief, if you reject his love for you. Here I lie. Can you find it in your heart to say: 'I despise you'?"

"No, no!" Tony replied, her voice suddenly consoling. Her tears had stopped, and compassion and pity welled up within her. Lord, how very much he must love her to take this so far, when all it aroused in her was a queer feeling of indifference. Was it possible that this was happening to *her*? You read about this sort of thing in novels, but now here in the flesh was a man in a frock coat, on his knees, begging. The thought of marrying him had simply seemed absurd, because she found Herr Grünlich silly. But, by God, at that moment he was not silly at all. There was such sincere anguish in his voice and in his face, such honesty and despair in his pleas. . . .

"No, no," she repeated, so touched that she bent down to him, "I don't despise you, Herr Grünlich. How can you say such a thing? Now, do stand up, please."

"You do not wish to slay me?" he asked again.

And in a comforting, almost maternal tone, she repeated, "No, no."

"You've given your word!" Herr Grünlich cried, jumping to his feet. But the moment he saw Tony pull back in shock, he was on his knees again and, to calm her, said in an anxious voice, "Fine, fine. . . . Not another word, Antonie. Enough for now about all this, I beg you. We shall speak of it again, some other day. Some other day. But farewell for now. I shall return. Farewell."

He quickly got to his feet, grabbed his large gray hat from the table, kissed her hand, and hurried out through the glass door.

Tony watched him pick up his cane in the columned hall and disappear down the corridor. Totally confused and exhausted, she stood there in the middle of the room, her moist handkerchief dangling from a limp hand.

4

CONSUL BUDDENBROOK said to his wife: "If only I could think of some reason, however delicate, Tony might have for deciding against this alliance. But she is a child, Bethsy; she enjoys her fun, dancing at balls, being courted by young men, relishes it all, because she knows she's pretty and comes from a good family. Of course, it may be that secretly, unconsciously, she is looking on her own—but I know her, she hasn't found her own heart yet, as the saying goes. And if you were to ask her, she would toss her head and think long and hard—and there wouldn't be anyone. She is a child, a chickadee, a flighty young thing. If she would say yes, she could take her place in the world, set herself up quite nicely, which is what she really wants, and within a matter of days she would love her husband. He's no Apollo, heaven knows, no Apollo. But he is certainly more than presentable, and there's no use demanding a sheep with five legs, if you'll permit me a businessman's turn of phrase. And if she wants to wait until someone comes along who is both handsome and a good match—well, God help us all! Tony Buddenbrook can always find something. Of course, on the other hand . . . there is some risk, and, to use another business expression, just because you cast a net doesn't mean you'll catch any fish. I had a long talk with Herr Grünlich yesterday morning—he is indeed a most insistent suitor—and I saw his books, he spread them out for me himself. Books, my dear Bethsy, worthy of framing! I told him how delighted I was. Still a young enterprise—but he is doing quite well, quite well. His assets come to about 120,000 thalers, and that is obviously only the start, for he turns a tidy profit every year. And I asked the Duchamps, too, and what they said didn't sound bad. Although they are not familiar with his circumstances, he lives like a gentleman, moves in the best society, and it is well known that his business is flourishing, branching out in all directions. And what I've learned from several other people in Hamburg—from Kesselmeyer the banker, for instance—was quite satisfactory as well. In brief, Bethsy, I can only sincerely wish that this marriage take place, to the benefit of both our family and the firm. Heaven knows, I am very sorry that the child finds herself in such a difficult position, besieged on all sides, walks around depressed and not talking to anyone. But I simply cannot bring myself to reject Grünlich out of hand. And one more thing, Bethsy, and I cannot say it too often: in the last few years we have, Lord knows, not been expanding to any appreciable extent. Not that things have been going badly, God forbid—no, hard work does have its honest reward. The business goes on quietly—all too quietly, and even that is only because I exercise great prudence. We have not moved ahead, not really, since Father passed on. These are definitely not good times for merchants. In brief, there is little cause for rejoicing. Our daughter is of a marriageable age and has the opportunity of making a match that anyone can see is both advantageous and honorable—and she should do it! It is not advisable to wait, not advisable, Bethsy! Do have a talk with her. I tried my best to persuade her this afternoon."

Tony was under siege, the consul was right about that. She no longer said no, but—God help her—neither could she bring herself to say yes. She herself didn't even understand why, struggle as she might, she could not give her consent.

Meanwhile her father would take her aside for a serious word, or her mother would ask her to have a seat beside her and then press her finally to make a decision. Uncle Gotthold and his family had not been told about all this, because they always seemed somehow to snicker at life on Meng Strasse. But Sesame Weichbrodt had heard about the whole affair and offered good advice, impeccably enunciated. Even Mamselle Jungmann said, "Tony, my child, there's nothing to worry about, you'll still be in the best society." And Tony could not visit that silk salon she so admired in the villa beyond the Burg Gate without Madame Kröger's starting in: "*A propos*, I've heard something about an affair. I do hope you'll listen to reason, child."

One Sunday, as she was sitting in St. Mary's with her parents and brothers, Pastor Kölling expanded in strong words on a text that said that a woman should leave father and mother and cleave to her husband—and suddenly became so emphatic that Tony stared up at him in alarm to see if he might be looking at her. But no, thank God, his head was turned in the other direction and he was just preaching away in general across the throng of worshipers; and yet it was only too clear that this was a new assault and that every word was meant for her. For a young woman, a mere child who as yet had neither will nor wisdom of her own, to oppose the loving advice of her parents was an offense such as the Lord would spew from His mouth—and at this last phrase, one of those that Pastor Kölling greatly admired and used with enthusiasm, Tony saw him make a dreadful sweep of his arm and turn to look right through her. Tony saw her father, who was sitting next to her, raise one hand, as if to say, "Not so rough . . ." But there was no doubt that Pastor Kölling was in collusion with him or her mother. She turned red and cowered in her seat, feeling as if every eye were watching her. The next Sunday, she flatly refused to go to church.

She wandered the house not saying a word, seldom laughed, completely lost her appetite; and sometimes she would heave a great heartbreaking sigh, as if wrestling with a decision, and then gaze wretchedly at her family. You couldn't help pitying her. She even lost weight—and the glow in her cheeks.

At last the consul said: "This can't go on, Bethsy, we can't mistreat the child. She has to get away for a while, calm down, and collect her thoughts. You'll see, she'll come to reason. I can't leave the office, and the children's vacation is almost over . . . but we can all get along quite well here at home. Old Schwarzkopf from Travemünde happened to stop by yesterday—Diederich Schwarzkopf, the harbor pilot. I dropped a few hints, and it turned out he would be happy to have the lass stay with them a while. I'll pay him a little something for it. She'll have a nice, cozy place to stay, can go swimming and get some fresh air and sort things out. Tom can ride with her, so everything is arranged. And the sooner the better. . . ."

Tony was delighted with the idea, and said so. True, she hardly ever saw Herr Grünlich, but she knew he was in town, negotiating with her parents and waiting. Good Lord, he could appear at any moment—stand there shouting and begging. She would feel much safer in a strange house in Travemünde. So she packed her trunk quickly and cheerfully, and on the last day of July she climbed aboard the majestic Kröger equipage with Tom as her chaperon, said her goodbyes in the best of moods, and gave a great sigh of relief as they drove out through the Burg Gate.

5

THE ROAD TO TRAVEMÜNDE goes straight ahead, then comes a ferry, and then it's straight ahead again—they both knew the way well. The gray road glided swiftly along as the hoofs of Lebrecht Kröger's massive Mecklenburg bays rang out hollow and regular, but the sun burned hot and the unexciting landscape was veiled in dust. They had eaten an early dinner at one o'clock and had departed at two on the dot, which meant they would arrive shortly after four—because, if a trip took four hours in a hired carriage, the Krögers' driver, Jochen, made a point of doing it in two.

Tony fell into a dreamy half-sleep, her head nodding under a big, flat straw hat and a gray parasol, which she had propped against the folded-back carriage top. Her twine-gray parasol was trimmed with cream-colored lace and matched her simple, close-fitting dress; she had daintily crossed her feet in front of her to show off her white stockings and the crisscross lacing on her shoes. She leaned back, elegant and comfortable, as if born to ride in this carriage.

Tom, an impeccably dressed twenty-year-old in a blue-gray suit, had shoved his straw hat back and was smoking Russian cigarettes. He was not very tall, but his mustache had begun to grow out thick and dark, darker than his hair and eyelashes. With one eyebrow raised slightly as always, he gazed out across the clouds of dust and passing roadside trees.

Tony said, "I've never been so happy to go to Travemünde in all my life—for all kinds of reasons. Don't make fun of me, Tom. I wish I could leave a certain set of gold muttonchops several miles farther behind me. And it will be a whole new Travemünde, right on Front Row with the Schwarzkopfs. I won't pay any attention to the social whirl at the spa. I know all that quite well enough already. And I'm not in the mood for it anyway. Besides, it's all so public, and there's certainly nothing shy about the man. Just watch, he'll pop up one day right beside me, smiling his gracious smile."

Tom threw his cigarette away and took another from his case, its lid decoratively inlaid with a scene of wolves attacking a troika—the gift of one of the consul's Russian clients. Tom had a passion for these little strong cigarettes with a yellow mouthpiece; he smoked one after another and had the bad habit of inhaling the smoke deep into his lungs and slowly letting it cascade out as he spoke.

"Yes," he said, "as far as that goes, the spa gardens are teeming with people from Hamburg. Consul Fritsche, who recently bought the place, is one himself. Business is splendid at present, Papa says. All the same, you'll miss out on quite a few things if you don't join in just a little. Peter Döhlmann will be there, of course; he's never in town this time of the year; his business just trots along on its own like an old hound dog, I guess. Strange. Well . . . Uncle Justus is sure to come out on Sundays and pay a visit to the roulette tables. And then there's the Möllendorpfs and the Kistenmakers—all at full strength, I would think—and the Hagenströms. . . ."

"Ha!—Naturally. How could we do without Sarah Semlinger."

"Her name's Laura, my girl, let's be fair."

"And Julie, of course. They say Julie's going to announce her engagement to August Möllendorpf this summer, and Julie is *sure* to do it. And then they'll be accepted at last. You know, Tom, it's simply outrageous, the way these families just move into town. . . ."

"Yes, but, good Lord, Strunck & Hagenström have built up a fine business; and that's the main thing."

"But of course! And we all know how they've built it up. With their elbows, do you hear—not an ounce of culture or refinement. That Hinrich Hagenström. Grandfather said he could make oxen give milk, those were his very words."

"Yes, yes, yes, but what's the difference. The main thing is that he's making money. And as far as the engagement goes, it's a very nice piece of business, too. Julie ends up a Möllendorpf, and August moves into a pretty job."

"Oh, you just want to annoy me, Tom, that's all. I loathe those people."

Tom began to laugh. "Good Lord, we'll have to get used to them all the same, you know. As Papa said recently, they're the up-and-coming families—whereas the Möllendorpfs, for example. And one can't deny that the Hagenströms are hard workers. Hermann is already indispensable in the firm, and Moritz graduated at the top of his class, despite his bad lungs. They say he's very clever and is going to study law."

"How nice, Tom. But I'm glad that there are at least some other families that don't have to kowtow to them, and that, for instance, we Buddenbrooks . . ."

"Now, now," Tom said, "let's not boast. Every family has its weak points." And with a glance at Jochen's broad back, he lowered his voice. "Lord only knows, for example, what's going on with Uncle Justus. Papa just shakes his head when he speaks of him, and Grandfather Kröger has had to help out a couple of times now with some very large sums, I think. And things are not quite what they should be with our cousins, either. Jürgen is supposed to go to university, but he still hasn't taken his finals. And I've heard Dahlbeck & Co. in Hamburg is not at all satisfied with Jakob. He can never make ends meet, despite the big allowance he gets; and what Uncle Justus won't give him, Aunt Rosalie will. No, I think it's best we not cast any stones. And if you want to balance the scales with the Hagenströms, then you had best marry Grünlich."

"Did I get into this carriage with you to talk about him? Yes, yes, I probably ought to marry him. But I don't want to think about that now. I simply want to forget it. And so now we're on our way to the Schwarzkopfs'. As far as I know, I've never met them. They're nice people, you say?"

"Oh, Diederich Schwarzkopf—now, there's a right tol'rable ol' gent. Not that he always talks that way, only when he's had more than five glasses of grog. He was visiting the office once, and we all went down to the Seaman's Guild together. He drank like a fish. His father was born on a Norwegian ship, and ended up a captain on the same line. Diederich has had a good education; harbor pilot is a very responsible and rather well-paid position. He's an old salt, but always polite to the ladies. Watch out, he'll try to flirt with you."

"Pooh! And his wife?"

"I don't know his wife myself. She's pleasant enough, I'm sure. And there's a son, too, who was one or two years ahead of me in school and is at university, I think. Look, there's the sea! Less than fifteen minutes now . . ."

They drove down an avenue lined by beech trees, right beside the sea, which lay blue and peaceful in the sun. Then came the round, yellow lighthouse, and for a while they watched the bay and the breakwater, the red roofs of the little town and its little harbor, the sails and tackle of the boats. Then they passed the first houses, left the church behind them, and rolled along Front Row, until they reached a pretty little house that had a porch overgrown with grapevine.

Captain Schwarzkopf was standing at the door, and as the carriage approached he doffed his seaman's cap. He was a stocky, broad-shouldered man with a red face, watery-blue eyes, and a frosted, bristly beard that ran in a fan shape from ear to ear—but the firm red curve of his upper lip was clean-shaven. There was dignity and honesty in his mouth, which was turned down around a wooden pipe. A white piqué vest shimmered under an open coat trimmed with gold braid. He stood there, legs set wide apart, and had something of a paunch.

"It's a genuine honor for me, mamselle. Suits us just fine that you're willing to put up with us for a time." He carefully helped Tony out of the carriage. "My compliments, Herr Buddenbrook. The consul's doing well, I hope? And your good mother? It's a genuine pleasure. Well, come on in, lady and gent. My wife's put together something like a little snack. Just head on down to Pedderson's Inn," he said to the driver, who had carried their baggage into the house, "your horses'll be nicely taken care of there. You are spending the night with us, aren't you, Herr Buddenbrook? So, and why not? The horses'll have to catch a bit of breath at least, and you won't make it back to town before dark."

"You know, staying here will be at least as pleasant as at the spa hotel," Tony said, fifteen minutes later, as they took their coffee on the veranda. "The air is simply marvelous! You can smell the seaweed from here. I'm so dreadfully happy to be in Travemünde again."

She could look out between the vine-clad columns of the porch onto the wide river shining in the sun, its boats and docks, and on across to the ferry landing on Priwall, the peninsula that jutted out from Mecklenburg. The big, bowl-shaped cups rimmed with blue were so unusual, so crude in comparison with their dainty old porcelain at home; but the table looked inviting—a bouquet of wildflowers had been set at Tony's place—and the trip had made her hungry.

"Yes, Mamselle will see, she'll get to feeling better here," the mistress of the house said. "She's looking just a tad peaked, if I might put it that way. That's what comes of city air, and, then, all those balls and parties. . . ."

Frau Schwarzkopf, the daughter of a pastor from Schlutup, looked to be about fifty; she was a head shorter than Tony and rather slight of build. Her hair was black, smooth, and freshly put up in a large-meshed net. She wore a dark brown dress trimmed with white crocheted cuffs and a small collar. She was tidy, gentle, and friendly, and warmly recommended her homemade raisin bread, which lay in a boat-shaped basket, surrounded by cream, sugar, butter, and honey still in the comb. The breadbasket was trimmed with pearl embroidery, the handiwork of Meta, who was sitting beside her mother, a polite little eight-year-old in a plaid frock and with flaxen hair tied up in a stiff pigtail.

Frau Schwarzkopf apologized for the room that was to be Tony's and that she had already used to freshen up a bit. It was furnished so simply. . . .

"Pooh, sweet as it can be," Tony said. It had a view to the sea, that was the main thing. And with that she dipped her fourth slice of raisin bread in her coffee. Tom was talking with the old man about the *Wullenwever*, which was in town for repairs.

Suddenly a young man of about twenty came up onto the porch, book in hand. He doffed his gray felt hat, blushed, and made a somewhat awkward bow.

"Well, my lad," the pilot captain said, "you're late getting home." Then he introduced him to them. "This is my son"—and he mentioned the name, but Tony did not catch it. "Studying to be a doctor, spending his vacation here with us."

"Pleased to meet you," Tony said, just as she had been taught. Tom stood up and shook hands. Young Schwarzkopf bowed again, put his book down, and blushed as he took a seat at the table.

He was of average height, rather slender, and as blond as could be. The beginnings of a mustache were barely visible and as colorless as the short-cropped hair on his longish head; all of which was a perfect match for his extraordinarily pale complexion—skin like translucent porcelain that turned red at the slightest provocation. His eyes were a somewhat darker blue than his father's, but they had the same kindly, if not lively, way of appraising things; the features of his face were regular and rather pleasing. As he began to eat, he displayed a set of unusually well-formed, closely set teeth so shiny that they sparkled like polished ivory. And he was dressed in a gray, high-buttoned jacket with flaps over the pockets and an elastic band across the back.

"Yes, I really must apologize for being so late," he said. He spoke somewhat ponderously and his voice was a little scratchy. "I've been reading out on the beach and simply didn't keep track of the time." He fell silent, but as he chewed, he would glance now and then at Tony and Tom, checking them over.

Later, when at Frau Schwarzkopf's urging Tony helped herself to more, he said, "You can trust that honey, Fräulein Buddenbrook. It's a pure product of nature. You know what you're eating there. You have to eat right, you know. This sea air will cause you to lose weight. It accelerates the metabolism. And if you don't eat enough, you'll just waste away." He had a naïve and agreeable way of bending forward when he spoke, though sometimes he might not be looking at the same person he was talking to.

His mother listened to him fondly, and then searched Tony's face for the impression his words had made.

But old Schwarzkopf said, "Don't go putting on airs, doc, with your metabolism. We don't want to know about it." And the young man laughed and looked again at Tony's plate—and blushed.

The harbor pilot mentioned his son's first name several times, but Tony could never quite catch it. It was something like "Moore" or "Mort"—it was impossible to tell, given the old man's broad Plattdeutsch accent.

The table had been cleared; Diederich Schwarzkopf was sitting there comfortably squinting into the sun, his jacket wide open to reveal his shimmering vest, he and his son had lit their stubby wooden pipes, and Tom was occupied with his cigarettes—and now the young men found themselves engaged in lively reminiscences of their school days, even Tony joined in with enthusiasm. They quoted Herr Stengel: "You were asked to draw a line, and what have you done? You have made a stroke!" What a shame Christian wasn't there; he could have done it much better.

At one point Tom pointed to the vase of wildflowers in front of Tony and remarked, "Herr Grünlich would say: Those add a rare, ornamental touch."

Tony, red with rage, poked him in the ribs, and her eyes glided shyly in the direction of young Schwarzkopf.

Coffee had been served unusually late, and they went on sitting there for a long time, too. It was already half past six, and the Priwall peninsula had begun to sink beneath the oncoming dusk, when the old captain finally rose from the table. "Well, you'll have to excuse me, ladies and gents," he said. "I've got some things to do down at the pilots' office. We'll eat at eight, if that's all right by you. Or maybe even a little later for once—what do you think, Meta? But, say now"—and he used that first name again—"don't just sit around here doing nothing. Why don't you go occupy yourself with your bones. Mamselle Buddenbrook'll be wanting to unpack, I suppose. Or you two young folks can take a walk along the beach if you like. Just don't get in their way, son."

"Good heavens, Diederich, why can't the lad sit here for a while if he likes," Frau Schwarzkopf said, remonstrating gently. "And why shouldn't he join them on the beach if he wants to? He's on vacation, Diederich. Why shouldn't he enjoy spending some time with our visitors?"

6

WHEN TONY AWAKENED the next morning in her little, tidy room with its chintz-covered furniture, she had that prickly, happy feeling one has when one opens one's eyes and finds life has begun a new chapter.

She sat up, wrapping her arms around her knees and throwing back her tousled head, squinted into the narrow, blinding streak of daylight pouring into the room through the closed shutters, and lazily unpacked all yesterday's adventures.

She gave barely a thought to Herr Grünlich. The city, that ghastly scene in the landscape room, her parents' and Pastor Kölling's reprimands—that all lay far behind her. She would wake up every morning here without a care in the world. These Schwarzkopfs were marvelous people. Yesterday evening there had even been orange punch and a toast to the fine time they would spend together. They had had such fun. Old Schwarzkopf had entertained them with sea yarns, and the younger one had told them about Göttingen, where he was studying. But how odd that she still didn't know his first name. She had paid close attention, but it had not been mentioned once during dinner, and it hadn't seemed quite proper to ask at that point. She concentrated hard—Lord, what was young Schwarzkopf's name? Moore . . . Mort . . . ? Whatever it was, Moore or Mort, she had liked him. He had such a good-natured, mischievous laugh, and when he had asked for water by using a couple of letters with some numbers added, his father had been simply furious. Yes, that was the scientific formula for water—though not for *this* water, because the formula for the liquid of Travemünde would be much more complicated. Why, you might discover a jellyfish in it any second. The authorities, now, they had their own definition of pure water. And this earned him another rebuke from his father, for speaking in such disparaging tones about the authorities. Frau Schwarzkopf had kept searching Tony's face for some sign of admiration, and she had to admit that he was very amusing, so learned and funny at the same time. He had paid rather a lot of attention to her, the young man had. She had complained that when she ate her head always got hot, that she thought she had too much blood. And what was his answer? He had eyed her critically and said: Yes, the arteries at her temples were swollen, but that did not rule out that she might not have enough blood or blood corpuscles in her head. She might even have a *touch* of anemia.

The cuckoo jumped from its little wooden house and gave four bright, mellow calls. "Seven, eight, nine"—Tony counted along—"on your feet!" And with that she sprang from her bed and threw open the shutters. The sky was lightly overcast, but the sun was shining. She looked out across the Leuchtenfeld flats and the lighthouse to the ruffled sea, bordered on the right by the curving coast of Mecklenburg and then extending out in bands of green and blue until it merged with the hazy horizon. I'll go swimming later, Tony thought, but first a good breakfast, so that my metabolism doesn't make me waste away. And she made quick, happy work of washing and dressing.

It was a little after nine-thirty when she left her room. The door to the room where Tom had slept stood open; he had ridden back to town very early. Even upstairs here, where there were only bedrooms, Tony could smell coffee—that seemed to be the little house's characteristic odor, and it grew stronger as she came down the staircase with its simple, unbroken wooden railing and followed the hallway that led past the parlor, the dining room, and the harbor pilot's private office. Feeling fresh and in the best of moods, she walked out onto the porch in her white piqué dress.

Frau Schwarzkopf was sitting with her son at the coffee table, which had already been partially cleared. She was wearing a blue-checked apron over her brown dress. There was a basket of keys in front of her.

"A thousand pardons for not waiting for you, Mamselle Buddenbrook," she said as she stood up. "We get up early, we simple folks do. There's a hundred things to be done. Schwarzkopf is in his office already. But you won't take it amiss, will you, mamselle?"

Tony made her own apologies. "You mustn't believe I always sleep this late. I'm quite ashamed of myself, but that punch last night . . ."

And the young man of the house began to laugh. He was standing behind the table now, his stubby pipe in his hand, a newspaper spread open before him.

"Yes, it's your fault," Tony said. "Good morning. You kept toasting glasses with me. But all I deserve now is some cold coffee. I should already have had my breakfast and taken my swim."

"No, such an early swim wouldn't be good for a young lady. The water was still quite cold at seven this morning, you know—fifty-two degrees. A little bracing coming from a warm bed."

"And how would you know if I like lukewarm water, monsieur?" And Tony took her place at the table. "You've kept the coffee warm for me, Frau Schwarzkopf. But I can certainly pour it for myself, many thanks."

The mistress of the house watched her guest take the first bite. "And Mamselle slept well her first night here? Heaven knows, the mattress is just seaweed—we're simple folk. But now enjoy your breakfast and the rest of the morning. I'm sure Mamselle had plans to meet some of her friends on the beach? If you'd like, my son can walk you there. I'm sorry I can't spend more time with you, but I really *must* look after lunch. We'll be having bratwurst. We'll do our best to feed you."

"I'll just have some of the honeycomb," Tony said, when the two were alone. "After all, you know what you're eating there."

Young Schwarzkopf stood up again and laid his pipe on the porch railing.

"Oh, go ahead and smoke. Really, it doesn't bother me in the least. By the time I get to the breakfast room at home, it always smells of Papa's cigar smoke. Tell me," she suddenly asked, "is it true that an egg is as nutritious as a quarter-pound of meat?"

He blushed all over. "Are you trying to tease me, Fräulein Buddenbrook?" he asked with a laugh that was half annoyance. "My father rapped my knuckles last night for putting on airs with my scientific lingo, as he put it."

"It was only a harmless question!" In her dismay, Tony stopped eating for a moment. " 'Putting on airs'—how could anyone say that? I really would like to know. Lord, I'm such a silly goose, you see. I was always Sesame Weichbrodt's laziest student. It just seems to me that you know so much. . . ."—But a voice inside her said: Putting on airs? One finds oneself among strangers, shows oneself from one's best side, chooses one's words, and tries to please—that's quite normal.

"Well, then, they are more or less the same," he said, flattered. "Certain nutrients, you see . . ."

And as Tony went on eating her breakfast and young Schwarzkopf smoked his pipe, their small-talk turned to Sesame Weichbrodt, Tony's years at the boarding school, her friends Gerda Arnoldsen, who had returned to Amsterdam, and Armgard von Schilling, whose white farmhouse you could see here from the beach, at least if the weather was clear.

When she finished eating, Tony dabbed her mouth with her napkin and asked, pointing to the newspaper, "Anything new there?"

Young Schwarzkopf laughed and shook his head in mock sympathy. "No, no. How could there be anything new there? This local *Advertiser* is a pitiful rag, really."

"Oh? But Papa and Mama have always had it delivered."

"Yes, well," he said with a blush, "I read it, too, as you can see, simply because there's nothing else. But that Consul Such-and-such, wholesaler of whatever, is planning to celebrate his silver anniversary is not exactly earthshaking news. Yes, yes—you laugh. But you should read other papers sometime, the Königsberg *News* or the Rhine *Gazette*. You'd find something quite different in them. Whatever the King of Prussia may say."

"And what does he say?"

"Yes, well . . . but, no, unfortunately I cannot repeat that to a lady." And he blushed again. "He has spoken rather ungraciously about that part of the press," he continued with a forced ironic smile that, for a moment at least, touched Tony to the quick. "They don't speak all too highly of the government, you see, of the nobility, the clergy, and the Junkers. And they're very clever at leading the censors around by the nose."

"Well, and what about you, don't you speak highly of the nobility?"

"Me?" he asked in embarrassment.

Tony stood up. "Well, let's talk about that some other time. How would it be if I took a walk on the beach? You see, the sky is almost all blue now. It won't rain anymore today. I can't wait to jump into the ocean again. Would you like to walk down with me?"

7

SHE HAD DONNED her large straw hat and put up her parasol, because it was uncomfortably hot despite the sea breeze. Wearing his gray felt hat and carrying his book, young Schwarzkopf strode along beside her, and from time to time he threw a sidelong glance her way. They walked along Front Row, and strolled through the spa gardens, the gravel paths and rose beds still and shadeless in the hot sun. The band shell, hidden behind evergreens, stood silent beside the pump room, and across the way was the pastry shop and the two Swiss-style lodges separated by a long central building. It was eleven-thirty now; all the hotel guests must already have gone to the beach.

They crossed the children's playground with its benches and large set of swings, passed close by the bathhouse with hot springs, and then moved slowly across the Leuchtenfeld flats. The sun brooded over the grass, sending up the hot, spicy odor of clover and weeds, while buzzing blue flies sped through the air or simply hovered there. The sea roared in a muffled monotone, and little whitecaps sparkled now and then in the distance.

"What is that you're reading?" Tony asked.

The young man took the book in both hands and ruffled the pages from back to front with his thumb.

"Oh, nothing for you, Fräulein Buddenbrook. It's all blood and guts and misery. Look, this is about edema of the lungs—what people call 'catarrh.' And what happens is, the pockets of the lungs fill up with a kind of watery fluid, which is highly dangerous, common in cases of pneumonia. If it gets very bad, the patient can't breathe, and then simply dies. And it's all described in a very cool and superior way."

"Oh, phooey! But I suppose if one wants to be a doctor . . . Just you wait, I'll see to it that you become our family doctor when Grabow retires someday."

"Ha! And what are you reading, Fräulein Buddenbrook, if I might ask?"

"Do you know Hoffmann?" Tony asked in return.

"The fellow with the choirmaster and the golden pot? Yes, that's very pretty stuff. But, you know, it's probably more for the ladies. Men have other things to read nowadays."

"And now I have to ask *you* something," Tony said, after they had taken a few more steps—she had decided she must. "And that is, just what is your first name, really? I haven't been able to catch it any time it's been mentioned . . . and it's making me downright nervous. I've been racking my brains. . . ."

"You've been racking your brains about it?"

"Yes, and now don't make it any worse than it already is. It's probably not proper for me to ask, but I am curious, of course. Although I don't suppose there's any reason I'd ever need to know it."

"Well, my name is Morten," he said, and blushed redder than ever.

"Morten? That's a pretty name."

"What? Pretty?"

"Yes, for heaven's sake. It's certainly prettier than if your name was Jack or Joe. There's something special about it, something exotic."

"You're a romantic, Mademoiselle Buddenbrook. You've been reading too much Hoffmann. Well, it's actually very simple. My grandfather was half Norwegian, and his name was Morten. And I was christened after him. That's the whole story."

Tony carefully waded up through the tall, sharp rushes bordering the exposed beach. And now the row of wooden beach pavilions, with their little round roofs lay before them, and beyond that, closer to the water, the wicker beach chairs with families encamped around them in the warm sand: ladies with pince-nez tinted blue and library books; gentlemen in light-colored suits, lazily drawing figures in the sand with their walking sticks; tanned children under immense straw hats—shoveling, tumbling, digging for water, baking pies in wooden plates, burrowing tunnels, wading up to their naked knees in the low surf, sailing little ships. The large wooden swimming pier jutted out into the water on their right.

"We're heading straight for the Möllendorpf pavilion," Tony said. "Let's turn off a little."

"Certainly—but you probably want to join your fine friends. I'll just go sit on those stones back there."

"Join them? Yes, yes, I suppose I will have to say hello. But I really haven't the least desire to, I assure you. I came here to get away, to find some peace."

"To get away? From whom?

"Why—from . . ."

"Fräulein Buddenbrook, there's one more thing I have to ask *you* . . . but later, when we have more time and an opportunity presents itself. But now allow me to say adieu and go sit there on those stones."

"Don't you want me to introduce you, Herr Schwarzkopf?" Tony asked pointedly.

"No, oh no . . ." Morten hastily replied. "Thanks so much. I don't think I'd fit in very well, you see. I'll just go sit back there on those stones."

And while Morten Schwarzkopf moved away to the right, in the direction of the swimming pier and some boulders lapped by the surf, Tony walked ahead toward a rather large group of people that had gathered around the Möllendorpfs' pavilion and that included Möllendorpfs, Hagenströms, Kistenmakers, and Fritsches. Except for Consul Fritsche from Hamburg, who owned all this, and Peter Döhlmann, the *suitier*, there were only women and children—this was a workday, and most of the men were in their offices in town. Consul Fritsche, an older gentleman with a distinguished clean-shaven face, was standing up in the pavilion, busily directing a telescope at a sailboat visible in the distance. Sporting a broad-brimmed straw hat and a round-cut nautical beard, Peter Döhlmann was chatting with the ladies, who were either lying on plaid blankets or sitting on little canvas stools. These included: Frau Möllendorpf, née Langhals, who was toying with a long-handled lorgnette, her gray hair flying in all directions; Frau Hagenström, plus Julie, who had never grown all that much, but already wore diamond earrings like her mother; Frau Kistenmaker and her daughters; and Frau Fritsche, a small wrinkle-faced lady, who wore a bonnet and was in charge of the spa's entertainments. Sunburned and exhausted, she was forever worrying about sailing excursions, raffles, children's parties, and galas. The woman who read aloud for them sat off at some distance. The children were playing in the water.

In the last few years Kistenmaker & Sons had been prospering, and had begun to replace C. F. Köppen as the fashionable firm from which to buy wine. The two sons, Eduard and Stephan, were old enough to work in their father's office. Consul Döhlmann displayed none of the fine manners that were the mark of a man like Justus, for instance; he was an ordinary *suitier*, who made a specialty of being amiably down-to-earth and who permitted himself extraordinary social liberties because he knew that the ladies in particular regarded him as a character and enjoyed his loud, easygoing audacity. At a banquet given by the Buddenbrooks one evening, when the next course was much too long in coming and the hostess was beginning to show her embarrassment and the guests were growing ill-humored, he put everyone at ease again by roaring across the table in booming Plattdeutsch, "Hope it ain't me they're waitin' for, Frau Buddenbrook!"

And in that same gruff, reverberating voice he was now telling dubious anecdotes, spiced with dialect idioms. Frau Möllendorpf was beside herself with laughter and kept crying in exhaustion, "Good Lord, Herr Döhlmann, stop that this minute!"

Tony was received coldly by the Hagenströms, but all the others greeted her with great cordiality. Even Consul Fritsche came hurrying down the steps of the pavilion—he hoped that at least next year the Buddenbrooks would return to help swell the population of his spa.

"Your servant, as always, mamselle," Consul Döhlmann said, employing his most refined enunciation, because he knew that Fräulein Buddenbrook did not particularly care for his manners.

"Mademoiselle Buddenbrook!"

"You did come."

"How delightful."

"And when did you arrive?"

"And what an inchanting dress!"—It was the rage to say "inchanting."

"And where are you staying?"

"With the Schwarzkopfs?"

"The harbor pilot?"

"How original."

"Yes, it's simply dradfully original."—It was the rage to say "dradfully."

"You're staying in town?" Consul Fritsche, the owner of the spa, repeated his question, without letting it be known that his feelings were hurt.

"So we'll not have the pleasure of your company at the next gala?" his wife asked.

"Oh, you're staying in Travemünde for only a short while?" another lady responded.

"Don't you think, my dear, that the Buddenbrooks are just a bit too exclusive?" Frau Hagenström asked in a very low voice of Frau Möllendorpf.

"And you've not had your swim yet?" someone inquired. "Which of our young ladies hasn't been swimming yet today? Marie, Julie, Louise? But of course your friends will join you, Fräulein Antonie."

Several young women emerged out of the group, ready for a swim with Tony. And there was no talking Peter Döhlmann out of accompanying the ladies along the beach.

"Heavens, do you remember how we used to walk to school together?" Tony asked Julie Hagenström.

"Y-yes. And you were always doing something naughty," Julie said with an indulgent smile.

They walked toward the pier, taking the boardwalk laid well above the waterline; and as they passed the boulders where Morten Schwarzkopf was sitting reading, Tony quickly nodded to him several times from a distance.

Someone asked, "Who was that you were nodding to?"

"Oh, that's young Schwarzkopf," Tony said. "He escorted me down to the beach."

"The harbor pilot's son?" Julie Hagenström asked, her bright black eyes sending a sharp glance over to where Morten was sitting and watching the elegant swimming party, his face betraying a certain melancholy.

But in a loud voice Tony said, "What a shame that August Möllendorpf isn't here. Afternoons on the beach must be awfully boring."

8

AND SO BEGAN Tony Buddenbrook's summer vacation—a few lovely weeks, more pleasant and amusing than any she had ever spent in Travemünde. A weight had been lifted from her, and she blossomed—her words and gestures were as carefree and saucy as ever. The consul came to Travemünde with Tom and Christian every Sunday, and he was pleased with what he saw. They would dine at the table d'hôte, sit under the awnings of the pastry shop, drinking coffee and listening to open-air concerts, or watch the festive crowd of people like Justus Kröger and Peter Döhlmann play roulette in the grand salon. The consul never gambled.

Tony swam, sunned, ate bratwurst with ginger gravy, and took long walks with Morten—down the beach road to the next town, along the shore to the Temple of the Sea with its panorama of the coastline, or up the path to the little woods on the hill behind the spa hotel, where the big dinner bell was hung. Or they rowed across the Trave to Priwall, where they looked for amber.

Morten was an entertaining escort, although he could be a little heated and dogmatic in his views. He never failed to have some stern and righteous opinion on every topic, even if he blushed when he gave it. With angry, awkward gestures, he would declare all members of the nobility to be wretched idiots, and that grieved Tony, and she scolded him for it. But she was very proud of how openly he confided to her thoughts that he concealed from his parents.

One day he said, "There's something else I must tell you: I have a complete skeleton in my room in Göttingen. You know, all the human bones, more or less held together with wire. Well, I've dressed my skeleton in an old police uniform. Ha! Isn't that magnificent? But for God's sake, don't tell my father!"

Tony did of course spend some time with her friends from town on the beach or in the hotel garden, and she was taken along on sailing parties or invited to this gala or that. And then Morten would go sit "on the stones." Since that very first day, those stones had become a fixed phrase for them: "to sit on the stones" meant "to be lonely and bored."

One rainy day—the ocean was hidden in all directions by a veil of gray drizzle that merged with the low-hanging sky and made the beach soggy and the paths a sea of puddles—Tony said, "We'll both have to sit on the stones today, either on the porch or in the parlor. I have no choice but to listen to you play some of your student songs, Morten, though I find them awfully boring."

"Yes," Morten said, "let's take a seat. But, you know, when you're along, they're not stones at all." He didn't say such things when his father was present, by the way; his mother was allowed to hear them, though.

"What now?" the harbor pilot asked, when Tony and Morten both got up from lunch as if they were about to go off somewhere together. "Just where are you young folks headed?"

"Well, I was going to escort Fräulein Antonie to the Temple of the Sea."

"Oh, you were, were you? Tell me, my son, might it not be a better plan if you'd go up to your room and memorize your nerve system? By the time you get back to Göttingen you'll have forgotten everything."

But Frau Schwarzkopf said in her mild way, "Good heavens, Diederich, why shouldn't he go along? Let him be. He's on vacation. Can't he enjoy our visitor with the rest of us?"—And so they went for their walk.

They strolled along the beach, right next to the water, where it is easy to walk because the sand is smooth and hard after high tide, where little ordinary white shells are scattered about, and the other kind, too—larger and longer, iridescent—and here and there you find wet yellow-green seaweed with berries like hollow balls that pop when you squeeze them, and jellyfish, the simple translucent kind, and the reddish yellow poisonous ones that sting you on the legs when you're swimming.

"Do you want to know just how stupid I used to be?" Tony asked. "I wanted some of those pretty, colored stars that jellyfish have inside. So I wrapped a whole bunch of jellyfish in my handkerchief and laid them out neatly in the sun on the balcony, so that they'd dry up. And then only the stars would be left. Right . . . And when I went back to look, there was just a big wet spot that smelled like rotting seaweed."

They walked, and the long waves rolled and murmured rhythmically beside them; the fresh salty wind blew free and unobstructed in their faces, wrapped itself around their ears, and made them feel slightly numb and deliciously dizzy. They walked along in that wide, peaceful, whispering hush of the sea that gives every sound, near or far, some mysterious importance.

On their left were broken cliffs of clay, with boulders that kept jutting out at new angles, hiding the curve of the shoreline. At one point the beach turned rocky, and they climbed up into the woods to reach the path that led to the Temple of the Sea—a round pavilion of logs and planks, its interior full of carved inscriptions, initials, hearts, and poems. Tony and Morten sat down on a wooden bench at the back of one of the little niches that faced the sea and had the same woody smell as the changing cabins at the pier.

It was very still and solemn up here at this time of the afternoon. A few birds were chattering and the gentle sough of the trees blended with that of the sea, which lay spread out far below—the rigging of a ship visible in the distance. Protected from the wind that had played about their ears until now, they were suddenly caught up in the mood of pensive silence.

Tony wanted to know: "Is it coming or going?"

"What?" Morten asked in his ponderous voice. But then, as if awakening from some profound reverie, he quickly said, "Going. That's the *Bürgermeister Steenbock*, heading for Russia. I wouldn't want to be on it," he added after a pause. "Things there must be even more atrocious than they are here."

"Oh," Tony said, "and now you're about to start in on the nobility again, Morten, I can see it in your face. That's not very nice of you. Have you ever known a single one?"

"No!" Morten cried, close to rage. "Thank God!"

"Right, so you see? But I have. Just a girl of course, Armgard von Schilling, who lives over there, the one I told you about. Well, now, she had a kinder heart than you or I, she hardly knew what her *von* meant, she ate plain old sausage and talked about her cows."

"Of course there are exceptions, Fräulein Tony," he said heatedly. "But listen to me now. You're a young lady, and you see everything from a personal angle. You know a young noblewoman and say: My, what a fine person she is. Of course. But you don't have to know a single one of them to condemn the lot. It's a matter of principle, you see, it's the institution itself. So what do you have to say to that? Nothing. How can anyone, simply by virtue of being born noble and special, look with disdain down at us others, who no matter what we achieve can never reach their heights?" Morten spoke out of naïve and goodhearted outrage. He tried to make little gestures with his hands, saw himself how awkward they were, and gave that up. But he went on speaking. He was rolling now. He sat bent forward, one thumb wedged between the buttons on his jacket, a kind but defiant look in his eyes. "We are the bourgeoisie—the third estate, as they call us now—and what we want is a nobility of merit, nothing more. We don't recognize this lazy nobility we now have, we reject our present class hierarchy. We want all men to be free and equal, for no one to be someone else's subject, but for all to be subject to the law. There should be an end of privileges and arbitrary power. Everyone should be treated equally as a child of the state, and just as there are no longer any middlemen between the layman and his God, so each citizen should stand in direct relation to the state. We want freedom of the press, of employment, of commerce. We want all men to compete without any special privileges, and the only crown should be the crown of merit. But we have been enslaved, bound and gagged. . . . What was it I was going to say? Oh yes, now pay attention. Four years ago they renewed the Confederation's laws dealing with the university and the press—fine laws those are! No truth can be written or taught that might not agree with the established order of things. Do you understand? Truth is suppressed, cannot get a hearing. And why? For the sake of an antiquated, idiotic, enfeebled class that, as everyone knows, will have to be done away with sooner or later. I don't think you have any notion of how beastly that is. Force—the application of dumb, brutal, instantaneous force by the police—without any understanding of intellectual matters, of new ideas. But apart from all that, I have just one thing to say: The King of Prussia committed a great injustice back then, in 1813, during the French occupation. He called us to arms and promised us a constitution. And we came, and we liberated Germany."

Tony, who had been watching him, chin in hand, from the side, wondered for one brief, solemn moment if he really might have helped drive out Napoleon.

"But do you suppose he honored his promise? Oh no! Our present king is a fine orator, a dreamer, a romantic like you, Fräulein Tony. For there is one thing we must keep in mind: if philosophers and poets have finally put aside or dismissed some idea, some point of view, some principle, a king is sure to come along who has just discovered it, who believes it to be the latest and best idea, something he has to believe and act on. That's how things are in a monarchy. Kings are not just men, they are perfectly mediocre men, always bringing up the rear several miles behind. Ah, Germany is just like some student in a fraternity back in the days of the Wars of Liberation, some brave and enthusiastic young fellow, who has turned into a wretched philistine."

"Yes," Tony said, "that's all very fine. But let me ask you one thing. What does it matter to you? You're not even a Prussian."

"Ah, it's all the same, Fräulein Buddenbrook—and, yes, I intentionally used your last name. Actually I should call you *Demoiselle* Buddenbrook, to do you full justice. Do people here enjoy any more freedom, equality, or fraternity than in Prussia? Barriers, social distance, aristocracy—here as well as there. Your sympathies are with the nobility—and do you want me to tell you why? Because you're an aristocrat yourself. Ah yes, didn't you know that? Your father is a great sovereign, and you are a princess, separated by an abyss from all us others, who don't belong to your circle of ruling families. Sure, you can go for a walk along the shore with one of us for a little relaxation, but when you return to that circle of the chosen with their privileges, then it's off to sit on the stones." His voice had grown strangely impassioned.

"Morten," Tony said sadly, "you really *were* angry when you went to sit on the stones. I asked you to let me introduce you. . . ."

"Oh, you're taking it all too personally again, like the young lady you are, Fräulein Tony. I'm speaking in general. I said that there is no more equality among people here than in Prussia. But if I were to speak personally," he went on now in a more gentle voice, but that strange passion had not gone out of it, "then I would not be speaking about the present, but about the future, perhaps, when as Madame Such-and-such you will vanish for good and all into your elegant world and . . . it's off to sit on the stones for the rest of one's life."

He fell silent, and Tony was silent, too. She was no longer looking at him, but in the other direction, at the plank wall beside her. There was a rather long, uneasy pause.

"Do you remember," Morten began again, "how I once told you that there was a question I wanted to ask you? Yes, well, you should know that it's something I've been thinking about since the afternoon you first arrived. Don't guess. You can't possibly know what it is. I'll ask some other time, when the opportunity presents itself; there's no hurry, it really is none of my business, I'm merely curious. No, for today I'll just let you in on a secret . . . something quite different. Look at this."

Morten pulled out the end of a narrow, gaily striped ribbon from his jacket pocket, and gazed with both expectation and triumph into Tony's eyes.

"It's very pretty," she said, not understanding. "What does it mean?"

"It means that I belong to a fraternity in Göttingen—and now you know. I have a cap with these colors, too, but while I'm on vacation, my skeleton is wearing it along with his police uniform. Because I wouldn't dare be seen with it here, you see. I can depend on you not to say anything, can't I? If my father ever learned about this, it would be a disaster."

"Not a word, Morten. No, you can count on me. But I don't really know anything about what it means. Have you all sworn to overturn the nobility? What is it you want?"

"We want freedom!" Morten said.

"Freedom?" she asked.

"Why, yes, freedom, you know, freedom," he repeated, gesturing somewhat awkwardly but enthusiastically toward the sea—not in the direction where the coast of Mecklenburg hemmed in the bay, but to the open water, where ruffling bands of green, blue, yellow, and gray grew thinner and thinner, extending as far as the eye could see toward the grand blur of the horizon.

Tony followed the gesture with her eyes, and they gazed together into the same distance—it would not have taken much for their two hands, lying side by side on the bench, to have joined. They said nothing for a long time. And while the sea murmured ponderously and peacefully below, Tony suddenly felt herself united with Morten in a great, vague, yearning, intuitive understanding of what "freedom" meant.

9

"Isn't it remarkable, Morten, how you can't get bored at the beach? Try lying on your back for three or four hours anywhere else—not doing anything, not thinking about anything."

"Yes, yes. Although I must admit that I used to be bored now and then, Fräulein Tony; but that was several weeks ago."

Autumn arrived, the first strong winds had begun to blow. Gray, thin, tattered clouds scudded across the sky. The dark, tossing sea was dotted everywhere with foam. Great waves rolled toward the shore with inexorable, appalling, silent power, pitched forward majestically, the swells shining like dark green metal, and plunged raucously onto the sand.

The season was definitely over. There were only a few wicker chairs left on the deserted section of the beach that had been populated by the crowd of bathers—even some of the pavilions had been dismantled. But Tony and Morten spent their afternoons in the remote spot where the yellow clay cliffs began and the waves flung their spray high against Seagull Rock. Morten had built her a tall fortress of firmly packed sand; and there she lay on her back in her soft gray fall jacket with large buttons, her feet crossed to reveal her strap shoes and white stockings. Morten lay on his side, turned toward her, his chin propped in one hand. Now and then a gull would dart across the open water, shrieking in its search for prey. They watched as walls of water streaked green with sea-grass moved toward the cliffs, only to burst against the boulders opposite them—in a wild, eternal, deafening tumult that swallowed every word and destroyed all sense of time.

Finally Morten stirred as if rousing himself and asked, "And so you'll be leaving soon, Fräulein Tony?"

"No . . . why?" Tony responded absent-mindedly, not really comprehending his question.

"Well, good Lord, it's the tenth of September. My vacation will soon be over in any case. How long can this last? Are you looking forward to parties in town? So tell me—I suppose the gentlemen you dance with are very charming? No, that's not what I wanted to ask. There's just one question I want you to answer," he said, shifting his chin in his hand and gazing at her with sudden resolve. "It's the question I've been saving for so long now, you remember? Well, then—who is Herr Grünlich?"

Tony winced, looked straight at him, and then let her eyes wander about like someone reminded of a distant dream. At the same time she felt reawakening within her the same emotion that she had toyed with during the days of Herr Grünlich's courtship: a sense of personal importance.

"*That's* what you wanted to know, Morten?" she asked solemnly. "Well, then, let me tell you. I felt terribly embarrassed, I assure you, when Thomas mentioned that name my first afternoon here; but since you've already heard it anyway . . . Enough.—Herr Grünlich, Bendix Grünlich, is a business friend of my father, a well-to-do merchant from Hamburg, who came to town and asked for my hand. Oh no!" she said, hastily countering a gesture Morten had made. "I refused him, I could not bring myself to consent to his proposal of marriage."

"And why not, if I might ask?" Morten said ineptly.

"Why not? Good Lord, because I couldn't *stand* him!" she cried, close to fury. "You should have seen him, the way he looked, the way he acted. He had these gold muttonchops—totally unnatural. I'm sure he curls and powders them with the same dust they use to gild walnuts at Christmas. And he was devious besides. He fawned on my parents, shamelessly echoed their every word."

Morten interrupted her: "But there's one more thing you have to tell me. What does . . . what does 'Those add a rare, ornamental touch' mean?"

Tony broke into a nervous giggle. "Yes, that's just how he talked, Morten. He didn't say: 'Those look lovely,' or 'That works nicely in this room,' but 'That adds a rare, ornamental touch.' That's just how silly he was, I swear. And unbelievably persistent. He wouldn't let me alone, although I never treated him with anything but sarcasm. There was one scene when he came close to tears. I ask you—a man who weeps?"

"He must have admired you greatly," Morten said softly.

"But what concern is that of mine?" she cried in amazement, turning to him on her pile of sand.

"You are cruel, Fräulein Tony. Are you always cruel? Tell me—you couldn't stand this Herr Grünlich, but have you ever been fond of anyone else? Sometimes I think: Does she have a cold heart? But there is one thing I must tell you . . . something so true that I can swear to it: there is nothing silly about a man who weeps because you will have nothing to do with him. That's all. I am not sure, not sure in the least, that I might not do the same. You see, you're a spoiled, elegant creature. Do you always mock the people who lay themselves at your feet? Do you really have a cold heart?"

And now, after her brief, initial gaiety, Tony's upper lip began to quiver. She stared at him with large, sad eyes that slowly began to glisten with tears, and said, "No, Morten, do you believe that of me? You mustn't believe that of me."

"I don't, I don't believe it!" Morten cried with a laugh that betrayed both his deep affection and barely stifled exultation. He rolled over now so that he was lying close beside her on his stomach; and, propping himself on his elbows, he took one of her hands in his, and his kindly steel-blue eyes gazed deep into hers with rapturous fervor. "And you . . . you won't mock me if I tell you that . . ."

"I know, Morten," she interrupted him, very softly, staring down at her free hand, her fingers slowly sifting the soft, white sand.

"You know! And what about you . . . *you*, Fräulein Tony?"

"Yes, Morten. I think a great deal of you, too. I'm very fond of you, fonder than of anyone else I know."

He sat up and attempted a few gestures with his arms, not really knowing what to do. He leapt to his feet, but immediately sat back down and cried in a wavering voice that first faltered, broke, and then, in its joy, found itself again, "Ah, thank you, thank you! You see, I'm happier now than I have ever been in my life." He began to kiss her hands.

Suddenly he said more softly, "You'll soon be going back to town, Tony, and my vacation is over in two weeks as well and I'll be returning to Göttingen. But will you promise me that you won't forget our afternoon here on the beach—until I come back, have become a doctor, and can plead our cause with your father, however difficult that may be? And that in the meantime you won't pay any attention to any Herr Grünlichs? Oh, it won't be long, you'll see. I'll work like, like . . . and it won't be hard at all."

"Yes, Morten," she said happily and dreamily, gazing at his eyes, at his mouth and his hands, which were holding her own.

He pulled one of them closer to his chest and asked in a subdued, pleading voice, "And to seal that promise, won't you . . . may I not . . ."

She didn't answer, didn't even look at him—but silently moved the upper part of her body a little closer to him on their cushion of sand, and Morten kissed her slowly and formally on the mouth. Then they both looked down in different directions at the sand—embarrassed beyond measure.

10

Dearest Demoiselle Buddenbrook,

How long it has been since the undersigned was last permitted a glimpse of that most enchanting of faces. These few lines are penned to say that that same face has not ceased to float before his mind's eye, that during all the suspense and anxiety of the last weeks he has never ceased to recall how last he saw it on that precious afternoon in your parents' salon, when you let slip that half-promise with such modesty, and yet to what blissful effect. Long weeks have passed, during which you have withdrawn from the world, seeking to collect and know your thoughts, and one would presume that one may now hope one's period of trial is past. The undersigned makes bold, dearest demoiselle, deferentially to send you this little ring, enclosed as a pledge of his undying tenderness. With his most devoted compliments and kissing your hand most affectionately, he remains

Your most obedient servant,

Grünlich

Dear Papa,

Heavens, I am so angry! I just received the enclosed letter and ring from Grünlich, and my head hurts I am so upset, and I know no other course than to send them both back to you. Grünlich *refuses* to understand, and his poetic description of my "promise" is simply not true, and I implore you immediately to make it very clear to him that I am *a thousand times less* inclined to consent to his proposal than I was six weeks ago, and that he should finally leave me in peace—*he really is making a fool of himself.* I know I can tell you, my dearest father, that I have pledged my heart to someone else, who loves me and whom I love beyond anything I can say. Oh, Papa, I could write pages and pages about him. I am speaking of Morten Schwarzkopf, who intends to become a doctor and, as soon as he is one, to ask for my hand. I know that by family custom I should marry a merchant, but as a scholar Morten is an equally respectable gentleman. He is not wealthy, something I know is important for you and Mama, and I may be young, but I do know one thing, dear Papa: that life has taught many people that riches do not always make for happiness. With a thousand kisses I remain

Your obedient daughter

Antonie

P.S. The ring is not quality gold, and it is rather small, I notice.

My dear Tony,

Your letter duly received. As regards its contents, I should tell you that I did not fail dutifully to communicate to Herr Grünlich your view of the situation in an appropriate manner. The result of which, however, truly shocked me. You are a grown young lady and find yourself at such a serious crossroads in life that I do not scruple to point out the consequences that might result from any frivolous step on your part. Upon hearing what I had to say, Herr Grünlich became quite desperate, crying that he loved you so much and the pain of losing you would be so great that he was prepared to take his own life if you were to persist in your decision. Inasmuch as I cannot take seriously what you have written about another attachment, I would ask you to master your agitation about the ring you were sent and to weigh all this most seriously one more time. My Christian convictions, dear daughter, tell me it is our duty to have regard for the feelings of others, for we do not know whether one day you may not be held answerable before the Highest Judge because the man whom you have stubbornly and coldly scorned has been guilty of the sin of taking his own life. I would like you to recall, however, something that I have impressed upon you often enough in conversation, and which the present occasion allows me to repeat in writing. For, although the words we speak are more vivid and immediate, the written word has the advantage of having been chosen with great care and is fixed in a form that its author has weighed and considered, so that it may be read again and again to cumulative effect. We are not born, my dear daughter, to pursue our own small personal happiness, for we are not separate, independent, self-subsisting individuals, but links in a chain; and it is inconceivable that we would be what we are without those who have preceded us and shown us the path that they themselves have scrupulously trod, looking neither to the left nor to the right, but, rather, following a venerable and trustworthy tradition. Your path, it seems to me, has been obvious for many weeks now, its course clearly defined, and you would surely not be my daughter, the granddaughter of your grandfather, who rests now in God, indeed would not be a worthy link in our family's chain if, of your own accord and out of stubbornness and frivolity, you seriously intended to follow an aberrant path of your own. I beg you, my dear Antonie, to ponder these things in your heart.

The most heartfelt greetings as well from your mother, Thomas, Christian, Clara, and Klothilde (who has spent the last few weeks at Grudging with her father), and from Mamselle Jungmann as well. We all look forward to the moment when we may embrace you once again.

As always with love,

Your Father

11

It was pouring rain. Heaven, earth, and sea melted into one another, while gusts of wind picked up the rain and drove it against the windows until drops became streams that ran down the panes, making it impossible to see out. From the chimneys came voices of lament and despair.

Shortly after lunch, when Morten Schwarzkopf stepped out on the porch with his pipe to have a look at the skies, he discovered a gentleman standing there in a long, narrow, yellow-plaid ulster and a gray hat; a closed carriage, its top glistening with rain and its wheels spattered with mud, stood waiting in front of the house. Morten stared in bewilderment at the gentleman's pink face—and muttonchops that looked as if they had been powdered with the same dust used to gild walnuts at Christmas.

The gentleman in the ulster looked at Morten as if he were a servant—eyes squinted slightly but not really seeing him—and asked in a gentle voice, "Might I speak with the harbor pilot?"

"But of course," Morten stammered, "I think my father is . . ."

And now the gentleman fixed his eyes on him—eyes as blue as a goose's.

"Are you Herr Morten Schwarzkopf?" he asked.

"Yes, sir," Morten replied, trying to give his face a stern, determined look.

"Why, look, it is indeed!" the gentleman in the ulster remarked, and then continued: "Would you be so good as to announce me to your father, young man. My name is Grünlich."

Morten led the gentleman across the porch and down the hall, opened the door to his father's office, and returned to the parlor to inform his father, who now left the room. The younger Schwarzkopf sat down at the round table, propped his elbows on it, and, without so much as a glance at his mother, who was busy darning stockings by the dim light of the window, appeared to immerse himself in the "pitiful local rag," whose only news was Consul Such-and-such's silver anniversary. Tony was resting upstairs in her room.

The harbor pilot entered his office with the bearing of a man satisfied with the hearty lunch he has just eaten. His uniform jacket was unbuttoned, revealing the full curve of his white vest. His frosty sailor's beard contrasted sharply with his red face. His tongue was contentedly wandering among his teeth, causing his dignified mouth to assume the most extraordinary positions. He gave a brief, jerky bow, as if to say: "That's how it's done."

"Good afternoon," he said. "At your service, sir."

For his part, Herr Grünlich made a very deliberate bow, and said softly, while turning the corners of his mouth down just a little, "Huh-uh-hmm."

The office was a rather small room, with wainscoting a few feet up the walls, the rest unpapered plaster. The curtains at the window, where rain drummed incessantly, were yellow with smoke. To the right of the door was a long rough desk covered with papers, and above it was pinned a large map of Europe and a smaller map of the Baltic. A trim model ship under full sail hung from the middle of the ceiling.

The harbor pilot motioned for his guest to take a seat near the door, on the sofa covered with cracked black oilcloth, and sat down himself in a wooden armchair, folding his hands across his stomach. Herr Grünlich sat at the edge of the sofa—back straight, hat on knee, ulster still buttoned tight.

"To repeat," he said, "my name is Grünlich, from Hamburg—*Grünlich.* By the way of introduction, might I mention that I call myself a close business friend of Consul Buddenbrook the wholesale merchant."

"My pleasure. It's an honor to meet you, Herr Grünlich. But won't you make yourself a little more comfortable? A glass of grog after your trip? I'll just tell the kitchen. . . ."

"I take the liberty of informing you," Herr Grünlich said very calmly, "that my time is limited, that my carriage awaits, and that I have had no choice but to come here to speak but a very few words with you."

"At your service, sir," Herr Schwarzkopf said again, a little intimidated—and now came a pause.

"Herr Captain," Herr Grünlich began, setting his head back a little and giving it a determined shake. But then he fell silent again to enhance the effect of this form of address; he closed his mouth firmly, as if tugging the strings tight on a purse.

"Herr Captain," he repeated, and then quickly went on, "the matter that has brought me here directly concerns the young lady who has resided in your home for some weeks now."

"Mamselle Buddenbrook?" Herr Schwarzkopf asked.

"Indeed," Herr Grünlich replied—his voice devoid of expression, his head lowered, and little hard lines forming at the corners of his mouth. "I . . . find myself constrained to reveal to you"—his voice took on a casual lilt now, and his eyes wandered about the room, fixing briefly with great attention on each point before taking a final leap to the window—"that some time ago I asked for the hand of Demoiselle Buddenbrook in marriage, that I possess the fullest consent of both parental parties, and that, although a formal betrothal has not yet taken place, the young lady has acknowledged in unambiguous terms my claim to her hand."

"Good God, you don't say?" Herr Schwarzkopf replied cheerily. "I didn't know a thing about it. Congratulations, Herr . . . Grünlich, my heartiest congratulations. You've got a good thing there, something really solid."

"Much obliged," Herr Grünlich said, laying cold emphasis on both words. "But what brings me here to you," he continued in that same high lilting voice, "as regards this matter, my good Herr Captain, is the fact that certain grave *difficulties* have newly arisen to hinder this alliance, and that these difficulties . . . have their source in your household—?" He gave an interrogatory lift to these last words, as if to say, "Can what these ears have heard really be possible?"

Herr Schwarzkopf's sole reply was to raise his gray eyebrows very high and grab both arms of his chair in his tanned, hairy sailor's hands.

"Yes. Indeed. So I hear," Herr Grünlich said with grim certainly. "*I hear* that your son—a *studiosus medicinae*, I believe—has allowed himself—quite out of ignorance, of course—to encroach upon my rights. *I hear* that he has used the young lady's presence here to wrest from her certain promises. . . ."

"What?" the harbor pilot shouted, grabbing even more tightly to the arms of his chair and then jumping up. "Well, we'll soon see . . . By God, we'll just see about that." And he was at the door in two strides; he flung it open and called down the hall in a voice that would have outboomed the wildest seas, "Meta! Morten! Come here! Come in here, both of you!"

"It would cause me keen regret," Herr Grünlich said with a delicate smile, "if in exerting my prior claims I may be countering your own paternal intentions, Herr Captain."

Diederich Schwarzkopf whirled around and stared hard at him, wrinkles forming all around his sharp blue eyes, as if he were trying in vain to understand this remark.

"Sir!" he said in a voice that sounded as if his throat had just been seared by a strong pull of grog. "I'm a simple man and don't know much about innuendies [*sic*] and other such refinements, but if you just might be implying . . . Well, all I have to say to you is that you're barking up the wrong tree and are badly mistaken about my principles. I know who my son is, and I know who Mamselle Buddenbrook is, and there's too much self-respect and too much pride in these old bones, sir, for me to be having any paternal intentions. Ah, so here you are—well, speak up and answer me! What is going on here, huh? What is this I've just heard?"

Frau Schwarzkopf and her son were standing in the doorway—the former quite unsuspecting and busy setting her apron to rights, Morten with the look of an impenitent sinner. Herr Grünlich had not risen when they entered—by no means—but just sat there calmly in his buttoned-up ulster, holding his straight-backed pose on the edge of the sofa.

"So you have been behaving like a silly fool?" the harbor pilot snapped at Morten.

The young man kept one thumb wedged between the buttons of his jacket; he scowled, even puffed out his cheeks in defiance. "Yes, Father," he said, "Fraülein Buddenbrook and I . . ."

"Well, I've got just one thing to say to you—that you're an idiot, a nincompoop, a silly ass. And it's back to Göttingen with you tomorrow, do you hear, tomorrow morning! And this whole thing is childishness and damn tomfoolery. And there's an end to it!"

"Diederich, good heavens," Frau Schwarzkopf said, folding her hands. "You can't just brush it off like that! Who knows . . ." She stopped right there, and in her face they saw a beautiful dream collapsing in ruins.

"Would the gentleman like to speak with the young lady?" the harbor pilot said in a gruff voice, turning to Herr Grünlich.

"She's in her room. She's sleeping," Frau Schwarzkopf explained, her voice filled with compassion.

"I'm sorry to hear that," Herr Grünlich said with a little sigh of relief and stood up. "But I must repeat in any case that my time is limited, and that my carriage awaits. Permit me," he went on, executing a full sweep of his hat in Herr Schwarzkopf's direction, "to express to you, Herr Captain, my fullest satisfaction with and appreciation for your manly, high-principled conduct. My compliments. It was an honor. Adieu."

Diederich Schwarzkopf did not offer to shake hands; he simply let his heavy frame jerk forward briefly, as if to say: "That's how it's done."

Herr Grünlich strode with measured steps between Morten and his mother and out the door.

12

THOMAS APPEARED with the Krögers' carriage. This was the day.

The young man arrived about ten o'clock in the morning and had a bite to eat with the family in the parlor. They sat there together as they had on that first day; except that summer was over and it was too cold and windy to sit out on the porch—and that Morten wasn't there. He was in Göttingen. Tony and he hadn't even been able to say a real goodbye. The harbor pilot had stood beside them and said: "Well, there's an end to it."

At eleven o'clock brother and sister climbed into the carriage—Tony's large trunk was already strapped on at the rear. She was pale, and even in her soft fall jacket she shivered from the cold, from exhaustion, the excitement of the journey, and a sadness that from time to time would suddenly rise up and expand painfully inside her chest. She kissed little Meta, squeezed Frau Schwarzkopf's hand, and nodded to Herr Schwarzkopf who said, "Now, don't go forgetting us, mamselle. And no harm meant, eh? So, then, have a good trip and give my best to your good father, the consul, and his wife."

Then the door catch snapped into place, the heavy bays pulled, and the three Schwarzkopfs waved their handkerchiefs.

Tony tucked her head into a corner of the carriage and gazed out the window. The sky was overcast with white clouds, the Trave broken by little waves scurrying before the wind. Now and then little drops pricked at the windowpane. At the entrance to Front Row people were sitting on their stoops and mending nets; barefoot children came running up, curious to have a peek into the carriage. *They* would be staying here.

Once the carriage had left the last houses behind, Tony bent forward to have a final look at the lighthouse; then she leaned back and closed her tired, burning eyes. She had hardly slept all night she was so upset, had risen early to finish packing her trunk, and hadn't wanted any breakfast. Her mouth tasted dry and stale. She felt so weak that she didn't even try to hold back the tears that slowly welled into her eyes again and again.

She had only to close her eyes and she was back on the porch in Travemünde. She saw Morten Schwarzkopf—he was so real, and he spoke to her, bending forward in that special way of his, now and then turning his kind, probing eyes to gaze at someone else; he smiled, and wasn't even aware of how beautiful his teeth were. And it made her feel quite calm and serene. She could recall everything, all their many conversations, everything he had said, everything she had learned, and she found happy consolation in her solemn promise that she would keep all this in her heart forever as something sacred and inviolable. That the King of Prussia had committed a great injustice, that the local *Advertiser* was a pitiful rag, even that they had renewed the Confederation's laws dealing with universities four years ago—those would be cherished and consoling truths, a secret treasure that she could enjoy whenever she liked. In the middle of the street, at home with her family, at the dinner table—she would think of them. Who knew? Perhaps she would follow the path laid out for her and marry Herr Grünlich, she didn't care one way or the other. But whenever he would speak to her, she would suddenly be able to think: "I know something you don't. The nobility, as an institution, is despicable."

She smiled contentedly to herself. But then, suddenly, in the sound of the wheels she heard with perfect, unbelievably vivid clarity the sound of Morten's voice; she could make out every word he said in his kindly, somewhat ponderous and scratchy voice, heard it with very own ears—"We'll both have to sit on the stones today, Fräulein Tony"—and that brief memory overwhelmed her. She felt her chest contract with pain and grief, she didn't try to stop the burst of tears. Tucked in her corner, she held her handkerchief to her face with both hands and wept bitterly.

Thomas gazed somewhat helplessly out onto the road, a cigarette in his mouth. "Poor Tony," he said at last, patting her jacket sleeve. "I feel so very sorry for you. . . . I really do understand, you know. But what else is there to do? We simply have to get through it. Believe me, I know what it is."

"Oh, you don't know anything, Tom," Tony sobbed.

"Now, don't say that. It's absolutely certain, for example, that I'll be going to Amsterdam at the start of next year. Papa has found a position for me, with Kellen & Co. I'll have to say goodbye for a long, long time."

"Oh, Tom, saying goodbye to your parents and sisters and brothers—that's nothing!"

"Right," he said, drawing out the word somewhat. He sighed, as if he wanted to say more, but then he was silent. Letting his cigarette wander from one corner of his mouth to the other, he lifted an eyebrow and tilted his head to the side. After a while he tried again. "It won't last forever. Things take care of themselves. You'll forget. . . ."

"But I don't want to forget!" Tony cried in despair. "Forget? Is that any comfort?"

13

THEN CAME THE FERRY, then Israelsdorfer Allee, then Jerusalem Hill, Castle Yard. The carriage passed through the Burg Gate, on its right the towering walls of the prison; it rolled down Burg Strasse and crossed the Koberg. Tony looked at the gray gabled buildings, the oil lamps strung across the streets, the Holy Ghost Hospital—the lindens out front had lost most of their leaves already. Good Lord, it was all just as it had been before. It had stood here, immutable and venerable, and all the while she had thought of it as an old, easily forgotten dream. These gray gables were tradition, something old and trustworthy, and they had taken her back in, and here she would live again. She was not crying now; she looked about her with curiosity. The pain of parting was almost numbed by these streets and these old familiar faces. At that moment—the carriage was rattling along Breite Strasse—Matthiesen the grain hauler passed them and doffed his homely top hat with a deep sweep of his hand, and his gruff face was so full of respect it seemed to say, "I swear I'm at the bottom of the ladder."

The carriage turned onto Meng Strasse, and the heavy bays came to a halt, snorting and stamping, in front of the Buddenbrook house. Tom attentively helped his sister climb down, while Anton and Lina came hurrying out to unstrap the trunk. But they had to wait before they could enter the house. Three huge delivery wagons were lined up, moving slowly, one after another, into the passage; each was stacked high with full sacks of grain, all of them stamped "Johann Buddenbrook" in large black letters. They rumbled and swayed ponderously along the large echoing passageway and down the low steps into the courtyard. Some of the grain was to be unloaded in the back building, and the rest would find its way to the "Whale," the "Lion," or the "Oak."

The consul emerged from his office, his quill behind one ear, just as brother and sister entered the passage, and he stretched his arms out to his daughter. "Welcome home, my dear Tony!"

She kissed him, and she looked up at him, and in her eyes, still red from weeping, was something close to shame. But he was not cross, said nothing whatever about it. He only remarked, "It's late, but we've kept second breakfast waiting for you."

Elisabeth, Christian, Klothilde, Clara, and Ida Jungmann were standing together on the landing to greet her.

TONY SLEPT long and hard that first night on Meng Strasse, and the next morning, September 22, she came down to the breakfast room refreshed and relaxed—it had just struck seven. Only Mamselle Jungmann was already up, making coffee for breakfast.

"My, my, Tony dear," she said, turning around, her small brown eyes still puffy with sleep. "Up so early?"

Tony sat down at the secretary—its top was rolled back; she clasped her hands behind her head and stared for a while out into the courtyard, its black cobblestones glistening with rain, and at the damp garden, its green turned to yellow now. Then she began to rummage through the visiting cards and correspondence on the secretary.

Right next to the inkwell lay the familiar large gilt-edged notebook with its embossed cover and pages of various kinds of paper. There must have been some need for it yesterday evening, but the strange thing was that Papa had not slipped it into its leather case as usual and locked it in its special drawer.

She picked it up, started paging through, and soon found herself absorbed in reading. The entries she read were mostly simple matters that she knew well; yet each writer had picked up where his predecessor had left off, instinctively adopting the same stately, unexaggerated chronicle style, which in its very discretion spoke all the more nobly of a family's respect for itself, its traditions and history. This was nothing new to Tony; she had been allowed to study these pages several times before. But the contents had never made an impression on her the way they did this morning. The reverent importance given to even the most modest events pertaining to the family's history was inspiring. Propping her elbows on the secretary, she read with growing enthusiasm, with pride and high seriousness.

No event had been omitted from even her own brief past: her birth, her childhood illnesses, her first day of school, her enrollment in Mademoiselle Weichbrodt's boarding school, her confirmation. All of it had been entered in the consul's small, hurried commercial hand, with an almost religious respect for facts—for was not even the most insignificant event the will and work of God, who wonderfully guided the destinies of this family? And what else might be recorded here after her own name, given to her in honor of her grandmother Antoinette? Future members of the family would bring to the task the same piety with which she now followed past events.

She leaned back with a sigh, her heart pounding solemnly. She felt in awe of herself; the old, familiar feeling of her personal importance coursed through her, but heightened now by the spirit of what she had just read—she almost shuddered at the thrill. "Links in a chain," Papa had written. Yes, yes! And as a link in that chain, she had a higher, more responsible importance—she was called to help shape, by deeds and personal resolve, the history of her family.

She paged back to the end of the large notebook, where on a coarse folio page the whole genealogy of the Buddenbrooks was recapitulated in the consul's hand—with parentheses, rubrics, and clearly recorded dates: from the marriage of their earliest ancestor to Brigitta Schuren, a pastor's daughter, to the wedding of Consul Johann Buddenbrook and Elisabeth Kröger in 1825. From this marriage, it noted, had sprung four children, each listed, one below the other, by his or her baptismal name, with year and day of birth. There was already an entry after the name of the elder of the sons, stating that he had become an apprentice in the family business at Easter, 1842.

Tony gazed for a long time at her own name and the open space after it. And then, suddenly, she flinched and swallowed hard, her whole face a play of nervous, eager movement, her lips quickly touching for just a moment—and now she grabbed the pen, plunged rather than dipped it into the inkwell, and, crooking her index finger and laying her flushed head on her shoulder, wrote in her own clumsy hand, slanting upward from left to right: "Engaged on 22 September 1845 to Herr Bendix Grünlich, merchant from Hamburg."

14

I SHARE YOUR OPINION completely, my good friend. It is an important question and one that must be resolved. To be brief: the traditional cash dowry for a young woman from our family is seventy thousand marks."

Herr Grünlich cast his future father-in-law the brief, sidelong glance of a shrewd businessman. "Indeed," he said—and that "indeed" lasted as long as it took for his fingers to glide thoughtfully down his left golden muttonchop. He let go of its tip at the exact moment the "indeed" came to an end. "Dear Father," he continued, "you know, I'm sure, the deep respect in which I hold time-honored traditions and principles. But in the present case, is not this fine regard for tradition somewhat exaggerated? A firm grows, a family prospers; in short, conditions change and improve."

"My good friend," the consul said, "you see in me a fair-dealing man of business. Good heavens, you didn't even allow me to finish what I was about to say, otherwise you would have known that I am quite ready and willing to oblige you as present circumstances allow and will add another ten thousand to the seventy without further ado."

"Eighty thousand, then," Herr Grünlich said; and his mouth moved as if to say, "Not all that much, but it will do."

They came to a most amiable agreement, and as he stood up the consul contentedly jiggled the heavy bundle of keys in his trouser pocket. Only after raising the sum to eighty thousand had he in fact matched the "traditional cash dowry."

And now Herr Grünlich took his leave and departed for Hamburg. Tony was aware of little change in her daily life. No one objected to her dancing at the Möllendorpfs', Langhalses', or Kistenmakers', or in her own home; no one prevented her from ice-skating on Castle yard or in the bottoms down by the Trave, or from receiving the compliments of young men. In the middle of October she was invited to attend the party given by the Möllendorpfs in honor of the engagement of their eldest son to Julie Hagenström. "Tom," she said, "I'm not going. It's so disgusting." But she went anyway and had a wonderful time.

And besides, the stroke of her pen that added to the family's history had brought with it permission to go with her mother, or alone, to all the shops in town and place orders in grand style for her trousseau—an *elegant* trousseau. For days on end, two seamstresses sat beside the breakfast-room window, hemming, embroidering monograms, and eating lots of country bread and green cheese.

"Has the linen come from Lentföhr, Mama?"

"No, my child, but here are two dozen tea napkins."

"That's nice. But he did promise to send it by this afternoon. Good heavens, the sheets have to be hemmed."

"Mamselle Bitterlich was asking about the lace for trimming the pillowcases, Ida."

"In the linen cupboard in the entrance hall, dearest Tony."

"Lina!"

"You could jump up and fetch them yourself, sweetheart."

"O Lord, if I'm getting married just so I can run up and down stairs . . ."

"Have you thought yet about the fabric for your wedding dress, Tony?"

"*Moiré antique*, Mama! I'll not get married unless it's *moiré antique*."

And so October passed, and November, too. Herr Grünlich appeared at holiday time to spend Christmas Eve with the Buddenbrook family, and he didn't turn down the invitation to join the celebration at the old Krögers', either. His behavior toward his bride was characterized by all the delicacy they had correctly expected of him. No overblown courtliness, no social embarrassment, no tactless displays of affection. Their engagement had been sealed in the presence of Tony's parents by the discreet kiss he had dabbed against her brow. At times Tony found it astonishing how little his present happiness seemed to correspond to the despair he had exhibited as long as she had refused him. He regarded her with little more than the air of a satisfied owner. Now and then, to be sure, if he happened to be alone with her, his mood could change and he would tease and joke with her, might even try to pull her onto his knee and brush his whiskers against her face, asking in a quivering, jolly voice, "Have I really nabbed you? Have I really managed to catch you?" And then Tony would reply, "Good Lord, you're forgetting yourself, sir!" and cleverly extricate herself.

Herr Grünlich returned to Hamburg shortly after Christmas, because his flourishing business was unrelenting in its demands on his personal attention; and the Buddenbrooks silently agreed with him that Tony had had sufficient time to make his acquaintance before their engagement.

The question of where they would live was settled in an exchange of letters. Tony was so looking forward to life in a big city and had expressed her desire to live in the heart of Hamburg—where Herr Grünlich's office also happened to be located, on Spitaler Strasse. By sheer manly persistence, however, the bridegroom managed to obtain permission to purchase a villa on the outskirts of town, in Eimsbüttel—a romantic and secluded spot, an idyllic little nest so perfect for newlyweds, *procul negotiis*, far from business. No, he really had not entirely forgotten his Latin.

December passed, and then, early in January of '46, the wedding took place. There was a splendid party on the eve of the wedding, to which half the town was invited. Tony's friends—including Armgard von Schilling, who had arrived in town in a towering carriage—joined Tom's and Christian's friends—including Andreas Gieseke, the son of the fire chief, now *studiosus iuris*, as well as Stephan and Eduard Kistenmaker of Kistenmaker & Sons—and they all danced together in the dining room and out in the corridor, both of which had been strewn with talcum for the occasion. Peter Döhlmann was the life of the party when it came to breaking crockery for good luck, and he smashed every piece of pottery he could get his hands on against the flagstones in the passageway.

Frau Stuht from Glockengiesser Strasse had yet another opportunity to move in the best social circles when she joined Mamselle Jungmann and the seamstress in helping Tony dress for her wedding. She had, God strike her, never seen a more beautiful bride, and, fat as she was, she got down on her knees to tack the little sprays of myrtle to the *moiré antique*, all the while gazing up at Tony with admiring eyes. This was done in the breakfast room. Herr Grünlich waited in his long-tailed coat and silk vest outside the door. His pink face displayed a serious and correct expression; a little powder was visible on the wart at the left side of his nose, and his tawny, golden whiskers had been painstakingly curled.

The family had gathered upstairs in the columned hall, where the ceremony was to take place—and a handsome group they were. There sat the old Krögers, getting a little frail now, but distinguished personages as always. There was Consul Kröger and his sons, Jürgen and Jakob, who had come from Hamburg, as had the Duchamps relatives. There was Gotthold Buddenbrook and his wife, née Stüwing, with Friederike, Henriette, and Pfiffi, all three of whom were unlikely to marry now, sad to say. The Mecklenburg branch of the family was represented by Klothilde's father, Herr Bernhardt Buddenbrook, who had come all the way from Grudging and stared wide-eyed at the unbelievably splendid home of his rich relatives. The Frankfurt side of the family had merely sent gifts—the trip really was too long and difficult. But in their place were two other guests, the only ones who were not members of the family: Dr. Grabow, their physician, and Mamselle Weichbrodt, who was like a mother to Tony. Sesame Weichbrodt appeared in her black dress, but on her bonnet were brand-new green ribbons draping the curls at her ears. When Tony appeared in the columned hall at Herr Grünlich's side, Sesame stretched herself as tall as she could and kissed the bride's brow with a little popping sound, exclaiming, "Be heppy, you *good* chawld!" The family was proud of the bride; Tony looked pretty, cheerful, and quite at ease, though a little pale with curiosity and the excitement of the journey ahead.

The hall was decorated with flowers, and an altar had been set up on the right side. Pastor Kölling from St. Mary's performed the ceremony and sternly and specifically admonished *temperance* in all things. Everything went as custom demanded. Tony managed a naïve and goodhearted "I do," whereas Herr Grünlich first said "huh-uh-hmm" to clear his throat. Then followed an extraordinarily good and hearty meal.

While the guests, with the pastor as the focal point, were still eating upstairs, the consul and his wife accompanied the young couple, who had dressed now for their journey, out into the cold air, misty with snow. The great coach, packed full with trunks and bags, pulled up to the door.

After Tony had repeated several times her conviction that she would return home for a visit very soon and that her parents would not be long in making a trip to Hamburg, either, she climbed blithely into the coach and let her mother carefully tuck the warm fur blanket around her. Her husband took his seat as well.

"And, Grünlich," the consul said, "those new laces are in the little handbag on top? You'll slip them under your overcoat just before Hamburg, won't you? These customs taxes—one must try to avoid them whenever one can. Farewell. Farewell, my dear Tony. God be with you."

"You will find rooms in a good inn in Ahrensburg, won't you?" Elisabeth asked.

"Already reserved, dear Mama, already reserved," Herr Grünlich replied.

Anton, Lina, Trina, and Sophie said their goodbyes to "Madam Grünlich."

They were just about to slam the coach door shut when Tony suddenly decided to make an unexpected move. Despite all the trouble it caused, she unwound herself out of the fur blanket again, scrambled ruthlessly over Herr Grünlich's knees, amid his mumbled protests, and gave her father an impassioned hug.

"Adieu, Papa. My good Papa." And she whispered very softly, "Are you proud of me?"

The consul pressed her tight against him for a moment, not saying a word, then pushed her back just a little and shook both her hands, giving them an affectionate squeeze.

And now everything was ready. The door slammed shut, the driver cracked his whip, and the horses pulled so hard at their reins that the windowpanes rattled. Elisabeth let her little batiste handkerchief flutter in the wind until the coach began to disappear into the snowy mist as it rumbled off down the street.

The consul stood lost in thought beside his wife, who gave her fur cape a graceful tug, pulling it more tightly around her shoulders.

"There she goes, Bethsy."

"Yes, Jean, the first to leave us. Do you think she'll be happy with him?"

"Ah, Bethsy, she is at peace with herself, and that is the most solid kind of happiness we can ever achieve on earth."

They returned to their guests.

15

THOMAS BUDDENBROOK walked down Meng Strasse as far as "Five Houses." He avoided going around by way of Breite Strasse, because he didn't want to be constantly tipping his hat to all the acquaintances he would have to greet. With both hands in the wide pockets of his warm, dark gray overcoat, he walked along, deep in thought, and the hard crystalline crust of the snow sparkled and crunched under his boots. Where he was going and why., was something no one else knew anything about. The sky was a cold, bright blue, and the air had a sharp, crisp bite to it, twenty degrees—still, clear, wintry weather, a perfect February day.

Thomas walked past Five Houses, crossed Becker Grube, and entered a narrow alley that came out onto Fischer Grube, which ran steeply downhill to the Trave, parallel to Meng Strasse. He followed it a short distance before stopping at a small house—a flower shop with a narrow door and a window decorated with a few meager pots of lilies arranged in a row on a shelf of green glass.

He entered, and the brass bell above the door yelped like a vigilant puppy. Inside, the young salesgirl was standing at the counter talking to a small, fat elderly woman in a Turkish shawl, who was trying to make a selection from among some pots of flowers—examining each closely, smelling it, finding something wrong, chattering away, and all the while constantly wiping her mouth with her handkerchief. Thomas Buddenbrook greeted her politely and stepped aside. She was a poor relation of the Langhalses, a kindly, talkative old maid who, although she bore the name of one of the finer families, did not belong to their social circle, who was invited for coffee but never to the great banquets and balls, and who was known to all the world, with few exceptions, as "Aunt Lottie." As she turned toward the door with her flowerpot now wrapped in tissue paper under her arm, Thomas greeted her a second time and said to the salesgirl in a loud voice, "Give me a few roses, please. No, it doesn't matter what kind, La France is fine."

Then, when Aunt Lottie had closed the door behind her and vanished, he said more softly, "You can put those away now, Anna. Hello, my little Anna. Yes, here I am, but I've come with a heavy heart today."

Anna was wearing a white apron over her simple black dress. She was extraordinarily pretty and as delicate as a gazelle. Her face had something almost Malaysian about it: slightly prominent cheekbones, narrow black eyes that shimmered gently, and a smooth lemony complexion that one would look far and wide to find anywhere. Her small hands were that same lemony color—remarkably beautiful hands for a salesgirl.

She walked around the right end of the counter, back to the part of the shop that couldn't be seen from the window. Thomas followed her behind the counter, bent down, and kissed her lips and eyes.

"You're frozen through, poor thing," she said.

"Twenty degrees," Tom said. "I didn't even notice—it was a rather sad walk here today."

He sat down on the counter, holding her hand in his, and went on: "Now, listen to me, Anna. We're going to be sensible, aren't we? The day is here."

"O Lord," she said miserably, so forlorn and fearful that she lifted her apron to her eyes.

"It had to happen someday, Anna. Now, don't cry. We're going to be sensible, right? What else can we do? We simply have to get through it."

"When?" Anna asked with a sob.

"Day after tomorrow."

"O Lord, why then? Why not another week yet? Please, just five days."

"That won't work, dear little Anna. It's all settled and arranged.

They're waiting for me in Amsterdam. I can't stay on another day, as much as I would like to."

"But it's so dreadfully far away. . . ."

"Amsterdam. Pooh! Not at all. And we can always *think* about each other, can't we? And I'll write. Just watch, I'll write as soon as I get there."

"Do you remember?" she said. "A year and a half ago? At the sharpshooters' fair?"

He interrupted her, remembering with delight: "God, a year and a half ago! I thought you were Italian. I bought a carnation from you and put it in my buttonhole. I still have it. I'll take it with me to Amsterdam. It was so hot and dusty out there on the meadow."

"Yes, and you brought me a glass of lemonade from the next booth. It seems like only yesterday. The smell of fritters frying and of all the people and . . ."

"But it was so beautiful. From the very first moment, we could see in each other's eyes that there was something special between us, couldn't we?"

"And you wanted to ride the carousel with me—but I couldn't. I had to sell flowers. The old lady would have given me what-for."

"No, you couldn't, I can see that perfectly now."

She said softly, "But that's the only time I've ever refused you anything."

He kissed her again on the lips and eyes. "Adieu, my dear, good little Anna. Yes, it's time we started to say goodbye."

"Oh, but you'll come tomorrow, too, won't you?"

"Yes, sure, at about the same time. And the day after, early in the morning, if I can get away somehow. But now I just want to say one thing, Anna. I'm going rather far away—it's true, Amsterdam is a long way off. And you'll be staying here. But don't do anything to demean yourself, Anna, do you hear? Because you haven't so far, indeed you haven't."

She wept into her apron, holding it up to her face with one hand.

"And what about you?"

"God only knows, Anna, how things will turn out. We aren't

young forever. You're a clever girl—you never said anything about marriage and that sort of thing."

"No, heaven forbid that I'd ask anything like that of you."

"Time carries us along. And someday, if I live that long, I'll take over the firm, and make a good match. You see, I'm being quite frank with you, now that we're saying goodbye. And things will work out for you, too. I wish you every happiness, my dear, good little Anna. But don't do anything to demean yourself, you hear? Because you have *not* so far, indeed you haven't."

It was warm in the shop, the damp odor of soil and flowers hung in the air. Outside, the winter sun was about to set. Dusk glowed in the sky beyond the river—delicate, pure, pale, like something painted on fine china. Their chins hidden in the turned-up collars of their overcoats, people hurried past the window, not even noticing the two of them saying their goodbyes in one corner of the little flower shop.

PART FOUR

1

30 April 1846

Dearest Mama,

A thousand thanks for your letter telling me about Armgard von Schilling's engagement to Herr von Maiboom of Pöppenrade. Armgard sent an announcement herself (very elegant, edged in gold) and a letter saying how enchanted she is with her bridegroom. He's apparently a very handsome and elegant man. How happy she must be! Everyone's getting married; I got an announcement from Eva Ewers in Munich, too. She's getting the director of a brewery.

But now there's something I must ask you, dear Mama. Why haven't we heard a thing yet about a visit from the Buddenbrook family? Are you waiting for an official invitation from Grünlich, maybe? If so, it's hardly necessary, he hasn't given it a thought, I don't suppose, and when I do remind him, he says, Yes, yes, child, your father has other things to do. Or do you imagine that you'd be disturbing me, perhaps? No, really, not in the least. Or are you afraid you'd only make me homesick? Good heavens, I'm a sensible woman, with both feet planted firmly in life, I've matured.

I just returned from coffee with Madame Käselau, a neighbor. They're pleasant people, and our neighbors on the left, the name is Gussmann (but our houses are rather far apart), are sociable, too. And there are regular visits from a couple of good friends who also live out here: Dr. Klaassen (I'll have to tell you more about him later) and Kesselmeyer the banker, Grünlich's closest friend. You can't imagine what a funny old man he is! He has close-trimmed white whiskers and salt-and-pepper hair on top of his head that looks like goose down and flutters in the breeze. He makes funny motions with his head, like a bird, and is something of a chatterbox, I call him "the magpie"; but Grünlich has forbidden me to say that, because magpies are thieves and Herr Kesselmeyer is an honest man. He walks all hunched over and rows with his arms. The goose down reaches only about halfway down the back of his neck, and his nape is bright red and all wrinkly. He has such a merry way about him. Sometimes he pats my cheek and says, What a good little wife, Grünlich can count his blessings that he got you! And then he pulls out his pince-nez (he always carries three of them, on long cords that dangle at his white vest and get all tangled up), sets it on his nose, which he wrinkles up tight, and stares at me pleased as punch, with his mouth wide open, so that I simply have to laugh at him. But he's not at all offended.

Grünlich is very busy, leaves for town in our little yellow buggy early every morning and doesn't get back till late. Sometimes he will sit down with me and read his newspaper.

When we do go out in society—to see Kesselmeyer, or Consul Goudstikker on the Alster Damm, or Senator Bock on Rathaus Strasse—we have to hire a carriage. I have begged Grünlich often enough to buy us a coupé, because we really do need it out here. He has more or less promised me he would, but strangely enough he doesn't like to go out in society with me at all, and apparently he doesn't even like it when I talk with people in town. Can it be he's jealous?

Our villa, which I've already described in detail to you, dear Mama, is really very pretty, and the new furniture has made it even lovelier. You would find the salon on the mezzanine absolutely flawless: all in brown silk. The adjoining dining room is very prettily wainscoted; the chairs cost twenty-five marks *courant* apiece. I'm sitting in the *pensée* room, which serves as our sitting room. And then there's a smoking and billiard room, as well. The salon on the other side of the hallway on the ground floor has new yellow blinds and looks very elegant. The bedrooms, bathrooms, dressing rooms, and servants' quarters are all upstairs. We even have a little groom for the yellow buggy. And I'm fairly satisfied with our two maids. I don't know if they're entirely honest; but thank God I don't have to count every penny. In brief, everything as befits our family name.

And now, Mama, comes the most important thing, which I've saved till last. For some time now I've been feeling a bit strange, you know, not exactly ill and yet not really well. And so I happened to mention this to Dr. Klaassen. He's a tiny little man with a big head, with an even bigger floppy hat. He carries a cane walking stick with a round bone handle, and he always presses it up against his long beard, which is almost green, he's been dying it black so long. Well, you should have seen him! He didn't say a thing, just set his spectacles to rights, winked one little red eye, nodded his potato of a nose at me, giggled, and looked me up and down so impertinently that I didn't know what to do. Then he examined me and said that everything was going splendidly, but that I should drink mineral water, because I might be just a *bit* anemic. Oh, Mama, do tell Papa, but very circumspectly, so that he can enter it in the family history. I'll write more about it as soon as possible.

My fondest greetings to Papa, Christian, Clara, Thilda, and Ida Jungmann. I recently wrote a letter to Thomas in Amsterdam.

Your dutiful daughter,

Antonie

2 August 1846

My dear Thomas,

I was delighted to hear the news that you and Christian were able to meet in Amsterdam, I'm sure you had some very enjoyable days together. I have not yet heard anything about your brother's further journey to England via Ostende, but I pray God that everything went well. It may not yet be too late, now that Christian has decided to abandon his scientific pursuits, for him to learn something useful from his employer, Mr. Richardson, and I hope his mercantile career may be blessed with success. Mr. Richardson (of Threadneedle Street) is, as you know, a close business friend of our house. I consider myself lucky to have placed both my sons in firms with whom we have cordial ties. You have already experienced the advantages of such a relationship. I take great satisfaction in the fact that Herr van der Kellen has already raised your salary this quarter and wants to make provision for your earning other commissions as well. I am confident that, by dint of your own hard work, you have proved yourself worthy of the accommodating spirit he has shown and that you will continue to do so.

It grieves me, nevertheless, to hear that your health is not of the best. What you write about the state of your nerves reminds me of my own youth, when I was working in Antwerp and was forced to go to Ems for the waters. If something similar should prove necessary for you, my son, I am, but of course, ready to come to your assistance in both word and deed, although I am avoiding such expenses for the rest of us, given the current state of political unrest.

Your mother and I did, however, take a trip to Hamburg in the middle of June to visit your sister Tony. Her husband had not invited us to come, but received us very cordially all the same and was so devoted in his attentions during the two days we spent with him that he neglected his own business and hardly left me time to visit the Duchamps in town. Antonie was then in her fifth month; her doctor assures us that everything is taking a normal and highly satisfactory course.

I would now like to mention a letter from Herr van der Kellen, from which I learned to my delight that you are also received privately as a most welcome guest within the circle of his family. You are now at an age, my son, when you are beginning to harvest the fruits of the upbringing your parents have been pleased to give you. It may serve you in good stead when I say that at your age I took special care, both in Bergen and in Antwerp, to be pleasant and useful to my employers, which always proved to be to my great advantage. Quite apart from the honor and pleasure of a closer association with one's employer's family, one acquires an advocate in the person of his wife, if the occasion should ever arise—and though such occasions are to be avoided if at all possible, they may nevertheless occur—that, through some oversight in the office or for some other reason, one's employer is less satisfied with one's work than one might wish.

As to your future business plans, my son, I am greatly pleased by the lively interest they reveal, though I cannot fully concur in them. You proceed on the assumption that there is a natural and enduring market for the products native to our city's environs, such as grain, rapeseed, hides and furs, wool, oil, linseed cake, bonemeal, etc., and you would particularly like to apply yourself to that trade, apart from our present consignment venture. At one time, when the competition in that trade was still relatively small (though in the meantime it has grown considerably), I also occupied myself with the same idea and, as time and opportunity permitted, made some experiments in that regard. The primary purpose of my trip to England was to investigate possible connections for such an enterprise. I even traveled as far as Scotland, making the acquaintance there of several people who have since proved valuable to the firm, but I soon recognized the precarious state of the export business there, with the result that I gave up any further cultivation of the idea, particularly because I have always kept in mind the admonition of our forefather and founder of our firm: "My son, show zeal for each day's affairs of business, but only for such that make for a peaceful night's sleep."

I intend to hold that principle sacred to the end of my days, although now and then one may entertain doubts when confronted with people who apparently have better success without such principles. I am thinking of Strunck & Hagenström, who are experiencing notable expansion, while the course of our own affairs remains all too peaceful. As you know, following the losses incurred upon the death of your late grandfather, the firm has not grown, and I pray God that I can pass the business on to you in at least its present condition. I have an experienced and prudent helper in Marcus, our chief clerk. If only your mother's family knew how to count their pennies a bit better; that inheritance will be of great importance to us!

I am quite overwhelmed at the moment with business and civic affairs. I have been made an alderman on the Bergen Line board of directors, and have been chosen as a committee member for the Finance Department, the Chamber of Commerce, the Auditing Committee, and the St. Anne Poorhouse, one after another.

Warmest greetings from your mother, Clara, and Klothilde. Several gentlemen—Senator Möllendorpf, Dr. Oeverdieck, Consul Kistenmaker, Gosch the broker, C. F. Köppen, Herr Marcus from the office, and Captains Kloot and Klötermann—have all asked me to send their greetings. God bless you, my son. Work, pray, and save.

With affectionate regards,
Your *Father*

8 October 1846

Dear and honored parents,

The undersigned finds himself in the agreeable position of reporting to you the happy news of the birth of a daughter, delivered of his beloved wife, Antonie, some thirty minutes ago. It is a girl, by God's will, and I can find no words to express the joy that presently moves me. Both the child and her dear mother are in excellent health, and Dr. Klaassen indicated that he was quite satisfied with how matters progressed. Even Frau Grossgeorgis, the midwife, says that it was nothing at all. My elation obliges me to lay down my pen. Commending myself to my most worthy parents, I remain with respectful affection,

B. Grünlich

If it had been a boy, I had a very pretty name all picked out. I would prefer to call her Meta, but Grünlich is for Erika.

T.

2

WHAT IS WRONG with you, Bethsy?" the consul asked as he sat down at the table, removing the plate that covered his soup. "Are you ill? What's wrong? You look as if you're not feeling well."

The company seated around the table in the spacious dining room had grown very small. On normal days, besides the consul and his wife, there were only Mamselle Jungmann, ten-year-old Clara, and skinny Klothilde, meekly and silently eating away. The consul looked around the table—nothing but long, worried faces. What had happened? He was nervous and anxious himself, because the awkward situation in Schleswig-Holstein had set the stock market in turmoil. But there was some other turmoil in the air here. Later, when Anton left to fetch the meat course, the consul learned what had happened. Trina—their cook, Trina, who until now had always been a loyal and solid girl—was suddenly showing clear signs of revolt. Much to Elisabeth's displeasure, Trina had taken up of late with a butcher's apprentice—in a kind of intellectual alliance, it seemed—and this bloody fellow had to have been the reason her political views had changed so disastrously. Madame Buddenbrook had felt it necessary to reprimand her for a shallot sauce that had turned out badly, whereupon Trina had set her bare arms on her hips and expressed herself as follows: "Just you wait, madame, twon't be long now and things're gonna be reg'lated different. Then *I'll* be asittin' up on the sofa in a silk dress, and *you'll* be waitin' on me, 'cause . . ." It went without saying that she had been let go at once.

The consul shook his head. He had been witness of late to all sorts of disquieting incidents himself. To be sure, the older grain haulers and warehouse workers were solid enough fellows not to let notions be put in their heads. But among the younger ones a few had shown by their conduct on one occasion or other that this new rebellious spirit had wormed its way into them. Last spring there had been a riot in the streets, although a new constitution commensurate with the demands of the times was already being drafted, and, indeed, despite the objections of Lebrecht Kröger and a few other obstinate old men, it had been adopted as the basic law of the city by decree of the senate. Elections had been held, and a representative assembly had met. But still there was no peace. The world was being turned upside down. Everyone wanted to revise the constitution and amend the qualifications for voting—and the old citizens were wrangling. "Retain restricted voting rights!" one side said, including Consul Johann Buddenbrook himself. "Universal franchise," said the others, including Hinrich Hagenström. And then there was yet another group who cried, "Universal restricted franchise," and some of them perhaps even knew what they meant by it. And the air was full of notions such as the abolition of the difference between citizens and inhabitants, or the easing of qualifications for citizenship, even for non-Christians. No wonder, then, that the Buddenbrooks' Trina had taken a fancy to the sofa and a silk dress. Oh, but worse was to come. Things threatened to take a dreadful turn.

It was an early October day in 1848; a few light clouds drifted across a blue sky and were turned silvery white by a sun that had lost much of its strength—indeed, the fire was crackling behind the tall, shiny grate of the stove in the landscape room.

Little Clara, whose hair was a darker blond now and whose eyes were rather stern, was sitting with her embroidery beside the sewing table at the window, and Klothilde had taken a sofa seat next to Elisabeth to do her needlework. Although Klothilde Buddenbrook was not much older than her married cousin—she had just turned twenty-one—there were already pronounced lines in her long face, and her hair, which had never been blond but more a mousy gray, was parted and drawn back tight to complete the picture of an old maid, a state with which she was quite content and which she did nothing to remedy. Perhaps she felt some need to grow old early, to move beyond all the doubts and hopes as quickly as possible. Since she was absolutely penniless, she knew that no one would be found in all the world to marry her, and so she looked humbly toward a future in some little parlor, living on a small pension that her powerful uncle would procure for her from the funds of some charitable foundation for poor women of good family.

Madame Buddenbrook was busy reading two letters. Tony wrote about how little Erika was thriving happily, and Christian was eager to report about his life and doings in London, though without any mention of his work in Mr. Richardson's office. Now approaching her mid-forties, Elisabeth bitterly complained about how fair women were doomed to age so quickly. The delicate complexion that went so well with her reddish hair had lost its glow over the years, despite all the lotions she had applied; and even her hair would have begun its inexorable turn to gray if she had not prevented the worst for now by applying a tinting remedy, available, thank God, from Paris. Elisabeth was determined never to be a white-haired lady. And if the day should arrive when dye no longer sufficed, she would wear a wig of the same color as the hair of her youth. Set atop her always artfully coiffed hair was a small silk bow, surrounded by white lace: the beginning, the least hint, of a matron's cap. Her silk skirt billowed wide around her, her bell-shaped sleeves were lined with stiff muslin. And as always a pair of gold bracelets tinkled softly at her wrist. It was three o'clock in the afternoon.

Suddenly they heard the noise of shouts and screams, some kind of insolent yowling, plus whistles and the stamping of a great many feet on pavement—coming closer now and growing.

"Mama, what's that?" Clara asked, looking first into the "spy" and then out the window. "All those people . . . what are they doing? Why are they so happy?"

"My God!" Elisabeth cried, leaping up and nervously casting her letters aside. She hurried to the window. "Can it be . . . Oh my God, it's the revolution, it's the masses."

The fact was that there had been unrest in the streets all day. That same morning, the display window of Benthien Clothiers had been shattered by a stone, although God only knew what Herr Benthien's window had to do with politics.

"Anton?!" Elisabeth cried in a tremulous voice into the dining room, where the butler was busy with the silver. "Anton, go downstairs and bolt the front door. The masses are here. . . ."

"Yes, Madame Buddenbrook," Anton said. "But do I dare risk it? I'm a house servant, and if they see me in my livery . . ."

"Wicked people," Klothilde said in sorrow, drawing out the words, but without putting her needlework down. At that moment, the consul came striding down the columned hallway and entered through the glass door. He had his hat in hand and his overcoat was flung over his arm.

"You're going out there, Jean?" Elisabeth asked in horror.

"Yes, my dear, I have to attend a council meeting."

"But the masses, Jean, the revolution . . ."

"Oh, good Lord, it isn't as serious as that, Bethsy. We are in God's hands. They've already moved past the house. I'll go out through the back building."

"Jean, if you love me at all—do you really intend to expose yourself to danger, to leave us alone here? Oh, I'm so afraid, I'm so afraid."

"Dearest, I beg you, don't get overwrought like this. The people will kick up a bit of a rumpus in front of the town hall or on the market square. And it may cost the government a few windowpanes, that's all."

"*Where* are you going, Jean?"

"To a council meeting. I'm late already, I was delayed in the office. It would be disgraceful if I were to miss the meeting. Do you imagine this will stop your father—old as he is?"

"Yes, well, then, go with God, Jean. But be careful, I beg you, do take care. And keep an eye on my father. If something were to happen to him . . ."

"Not to worry, my dear."

"When will you be back?" Elisabeth called after him.

"Oh, around four-thirty, five o'clock. It depends. There are some important items on the agenda—it all depends."

"Oh, I'm so afraid, I'm so afraid," Madame Buddenbrook said once more, glancing helplessly about and pacing back and forth in the room.

3

CONSUL BUDDENBROOK strode hurriedly across his extensive property. As he emerged on Becker Grube, he heard footsteps behind him and spotted Gosch the broker, a picturesque figure wrapped in a long coat, who was also heading up the steep hill for the meeting. Doffing his Jesuit hat with one long, skinny hand and smoothly executing a gesture of deference with the other, he said in a stifled but fierce voice, "My salutations . . . Consul Buddenbrook."

Siegismund Gosch the broker was a bachelor, about forty years old, and, despite appearances, the most honest and kindhearted man in the world; but he was an aesthete, an original thinker. His clean-shaven face was marked with sharp features—an arching nose, a jutting pointed chin, and a wide, down-turned mouth, its thin lips pressed tight, giving him a wicked look. He strove to give the impression of being a wild, handsome, scheming devil, to play the role of a wicked, crafty, interesting villain, somewhere between Mephistopheles and Napoleon—and he pulled it off rather well. His gray hair was combed down over his brow for sinister effect. He regretted not being hunchbacked. He was an exotic and attractive character among the bourgeois inhabitants of the old commercial town. And yet he was one of them, because he managed his small, respectable brokerage business in the best, modest middle-class fashion. But in his dark, narrow office there was a large bookcase filled with poetical works in all languages, and it was rumored that for the last twenty years he had been working on a translation of the complete plays of Lope de Vega. On one occasion he had played Domingo in an amateur production of Schiller's *Don Carlos.* It had been the highpoint of his life. No vulgar word had ever passed his lips, and he even spoke the kind of phrases common in business conversation with clenched teeth and a face that seemed to say: "Scoundrel, ha! I curse thy forebears in their graves!" He was, in many ways, the heir and successor to Jean Jacques Hoffstede; except that there was something more somber and pathetic about him, and he was totally incapable of the droll joviality that old Johann Buddenbrook's friend had managed to salvage from the previous century. At the exchange one day, he lost six and a half thalers *courant* at one blow on two or three stocks he had bought on speculation. His dramatic sensitivities overcame him and he gave a performance. He sank down onto a bench in the pose of a man who has lost the battle of Waterloo, pressing a clenched fist to his brow, rolling his eyes blasphemously, and repeating several times over: "Ha, curses!" He was, in reality, bored by the small, steady, secure commissions he made on the sale of this or that piece of real estate, but this loss, this tragic blow that heaven had struck against him, the great schemer, was pure joy, a source of happiness on which he feasted for weeks afterward. If someone said, "I hear you've been unlucky, Herr Gosch. I'm very sorry," he would reply, "Oh, worthy friend, *uomo non educato dal dolore riman sempre bambino*!" As might be expected, no one understood this. Was it from Lope de Vega? But one thing was certain—Siegismund Gosch was a learned and remarkable man.

"What times we live in," he said to Consul Buddenbrook and bent down over his cane as they made their way up the street, side by side. "Times of tempest and trouble."

"You're right about that," the consul replied. "The times are troubled. Things will be tense at today's meeting. Restricted voting rights . . ."

"Oh no, listen," Herr Gosch went on. "I've been out and about all day. I have been observing the rabble. There are splendid fellows among them, their eyes flaming with hatred and excitement."

Johann Buddenbrook broke into a laugh. "You certainly are something, my friend. You seem to take some sort of pleasure in this, don't you? No, if you'll permit me, it's all childishness. What do these people want? A bunch of ill-mannered young fellows who are taking this opportunity to kick up something of a rumpus."

"True enough. And yet one cannot deny—I was there when Berkemeyer the butcher's apprentice threw the stone at Herr Benthien's window. He was like a panther!" Herr Gosch spoke this last word with his teeth clenched especially tight, and then continued, "Oh, one cannot deny that the whole affair has its sublime side. At last, something different, you see, something out of the ordinary, powerful—a savage storm, a tempest. Ah, the masses are ignorant, I know that. And yet my heart, this heart of mine, is with them." They were now almost at the door of the austere yellow building where the council held its meetings in the ground-floor assembly room.

This room was part of a beer-and-dance hall that belonged to the widow Suerkringel, but it was made available to the gentlemen of the council on certain days. The main entrance led into a narrow, stone-paved hallway, on the right of which was the restaurant, smelling of beer and food, and on the left a door of green-painted planks, with neither handle nor lock, and so narrow and low that no one would have expected such a large room behind it. The room was cold, bare, barnlike, with whitewashed walls and ceiling, exposed beams, and three rather high, curtainless windows, the panes divided in four by green crosses. Opposite the windows, ranks of seats rose to form an amphitheater, at the bottom of which stood a table, covered by a green cloth and furnished with a large bell, documents, and writing utensils for the chairman, recording clerk, and whatever members of the senate delegation might be present. On the wall across from the door were several high racks hung with coats and hats.

As the consul and his companion passed one behind the other through the narrow door into the hall, they were met with a confusion of voices. The room was filled with men with hands thrust into their trouser pockets, crossed behind their backs, or thrown into the air—all standing in little groups and arguing. Of the 120 members of the council, it looked as if about a hundred had gathered. A number of the representatives from the countryside had decided to stay at home, given current circumstances.

Closest to the door stood a group of less important men: two or three shopkeepers; a high-school teacher; Herr Mindermann, the orphanage director; and Herr Wenzel, the well-liked barber. Herr Wenzel—a small sturdy man with an intelligent face, a black mustache, and red hands—had shaved the consul that very morning, but here he was his equal. He shaved only men from the best circles—shaved nothing but Möllendorpfs, Langhalses, Buddenbrooks, and Oeverdiecks—and he owed his election to the council to his omniscience in local affairs, to his affability and good manners, to his obvious self-confidence despite his lower social status.

"Have you heard the latest, Consul Buddenbrook?" he shouted to his patron, his eyes anxious and earnest.

"What is it I should know, my dear Wenzel?"

"Something no one could have known anything about this morning, beg the consul's pardon. The latest word is that the mob isn't headed for the town hall or the market square. They're coming here to threaten the council. Rübsam the newspaper editor is the instigator."

"Oh my, impossible!" the consul said. He pushed his way between two groups at the front, to the middle of the room, where he saw his father-in-law standing with two senators, Dr. Langhals and James Möllendorpf. "Is it really true, gentlemen?" he asked, shaking their hands.

And, indeed, the whole council was talking about it: the rioters were heading this way, were already within earshot.

"Rabble!" Lebrecht Kröger said with cold disdain. He had come in his equipage. Under normal circumstances, the tall, distinguished figure of the former "cavalier à la mode" would have revealed that he was beginning to bend beneath the burden of his eighty years; but today he stood quite erect, his eyes half closed, the corners of his mouth turned down in elegant disdain, the short tips of his white mustache turned straight up. Two rows of jeweled buttons sparkled on his black velvet vest.

Not far from this group could be seen Hinrich Hagenström—a portly, square-framed gentleman, whose reddish beard was turning gray; his frock coat was open, and a heavy watch chain was draped across his blue-checkered vest. He was standing with his partner, Herr Strunck, and made no effort to greet the consul.

And then there was Benthien the clothier, a prosperous-looking man, who had gathered a large number of men around him, describing for them in exact detail what had happened to his windowpane. "A brick, half a brick, gentlemen! Crashed right through and landed on a role of green ribbed silk. Riffraff! And now the government will deal with them."

From some corner of the room came the incessant voice of Herr Stuht from Glockengiesser Strasse, a black coat pulled on over his woolen shirt, who was deeply involved in the discussion and kept repeating with great indignation, "Outrageous infamy!" (He pronounced it "iffamy," however.)

Johann Buddenbrook worked his way about the room, greeting first his old friend C. F. Köppen, and then the latter's competitor, Consul Kistenmaker. He shook Dr. Grabow's hand and exchanged a few words with Gieseke, the chief of the fire department, with Voigt the contractor, with Dr. Langhals, today's presiding chairman and brother of the senator, with merchants, teachers, and lawyers.

The meeting had not yet been opened, but the debate was extraordinarily lively. The gentlemen cursed Rübsam—ink-slinger and editor—who they all knew had incited the mob. But to what end? They had assembled to determine whether to retain restricted voting rights or to introduce universal franchise. The senate had already proposed the latter. But what did the masses want? They wanted their hands on these gentlemen's throats, that was all. Damn it, this was the unholiest mess in which these gentlemen had ever found themselves. They surrounded members of the senate delegation to hear their opinions. They also surrounded Consul Buddenbrook, who was sure to know how Mayor Oeverdieck felt about the matter, because the previous year Senator Dr. Oeverdieck, a brother-in-law of Consul Justus Kröger, had become president of the senate and mayor—and that meant that the Buddenbrooks were now related to the mayor, which greatly enhanced the esteem in which they were held.

There was a sudden surge in the tumult outside—the revolution had reached the windows of the assembly hall. The excited exchange of opinions inside stopped short. Hands folded over their stomachs and, mute with shock, they stared at one another or toward the windows, where they could see raised fists and hear boisterous hoots, inane and deafening yowls that filled the air. But then, quite unexpectedly, as if the rebels were suddenly appalled at their own behavior, it was as quiet outside as it was in the hall; and the deep hush that fell over everything was broken only by the sound of one word, spoken slowly and with cold intensity, emanating from somewhere in the bottom rows, where Lebrecht Kröger had taken his seat: "Rabble!"

And from some other corner, a hollow, indignant voice echoed, "Outrageous iffamy!"

And suddenly the trembling, hasty, furtive voice of Benthien the clothier floated out over the assembly: "Gentlemen, gentlemen. Listen to me. I know this building well. There is a trapdoor in the attic—I used to shoot cats through it as a boy. We can easily climb out onto the next roof and save our skins."

"Base cowardice," Gosch the broker hissed between his teeth. Head lowered and arms crossed, he was leaning on the speaker's table and staring grimly at the windows.

"Cowardice, sir? What do you mean? Good God, they're throwing bricks. And I've had a bellyful of it."

At that moment the sound outside swelled again, but instead of returning to its initial fever pitch, it rumbled low and steady in a patient singsong, almost a merry buzz, broken now and then by whistles and what were clearly shouts of "The vote!" and "Our rights!" The council listened attentively.

"Gentlemen," Dr. Langhals, the presiding chairman, said after a while, in a subdued voice audible to the whole assembly, "I assume I have your consent to open this meeting?"

But even this humble request received not the least support from any quarter.

"Ain't gonna get me to agree to that," someone said with the kind of honest resolve that brooks no objection. It was Pfahl, a farmer from the Ritzerau district, deputy for the village of Klein Schretstaken. No one could recall ever having heard his voice in debate before; but in the present situation the opinion of even the simplest man carried great weight. With sure political instinct, the intrepid Herr Pfahl had given voice to the view of the entire council.

"Heaven help us," said Herr Benthien in exasperation. "They

can see the top rows of seats from the street. People are throwing bricks. Good God! No, no—I've had a bellyful."

"That damn door is so small," Köppen the wine merchant blurted out in despair. "If we try to get out, we'll more'n likely get squeezed to death."

"Outrageous iffamy," Herr Stuht said in a hollow voice.

"Gentlemen," the chairman began insistently again, "I beg you to reconsider. I am required to present the final minutes of this meeting to the mayor within three days. And the town expects them in print, too. I would at least like to proceed to a vote as to whether the meeting is to be opened."

But although a few gentlemen agreed with the chairman, no one was prepared to move the order of the day. It was pointless to call for a vote. The mob should not be incited further. No one knew just what the mob wanted—so it was better not to antagonize it by a decision one way or the other. They had better wait, not make any moves. The clock of St. Mary's struck half past four.

They bolstered one another in their decision to wait it out patiently. They began to get used to the noise outside—it swelled, ebbed, paused, started up again. They began to calm down, to make themselves comfortable on the lower rows of benches and chairs. Native enterprise began to stir among these industrious men—here and there a business conversation was ventured, here and there a deal was even struck. The brokers sat down with the wholesalers. These beleaguered gentlemen chatted like people sitting out a violent thunderstorm together, speaking of this and that, but pausing now and then with serious and respectful faces to listen to the thunder. Five o'clock came, five-thirty—dusk fell. Now and then someone might sigh that his wife had coffee waiting for him at home, which Herr Benthien would take as a cue to mention the trapdoor again. But most of them agreed with Herr Stuht, who declared with a fatalistic shake of his head, "I'm too fat for that!"

Recalling his wife's admonition, Johann Buddenbrook stayed close to his father-in-law, and, eyeing him anxiously, he finally asked, "I hope this little adventure isn't upsetting you Father, is it?"

Two disquietingly swollen bluish veins had appeared on Lebrecht

Kröger's brow, just below his snow-white toupee, and while one aged, aristocratic hand played with the iridescent buttons on his vest, the other, the one with a large diamond ring, lay trembling on his knee.

"Poppycock, Buddenbrook!" he said with a strange weariness. "I'm bored, that's all." But then he betrayed himself by suddenly hissing, "*Parbleu*, Jean. What we ought to do is use some powder and lead to teach this infamous riffraff a little respect. It's a mob! Rabble!"

The consul murmured soothingly, "Yes, yes, you're right there, it's a rather undignified farce. But what can we do? Just keep our composure. Evening's coming on. They'll be leaving soon."

"Where's my carriage? I demand my carriage!" Lebrecht Kröger commanded, beside himself now. His rage exploded, his whole body was quivering. "I ordered my carriage for five o'clock. Where is it? There's not going to be a meeting, so what am I doing here? I am not about to be made a fool of. I want my carriage. Are they insulting my coachman? Go have a look, Buddenbrook."

"My dear father, for heaven's sake, calm down. You're getting yourself excited, which is not good for you. But of course I'll go out and see about your carriage. I've had enough of the situation myself. I'll speak to those people, ask them to go home."

And although Lebrecht Kröger protested—suddenly commanding in a cold, disdainful voice, "Do not compromise yourself, Buddenbrook. Wait, stay here!"—the consul strode rapidly across the room.

Just before the consul reached the narrow green door, Siegismund Gosch caught up with him, grabbing his arm with a bony hand and asking in a horrible whisper, "Whither now, Herr Buddenbrook?"

The broker's face was a maze of a thousand deep lines of worry. His pointed chin was thrust upward toward his nose in a look of wild determination, his gray hair hung ominously over brow and temples, his head was tucked so deep into his shoulders that he had finally succeeded in looking like a hunchback—and he exclaimed, "Behold me now, prepared to speak unto the people."

The consul said, "No, it's better that I should do that, Gosch. I probably have more acquaintances out there than you."

"So be it," the broker responded in a flat voice. "You are a greater man than I." But now, with a rising voice, he continued, "But I shall accompany you, I shall stand at your side, Consul Buddenbrook. Though the rage of unchained slaves may rend this body to shreds . . ."

And as they went through the door, he said, "Oh, what a day! What a night!" Never had he been so happy as at that moment.

"Behold, Herr Buddenbrook—the people!" They had passed down the hallway and, emerging through the main entrance, they stood now at the top of three narrow steps that led down to the sidewalk. And were greeted by a strange sight. The street itself was otherwise deserted, with only a few curious faces silhouetted against the light in the windows of the buildings, all staring down at the black mass of insurgents below. The crowd, however, was not much larger than the group assembled in the hall and consisted of young workers from the docks and warehouses, porters, schoolchildren, a few sailors from merchant ships—men and boys who lived in the alleys, lanes, mews, and courts of the less prosperous parts of town. Also present were three or four women, who apparently expected the enterprise to yield results similar to those envisioned by the Buddenbrooks' own cook. Several insurrectionists had grown weary of standing and had sat down on the curb, feet in the gutter, to eat their sandwiches.

It would soon be six o'clock, but although twilight was well advanced by now, the oil lamps still hung unlit on their chains above the street. This was an obvious and unprecedented disruption of public order, and for the first time that day Consul Buddenbrook truly lost his temper—and began to speak in curt and angry tones. "Folks, what sort of foolishness are you up to now?"

The picnickers leapt to their feet. Those at the rear, on the other side of the street, stood on tiptoe. A few of the dockworkers, employees of the consul, removed their caps. They stood there attentively, nudging each other and whispering: "That's Consul Buddenbrook. Consul Buddenbrook's gonna give a talk. Shut your mouth, Krischan, I've seen him get madder than hell! That's Gosch the broker. Lookathat! What an ass! Has he finally gone off the deep end?"

"Corl Smolt," the consul began again, directing his small, deep-set eyes at a bowlegged warehouse worker in his early twenties, who was standing directly below the stairs, with hat in hand and a mouth full of bread. "Now, speak up, Corl Smolt! It's high time. You've been yowling all afternoon."

"Well, Consul, sir," Corl Smolt managed, still chewing. "Things is . . . sorta . . . come to a pass. We're makin' a revolution."

"What sort of malarkey is that, Smolt!"

"Well, Consul, sir, you may well say that, but things is come to a pass. We ain't satisfied no more. We're demandin' a new 'rangement. Tain't nothin' more'n that, plain and simple."

"Now listen here, Smolt, and the rest of you! Whoever's got any sense left will head on home and forget all this about revolution and upsetting public order."

"The sacred public order," Herr Gosch interrupted with a hiss.

"Public order, I said!" Consul Buddenbrook concluded. "The lamps haven't even been lit yet. That's carrying revolution just a bit too far."

But Corl Smolt had swallowed his mouthful by now, and, with the crowd behind him, he stood there, legs set firmly apart, and offered his objections. "Well, Consul, sir, you may well say that. But it's 'cause of the gen'ral frenchies."

"Good Lord, you imbecile," the consul shouted, so indignant now that he forgot to speak in Plattdeutsch. "What asinine absurdity."

"Well, Consul, sir," Corl Smolt said, somewhat intimidated now. "That may be as may be. But there's gonna be a revolution, sure as rain. There's revolution everywhere, in Berlin and Paree. . . ."

"Smolt, what is it you really want? Speak up, out with it!"

"Well, Consul, sir, that's just what I'm sayin'. We want a republic, plain and simple."

"But, you nincompoop—you already *have* one."

"Well, Consul, sir, then we want 'nother besides."

Several of those standing around him who knew better began to laugh haltingly, then heartily; and although only a few people had actually heard Corl Smolt's reply, the merriment spread until the whole throng of republicans broke into broad, amiable laughter. A few curious faces now appeared at the windows of the assembly hall—some of the gentlemen had beer mugs in their hands. The only person disappointed and grieved by this turn of affairs was Siegismund Gosch.

"So, then, folks," Consul Buddenbrook said at last, "I think it'd be best if we all went home now."

Corl Smolt, totally dumbfounded at the effect his words had produced, replied, "Well, Consul, sir, that's about it, and so we'll let it rest for now, and 'm mighty happy to see you ain't took it amiss, Consul, sir, so we'll be seein' you, Consul, sir. . . ."

In the best of moods now, the crowd began to disperse.

"Smolt, wait a minute," the consul shouted. "Tell me, have you seen the Krögers' carriage, the barouche that should have come in by way of the Burg Gate?"

" 'sindeed, Consul, sir. It's come. It's down below somewheres, turned in at the consul-sir's own place, it did."

"Fine; then run down there quick, Smolt, and tell Jochen he's to drive up here. His master wants to go home."

"Yes, sir, Consul, sir!" And, setting his cap back on his head and pulling its leather bill down over his eyes, Corl Smolt ran off down the street, teetering on his bowlegs.

4

When Consul Buddenbrook and Siegismund Gosch returned to the meeting room, it presented a much cozier scene than fifteen minutes before. Two large paraffin lamps had been lit on the speaker's table, and the yellow light revealed gentlemen standing in groups, pouring bottles of beer into shiny mugs, toasting one another, and chatting noisily and jovially. Frau Suerkringel—the widow Suerkringel—had paid them a call, adopting them all in her openhearted fashion and persuading them that, since the siege could last a while yet, a little refreshment might be in order—and she made good use of the troubled times to sell a considerable quantity of her pale but strong beer. And just as the two negotiators entered, the serving boy, clad in shirtsleeves and a good-natured smile, was dragging in another round of bottles; and although the evening was now well advanced and it was much too late to give any attention to the revision of the constitution, no one was inclined to interrupt the get-together and go home. It was too late for coffee in any case.

After the consul had shaken hands with several well-wishers who congratulated him on his success, he hurried over to his father-in-law. Lebrecht Kröger appeared to be the only man whose mood had not improved. He sat there on his chair—erect, cold, and aloof—and in response to the news that his carriage was waiting for him, he replied in a scornful voice that quivered more from bitterness than age, "The rabble deigns to permit me to return home, do they?"

With stiff movements that betrayed nothing whatever of the charm and grace that he had always been known for, he let someone lay his fur coat over his shoulders, and when the consul offered to accompany him, he managed only a listless "*Merci*," and slipped his arm under his son-in-law's.

The majestic carriage, with two large lanterns on its box, halted at the door outside, where, much to the consul's profound satisfaction, the streetlamps were being lit. They both climbed in, and the carriage rolled off through the streets. Lebrecht Kröger sat on the consul's right, a blanket spread over his knees; he did not lean back, but held himself bent forward at a slight angle with his eyes half closed; he said not a word, and beneath his white mustache two deep folds ran from the corners of his mouth to the tip of his chin. Fury at being humiliated gnawed at him, devoured him. He gazed with dull, cold eyes at the empty cushions opposite them.

The streets were livelier than on a Sunday evening—everyone was in a holiday mood it seemed. The common folk, delighted at the happy outcome of their revolution, strolled about in an exuberant mood. Some were even singing. Here and there small boys threw their caps in the air and shouted "Hurrah!" as the carriage passed.

"I really think you've let all this affect you far too much, Father," the consul said. "When one considers what buffoonery the whole thing was—a farce." And, trying to evoke some reply or comment from the old man, he began vigorously to address the general topic of revolution. "If the unpropertied masses would only realize how little they are helping their own cause these days. Oh, good Lord, it's the same everywhere. I had a brief conversation with Gosch the broker this afternoon—such a bizarre man, who sees everything with the eyes of a poet and dramatist. You see, Father, the revolution in Berlin was rehearsed at the tea tables of aesthetes, and then had to be carried out by the people, at the risk of their own skins. But will it be worth the cost they've been asked to pay?"

"I would appreciate it if you would open the window on your side," Herr Kröger said.

Johann Buddenbrook threw him a quick glance, then hurriedly lowered the pane. "Aren't you feeling well, Father?" he asked worriedly.

"No. Not at all," Lebrecht Kröger replied sternly.

"You need a bite to eat and some rest," the consul said, and then he tucked the blanket more tightly around his father-in-law's knees, just for something to do.

Suddenly—the equipage was rattling down Burg Strasse now—something horrible happened. About fifteen yards on this side of the walls of the gate, which was just emerging from the shadows, they passed a band of noisy urchins at play—and a rock flew through the open window. It was a perfectly harmless stone, no bigger than a hen's egg, flung from the hand of some Krischan Snut or Heine Voss in celebration of the revolution—certainly not out of malice and presumably not even aimed at the carriage. It entered soundlessly through the window, bounced soundlessly against the heavy padding of furs on Lebrecht Kröger's chest, rolled just as soundlessly to the soft blanket on his knees, and finally came to rest on the floor.

"Clumsy brats," the consul said angrily. "Has everyone gone mad this evening? But it didn't hurt you did it, Father?"

Old man Kröger was silent, terrifyingly silent. It was too dark in the carriage to make out the expression on his face. He sat there with his back not touching the seat—straighter and stiffer than before. But then, from somewhere deep within, came one cold, heavy, slow word: "*Rabble.*"

Worried that he might upset the old man even more, the consul did not reply. The carriage rolled through the echoing tunnel of the gate and onto the broad avenue; within three minutes they were alongside the wrought-iron fence with gilt-tipped railings that bounded the Kröger estate. Two lanterns topped with golden knobs were burning brightly at each side of the wide entrance to the chestnut-lined drive that led up to the terrace. The consul was horrified by what the light revealed of his father-in-law's face. It was yellow, ragged, deeply furrowed. The cold, hard, disdainful set of the mouth had given way to the feeble, skewed, limp, stupid grin of an old man. The carriage pulled to a halt by the terrace.

"Help me," Lebrecht Kröger said—although the consul had already climbed out and pulled away the blanket and was offering the support of his arm and shoulder. He guided him slowly along a few steps of gravel walk to the glistening white stairway that led to the dining room. At the base of the stairs the old man's knees buckled. His head fell so hard against his chest that his lower jaw clattered loudly against his upper teeth. His eyes rolled back, and snapped.

Lebrecht Kröger, the cavalier à la mode, had joined his fathers.

5

ONE YEAR and two months later—it was January, 1850—on a morning misty with snow, Herr and Madame Grünlich and their little three-year-old daughter were sitting at breakfast in their dining room—wainscoted in light-brown woods, on chairs that had cost twenty-five marks *courant* apiece.

The panes of both windows were almost opaque with fog, and only blurred, naked trees and shrubs were still visible outside. The room was filled with a gentle, slightly fragrant warmth from the blaze burning in the low, green-tiled stove that stood in one corner, next to the door leading to the *pensée* room filled with foliage. Directly opposite, portieres of some green fabric had been pulled back to reveal the brown silk salon and a tall glass door—its cracks stuffed with rolls of cotton batting—with a view to the little terrace, which was now lost in the whitish-gray fog. A third door off to one side led out to the hallway.

An embroidered green runner ran across the snow-white cloth of woven damask spread over the round table, which was set with gold-rimmed porcelain of such transparency that here and there it shimmered like mother-of-pearl. A samovar hummed. Rolls and slices of sweet bread lay in a shallow basket of fine silver shaped like a large, jagged-edged leaf rolled back on itself. Under the bell of one crystal dish was a mountain of rippled balls of butter, under another could be seen various kinds of cheese—yellow, white, and marbled green. There was even a bottle of red wine set before the master of the house, for Herr Grünlich ate a full breakfast.

His side-whiskers had been freshly curled, and his face was especially pink this early in the morning. Dressed in a black coat and light trousers in a large check, he sat with his back to the salon and was dining on a lightly grilled chop. His wife found his English-style breakfast quite elegant, but also so disgusting that she could never bring herself to abandon her usual bread and soft-boiled egg for it.

Tony was in her dressing gown; she was mad about dressing gowns. She found nothing more elegant than a tasteful negligee, and since she had never been permitted to give free rein to this passion in her parents' home, she indulged herself all the more as a married woman. She owned three of these supple, clinging garments, and had found that designing them required more taste, refinement, and imagination than was ever needed for a ball gown. This morning she was wearing her dark-red dressing gown, its color exactly matched to the tones of the wallpaper above the wainscoting, its texture softer than the softest cotton, and its large-flowered print embroidered everywhere with sprays of tiny glass pearls in the same hue. Dozens of red velvet ribbons ran down in a straight row from neckline to hem.

She wore a dark red velvet bow in her heavy, ash-blond hair, which fell in curls over her brow. Although she was quite aware that she had already achieved the highpoint of her beauty, her slightly protruding upper lip had the same childish, naïve, and saucy effect as ever. The lids of her grayish blue eyes were pink from a splash of cold water. Her hands—those white, somewhat short, but delicately shaped fingers of the Buddenbrooks, with small wrists enclosed by the velvet cuffs of her sleeves—handled knife, fork, and cup with movements that for some reason seemed a little abrupt and hasty.

Next to her little Erika sat in a towerlike highchair—a well-nourished child with short blond curls, dressed in a funny, formless pale blue jacket of knitted wool. She held her cup clasped in both hands; her face vanished into the cup, and she gulped at her milk, pausing now and then for little enthusiastic sighs.

Frau Grünlich now rang the bell; and Thinka, the housemaid, entered from the hallway and was told to lift the child from her tower and take her to the nursery.

"You can take her for a half-hour walk outside, Thinka," Tony said. "But no longer than that, and put on her heavier jacket, do you hear? It's wet and foggy." And now she was alone with her husband.

"You're being ridiculous," she said after a long, silent pause, obviously picking up an interrupted conversation. "Can you give me any good reason why not? Tell me! I *cannot* always be taking care of the child."

"You're not fond of children, Antonie."

"Fond of children . . . fond of children. There's not enough time. I have all I can do with keeping up the house. I wake up with twenty things that have to be done that day, and go to bed with forty more that still need to be done."

"There are two maids. A young woman like yourself . . ."

"Two maids, fine. Thinka has to wash up, straighten up, clean, serve. The cook has more than enough to do. You have to have your chops for breakfast. Think about it, Grünlich. Sooner or later, Erika is going to have to have a nurse, a governess."

"It is beyond our current means to employ a governess for her now."

"Our means! O Lord, you *are* being ridiculous. Are we beggars? Do we have to do without necessities? It seems to me that I brought eighty thousand marks into this marriage."

"Oh, you and your eighty thousand."

"Yes indeed. You speak so lightly of it—it was of no importance to you, you married me for love. Fine. But do you still love me at all? You simply ignore my perfectly legitimate wishes. The child is not to have a governess. And we don't even speak of the coupé anymore, although it's as necessary as our daily bread. Why do you have us living out here in the country if it is beyond our *means* to have a carriage so that we can move about properly in society? Why don't you ever want me to go into town? What you'd like best is for us to bury ourselves here for good and all, and for me never to see another human face. You're a crosspatch!"

Herr Grünlich poured red wine into his glass, lifted the crystal bell, and began on the cheese. He offered no reply whatever.

"Do you love me at all?" Tony asked again. "Your silence is so rude that I feel I am quite within my rights to remind you of a certain scene in our landscape room at home. You cut quite a different figure back then. From the first day of marriage the only time you've spent with me has been in the evening—and that only to read your paper. At least you paid some regard to my wishes at the beginning. But even that stopped a long time ago. You're neglecting me."

"And what about you? You're driving me to ruin."

"*Me?* I'm driving you to ruin?"

"Yes. You're ruining me with your lassitude, your love of being waited upon, your extravagance."

"Oh, don't criticize me just because I was raised properly! I never had to lift a finger at my parents' home. And I've worked very hard to learn how to run a house, and the least I can demand is that you not deny me the most basic kind of assistance. Father is a rich man; he would never have dreamed that I could lack for domestic help."

"Then you can wait for your third servant until those riches do us some good."

"Is that what you want? For Father to die?! I'm saying—we are wealthy ourselves and I certainly did not come empty-handed into this marriage."

Herr Grünlich had a mouthful he was about to chew, but he smiled—a superior, melancholy smile—and said not a word. This confused Tony.

"Grünlich," she said more calmly now, "that smile—and the way you talk about our means. Am I wrong about our current situation? Has business been bad? Have you . . . ?"

At that moment there was a knock, a brief drum roll, on the door to the hallway—and Herr Kesselmeyer appeared.

6

AS A FRIEND of the family, Herr Kesselmeyer entered the house unannounced, and stood now without coat and hat at the dining-room door. He looked exactly the way Tony had described him in her letter to her mother. He was rather short and square-built, neither fat nor thin. He wore a black coat, slightly shiny with wear, matching short, tight trousers, and a white vest across which hung a thin watch chain with two or three dangling cords for his pince-nez. His white, close-cropped beard stood out against his red face, but his upper lip was clean-shaven, revealing a small, comical, and mobile mouth, with only two teeth left in his lower jaw. Herr Kesselmeyer stood there somewhat confused, his hands buried in his pockets, musing absent-mindedly, his two yellow cone-shaped canines pressed to his upper lip. The salt-and-pepper down on his head fluttered softly, although there was not the slightest draft.

Finally he pulled his hands from his pockets, let his lower lip hang free, and with difficulty freed one of his eyepieces from the general tangle on his chest. Then he set the pince-nez firmly on his nose with a most bizarre grimace, inspected husband and wife, and remarked, "Aha."

It must be noted at once that he used this exclamation with extraordinary frequency, but that he could employ it with great and strange variety. He might lay his head back, wrinkle his nose, open his mouth wide, and fidget in the air with his hands—and the sound was long, nasal, and metallic, much like the clang of a Chinese gong. Or, apart from all other nuances, he might toss it away quite casually—a brief, soft, offhanded "Aha," whose effect was still more comical because he formed his vowels in a murky, nasal fashion. Today he merely gave a quick jerk of his head and added a fleeting, cheerful "Aha" that seemed to arise from a vast reservoir of good spirits—and yet that impression was not to be trusted, for it was a known fact that, the merrier his behavior, the more dangerous was banker Kesselmeyer's mood. He might leap about and exclaim a thousand "Aha"s, set his pince-nez to his nose, then let it fall again, or flail his arms and chatter away, obviously incapable of controlling his exaggerated silliness—and then you could be sure that something wicked was eating away at him.

Blinking his eyes, Herr Grünlich gazed at him with undisguised mistrust. "Here so early?" he asked.

"Aha, yes," Kesselmeyer replied and shook one of his little, red, wrinkly hands in the air as if to say: Just be patient, I have a surprise. "I need to speak with you. To speak with you without delay, my friend." His manner of speech was even more ridiculous. He turned each word over in his little, toothless, mobile mouth before uttering it with incredible effort. He rolled his "r"s as if his throat were greased. Herr Grünlich went on blinking with increasing suspicion.

"Come in, Herr Kesselmeyer," Tony said. "Sit down here. How nice that you've come. Listen here, please. You can be our referee. I've been having an argument with Grünlich. Now, tell me: ought a three-year-old child have a governess, or not? Well?"

But Herr Kesselmeyer seemed to pay no attention to her. He did sit down, but now, opening his mouth as wide as possible and wrinkling his nose, he began to scratch at his close-cropped beard with his index finger—the sound alone could make a person nervous—all the while peering over his pince-nez with an indescribably jaunty air, inspecting the elegantly set breakfast table, the silver breadbasket, the label on the wine bottle.

"You see," Tony continued, "Grünlich claims I'm driving him to ruin."

At this point Herr Kesselmeyer looked at her, then at Herr Grünlich, and then burst into riotous laughter. "You're driving him to ruin?" he cried. "You're—driving—you're—you're ruining him? O God! Good God! Well, I never! That's very funny! That's quite, quite, *quite* funny." Which was followed by a flood of various "aha" sounds.

Herr Grünlich fidgeted nervously back and forth in his chair. He alternated between running one long finger inside his collar and letting both hands glide through his golden muttonchops.

"Kesselmeyer!" he said. "Contain yourself. Have you lost your senses? Stop that laughing. Would you like some wine? A cigar? What are you laughing about?"

"What am I laughing about? Yes, please do give me a glass of wine, give me a cigar. What am I laughing about? So you think that your wife is driving you to ruin, do you?"

"She is all too inclined to luxury," Herr Grünlich said with annoyance.

Tony did not dispute this in the least. Leaning back calmly, laying her hands in her lap among the velvet bows of her dressing gown, she shoved her upper lip forward saucily and said, "Yes. That's just how I am. That's obvious. I take after Mama. All the Krögers have been partial to luxury."

She would have declared with equal composure that she was flighty, quick-tempered, and vindictive. Given her pronounced sense of family, any notion of free will or self-determination was alien to her, so that she knew and could acknowledge the traits of her character with almost fatalistic equanimity, even her faults, and had no intention of correcting any of them. She believed, without knowing it, that absolutely every character trait was a family heirloom, a piece of tradition, and therefore something venerable and worthy of her respect, no matter what.

Herr Grünlich had finished his breakfast, and the odor of two cigars blended with the warm air from the stove.

"Isn't it drawing all right, Kesselmeyer?" his host asked. "Here, have another. I'll just pour you a little more wine. You wanted to speak with me, did you? Is it urgent? Something important? Do you find it rather warm in here? We'll ride into town together later. It's cooler in the smoking room, by the way." But Herr Kesselmeyer's response to all such attempts was merely to wave a hand in the hair, as if to say: That gets us nowhere, my friend.

Finally they rose, and while Tony remained behind to supervise the maid's clearing of the table, Herr Grünlich led his colleague into the *pensée* room. His head was bowed, and, lost in thought, he twirled the tip of his left muttonchop in his fingers; rowing wildly with his arms, Herr Kesselmeyer now followed him into the smoking room and they disappeared.

Ten minutes passed. Tony had gone into the salon for a moment, feather-duster in hand, to give the gleaming walnut top of the secretary and the curved legs of the table her personal attention, and now she slowly walked back through the dining room to the sitting room. She moved calmly and with undeniable dignity. Demoiselle Buddenbrook had obviously lost none of her self-confidence as Madame Grünlich. She held herself quite erect, her chin tucked slightly, viewing the world from on high. She held her enameled basket of keys in one hand and slipped the other into the side-pocket of her dark red dressing gown, letting herself be caught up in the play of its long, soft folds; but the naïve and innocent expression of her mouth betrayed her—this great dignity was a childish, harmless game.

In the *pensée* room she wandered about with the little brass sprinkling can, watering the black earth of the various plants. She loved her palm trees very much, they added such splendid elegance to the house. She cautiously fingered a new sprout on one of the thick, round stems, tenderly inspected the majestically spreading fronds, and trimmed a yellow tip here and there with the scissors. Suddenly she stopped to listen. The conversation in the smoking room, which had grown quite lively in the last few minutes, had now become so loud that she could understand every word from here, despite portieres and the heavy door.

"Stop shouting! Control yourself, for God's sake!" she heard Herr Grünlich yell, but his soft voice could not take the strain and broke, ending in a squeak. "Here, have another cigar," he added now, with desperate gentleness.

"Yes, thank you, I'd love one," the banker replied; and now a pause ensued, during which Herr Kesselmeyer apparently lit it. And then he said, "In short, will you or won't you? One or the other."

"Give me an extension, Kesselmeyer."

"Aha? No, no . . . *no*, my friend, no chance. Not even subject to debate."

"Why not? What's your rush? Be reasonable, for heaven's sake. You've waited this long . . ."

"But not a day more, my friend! All right, let's say eight days, but not an hour longer. But, be frank, is there anyone who still has confidence in . . ."

"No names, Kesselmeyer!"

"No names? Fine. Is there anyone who still has confidence in your estimable father-in- . . ."

"Don't even allude to him. Good God, don't be so foolish!"

"Fine, no allusions. Is there anyone who still has confidence in a well-known firm, upon which your credit, my friend, stands or falls? How much did that firm lose on that bankruptcy in Bremen? Fifty thousand? Seventy, a hundred? Or more? It was involved, very heavily involved—it's the talk of the town. Which all contributes to the general mood. Yesterday the firm of . . . Fine, no names. Yesterday said firm was solid and, without knowing it, protected you completely from any and all pressures. But today that firm is shaky, and B. Grünlich is the shakiest of the shaky. You do see that? Haven't you noticed? You'd be the first to sense such shifts. How have people been treating you? How do they look at you? Bock and Goudstikker have been uncommonly obliging and trusting, I suppose? And how has the bank reacted?"

"They've granted me an extension."

"Aha? But you're lying, aren't you? I know that what you got yesterday was a kick in the pants, wasn't it? A very, very stimulating kick? Well, look at that—there's no need to be embarrassed. Of course, it's in your best interest to have me believe that the others are as calm and trusting as ever. No, no, my friend. Write the consul. I'll wait one week."

"A partial payment, Kesselmeyer."

"Partial payment, my foot! One accepts partial payments to make sure in advance that someone is indeed reasonably solvent. But do I need to make any experiments in *that* regard? I know perfectly well how things stand with *your* solvency. Aha, aha. Partial payment—that is really quite, quite funny."

"Lower your voice, Kesselmeyer. Don't keep laughing like that, damn it. My situation is so serious—yes, I admit it, it is serious; but I have a lot of deals in the making. It can all turn out fine. Now, listen, listen carefully. Give me an extension and I'll sign you a note at twenty percent."

"No, nothing doing. That's quite absurd, my friend. No, no, I'm a man who likes to sell at the right time. You offered me eight percent, and I gave you your extension. You offered me twelve and sixteen percent, and I gave you an extension each time. But you could offer me forty now, and I wouldn't think of extending, would not give it one thought, my friend. Now that the Westfahl Brothers have fallen on their noses in Bremen, everyone at the moment is trying to protect himself and disengage his interests from those of the aforementioned firm. As I said, I am a man who likes to sell at the right time. I kept your notes as long as Johann Buddenbrook was sure to be good for them. And meanwhile I could add the unpaid interest to the capital and raise the percent. But you hold on to something only as long as it is rising in value or at least steady. And when it begins to fall, you sell. Which is to say, I want my capital."

"Kesselmeyer, have you no shame!"

"Aha, aha, 'shame'—now, I find that quite funny. What would you have me do? You're going to have to turn to your father-in-law in any case. The bank is ranting, and, for that matter, you're not exactly without stain."

"No, Kesselmeyer, I implore you, just calm down and listen to me. Yes, let me be candid, I will admit quite openly to you that my situation is serious. You and the bank are not the only ones. My promissory notes are being called in. Everyone seems to be in collusion."

"But of course. Given the circumstances—it's best done all at once."

"No, Kesselmeyer, listen to me. Be kind enough to take another cigar."

"I'm not even half finished with this one. Enough of your cigars. Pay up."

"Kesselmeyer, don't drop me. You're a friend, you've eaten at my table."

"And you haven't eaten at mine, my friend?"

"Yes, yes . . . but don't cut off my credit now, Kesselmeyer."

"Credit? You want *more* credit? Are you in your right mind? A new loan?"

"Yes, Kesselmeyer, I implore you . . . just a little, a bagatelle. All I have to do is make a few payments and advances here and there, and patience and respect will be restored. Keep me afloat, and you'll make a lot of money. As I said, I have all kinds of deals in the making. It can all turn out fine. You know that I'm industrious and inventive."

"Right—a dandy, a bungler, that's what you are, my friend. Would you be kind enough to tell me where you're going to find anything at this point? Is there a bank out there in the world somewhere, perhaps, that will put one thin dime on the table for you? Or another father-in-law, maybe? Ah no, your great coup is already behind you. That sort of thing comes along just once. My respects, for that. No, no, my highest respects."

"Speak a little softer, damn it."

"You're a bungler! Industrious and inventive . . . indeed, but always to the benefit of others. You certainly don't have any scruples, and yet it's never got you anywhere. You play some tricks, pilfer yourself some capital—and end up paying me sixteen percent instead of twelve. You pitched your honesty overboard, and gained nothing in return. You have the conscience of the butcher's dog, but you're a loser, a dolt, a poor fool. There are people like that; I find them quite, quite funny. Why are you so afraid, really, to go at last to the aforementioned gentleman with the whole story? Does it make you uneasy? Because things were not quite as proper as they should have been four years ago? Not quite tidy, is that it? Are you afraid that a certain matter . . . ?"

"All right, Kesselmeyer, I'll write. But what if he refuses? Lets me drop?"

"Aha, aha! Then we'll have a little bankruptcy, a very funny little bankruptcy, my friend. Which doesn't bother me in the least. I've more or less covered my investment with the interest you've managed to scratch together now and then. And I'll have first rights over what assets are left. So you can be sure that I'll not come up short. I know all I need to know about you, my good man. I already have an inventory right here in my pocket. Aha! I'll make very sure that no little silver breadbaskets and dressing gowns are stashed away."

"Kesselmeyer, you've eaten at my table. . . ."

"Enough about your table. I'll come for my answer in eight days. I'm *walking* into town. A little exercise would do me a great deal of good. Good morning, my friend. A very good morning."

And it looked as if Herr Kesselmeyer was departing—and, indeed, he did. The sound of his strange, shuffling steps in the hallway conjured up the picture of his departure, arms rowing.

When Herr Grünlich entered the *pensée* room, Tony was standing there with the bronze watering can in her hand. She looked him straight in the eye.

"Why are you standing there? What are you staring at?" he asked, baring his teeth, tracing vague designs in the air with his hands, rocking his upper body back and forth. His pink face was incapable of turning totally pale. It was splotched with red, as if he had scarlet fever.

7

CONSUL JOHANN BUDDENBROOK arrived at the villa at two in the afternoon; dressed in a gray overcoat, he entered the Grünlichs' salon and embraced his daughter with a certain painful fervor. He was pale and looked older. His small eyes lay deep in their sockets, his large nose jutted out sharply between his fallen cheeks, his lips seemed to have grown thinner, and what had once been curly side-whiskers running from his temples to mid-cheek was now a beard that covered his chin and lower jaw and extended halfway down over his stiff collar and necktie—and it was as gray as the hair on his head.

The consul had just gone through several difficult and exhausting days. Thomas had fallen ill, was hemorrhaging at the lung; he had received news of his son's misfortune in a letter from Herr van der Kellen. He had left the office in the prudent hands of his chief clerk, and hurried off to Amsterdam with all deliberate speed. It turned out that his son's illness had not involved any immediate danger, but that it was very wise to send him at once to a health spa in the mountains in the south of France; and as luck would have it, Herr van der Kellen's young son had also been planning a vacation, and as soon as Thomas was up to it, the two young men left together for Pau.

But no sooner had the consul returned home than he had been met with another blow, which for the moment had shaken his firm to its foundations: the bankruptcy in Bremen, which had meant the loss of eighty thousand marks in "cold cash." And how? Discounted checks drawn on the Westfahl Brothers had bounced—liquidation had already begun. Not that he had been unable to cover them; the firm had at once shown what it could do, without any hesitation or embarrassment. But that had not prevented the consul from having to experience the sudden cold reserve and mistrust that such a calamity, such a drain on capital, usually elicits from banks, "friends," and foreign firms.

Well, he had pulled himself erect, had taken stock of the situation, confronted it calmly, and begun to set things in order. But then, in the middle of that battle, in the middle of all the dispatches, letters, and calculations, this had befallen him as well. Grünlich, B. Grünlich, his daughter's husband, was insolvent, and in a long, confused letter that was one endless lamentation, he had begged, implored, whined for help in the amount of 100,000 to 120,000 marks. The consul had briefly explained the situation to his own wife, though sparing her the worst details, and in a cold, noncommittal letter he informed Herr Grünlich that he would meet with him, together with his banker, Herr Kesselmeyer, at the former's home—and left for Hamburg.

Tony received him in the salon. She loved to receive visitors in the brown silk salon and decided to make no exception in her father's case, for although the exact nature of the current situation was unclear to her, she had a keen and solemn sense of its importance. She looked pretty but serious, and was wearing a pale gray dress with lace at the bodice and cuffs, belled sleeves, a hoop skirt with a long train, all in the latest fashion, and a small diamond clasp at the throat.

"Hello, Papa, it's so good to see you again *at last*. And how is Mama? Have you had good news from Tom? Take off your coat, and do sit down, dear Papa. Would you like to freshen up? I have had the guest room made ready for you. Grünlich is just finishing dressing."

"Let him be, child; I'll wait for him down here. You know, don't you, that I've come to have a talk with your husband, a very, very serious talk, my dear Tony? Is Herr Kesselmeyer here?"

"Yes, he is, Papa, he's sitting in the *pensée* room, looking at our album."

"Where is Erika?"

"Upstairs, with Thinka in the nursery. She's doing very well.

She's giving her doll a bath. Not with water, of course—it's a wax doll. So she just pretends."

"But of course." The consul sighed and continued, "I suppose I cannot assume that you have been informed, my dear child, about the situation . . . about your husband's situation."

He had sat down in one of the easy chairs set around the large table, whereas Tony made a little stool for herself of three silk pillows, piling one atop another, at his feet. The fingers of her right hand toyed carefully with the diamonds at her throat.

"No, Papa," Tony replied, "I must admit I know nothing at all. Good heavens, I'm such a silly goose, you know. I have no idea. I did happen to hear a little of a recent conversation between Kesselmeyer and Grünlich. But at the end it sounded to me as if Herr Kesselmeyer was just joking again. He always says the most ridiculous things. And I did hear your name mentioned once or twice."

"You heard them mention my name? In what connection?"

"Oh, I don't know what the connection was, Papa. Grünlich has been very cross the last few days, absolutely insufferable, I must say! Until yesterday. Yesterday he was very sweet, asked me ten or twelve times whether I loved him, and if I would put in a good word for him if he asked something of you."

"Ah . . ."

"Yes. He told me that he had written you, that you'd be coming. And it's so good to have you here. It's all a bit mysterious. Grünlich has set up the big green card table—there are all kinds of papers and pencils on it—where you're supposed to have a conference with him and Kesselmeyer."

"Listen to me, my dear child," the consul said, stroking her hair. "I have to ask you something, something very serious. Now, tell me: you do love your husband with all your heart, don't you?"

"Of course, Papa," Tony said with a dissembling, childlike face, the same one she used to wear if someone asked her, "Now, you won't tease the old woman who sells dolls again, will you, Tony?" The consul said nothing for a moment or two.

"You love him so much," he asked again, "that you could not live without him, no matter what, is that right? Even if, should it be God's will, his situation were to change and he were no longer in a position to surround you with all these things?" And he let his hand wander hastily over the furniture and portieres, the gilt table-clock on the mirrored whatnot stand—and finally down over her dress.

"Of course, Papa," Tony repeated in the reassuring tone that she almost always used if someone spoke to her about serious things. She looked past her father's face to the window, where a heavy veil of delicate mist was descending soundlessly. Her face had the same wide-eyed expression that children put on when someone reading a fairy tale to them is tactless enough to insert some general remarks on morals and duty—a mixture of embarrassment and impatience, piety and boredom.

For one whole minute, the consul watched her silently, opening and closing his eyes as he pondered all this. Was he satisfied with her answer? He had weighed the matter well both at home and on his way here.

It is easy to understand that Johann Buddenbrook's first and most candid impulse was to do everything possible to avoid a payment in any amount to his son-in-law. But when he recalled how strongly he had advocated this marriage, to use a mild term, when he remembered the look the child had given him as she said goodbye after her wedding and asked him, "Are you proud of me?"—then he had to admit his own rather heavy guilt in regard to his daughter's situation and to tell himself that this matter would have to be decided entirely as she wanted. He was well aware that she had not agreed to the marriage out of love, but he thought it possible that four years of a life together and the birth of a child might have changed a great many things, that Tony might feel bound to her husband now, body and soul, and reject any notion of separation for reasons both Christian and worldly. In that case, the consul decided, he would have to make the best of it and hand over whatever sum was necessary. To be sure, honor and duty, both as a Christian and as a wife, demanded that Tony follow the spouse entrusted to her into any misfortune, no matter what; but if it became evident that this was indeed her decision, then he did not feel justified in asking her to forgo, through no fault of her own, all the amenities and comforts of a life she had known since earliest childhood; he would be duty-bound to avoid a catastrophe and to keep B. Grünlich afloat no matter what the cost. In brief, the upshot of all his reflections was a desire to take his daughter and her child home with him and let Herr Grünlich go his way. God forbid that such an awful thing should happen. But just in case, he had given much thought to the section of the legal code that permitted divorce should a husband prove incapable of supporting his wife and children. And above all, he had to sound out his daughter's true feelings.

"I can see," he said, continuing to stroke her hair, "I can see, my dear child, that you are moved by fine and worthy principles. All the same . . . I cannot assume, I'm sorry to say, that you see these matters as they must be seen: that is, as fact. I have not asked you what you *might* do in such-and-such a case, but, rather, what you *will* do, here and now. I have no idea what you may know or suspect about the present situation. But it is my sad duty to tell you that your husband has been obliged to stop all payments and is no longer able to carry on his business. You do understand me, don't you?"

"Grünlich is bankrupt?" Tony asked softly, rising halfway from her pillows and quickly grasping her father's hand.

"Yes, my child," he said earnestly. "You hadn't suspected it?"

"I didn't suspect anything definite," she stammered. "Then Kesselmeyer wasn't joking?" she continued, staring down at her brown carpet. "O God!" she suddenly cried and sank back onto her pillows. And at that moment everything locked inside the word "bankrupt" suddenly opened up before her, all the vague, terrible things that she had felt as a small child. Bankrupt—that was something more ghastly than death, it was chaos, collapse, ruin, disgrace, humiliation, despair, and misery. "He's bankrupt," she said again, so cast down and crushed by that fateful word that the idea never occurred to her that there might be some help, not even from her father.

He watched her, his eyebrows raised—his small, deep-set eyes weary and sad, but also betraying the extraordinary suspense of this moment. "And so I'm asking you, my dear Tony," he said gently, "if you are prepared to follow your husband into poverty?" He realized at once that he had instinctively chosen the cruel word "poverty" in order to intimidate her, and quickly added, "He can always work his way up again. . . ."

"Of course, Papa," Tony answered. But she broke into tears nonetheless. She sobbed into her batiste handkerchief trimmed with lace and bearing the monogram AG. She still cried just as she had as a child—openly and without any posturing. The way her upper lip quivered was inexpressibly touching.

Her father continued to probe her with his eyes. "And you are quite serious about that, my child?" he asked. He felt as helpless as she.

"But don't I have to?" she sobbed. "I have to."

"Certainly not," he said vigorously. But, feeling guilty, he immediately corrected himself: "I certainly would not force you to do so, my dear Tony. If it were the case, however, that your feelings do not bind you unswervingly to your husband . . ."

She looked at him with tearful, uncomprehending eyes. "What do you mean, Papa?"

The consul twisted back and forth a little, and found a way out. "My dear child, believe me when I say that I would find it very painful to see you exposed to all the hardships and insults that would result from your husband's misfortune, which would mean immediately dissolving both his business and your household. It is my wish to spare you the initial unpleasantnesses and to take you and our little Erika home for now. Am I right to think you would be grateful for that?"

Tony was silent for a moment and dried her tears. She first breathed fussily on her handkerchief and then pressed it to her eyes to keep them from turning red. And then she asked in a firm tone, but without raising her voice, "Papa, is Grünlich to blame? Are his misfortunes the result of his own carelessness and dishonesty?"

"That's very likely," the consul said. "That is . . . no, I don't really know, my child. I told you that I still have to discuss the matter with him and his banker."

Tony did not appear to have paid any attention to his answer. She was resting against her silk pillows, an elbow on one knee, her chin in her hand, her head sunk low—but she let her eyes drift up, dreamily scanning the room. "Oh, Papa," she said softly, her lips barely moving, "looking back now, wouldn't it have been better if . . ."

The consul could not see her face; but it bore the same expression it had on many a summer evening, when she would lean against the little window of her room in Travemünde. Her arm was resting on her father's knee now, her hand dangling limply in the air. But that hand betrayed an infinitely sad and soft surrender to memories, to sweet longings that drifted into the distance.

"Better?" Consul Buddenbrook asked. "If none of this had happened, my child?" He was ready to admit with all his heart that it would have been better if this marriage had not taken place.

But Tony only sighed and said, "Oh, never mind." She seemed to be wrapped up in thoughts that swept her so far away that the word "bankrupt" was as good as forgotten.

The consul felt it necessary to put into words things he would rather have merely agreed to. "I think I can guess your thoughts, dear Tony," he said. "And I do not hesitate, for my part, to admit that at this moment I sincerely regret the step that seemed to me so wise and beneficial four years ago. I truly believe, before God, that I am guilty of no sin. I believe I did my duty in trying to arrange for you a life suitable to your station. Heaven has decided otherwise. Please don't think that your father acted out of carelessness or gambled with your happiness without due thought. Grünlich approached me as a man with the best recommendations—a pastor's son, a Christian and urbane man. Later, I made inquiries as to his business, and the responses sounded as favorable as could be. I examined his circumstances. All that is still murky to me—murky and needs to be explained yet. But you don't blame me, do you?"

"No, Papa. How could you even say that? You mustn't take it to heart so. Poor Papa, you look so pale—should I have a cordial brought for you?" She had laid her arm around his neck and kissed him now on the cheek.

"No thanks," he said. "There, there. It's all right, thanks. Yes, the last few days have been exhausting. But what's a man to do? I've had a great deal of worry. These are trials sent by God. But that doesn't mean I don't feel some guilt about you, my child. Everything depends now on the question I've already put to you, but which you have not yet answered adequately. Tell me frankly, Tony—have you learned to love your husband over the years of marriage?"

Tony began to weep again. Holding her batiste handkerchief to her eyes with both hands now, she managed to say amid her sobs, "Oh! How can you ask, Papa? I never loved him. I've always loathed him. Don't you know that?"

It would be difficult to describe the play of emotions on Johann Buddenbrook's face. There was shock and sadness in his eyes, but he pressed his lips together hard, creating folds along his cheeks and at the corners of his mouth, an expression he usually reserved for the completion of a profitable business deal. He said softly, "Four years . . ."

Tony's tears suddenly ceased. Her moist handkerchief still in her hand, she sat upright on her pillows and said angrily, "Four years. Yes! And sometimes during those four years he would spend an evening with me, reading his paper."

"But God gave you both a child," the consul said, deeply touched.

"Yes, Papa. And I love Erika very much. Although Grünlich claims I'm not fond of children. I would never part with her, never. But Grünlich—no! Grünlich—no! And now he's bankrupt. Oh, Papa, if you want to take me and Erika home with you, I'd be so happy! So now you know."

The consul pressed his lips together again; he was thoroughly satisfied. He still had not addressed the main point, true—but given the resolve that Tony had now shown, there was not much risk involved.

"All the same," he said, "you seem to have fully forgotten, my child, that help might be possible. And by that I mean from your father, who has already admitted that he cannot help feeling some guilt in this matter. And in case, well, in case you would want him to, expect him to . . . he would intervene, would prevent a total collapse and cover your husband's debts as best he could to keep the business afloat."

He watched her intently, and the look on her face filled him with satisfaction—it was a look of disappointment.

"How much are we talking about, in fact?" she asked.

"What does that have to do with it, my child? It's a large sum, a very large sum." And Consul Buddenbrook nodded several times, as if staggered by the burden of even thinking of such a sum. "Moreover," he continued, "I cannot conceal from you that the firm has suffered other losses, quite apart from this matter, and that losing such a sum would be a blow from which it would recover with very, very great difficulty. I mention that in no way to . . ."

He did not finish. Tony had jumped up, had even taken a few steps backward, and, with her damp lace handkerchief still trailing in her hand, she cried, "Good! Enough! Never!"

She looked almost heroic. The word "firm" had hit its mark. It was highly likely that it was a more decisive factor than her dislike of Herr Grünlich.

"You shall *not* do it, Papa!" she went on, quite beside herself. "Do you want to go bankrupt, too? Enough! Never!"

At that moment the door to the hallway opened a little hesitantly, and Herr Grünlich entered.

And the manner in which Johann Buddenbrook stood up now, said: "That's settled."

8

HERR GRÜNLICH'S FACE was splotched with red, but he was impeccably dressed. He wore a dignified black pleated coat and pea-colored trousers, much like those he had worn for his first visit to Meng Strasse. He stood there in a limp pose, his eyes directed to the floor, and in a faint, languid voice he said, "Father . . ."

The consul bowed coldly and set his necktie to rights with a few energetic tugs.

"Thank you for coming," Herr Grünlich added.

"It was my duty, my friend," the consul replied. "But I fear it will be the only thing I can do for you."

His son-in-law threw him a quick glance, and his pose went even limper.

"I hear," the consul continued, "that your banker, Herr Kesselmeyer, is waiting for us. Which room have you chosen for our discussion? I am at your disposal."

"Please be kind enough to follow me," Herr Grünlich murmured.

Consul Buddenbrook kissed his daughter on the brow and said, "Go up to your child, Antonie." With Herr Grünlich skittering now ahead, now behind him and then pulling back the portieres, he strode across the dining room and into the sitting room.

Herr Kesselmeyer was standing at the window, and as he turned around the salt-and-pepper down on his skull first rose and then gently fell back in place.

"Herr Kesselmeyer . . . Consul Buddenbrook, my father-in-law," Herr Grünlich said with meek gravity. The consul's face was rigid.

Herr Kesselmeyer bowed, his arms dangling at his sides, both canines fixed against his upper lip; then he said, "Your servant, Consul Buddenbrook. I take sincere pleasure in having the opportunity to meet you."

"Please excuse us for having made you wait, Kesselmeyer," Herr Grünlich said. He was equally courteous to them both.

"Shall we get down to business?" the consul remarked, turning from one to the other.

Their host hastened to respond, "Gentlemen, please . . ."

As they moved into the smoking room, Herr Kesselmeyer remarked cheerfully, "You had a pleasant journey, I hope, Consul Buddenbrook? Aha, rain? Yes, a bad time of year, a dreary, dirty time of the year. If only we had a bit of frost, a bit of snow. But no—just rain and filth. Quite, quite disgusting."

"What an odd man," the consul thought.

In the middle of the little room, papered in a dark floral pattern, there stood a sturdy rectangular table, covered with green baize. The rain was picking up outside. It was so dark that Herr Grünlich quickly lit the three candles that stood in a silver candelabrum on the table, whose green surface was covered with bluish business correspondence stamped with the names of various firms and stacks of other papers, some torn and soiled, with visible dates and signatures. There was also a thick ledger, a sand-holder, and a pewter inkstand, studded with nicely sharpened quills and pencils.

Herr Grünlich did the honors with the silent, tactful, reticent gestures of someone directing guests at a funeral. "Dear Father, please, take the armchair," he said gently. "Herr Kesselmeyer, would you be so kind as to sit here?"

At last everything was in order. The banker sat across from his host, while the consul presided from his armchair at the long side of the table; the back of his chair rested against the door to the hallway.

Herr Kesselmeyer bent forward, let his lower lip hang free, disentangled a pince-nez from his vest, and, wrinkling his nose and opening his mouth wide, set it in place. First he scratched his close-cropped beard—the sound alone could make a person nervous—

then set his hands on his knees, nodded toward the papers, and remarked cheerfully, "Aha, so here's the whole mess."

"You will permit me, won't you, to take a closer look at the state of your affairs?" the consul said, reaching for the ledger.

But suddenly Herr Grünlich reached across the table, protecting the ledger with both hands—threaded with strong blue veins and visibly trembling—and cried in an agitated voice, "One moment, one moment, please, Father. Do let me make a few introductory remarks. Yes, you shall have your look at the state of my affairs, nothing can escape your eyes. But believe me when I say it will be a look into the affairs of an unfortunate, not a guilty, man. You see in me a man, Father, who has struggled tirelessly against fate, but who has at last been struck down. And with that in mind . . ."

"We shall see, my friend, we shall see," the consul said with obvious impatience; and Herr Grünlich pulled his hands back and let destiny take its course.

Long, dreadful minutes passed in silence. The three gentlemen sat huddled in the flickering candlelight, hemmed in by four dark walls. There was no perceptible movement except the rustle of papers under the consul's hand. The only other sound was the rain falling outside.

Herr Kesselmeyer had thrust his thumbs into the armholes of his vest, and while the rest of his fingers played the piano on his shoulders, he gazed with unutterable amusement at the other two men. Herr Grünlich did not lean back in his chair, but kept his hands on the table and stared gloomily straight ahead, although now and then his eyes shifted for a nervous sidelong glance at his father-in-law. The consul paged through the ledger, following the columns of numbers with a fingernail; he compared entries and jotted down little, indecipherable numbers with a pencil. His weary face reflected his dismay at the state of affairs revealed by this "closer look." Finally he laid his left hand on Herr Grünlich's sleeve and said in shock, "You poor man."

"Father—" Herr Grünlich blurted out. Two large tears rolled down the pitiful man's cheeks and into his golden muttonchops. Herr Kesselmeyer followed the course of these two drops with intense interest; he even raised himself up a little to stare open-mouthed directly into Grünlich's face. Consul Buddenbrook was deeply moved. Softened by the misfortune he had himself encountered, he felt compassion carrying him away; but he quickly mastered his emotions.

"How is it possible?" he said with a despondent shake of his head. "Within just a few years."

"Child's play!" Herr Kesselmeyer responded cheerfully. "A man can go to the dogs in high style in four years. One need only think of how jauntily the Westfahl Brothers were skipping about not long ago."

The consul stared at him, blinking—but he neither saw nor heard him. He had told them nothing of the real thoughts gnawing away inside him. Bewildered and suspicious, he asked himself why, why had all this happened just now? B. Grünlich's present misfortune could just as easily have overcome him two or three years before—that was evident at first glance. But he had enjoyed inexhaustible credit: banks had provided him with capital, again and again he had received the endorsements of solid firms like those of Senator Bock and Consul Goudstikker, his promissory notes had been treated as if they were cash. And then had come a collapse on all sides, a total withdrawal of trust as if by prearrangement, everyone joining in the attack on B. Grünlich with complete and ruthless disregard for even common business courtesy. But why now, now, now?—And the head of the firm of Johann Buddenbrook knew quite well what he meant by "now." He would have been very naïve not to have known that the reputation of his own firm necessarily enhanced his son-in-law's prospects, once the engagement to Antonie was announced. But had Grünlich's credit really depended so completely, so blatantly, so exclusively on his own? Had Grünlich in fact been a nobody? But what about the inquiries the consul had made, the books he had examined? However matters stood, he was firmer than ever in his resolve not to lift a finger to help. It seemed they were all sadly mistaken. So B. Grünlich had known how to create the illusion that Johann Buddenbrook stood behind him, had he? That was a dreadful misconception, and apparently widely held, and he would have to put a stop to it once and for all. And this Kesselmeyer was in for a surprise, too. Did that buffoon have no conscience at all? It was plain as day from the way he had kept extending more and more credit to Grünlich—long after he had become insolvent and at ever more bloodthirsty rates of interest—that he had shamelessly speculated on the probability that he, Johann Buddenbrook, would not let his daughter's husband be ruined.

"Be that as it may," he said curtly, "let us come to the point. If I were to render expert opinion as a businessman, I regret that I would have to say these are the ledgers of an unfortunate man, true, but of a very guilty man as well."

"Father—" Herr Grünlich stammered.

"That is not a form of address I take *any* pleasure in hearing," the consul replied quickly and harshly. "Your claims against Herr Grünlich, sir," he continued, turning momentarily to the banker, "total sixty thousand marks."

"Together with unpaid interest it comes to 68,755 marks and 15 shillings," Herr Kesselmeyer replied amiably.

"Indeed. And you are not prepared under any circumstances to grant an extension?"

Herr Kesselmeyer simply broke into laughter. He laughed with his mouth open, in good-natured spasms, without any trace of mockery, all the while gazing straight at the consul, as if urging him to join in as well.

Johann Buddenbrook's small, deep-set eyes darkened, and a sudden flush around the edges spread down to his cheekbones. He had asked merely for form's sake, knowing quite well that an extension by this one creditor would make no significant difference in any case. But he was indignant at the shameful way the man had refused. With one sweeping gesture, he shoved aside all the papers in front of him, laid his pencil on the table with a flick of the wrist, and said, "Then I hereby state that I am unwilling to have anything further to do with this matter."

"Aha!" Herr Kesselmeyer cried, waving his hands in the air. "That's what I call straight talk, spoken with dignity. The consul wants to settle things quite simply. No long-winded speeches. Short and sweet."

Johann Buddenbrook did not even look at him, but turned calmly to Herr Grünlich and said, "I cannot help you, my friend. Things will have to take their course. I do not see myself in a position to alter that. Pull yourself together and seek comfort and strength in God. I must consider our discussion at an end."

Surprisingly, Herr Kesselmeyer's expression turned quite serious, and the effect was very odd; but then he nodded encouragingly to Herr Grünlich, who sat there immobilized, except that he was wringing his long hands so violently that the knuckles cracked.

"Father . . . Consul Buddenbrook," he said in a quavering voice, "surely you do not, you cannot, want me to end in ruin and misery. Listen to me. The total deficit comes to 120,000. You can save me. You are a rich man. You may regard the sum, if you wish, as a final settlement, as your daughter's inheritance, as an interest-bearing loan. I will work. You know that I am industrious and inventive."

"I have spoken my final word," the consul said.

"If I may be so bold—is it because you *cannot* pay?" Herr Kesselmeyer asked, wrinkling up his nose and staring through his pince-nez. "If I might make a suggestion, Consul Buddenbrook, this would be an excellent opportunity to prove the strength of the firm of Johann Buddenbrook."

"You would do well, sir, to leave any concern about my firm's reputation to me. I have no need to throw my money in the nearest ditch to prove the firm's solvency."

"Surely not, surely not! Aha—ditch, now that's quite funny. But do you not think, Herr Buddenbrook, that your son-in-law's bankruptcy might not mistakenly tend to put your own situation in a bad light?"

"I can only urge upon you once again that my reputation in the business world is my own concern," the consul said.

Herr Grünlich stared helplessly at his banker and then began again: "Father, I beg you, consider what it is you're doing. Are we speaking here of me alone? Oh, it may well be that I, *I*, shall be ruined. But your daughter, my wife, whom I love so much, whom to win I battled long and hard . . . and our child, our own innocent child—shall they be ruined as well? No, Father, I could not bear it. I would kill myself. Yes, with this very hand, I would kill myself. And may heaven then declare you innocent of any guilt."

Johann Buddenbrook leaned back in his armchair—he was pale

and his heart was pounding. For the second time the storm of this man's emotions rushed over him, and there certainly seemed something genuine about the way he expressed them; it was the same awful threat he had heard that day when he told Herr Grünlich about the letter his daughter had sent from Travemünde, and once again a shudder passed through him—like any man of his generation, he felt a fanatical reverence for all human emotions that stood at odds with his sober and practical outlook as a man of business. But the attack lasted no longer than a second. "A hundred and twenty thousand marks," he repeated to himself. And then, calmly and firmly, he said aloud, "Antonie is my daughter. I will see to it that she does not suffer through no fault of her own."

"What do you mean by that?" Herr Grünlich asked, slowly stiffening.

"You will learn soon enough," the consul replied. "For now, I have nothing further to add." And with that he stood up, squared his chair back into its place, and turned toward the door.

Herr Grünlich sat there silent, stiff, bewildered—his mouth twitched from side to side, but he was unable to wrench a single word from it. But with this final and conclusive action by the consul, Herr Kesselmeyer's good cheer returned—indeed, it grew more intense and dreadful, until it burst all bounds. His pince-nez fell from his nose, which lurched upward between his eyes, and his tiny mouth, distorted by those two lonely yellow canines, threatened to rip apart. His little red hands rowed in the air, the down on his skull fluttered; and, framed by his white, close-cropped beard, his whole face, twisted and deformed by this excess of mirth, turned vermilion.

"Aa-hah!" he cried, his voice cracking. "I find all this really quite, quite funny! But you really should reconsider, Herr Buddenbrook, before tossing such a charming, such a priceless specimen of a son-in-law into the ditch. Such industry and invention will not be found a second time on God's good, wide earth. Aha! Once before, only four years ago, with the knife already at our throat, with the rope around our neck—suddenly the floor of the exchange was filled with shouts announcing an engagement to Mademoiselle Buddenbrook, before it had ever occurred. My respect! No, no, my deepest, deepest respect."

"Kesselmeyer," Herr Grünlich screeched, his hands clutching the air as if he were fending off a ghost; then he ran to a corner of the room, sat down on a chair, and buried his face in his hands, bending over so deep that the tips of his muttonchops lay across his thighs. Several times he even pulled his knees up in a crouch.

"And how did we manage that?" Herr Kesselmeyer continued. "How did we actually go about snapping up both the daughter and the eighty thousand marks? Oho! It can be arranged—even if one has no more than a pennyworth of industry and invention, it can be arranged. If Papa is to come to the rescue, one presents him with very pretty books—charming, tidy books with everything in tip-top order. Except, of course, that they don't quite correspond to crude reality. Because in crude reality, three-quarters of that dowry is already promissory notes."

The consul stood at the door, pale as death, the knob in his hand. Shivers of horror ran down his back. Was he really trapped in this little dimly lit room with a swindler and a vicious ape gone mad?

"Sir, I abhor your words," he managed to say, still rather unsure of himself. "I abhor your insane slander all the more because it is directed at me as well—and I did not thoughtlessly lead my daughter into this misfortune. I made serious inquiries about my son-in-law. The rest was God's will."

Determined not to hear any more, he turned and opened the door.

But Herr Kesselmeyer shouted after him, "Aha? Inquiries? And of whom? Of Bock? Goudstikker? Petersen? Massmann & Timm? They were all in on it. They were all in up to their ears. They were only too glad to see a marriage that would provide them some security."

The consul slammed the door behind him.

9

DORA, the not entirely honest cook, was busy in the dining room.

"Ask Madame Grünlich to come down," the consul ordered.

"Get ready to leave, my child," he said when Tony appeared. He walked across into the salon with her. "Get ready as quickly as you can and see to it that Erika is ready to travel, too. We are going into the city. We shall spend the night at an inn and then leave for home tomorrow."

"Yes, Papa," Tony said. Her face was flushed; she looked bewildered, distraught. Not knowing what sort of preparations she should make, she let her hands flutter about uselessly at her waist—she truly could not grasp the reality of what was happening to her.

"What should I take with me, Papa?" she asked with nervous excitement. "Everything? All my clothes? Or just one or two trunks? Is Grünlich really bankrupt? O God! But I can take my jewelry, can't I? Papa, the maids will have to be discharged. I can't pay them. Grünlich was supposed to give me my housekeeping money today or tomorrow."

"Let it be, my child. All those things will be handled here. Take only what you absolutely need. One trunk—a small one. We will send for your things. Step lively, do you hear? We have . . ."

At that moment the portieres were thrown open wide and Herr Grünlich entered the salon. With tripping steps, his arms widespread, his head tilted to one side in the pose of a man who wishes to say, "Here I am! Slay me if you will!," he flew to his wife and sank on both knees in front of her. He was pitiful to look at.

His tawny golden muttonchops were disheveled, his coat was all wrinkled, his necktie askew, his collar stood open, and little drops of sweat stood out on his brow.

"Antonie!" he said. "Behold me here. Do you have a heart, a feeling heart? Hear me out. You see before you a devastated man, a man who will perish, if—indeed, a man who will surely die of grief, if you reject his love for you. Here I lie. Can you find it in your heart to say: 'I despise you?' 'I am leaving you'?"

Tony wept. It was exactly the same as that day in the landscape room. She saw that same face distorted with fear, those pleading eyes directed up at her, and once again she was amazed and moved to see that there was no pretense in his pleas, that his fear was genuine.

"Get up, Grünlich," she said, sobbing. "Please, get up." And she tried to pull him up by the shoulders. "I do not despise you. How can you say such a thing." In total helplessness, not knowing what else to say, she turned to her father. The consul took her hand, bowed to his son-in-law, and moved with her toward the hallway door.

"You're leaving?" Herr Grünlich cried, leaping to his feet.

"I have already told you," the consul said, "that I cannot be responsible for allowing my child to suffer such misfortune through no fault of her own. And, might I add, neither can you. No, sir, you have forfeited your rights to my daughter. And you should thank your Creator that the heart of this child has remained so pure and unsuspecting that, in leaving you, she does not despise you. Farewell."

At this point Herr Grünlich lost his head. He had wanted to speak of a brief separation, of a reunion and a new life together, and perhaps even to salvage the inheritance. But all his careful planning, all his industry and invention were at an end. He could have picked up the large, unbreakable bronze plate from the mirrored whatnot stand, but instead he grabbed the fragile, ornate vase beside it and dashed it to the floor, breaking it in a thousand pieces.

"Ha! Fine! Fine!" he screamed. "Get out! Do you think I'll weep great tears for you, you goose? No, no, you're wrong there, my dear. I only married you for your money, but since it wasn't nearly enough, you can just go on home. I'm fed up with you—fed up—fed up!"

Johann Buddenbrook led his daughter out in silence. But the consul returned alone again and walked over to Herr Grünlich, who was standing at the window staring out into the rain, his hands behind his back. He touched him softly on the shoulder, and softly admonished him, "Pull yourself together. *Pray!*"

10

THE ATMOSPHERE in the big house on Meng Strasse remained subdued for some time after Madame Grünlich returned home with her little daughter. Everyone moved about rather gingerly and no one liked to speak about "it"—except the person who had played the leading role in the affair, who felt completely in her element and, unlike the others, spoke of it with gusto.

Tony moved into the rooms on the third floor that her parents had occupied when the old Buddenbrooks were alive. She was somewhat disappointed when her papa would not hear of hiring a separate maid for them; and she spent a half-hour in pensive reflection the day he gently explained to her that her only proper course of action for now was to live a private life apart from the social whirl of the town, for, although by all ordinary standards she was an innocent victim of the fate that God had sent to test her, her position as a divorced woman demanded the greatest discretion at present. But Tony had the lovely knack of being able to adapt readily to any situation in life simply by tackling its new possibilities. She was soon enjoying her role of "innocent woman afflicted by tragedy"; her wardrobe was dark now, her pretty ash-blond hair was parted and neatly drawn back, just as she had worn it in her youth; and, to compensate for her lack of social pleasures, she found inexhaustible joy and great dignity in the gravity and importance of her new situation and provided the household with her views on marriage, Herr Grünlich, and life and destiny in general.

Not everyone offered her the opportunity. Elisabeth was convinced that her husband had acted as correctly as duty demanded; but whenever Tony began to speak, she would simply lift her lovely white hand and say, "*Assez*, my child. I do not wish to hear about the matter."

Clara, now twelve years old, understood nothing of what had happened, and Cousin Thilda was just as dense. "Oh, Tony, how sad," was all she knew to say, drawing out the syllables in amazement. But the young wife found an attentive audience in Mamselle Jungmann, who at age thirty-five was proud of having grown gray in service to the best circles of society. "You need have no fears, Tony, my child," she said. "You are still young and will marry again." And she also devoted much loyalty and love to raising little Erika, telling her the same stories and anecdotes the consul's children had heard fifteen years before—particularly about an uncle in Marienwerder who had died of the hiccups because "his heart got squashed."

But most of all Tony loved to chat with her father over dinner, or at breakfast early each morning. Her attachment to him had suddenly become much deeper than ever before. She had always been in awe of his powerful position in the town, of his diligent, sober, stern, and pious competence, had felt more respect than tenderness for him, but during the stormy scene in her salon, he had shown her his human side; it had touched her and filled her with pride that he had found her worthy of a serious, confidential discussion of the matter, that he had put the decision in her hands, and that he, who had always been so unimpeachable, had admitted almost humbly that he did not feel guiltless in what had happened to her. Certainly such a thought would never have occurred to Tony on her own; but since he had said it, she believed it, and her feelings for him had grown softer and tenderer. The consul's view of the matter had not changed, either—in the wake of this terrible misfortune, he believed he owed his daughter twice as much love.

Johann Buddenbrook had taken no steps against his unscrupulous son-in-law. True, Tony and her mother had learned from several conversations just what dishonest means Herr Grünlich had employed to get his hands on the eighty thousand marks, but the consul was wary of having the matter made public or, worse, turned over to the courts. His pride as a man of business had been grievously wounded, and he wrestled in silence with the disgrace of having been swindled so badly.

Nevertheless, as soon as B. Grünlich had declared bankruptcy—causing not inconsiderable losses to various firms in Hamburg—the consul energetically prosecuted for divorce. And it was primarily that suit, the thought that she herself was the middle point of a real suit, that filled Tony with an indescribable sense of her own worth.

"Father," she said—because during such conversations she never called the consul Papa—"Father, how is our case going? You do think, don't you, that it will turn out well? The statute is perfectly clear; I've studied it myself: 'the incapacity of the husband to support his family.' The judges must surely recognize that. If there had been a son, however, Grünlich would retain custody."

On another occasion she said, "I have given a great deal of thought to the years of my marriage, Father. And, you know, *that* was why the man wouldn't live in the city, though I so much wanted to. *That* was why he never liked for me to go into town or move in society. The danger was much greater there than in Eimsbüttel that I might somehow learn just how matters stood with him. What a scoundrel!"

"It is not for us to judge, my child," the consul replied.

And, once the divorce was granted, she assumed a serious face and approached him, saying, "You did enter it in the family records, didn't you, Father? No? Oh, then surely I should. Please, give me the key to the secretary."

And right beneath the lines that she had entered after her name four years before, she resolutely and proudly wrote: "This marriage was dissolved by law in February of 1850."

Then she laid her pen down and pondered for a moment. "Father," she said, "I know very well that all this leaves a blot on our family history. Yes, it does—I have given it a great deal of thought. It's the same as if there were a splotch of ink on this page. But don't worry, it's up to me to see that it is erased. I am still young. Don't you think that I'm still rather pretty? Although, when Madame Stuht saw me again, she said, 'O Lord, Madame Grünlich, you've grown so old!' Well, one can't spend one's whole life being the silly goose I once was. Life sweeps one along with it. No. And so, in short, I shall marry again. You'll see, it will all be made good again by a new, advantageous match. Don't you think?"

"That's in God's hands, my child. But it is not at all proper to speak of such things at present."

From this point on, moreover, Tony began to use a certain phrase frequently: "After all, life is like that. . . ." And at the word "life" she would open her eyes wide in a pretty but serious sort of way to indicate what deep insight she now had into human life and human fate.

When Thomas returned home from Pau in August that same year, the table in the dining room was enlarged still further, and Tony had a new chance to speak her mind. She loved and respected her brother with all her heart—after all, he had recognized and appreciated her sorrow that day, coming home from Travemünde. And she knew that someday, in the distant future, he would be head of the firm and of the family.

"Yes, yes," he said, "we both have been through a lot, Tony." Then he lifted an eyebrow and let his Russian cigarette wander from one corner of his mouth to the other—thinking, presumably, about the little flower-shop girl with the Malaysian face, who had recently married the son of the woman who owned the shop on Fischer Grube and was now running it all on her own.

Thomas Buddenbrook, though still a little pale, was a strikingly elegant man. It certainly looked as if the last few years had rounded out his education. There was something almost military about him—he was short but square-built with broad shoulders, he brushed his hair in little hilly waves over his ears, he had now trimmed his mustache in the French fashion, the pointed ends twirled with hot tongs so that they stood straight out to each side. But both the bluish veins visible at his temples where his hair was waved back on each side and his tendency to take a chill—despite all Dr. Grabow's valiant efforts to counteract it—indicated that his constitution was not especially robust. Still, in the finer details of his physical appearance—the chin, the nose, and especially the hands, those marvelous, genuine Buddenbrook hands—he had grown more and more to resemble his grandfather.

When he spoke French it had a distinctively Spanish ring, and he amazed everyone with his fondness for certain modern writers who specialized in satire and polemics. The only person in town who showed any understanding for his taste in literature was Herr Gosch the broker; his father was most stern in his condemnation of it. But that in no way affected the look of pride and joy that appeared in the consul's eyes when he thought of his eldest son. With great and deep pleasure he welcomed him back to his office as a colleague, and indeed began to take renewed interest himself in their work there—particularly after the death of Madame Kröger, which occurred at the end of the year.

They bore the old lady's loss with appropriate composure. She was old as the hills and very lonely toward the end. God took her, and the Buddenbrooks received a lot of money, a nice round sum of one hundred thousand thalers *courant*, which increased the firm's working capital in a most timely fashion.

A second result of her death was that the consul's brother-in-law, Justus Kröger, who was weary of a long string of business setbacks, sold out and retired the moment he had his inheritance in hand. Justus Kröger, the debonair *suitier*, the son of the old cavalier à la mode, was not a very happy man. He was too easygoing, too generous of heart ever to attain a solid and undisputed position in the world of business; he had already spent a considerable portion of the money he had now inherited from his parents; and of late, his elder son, Jakob, was seriously adding to his worries.

That young man had apparently chosen immoral companions in the big city of Hamburg, had cost his father immense sums over the years; and when the day came on which Consul Kröger cut off his funds, his wife, a weak and softhearted woman, secretly sent her dissolute son more money, creating a sad state of discord between husband and wife. And, to cap it all, at almost the same time that B. Grünlich went bankrupt, something even worse happened at Dahlbeck & Co., where Jakob worked in Hamburg. There had been a breach of trust, a transgression. It was not talked about, certainly no one asked Justus Kröger anything about it—but it was common knowledge that Jakob would soon be sailing for New York, where he had found a job as a traveling salesman. He was seen in town once before he left: a foppishly dressed young fellow with an unwholesome look about him. He had come to get more money from his mother, beyond what his father had already given him for the trip.

In short, then, things had come to such a pass that Consul Justus spoke about "my son," as if he had only one heir, Jürgen—who, although he had never been guilty of any misdemeanors, seemed of rather limited mental capacities. He had graduated from high school only with great difficulty and had since been in Jena, where he was studying law, with neither much joy nor success, it appeared.

Johann Buddenbrook was greatly grieved by these less than admirable developments in his wife's family and was therefore all the more anxious about his own children. He was justified in placing the fullest confidence in the earnest competence of his elder son. As for Christian, Mr. Richardson had written that, although the young man had shown a true talent for making the English language his own, he had not shown sufficient interest in business and evidenced all too great a weakness for the amusements of the metropolis—the theater, for example. Christian's own letters expressed a lively interest in travel, and he begged ardently for permission to accept a position "out there"—which meant in South America, in Chile perhaps. "Wanderlust, nothing more," the consul said and demanded that he at least finish his fourth year perfecting his mercantile knowledge with Mr. Richardson. At which point several more letters were exchanged concerning his plans, and in the summer of 1851 Christian Buddenbrook did indeed sail for Valparaiso, where he had found a position. He left directly from England without first returning home.

Apart from his concern about his two sons, the consul was also pleased to notice with what resolve and self-assurance Tony defended her position in town as a born Buddenbrook—especially when it was to be expected that, as a divorced woman, she would have to overcome all sorts of maliciousness and prejudices among the other families.

"Oh!" she cried, returning home from a walk with a red face and tossing her hat on the sofa in the landscape room. "That Möllendorpf woman, or Hagenström, or Semlinger, or whatever, that

Julie, that creature! What do you think happened, Mama? She didn't even greet me—no, she did not greet me. She was waiting for me to greet her first. What do you say to that! I walked right past her on Breite Strasse with my head held high and looked straight at her."

"Don't go too far, now, Tony. No. Everything has its limits. Why couldn't you greet Madame Möllendorpf first? You two are the same age, and she is a married woman, just as you once were."

"Never, Mama. Good Lord, the dregs!"

"*Assez*, my dear. Such indelicate expressions."

"Oh, it's very easy to get carried away."

Her hatred of this particular "upstart family" was nursed by the mere thought that the Hagenströms might now feel justified in thinking they could look down on her, but no less by the family's flourishing prosperity. Old Hinrich had died at the beginning of 1851, and his son Hermann—Hermann with the lemon buns and the slaps—was now carrying on his father's very profitable export business at the side of old Herr Strunck; and within a year he married the daughter of Consul Huneus, the richest man in town, whose wholesale lumber business had enabled him to leave each of his three children two million marks. Hermann's brother, Moritz, had been an unusually successful student—despite his bad lungs—and established a law office in town. He was considered to be very astute and sly—indeed, to be a man of taste and wit—and he quickly built up a sizable practice. There was nothing of his Semlinger heritage about him, but he did have a yellow complexion and pointed gap-teeth.

She even had to keep her head held high in her own family. Ever since Uncle Gotthold had retired from business to spend his days walking around his modest home in trousers that were too short and too baggy, eating cough drops from a tin box—he loved his sweets—his attitude toward his more privileged stepbrother had grown milder and more tolerant with the years, though that did not preclude his taking a certain quiet satisfaction in Tony's ill-fated marriage, inasmuch as he himself had three unmarried daughters. And speaking of his wife, née Stüwing, and particularly of those three young women—now aged twenty-six, twenty-seven, and twenty-eight—they showed an almost extravagant interest in their cousin's misfortunes and divorce—indeed, a much livelier one than they had exhibited at the time of her engagement and marriage. On "children's day," which since the death of Madame Kröger was held each Thursday on Meng Strasse, Tony had no easy time of it holding her own against them.

"Good heavens, you poor thing," said Pfiffi, the youngest, who was short and plump and who with each word would give a funny little jiggle, while drops of moisture collected at the corners of her mouth. "So the decree has come through, then? And so you're right back where you were before, aren't you?"

"Oh, on the contrary," said Henriette, who, like her older sister, was taller and skinnier, extraordinarily so. "You're in much sadder shape than if you had never married at all."

"I certainly agree," Friederike chimed in. "In *that* case it's ever so much better *never* to marry."

"Oh no, dear Friederike," Tony said, tossing her head back and giving herself time to come up with a polished and trenchant reply. "Surely you're in error there, aren't you? One has in any case learned something about life, don't you know. One is no longer such a silly goose. And, then, of course, I have a much better prospect of marrying again than so many others, who have yet to be married even once."

"So?" her cousins said in unison. They hissed their "so" with a great deal of "s" to make it all the more biting and skeptical.

Sesame Weichbrodt, however, was much too kind and tactful ever to mention the matter. Tony would visit her former guardian in her little red house, Mühlenbrink 7, still a lively place occupied by a number of young ladies, although the boarding school itself was slowly beginning to go out of fashion; and the energetic old maid was occasionally invited to Meng Strasse for roast venison or stuffed goose. Then, deeply moved, she would stand on her tiptoes and place an expressive kiss on Tony's brow, making a soft popping sound. Her untutored sister, Madame Kethelsen, however, had recently begun to go rapidly deaf and so had understood almost nothing at all of Tony's misfortune. At increasingly inopportune moments, she would, out of pure ignorance, wail her loud, hearty laugh, which meant that Sesame was constantly required to rap on the table and cry, "Nally!"

The years slipped by. The traces of what had befallen Consul Buddenbrook's daughter grew more and more blurred, both in town and in the family. Tony herself was reminded of her marriage only if now and then some trait in sturdy little Erika's healthy face would remind her of Bendix Grünlich. But her wardrobe was all bright colors again, she let her hair fall in little curls over her forehead, and she was once again busy with her round of social visits.

She was quite glad, nonetheless, to seize the opportunity of getting away from town every summer for a while—unfortunately the consul's health now demanded he take such therapeutic trips.

"You can't imagine what it means to grow old," he said. "I get a coffee stain on my trousers and can't brush it out with cold water without immediately having a violent attack of rheumatism. And to think of the things I could do when I was young." He also had occasional dizzy spells.

They went to Obersalzbrunn, to Ems and Baden-Baden, to Kissingen, and from there they even made a delightful educational trip to Munich by way of Nuremberg, and from there to Ischl and the Salzburg area, then on to Vienna, Prague, Dresden, Berlin, and finally home. And although Madame Grünlich had recently begun to suffer from a nervous stomach condition that required she take the waters and subject herself to rigorous courses of treatment, she found these trips a very welcome change, because she could not hide the fact that she was a little bored at home.

"But, good heavens, life is like that after all, Father," she said, thoughtfully studying the ceiling. "True, I have learned something about life, but that just makes the prospect of sitting around here at home like a silly goose all the more depressing. Although I certainly hope you don't think I'm not glad to spend time with all of you, Papa—that would be the worst ingratitude, I'd deserve to be horsewhipped. But, after all, life is like that, you know."

Her chief and most constant annoyance, however, was the religiosity that pervaded her parents' spacious house—because with each added year and each new ailment the consul's pious leanings grew increasingly more fervent, and his wife, too, was developing a taste for such things as she grew older. Grace before meals had always been the custom at the Buddenbrook table; but for some time now the family and servants had been required to assemble in the breakfast room each morning and evening to hear a passage of scripture read by the master of the house. In addition to which, the visits of pastors and missionaries were growing more frequent from year to year. Throughout the universe of Lutheran and Reformed clergy committed to both foreign and home missions, the stately patrician house on Meng Strasse had, for some time now, become known as a safe spiritual harbor—and one where, by the way, the food was excellent. From all quarters of the Fatherland, long-haired gentlemen dressed in black would occasionally drop by for a few days, certain that there would be godly conversation, nourishing meals, and contributions in hard cash to be applied to holy purposes. The preachers in town likewise came and went as friends of the house.

Tom was much too discreet and prudent to let anyone ever notice his smirks, but Tony was quite open in her mockery, making a point, sad to say, of casting these gentlemen in a ridiculous light whenever the opportunity presented itself.

On those occasions when Elisabeth was suffering from a migraine, it was Madame Grünlich's task to look after the household and make up the menu. One day, one of these visiting preachers, whose appetite was a source of general mirth, happened to be a guest in their home, and she maliciously ordered "bacon soup," a local specialty consisting of broth and sour herbs into which an entire dinner was then dumped: ham, potatoes, prunes, pears, cauliflower, peas, beans, beets, plus a kind of fruit sauce and other ingredients—a dish that no one in the world could enjoy unless he had grown up with it.

"Do you like it? Do you like it, pastor?" Tony kept asking. "No? Oh, heavens, who would have thought you wouldn't." And then she made a downright roguish face, letting the tip of her tongue play along her upper lip the way she always did when she had thought of some clever prank—or carried it out.

The fat gentleman laid his spoon down in resignation and said, all unsuspecting, "I shall wait for the next course."

"Yes, there will be a little dessert," Elisabeth quickly said, because "a next course" was unthinkable after bacon soup; and, despite a few fritters with apple jelly, the cheated parson had to leave the table still hungry—while Tony sat there giggling to herself and, with amazing self-control, Tom lifted one eyebrow.

Another time, Tony happened to be standing in the entrance hall speaking with the cook about household matters when the bell rang in the vestibule—Pastor Mathias from Cannstatt, who once again was spending a few days with them, had just returned from his walk. Waddling to the door in her rustic way, Stina let him in, and the pastor asked her affably and condescendingly, "Doest thou love the Master?" Perhaps it was his way of testing her piety, or perhaps he intended to give her a little something for faithfully professing her Saviour.

"Well, now, Rev'rund," Stina said hesitantly, blushing and wide-eyed, "which one y' mean? The old 'un or the young 'un?"

Madame Grünlich did not miss the chance of telling this story at the dinner table that evening for all to hear, so that even Elisabeth broke into her spluttering Kröger laugh.

The consul, to be sure, gazed sternly and indignantly at his plate.

"A slight misunderstanding," Pastor Mathias said in confusion.

11

WHAT NOW FOLLOWS occurred on a Sunday afternoon late in the summer of 1855. The Buddenbrooks were sitting in the landscape room, waiting for the consul, who was still dressing downstairs. They had invited the Kistenmaker family to join them for a leisurely stroll to the public gardens outside the city gates—everyone was going, except Clara and Klothilde, who went to a friend's house each Sunday afternoon to knit stockings for little black children. They planned to have coffee and perhaps, if weather permitted, to go for a row on the river.

"Papa can drive a person to tears," Tony said, choosing strong words as was her habit. "Why can't he ever be ready on time for things? He sits there at his desk, and sits, and sits, he simply *must* finish this or that. Good Lord, perhaps it really is necessary, I'm not saying it isn't—although I doubt we would have to declare bankruptcy if he would lay down his pen fifteen minutes sooner. Fine, and then, when he's already ten minutes late, he remembers what he's promised and comes bounding up the stairs, taking them two at a time, although he knows that it causes him heart congestion and palpitations. It's the same for every party, every time we go out. Can't he remember to leave himself some time? Can't he break off work when he's supposed to and then walk slowly up the stairs? It's quite irresponsible of him. I would give my husband a serious talking-to, Mama."

Dressed in shimmering silk, which was all the rage, Tony was sitting on the sofa beside her mother, who was wearing a gown of heavy gray ribbed silk, trimmed with black lace. She was also wearing a bonnet of lace and starched tulle, with lappets that fell down over her chest and a satin bow that tied under her chin. Her hair was parted and pulled back smooth—and it was the same reddish blonde as always. She was holding a reticule in her white hands lined with delicate blue veins. Next to her, Tom was leaning back in his easy chair, smoking a cigarette; Clara and Thilda sat facing one another on the window seat. It was incredible that, although poor Klothilde partook daily of large quantities of strong nourishment, it was all to no avail. She was growing skinnier and skinnier, and even her totally shapeless black dress could not hide that fact. In the center of her silent, gray face, right below the line of the part in her smoothed-back, ashen hair, sat a straight nose, which had large pores and ended in a little bulb.

"It's surely going to rain, don't you think," Clara asked. The young lady had the habit of never lifting her voice at the end of a question, and now she gazed directly at each of them with a determined and rather stern look. A little white starched turndown collar and cuffs were the only trim on her brown dress. She sat very erect, her hands folded in her lap. She was the person the servants feared the most, and of late she had been leading morning and evening services, because the consul could no longer read aloud without getting a headache.

"Are you taking your new *bashlyk* along for this evening, Tony!" she asked as her second question. "It's going to rain. What a shame—it will be ruined. I think it would be better if you put off your walk."

"No," Tom replied. "The Kistenmakers are coming. It doesn't matter. The barometer fell much too quickly—there'll be a sudden shower, a little downpour, it won't last long. Papa isn't ready yet. Which is fine—we can wait until it passes."

His mother raised her hand in protest. "You don't think we'll have a thunderstorm, do you, Tom? Oh, you know how they frighten me."

"No," Tom said. "I was speaking with Captain Kloot down at the docks this morning. He's never wrong. There'll just be a quick downpour—not even a strong wind."

The dog days had come late—it was already the second week in September—and summer lay over the city more oppressively than in July. The wind came from the south-southwest, and a strange, deep blue sky shimmered above the gables, but faded toward the horizon, as if this were the desert. After sundown the houses and sidewalks were like ovens, radiating heat in the narrow, stuffy streets. But today the wind had shifted around to the west, and simultaneously the barometer had plummeted. Much of the sky was still blue, but a bank of leaden clouds, thick and soft as pillows, was slowly approaching.

Tom added, "It would certainly be a good thing if it did rain. We'll swelter if we have to march off in this heat—it's quite unnatural. I never saw anything like it in Pau."

At that moment Ida Jungmann entered the room, holding little Erika by the hand. The child looked very droll somehow in her freshly starched cotton frock, and she gave off an odor of starch and soap. She had Herr Grünlich's rosy face and eyes; but her upper lip was all Tony's.

Kindly Ida's hair was quite gray now, almost white, although she was barely over forty. But it was in the family—even the uncle who had died of hiccups had had white hair at thirty. But her little brown eyes were as loyal, bright, and alert as ever. She had been with the Buddenbrooks for twenty years now and was proud of how indispensable she was. She supervised the kitchen, the pantry, the china and linen cupboards, she did the important shopping, she read aloud to little Erika, made clothes for her dolls, helped her with her homework, and every noon, armed with a sandwich made with French bread, she met her at school so that they could walk along the Mühlenwall. Every lady in town said, either to Elisabeth Buddenbrook or to her daughter: "What a treasure your Mamselle Jungmann is, my dear. Heavens, she's worth her weight in gold, let me tell you. Twenty years—and she'll be hale and hearty at sixty or more, these raw-boned types always are. And then those loyal eyes. I envy you, my dear." And Ida Jungmann had her self-respect, too. She knew who she was, and if some ordinary servant girl sat down with her ward on the same bench with her along the Mühlenwall and started a conversation as if they were equals, Mamselle Jungmann would say, "Erika dear, I feel a draft," and depart.

Tony pulled her little daughter to her and kissed her on one of her rosy cheeks, and Elisabeth reached out to her with an upturned palm and a preoccupied smile—she was watching the sky, as it turned darker and darker. Her left hand played nervously with the sofa pillows, and her pale eyes drifted uneasily to the window.

Erika was permitted to sit next to her grandmother, and Ida took a seat on an armchair, without touching her back to it, and began to crochet. They sat a while in silence and waited for the consul. The air was stuffy. The last swatch of blue had vanished, and the dark-gray sky dipped low, swollen and heavy. The colors in the room, the hues in the landscapes of the wall coverings, the yellow of the furniture and curtains, were dulled now; the subtle shades in Tony's dress no longer shimmered—even eyes had lost their brightness. And the wind, the west wind, which had been playing in the trees in St. Mary's Cemetery and driving the dust in little whirlwinds along the dark streets, no longer stirred. For one brief moment everything was completely still.

Then suddenly something happened—a soundless, terrifying something. It felt as if the humidity had doubled; in less than a second the atmospheric pressure rose rapidly, alarmingly, oppressing heart and brain and making breathing difficult. A swallow fluttered so low over the street that its wings seemed to brush the cobblestones. And this knot of pressure, this tension, this growing constriction of the body would have been unbearable if it had lasted a split second longer, if the shift, the release had not followed, a break that liberated them, an inaudible crack somewhere—though they all thought they had heard it. And at that same moment, the rain was falling in sheets, almost as if not a single drop had preceded it, and water gushed and foamed in the gutters, lapping up over the sidewalks.

Thomas's illness had made him accustomed to watching closely the signals of his nerves, and during that strange moment he bent over, tossed his cigarette away, and brushed his head with his hand. He looked around the room to see if anyone else had noticed or felt what he had. He thought perhaps his mother had sensed something, but the others seemed not to have been aware of anything.

Elisabeth looked out into the veil of rain that completely hid St. Mary's now and sighed, "Thank God."

"Well, now," Tom said, "things will cool down in two minutes. But the trees will still be dripping wet—we can drink coffee on the veranda. Open the window, Thilda."

The sound of rain thrust its way into the room. It was a downright racket—it dashed, splashed, babbled, and foamed. The wind had picked up again and played merrily among the heavy curtains of water, ripped them open, and shoved them about. It grew cooler by the minute.

Then Lina, their maid Lina, came running down along the columned hall and burst into the room so violently that Ida Jungmann tried to calm her down by crying reproachfully, "Good heavens, I must say!"

Lina's expressionless blue eyes stared wide and her jaws worked a while without making a sound. "Oh, Madame Buddenbrook, oh no. You gotta come quick. Oh, good God, no, I've taken such a fright!"

"Oh, fine," Tony said, "now what has she smashed to smithereens? It's probably some of the good china. I mean, Mama, your household help . . ."

But, frightened as she was, the girl blurted it out, "Oh no, Madame Grünlich, ma'am. If only it was that. But it's the master. I was bringin' him his boots, and there sits Herr Buddenbrook, sittin' up in his chair, and he can't talk but jist keeps gulpin' away, and I don't think Herr Buddenbrook's doin' so good, 'cause he's jist too yella in the face."

"Get Grabow!" Thomas shouted and pushed his way out the door.

"My God! Oh my God!" Elisabeth cried, pressing her hands to her face and dashing out.

"Get Grabow, send a carriage, at once!" Thomas repeated breathlessly.

They all flew down the stairs, through the breakfast room, into the bedroom.

But Johann Buddenbrook was already dead.

PART FIVE

1

GOOD EVENING, Justus," Elisabeth Buddenbrook said. "How are you? Please, have a seat."

Consul Kröger gave her a hasty, tender embrace and shook the hand of his oldest niece, who also happened to be in the dining room. He was about fifty-five years old and now sported, in addition to his little mustache, a set of heavy, bushy whiskers that left his chin bare. Sparse strands of hair had been carefully combed across his broad, pink bald head. The sleeve of his elegant frock coat was trimmed with a wide band of mourning crape.

"Have you heard the latest, Bethsy?" he asked. "Yes, Tony, this would interest you especially. To put it briefly, the property outside the Burg Gate has been sold. To whom? Well, not to just *one* person, but to two. It will be divided, the house torn down, then the lot split by a fence, and Benthien the clothier will build his doghouse on the right and Sörenson his on the left. Well, it's in God's hands."

"How outrageous," Frau Grünlich said, folding her hands in her lap and gazing at the ceiling. "Grandfather's lot. Well, that certainly makes a botch of the property. The charm was in the extensive grounds—far too extensive, of course, but that was what made it so elegant. The large gardens stretching down to the Trave, and the house set back from the road, and the driveway bordered with chestnuts. So it's to be divided. Fine. Benthien will stand at his front door, smoking his pipe, and Sörenson at his. Yes, I agree with you, Uncle Justus, it's in God's hands. There's probably no one elegant enough to occupy the whole property. It's a good thing that Grandpapa never lived to see it."

Tony would have liked to express her outrage in stronger, franker terms, but the air of mourning still lay heavy over the room. The consul had been dead for two weeks now—it was half past five in the afternoon of the day on which the will was to be read. Madame Buddenbrook had invited her brother to Meng Strasse to join with Thomas and Herr Marcus, the chief clerk, in a discussion of the provisions in the deceased's will and of the general financial situation; and Tony had let it be known that she would likewise be taking part in the conference. She owed both the firm and the family that much, she had said, and she was anxious to give the meeting the character of a formal family council. She had drawn the curtains, and although the two paraffin lamps on the dining table provided sufficient light, she had lit every candle on the tall gold-plated candelabra. The dining table was pulled out to its full extent and covered with a green cloth, and Tony had made sure that plenty of writing paper and sharpened pencils had been distributed around it—though no one was exactly sure what they might be needed for.

Her black dress made her look young and slender. Although she perhaps felt the grief of the consul's death more than the others, after having been so close to him in recent years, and although she had twice shed bitter tears today at the thought of him, it was probably the prospect of a little family council, of an earnest little conference in which she would play a dignified role, that gave such a glow to her pretty cheeks, such liveliness to her eyes, such a sense of satisfaction and importance to her movements. Her mother, however, did not look well; she was exhausted by grief, apprehension, and the thousand sad formalities of a funeral. Framed by a black lace bonnet, her face looked paler than ever, and her bright-blue eyes were dulled. But there was not a strand of white to be seen in her smoothly parted, reddish blonde hair. Was that still the Parisian tint, or was it a wig now? Only Mamselle Jungmann knew, and she would never have betrayed the secret, even to the other ladies of the house.

They were sitting at one end of the dining room table and waiting for Thomas and Herr Marcus to arrive from the office. The painted gods atop their pedestals stood out white and proud against the sky-blue background.

Elisabeth said, "The thing is, my dear Justus, I asked you to come because—to be brief, it's about Clara, our youngest. My dear, departed Jean left it to me to choose a guardian. The girl will require one for another three years yet. I know that you do not like to be burdened with extra responsibilities; you have your duties to your wife and your sons. . . ."

"To my son, Bethsy."

"Yes, yes, Justus, but as Christians we must be merciful—as we forgive our debtors, the prayer says. We must always remember our gracious Father in heaven."

Her brother gave her a somewhat puzzled look. Until now, such phrases had been known to come only from the mouth of the late consul.

"But enough," she continued. "There are as good as no obligations involved. I should like to ask you as a favor to be her guardian."

"With pleasure, Bethsy, I'll do it gladly. Might I not see my ward? She's a good child, though a little too serious."

Clara was called. And when she entered, black and pale, she moved with slow reserve. Since her father's death, her days had been spent alone in her room in almost ceaseless prayer. Her dark eyes were inert; she seemed frozen with grief and the fear of God.

Uncle Justus, still a gallant man, strode toward her and almost bowed as he took her hand and spoke a few well-chosen words. After returning her mother's kiss with rigid lips, she left again.

"And how is dear Jürgen doing?" Elisabeth said, picking up the conversation again. "How does he like it in Wismar?"

"Fine," Justus Kröger replied, sitting down with a shrug. "I think he's found his place at last. He's a good lad, Bethsy, an honorable lad. But when he failed his exams a second time, it was probably for the best. He didn't enjoy the law, and his position with the post office in Wismar is quite suitable. But tell me, I hear Christian will be coming home."

"Yes, Justus, he's coming, and may God protect him at sea. Oh, it takes such a dreadfully long time. Although I wrote him the very next day after Jean's death, he still doesn't have the letter. And then it will take another two months, I suppose, for his ship to sail all that way. But he has to come, I truly need him, Justus. Tom says that Jean would never have permitted him simply to abandon his post in Valparaiso. But I ask you, it's almost eight years now since I've seen him—and under the circumstances. No, I want them all with me now, at this difficult time. It's only natural for a mother to want that."

"Of course, of course," Consul Kröger said, for tears had come to her eyes.

"And Thomas agrees with me now," she continued, "because where would Christian be better off than in his own father's firm, in Tom's firm? He can live here, work here. Oh, I worry constantly that the climate there may be bad for him."

And now Thomas Buddenbrook, accompanied by Herr Marcus, entered the dining room. Friedrich Wilhelm Marcus, long-time chief clerk of the late consul, was a tall man; today he wore a long-tailed brown coat with mourning crape. He spoke very softly, hesitantly, almost stuttered as he considered each word for a second; and he had a habit of extending the first two fingers of his left hand and slowly, cautiously stroking the unkempt, reddish brown mustache that hid his mouth; or sometimes he would carefully rub his hands together while his round, brown eyes wandered off discreetly to one side, lending him a confused and distracted look—whereas in fact he was always studiously analyzing the matter at hand.

Thomas Buddenbrook was now head of a large concern at a very young age, and there was a dignity in his face and in his carriage. But he was pale, and his hands in particular were as white as the cuffs visible at the end of his black sleeves, almost frosty white; and his carefully manicured oval fingernails had the bluish tone they sometimes took on when his hands were this cold and dry. On one finger could be seen the bright green gemstone of the large signet ring he had now inherited. Sometimes he would unconsciously cramp his hands a little, and at that moment they expressed something indescribable—a dismissive sensibility, an almost anxious reticence, that was somehow ill-suited to him and quite untypical of the effect broad, stolid Buddenbrook hands had always made, even given their long, delicate fingers.

Tom's first concern was to open the folding doors to the landscape room to get the benefit of the warmth of the fire burning behind the wrought-iron grate of the stove there. Then he shook hands with Consul Kröger, sat down at the table beside Herr Marcus, and, raising an eyebrow, looked across in some surprise at his sister Tony. But the way she tossed her head back and pressed her chin to her chest stifled any comment he might have made about her presence.

"We cannot call you Consul Buddenbrook yet, I suppose?" Justus Kröger asked. "Are the Netherlands still waiting in vain for you to represent them, Tom, my boy?"

"Yes, Uncle Justus; I thought it better this way. You see, I could have taken on the consulate at once, right along with all my other duties. But, first of all, I'm still rather young—and, then, I had a talk with Uncle Gotthold, and he was very happy to accept the position himself."

"Very wise, my boy. Very politic. The gentlemanly thing to do."

"Herr Marcus," Elisabeth said, "my dear Herr Marcus." And she stretched out a hand to him, the palm turned up as far as possible, which he then slowly took with a cautious, polite, sidelong glance. "I asked you to come up because—but, then, you know what this is about, and I know that you are in agreement with us. My late husband expressed the wish in his last testament that, upon his passing, you would no longer be employed as an outsider, but would offer your steadfast services and proven abilities to the firm as a partner."

"But of course, certainly, Madame Buddenbrook," Herr Marcus said. "I give you my most humble assurances that I am deeply grateful and know to appreciate the honor which you have tendered my person, inasmuch as such resources as I may bring to the firm are but limited indeed. Before God and my fellow man, I know no better course than to accept with gratitude the offer which you and your son have made me."

"That's fine, Marcus, and my hearty thanks for your willingness to assume some of the responsibilities that otherwise might prove too much for me," Thomas responded quickly, and casually offered his partner a hand across the table—for the matter had been settled for some time, and all this was a mere formality.

"Fast friends are fast parted—so, now, don't spoil our little chitchat here, you two," Consul Kröger said. "Shall we work our way through the provisions now, children? I only have to keep an eye on my ward's dowry, the rest is no concern of mine. Have you a copy of the will there, Bethsy? And you, Tom, have you worked up some rough figures?"

"I have those in my head," Thomas said, leaning back, staring across to the landscape room and letting his yellow pencil sweep back and forth over the tabletop—and now he began to explain how matters stood.

The truth was that the consul had left behind a much more considerable fortune than anyone would have imagined. To be sure, his eldest daughter's dowry had been forfeited, and the losses the firm had suffered in that bankruptcy in Bremen in 1851 had been a heavy blow. The unrest and conflicts in both 1848 and the present year of 1855 had cost the firm as well. But the Buddenbrook share in the Kröger estate of 400,000 marks *courant* had come to 300,000—because Justus had already spent most of his inheritance. And although Johann Buddenbrook was forever complaining in typical businessman's fashion, all the losses had been balanced out over the past fifteen years by a profit of some 30,000 thalers *courant*. Apart from real estate, then, the family fortune came to some 750,000 marks *courant*, in round numbers.

Even Thomas, with all his access to the daily course of business, had been left in the dark by his father about the size of the estate. His mother accepted the sum with calm discretion. Tony gazed straight ahead with the most charming and uncomprehending dignity, although she was unable to suppress a look of anxious doubt that said: "Is that a lot? Really a lot? Are we very rich now?" Herr Marcus sat there and slowly—and absent-mindedly, or so it seemed—rubbed his hands. And Consul Kröger was obviously bored. But the mere naming of this sum filled Tom with a nervous, compelling pride that almost made him look out of sorts.

"But we ought to have made a million long before this," he said, his voice edgy with excitement, his hands trembling. "In his best days, Grandfather had a good 900,000 at his disposal. And what efforts we have made since then—all the sweet triumphs, the fine coups now and then. Plus Mama's dowry. And Mama's inheritance. But it is constantly being split up. Good Lord, it's the nature of things, I suppose. Do forgive me if at this moment I speak only from the viewpoint of the firm and not of the family—but these dowries, these disbursements to Uncle Gotthold and to Frankfurt, these hundreds of thousands that had to be withdrawn from our capital. And in those days, the head of the firm had only a stepbrother and a sister, only those *two*. But enough of all that. We have our work cut out for us, Marcus."

The longing for action, victory, and power, the urge to force good fortune to its knees, blazed in his eyes briefly and fiercely. He felt the whole world looking expectantly at him to see if he would know how to further the interests of both the old firm and the family, and not just preserve their prestige. On the floor of the exchange he had seen the sidelong glances measuring him, had seen the jovial, skeptical, and slightly mocking eyes of businessmen that seemed to ask: "So you think you can bring it off, too, my boy?" And he thought, "I can."

Friedrich Wilhelm Marcus cautiously rubbed his hands. And Justus Kröger said, "Steady now, Tom, my boy, steady. The times aren't what they once were, when your grandpapa was supplying the Prussian army."

And now began a lengthy discussion of the larger and smaller bequests in the will, in which they all took part—with Consul Kröger keeping everyone in a good mood by constantly calling Tom "His Highness the Reigning Prince" or saying things like: "But of course the warehouses will remain with the Crown, as tradition dictates."

On the whole, as was to be expected, the will's provisions were aimed at keeping the estate together as best as possible, making Frau Elisabeth Buddenbrook virtually the universal heir and retaining all assets within the business—in which regard, Herr Marcus gave notice that as a partner he would be strengthening the firm's capital by 120,000 *courant*. Thomas's private fortune was tentatively set at 50,000, and an equal sum was put aside for Christian, should he at some point establish himself independently. Justus Kröger was all ears when the following clause was read: "The fixing of the sum to be applied as a dowry for my dearly beloved younger daughter, Clara, in the event of her marriage is left to the judgment of my dearly beloved wife." "Let's say 100,000," he suggested, leaning back, crossing his legs, and using both hands to turn up the ends of his short mustache. He was fairness personified. But they decided on the traditional sum of 80,000 marks *courant*.

"Should my dearly beloved elder daughter, Antonie, enter into a second marriage," the will continued, "and in light of the fact that 80,000 marks *courant* were already expended for her first marriage, the dowry may not exceed the sum of 17,000 thalers *courant*." Frau Antonie pushed back the sleeves of her blouse with a graceful though impatient gesture, stared up at the ceiling, and cried, "Grünlich—ha!" It sounded like a war cry, a little trumpet blast. "Do you know the facts in the case, Herr Marcus? We are sitting quite innocently in the garden one afternoon, by the 'Portal.' You know what I mean by the 'Portal,' do you not, Herr Marcus? Fine. And who should appear but this person with golden muttonchops. What a scoundrel."

"Yes, yes," Thomas said. "We'll speak of Herr Grünlich later, all right?"

"Fine, fine; but you must admit I'm right, Tom. You're a clever fellow, and although I was a silly goose not so very long ago, it's been my experience, you know, that things do not always turn out fairly and squarely in life."

"Yes," Tom said. And they moved on to other details, noting the instructions about the large family Bible, the consul's diamond studs, and a great many other small items.

Justus Kröger and Herr Marcus stayed for supper.

2

IN EARLY FEBRUARY, 1856, after an absence of eight years, Christian Buddenbrook returned to his hometown, arriving in the post coach from Hamburg. He was dressed in a yellow plaid suit that certainly hinted at the tropics and carried a swordfish sword and a long stalk of sugarcane. He looked half embarrassed and half preoccupied as he stiffly returned his mother's embrace.

He had the same look the morning after his arrival, when the family walked to the cemetery outside the Burg Gate to lay a wreath on the grave. They all stood together on the gravel path in front of the huge grave cover with the family crest chiseled into the stone and surrounded by the names of those who rested there; rising behind it was a marble cross silhouetted against the little woods, leafless now in winter. They were all there, except Klothilde, who had gone to Grudging to nurse her sick father.

Tony laid the wreath over the golden letters of her father's name, which had only recently been added to the stone, and despite the snow she knelt down on the grave to pray softly; her black veil fluttered about her, and her broad skirt lay spread out beside her in soft, picturesque folds. God alone knew how much of this molded pose was grief and piety—and how much was the vanity of a pretty woman. Thomas was not in the mood to think about that. Christian, however, gazed at his sister from one side with a mixture of mockery and misgiving, as if he wanted to say, "Can you really justify that? Won't you be ashamed, too, when you stand up again? How unpleasant!" Tony caught his look as she got up, but she wasn't embarrassed in the least. She tossed her head back, set her veil and skirt to rights, and with dignified self-composure turned to leave—which was an obvious relief to Christian.

Given his fanatical love of God and the crucified Saviour, the late consul was probably the first of his lineage to know and cultivate feelings that were out of the ordinary, more differentiated, alien to his solid middle-class heritage. But his two sons were the first Buddenbrooks who were uneasy and frightened by the naïve and frank display of such feelings. To be sure, Thomas felt the pain of his father's death more acutely than his grandfather had felt the loss of his. But he was not the sort to sink to his knees beside a grave; no, he was not like his sister, not like Madame Grünlich, who loved to lay her head on the table, after the main course and before dessert, and sob like a child, her words blending with her tears as she recalled the person and personality of her dear, departed father. Tom responded to such effusions with tactful gravity, with reserved nods and composed silence. And yet, at moments when no one had so much as mentioned his dead father, tears would slowly fill his eyes—with no change at all in his facial expression.

Christian had a different reaction. He simply could not maintain his composure whenever his sister broke into one of her naïve and childish outbursts. It was clear he wanted to hide from them—he would bend down over his plate, turn his head away, even interrupt her in a low, tormented voice, saying over and over, "Good God, Tony!"—and his large nose would screw up into a thousand wrinkles. In fact, the moment conversation turned to his late father, he was obviously embarrassed and uneasy, and it seemed that he feared not just some indelicate expression of deep or solemn emotion, but that he feared and avoided all feeling.

No one had seen him shed a tear over the death of his father. And his long absence alone did not explain it. The strangest thing was, however, that, in contrast to his customary distaste for such remarks, he was forever pulling his sister Tony aside and asking her again to tell him in vivid, precise detail about the events of that dreadful afternoon—and Madame Grünlich had a wonderful gift for lively narration.

"So he looked yellow?" he asked for the fifth time. "What did the maid scream when she burst in on you? His face was all yellow, you say? And he wasn't able to say anything before he died? What did the maid say? He could only just go 'Uh! Uh!'?" He fell silent, said nothing for a long time, and, lost in thought, let his little, round, deep-set eyes travel rapidly around the room. "Horrible," he said, visibly shuddering as he stood up. And then he paced back and forth, his eyes growing more and more restless and brooding—while Tony sat there puzzled that her brother, who for some incomprehensible reason seemed mortified at any mention of her grief over her father's death, could repeat over and over with a kind of dreadful intensity the man's final death cries, which he had taken great trouble to learn from Lina their maid.

Christian had certainly not grown any handsomer. He was gaunt and pale. His skin was stretched tight across his skull, his large, fleshless nose with its distinct hump protruded sharply between his cheekbones, and his hair had thinned quite noticeably. His neck was thin and too long, and his skinny legs were conspicuously bowed. His stay in London seemed to have influenced him the most, and since he had associated mainly with Englishmen in Valparaiso, his whole look was English somehow—and it suited him rather well. You could see it in the comfortable cut and durable wool of his suits, in the broad, solid style of his boots, and in the way his bushy reddish blond mustache drooped over his mouth, giving him a somewhat sour expression. His hands, with their round, clean, closely clipped nails, had turned the dull, porous white that hot climates can cause—and even they, for some inexplicable reason, looked English.

"Tell me," he said out of the blue, "have you ever had that feeling? It's hard to describe—you're trying to swallow something that's hard and it goes down the wrong way and it hurts all the way down your back?" And as he spoke, his nose was all tense little wrinkles again.

"Yes," Tony said, "that's perfectly normal. You take a drink of water."

"Really?" he asked, dissatisfied. "No, I don't think we mean the same thing." And a serious look shifted uneasily back and forth across his face.

But he was the first person in the house to put aside mourning and suggest life be a bit freer again. He had not forgotten his knack for imitating the late Marcellus Stengel, and could talk in that voice for hours. One day at dinner, he asked about the local theater, whether the company was any good and what was playing.

"I don't know," Tom said, with exaggerated indifference in his voice, trying not to be impatient. "I don't worry about such things these days."

But Christian completely missed the point and began talking about the theater. "I can't tell you how I love the theater. The mere mention of the word 'theater' makes me happy. I don't know whether you know the feeling? I could sit there silently for hours, just gazing at the closed curtain. It makes me feel like I did as a child when we would come in here for our Christmas presents. Or the sound of the orchestra tuning up. I could go to the theater just to hear that. And I especially love the love scenes. Some of the heroines have a way of holding their lover's head between their hands like this. . . . Actors in general, really. I spent a lot of time with actors in London, and in Valparaiso, too. At first, I was proud as Punch just to be able to talk with them in completely everyday kinds of settings. I pay attention to their every gesture on the stage. It's very interesting. An actor says his final line, turns around very calmly, and walks off very slowly, and sure of himself, not the least bit self-conscious, even though he knows that the eyes of the entire audience are on his back. How can they do that? I used to think constantly of what it must be like to be backstage. But now I'm really quite at home there, let me tell you. Just imagine, one evening at an operetta—it was in London—the curtain went up when I was still out on the stage. I was talking with Fräulein Wasserklosett; actually her name was Miss Waterhouse, a very pretty girl. Well, and then—suddenly—there's the audience in front of me. My God, I don't know how I got off that stage."

Madame Grünlich was more or less the only person at the table to laugh; but Christian went right on talking, his eyes wandering here and there. He talked about English café-concert singers, told them about a woman in a powdered wig who banged the floor with a long staff and sang a song titled "That's Maria!" "Because Maria, you see, Maria's a scandalous girl, the worst of 'em all. If somebody's done something naughty, that's Maria. Maria's the worst of the lot, you see, Maria's simply depraved." And he spoke the final word in a dreadful voice, wrinkling up his nose and raising his right hand with his fingers cramped in horror.

"*Assez*, Christian," Madame Buddenbrook said. "This doesn't interest us in the least."

But Christian's eyes drifted absent-mindedly past her, and he probably would have stopped even had she not objected. His little, round, deep-set eyes were roaming restlessly about the room, and he seemed to have sunk into a deep, uneasy reverie, thinking of Maria and her depravity.

Suddenly he said, "You know, it's strange—sometimes I feel like I can't swallow. No, now don't laugh. I'm being quite serious. The thought occurs to me that I can't swallow, and then I really can't. What I've eaten is clear at the back of my mouth, but these muscles here, along the neck—they just won't work. They won't obey my will, you see. Or, better, the fact is: I can't bring myself to actually will it."

Quite beside herself now, Tony cried, "Good heavens, Christian, what silly nonsense. You can't make up your mind whether to swallow. No, you're just being ridiculous. What are you talking about?"

Thomas said nothing. But his mother said, "It's your nerves, Christian. It was high time you came home. The climate out there would surely have made you ill."

After dinner he sat down at the little harmonium in the dining room and imitated a concert pianist. He pretended to throw his hair back, rubbed his hands, looking first at the floor and then at the ceiling. And now, without working the bellows—he couldn't play at all and was totally unmusical, like most Buddenbrooks—he bent down eagerly and began soundlessly to belabor the bass register, executing insane passages; he threw his head back, stared at the ceiling, and banged at the keyboard energetically and triumphantly with both hands. Even Clara burst into laughter. The imitation was convincing, full of passion and subterfuge, irresistibly comic, with a touch of the eccentric burlesque that the English and Americans do so well—yet never for a moment unpleasant, because Christian was enjoying himself much too much.

"I've always been a great concertgoer," he said. "I love to watch how the performers handle their instruments. Yes, it must be absolutely wonderful to be an artist."

He started all over again—and then suddenly broke off. He turned serious, abruptly, surprisingly, as if a mask had fallen from his face. He stood up, ran his hand through his sparse hair, moved to another chair, and there he sat, silent, foul-humored, with edgy eyes and a look on his face as if he were listening to some mysterious sound.

"You know, I find Christian somewhat odd at times," Madame Grünlich said one evening when she was alone with her brother Thomas. "What's he really saying? He goes into such strange detail about things, it seems to me. How should I put it? He sees things from a very peculiar angle, doesn't he?"

"Yes," Tom said, "I know exactly what you mean, Tony. Christian is terribly indiscreet—it's hard to put it in words. He lacks what one could call balance, personal balance. On the one hand, he is incapable of keeping his composure when other people are tactless and naïve. He is no match for them, doesn't understand how to gloss over things, and completely loses self-control. But, on the other hand, it's the way he loses self-control—suddenly starts chatting away, blurting out to all the world the most unpleasant and intimate things. It sometimes borders on the uncanny. It's almost like someone delirious with fever, isn't it? They fantasize in exactly the same way, regardless of the consequences. Oh, it is merely a matter of Christian's worrying too much about himself, about what is going on inside him. He has a regular mania sometimes for dragging up the most insignificant things from deep within him and talking about them—things that a reasonable man doesn't even think about, doesn't want to know about, for the very simple reason that he is too embarrassed to share them with anyone else. There's something so shameless about that sort of unrestrained talk, Tony. You see, someone else might say that he loves the theater, too; but he would do it with a different emphasis, offhandedly, more modestly, in fact. But Christian proclaims it in a tone of voice that says: 'Isn't my obsession with the theater something terribly strange and interesting?' He struggles to find the right words, he acts as if he were wrestling with himself to express something unusually obscure or supremely refined.

"I want to tell you something," he continued after a pause, during which he tossed his cigarette through the wrought-iron grate into the stove. "I have occasionally given some thought to that sort of useless curiosity and preoccupation with one's self—because I tended to be that way myself at one time. But I realized that it left me unstable, erratic, out of control. And for me the important thing is control and balance. There will always be people for whom this sort of interest in oneself, this probing observation of one's own sensibilities, is appropriate—poets, for instance, who are capable of expressing the inner life, which they prize so much, with assurance and beauty, thereby enriching the emotional life of other people. But we are just simple merchants, my dear; our self-observations are dreadfully petty. At the very best, all we are capable of saying is that we take some special delight in hearing the orchestra tune up, or that we sometimes can't bring ourselves to swallow. But what we should do, damn it, is to sit ourselves down and accomplish something, just as our forebears did."

"Yes, Tom, that's exactly how I see it, too. When I think of how these Hagenströms are prospering. Good heavens, what dregs—that's what they are. Mother doesn't like me to use the word, but it's the only one that fits. Do they think, maybe, that there are no longer any other elegant families in town except them? Ha! That makes me laugh, you know. It really makes me laugh."

3

THE HEAD OF THE FIRM of Johann Buddenbrook had measured his brother with a long, probing look on his arrival, had watched him in passing during the next few days, quite unobtrusively. And with that, although his conclusions could not be read from his calm and discreet expression, his curiosity had apparently been satisfied, his mind made up. He spoke to him in a casual way about casual matters as a member of the family, and he enjoyed himself as much as the others whenever Christian gave a performance.

Eight days later, he said to him, "And so we'll be working together, my boy, right? As far as I know, you're in agreement with Mama's wish, aren't you? Well, as you know, Marcus is my partner now, with a percentage share in the business matching the amount of capital he put in. It seems to me that as my brother you should assume more or less the position of chief clerk that he held before, at least in a representative sense, for appearance's sake. As far as the actual work goes, I'm not sure how much progress you've made in your knowledge of commercial matters. It seems to me you've been loafing a bit thus far, am I right? In any case, taking care of our correspondence in English would probably be most to your liking. But I must ask one thing of you, my friend. In your position as the brother of the owner, you will of course have a privileged place among the other employees. But I need not tell you, need I, that you will impress them much more by behaving as an equal and energetically doing your duty, than by making use of your prerogatives and taking liberties. Which means keeping office hours and keeping up appearances, all right?"

And then he made a suggestion as to the matter of salary, which Christian accepted without giving it a thought, much less haggling over it—the absent-minded chagrin on his face revealed very little greed and a great desire to settle the issue quickly. The next day Thomas introduced him in the office, and Christian's professional life with the firm began.

The business had continued on its solid course, uninterrupted by the consul's death. But it soon became clear that, once the reins had passed into Thomas Buddenbrook's hands, a fresher, more inventive, more enterprising spirit pervaded the firm. Now and then a little risk was taken, now and then the firm's credit, which had been merely a theoretical luxury under the old regime, was put to work and made the most of. The gentlemen on the exchange nodded to one another and said, "Buddenbrook is out to make money, and how!" But they thought it was a very good idea that Thomas also had to drag trusthworthy Friedrich Wilhelm Marcus behind him like a ball and chain. Herr Marcus's influence provided the crucial element of restraint in all their dealings. He would carefully stroke his mustache with two fingers, compulsively rearrange his writing utensils and the glass of water that always stood on his desk, examine each issue from several sides, always with a wool-gathering look on his face; and he also had the habit of crossing the courtyard to the scullery, five or six times a day during office hours—where he would hold his head under the tap to refresh himself.

"Those two complement one another," the heads of the larger firms would say—Consul Huneus to Consul Kistenmaker, for instance; and the same opinion was repeated by the dock and warehouse workers or other humbler citizens. The whole town, in fact, took an interest in how young Buddenbrook would "tackle the job." Even Herr Stuht on Glockengiesser Strasse told his wife, who always moved in the best circles, "Lemme tell you, those two com'lement each other real good."

But there was no doubt whatever that the "personality" of the business was the younger of the two partners. That was evident, if from nothing else, from his skill in dealing with their employees, with the ship captains, the supervisors in the warehouses, the wagon drivers and warehouse hands. He could speak quite naturally with them in their Plattdeutsch, and still maintain an unapproachable distance. But if Herr Marcus asked some honest laborer, "Catch my drift?," it sounded so preposterous that his partner, who sat across the desk from him, would simply start laughing—a sign for the whole office to join in the mirth.

Filled with a desire to preserve and enhance the luster of the firm in a manner commensurate with its proud old name, Thomas Buddenbrook loved to throw himself into the daily battle, because he knew quite well that he owed many a profitable deal to his self-assurance and elegance, his winning charm, and his polished tact in conversations.

"A businessman cannot be a bureaucrat," he told his former schoolchum Stephen Kistenmaker—of Kistenmaker & Sons—who was still Tom's friend, though hardly his match intellectually, and listened to his every word in order to pass it on as his own opinion. "It takes personality, and that's *my* specialty. I don't think great things can ever be accomplished from behind a desk—at least none that would give me any pleasure. Calculations from behind a desk don't lead to success. I need to see how things are going with my own eyes, direct them with a gesture, a spoken word, to control them on the spot by dint of my own will, my talent, my luck or whatever you want to call it. Sad to say, that kind of personal involvement by the businessman is going out of fashion. Time marches on, but she leaves the best behind, it seems to me. Markets are easier and easier to open up, we get our price quotes faster and faster. The risks grow less and less—and so do the profits. Yes, it was different in the old days. My grandfather, for instance, a fine old gentleman in a powdered wig and pumps, rode in a coach-and-four to southern Germany as a contractor for the Prussian army. And he turned his charm on everyone, put all his arts to work, and made an incredible profit, Kistenmaker. Ah, I almost fear that as time goes on the businessman's life will become more and more banal."

Those were his sentiments, and for just that reason he loved the kind of business that sometimes came his way when he was out for a walk with his family, for instance, and he would drop by a mill for a casual chat with the miller, who felt quite honored by the visit, and *en passant* concluded a profitable deal with him. That sort of thing was quite foreign to his partner.

As for Christian, he appeared at first to throw himself into his work with zest and pleasure; indeed, he seemed to take increasing satisfaction in it; for several days he ate with a good appetite and had a way of smoking his stubby pipe and squaring his shoulders inside his English jacket that expressed just how comfortable and satisfied he felt. He would go down to the office at about the same time as Thomas and take his seat beside Herr Marcus and catercorner from his brother—in the same kind of adjustable armchair the two partners used. First he read the *Advertiser* and contentedly finished smoking his morning cigarette. Then he pulled a bottle of old cognac from his lower desk drawer, stretched his arms to give himself a little more elbowroom, said, "Well, now," and went to work in the best of moods, while his tongue wandered here and there among his teeth. His English correspondence was exceptionally polished and effective, for he wrote English just as he spoke it—it rolled along in an effortless, simple, unconstrained, nonchalant stream.

And, as was his habit, he verbalized his good mood for the rest of the family. "The businessman's calling is indeed a fine, a truly gratifying one," he said. "Solid, satisfying, dynamic, comfortable. I was surely born for it! And now that I'm a member of the firm, you know—well, to be brief, I feel better than I ever have before. You go to the office fresh each morning, read the paper, have a smoke, think of this and that and how good life is, drink a cognac, and do a bit of work. Then comes the noon break, you dine with your family, relax—and it's back to work. You write your letters on the firm's fine, smooth, immaculate stationery, with a good pen, you have first-rate equipment—a ruler, a letter opener, rubber stamps—all as it should be. And then you diligently deal with matters, one after another, until you finally pack your things away. There's always tomorrow. And when you come upstairs for supper you feel thoroughly satisfied with yourself, every muscle in your body is satisfied. Even your hands feel satisfied."

"Good heavens, Christian," Tony cried. "You're being ridiculous—your hands feel satisfied."

"Yes, really! You don't know the feeling? I mean . . ." And he grew quite agitated trying to express himself, to explain. "You close your fist, you know, and your hand's not especially strong, because you're weary from work. But it's not damp, either, it doesn't irritate you. It feels good and comfortable. It's a feeling of self-satisfaction. You can sit there quite still without being bored."

No one said anything. Until Thomas commented quite indifferently, to hide his distaste, "It seems to me that one doesn't work in order to . . ." But he broke off; he was not going to repeat Christian's remarks. "At least, I have other goals in mind," he added.

Christian, however, whose eyes were wandering again, ignored this, because he was already lost in thought, and very soon he began to tell a tale of murder and passion that he had himself witnessed in Valparaiso. "But then the fellow pulls out a knife, and . . ." For some inexplicable reason Thomas did not greet these stories, of which Christian had a great many, with applause—although Madame Grünlich found them delightfully amusing, while her mother, Clara, and Klothilde pulled back in horror, and Mamselle Jungmann and Erika simply sat there listening with their mouths open. Thomas's usual reaction was to interject cool, ironic comments, giving the clear impression that he thought Christian was exaggerating and showing off—which was certainly not the case, although he did tell his tales with colorful verve. Could it be that Thomas did not like the idea that his younger brother had traveled and seen more than he? Or was he disgusted by his brother's glorification of disorder and exotic violence in these blood-and-thunder stories? Certainly Christian was not in the least bothered by his brother's disapproval of them; he was all too preoccupied with his descriptions to notice whether they were a success or failure with the others—and after he finished his eyes would roam about the room in absent-minded reverie.

And if over time the relationship between the two Buddenbrooks did not turn out all that well, Christian was not the one to whom it would have occurred to feel or show any sort of malice toward his brother, to presume to judge him, or even to form a critical opinion about him. In his silent matter-of-factness, he left no doubt that he recognized his elder brother's superiority, his greater expertise, competence, and respectability. But it was just such unbounded, nonchalant, peaceable subordination that annoyed Thomas, because on any given occasion Christian was so blithely docile that it appeared as if he set no value whatever in superiority, competence, seriousness, or respectability.

He seemed not even to notice that the head of the firm increasingly responded to him with silent animosity—for which he had his reasons. Unfortunately Christian's zeal for commerce began to dwindle after his first week on the job, and even more decisively after his second. This manifested itself in his preparations for work—reading the paper, smoking his after-breakfast cigarette, drinking his cognac—which at first had looked like a refined and artfully prolonged anticipation of the tasks ahead, but which now took more and more time and finally stretched out over the entire morning. And then, as a matter of course, Christian began to disregard the constraint of office hours, to appear later and later each morning, puffing on his after-breakfast cigarette, before finally starting his preparations for work; he would then go to the Club for his midday meal and not return until rather late, sometimes not before evening, sometimes not at all.

The Club, whose members were primarily unmarried businessmen, occupied a few private rooms on the second floor of a wine restaurant—a place where one could take one's meals and gather informally for harmless, and often not so harmless, amusements—including roulette. Even several somewhat debonair family men, like Consul Kröger and of course Peter Döhlmann, were members; and Police Chief Cremer was always "Johnny-on-the-spot." That was Dr. Geiseke's phrase—Andreas Gieseke, the son of the fire chief and Christian's old schoolchum, who had set up a law practice in town and with whom the younger Buddenbrook quickly struck up a renewed friendship, despite Andreas's reputation as a rather wild *suitier*.

Christian—or Krischan, as he usually was called, for good or ill—knew them all as friends or acquaintances from the old days—most of them had been students of the late Marcellus Stengel—and he was received with open arms, for, although neither the merchants nor the professionals considered him a great intellect, they recognized his amusing social gifts. And, indeed, he gave his best performances there, told his very best stories. He did his concert-pianist imitation at the Club's piano, he parodied English and American actors and opera singers, and, in his inoffensive and always entertaining way, he obliged them with stories about his affairs with women all over the world. No doubt about it, Christian Buddenbrook was a *suitier*. He told of amorous adventures he had had on ships, on trains, in Sankt Pauli, in Whitechapel, in the jungle. He charmed and captivated them with stories that flowed in an effortless stream, spoken in a slightly plaintive, languid voice and delivered in the harmlessly risqué fashion of an English comedian. He told a story about a dog that had been sent in a box from Valparaiso to San Francisco, and was mangy to boot. God only knew what the point of the anecdote was, but it was incredibly funny when he told it. And while everyone around him was convulsed with laughter, there he would sit—a man with a large hooked nose, a scrawny and overlong neck, and thinning reddish-blond hair—and, as a restless and inexplicably serious look spread over his face, he would cross one skinny, bowed leg over the other and let his little, round, deep-set eyes pensively scan the room. It almost seemed as if they were laughing at his expense, laughing at him. But that never occurred to Krischan.

At home, his favorite stories were about his office in Valparaiso, about the extreme heat that was the rule there, and about a young fellow from London named Johnny Thunderstorm, a gentleman of leisure, whom he had "never seen do a lick of work, goddamn if I did," but who nevertheless had been a very clever businessman. "Good God," he said, "you wouldn't believe the heat. Well, the boss would come into the office, and there we were, all eight of us, lying around like flies and smoking cigarettes to keep the mosquitoes away at least. Good God, 'Well, gentlemen?' said the boss. 'You're not working today?' 'No, sir,' Johnny Thunderstorm said. 'As you can see, sir.' And then we'd all blow cigarette smoke in his face. Good God!"

"Why do you constantly use the expression 'Good God'?" Thomas asked in annoyance. But that was not really what upset him. He felt as if Christian only told this story with such relish because it gave him an opportunity to scorn and ridicule work.

At which point their mother discreetly changed the subject.

"There are so many ugly things in this world," Elisabeth Buddenbrook, née Kröger, thought to herself. "Even brothers can hate or despise each other; that does happen, as awful as it may sound. But no one ever speaks of it. They gloss over it. It's best to know nothing about it."

4

IT HAPPENED one sad night in May—Uncle Gotthold, Consul Gotthold Buddenbrook, age sixty, was taken with a heart attack and died an agonizing death in the arms of his wife, née Stüwing.

The son of poor Madame Josephine, who had come up short in life when compared with his more powerful latter-day siblings, born of Madame Antoinette, had long since made peace with his fate, and in his later years, especially after his nephew had transferred the Dutch consulate to him, had eaten his cough drops from their tin box without bearing any grudges whatever. It was the ladies, rather, who with a kind of general and diffuse hostility tenderly nursed and cultivated the old family feud—not so much his kindly and obtuse wife as his three spinster daughters, who could not look at Elisabeth, or Antonie, or Thomas without a little spark of spite flaring in their eyes.

On Thursdays, the traditional "children's day," they would all gather at the stroke of four in the large house on Meng Strasse to have a late dinner and to spend the evening together. Sometimes even Justus Kröger and his family would appear, or Sesame Weichbrodt with her uneducated sister. And on those occasions the Ladies Buddenbrook from Breite Strasse would bring the conversation around to Tony's bygone marriage in the hope of egging Madame Grünlich into using some strong language, while they hastily exchanged pointed glances. Or they would make general remarks about how undignified and vain it was to dye one's hair, or inquire all too sympathetically about how Jakob Kröger, Elisabeth's nephew, was doing. And they made jokes at the expense of poor innocent, patient Klothilde, the only person who truly had reason to feel inferior to them—and the jokes were certainly not as harmless as the ones to which the penniless, hungry woman was subjected daily by Tom or Tony, and to which she responded with her usual methodical, perplexed good humor. They sneered at Clara's rigidity and bigotry; they quickly discovered that Thomas was not on the best terms with Christian and that, thank God, they didn't have to pay any attention to Christian because he was a buffoon, a ridiculous man. As for Thomas himself, they could not find any weak points in the man, and he always regarded them with an indulgent indifference that implied, "I understand you, and I feel sorry for you." And so they treated him with a respect tinged with venom. But they could not help remarking that little Erika, so pink and pampered, was far behind in her growth, alarmingly so. And, to cap it all, Pfiffi, with a little jiggle and drops of moisture at the corners of her mouth, would comment on the child's extraordinary resemblance to that swindler Grünlich.

But now they stood in tears beside their mother around their father's deathbed, and although it seemed to them that even his death was somehow the fault of their relatives, a message was sent to Meng Strasse.

It was the middle of the night when the bell above the front door echoed across the large entrance hall, and since Christian had come home late and was not feeling well, Thomas set out alone in the spring rain.

He arrived just in time to see the old gentleman's last twitches and convulsions, and then he stood there for a long while beside the deathbed, his hands folded, gazing down at the short figure visible under the sheets, and he stared at the dead face with its soft features and white whiskers.

"You never had things very good, Uncle Gotthold," he thought. "You learned too late to make concessions, to make allowances. But they are necessary. If I had been like you, I would have married my shop girl years ago. But one must keep up appearances. And did you ever really want things to be any other way? You were stubborn, though, and probably thought that there was something idealistic in being stubborn. You had too little momentum and imagination, too little of the idealism that enables a man to cherish, to nurture, to defend something as abstract as a business with an old family name—and to bring it honor and power and glory. That requires a quiet enthusiasm that is sweeter and more pleasant, more gratifying than any secret love. You lost your sense of poetry, although you were brave to love and marry against your father's wishes. You had no ambition, Uncle Gotthold. Our family name is an ordinary name, I'll grant you, and one nurtures it by helping a grain business flourish, and by making oneself powerful, respected, and loved in a little corner of the world. Did you think: 'I'll marry my Stüwing because I love her, and hang the practical considerations—those are nothing but petty, philistine details'? Oh, but we've all traveled about and learned enough to know only too well that the limits set to our ambitions are narrow and pathetic—when viewed from the outside or from on high. But everything in this world is comparative, Uncle Gotthold. Didn't you know that one can be a great man in a small town? That a man can be a Caesar in an old commercial city on the Baltic? That takes a little imagination, I'll grant, a little idealism—and that's what you lacked, whatever you may have believed about yourself."

And Thomas Buddenbrook turned away. He walked to the window and, with his hands behind his back and a little smile on his intelligent face, he looked out at the dimly lit Gothic façade of the town hall shrouded in the rain.

IT LAY in the nature of things that the office and title of the Royal Dutch Consulate, which Thomas might have claimed for himself at the death of his father, now in fact devolved upon him. And, to Tony's boundless satisfaction, the curved coat-of-arms, with its lions, crest, and crown, hung once again on the gable of the house on Meng Strasse, right under the motto *Dominus providebit.*

In June that year, shortly after all this had been settled, the young consul set out on a business trip to Amsterdam, unsure how long he would be gone.

5

DEATHS TEND TO TURN eyes and hearts toward heaven, and no one was surprised now to hear from the lips of Madame Buddenbrook a few very pious phrases that would not have been expected of her before the demise of her husband.

But it soon turned out that this was not a temporary phenomenon, and it quickly become known around town that the consul's wife, who as she had grown older had shown some sympathy for her late husband's spiritual inclinations in the last years of his life, now intended to honor his memory by making his religious views totally her own. She strove to fill the spacious house with the same spirit that had inspired the deceased: a gentle Christian gravity that did not exclude a refined gladness of heart. The morning and evening services continued in expanded form. The family gathered in the dining room, while the servants stood in the columned hall, and Elisabeth or Clara read a passage from the large family Bible with its huge, funny letters; then a few verses were sung from the hymnal, accompanied by Madame Buddenbrook on the harmonium. The Bible passage was often replaced by a reading from a book of sermons or from one of the edifying, black-bound, gilt-edged volumes of which there were many in the house, with titles like *The Jewel Box, Psaltery, Holy Hours, Morning Chimes, The Pilgrim's Staff*, and whose unrelenting tender affection for the sweet Baby Jesus tended to be somewhat cloying.

Christian did not often attend services. Thomas seized an opportunity one day to raise a cautious objection to the practice, half in jest, but was rebuffed with gentle dignity. And as for Madame Grünlich, her behavior, unfortunately, was not always quite correct. A visiting preacher happened to be a guest in the Buddenbrook household one morning when a solemn, devout, and heartfelt tune was struck up to which they were required to sing the following words:

I am a lowly scavenger,
A crippled, limping sinner,
Foul, rancid sin I did prefer,
And gorged it down for dinner.
O Lord, please cast a bone of grace
Before this dog so lowly;
This bestial sinner first abase,
To rise then clean and holy.

And Frau Grünlich was so overcome with spasms of contrition that she tossed her hymnal aside and left the room.

But Madame Buddenbrook demanded much more of herself than of her children. She founded a Sunday school, for example. On Sunday mornings, the doorbell on Meng Strasse was rung only by little grammar-school girls—by Stina Voss, who lived near the wall; or Mika Stuht, from Glockengiesser Strasse; and Fika Snut, from down by the river, or on Kleine Gröpel Grube, or on Engelswisch—it all depended. Their towheads tamed by water and comb, they paraded through the large entrance hall and into the brightly lit garden room, which had not been used as an office for some time and was now fitted out with benches facing a little table on which was placed a glass of sugar-water and behind which sat Madame Buddenbrook, née Kröger, in a dress of heavy black satin, her white, genteel face framed by an even whiter lace cap, who proceeded to catechize them for an hour.

She also founded her "Jerusalem Evenings"—which Clara and Klothilde were required to attend, as was Tony, whether she wished to or not. Once a week about twenty ladies, who were of an age when it is time to look around for a good spot in heaven, sat at the extended table in the dining room; and by the light of lamps and candles they drank tea or "bishop's punch," ate delicate sandwiches and pudding, read hymns and sermons to one another, and did needlework that would be sold at a bazaar at year's end, the profits from which would be sent to Jerusalem for missionary purposes.

This pious fellowship was made up primarily of ladies from Madame Buddenbrook's social circle, including Mesdames Langhals, Möllendorpf, and Kistenmaker, although some older ladies, whose views were more secular and profane, like Madame Köppen, made fun of their friend Bethsy. Other members were the wives of the town's several preachers, the widow of Gotthold Buddenbrook, née Stüwing, and Sesame Weichbrodt accompanied by her uneducated sister. There is neither rank nor privilege before Christ, however, and so other, more humble oddities also took part—for example, a small, wrinkled creature, her riches consisting entirely of piety and crochet patterns, who lived in the Holy Ghost Hospital and was named Himmelsbürger. She was the last of her line, "the last Himmelsbürger," she would say dolefully, running her needle up under her bonnet to give her head a scratch.

Two other members were even more remarkable—a pair of twins, two quaint old maids dressed in very faded frocks and shepherdess hats from the last century, who wandered about town, hand in hand, doing good deeds. Their name was Gerhardt and they claimed to be direct descendants of Paul Gerhardt. It was said that they were not destitute by any means, but that they gave everything to the poor and lived in great poverty. "My dears," Madame Buddenbrook remarked, feeling somewhat ashamed of them, "God reads our hearts, but your clothes are less than suitable—one must have some regard for one's appearance." But, filled with all the indulgent affection and sympathetic superiority that the lowly feel for the great who are in search of salvation, they would simply kiss the brow of their elegant friend—who could not renounce her status in this world. They were not stupid women at all; and shining softly in their little, ugly, shriveled parrot faces were enigmatic brown eyes that gazed at the world with a strange, gentle look of wisdom. Their hearts were full of marvelous and mysterious knowledge. They knew that in our last hours all our loved ones who have gone before come to gather us to them with hymns and blessings. They spoke the word "Lord" with the pristine ease of the first Christians, who with their own ears had heard the Master say, "Yet a little while and ye shall see me." They had the strangest theories about premonitions and the inner light, about how thoughts could wander through the world and be transferred from person to person—and, indeed, one of them, Lea, was deaf and yet always knew immediately what people were saying.

Because Lea Gerhardt was deaf, it was customary for her to read aloud on Jerusalem Evenings—the ladies thought she read most beautifully and touchingly. From her bag she would extract an ancient book that was considerably—in fact, ridiculously—longer than it was wide and bore on its first page an etching of her ancestor—with chubby cheeks no human ever had—and, holding it up in both hands, she would read very loudly so that she, too, might hear some of it, in a dreadful voice that sounded like the wind trapped in a chimney: "Though Satan should devour me . . ."

"Well, now," Tony Grünlich thought, "what sort of Satan would want to devour you?" But she said nothing, just went on devouring her own pudding and wondering if there would ever come a day when she would be as ugly as the two Miss Gerhardts.

She was not happy; she was bored and annoyed by all these pastors and missionaries, whose visits had grown ever more frequent, it seemed, since the consul's death, and who, in Tony's opinion, had far too much to say in the house and received far too much money. This latter point concerned Thomas, too; but he held his peace about it, whereas his sister now and then would mutter something about those who devour widows' houses and make long prayers.

She bitterly despised these gentlemen in black. As a mature woman who had learned something about life and was no longer a silly goose, she found herself incapable of believing in their spotless sanctity. "Good heavens, Mother," she said, "I know one should not speak evil of one's neighbor—I do, really. But one thing must be said nonetheless, and I would be surprised if life has not taught it to you as well. Not everyone who goes about in long clothing and cries, 'Lord, Lord!' is without blemish."

It was unclear how Thomas felt about these truths, which his sister preached with such prodigious energy. Christian, however, had no opinion whatever; he confined himself to wrinkling up his nose and observing these gentlemen in order to imitate them later at the Club or for his family.

But it is true that Tony suffered the most from their sanctified guests. One day it verily came to pass that a missionary named Jonathan, who had served in both Syria and Arabia, a man with large, reproachful eyes and drooping, melancholy jowls, stepped up to her and demanded with mournful gravity that she decide whether the curls on her forehead, being the work of a curling iron, were consistent with Christian humility. Oh, he had no idea of Tony Grünlich's sarcastic rhetorical powers. She was silent for several seconds, but you could see her brain working. Then it came to her. "Might I beg you, reverend sir, to worry about your own curls." And she sailed away with her shoulders held high, her head tossed back, and her chin pressed lightly to her chest. Pastor Jonathan possessed very little hair on his head—indeed, one could say his skull was bare.

She once had an even greater triumph—over Pastor Trieschke from Berlin, whose nickname was Teary Trieschke, because every Sunday he would begin to weep at some point in his sermon. Teary Trieschke, who was notable for a pale face, red eyes, and the facial bone-structure of a horse, had spent eight or ten days at the Buddenbrooks', taking turns with Klothilde as the winner in the eating contest, and now found occasion to fall in love with Tony. Not with her immortal soul, oh no, but with her upper lip, her full head of hair, her pretty eyes, and her fine figure. And this man of God, who had a wife and numerous children in Berlin, was impudent enough to commission Anton to climb to Madame Grünlich's bedroom on the third floor and deliver a letter, a persuasive hodgepodge of Bible verses and strangely obsequious endearments. She found it as she was preparing for bed, read it, and marched with a firm stride downstairs to Madame Buddenbrook's bedroom on the mezzanine, where, without the least embarrassment, she read the cleric's epistle in a loud voice. From then on, Teary Trieschke was no longer welcome on Meng Strasse.

"They're all like that," Madame Grünlich said. "Ha! All of them.

Heavens, what a goose I used to be, what a silly goose, Mama. But life has robbed me of my trust in my fellow man. Most of them are scoundrels. Yes, it's true, sad to say." And, raising her shoulders and directing her gaze heavenward, she added, "Grünlich!" And the name sounded like a fanfare, as if she had given a little blast on a trumpet.

6

SIEVERT TIBURTIUS was a small, narrow-shouldered man with a large head and a scraggly long blond beard that he parted in two strands and that for comfort's sake he would sometimes lay to the sides, one strand to each shoulder. His round head was covered with countless tiny, woolly curls. His large ears stood way out, their rolled edges tucked inward and extending to points like a fox's. His nose looked like a little flat button between his protruding cheekbones, and his gray eyes squinted and blinked in all directions a little stupidly, although at certain moments they could unexpectedly grow larger and larger, sticking out until they almost popped.

Pastor Tiburtius came from Riga and, after serving for several years in central Germany, had stopped off in town on his way home, where a pulpit had been offered him. Furnished with recommendations from a fellow clergyman, who had once enjoyed his share of the mock-turtle soup and ham with shallot sauce on Meng Strasse, he stopped to pay Madame Buddenbrook his respects and was invited to spend the rest of his stay, which would take a few days yet, in the spacious guest room along the corridor on the second floor.

But he stayed longer than expected. Eight days passed, and he still had not seen this or that interesting sight—the dance of death and the apostles on the clock of St. Mary's, the town hall, the Seaman's Guild, or the sun with movable eyes that hung inside the cathedral. Ten days passed, and he frequently mentioned his departure; but at the first word urging him to stay on, he would delay leaving again.

He was a better man than the Reverend Jonathan or Teary

Trieschke. He was not in the least interested in the curls on Tony's forehead and he wrote her no letters. But he was all the more attentive to Clara, her younger and more serious sister. In her presence—when she spoke, when she came or went—his eyes might unexpectedly grow larger and larger, protruding until they almost popped. He spent nearly his whole day with her, engaging her in religious and secular conversation or reading aloud to her in his high, cracking voice that bumped along in the droll accents of his Baltic homeland.

The very first day, he said, "Mercy me, Madame Buddenbrook, what a treasure, what a blessing from God you have in your daughter Clara. She is truly a splendid child."

"How right you are," Elisabeth replied. But he repeated this so often that her pale blue eyes began to look him up and down, discreetly examining him, and she brought him around to speaking in more detail of his family, his circumstances, and his prospects. It turned out that he came from a merchant family, that his mother had gone to her heavenly reward, that he had no brothers or sisters, and that his aged father had retired on an adequate income—the principal of which would one day belong to Pastor Tiburtius, although his ministerial duties alone would assure him a sufficient income.

As for Clara Buddenbrook, she was now eighteen years old and had grown to be a woman of austere and peculiar beauty—her dark hair was parted and pulled back smooth, her brown eyes were stern and yet somehow dreamy, her nose was slightly arched, her mouth closed a little too firmly, and her figure was tall and slender. At home, she was closest to her poor and equally pious cousin Klothilde, whose father had died recently and who was toying with the idea of "establishing" herself—which meant taking the few pennies and sticks of furniture that she had inherited and finding lodgings somewhere. Clara had none of Thilda's patient, methodical, and hungry humility. On the contrary, her voice tended to assume a somewhat domineering tone when she spoke with the servants—or with her brothers and sister and mother, for that matter; there was something imperious about that alto sound, which she knew only to lower to emphasize her point, but never to raise at the end of a question, and it often took on a curt, hard, impatient, haughty timbre—especially on days when Clara had her headaches.

Before the death of the consul had shrouded the entire family in mourning, she had participated with unapproachable dignity in the social life of her parents' home and attended parties in the homes of those of equal rank. Elisabeth had watched her and could not deny that, despite a handsome dowry and Clara's domestic talents, she would have a difficult time marrying the child off. She could not picture any of the skeptical, claret-drinking, jovial young merchants from their social circle taking his place at the side of her serious and God-fearing daughter, but she could definitely imagine a man of the cloth. And since that idea gave her considerable pleasure, Pastor Tiburtius's delicate overtures were received with nicely tempered cordiality.

And, indeed, matters proceeded with great precision. On a warm, cloudless July afternoon, the family went for a walk. Madame Buddenbrook, Antonie, Christian, Clara, Thilda, Erika Grünlich, and Mamselle Jungmann—with Pastor Tiburtius in their midst—strolled to a country inn some distance beyond the Burg Gate, to sit at wooden tables under the trees and enjoy an afternoon snack of strawberries, sour cream, or groat pudding. And afterward, they wandered in the large gardens that stretched down toward the river, walking in the shade of all sorts of fruit trees, among currant and gooseberry bushes, between beds of asparagus and potatoes.

Sievert Tiburtius and Clara Buddenbrook held back a little. He was much shorter than she and had now taken off his floppy black straw hat and laid his parted beard on his shoulders, one strand to each side; and drying his brow with his handkerchief now and then, he engaged her in deep and gentle conversation, during the course of which they both came to a halt at one point and in a calm, serious voice Clara gave her consent to his proposal.

They all returned home to the pensive stillness of Sunday evening; and Madame Buddenbrook was sitting alone and rather weary in the landscape room when Pastor Tiburtius joined her, taking his seat in the summer twilight, and engaged her in deep and gentle conversation.

When he had finished, Madame Buddenbrook said, "Enough, my

good Pastor Tiburtius. Your offer coincides with my own maternal wishes, and you certainly have not made a bad choice, I can assure you of that. Who would have thought that first your visit and then your longer stay here in our house would be so wonderfully blessed. I will not give you my final answer today, because it is only proper that I first write my son the consul, who as you know is in the Netherlands at present. You will depart for Riga tomorrow to assume your new duties, as God grants you life and health to do so, and we intend to spend a few weeks at the shore ourselves. You will receive word from me very soon, and God grant that we all shall see one another again."

7

Amsterdam, 20 July '56
Hotel Het Haasje

My dear Mother,

Your informative letter has just reached me, and I hasten to thank you most warmly for the consideration you have shown in asking my consent in the matter at hand; it goes without saying that I am not only happy to give it, but wish also to add my heartiest congratulations, being fully confident as I am that both you and Clara have made an excellent choice. I am familiar with the fine old name Tiburtius, and I am almost certain that Papa had business relations with Herr Tiburtius senior. Clara will at any rate find herself in pleasant surroundings, and the duties of a pastor's wife are well suited to her temperament.

If I understand correctly, Tiburtius has now departed for Riga and is to visit his fiancée in August? Well, that will certainly make for festive times on Meng Strasse—even more festive than any of you might expect, because you have no idea what special reasons I have for being so delightfully surprised by news of Mademoiselle Clara's engagement and for looking forward to what will be a very happy gathering. Yes, my dear good Mama, in submitting my solemn consent from here on the Amstel for Clara to enjoy future earthly happiness on the Baltic, I do so on one simple condition—that by return post I may receive from your pen just such a solemn consent to just such a happy enterprise. I would give three gold guldens to see your face, and even more to see our gallant Tony's face, as you read these lines. But now let me come to the point.

My tidy little hotel is in the heart of the city, not far from the exchange, and has a lovely view of a canal; and the business I came here to attend to (primarily to establish a new and valuable connection, which as you know I always prefer to do in person) proceeded as I had hoped from the very first day. I have retained numerous acquaintanceships from my apprentice days here in the city, and although many families are now at the seashore, social obligations have laid claim to much of my time. I attended small evening affairs at the van Henkdoms' and the Moelens', and I had not been here three days before I had to don my finery to attend a banquet given in my honor, arranged quite out of season, by Herr van der Kellen, my former chief. And the lady I escorted to the table was—would you care to guess? Fräulein Arnoldsen, Tony's roommate from boarding school, whose father, a notable merchant and an almost even more notable virtuoso on the violin, was likewise present, as were his married daughter and her husband.

I can recall quite well that Gerda—you will permit me to use her first name—made a very strong, indeed indelible, impression on me even when she was still just a girl attending Mademoiselle Weichbrodt's school on Mühlenbrink. But now I have seen her again: taller, more beautiful, more mature and intelligent than ever. Spare me, please, any further description of her person, which might tempt me to become all too impetuous—you shall all soon be able to meet her face to face.

You may well imagine that many topics of conversation offered themselves as we dined; but no sooner was the soup course ended than we left old anecdotes behind and proceeded to more serious and fascinating subjects. I could not hold my own in matters musical, since, sadly, we Buddenbrooks know all too little about them; but I was more at home when speaking of Dutch painting, and we understood one another quite well when it came to literature.

Indeed, time took wing. After dinner I had her introduce me to Herr Arnoldsen senior, who responded with special politeness. Later, in the salon, he played several concert pieces, and Gerda performed as well. She looked so splendid, and although I have no notion of the finer points of violin playing, I do know that she was able to make her instrument (a genuine Stradivarius) sing—indeed, it almost brought tears to one's eyes.

The following day I visited the Arnoldsens on Prinz Hendrik Kade. I was first received by an elderly lady who serves as a social companion and with whom I was forced to speak French; but then Gerda arrived and we chatted away, as we had the evening previous, for a good hour or more; except that this time we found ourselves drawn even closer to one another and strove to understand and know one another better. We spoke again of you, dear Mama, and of Tony, about our fine old town, and about my own occupation.

I made my decision that very day, and it was: this woman or none, now or never! I met her again on the occasion of a garden party given by my friend van Svindren; I was invited to a musical soirée at the Arnoldsens', and in the course of the evening I ventured to sound the lady out with something close to a declaration, to which she responded very encouragingly. And only five days ago, I paid a morning visit to Herr Arnoldsen to ask permission to sue for his daughter's hand. He received me in his private office. "My dear consul," he said, "you are most welcome to try, as difficult as it will be for this old widower to separate himself from his daughter. But she? She has thus far held firm in her resolve never to marry. Do you have a chance?" And he was quite amazed when I replied that Fräulein Gerda had indeed already given me some cause for hope.

He gave her several days to consider the matter, and I believe that out of pure selfishness he even advised against it. But to no avail. I am the man she has chosen, and as of yesterday afternoon we are officially engaged.

No, my dear Mama, I am not asking you for a written blessing of our union, for I shall be leaving for home the day after tomorrow. But I am bringing with me the promise that all three Arnoldsens—Gerda, her father, and her married sister—will visit us in August. And then you will have no choice but to admit that she is the right woman for me. For you surely cannot object that Gerda is only three years younger than I, can you? You never expected, I hope, that I would bring home some young thing from the Möllendorpf-Langhals-Kistenmaker-Hagenström circle.

And as far as the "match" goes—ah, I'm almost afraid that Stephen Kistenmaker and Hermann Hagenström and Peter Döhlmann and Uncle Justus and the whole town will all give me sly winks when they hear of this match—because my future father-in-law is a millionaire. Good Lord, what is there to say? There are so many mixed emotions in all of us that can be read one way or the other. I adore Gerda Arnoldsen, ardently adore her, but I am not in the least inclined to delve deeper into myself to determine whether and to what extent the large dowry—a sum that someone cynically whispered in my ear on that first evening—contributed to my adoration. I love her, but it only makes me that much happier and prouder that at the same time I shall be gaining a significant source of capital for our firm.

Dear Mother, I shall now conclude this letter, which has grown much too long, given the fact that we shall be able to speak of my good fortune within a few days. I wish you a pleasant and refreshing stay at the shore and beg you to extend my warmest greetings to our entire family.

Your loving and obedient son,

T.

8

AND, INDEED, it was a busy, festive summer for the Buddenbrook household that year.

Thomas was back on Meng Strasse by the end of July, but, like other gentlemen whose business kept them in town, he visited his family at the shore several times. Christian, however, had decided he needed a full vacation and complained of a vague pain in his left leg, which Dr. Grabow had no idea how to treat, giving Christian cause to describe his symptoms in that much greater detail.

"It isn't a pain, you can't really call it that," he struggled to explain, rubbing his hand up and down his leg, wrinkling his nose, and letting his eyes roam about. "It's an ache, a constant, faint, unsettling ache along the whole leg, and up my left side, the side where the heart is. Strange, I do find it strange. What's your opinion, Tom?"

"Yes, yes," Tom said, "but you can relax here and swim in the sea."

And then Christian would walk down to join the others gathered on the shore and tell stories until the whole beach echoed with laughter, or he would go play roulette in the grand salon with Peter Döhlmann, Uncle Justus, Dr. Gieseke, and several *suitiers* from Hamburg.

And, as always when they were in Travemünde, Consul Buddenbrook joined Tony for a visit with the old Schwarzkopfs on Front Row. " 'nd a good day to you, Madame Grünlich," the harbor pilot said, so delighted he went right on speaking Plattdeutsch. "So you're still acomin' to the shore? Been a dreadful long time now, but those were damn nice days back then. And our Morten's a doctor in

Breslau now, too, and has built hisself a fine practice, the scamp has." Then Frau Schwarzkopf bustled about and made coffee, and they had an evening snack on the porch just as in the old days—except that they were all a good ten years older now and that Morten was not there, nor little Meta, who had married the chief magistrate of the town of Haffkrug; except that the pilot, rather deaf and very white-haired now, had retired; except that the hair in his wife's hairnet was all gray, too; except that Madame Grünlich was no longer a silly goose, but had learned something about life—which did not prevent her from helping herself to the honeycomb and remarking, "That's a pure product of nature. You know what you're eating there."

In early August, however, the Buddenbrooks returned to town, as did most of the other families; and then came the great moment when, almost simultaneously, Pastor Tiburtius arrived from Russia and the Arnoldsens from Holland to begin their extended visits on Meng Strasse.

It was a very beautiful scene when for the first time the consul led his fiancée into the landscape room to meet his mother, who rose and greeted her with outstretched arms, her head laid to one side. Gerda, who strode across the pastel carpet with an easy, proud charm, was tall and full-figured. With her heavy chestnut hair, close-set brown eyes amid delicate bluish shadows, and broad shiny teeth that dazzled when she smiled, with her strong, straight nose and a mouth of truly noble shape, she was, at age twenty-seven, a woman of elegant, exotic, enthralling, and enigmatic beauty. Her face was soft and white, its expression a little arrogant; but she bent her head down nevertheless when Madame Buddenbrook took it between both hands with gentle affection and kissed her unblemished, snow-white brow. "Yes, welcome to our house and to our family, as our dear, beautiful, blessed daughter," she said. "You will make him very happy. I can see already that you have made him happy, can I not?" And with her right hand she pulled Tom to her to give him a kiss as well.

Never, or at best perhaps in their grandfather's day, had such a gathering of good cheer filled the large house, which had more than enough room for them all. Only Pastor Tiburtius had, in his modesty, chosen a room off the billiard room in the back building;

the others distributed themselves among unoccupied rooms on the ground floor, or off the columned hall, or upstairs on the second floor: lovely Gerda; Herr Arnoldsen, an agile, witty man in his late fifties, with a gray goatee and genial vigor in every movement; his elder daughter, a lady who did not look to be in the best of health; his son-in-law, an elegant man of the world who had Christian introduce him to the town and the Club.

Antonie Grünlich was happy—more than happy—that at present Sievert Tiburtius was the only clergyman in her parental home. Her beloved brother's engagement, the fact that of all people it was her friend Gerda who had been chosen, the brilliant match itself, which would bring new radiance to the family name and the firm, the three hundred thousand marks *courant* she had heard rumored as the dowry, the notion of what the town and other families, in particular the Hagenströms, would say—it all contributed to keep her in a state of constant delight. At least three times an hour she would give her future sister-in-law an enthusiastic hug.

"Oh, Gerda," she cried, "I love you, you know. I've always loved you. I know, of course, that you can't stand me. You've always hated me, but . . ."

"Oh, please, Tony," Fräulein Arnoldsen said, "what would ever have caused me to hate you, might I ask? What awful thing did you ever do to me?"

But for some reason, whether it was from an excess of delight or the pure love of hearing herself talk, Tony stubbornly insisted that Gerda had always hated her, whereas she, for her part—and her eyes would fill with tears—had always repaid that hate with love.

She also took Thomas aside and said to him, "You've done well, Tom—good Lord, how well you've done. To think that *Father* never lived to see it—it simply makes me want to weep, you know. Yes, this truly makes up for a great many things. And not least for our trouble with that person whose name I do not gladly let pass these lips." And then it occurred to her to pull Gerda into an empty room and tell her everything, down to the most dreadful detail, about her marriage to Bendix Grünlich. She also chatted long hours away recalling their days together at boarding school, their bedtime conversations, Armgard von Schilling in Mecklenburg, and Eva

Ewers in Munich. She showed almost no interest at all in Sievert Tiburtius and his engagement to Clara; but that was not something to which the two of them aspired. Most of the time they sat quietly holding hands and speaking softly and earnestly about the beautiful future before them.

Since the Buddenbrooks' year of mourning was not yet over, the two engagements were celebrated only within the family. Gerda Arnoldsen's fame spread quickly through the town nonetheless—indeed, she was the main topic of conversation on the exchange, at the Club, in the theater, in society in general. "Tip-top," the *suitiers* remarked, clicking their tongues—this was the latest term from Hamburg for something exquisite, be it a red wine, a cigar, a dinner, or a business coup. But among the solid, honest, and respectable citizens were many who shook their heads and said, "Peculiar, the way she dresses, and her hair, her posture, that face. Really a bit too peculiar." Sörenson the merchant put it this way: "There's a certain something about her . . ." and he turned his head to one side and made a face, as if someone were proposing a shady deal on the exchange. But it was just like Consul Buddenbrook—he was a little pretentious, Thomas Buddenbrook was, a little . . . different. Different from his forebears. Everyone knew, and Benthien the clothier in particular knew, that not only his fine and fashionable clothes—and he had an extraordinary wardrobe: overcoats, jackets, hats, vests, trousers, and cravats—came from Hamburg, but his underwear as well. It was said that he changed his shirt every day, sometimes twice a day, and that he perfumed his handkerchief and even his mustache, trimmed à la Napoleon III. And it was all done, not for the sake of the greater renown of the firm—the house of Johann Buddenbrook had no need of that—but out of a personal propensity for things refined and aristocratic, or whatever the devil you called all that. And then the way he would slip in those quotes from Heine and other poets, even when talking about the most practical matters, about business or civic issues. And now this woman for a wife. No, there was even "a certain something about him," about Consul Buddenbrook. Of course, this was said with all due respect, because the family enjoyed the best of reputations, and the firm the finest credit; and the head of the firm was an able and charming man, who loved his town and would serve it most admirably as time went on. Certainly, it was a damn fine match; word had it that it came to one hundred thousand thalers *courant* . . . but all the same. And among the ladies were several who found Gerda Arnoldsen simply "silly"—a word, it will be recalled, that implied very severe condemnation.

The one person, however, who worshipped Thomas Buddenbrook's fiancée with a fierce passion from the first moment he saw her on the street was Gosch the broker. "Ah!" he would exclaim at the Club or at the Seaman's Guild, lifting his glass of punch and screwing his crafty, villainous face into a horrible grimace. "What a woman, gentlemen. Hera and Aphrodite, Brunhilda and Melusina all wrapped up in one." And then he would abruptly add, "Ah, life is truly beautiful!" and stare up at the model sailboats and huge fish hanging from the ceiling of the old guild hall. And none of the good citizens sitting near him on the heavy, carved wooden benches, drinking their pints, understood what the advent of a Gerda Arnoldsen meant in the modest life of Gosch the broker, who longed for extraordinary events.

Since, as noted, they were under no obligation to celebrate in any grand style, the little group gathered on Meng Strasse had that much more time to become better acquainted. With Clara's hand in his, Sievert Tiburtius talked about his parents, his youth, and his plans for the future; the Arnoldsens told about the history of their family, which had originated in Dresden and only one branch of which had been transplanted to Holland. And then Madame Grünlich demanded the key to the secretary in the landscape room, and with a very serious face she returned bearing the writing case with the family papers, in which Thomas had already entered the most recent events. With great dignity she told the history of the Buddenbrooks, beginning with the merchant tailor from Rostock who had done very well. She read old festive poems:

Simplest beauty, ablest talent,
Grace your children, and we view
Foam-born Venus and her gallant
Vulcan wed in love anew.

And she winked at Tom and Gerda and let her tongue play along her upper lip. Nor, out of respect for history, did she omit the incursion made on the family by a personage whose name she did not gladly let pass her lips.

The usual guests, however, appeared on Thursday at four o'clock. Justus Kröger and his weak-willed wife came. They continued to live very much at odds, because she was still supporting her spoiled and disinherited son, Jakob, in America with money she saved from her household allowance—and served her husband almost nothing but buckwheat porridge. There was nothing anyone could do. The Ladies Buddenbrook from Breite Strasse arrived, and their love of truth demanded that they point out that Erika Grünlich had still not grown, that she looked more and more like her swindler father, and that there was something *rather* showy about the way the consul's future bride did her hair. And even Sesame Weichbrodt came—who stood on her tiptoes, kissed Gerda's brow with a soft popping sound, and said with deep emotion, "Be heppy, you good chawld!"

At dinner Herr Arnoldsen gave one of his very witty toasts in honor of the two engaged couples, and later, as they drank coffee, he played the violin like a gypsy, with savage passion and dexterity. Even Gerda got out her Stradivarius—she never traveled without it—and added her own sweet cantilena above his solo; they played flamboyant duets, standing together beside the harmonium in the landscape room, where once the consul's grandfather had piped little graceful melodies on his flute.

"How sublime," Tony said, leaning far back in her easy chair. "O Lord, I find it simply sublime." And with her eyes gazing heavenward, she gave fervent expression to her honest emotions, and earnestly, slowly, weightily, she said, "No, no, you all know how it is in life. Not everyone is granted such a talent. Heaven denied me such a gift, you see, although many a night I pled for it. I'm a goose, a silly goose. Yes, Gerda, let me tell you—I'm older than you and have learned something of life. You should fall to your knees daily and thank your Creator that in His grace He has imbrued you with such gifts."

"Im*bued*," Gerda said with a smile, displaying her lovely, white, broad teeth.

Later, they gathered together to eat sabayon and deliberate what all had to be done in the near future. It was decided that, at the end of the month or in early September, both Sievert Tiburtius and the Arnoldsens would return home. Clara's wedding would be a grand affair celebrated in the columned hall shortly after Christmas, whereas the nuptials in Amsterdam, which Madame Buddenbrook planned to attend—"if God granted her life and health"—would be delayed until early in the new year, giving them all a little breather. Tom opposed this arrangement, but to no avail. "Please," Elisabeth said, laying a hand on his arm, "Sievert should have precedence."

The pastor and his bride decided against a honeymoon. But Gerda and Thomas had already agreed on a trip across northern Italy to Florence. They would be gone about two months; meanwhile Antonie would work with Jakobs the upholsterer on Fisch Strasse to redecorate a charming little house on Breite Strasse, which had belonged to a bachelor who had recently moved to Hamburg, and which the consul was already arranging to buy. Oh, Tony would handle that very much to their satisfaction. "It will be so elegant—you'll see," she said. And they were all quite sure of that.

Christian paced about the room on his thin, bowed legs, wrinkling his large nose and listening to this discussion of weddings, trousseaus, and honeymoons. He could feel that ache, that vague ache in his left leg, and his little, round, deep set eyes were serious, restless, and pensive as he studied the two couples holding hands. Finally he turned to his poor cousin, sitting there amid all these happy people—a silent, skinny old maid, still hungry despite dinner and dessert—and in the voice of Marcellus Stengel he said, "Well, Thilda. Let's get married right away, too; separately, I mean."

9

SOME SEVEN MONTHS later, Consul Buddenbrook returned with his wife from Italy. It was five in the evening, and Breite Strasse lay under March snow as their carriage pulled up in front of the simple, painted façade of their house. A few children and adults stopped to watch the new arrivals climb out. Frau Antonie Grünlich stood at the front door—proud of the arrangements she had made. Behind her were the two maids she had expertly chosen for her sister-in-law; they stood in their white caps and heavy, striped skirts, at the ready, their forearms bare.

Flushed with joy and hard work, Tony ran down the low steps and, smothering Gerda and Thomas with hugs as they emerged wrapped in furs from their baggage-laden carriage, she pulled them into the entryway.

"Here you are. Here you are, you lucky people, you world travelers, you. Hast thou seen the house, its roof, its pillars high? Gerda, you're more beautiful than ever; here, let me give you a kiss. No, on the mouth. Right! Hello, dear old Tom, you get a kiss, too. Marcus told me that everything has gone quite well in your absence. Mother is waiting for you on Meng Strasse. But first make yourselves comfortable. Would you like tea? Or a bath? It's all ready for you. You'll have no complaints. Jakobs spared no effort, and I've done what I could, too."

They walked together into the entrance hall, while the maids helped the coachman drag their trunks in. Tony said, "For the time being you'll not have much need for these rooms here on the ground floor. For the time being," she repeated, letting the tip of her tongue play along her upper lip. "This is a pretty one here, though," and she opened a door directly on the right of the vestibule. "That's ivy at the windows, simple wooden furniture, oak. And back there, on the other side of the hall, is another, larger room. Here on the right are the kitchen and the pantry. But let's go upstairs. Oh, I want to show it all to you."

They climbed the gentle flight of stairs covered with a broad, dark-red runner. Behind the glass door that opened onto the second floor was a small hallway. Off it lay the dining room, where a samovar stood simmering on the heavy round table, and carved walnut chairs with cane seats and a massive buffet had been set along the walls, covered in a dark-red damasklike fabric. A comfortable sitting room done in gray fabric was separated by portieres from a small salon with a bay window and easy chairs upholstered in green-striped rep. An entire quarter of the floor was taken up by a salon with three windows.

They now crossed the hallway to the bedroom, which lay on their right and had flowered curtains and two huge mahogany beds. Tony moved to a small, openwork door at the back of the room and pushed on its latch—revealing a spiral staircase that led down to the ground floor, to the bath and the maids' rooms.

"It's very pretty. I think I shall stay," Gerda said and sank with a sigh of relief into an easy chair beside one of the beds.

The consul bent down to her and kissed her brow. "Tired? But it's true, I wouldn't mind a chance to freshen up a bit myself."

"And I'll see about the tea," Frau Grünlich said. "I'll wait for you in the dining room." And she left.

When Thomas came across the hall, tea was steaming in Dresden-china cups. "Here I am," he said. "Gerda would like to rest for half an hour. She has a headache. We'll go to Meng Strasse later. Is everyone well, my dear Tony? Mother, Erika, Christian? Well, then," he continued, turning on his finest charm, "our warmest thanks—Gerda's, too—for all your efforts, my dear. You've made it all so pretty! All we lack are a couple of palm trees to put at my wife's bay window, and a few suitable oil paintings, which I'll look around for. But now tell me, how are you? And what have you been doing all this time?" He had pulled a chair over for his sister and now slowly drank his tea and ate a cookie while she spoke.

"Oh, Tom," she replied. "What is there for me to do? My life is behind me now. . . ."

"Nonsense, Tony. You and your talk of life. But we've been rather bored, I take it?"

"Yes, Tom, I'm bored something awful. Sometimes I could weep with boredom. I've enjoyed decorating your house for you, and don't think I'm not glad you're back. But I'm not happy at home. God strike me if that's a sin. I'm in my early thirties now, but I'm not yet so old that my dearest friends should be the last Himmelsbürger or the ladies Gerhardt or one of mother's men in black who devour widows' houses. I don't trust them, Tom. They're wolves in sheep's clothing, a generation of vipers. We're all weak human beings with sinful hearts, and if they want to look down on me as a miserable worldly woman, why, I'll just laugh in their faces. I've always been of the opinion that all men are equal, and that we don't need any middlemen between us and our God. You know my political principles, too. I want each citizen to stand in direct relation to the state."

"So you're feeling a little lonely, is that it?" Thomas asked to bring her back to the point. "But, now, listen here, you have Erika, don't you?"

"Yes, Tom, and I love that child with all my heart, although there was a certain person who claimed I am not fond of children. But, you see . . . I'm being frank with you, I'm a straightforward woman who says what she feels in her heart, and I have no use for a lot of pretty words."

"Which is very pretty of you, Tony."

"To be brief—the sad thing is that the child reminds me all too much of Grünlich. Even the Buddenbrooks from Breite Strasse say that she looks very much like him. And, then, whenever she's standing right there in front of me, I'm forced to think: You're an old woman with a grown daughter, and your life is behind you. For a few years you stood in the thick of things, but now you'll live to be seventy or eighty, sitting here listening to Lea Gerhardt read to you. The thought makes me so sad, Tom, that I can feel it as a pressure right here, just sitting in my throat. Because I still feel young, you know, and I want so much to get back into the thick of life. And besides, it's not only that I'm uncomfortable at home, but in town, too. You can't suppose I've been struck blind and can't see how things stand. I'm not a silly goose anymore and I've got eyes in my head. I'm a divorced woman, and it's only too clear that they make sure I feel it. Believe me, Tom, it still lies heavy on my heart that I have left such a stain on our name, even if it was no fault of my own. Do what you will, you can earn lots of money, become the most important man in town—people will always say, 'Yes. But did you know his sister is divorced?' Julie Möllendorpf, née Hagenström, never greets me. Well, she really is a goose! But it's the same with all the families. And yet, Tom, I simply can't stop hoping to make up for it all someday. I am still young. And still rather pretty, am I not? Mama can't give me all that much, but it's still a nice tidy sum of money. What if I were to marry again? To be frank, Tom, it's my most fervent wish. Then everything would be set right again, the stain would be washed away. O Lord, if I could only make a match that would be a credit to our name and set myself up on my own again. Do you think it's entirely out of the question?"

"By no means, Tony. Oh, not at all. I've never stopped assuming you would. But it seems to me that the most necessary thing is for you to get away for a bit—you need a little change of scenery."

"That's it!" she said eagerly. "And now I must tell you a story."

Very pleased with his own suggestion, Thomas leaned back in his chair. He was already smoking his second cigarette. Dusk had begun to fall.

"Well, then, while you were gone I almost accepted a position—a position as a social companion in Liverpool. Would that have shocked you? But all the same, a little questionable, right? Yes, yes, it would probably have been undignified. But it was my most ardent wish just to get away. But the whole thing fell apart. I sent Mrs. Whatever my photograph and she had to dispense with my services—I was too pretty. There was a grown son in the house. 'You are too pretty,' she wrote. I've never been more amused in all my life."

And they both laughed very heartily.

"But now something else has come along," Tony continued.

"I've received an invitation, an invitation to visit Eva Ewers in Munich. Oh yes, by the way, her name is Eva Niederpaur now, and her husband is a brewery director. Well, she has asked me to come for a visit, and I'm thinking of taking advantage of the offer very soon. Or course, Erika couldn't come along. I'd place her in Sesame Weichbrodt's boarding school. She'd be looked after very nicely there. Would you have any objections?"

"None at all. In any case, what you need are some new surroundings."

"Yes, that's it precisely!" she said with gratitude. "But, now, what about you, Tom? I've been talking about nothing but myself. What a selfish woman I am. So tell me all. Good Lord, how happy you must be!"

"Yes I am, Tony," he said emphatically. There was a short pause. He first exhaled and let the smoke drift across the table, then continued, "First of all, I'm very happy to be married and to have set up a household of my own. You know me—I would have made a very bad bachelor. That sort of life smacks of loneliness and indolence, and I have my own ambitions, as you well know. I don't believe I've reached the endpoint of my career, either in business or, if I may make light of it, in politics. But a man first wins the world's trust as master of his own house, as a family man. And yet, Tony, it all hung by the merest thread. I am a bit choosy. For a long time I didn't think it possible I would ever find the right woman. But one look at Gerda decided me. I saw at once that she was the only one, she and no one else. Although I know that a lot of people here in town are upset with me about my choice. She's a wonderful creature—there are very few like her on earth. I'll grant, she's very different from you, Tony. You're not as complex, you're more natural. Madame Antonie is simply more vivacious," he went on, suddenly striking a lighter tone. "And Gerda has her share of high spirits, too—she surely proves that when she plays her violin. But she can be a little cold sometimes. In short, she can't be measured by ordinary standards. She's an artist by nature—a unique, puzzling, ravishing creature."

"Yes, yes, she is," Tony said. She had been giving serious attention to what her brother was saying. Evening had fallen, and no one had thought to light a lamp.

The door to the hallway opened, and a tall, erect figure stood before them, surrounded by twilight and dressed in a pleated, flowing robe of snow-white piqué. Heavy chestnut hair framed the white face, and bluish shadows brooded in the corners of the brown, close-set eyes.

It was Gerda, the mother of future Buddenbrooks.

PART SIX

1

THOMAS BUDDENBROOK almost always ate an early breakfast alone in the pretty dining room. His wife usually left her bedroom only later in the day, because most mornings she suffered from a migraine headache, or was generally indisposed. The consul then left at once for Meng Strasse, where the firm's offices were still located, ate a second, late breakfast with his mother, Christian, and Ida Jungmann, and did not see Gerda until four in the afternoon, at dinner.

The commotion of daily business kept the ground floor of the old house bustling with life; but the upper floors of the large house on Meng Strasse were now quite deserted and lonely. Little Erika had been enrolled as a boarding student at Mademoiselle Weichbrodt's school; poor Klothilde had moved her four or five pieces of furniture to an inexpensive room in the home of Frau Dr. Krauseminz, a high-school teacher's widow; even Anton the butler had left the house, to work at the younger Buddenbrooks', where he was needed; and if Christian was at the Club, four o'clock found Madame Buddenbrook and Mamselle Jungmann sitting all by themselves at the round table, which, without a single extra leaf, now looked quite lost among all the gods in the large dining room.

With the death of Johann Buddenbrook, normal social life had also died on Meng Strasse, and apart from the visit of an occasional clergyman Elisabeth entertained no guests other than the members of her family, who gathered on Thursday evenings. Her son, however, and his wife already had their first dinner party behind them, with tables set in both the dining and sitting rooms, with cook, footmen, and wine from Kistenmaker's—an affair that began at five in the evening, with odors and sounds still lingering when the clock struck eleven. All the Langhalses, Hagenströms, Huneuses, Kistenmakers, Oeverdiecks, and Möllendorpfs—whether business or professional men, couples or *suitiers*—had attended the party, which concluded with whist and several earfuls of music and was praised in the highest terms on the exchange for a good week afterward. And it was more than evident that the consul's young wife knew how to entertain in style. That same evening, as they stood alone in the sitting room by the dim light of candles burning low now among furniture shoved this way and that—and enveloped in the sweet, heavy, thick odor of fine foods, perfumes, wines, coffee, cigars, and flowers that had adorned both the ladies and the tables—the consul squeezed her hands and said, "Well done, Gerda. We certainly have nothing to be ashamed of. This sort of thing is important. I have no great desire to throw a ball and have young people leaping around in here—there's not room enough, anyway. But the more staid and settled folks should eat well at our table. A dinner like this costs a little more, but it's money well invested."

"You're right," she replied, arranging the laces at her bodice, beneath which her breasts shimmered like marble. "I definitely prefer dinners to balls myself. A dinner has such an extraordinarily soothing effect. I had been playing my violin this afternoon and was feeling a bit odd. But now my brain is so numb that I could be struck by lightning and not bat an eyelash."

WHEN THE consul sat down beside his mother for late breakfast at about eleven-thirty the next morning, she read the following letter to him:

Munich, 2 April 1857
Marienplatz 5

My dear Mama,

I beg your pardon, I'm truly ashamed for not having written yet, even though I've been here for eight days now; my time has been taken up with all the things there are to see here—

but more of that later. First I must ask how my dear family is doing—you and Tom and Gerda and Erika and Christian and Thilda and Ida. That's the most important thing.

Oh, what all haven't I seen in these last few days. There is the Pinakothek and the Glyptothek and the Hofbräuhaus and the Court Theater and the churches and so many other things. I shall have to tell you about them when I see you, otherwise I'll write my fingers to the bone. We've also taken a carriage ride through the Isar Valley, and for tomorrow we are planning an excursion to Lake Würm. There seems to be no end to it. Eva is very sweet to me, and Herr Niederpaur, the brewery director, is an easygoing man. We live on a very pretty square in the middle of town, with a well in the middle, just like on the marketplace at home, and our house is very close to the town hall. I've never seen such a house. It's all painted in bright colors, from top to bottom—with St. George slaying the dragon and old Bavarian princes in long robes and carrying shields and swords. Just imagine!

Yes, I am quite taken by Munich. The air here is said to be good for the nerves, and my digestion is doing quite nicely at the moment. I am really enjoying drinking lots of beer, especially since the water here is not all that healthy. There are too few vegetables and they use too much flour—in the sauces, for example, which are deplorable. The people here haven't the vaguest what a good loin of veal is, because the butchers hack everything into pathetic little pieces. And I miss fish very much. And it really is purest madness, these everlasting pickles and potato salad, all washed down with beer—the sounds that come from my stomach!

In fact, one first has to get used to a great many things, as you may well imagine—it's a foreign country, after all. There are the unfamiliar coins, and the problem of making yourself understood with common people—with the servants, for instance, because I speak too fast for them and they just speak gibberish. And then there's Catholicism; I hate it, simply have no use for it, as you know.

The consul began to laugh at this, leaning back against the sofa with a piece of bread and herb cheese in his hand.

"Yes, Tom, you may well laugh," his mother said, giving the tablecloth several raps with her middle finger. "But I am very pleased that she holds to the faith of her fathers and detests such unevangelical gimcrackery. I know that you discovered a certain sympathy for the papish church while you were in France and Italy, but that is not a matter of religion with you, Tom, it's something else, and I know what it is. We should be forbearing, I know, but making a game or hobby out of such things is reprehensible, and I pray God that as the years go by He may give both you and Gerda—whose faith I know is not exactly of the firmest—the seriousness necessary in such things. You will forgive your mother such remarks, I'm sure."

"Atop the well"—she went on reading—"which I can see from my window, is a madonna, and sometimes they crown her with wreaths, and then the common people kneel down with their rosaries and pray, which really looks quite pretty, but it is written: Enter into thy closet. You often see monks on the streets here, and they look quite distinguished. But just imagine, Mama, yesterday, on Theatiner Strasse, some high dignitary of the church rode past me in his carriage, he might have been the archbishop, an older man—well, the man leered at me from his carriage window as if he were a lieutenant of the guard. You know, Mother, that I don't set great store by your friends the missionaries and pastors, but Teary Trieschke is certainly nothing compared with that lecherous prince of the church."

"Shame, shame!" Elisabeth interjected in outrage.

"That's Tony all over," the consul said.

"What do you mean, Tom?"

"Why, you don't suppose she provoked him a little, just to test him? I know my Tony. And she was immensely amused by that 'leer'—which was probably all the old gentleman intended."

Madame Buddenbrook did not respond, but went on reading:

The day before yesterday, the Niederpaurs had a dinner party, which was absolutely lovely, although I couldn't always follow the conversation and I found the tone rather *équivoque* at times. There was even a tenor from the Court Opera, who sang some songs, and a young artist who begged me to let him do my portrait, which I declined, however, because I did not think it proper. I enjoyed myself best with Herr Permaneder—would you ever have thought someone could have a name like that? He's a hops merchant, a pleasant, amusing man, a bachelor in his best years. I sat beside him at dinner and stayed close to him the rest of the evening, since he was the only Protestant at the party, for, although he is a solid citizen of Munich, his family comes from Nuremberg. He assured me that he knew our firm's name quite well, and you can imagine, Tom, how pleased I was by the respectful way he said it. He also asked about us in some detail, how many brothers and sisters I had and such. He wanted to know about Erika and even about Grünlich. He visits the Niederpaurs on occasion, and I believe he'll be joining us on our trip to Lake Würm tomorrow.

And now adieu, dear Mama, I cannot write any more. If God grants me life and health, as you always say, I shall stay here another three or four weeks, and then I can tell you all about Munich when I'm home, because I really don't know where to start in a letter. But I like it here very much, that much I can say, except that one would have to train a cook to make proper sauces. You see, I am an old woman whose life is behind her and have nothing more to expect on this earth, but if God grants Erika life and health and she should ever marry someone here, I would have no objection, I must say.

At this point the consul stopped eating again and lay back against the sofa, laughing.

"She is priceless, Mother! There's no one like her for playing the hypocrite. I'm simply mad about her, because she's simply incapable of disguising her true feelings, doesn't come within a thousand miles of it."

"Yes, Tom," Elisabeth said, "but she is a good child and deserves all sorts of good things." Then she read the rest of the letter.

2

AT THE END OF APRIL, Frau Grünlich settled in at home again, and although she had once more left some portion of life behind her, and although the old routine began again and she had to attend services and listen to Lea Gerhardt read aloud on Jerusalem Evenings, she was apparently in a happy and hopeful mood.

Her brother the consul picked her up at the train station—she had come by way of Büchen—and the moment they drove into town through the Holsten Gate he could not resist complimenting her by saying that she was still the fairest in the family, except for Klothilde. To which she responded, "O Lord, Tom, I hate you—mocking an old lady like that."

But there was truth to it, nonetheless. Much to her advantage, Madame Grünlich had kept her looks, and to look at her—with her full head of ash-blond hair set in little cushioned waves at each side of the part, then combed back over her small ears and gathered at the top with a tortoiseshell comb; with the softness that still lingered in her gray-blue eyes; with her pretty upper lip, the perfect oval and delicate complexion of her face—one would have guessed her to be, not thirty, but twenty-three. She wore very elegant, dangling gold earrings, which, in a slightly different form, her grandmother had worn before her. A loose-fitting bodice of soft dark silk, with satin lapels and shoulders trimmed in lace, made her breast look enchantingly soft.

She was, as noted, in the best of moods, and every Thursday—when the party around the table included her brother and his wife, the Ladies Buddenbrook from Breite Strasse, Consul Kröger, Klothilde, and Sesame Weichbrodt with little Erika—she provided picturesque descriptions of Munich: the beer, the steamed dumplings, the artist who had wanted to paint her portrait, and the court carriages, which had made the greatest impression on her. She would also mention Herr Permaneder in passing, and if Pfiffi Buddenbrook or one of the others made some remark to the effect that such a journey was quite pleasant, of course, but that apparently it had resulted in nothing of practical consequence, Frau Grünlich would pass this over with unutterable dignity, laying her head back and yet somehow managing to tuck her chin against her chest.

It had become her custom, by the way, that whenever the vestibule bell echoed through the large entrance hall, she would hurry out to the landing to see who was coming. What could possibly be the point of that? Probably the only person who knew was Ida Jungmann, Tony's governess and confidante over the years, who every now and then would say something like, "You'll see, Tony, my child, he'll come. He surely doesn't want to look like a blatherskite."

The other members of the family had reason to be grateful to Antonie for her high spirits now that she was home again; the mood in the house had definitely been in need of improvement, particularly since the relationship between the head of the firm and his younger brother had not grown better over time, but, sadly, much worse. Their mother, Madame Buddenbrook, had anxiously followed this course of events, and it was all she could do just to mediate between the two. Christian responded with distracted silence to her suggestions that he be more regular about appearing in the office, and he greeted his brother's admonitions with pensive gravity and uneasy embarrassment, letting them pass over him without argument—and for a few days he would apply himself somewhat more zealously to the English correspondence. More and more, however, the older brother felt growing within him an irritable contempt for the younger, which was not diminished by the fact that, if he occasionally expressed such feelings, Christian offered no resistance, but simply let his eyes wander aimlessly and wistfully about.

The stress of business and the state of his own nerves made it impossible for Tom to listen with sympathy or even composure to

Christian's detailed descriptions of the ever-changing symptoms of his illness; and in talking to his mother or sister he would angrily call it "the silly upshot of a case of disgusting self-absorption."

The ache, the vague ache in Christian's left leg, had eased over time—after the application of various topical medications. But he still often had difficulty swallowing when eating, and of late this phenomenon had been accompanied by a temporary shortness of breath, an asthmatic condition, which for several weeks Christian believed to be consumption, the nature and symptoms of which he painfully attempted—with much wrinkling of his nose—to describe in minute detail for his family. Dr. Grabow was called in for consultation. He determined that both heart and lungs were working quite vigorously, but that the occasional shortness of breath could be traced to a sluggishness in certain muscles, and prescribed both the use of a fan to ease respiration and a greenish powder that one first ignited in order to breathe its fumes. Christian used the fan in the office as well, and when his brother objected to this, he replied that in Valparaiso every office-worker had had a fan because of the heat—"Johnny Thunderstorm . . . good God!" But then, one day, after a long session of serious and restive squirming in his office chair, he pulled his powder from his pocket and, upon lighting it, produced such potent, foul-smelling fumes that several people in the office began to cough and even Herr Marcus turned quite pale—and then came a dreadful argument, a public outburst, a scandal, which would have immediately led to a total break had not Madame Buddenbrook once more managed to smooth things over, appealing to reason and setting things right again.

But that was not the only problem. The consul was also disgusted by the life that Christian led outside the house, usually in the company of his old schoolchum Andreas Gieseke the lawyer. Thomas was not a prig or a spoilsport. He could recall only too well the sins of his own youth. He knew that his hometown, this town of ships and commerce, where highly respectable businessmen with incomparably principled faces strode along the sidewalks tapping their walking sticks, was no cradle of stainless morality. People compensated for long days spent sitting on office stools with more than just rich wines and rich foods. But a heavy cloak of rectitude hid such compensations—and if Consul Buddenbrook's first law was "Keep up appearances," in that respect he completely shared the creed of his fellow citizens. Andreas Gieseke was one of the "professionals" who had adapted themselves nicely to the comfortable existence of the "merchants"—and a notorious *suitier*, which was obvious just from looking at him. But, like the other pleasure-loving bons vivants, he understood how to put on the right face, to avoid public offense, and to maintain a reputation for absolute reliability in matters political and professional. His engagement to Fräulein Huneus had just been made public, and that meant that he would be marrying into the first rank of society—and would receive a considerable dowry. He showed a marked interest in civic affairs; indeed, he was so active that people said he had his eye on a particular seat in the town hall and that one day he would in fact sit in old Mayor Oeverdieck's chair.

Christian Buddenbrook, however, his friend, the same lad who had once resolutely marched up to Mademoiselle Meyer–de la Grange, handed her his bouquet, and said, "Your acting is simply beautiful, Fräulein"—Christian was by nature a much too naïve and reckless *suitier*, and, indeed, his long years of wandering had made of him a man as little inclined to curb his feelings as to employ discretion or maintain his dignity. The whole town was highly amused, for example, by his affair with a girl working as an extra for the summer theater, and Frau Stuht from Glockengiesser Strasse, the woman who moved in the best social circles, told any of the ladies who might wish to hear that Krischan had been seen again on the street with that girl from the Tivoli, in broad daylight.

Not that people held that against him—they were much too plodding and skeptical to show any signs of serious moral outrage. Christian Buddenbrook and perhaps Consul Peter Döhlmann—whose business was now languishing beyond repair and thus allowed him to proceed in much the same harmless fashion—both had a talent to amuse that was much prized, indeed indispensable, at all-male gatherings. But they were certainly not to be taken seriously; they did not count in matters of importance. It was significant that throughout the town—at the Club, on the exchange, on the docks—they were known by their first names: Krischan and Peter; and spiteful people, like the Hagenströms, felt no compunction about laughing, not at Krischan's tales and jokes, but at Krischan himself.

He paid no attention to it, or in his usual fashion he would shrug it off after a curiously anxious moment of thinking things over. His brother the consul, however, knew—he knew that Christian offered the family's adversaries an easy target, and that this was one target too many. Their relation to the Oeverdiecks was a distant one and would be quite useless after the mayor's death. The Krögers no longer played any role at all; they lived in seclusion and continued to have dreadful troubles with their son. Late Uncle Gotthold's bad marriage remained an embarrassment. The consul's sister was a divorced woman, even if one need not give up all hope that she might marry again. And his brother was considered a ridiculous fool. Busy men whiled away their leisure hours over his buffoonery, laughed at him—out of pity or scorn. He ran up far too many debts; and when he was out of money before the end of each quarter, he quite flagrantly let Andreas Gieseke pay his bills—a direct slap in the firm's face.

The fierce contempt in which Thomas held his brother—and the wistful indifference with which Christian bore it—found expression in all those trivial moments of life that can only manifest themselves among people thrown together in families. If, for example, conversation turned to the history of the Buddenbrooks, Christian could become wrapped up in a mood of high seriousness—which ill became him—and speak with love and admiration of his hometown and his forebears. The consul would immediately cut him off with an icy remark. He could not stand it. He despised his brother so much that he would not allow him to love the things he loved. He would have much preferred to hear Christian speak of them in his Marcellus Stengel voice. Thomas had read a book, some historical work, that had made a strong impression on him, and he praised it in stirring words. Christian was impressionable and easily influenced, always depending on others for his views; he would never have found such a book on his own. But he read it now, and, having been primed and made receptive by Tom's praise of it, he found it quite splendid himself, describing his reactions as precisely as possible. And from that moment the book was spoiled for Tom. He spoke of it with cold disregard. He pretended he had barely looked at it. He left it to his brother to admire it all by himself.

3

CONSUL BUDDENBROOK was returning to Meng Strasse from the Harmony, a gentlemen's reading club, where he had spent an hour after second breakfast. He crossed the rear of the property, striding quickly alongside the garden and down the paved passageway that cut between two overgrown walls and connected the back and front courtyards; he walked through the back entryway and called into the kitchen, asking if his brother were at home—they should let him know when he came in. Then he marched through the office, where at the mere sight of him people at their desks bent down deeper over their account books, and into his private office; he laid his hat and cane aside, pulled on his working coat, and sat down at his desk by the window, across from Herr Marcus. Two deep furrows were visible between his pale eyebrows. The yellow mouthpiece of a Russian cigarette he had already finished wandered nervously from one corner of his mouth to the other. He reached for paper and pen with such an abrupt jerk that Herr Marcus cautiously stroked his mustache with two fingers and slowly shifted his eyes to examine his partner's face; the younger workers looked at each other with raised eyebrows. The boss was angry.

After a half-hour in which there was no audible sound except the scratching of pens and the prudent coughs of Herr Marcus, the consul looked across the green windowsill and spotted Christian walking toward the office. He was smoking—he had just finished breakfast and a quick game at the Club. His hat was cocked a little low and he was swinging his yellow walking stick, the one from "out there," with the carved ebony bust of a nun on the knob. He was obviously in good health and the best of moods. He was humming some melody or other as he came into the office, said, "Morning, gentlemen," although it was a lovely spring afternoon, and added as he strode to his seat, "Have to get a bit of work done."

But the consul stood up and as he walked past he said, without looking at Christian, "Ah—a couple of words with you, my friend."

Christian followed him. They walked rather rapidly through the outer room. Thomas had crossed his hands behind his back, and involuntarily Christian did the same and turned his head toward his brother, so that his large nose, its bony hook set squarely between his hollow cheeks, jutted out above his drooping reddish-blond English mustache. As they moved across the courtyard, Thomas said, "I'll ask you to accompany me while I take some air in the garden, my friend."

"Fine," Christian replied. And then came a long silence, during which they followed the outside path, passing the rococo façade of the "Portal" and skirting the garden, which was just coming into bloom.

Finally the consul took a quick breath and said in a loud voice, "I am terribly angry—on your account."

"My account?"

"Yes. Someone at the Harmony told me about a remark you made yesterday evening at the Club—a remark so out of place, so indescribably tactless that I cannot find words for it. And the fiasco was soon complete—you were given the most dreadful dressing-down on the spot. Do you care to recall the incident?"

"Oh, now I know what you mean. Who told you all this?"

"What does that matter? Döhlmann. And, of course, he told me in a voice so loud that people who perhaps hadn't heard about it yet could gloat over it, too."

"Yes, Tom, I must tell you, I felt quite embarrassed for Hagenström."

"You felt . . . That's really too much. Now, listen to me!" the consul shouted, stretching both hands before him, palms up, and he tilted his head to one side, giving it a demonstrative and excited shake. "There you are surrounded by both business and professional men, where everyone can hear you, and you say, 'Seen in the light of day, actually, every businessman is a swindler'—you, who are a businessman yourself, a part of a firm that strives with might and main for absolute integrity, for a spotless reputation."

"Good heavens, Thomas, it was a joke. Although, actually . . ." Christian started to add, wrinkling up his nose and thrusting his head forward at a little angle. And, holding this pose, he walked a few more steps.

"A joke! A joke!" the consul shouted. "I think I can take a joke—but you saw for yourself how your joke was taken. 'Well, *I for one* think *very* highly of my profession.' That was Hermann Hagenström's answer. And there you sat—a man who has wasted his life away, who has no respect for his own profession."

"Yes, Tom, but what does one say then? I assure you that the whole mood was shot to hell. People were laughing as if they agreed with me. And there sits Hagenström, all dreadfully serious, and says, 'Well, *I for one* . . .' What a stupid fellow. I was truly embarrassed for him. I thought long and hard about it lying in bed last night, and it gave me such a strange feeling. I don't know whether you know it, it's . . ."

"Stop babbling, I beg you, stop babbling," the consul interrupted. His whole body trembled with anger. "I will admit, yes, I will admit that his answer perhaps did not fit the mood, that it was in bad taste. But one seeks out the proper audience for saying something like that—if it really must be said. But you don't lay yourself open to such an insolent dressing-down. Hagenström used the opportunity to get back, not at you, but at us, *us*. Surely you realize what he meant with his 'I for one,' don't you? He meant: 'Apparently you come by such notions in your brother's office, Herr Buddenbrook.' *That's* what he meant, you ass!"

"Well, 'ass' is a bit . . ." Christian said with a chagrined, anxious look on his face.

"In the final analysis, you do not belong just to yourself alone," the consul continued. "But I assure you it is a matter of total indifference to me if you personally make a ridiculous fool of yourself. And when *don't* you make a fool of yourself?" he shouted. He was white, and blue veins were clearly visible on his narrow temples, from which his hair fell back in two waves. He had lifted one pale eyebrow, and even the stiffened, long ends of his mustache showed his anger; and as he spoke he flung his words with dismissive gestures on the gravel path at Christian's feet. "And you are making a fool of yourself with your little love affairs, with your buffoonery, with your sicknesses, with your remedies for your sicknesses."

"Oh, Thomas," Christian said, shaking his head very seriously and lifting an index finger rather ungracefully, "as far as that goes, that's something you can't really understand. The thing is—a man has to come to terms with his own conscience, so to speak. I don't know if you know the feeling. Grabow prescribed a salve for the muscles here on my neck. Fine. And if I don't use it, forget to use it, I feel quite lost and helpless and get all nervous and anxious and unsure of myself, and when I'm in that state I can't swallow. But if I use it, then I feel I've done my duty and that everything is in order; my conscience is clear, and I feel calm and content, and swallowing is absolutely effortless. I don't think that the salve itself does it, you see. But the main thing, you understand, is that one idea can only be canceled by an opposing idea. I don't know if you know the feeling. . . ."

"Oh yes, yes!" the consul shouted and held his head in both hands for a moment. "Go ahead and do it! Do what you must, but don't talk about it. Don't babble on about it. Leave other people in peace with your disgusting sensibilities. You make a fool of yourself from morning till night with your indecent babblings. But let me tell you this, I'll repeat once more: I could not care less if you personally make a fool of yourself; but I forbid you, do you hear me, I *forbid* you ever to compromise the firm in the manner in which you did yesterday evening."

Christian offered no response to this, except that he slowly ran his hand through his thinning reddish-blond hair and his face turned serious and anxious, his eyes drifting about absent-mindedly, seeing nothing. He was doubtless still preoccupied with what he himself had last said. There was a long pause.

Thomas stalked away in silent desperation. "All businessmen are swindlers, you say," he began again. "Fine. Are you tired of your job? Do you regret having become a businessman? You once convinced Father to allow you to . . ."

"Yes, Tom," Christian said pensively, "but I would have much preferred to study. It must be very nice at a university, you know. You go to classes when you feel like it, quite voluntarily, you sit down and listen just like in the theater."

"Like in the theater. Oh, you belong in a *café chantant*, as the comedian. I'm not joking, I'm in dead earnest. I am quite convinced that that's your secret goal in life," the consul asserted. And Christian certainly did not contradict him—just looked wistfully about.

"And you have the audacity to make such a remark, when you haven't the vaguest, not the vaguest idea of what work is. Because you fill up your days with the theater and strolling about and buffooneries, creating a whole series of feelings and sensitivities and conditions to keep yourself occupied, to observe and nurse them, so that you can shamelessly babble on about them."

"Yes, Tom," Christian said, a little morosely, running his hand across his head again. "That's true; you've put it quite accurately. That's the difference between us, you see. You enjoy watching a play, too, and you once told me, just between us, that you had your little affairs, and there was a time when you preferred reading novels and poems and such. But you've always known how to reconcile that with regular work and a purpose in life. That's what I lack, you see. I get totally used up by the other things, all the junk, you see, and have nothing left for the respectable part of life. I don't know if you know the feeling, but . . ."

"So, then, you do understand!" Thomas shouted, stopping in his tracks and crossing his arms on his chest. "You admit it to your own shame, and yet you go on in the same old way. Are you a dog, Christian? Good God in heaven, a man has his pride! One doesn't go on living a life that one wouldn't even think of defending. But that's what you do. That's who you are. It's enough for you just to perceive something and understand it and describe it. No, my patience is at an end, Christian." And the consul took a step backward, lifting his arms violently so that they stood straight out at his sides. "It's at an end, I tell you. You draw your salary and never come to the office—although that's not what exasperates me. Go ahead and piddle your life away, just as you've done so far. But you compromise us, all of us, no matter where you are, where you go. You're an abscess, an unhealthy growth on the body of our family. You're a scandal to the whole town, and if this house were mine I would turn you out, I would show you the door!" he shouted, gesturing wildly across the garden, the courtyard, the large entryway. He could no longer contain himself—it was an explosion of all the rage he had stored up inside him.

"What is the matter with you, Thomas!" Christian said, now seized by a fit of anger himself—which looked rather odd on him. He stood there in a pose not unusual for bowlegged people, bent in a kind of question mark, his head, belly, and knees shoved forward, and his round, deep-set eyes, as large now as he could make them, had a flush around the edges that spread down to his cheekbones—just like his father's when he was angry. "How dare you speak like that to me," he said. "What have I ever done to you? I'll go, all on my own, you don't need to throw me out. Shame, shame!" he added as a heartfelt reproach and accompanied the words with a quick snapping movement of one hand, as if he were catching a fly.

Strangely enough, Thomas did not react with a more violent outburst, but silently lowered his head and started slowly back on the path around the garden. It seemed to have satisfied him, to have actually done him good, finally to have made his brother angry, to have at last enabled him to react vigorously and raise some protest.

"Believe me," he said quietly, his hands crossed behind his back again, "when I say this conversation has been painful for me, Christian, but it had to happen sometime. There is something awful about such scenes within a family, but we had to have it out once and for all. And now we can discuss these matters quite calmly, my boy. You're not happy in your present position, I see, right?"

"No, I'm not, Tom. You're right there. You see, at the start I was really quite content, and I do have things better here than I would in a strange office. But what I lack is independence, I think. I always envy you when I see you sitting there and working, and it really isn't work for you. You don't work because you *have* to—you're in charge, you're the boss, and you let others do your work for you. You make your calculations and supervise things and are quite free. That's something very different."

"Fine, Christian. Couldn't you have told me that before now?

Naturally you're free to go on your own and be more independent. You know that Father set aside a part of both our inheritances, fifty thousand marks *courant* apiece, for immediate use, and that of course I'd be ready to pay you your share on the spur of the moment for any reasonably sound investment. There are quite enough solid though financially straitened firms in Hamburg, or wherever, that could use a new flow of capital and would take you on as a partner. So let's give the matter some thought, each on his own, and speak to Mother, too, when the right moment comes. I have work to do now; and you might spend a few days taking care of the English correspondence."

"What do you think, for example, of H. C. F. Burmeester & Co. in Hamburg?" he asked as they walked across the entrance hall. "Import and export. I know the man. I'm sure he'd grab at the chance."

THIS HAPPENED in 1857, at the end of May. In early June Christian departed for Hamburg by way of Büchen—a heavy loss for the Club, the theater, the Tivoli, and for conviviality in general. All the *suitiers*, Andreas Gieseke and Peter Döhlmann among them, said goodbye to him at the train station, brought him flowers and even cigars, and laughed till their sides split—recalling, no doubt, all the stories that Christian had ever told them. Finally Andreas Gieseke, attorney-at-law, pinned a corsage made of gold paper to Christian's overcoat. This particular medal of honor came from a house down near the docks, an inn that hung a red lamp above the door each evening and was known for its easy sociability and the good times to be had there. It was awarded to Krischan Buddenbrook for distinguished service on the field of battle.

4

THE BELL RANG in the vestibule, and as was her habit of late, Frau Grünlich appeared on the landing to peer down over the white-enameled banister at the entry hall below. But no sooner had the door been opened than she abruptly leaned over farther still, then jerked back and, pressing her handkerchief to her mouth with one hand and gathering up her skirts with the other, sped back upstairs in a kind of low crouch. She met Mamselle Jungmann on the stairs to the third floor and whispered something to her in a strained voice. In terrified delight, Ida replied in Polish. It sounded like *My boshy kock hanna!*

Madame Buddenbrook happened to be sitting in the landscape room, crocheting with two large wooden needles—a shawl, a blanket, or something of that sort. It was eleven o'clock in the morning.

The maid suddenly came waddling down the columned hall, rapped at the glass door, and presented Elisabeth with a calling card. She took it, adjusted her glasses, which she wore when doing her needlework, and read. Then she looked back up at the maid's flushed face, read it again, and looked at the maid's face again. Finally she asked in a gentle but firm voice. "What is this, my dear? What does this mean?"

For the printing on the card read: "X. Noppe & Co." But both X. Noppe and the ampersand had been crossed out, leaving only the "Co."

"Well, madam," the maid said, "there's a gen'leman here, but he don't speak German, though he talks a blue streak."

"Ask the gentleman to come up," Elisabeth said, realizing now that it was "Co." who wished to be received. The maid left. Almost immediately the glass door opened again to admit a stocky figure that held back for a moment in the shadows at the far end of the room and in a kind of drawl said something that sounded like " 't's 'n honor."

"Good morning," Madame Buddenbrook said. "Won't you please come in?" And, propping herself with one hand on a sofa cushion, she rose slightly, since she was not yet sure whether manners required that she stand up.

"Hope y' don' mind . . ." the gentleman replied in a lilting drawl, and, bowing politely, he took two steps forward, came to another stop, and looked about as if searching for something—perhaps a place to sit or somewhere to put down his hat and cane, because he still had both with him, the latter topped by a curved, clawlike handle of deerhorn that measured a good foot and a half.

He was a man of about forty, portly, with short arms and legs. His brown loden coat was unbuttoned, revealing a bright, flowered vest that covered the gentle vault of his stomach and across which hung a gold watch chain with an entire bouquet of charms, a glittering collection of silver, coral, bone, and deerhorn trinkets. His trousers were an indefinite grayish green—and too short; they were apparently made of some strange stiff fabric, because the cuffs fell in unpleated circles around the short shafts of his broad boots. A pale blond, sparse mustache that hung like fringe over his mouth, a perfectly round head, a stump of a nose, and thinning, badly cut hair combined to make him look somewhat like a walrus. Between his chin and lower lip, the stranger wore a bristly goatee, which, in contrast to his drooping mustache, tipped slightly upward. His cheeks were so extraordinarily fat and puffy that they squeezed his eyes into two very narrow pale blue slits with lots of wrinkles at the corners. All this gave his pudgy face an expression that was a mixture of ferocity and simple, clumsy, touching bonhomie. His chin dropped in a straight line to join his narrow white necktie—the goiterous neck could never have endured a stiff high collar. The lower half of his face, cheeks and nose, the back of his head, the nape of his neck—it all merged like a pile of little shapeless pillows. The puffiness and swelling had stretched the skin on his face so tight that it was chapped and red in some places—just below the earlobes and at both sides of his nose, for instance. The gentleman held his cane in one short, white, fat hand, in the other his green Tyrolean hat trimmed with a chamois tuft.

Madame Buddenbrook had removed her glasses, but was still propped against the sofa cushion in a half-standing position. "How may I help you?" she asked politely but firmly.

In one decisive gesture, the gentleman laid his hat and cane on the lid of the harmonium; he rubbed his now unencumbered hands contentedly, gazing at Madame Buddenbrook with bright, puffy, but guileless eyes. He said, "Beg pardon, ma'am, for that callin' card there. Jist didn't have 'nother one handy. My name is Permaneder, Alois Permaneder, from Munich. You maybe heard my name mentioned, ma'am, by your daughter."

He said all this very loudly in his gnarled dialect, crudely accenting some syllables, suddenly eliding others—but with a confidential gleam in his narrow eyes, which said, "We'll get along all right."

Elisabeth had now stood up, and she walked toward him with her hands outstretched, her head tilted to one side. "Herr Permaneder. Is it really you? But of course my daughter told us about you. I know how very much you contributed to making her stay in Munich so pleasant and enjoyable. And now you find yourself here in our town?"

"Yup, 'nuff t' floor y'!" Herr Permaneder said, sitting down in the armchair to which Elisabeth had directed him with a polite gesture; feeling at home now, he began to rub his short, fat thighs with both hands.

"I beg your pardon?" Elisabeth said.

"Yup, 'nuff t' floor y'!" Herr Permaneder replied and stopped rubbing his knees.

"How nice," Madame Buddenbrook said, leaning back and putting her hands in her lap in feigned satisfaction—she had not understood one word.

Realizing this, however, Herr Permaneder bent forward and, drawing—God knows why—circles in the air, he said with all his might and main, "What I said was, you must be durn surprised, ma'am."

"Yes, yes, my dear Herr Permaneder, that's true," she replied amiably; and now that these matters were taken care of, a pause ensued.

But Herr Permaneder felt constrained to fill this pause with a groaning sigh, to which he added, "A pain 'n th' ol'!"

"Hmm, beg your pardon?" Madame Buddenbrook said, her pale eyes drifting off a little to one side.

"A pain 'n th' ol'!" Herr Permaneder said, in his loudest, roughest voice.

"How nice," Elisabeth said, smoothing things over; and that took care of that subject.

"Might I ask," she continued, "what has brought you here to us, sir? It's quite a distance from Munich."

"A li'l deal," Herr Permaneder said, twisting his short hand back and forth in the air. "Jist a tiny li'l deal, ma'am, with the Walkmühle Brewery."

"Oh, right, you are in hops, Herr Permaneder. Noppe & Co., is that right? I can assure you that I've heard many good things about your firm from my son the consul," Madame Buddenbrook said politely.

But Herr Permaneder brushed this aside. " 'tain't nothin' worth mentionin'. Main thing is, I been hank'rin' to pay my respects to you, lovely lady, and to see Frau Grünlich again. That's reason 'nuff to set out on such a long haul."

"Why, thank you," Madame Buddenbrook said cordially, stretching out a hand to him again, the palm turned upward as far as possible. "But now we should tell my daughter of your arrival," she added, standing up and walking toward the braided bell rope.

" 'sindeed. Hell's bells, 'm lookin' for 'ard to that," Herr Permaneder shouted, turning his whole easy chair around to face the door.

Elisabeth told the maid, "Please tell Madame Grünlich to come down, my dear." Then she came back to the sofa—and Herr Permaneder turned his chair around again.

" 'm lookin' for'ard to that," he reiterated absent-mindedly, while examining the wallpaper, the furniture, and the large inkwell of Sèvres porcelain on the secretary. Then he repeated several times,

"Pain in ol'. Reg'lar pain in th' ol'," rubbing his knee and sighing heavily for no apparent reason. This more or less occupied the time until Frau Grünlich appeared.

She had definitely spruced up a little—had put on a light-colored blouse and fixed her hair nicely. Her face was fresher and prettier than ever. The tip of her tongue played mischievously in the corner of her mouth.

"Why, Frau Grünlich! Why, howdy do! How y' been gettin' on all this while? What y' been doin' with yourself up in these parts? Jesus, 'm jist plum tickled. D'you ever think back on our li'l ol' Munich and our mountains? Yessir, we had ourselves some high time, wouldn't y' say? Hell's bells! So here we are again. Now who woulda thought!"

And Tony was just as effusive in her greetings, too; she pulled a chair over and started chatting with him about her weeks in Munich. The conversation flowed now without any problem, and Madame Buddenbrook followed it intently, nodding her encouragement to Herr Permaneder; each time she succeeded in translating some idiom or phrase into standard German, she would lean back against the sofa in satisfaction.

Herr Permaneder had to explain again for Frau Antonie his reasons for being in town, but he obviously set such little store by his "deal" that it appeared he was here for no purpose whatever. All the same, he inquired with great interest about her younger sister and two brothers, expressing loud regrets that both Clara and Christian were not home, because he had "been lookin' for 'ard mightily to meetin' the whole durn fam'ly."

He was quite vague about the length of his stay in town. But then Madame Buddenbrook remarked, "I'm expecting my son for late breakfast any moment now, Herr Permaneder. Would you care to give us the pleasure of your company and join us in a little bite?" And he accepted the invitation before she even finished—so readily, in fact, that he appeared to have been waiting for it.

The consul arrived. Having found no one in the breakfast room, he entered in haste, still wearing his office coat and looking a little weary and overworked—he wanted to remind them that it was time for a quick snack. But, lifting his head now, he was all attention.

One look at their exotic guest with his outlandish watch chain and his loden jacket and the chamois-tufted hat on the harmonium, one mention of a name he had often heard on Tony's lips, and one quick sidelong glance at his sister—and he turned on all his charm to greet Herr Permaneder. He did not even sit down, but immediately joined them to go down to the mezzanine, where Mamselle Jungmann had set the table and started the samovar humming—a genuine samovar, a gift from Pastor Tiburtius and his wife.

"Y'all got things right nice here," Herr Permaneder said as he sat down, gazing out over the selection of cold delicacies on the table. Now and then, at least in the plural, he addressed them with familiar pronouns—but his face was all innocence.

"The beer's not exactly Hofbräu, Herr Permaneder, but it's better than our local brew, at any rate," the consul said, pouring him some of the foaming brown porter he normally drank at this time of day.

"Thanks heaps, neighbor," Herr Permaneder said, chewing away, not even noticing the shocked look on Mamselle Jungmann's face. He was obviously only sipping at his porter, and so Madame Buddenbrook had a bottle of red wine brought in—which visibly cheered him up; and he began again to chat with Frau Grünlich. His paunch forced him to sit at some distance from the table with his legs spread wide, and most of the time he dangled one stout white hand at the end of its short arm over the back of his chair. The expression on his walrus face said that he was very much at home, almost annoyingly so. He had laid his round head to one side, and his guileless eyes sparkled in their little slits as he listened to everything Frau Grünlich said.

Since he had no experience with northern German cuisine, Tony daintily filleted his herring for him, all the while gladly sharing her observations about life in general. "O Lord, how sad it is, Herr Permaneder, that all the good and beautiful things in life pass by so quickly," she said, referring to her stay in Munich, and for a moment she put down her knife and fork and gazed pensively at the ceiling. Now and then she also made quaint, and totally untalented, attempts at speaking the dialect of Bavaria.

While they were eating, there was a knock at the door, and an apprentice from the office delivered a telegram. The consul read it, slowly twirling one tip of his long mustache in his fingers, and although he was plainly preoccupied with the message he was reading, he asked in a most casual tone, "And how is business, Herr Permaneder?" Then he turned to the apprentice and said, "That will do." And the young fellow disappeared.

"Lordy, neighbor," Herr Permaneder replied, turning now to the consul with the awkwardness of a man who has a thick, stiff neck and dangling his other arm over the back of his chair, " 'tain't much to write home 'bout, jist a lotta hard work. Now y' take Munich"—from the way he pronounced the name of his hometown, one could only guess what he meant—"Munich ain't no town for business. Folks want their peace 'n' a mugga beer. And y' certainly wouldn't read no telegram while you're eatin', sure as hell wouldn't. You got another kinda gittup 'n' go up this way, damn if y' don't. Thanks heaps, I'll have 'nother glass. Pain in th' ol'! My partner, Noppe, 's always wantin' to move to Nuremberg, 'cause they got a stock exchange up there 'n' some business smarts. But I ain't gonna leave good ol' Munich. Damned if I am. Pain in ol'! Y' see, we got comp'tition galore, galore! And our export trade's enough t' make a grown man cry. They say they'll be plantin' hops in Russia here shortly."

Suddenly he shot the consul an unusually swift glance and said, "All the same, 'tain't bad as it sounds, neighbor. It's a durn fine li'l business. We make a smart piece of money with the brewery that Neiderpaur's director of. It was jist a li'l deal, but we gave him a bitta credit and some cash money, too—at four p'cent—so he could expand his plant. And now they're doin' right good themselves and we sell 'em our hops and have a nice little income from the int'rest besides—'tain't bad at all," Herr Permaneder concluded; and, declining either cigarette or cigar, he asked if he could smoke his pipe. He pulled it out, a long horn-bowled affair, and from a cloud of smoke he went on talking to the consul about business, which soon led to politics and Bavaria's relations with Prussia, to King Max and Emperor Napoleon—all of it spiced here and there with Herr

Permaneder's totally obscure idioms. Whenever the conversation lagged, he would for no apparent reason emit hefty sighs and say things like: " 't's a hard pull!" or "Ain't that somethin'."

Mamselle Jungmann was so astounded that she forgot to chew what she had in her mouth. She was struck speechless and her shiny brown eyes stared at their guest; as was her habit, she held her knife and fork very erect on the table, waving them slightly back and forth. These rooms had never heard such sounds, never been filled with such pipe fumes—such slovenly, easygoing, formless manners were alien to them. After first making anxious inquiries about the trials that such a small evangelical congregation must necessarily endure amid all those papists, Madame Buddenbrook fell back into amiable incomprehension, and as the meal progressed Tony appeared to grow increasingly pensive and restless. The consul, however, was enjoying himself immensely; he persuaded his mother to have a second bottle of red wine brought up and extended a warm invitation for Herr Permaneder to pay a visit to Breite Strasse—his wife would be simply delighted to have him.

Three hours after his arrival, the hops dealer began to make preparations for departure—he knocked the ashes from his pipe, emptied his glass, declared something or other to be a "pain in th' ol'," and rose from the table. " 't's been an honor, good lady. You take care, now, Frau Grünlich. You take care of yourself, too, Herr Buddenbrook." Ida Jungmann winced and visibly blanched at that. "And a good day to you, missy." He had called her "missy."

Madame Buddenbrook and her son now exchanged glances. Herr Permaneder had announced his intention of returning to the modest inn down on the Trave where he had left his things.

"My daughter's friend and her husband are so far away in Munich," the old woman said, approaching Herr Permaneder, "that we will probably not have an opportunity to repay them for their hospitality soon. But, dear sir, it would please us greatly if you would stay with us as long as you're in town. You would be more than welcome here with us."

She held her hand out to him, and—lo and behold—Herr Permaneder accepted without a second thought. As quickly and eagerly as he had accepted her invitation to breakfast, he now agreed to this proposal and kissed the hands of both ladies—and what an odd figure he made. He collected his hat and cane from the landscape room and promised once again to have his bags brought here at once and to return at four o'clock after taking care of that bit of business.

With the consul in the lead, he descended the stairs now; but as they stood in the vestibule he turned and, shaking his head with quiet fervor, said, "No offense, neighbor, but your sister is one sweet customer. You take care, now." And, still shaking his head, he departed.

The consul felt an irresistible need to go back upstairs and see about the ladies. Ida Jungmann was already scurrying around the house somewhere gathering linens and getting one of the guest rooms on the corridor ready.

But Elisabeth was still at the breakfast table, her pale eyes fixed on a spot on the ceiling, her white fingers softly drumming the tablecloth. Tony was seated at the window, arms crossed; she looked neither to the right nor to the left, but stared straight ahead with a dignified, even stern air. Silence reigned.

"Well?" Thomas asked, standing in the door and taking a cigarette from his case with the troika on the lid. His shoulders bobbed with suppressed laughter.

"A pleasant man," Elisabeth responded innocuously.

"I quite agree," the consul said and turned quickly now—in a quite gallant but humorous way—to Tony, as if humbly asking her opinion. She said nothing. She stared sternly straight ahead.

"But it seems to me he should swear a little less," Elisabeth went on in some distress. "If I understood correctly, he referred frequently to hell and to a most indelicate pain."

"Oh, that's nothing, Mother, he doesn't mean anything by that."

"And perhaps a bit too nonchalant in his manners, Tom, don't you think?"

"O Lord, that's just the way people are in the south," the consul said, slowly exhaling smoke into the room and smiling at his mother. He also stole a glance at Tony, which his mother did not notice.

"You'll come to supper with Gerda, won't you, Tom? As a favor to me?"

"Gladly, Mother, I'd be delighted. To be honest, I expect to be frequently delighted by our visitor, don't you? He's certainly different from your pastors."

"To each his own, Tom."

"No argument there. I must go. Oh, by the way," he said, his hand on the doorknob, "you've made quite an impression on him, Tony. No doubt of it. Do you know what he called you just now downstairs? 'One sweet customer'—his very words."

But now Frau Grünlich turned around to him and said in a loud voice, "Fine, Tom, so you've told me. And I assume he didn't ask you not to. Though I'm not sure if it's proper for you to come bearing tales. But this much I do know, and I want to make it quite clear—what counts in life is not how things are expressed or pronounced, but what the heart feels and intends. And if you want to mock Herr Permaneder's dialect or if you think he's ridiculous . . ."

"What? But, Tony, it would never enter my mind. Why are you so upset?"

"*Assez*," Madame Buddenbrook exclaimed, and threw her son an earnest, imploring glance that said, "Go easy on her."

"Now, don't be angry, Tony," he said. "I wasn't trying to tease you. So, I'll be off now, and I'll give orders for one of the warehouse lads to bring those bags here. Till later, then."

5

HERR PERMANEDER moved into Meng Strasse and dined the following day with Thomas Buddenbrook and his wife; the next day, a Thursday, he became acquainted with Justus Kröger and his wife, with the Ladies Buddenbrook from Breite Strasse, who found him dradfully funny—they said "dradfully"—and with Sesame Weichbrodt, who was rather stern with him, as well as with poor Klothilde and little Erika, whom he gave a sack of "hore-hound," by which he meant candy.

He was a man of inexhaustible good cheer, despite his gloomy sighs, which meant nothing in particular and appeared to arise more from an excess of creature comfort. He had his pipe, his curious dialect, and his capacity for lingering on long after meals were over, always finding the most comfortable position possible to smoke, drink, and chat. And although he brought a totally new and strange tone to the quiet life of the old house, and although his whole being seemed somewhat out of sync, as it were, with its atmosphere, he disturbed none of its customary ways. He was faithful in attending morning and evening services, even asked permission to visit Madame Buddenbrook's Sunday school one morning, and went so far as to appear for a moment on a Jerusalem Evening so that he might be introduced to the ladies—though he withdrew in bewilderment when Lea Gerhardt began to read aloud.

His presence was quickly known all over town, and in the grand houses people were curious about the Buddenbrooks' Bavarian guest; but since Herr Permaneder had no connections with either those families or the men on the exchange, and since it was rather late in the season and most people were getting ready to go to the shore, the consul refrained from introducing him to society. But at every possible opportunity he devoted himself energetically to his guest. Despite all his business and civic duties, he took time to show him the medieval sights of the town—the churches, the gates, the wells, the market, the town hall, the Seaman's Guild—and to keep him well entertained at all times, even introducing him to his closest friends on the exchange. And when his mother took the occasion one day to thank him for sacrificing his time, he dryly remarked, "Yes, Mother, the things one must do."

Madame Buddenbrook offered no response at all to this, did not even smile or lower her eyes. She merely let her gaze drift away and asked a question about a totally different subject.

Her warm cordiality toward Herr Permaneder never varied—but the same could not be said of Tony's treatment of him. Within three or four days of his arrival, he had casually let it be known that he had concluded his business with the local brewery, and yet a good week and a half had passed since then. The hops dealer had attended two "children's days" now, and on both of those Thursdays, whenever Herr Permaneder said or did something, Frau Grünlich would cast a quick skittish glance around the circle of her family—at Uncle Justus, her Buddenbrook cousins, and Thomas—and then she would blush and sit there stiffly, not saying a word. Once she even left the room.

Both windows of Frau Grünlich's bedroom on the third floor were open, and the green blinds were stirring in the warm gentle wind of a clear June night. On the nightstand beside her four-poster, several burning wicks floated in a glass half filled with water and then topped with a layer of oil; they cast an even, dim light across the large silent room and along the high-backed upholstered armchairs protected by slipcovers of gray canvas. Frau Grünlich was in bed. Her pretty head was sunk in the soft pillows trimmed with lace, and her hands lay folded on the quilt. But so many thoughts filled her mind that her eyes could not close and, instead, slowly followed the movements of a large insect with a long abdomen that kept circling the bright glass with a million soundless beatings of its wings. On the wall beside the bed, between two old etchings of the medieval town, was a framed motto that read: "Commit thy ways unto the Lord." But is that any comfort when you are lying open-eyed at midnight and, alone and without advice from anyone, you must answer yes or no, must decide the one question that will determine the rest of your life—and not just your life alone?

Everything was very still—except for the ticking of the clock on the wall and an occasional cough from Mamselle Jungmann's room, which was separated from Tony's only by heavy portieres. There was still light in her room. The faithful Prussian woman was sitting erect at an extension table, directly under the hanging lamp, darning stockings for little Erika—whose deep, peaceful breathing was audible as well, because Sesame Weichbrodt's students were on vacation and she was home for the summer.

Frau Grünlich sat up a little with a sigh and propped her head in her hand.

"Ida?" she asked in a low voice, "are you still darning?"

"Yes, yes, Tony, my child," came Ida's voice. "Go to sleep now, you have to be up early in the morning and you need your rest."

"All right, Ida. And you'll wake me at six?"

"Six-thirty will be early enough. The carriage is to be here at eight. Go back to sleep so that you'll be fresh and pretty."

"Oh, I haven't slept a wink yet."

"Now, now, Tony, that's not being a good girl. You don't want to arrive in Schwartau all worn out, do you? Take seven sips of water, lie on your right side, and count to a thousand."

"Oh, Ida, please come in here for a little. I can't sleep, I tell you. I've so much to think about that my head aches. Would you come check, I think I'm running a fever, and then my stomach's back to its old tricks; or it's anemia, maybe, because the veins at my temples are quite swollen and throbbing so hard it hurts. They're full of blood, which of course does not rule out that there may be too little blood in my head."

She heard a chair being pushed back, and Ida Jungmann's bony, robust form, clad in a simple, unfashionable brown dress, emerged from between the portieres.

"My, my, Tony—fever, you say? Let me feel, my child. I'll fix a little compress."

And, moving to the dresser in her long, firm, somewhat manly strides, she took out a handkerchief and dipped it in the washbasin; returning to the bed, she laid it carefully on Tony's forehead and smoothed it out a couple of times with both hands.

"Thank you, Ida, that helps. Oh, please sit here on the edge of my bed for a while, my good old Ida. You see, I keep thinking about tomorrow. What should I do? It all just keeps spinning around in my head."

Ida sat down next to her, picked up her needle and the darning egg with the stocking stretched over it, and, with her head bent low, the smooth gray hair pulled back tight, and following her stitches with unwearying shiny brown eyes, said, "Do you think he'll ask tomorrow?"

"Of course, Ida. There's no doubt of it. He won't pass this chance by. Remember how it was with Clara? It was an excursion just like this. I could avoid it, you see. I could spend my time with the others and not even let him get near. But then it would all be over. He's leaving the day after tomorrow, he told me so, and he can't possibly stay on if nothing comes of this tomorrow. It *has* to be decided tomorrow. But what should I say, Ida, when he asks? You've never been married and so you don't really know about life, but you're a truthful woman with common sense, and you're forty-two now. Can't you give me some advice? I need it so badly."

Ida Jungmann let her darning fall to her lap. "Yes, yes, Tony, I've thought a lot about it myself. But what I think is that it's well-nigh"—Ida still used words like "well-nigh"—"past time for advising, my child. He can't possibly be leaving now without first speaking to you and your mama, and if you didn't want him, you should've sent him on his way afore this."

"You're right there, Ida; but I couldn't do that, because it simply has to be, that's all. The whole time I kept thinking, I can still pull back, it's not too late. And now here I lie in agony."

"Do you like him, Tony? Now, be honest."

"Yes, Ida. I'd be lying if I said I didn't. He's not handsome, but that's of no consequence in this life, and he's good to the bone, incapable of doing anything mean, believe me. When I think of Grünlich—Oh God! He was always saying how industrious and inventive he was, and cloaked his villainy in the most cunning ways. But Permaneder's not like that, you see. He is, I would say, too comfortable a man for that, he takes life too easy—which is, however, a fault in its own way, too. Because he'll certainly never be a millionaire, and he tends to just let things take their course, I think—he'll always just keep muddlin' through, as they say down south. But they are all like that down there, and that's what I wanted to say, Ida, that's the main thing. Because in Munich, when he was among people just like him, who talked like him and acted like him, I really loved him, thought he was so nice and natural and easygoing. And I noticed at once that the feeling was mutual—although that may have had something to do with his thinking I'm a rich woman, much richer, I'm afraid, than I really am. Because Mother can't give me much of a dowry, as you know. But that won't matter to him, I'm sure of that. He's not the sort of man who is out for a lot of money. But enough of that. What was I saying, Ida?"

"In Munich, Tony—but what about here?"

"Yes, here, Ida. You already know what I'm going to say. He's torn completely out of his own world, and comes here, where everyone is so different, so much more rigid and ambitious and dignified, so to speak. I'm often embarrassed for him here—yes, I'll admit it openly to you, Ida. I'm a truthful woman and I'm embarrassed for him, although that's perhaps sinful of me. You see, several times in conversation he merely said "don't" when he should have said "doesn't." People do that down south, Ida, it happens, even among educated people when they're feeling at their ease—and it doesn't hurt anyone, doesn't bother anyone, it just happens and no one's surprised. But here Mother glances at him out of the corner of her eye, and Tom raises his eyebrow, and Uncle Justus flinches and almost splutters, the way Krögers do when they laugh, and Pfiffi Buddenbrook gives her mother or Friederike or Henriette a *look*, and then I'm so ashamed that I'd just as soon leave the room, and can't even imagine I could ever marry him."

"Now, now, Tony. You'll be living with him in Munich."

"You're right, Ida. But first comes the engagement, and there'll be parties, and I ask you, if I'm going to be ashamed the whole time in front of my own family and the Kistenmakers and the

Möllendorpfs and the rest of them, because he's not all that elegant—Oh, Grünlich was much more elegant, but he was black internally, as Herr Stengel always used to say. Ida, my head is spinning. Could you please freshen my compress?"

Taking the cold compress with a sigh, she began again: "When all is said and done, it simply has to be. Because the point is, has always been, that I need to marry again and stop dawdling around here as a divorced woman. Oh, Ida, I've been thinking about the past so much of late, back when Grünlich first appeared and the scenes he made—it was scandalous, Ida. And Travemünde, too, the Schwarzkopfs," she said slowly, and her eyes rested dreamily for a while on the spot where Erika's stocking had been darned. "And then the engagement and our house in Eimsbüttel—it was elegant, Ida. When I think of my dressing gowns. I'll never have it like that again, not with Permaneder—but life has a way of making us more modest, you know. And then Dr. Klaassen, and my baby, and Kesselmeyer the banker. And then came the end—it was horrible, you have no idea how horrible. And once you've had such ghastly experiences in life . . . But Permaneder won't get involved in nasty things like that. It's the last thing I would expect of him, and we can rely on him when it comes to business, too. Because I really believe that he and Noppe have done very well for themselves with the Niederpaurs' brewery. And once I am his wife, Ida, you'll see. I'll make sure that he's more ambitious, puts out some effort and gets ahead, and is a credit to me and to all of us—that *is* his duty, after all, if he's going to marry a Buddenbrook."

She clasped her hands behind her head and gazed at the ceiling. "Yes, it's over ten years now since I accepted Grünlich. Ten years! And now I'm back in the same position—having to consent to someone's proposal. You know, Ida, life is dreadfully serious, it really is. But the difference is that back then there was such a to-do about it, and everyone was pushing me and torturing me, and now they're all so quiet and still about it, simply assuming that I'll say yes. Because you should know, Ida, that there's nothing festive or joyous about my engagement to Alois—I'm already calling him Alois, because it simply has to be. It's not even a matter of my happiness. But by marrying a second time, very calm and cool, simply as a matter of course, I'm making up for my first marriage. It's my duty, I owe that much to our family name. That's what Mother thinks, that's what Tom thinks."

"Come, come, Tony! If you don't want to marry him, and if he's not going to make you happy—"

"Ida, I know about life—I'm not a silly goose anymore. I have eyes in my head. It may be that Mother wouldn't exactly press me to do it—if there's any doubt about something, she always just looks right on past and says, '*Assez*.' But Tom wants me to. Don't try to tell me anything about Tom. Do you know what Tom thinks? He's saying to himself, 'Anyone! Anyone who is not absolutely unworthy. Because it's not a matter of a brilliant match this time, but solely of patching over the past as best we can with a second marriage.' That's what he thinks. And as soon as Permaneder arrived, Tom very quietly gathered information about his business, you can be sure of that, and when it turned out more or less favorable and solid, the question was resolved then and there. Tom is a politician, and he knows what he wants. Who showed Christian the door? That may be strong language, but that's how it was. And why? Because he compromised the firm and the family, and in Tom's eyes that's what I do, too, Ida—not with deeds and words, but simply by being a divorced woman. And he wants that to stop, and he's right. And God knows I don't love him any less for it, and I hope that he loves me in the same way. In all these years, I have longed for nothing else but to get back into the thick of life, because I am bored here with Mother—God strike me if that's a sin, but I'm barely thirty and I still feel young. Things fall out differently for people in life, Ida; you were gray at thirty, it's in your family, and there was your uncle Prahl, who died of the hiccups. . . ."

She reflected on all this from several angles that night, but every now and then she would say once more, "When all is said and done it simply has to be." And then she slept for five hours—a gentle, deep sleep.

6

A LIGHT FOG lay over the town as the large carriage, open on all sides, pulled onto Meng Strasse; but Herr Longuet, who owned the livery stable on Johannis Strasse and was doing the driving this morning, said, "Won't be more'n hour 'nd the sun'll be shinin' "—so there was no need to worry.

Madame Buddenbrook, Antonie, Herr Permaneder, Erika, and Ida Jungmann had breakfasted together; and now, ready for their excursion, they gathered one by one in the large entrance hall to wait for Tom and Gerda. Frau Grünlich was wearing a cream-colored dress with a satin scarf tied at the chin, and despite a short night's rest she looked splendid. The quandaries and questions seemed to be at an end, for as she slowly buttoned up her gloves and chatted with their guest, her face was calm, assured, almost solemn. She had rediscovered the mood that she had once known so well. She was filled with a sense of her own importance, the significance of the decision she was asked to make, the awareness that once again a day had come on which duty demanded that she act earnestly and decisively to alter her family's history—and her heart beat higher. Last night, in her dreams, she had seen the spot in the family records where she intended to enter the fact of her second engagement—a fact that would erase and render meaningless the black smudge contained within those pages. She was looking forward to the moment when Tom would appear and she would greet him with a dignified nod.

The consul and his wife arrived a little late—Gerda was not accustomed to being up and ready so early in the day. Tom looked good in his tan, small-checked suit with broad lapels that revealed the edge of his summer vest; he was cheerful and a smile came into his eyes at the sight of Tony's incomparable dignity. But, in curious contrast to her sister-in-law's glowing prettiness, Gerda's beauty was somehow unwholesome and enigmatic—and she was definitely not in the mood for a Sunday excursion. Presumably she had not had enough sleep. The rich lilac of her gown matched her heavy, dark chestnut hair in some very odd way and made her lusterless complexion look paler than ever; even the bluish shadows seemed deeper and darker in the corners of her close-set brown eyes. She coolly offered her mother-in-law her brow for a kiss, gave her hand to Herr Permaneder, but with a rather ironic look on her face, and, when Frau Grünlich clapped her hands and cried in a loud voice, "Gerda, oh, heavens, how *lovely* you do look!," she responded with only a dismissive smile.

She had a deep dislike of the kind of undertaking ahead of them today, especially in summer, and most especially on a Sunday. She lived in the twilight of her curtained rooms, seldom went out, and dreaded the sun, the dust, the common people in their Sunday best, the smell of coffee, beer, and tobacco. And most of all she loathed the *dérangement*, the heat, and the confusion. And when the arrangements had been made for this trip to Riesebusch Inn in Schwartau to show their guest from Munich a little something of the surrounding countryside, she had remarked offhandedly to Thomas, "Dearest, you know how I am. God made me for the quiet of everyday life, and not for bustle and novelty. You will make apologies for me, won't you?"

She would never have married him if she had not been certain of his virtual approval in such matters.

"Lord, yes, Gerda, you're right, of course. For the most part we just imagine that such excursions are amusing. But one goes along with it because one doesn't want to appear odd to the others, or to oneself. Everyone has that much vanity, don't you think? Otherwise one quickly finds oneself regarded as an unhappy loner and is held in less esteem. And one more thing, dear Gerda. We all have good reason to court Herr Permaneder a bit. I don't doubt you're well aware of the situation. Things are developing, and it would be a shame, a downright shame, if nothing came of it."

"I don't see, dearest, how my presence—but no matter. Since you wish it, that's how it will be. Let us endure these amusements."

"I would be much obliged."

They stepped out onto the street. And, indeed, the sun now began to pierce the morning fog; the bells of St. Mary's rang out the Sunday, and birdcalls filled the air. The coachman tipped his hat and Madame Buddenbrook gave a nod of excessive kindness and said, "Good morning, my good man," with the sort of patronizing benevolence that Thomas found embarrassing on occasion. "And now let us climb aboard, my dears," she continued. "Early services are just starting, but we shall lift our hearts and praise God in the glory of nature, isn't that right, Herr Permaneder?"

"Sure is, ma'am."

And, one after another, they climbed the two metal steps that led to the small door at the rear of the coach, which could have easily seated ten adults, and made themselves comfortable on pillows striped in the white and blue of Bavaria—doubtless in honor of Herr Permaneder. Then the door was slammed shut, and as Herr Longuet clicked his tongue and shouted various "gee"s and "haw"s, the coach rolled down Meng Strasse, followed the Trave on past Holsten Gate, and then turned off onto Schwartau Road.

Fields, meadows, stands of trees, farmsteads—and they searched the rising fog, growing bluer as it thinned, for the larks they could hear above them. Smoking his cigarettes, Thomas looked about attentively whenever they passed a field of grain and apprised Herr Permaneder of how each was doing. The hops dealer was in a truly youthful mood; he jauntily cocked his green hat with its chamois tuft, he balanced his cane with its huge deerhorn handle on the broad white palm of his hand, and even on his lower lip—a parlor trick that never quite succeeded, but was greeted with such great applause, particularly from little Erika, that he repeated it several times.

"Won't be the Zugspitz, don't s'pose, but we'll have to hoof it a bit, and we'll have a high ol' time, reg'lar field day, damn if we won't—ain't that right, Frau Grünlich?"

Then he began a lively account of mountain-climbing expeditions with backpacks and ice-axes, and was rewarded for his efforts by

Elisabeth Buddenbrook, who exclaimed "My word!" at several points. This train of thought somehow led him to express his regrets that Christian was not with them and to say that he had heard he was quite a hoot.

"That varies," the consul said. "But he's incomparable on occasions like this, that's true. We shall have crabs for lunch, Herr Permaneder," he went on, in high spirits himself. "Crabs and fresh shrimp from the Baltic. You've already sampled them a few times at my mother's table, but my friend Dieckmann, who owns the Riesebusch Inn, always serves the very best. And gingersnaps, the famous local specialty. Or has their fame not yet reached the banks of the Isar? Well, you'll soon see."

Frau Grünlich had the carriage stop two or three times so that she could pick poppies and cornflowers along the side of the road, and each time Herr Permaneder protested vehemently that he wanted to help her—but since he was a little nervous about climbing in and out, he refrained from doing so.

Erika reveled at every crow that took wing; and as a dependable governess Ida Jungmann responded to every mood of her young charge, not just outwardly but with childlike empathy. Dressed as always in an open raincoat and carrying an umbrella—even in the most settled weather—she now chimed in with her own frank, somewhat whinnying laughter. Gerda, who had not watched Ida grow old in service to the family, gazed at her with a kind of chilly amazement.

They were in the Duchy of Oldenburg now. They could see groves of beech in the distance. They drove into the village, passing through the little market square with its fountain, and then back out into the countryside, and after rolling over the bridge across the little Au River, they finally halted at the Riesebusch, a low, one-story inn, flanked on one side by a level lawn with sandy paths and rustic flower beds, behind which rose an amphitheater of woods. Crude sets of stairs formed from protruding roots and jutting rocks led from one tier to the next, and at each level white wooden tables, benches, and chairs were set out among the trees.

The Buddenbrooks were certainly not the only guests. A few stout maids and even a waiter in a greasy frock coat were marching at high speed across the lawn, bearing cold plates, lemonade, milk, and beer up to the tables, several of which were already occupied by scattered families with their children.

Herr Dieckmann, the innkeeper, appeared in his shirtsleeves and a yellow-embroidered cap to assist personally in handing the party down from their carriage. As Longuet drove the carriage off to unhitch, Elisabeth remarked to Dieckmann, "We shall first go for a little walk, my good man, and then, in an hour or so, we shall have our luncheon. Would you serve us at one of those tables there, please, but not too high up—on the second level, I think."

"Do your best, Dieckmann," the consul added. "We have a guest who's hard to please."

Herr Permaneder protested, "Damn 'f I am. Some rat-trap and a brew's fine by me."

Herr Dieckmann, however, did not quite understand what he'd said, and so began to rattle off his menu. "Anything you'd like, Consul Buddenbrook—crabs, shrimp, all kinds of cold cuts, cheeses, smoked eel, smoked salmon, smoked sturgeon."

"Fine, Dieckmann. You'll do it up right, I'm sure. And then we'll have—six glasses of milk and one mug of beer, if I'm not mistaken, Herr Permaneder?"

"One beer, six milks. Sweet milk, buttermilk, sour milk, Herr Buddenbrook?"

"Half sweet, half buttermilk, Dieckmann. In an hour or so." And now they proceeded across the lawn.

"Our first duty, Herr Permaneder, is to visit the spring," Thomas said. "The spring is the source of the Au, and the Au is the little river on which Schwartau lies. Back in the darkest Middle Ages, our own town was also situated on the Au, until it burned down—it wasn't a very permanent affair in those days, you see—and was rebuilt on the Trave. There are some rather painful memories connected with the name of that little river. When we were boys, we thought it great sport to pinch each other in the arm and ask, 'What's the name of Schwartau's river?' And the pinches hurt, of course, so we would reluctantly supply the correct answer. But look there," he said, interrupting himself—they were about ten steps from the base of the hill now—"someone's here ahead of us—the Möllendorpfs and the Hagenströms."

And, indeed, there on the third tier of the wooded terrace were the principal members of the two families, now related by marriage to their mutual advantage. Two tables had been joined together, and there they sat, eating and conversing breezily. Old Senator Möllendorpf presided—a pallid, diabetic gentleman with sparse white whiskers that ended in two points. His wife, née Langhals, was fidgeting with her long-handled lorgnette, and as always disheveled gray hair framed her face. Their son was there, too—August, a blond young man who exuded prosperity; with him was his wife, Julie, née Hagenström, who was sitting between her brothers, Hermann and Moritz—a short, energetic woman with large bright black eyes and equally large diamonds dangling from her earlobes. Consul Hermann Hagenström was beginning to get quite stout, for he lived very well, and it was said that he even started his day with *pâté de foie gras*. He sported a reddish blond, short-cropped beard and his flat nose—his mother's nose—lay conspicuously flat against his upper lip. Moritz still had his shallow chest and yellow complexion, and his pointed gap-teeth showed whenever he spoke in his lively way. Both brothers had their wives with them—lawyer Moritz had married several years before as well: a Fräulein Puttfarken from Hamburg, a lady with butter-colored hair and an exceptionally impassive, decidedly English-looking face, with beautiful and terribly regular features. Moritz Hagenström would never have compromised his reputation as a man of taste and wit by marrying an ugly girl. Also present were Hermann Hagenström's little daughter and Moritz's little son—two children dressed in white, who were already as good as engaged to one another, because the Huneus-Hagenström fortune was not to be scattered and lost. They were all eating scrambled eggs and ham.

They did not exchange greetings until the Buddenbrooks began climbing the stairs close by. Elisabeth gave an absent-minded and, so to speak, surprised nod; Thomas tipped his hat and moved his lips as if making some polite yet cool remark; and Gerda made an odd, formal bow. Herr Permaneder, however, was exhilarated by the climb and nonchalantly swung his green hat and called out in a loud, merry voice, "Right good mornin' to y'all." Madame Möllendorpf immediately reached for her lorgnette. For her part, Tony raised her shoulders just a little, laid her head back, trying all the while to tuck her chin against her chest, and greeted them as if from unattainable heights, her glance brushing past Julie Möllendorpf's broad-brimmed, elegant hat. At that moment her decision was irrevocably fixed for good and all.

"Thank the good Lord—and a thousand thanks to you, Tom—that we're not eating for an hour yet. I wouldn't want to have Julie watching my every bite. Did you see how she greeted us? As good as not at all. Although in my humble opinion her hat was in quite abominable taste."

"Well, I can't speak as to the hat. And as far as greeting goes, you weren't all that much more accommodating, my dear. But don't let it annoy you so—it causes wrinkles."

"Let it annoy me, Tom? Oh no. Those people may think they're the cream of the crop, but all anyone can do is laugh. What is the difference between me and that Julie, might I ask? Her husband didn't turn out to be a scoundrel, just a blatherskite, as Ida would say, and if she ever found herself in my situation, we would soon see whether she could ever find a second one."

"Does that imply that you'll find one yourself?"

"A blatherskite, Thomas?"

"It's much better than a scoundrel."

"It doesn't have to be either. But it's best we not speak of it."

"Right. We're falling behind. Herr Permaneder is an energetic climber."

The shady woodland path leveled out, and it was not long before they had reached the spring, a lovely, romantic spot where a wooden bridge crossed a small ravine with steep, creviced sides and overhanging trees with exposed roots. Elisabeth had brought along a collapsible silver cup, and they dipped it in a small stone basin just below the source, refreshing themselves with cool water that tasted of iron. Herr Permaneder was seized with a little attack of gallantry and insisted that Frau Grünlich first taste his drink for him. He was all gratitude, repeating over and over, "Now, ain't that nice." He chatted tactfully and attentively with Elisabeth and Thomas, as well as with Gerda and Tony and even little Erika. Gerda, who thus far had been slightly flushed with the heat and had walked nervously beside them, silent and stiff, began to come alive now; and, indeed, after they had returned at a faster pace to the inn and were sitting down at their table laden with food on the second level of wooded terraces, it was Gerda who, in the most charming phrases, expressed her regret that Herr Permaneder would be departing so soon, just when they were all becoming a little better acquainted, and when, as she had noted by way of example, there were fewer and fewer confusions or misunderstandings resulting from differences in dialect. She was even ready to assert that on two or three occasions her friend and sister-in-law, Tony, had managed "Y'all take care now!" with absolute virtuosity.

Herr Permaneder refrained from any comment that might have confirmed an imminent departure and instead devoted himself to the vast array of delicacies on the table—certainly not the daily fare below the Danube.

They took their time eating all these good things, although little Erika seemed most delighted by the tissue-paper napkins, which she considered incomparably more beautiful than the large linen ones they used at home, even sticking a few of them in her pocket as souvenirs—after first asking the waiter's permission. While the consul smoked cigarettes and Herr Permaneder puffed away on several very black cigars and drank his beer, the family sat chatting with their guest for quite a long time. But the remarkable thing was that no one said anything more about Herr Permaneder's departure—indeed, the future was left totally unmentioned. Instead, they reminisced and talked about the political events of the past few years. Herr Permaneder jiggled with laughter at the anecdotes that Madame Buddenbrook told about her late husband's role in the events of '48, and in return he reported about the revolution in Munich and about Lola Montez, in whom Frau Grünlich took an immense interest. Noon came and another hour passed, but it was not until Erika returned, all flushed from her expedition with Ida, her pockets stuffed full of daisies, lady's-smock, and grasses, and reminded them of the gingersnaps that still had to be bought, that they started off on a walk to the village—but only after Elisabeth, who was their hostess today, had paid the bill with a good-sized gold coin.

Orders were given at the inn to have the carriage ready in an hour, since they would want to rest for an hour or so before sitting down to dinner in town; and then they slowly strolled in the hot, dusty sunshine toward the low roofs of the village.

Shortly after passing the bridge over the Au, they arranged themselves quite naturally and of their own accord into three groups that were maintained for the rest of the way: at the head, given her long stride, was Mamselle Jungmann and beside her little Erika, who leapt about in untiring pursuit of small white butterflies; this pair was followed by Elisabeth, Thomas, and Gerda; and at some distance behind walked Frau Grünlich and Herr Permaneder. It was noisy at the head of the procession, because the little girl constantly shrieked with glee and Ida joined in, laughing in her singular deep, kindly whinny. The three in the middle were silent—all the dust had brought on another attack of Gerda's moody nervousness, and both Madame Buddenbrook and her son were lost in their own thoughts. Things seemed quiet at the rear, too, but in fact Tony and her Bavarian guest were engaged in subdued, intimate conversation. And what were they talking about? About Herr Grünlich.

Herr Permaneder had made the accurate observation that Erika was a "durn" sweet, pretty child, but that she bore almost no resemblance to her mother.

To which Tony responded, "She's her father all over, and is none the worse for it, one might say. Because externally Grünlich was a gentleman—to a tee. He had gold-colored muttonchops; quite original—I've never seen the like."

And although Tony had told him the story of her marriage in some detail when she was visiting the Niederpaurs in Munich, he queried her once again about the whole affair, squinting in anxious sympathy and inquiring in particular about the specifics of the bankruptcy.

"He was a wicked man, Herr Permaneder, otherwise my father would not have taken me away from him, you can be sure of that. Not everyone on this earth has a good heart—life has taught me that, you see, as young as I am, with only ten years of widowhood or whatever behind me. He was wicked, and Kesselmeyer, his banker, was even more wicked—and sillier than a puppy besides. But please don't misunderstand me—that does not mean that I consider myself an angel and free of all guilt. Grünlich neglected me, and when he did sit down with me, it was only to read his newspaper; he deceived me, just left me sitting there in Eimsbüttel—because if I had been in town I would have learned of the mess he had got himself into. But I am only a poor weak woman myself. I have my shortcomings, and I'm quite certain that I didn't always do the right thing. For example, I gave my husband good reason to worry and complain about my frivolousness and extravagance and new dressing gowns. But let me say one thing as well: I do have some excuse, and that is that I was a mere child when I married, a goose, a silly young thing. Can you believe, for instance, that it was only very shortly before my marriage that I learned that the Confederation's laws concerning the universities and the press had been renewed? Fine laws those were, by the way. Ah yes, it's sad but true—one has but one life to live, Herr Permaneder, and there's no starting all over again. There are so many things one would be wiser about."

She fell silent and looked anxiously down at the road. She had given him an opening—had done so quite skillfully, in fact, since it was now but an easy step to the idea that, although a whole new life was impossible, that did not exclude beginning again in a new and better marriage. Except that Herr Permaneder let the chance go by and confined himself to censuring Herr Grünlich in such strong terms that the goatee on his little round chin bristled.

"What a puny, disgustin' cuss! If I had that mangy dog here right now, I'd knock him into next week."

"Shame, shame, Herr Permaneder! No, you must stop that right now. We must forgive and forget, and 'Vengeance is mine, saith the Lord'—you need only ask mother. Heaven forbid! I have no idea where Grünlich may be now or how life has treated him, but I wish him the best, even if he perhaps does not deserve it."

They were in the village now, standing in front of a little house that also served as the bakery shop. They had stopped almost without knowing why. Although they had spoken only of silly, unimportant things, they were so absorbed in their conversation that their solemn eyes were oblivious to the fact that Erika, Ida, Elisabeth, Thomas, and Gerda had ducked through the ridiculously low door and vanished.

Next to them was a fence, enclosing a long, narrow flower bed where a few mignonettes were growing in the loose, black soil, which Frau Grünlich, her flushed face bent low, now began to plow with the tip of her parasol. Herr Permaneder, whose green hat with its chamois tuft had slipped down over his forehead, stood beside her and joined her in cultivating the bed with his deerhorn cane. His head was hung low, too, but his little, pale blue, puffy eyes were glistening, had even reddened a little, and he looked up at her with a mixture of devotion, distress, and apprehension—the drooping, frayed fringe of his mustache even took on the same expression.

"And so now, I s'pose," he said, "you're dreadful feared of gettin' married 'n' wouldn't ever try it again, 'm I right, Frau Grünlich?"

"How inept of him," she thought. "Am I supposed to agree to that?" But she answered, "Yes, dear Herr Permaneder, I will be frank with you. It would be difficult for me ever to consent to a proposal of marriage again, for life has taught me, you see, what a dreadfully serious decision that is. One must have the firm conviction that the gentleman is truly honest, and noble, and kindhearted."

And now he ventured to ask whether she considered him such a man.

To which she replied, "Yes, Herr Permaneder, I believe you are."

And now there followed a very few softly spoken words that constituted their engagement and gave Herr Permaneder permission to speak to Elisabeth and Thomas once they had returned home.

When the rest of the party, laden with large sacks of gingersnaps, emerged from the shop, Thomas let his eyes drift discreetly over their heads—they were both obviously very embarrassed. Herr Permaneder made no attempt to disguise the fact, but Tony hid her confusion behind a mask of almost majestic dignity.

They hurried to get back to their coach, because the sky had clouded over and the first drops of rain were falling.

As Tony had assumed, her brother had gathered precise information about Herr Permaneder's affairs shortly after his arrival. What he had learned was that X. Noppe & Co. was a smallish but quite solid firm, which, in conjunction with the joint-stock brewery headed by Herr Niederpaur, turned a tidy profit, and that Herr Permaneder's share, together with Tony's seventeen thousand thalers *courant*, would be sufficient for them to live a respectable life together, although it would be without luxury. Madame Buddenbrook had been informed of this; and that same evening, she joined Herr Permaneder, Antonie, and Thomas in the landscape room for a discussion in which all questions were resolved without difficulty—even those concerning little Erika. It was Tony's wish, to which her fiancé agreed in a touching scene, that Erika join them in Munich.

The hops dealer departed two days later—" 'cause otherwise Noppe'll start raisin' holy hell." In July, however, Frau Grünlich arrived in his beloved hometown, accompanied by Tom and Gerda, whom she then joined for four or five weeks in Bad Kreuth. Madame Buddenbrook, however, spent her summer vacation with Erika and Mamselle Jungmann on the shores of the Baltic. While they were in Munich, the two couples took the opportunity to have a look at the house on Kaufinger Strasse—very near the Niederpaurs', in fact—that Herr Permaneder was about to buy, with the intention of renting out most of it. It was a very curious old house—on opening the front door, you were confronted with a narrow stairway, which, like Jacob's ladder, ran straight up in a single flight, without a turn or a landing, to the second floor, where you then had to walk in either direction down a long corridor to the rooms at the front and back of the house.

In the middle of August, Tony returned home to devote the next few weeks to her trousseau. There were a great many things still left from her first marriage, but she had to buy some new items to supplement them. One day a package arrived from Hamburg, where she had ordered several things, and it contained a dressing gown—

trimmed, this time, not with velvet, of course, but with little cotton bows.

In late autumn Herr Permaneder reappeared on Meng Strasse—it was decided to delay things no longer. Just as Tony had expected, and indeed wanted, the wedding festivities were carried out with no great to-do. "Let's forget the pomp and ceremony," the consul said. "You are to be a married woman again, and it's simply as if you have never ceased to be one." Only a few engagement announcements were sent—although Madame Grünlich made sure that Julie Möllendorpf, née Hagenström, received one of them—and there was to be no honeymoon, since Herr Permaneder detested such "fuss 'n' bother" and Tony, who had recently returned from her summer vacation, thought the trip back to Munich would be quite long enough. This time the ceremony took place in St. Mary's rather than in the columned hall, with only the closest family attending. Tony wore her orange blossoms, which replaced the sprays of myrtle, with great dignity; and although Pastor Kölling's voice was somewhat weaker than on the first occasion, he still preached *temperance* in the strongest of terms.

Christian arrived from Hamburg, dressed very elegantly; he looked a little peaked, but he was in high spirits and declared that business and Burmeester were both "tip-top" and that he and Klothilde would probably have to wait to get married "in heaven—separately, I mean." And he arrived at the church much too late for the ceremony, because he had paid a visit to the Club. Uncle Justus was very touched and proved as generous as always, giving the newlyweds an extraordinarily beautiful sterling-silver epergne—despite the fact that he and his weak-willed wife almost went hungry at home, because she continued to use her household money to pay the debts of the disowned and outcast Jakob, who was living in Paris at present, so people said. The Ladies Buddenbrook from Breite Strasse commented, "Well, let's hope it lasts this time." What made this even more unpleasant was a general doubt that they hoped anything of the sort. Sesame Weichbrodt, however, stood on her tiptoes, kissed her former ward—now Frau Permaneder—on the brow with a soft popping sound, and said with her most warmly exaggerated vowels, "Be heppy, you *good* chawld."

7

WHEN CONSUL BUDDENBROOK left his bed each morning, he would descend to the ground floor via the spiral staircase hidden behind the little door, take his bath, and put his dressing gown back on—and by eight o'clock he was already engaged in civic affairs. Because at precisely that hour Herr Wenzel, the barber and member of the town council, would appear in his bathroom, a man with an intelligent face and red hands, in which he carried the tools of his trade and a basin of warm water fetched from the kitchen. The consul would sit down in a large armchair and lay his head back, Herr Wenzel would begin to lather his soap—and then there almost always ensued a conversation that started with the weather and how each had slept, but soon turned to events in the great, wide world, moved on to the town's domestic affairs, and generally concluded with very personal matters of business and family. All of which tended to prolong the process, because, whenever the consul spoke, Herr Wenzel would have to lift the razor from his face.

"Did you sleep well, Consul Buddenbrook?"

"Yes, thanks. Good weather today?"

"Below freezing and a little fog and snow, Herr Buddenbrook. The boys have fixed themselves up another slide, good thirty foot long, out in front of St. Jakob's, and I almost took a tumble as I was leaving the mayor's house. Damn those kids."

"Have you seen the papers?"

"Yes, the *Advertiser* and the Hamburg *News*. Nothing but Orsini and his bombs—gruesome. On the way to the opera, it was. Nice bunch of folks they have there."

"Well, I don't think it means much. The common folk aren't involved in it, and the only result is that they'll just double the police and increase the pressure on the press and the rest of it. He won't take any chances. Yes, things are always in a turmoil, true enough, and he's constantly having to come up with new schemes just to stay in power. But he has my respect—no matter what. Given *their* traditions, there's no way the man can be a blatherskite, as Mamselle Jungmann would say, and the way he managed the bakery fund and cheap bread, for instance, that impressed me no end. He does a great deal for the common people, no doubt of it."

"Yes, Herr Kistenmaker was saying the same thing just this morning."

"Stephan? We were speaking about it yesterday."

"And Friedrich Wilhelm of Prussia's doing poorly, Herr Buddenbrook. Things can't go on like this. People are saying the prince should be made regent for good and all."

"Oh, I'm anxious to see what happens there. He's already shown his liberal tendencies, Wilhelm has, and doesn't share his brother's secret disgust for the constitution. Ultimately, it's only grief that has worn him down, the poor man. Anything new from Copenhagen?"

"Not a thing, Herr Buddenbrook. They're not about to do it. The Confederation can declare the constitution for a united Holstein and Lauenburg to be illegal all they want. Those fellows up there are simply not about to abandon it."

"Yes, it's quite outrageous, Wenzel. They're simply daring the Bundestag to act—if only it were just a little more alert. Oh, these Danes! I can recall quite well how as a young lad one verse of a hymn always annoyed me, 'Jesus loves his children all, disdains not one most lowly,' which I took to mean 'this Dane's not one most lowly' and couldn't understand why he should be better than I. Don't laugh so hard, and watch that chapped spot there, Wenzel. Well, and here we are back again to the question of a direct railroad line to Hamburg. It's already cost a lot of diplomatic blood, and will cost a lot more before Copenhagen gives in."

"Yes, Herr Buddenbrook, and the stupid thing is that the Altona-Kiel Railroad Company is against it, and all Holstein, too, when you get down to it. Mayor Oeverdieck was saying that just this morning, too. They're dreadfully afraid of an economic boom in Kiel."

"That's understandable, Wenzel. A new connection like that between the Baltic and North Seas. And just you wait, those Altona-Kiel fellows won't stop their scheming against it. They're perfectly capable of building a competing line—East Holstein, Neumünster, Neustadt. No, sir, it's not out of the question. But we can't let ourselves be cowed, and we need a direct line to Hamburg."

"You need to get involved in the matter yourself, Herr Buddenbrook."

"Yes, well, as far as it's in my powers and to the extent I have any influence. I'm interested in railroad policy—it's a tradition with us. My father was on the board of directors of the Büchen Line as far back as '51, which is probably the reason I've been elected to it at age thirty-two. I've not done all that much to deserve it."

"Oh, now, Herr Buddenbrook, what about that speech you gave in the council?"

"Yes, I probably did make some impression with that, and there's no lack of good will, at any rate. I can only be grateful, you know, that my father, grandfather, and great-grandfather paved the way for me, and that a great deal of the trust and esteem they gained in this town have automatically fallen to me. Otherwise I couldn't move a finger. For example, just think of what all my father did after '48, and on through the beginning of this decade, for the postal system. Think back, Wenzel, how he prodded the council to merge the post with the Hamburg coach system, or in 1850 how he pushed the senate, which was so irresponsibly slow in those days, to join the Austro-German Postal Union. If we have lower postal rates these days—and stamps and book rates and mailboxes and a telegraph connection between Berlin and Travemünde—he's not the last person we have to thank for it, and if he and a few other people had not constantly urged the senate to act, we would have lagged behind the Danish and Thurn and Taxis postal services forever. And so, when I offer my opinion about such matters now, people listen."

"God knows they do, Herr Buddenbrook, you've never spoken a truer word. And as far as the Hamburg line goes—it wasn't three days ago that Mayor Oeverdieck said to me, 'Once we get to the point where we can purchase a suitable site for a station in Hamburg, we'll send Consul Buddenbrook. Consul Buddenbrook's better at such negotiations than many a lawyer.' Those were his very words."

"Well, that's very flattering, Wenzel. But put a little more lather here on my chin—it needs to be shaved cleaner. Yes, in point of fact, we need to get moving there. Not that I have anything against Oeverdieck, but he's getting up in years, and if I were mayor things would all move a little more quickly, I think. I can't tell you what satisfaction it gives me to see that they've finally begun work on the gas lanterns and are getting rid of those ghastly oil lamps hanging from chains. I must admit that I had a little something to do with that project. Oh, the things that need to be done! Because the times are changing, Wenzel, and we have a great many responsibilities in light of the new age ahead. When I think of my early boyhood—well, you know better than I how things looked around here back then. No sidewalks, grass growing a foot high between the cobblestones, and houses with bays and stoops and benches jutting out into the streets. And the buildings from the Middle Ages disfigured with all sorts of lean-tos, and just crumbling away—although people had money and no one was starving. But the city itself didn't have a penny and just muddled along, as my brother-in-law, Permaneder, would say, and repairs were out of the question. Those were happy, easygoing times back then, when my grandfather's crony good old Jean Jacques Hoffstede strolled about and translated little off-color poems from the French. But things couldn't go on like that forever. So much has changed and will have to go right on changing. We no longer have thirty-seven thousand inhabitants, but well over fifty now, as you know, and the whole nature of the town is changing. We have new construction and expanding suburbs and good streets, and we can afford to restore the grand monuments from our past. But those are mere externals. The most important matters still lie ahead of us, my good Wenzel. Which brings me right back to the *ceterum censeo* of my late father: the Customs Union. Wenzel, we have to join the Customs Union—that shouldn't even be an issue, and I need you all to help me fight for it. Believe me, as a merchant I know more about it than any diplomat, and in this case any fears about losing our independence and freedom are ridiculous. It would open up the interior, Mecklenburg and Schleswig-Holstein, to us, and that is all the more desirable since we no longer control the northern trade as completely as we once did. But enough—the towel, please, Wenzel," the consul concluded.

And then, after something was said about the current price of rye—fifty-five thalers and still falling, damn it—and perhaps a comment made about some event in the life of one of the town's families, Herr Wenzel vanished down the ground-floor hall to empty his shiny shaving bowl out on the cobblestones, and the consul climbed back up the spiral stairs to his bedroom, where Gerda was awake now. Then he would kiss her on the forehead and dress.

These little morning conversations with the astute barber acted as the prelude to busy, active days, filled to overflowing with thinking, speaking, dealing, writing, calculating, moving here and there about town. As a result of his travels, his knowledge, and his interests, Thomas Buddenbrook had the least provincial mind of any of the men around him, and he was certainly the first to realize the limits of the world in which he moved. But out in the broad expanses of his Fatherland, the renewal in public affairs that had accompanied the years of revolution had given way to a period of lethargy, stagnation, and regression much too dreary to occupy a lively mind. Thomas, however, had imagination enough to adopt as his personal precept the old maxim that all human endeavor is merely symbolic, and to place all his aspirations, abilities, enthusiasm, and active energies both at the service of this small community, where the name Buddenbrook placed him in the first ranks, and at the service of that name and the family firm he had inherited—indeed, he had imagination enough to take seriously his ambition of attaining greatness and power in this small sphere and at the same time to smile at himself for being so ambitious.

Anton always served him his breakfast in the dining room, and as soon as he had eaten he would finish dressing and walk to his office on Meng Strasse. He seldom stayed there much over an hour; he would write two or three urgent letters and telegrams, give an order here, an instruction there, nudging, as it were, the great wheel of industry and leaving its further revolutions to the watchful eye and sidelong glances of Herr Marcus.

He would appear and often speak at meetings and assemblies, spend some time under the Gothic arches of the exchange on the market square, make a tour of inspection along the docks and in the warehouses, negotiate with the captains of the ships he owned. Interrupted only by a quick second breakfast with his mother and by dinner with Gerda, after which he might spend a half-hour on the sofa with a cigar and a newspaper, he kept busy at his work until well into the evening—if not his firm's affairs, then customs, taxes, railroads, new construction, the post, the care of the poor. He even learned a thing or two about matters that were normally the concern of "professionals," and quickly showed that he had special talents in the arena of higher finance.

He was careful not to neglect his social duties. Granted, his punctuality in such matters left much to be desired. It never failed—his wife would be sitting, dressed and ready, in the carriage, and he would appear at the very last moment, a half-hour late, cry, "I'm sorry, Gerda—business," and hastily change into a frock coat. But when they arrived at the dinner or ball or soirée, he knew how to be an amiable conversationalist and show a lively interest in everything. And the entertainments he and his wife provided were the equal of those in other wealthy homes. His kitchen and wine cellar were considered "tip-top"; he was admired as a polite, attentive, tactful host; and the wit he displayed in his toasts was well above average. He spent his quiet evenings at home with Gerda, smoking and listening to her play the violin or reading a book aloud with her—German, French, or Russian stories that she had picked out.

He worked hard, and success was his. His standing in town grew, and, despite the capital lost through setting Christian up on his own and Tony's second marriage, the firm had several excellent years. Nevertheless, there were a few things that could sap his courage for hours on end, dulling the sharpness of his mind and casting him into gloom.

There was, for example, Christian in Hamburg, whose partner, Herr Burmeester, had died suddenly of a stroke in that spring of 1858. His heirs had drawn their money out of the business, and the consul strongly advised Christian not to continue with only his own funds, because he knew quite well how difficult it was to keep a large-scale business going once its capital was suddenly reduced. But Christian insisted on remaining independent and assumed both the assets and the liabilities of H. C. F. Burmeester & Co.—and it was to be feared that unpleasant events lay ahead.

And then there was the consul's sister Clara in Riga. It was perhaps no matter that her marriage with Pastor Tiburtius had not been blessed with children, particularly since Clara Buddenbrook had never wanted them and almost certainly had very few of the requisite maternal talents. But, to judge from her husband's letters, her health was not of the best; and the headaches from which she had suffered as a child now appeared with periodic regularity and had grown almost unbearable.

That was disquieting. And even at home, there was a third worry—the perpetuation of the family name was still not assured. Gerda responded to this issue with a sovereign indifference that came very close to repugnance. Thomas was distressed, but said nothing. His mother, Madame Buddenbrook, however, took the matter in hand, pulling Grabow aside to ask, "Just between us, doctor, something must be done, don't you think? A little mountain air in Bad Kreuth or a little sea air in Glücksburg or Travemünde doesn't seem to have had any effect. What do you suggest?" And since in this case his usual remedy of "a strict diet, a little squab, a little French bread" did not seem to be quite aggressive enough as a treatment, Grabow prescribed a trip to Pyrmont and Schlangenbad.

Those were three of his worries. And Tony? Poor Tony!

8

SHE WROTE:

> And she doesn't understand when I say "croquettes" because they call them "patties" here; and when she says "snappers" it isn't easy for an ordinary Christian to realize that she means "green beans"; and if I say "fried potatoes," she keeps yelling "Huh?" until I say "home fries," which is what they call them here, and "Huh?" means "Beg your pardon?" And she's the second maid already. I took the liberty of firing the first one, a girl named Kathi, because she was always rude; or at least it seemed to me that she was, although in hindsight I may have been mistaken, because one is never quite sure here whether people are being rude or friendly. My new maid, who is named Babette, which rhymes with "rabbit," is quite a pleasant-looking girl, with something Mediterranean about her, as is common here, with black hair and black eyes and teeth that one can only envy. And she's cooperative, even prepares some of our northern dishes, under my direction; yesterday, for instance, we had sorrel and raisins, but Permaneder was so upset with this vegetable dish of mine (although he did pick out the raisins with his fork) that he wouldn't speak to me the rest of the day, just grumbled to himself. And I can tell you, Mother, that life isn't always easy here.

If only it had been just "snappers" and sorrel that made Tony's life so bitter. But before the honeymoon was over, she had been struck a blow so unforeseen, so startling, so incomprehensible that it had robbed her of every joy in life. She could not get over it. This is what had happened.

The Permaneders had been living together in Munich as man and wife for several weeks when Consul Buddenbrook finally was able to convert into cash the amount specified in his father's will for his sister's dowry, a total of fifty-one thousand marks *courant*, which sum was then converted into guldens and was received intact by Herr Permaneder, who then transferred it to secure and profitable investments.

But then, without the least hesitation or embarrassment, he had turned to his wife and said, "Tony gal"—he called her "Tony gal"—"Tony gal, that'll do it. We don't need nothin' more. I've plugged away all my life, and now I want my peace 'n' quiet. Damn if I don't. We'll rent out the ground floor, and the third floor, and we've got ourselves a nice 'partment here, 'n' we can eat our ham hocks 'n' don't need all the rest of the fancy fiddle-faddle. And I can spend my evenin's at the Hofbräuhaus. I'm not much for puttin' on the dog or scrimpin' and sockin' away the money. I want to take things easy. So, startin' t'morrow mornin', I'm callin' it quits. I'm retirin'."

"Permaneder!" she had cried, and for the first time it had the throaty sound she had reserved for Herr Grünlich's name until now.

But all he said in reply was, "Oh, cut that out, and hush up now." And then an argument had unfolded that was so serious and violent that it could only undermine the happiness of any marriage at such an early stage. He remained the victor. Her passionate opposition was crushed beneath his desire for "takin' things easy," and the upshot of all this was that Herr Permaneder withdrew the capital he had invested in the hops business and it was now Herr Noppe's turn to draw a blue line through the "& Co." on his calling card. And, like the majority of his friends, he now spent his evenings at his regular table in the Hofbräuhaus, playing cards and drinking his three liters of beer, and he limited his modest business activities as a landlord to raising rents and quietly snipping coupons.

Madame Buddenbrook was simply informed of the matter. But Frau Permaneder's pain was evident in the letters she wrote her brother about what had happened. Poor Tony—her worst fears had been more than realized. She had known all along that Herr Permaneder had none of the industriousness that her first husband had displayed far too much of. But that he should so totally dash all the hopes she had shared with Mamselle Jungmann on the evening before her engagement, that he could fail so completely to recognize the obligations he had assumed in marrying a Buddenbrook—no, she had never dreamed of that.

But she had to make the best of things, and her family at home could see from her letters that she had resigned herself to her fate. Life drifted on rather monotonously with her husband and Erika, who went to school now; she took care of the household, remained on friendly footing with the people they had found to rent the floors above and below them, and with the Niederpaurs on Marienplatz. She wrote now and then about attending the Court Theater with her friend Eva, because Herr Permaneder didn't like that sort of thing. It also turned out that, although he had lived in his "good ol' Munich" for more than forty years now, he had never seen the inside of the Pinakothek.

The days passed—but for Tony any genuine joy in her new life had faded since the day when Herr Permaneder had received her dowry and retired. There was nothing to hope for. She would never be able to write home about some success, some turn for the better. Things would remain the way they were now—with no real worries, but limited and far from "elegant"—and they would never change for the rest of her life. She felt it as a burden. And from her letters it was clear that her mood, which was anything but elated, made it that much more difficult for her to adapt to life in southern Germany. She could deal with minor matters. She had learned to communicate with her maid and the delivery men, could say "patties" instead of "croquettes," and no longer served her husband chilled fruit soup after he had called it "revoltin' goo." But for the most part she remained a stranger in her new home, primarily because it was a source of constant and never-ending humiliation to realize that being a born Buddenbrook was not in the least remarkable here in the south. She wrote in one of her letters about how some bricklayer, holding a mug of beer in one hand and a radish by the tail in the other, had stopped her on the street and asked, " 'xcuse me, neighbor, got the time?"—and although she made a joke of it, the undertone of outrage was palpable, and there could be no doubt that she had tossed her head back and refused to answer the man with so much as a glance. It was not just this lack of a sense of reserve or formal manners, however, that she found alien and disagreeable; although she did not taste deeply of the life and temper of Munich, she was surrounded by the atmosphere of a large city full of artists and people who seemed to have nothing to do, and her own mood often made it difficult for her to breathe in such slightly decadent air, to bear all this with good humor.

The days passed—but then, suddenly, it looked as if there might be some happiness in store for her after all, the very same happiness for which they waited in vain on Breite Strasse and Meng Strasse. Not long after New Year's Day, 1859, the hope that Tony would be a mother for the second time became a certainty.

Her letters almost quivered with joy now and overflowed with high spirits and the sort of childish, momentous phrases she had not used for a long time. Madame Buddenbrook, who no longer liked to travel—apart from her summer journeys, which were more and more restricted to the shores of the Baltic in any case—wrote to say she was sorry that she would be unable to visit her daughter at this time, but assured her that God would lend His aid. Tom wrote to say that both he and Gerda would attend the christening, and Tony's head was full of plans for an *elegant* reception. Poor Tony! The reception turned out to be a very sad affair, and the christening, which in her mind's eye she had seen as a gala occasion for flowers, candies, and chocolate, was never to take place. The child, a little girl, was destined to experience a mere quarter-hour of existence—during which the doctor struggled in vain to keep the little ill-adapted organism functioning—and then was no longer a participant in life.

When they arrived in Munich, Consul Buddenbrook and his wife discovered that even Tony was not entirely out of danger. This delivery had been much more difficult for her than the first, and for several days she was unable to take any nourishment—she had always suffered from occasional nervous upsets of her digestion.

But in time she recovered, and the Buddenbrooks could depart with their minds at ease in that regard at least—though not without some apprehension, because it had been only too clear to them, and in particular to the consul's observant eye, that not even shared suffering had been able to bring husband and wife any closer together.

Not that Herr Permaneder did not have a good heart. He was terribly shaken at the sight of his lifeless child, and great tears fell from his swollen eyes and rolled down his pudgy cheeks and into his frayed mustache. And with heavy sighs he managed to say several times, "Oh my, what a pain, what a pain in th' ol'!" But as far as Tony could see, it was not long before he was "takin' things easy" again. His evenings at the Hofbräuhaus soon helped him over his suffering, and with the contented, kindly, half-grumpy, half-doltish fatalism expressed in those words "it's a pain in th' ol'," he "muddled" through.

From that point on, Tony's letters never lost a sense of hopelessness, which sometimes would even break into lament. "Oh, Mother," she wrote, "everything happens to me! First Grünlich and then the bankruptcy and then Permaneder's retirement and now this dead child. What have I done to deserve such misfortune!"

But when the consul read such letters in private at home, he could not help smiling, because, despite all the pain such words expressed, he could hear an undertone of almost comical pride, and he knew that Tony Buddenbrook, whether as Madame Grünlich or as Madame Permaneder, was still a child, that she met all these very adult experiences with something like incredulity, and that she experienced them with a child's gravity and a child's sense of importance and—most of all—a child's inner powers to overcome them.

She did not understand what she had done to deserve her suffering; for, although she sneered at her mother's great piety, she shared in it, believing that justice is rewarded on this earth. Poor Tony! The death of her second child was neither the last nor the hardest blow that she would have to bear.

As 1859 drew to a close, something dreadful happened.

9

IT WAS A LATE November day, a cold autumn day with a hazy sky that seemed to threaten snow, and with rolling swatches of fog that were pierced now and then by the sun, the kind of day when the northeast wind whistled spitefully as it swooped around the massive corners of the churches and offered pneumonia at bargain rates to the seaport's inhabitants.

It was close to noon when Consul Thomas Buddenbrook entered the breakfast room and found his mother bent over a piece of paper, her spectacles set firmly on her nose.

"Tom," she said, looking up at him and holding the paper to one side in both hands as if afraid to show it to him, "don't be alarmed. It's rather unpleasant news—I don't quite understand. It's from Berlin. Something must have happened."

"Let me see, please," he said curtly. His face turned pale, and for a moment the muscles at his temples stood out as he clenched his teeth. He stuck out his hand decisively, as if to say, "Be quick about it, please. Just the bad news, no long introductions."

Lifting one eyebrow and slowly twirling one long tip of his mustache in his fingers, he read what was written on the paper. It was a telegram. It said: "Don't be alarmed. Arriving in short order with Erika. All is over. Your unhappy Antonie."

"Short order . . . short order," he said crossly and shook his head as he glanced at his mother. "What does she mean by short order?"

"It's just her way of putting it, Tom. She doesn't mean anything in particular. She means 'at once' or something like that."

"And from Berlin? What is she doing in Berlin? How did she get to Berlin?"

"I don't know, Tom. I still don't understand it—the telegram arrived about ten minutes ago. But something must have happened, and we shall have to wait to find out what it is. God has a way of turning all things to good. Now sit down, my son, and eat."

He took his seat and mechanically poured some porter in the tall, heavy glass. "All is over," he repeated. "And signed 'Antonie'—what childishness."

Then he ate and drank in silence.

After a while his mother risked a remark—"Do you suppose it's about Permaneder, Tom?"

He shrugged, but didn't look up.

As he was leaving, his hand already on the doorknob, he said, "Yes, Mother, we'll just have to wait for her. Assuming she won't burst into the house in the middle of the night, it will probably be sometime tomorrow. Let me know, please."

MADAME BUDDENBROOK waited, hour after hour. She slept very poorly that night, even rang for Ida Jungmann, who now slept in the back room adjoining her own on the mezzanine, had her bring some sugar-water, and then sat up in bed doing needlework for quite a long time. Her nervous suspense continued as the morning slipped by. At late breakfast the consul explained that if Tony was coming she would have to arrive in Büchen on the three-thirty-three. As the afternoon wore on, Madame Buddenbrook sat at the window of the landscape room and tried to read—a book bound in black leather with a palm frond embossed in gold on the cover.

The day was much like the one before—cold, hazy, windy. The fire crackled behind the shiny wrought-iron grate. At every sound of wagon wheels, she would give a little jerk and peer out. And then, around four o'clock, when she was no longer paying any real attention and had almost forgotten her daughter, something stirred below in the house. She turned around to the window and wiped the moisture from the pane with her lace handkerchief—and, indeed, a carriage had stopped out front and someone was coming up the stairs.

She grasped both arms of her chair and stood up; but then she thought better of it and sank down again and, with an expression that almost seemed to fend her daughter off, she merely turned her head toward Tony, who was hurrying, almost flinging herself across the room— Erika had been left standing at the glass door, her hand in Ida Jungmann's.

Frau Permaneder was wearing a fur-trimmed shawl and a long, narrow felt hat with a veil. She looked very pale and shaken; her eyes were red, and her upper lip quivered just as it had when she had cried as a little girl. She raised her arms, let them fall again, and then slid to her knees beside her mother, hiding her head in the folds of the old woman's skirt and sobbing bitterly. This left the impression that she had rushed here straight from Munich, all in one breath—and now here she lay, exhausted but safe, her flight over.

Madame Buddenbrook was silent for a moment. "Tony," she then said in gentle reproach, and after carefully extracting the large pin that held Tony's hat in place and laying the hat on the window seat, she lovingly stroked her daughter's ash-blond hair with both hands, calming her. "What is wrong, child? What has happened?"

But she would have to be the soul of patience—it was some time before she was given an answer. "Mother," Frau Permaneder managed to say at last, "Mama." And that was all.

With her arm still around her daughter, Elisabeth lifted her head and saw her granddaughter standing at the glass door, one finger pressed to her lips in bewilderment. She reached out to her with her free hand and said, "Come, child. Come here and say hello to me. You've grown so big and you look so strong and healthy, and we should thank God for that. How old are you now, Erika?"

"Thirteen, Grandmama."

"My word! A young lady." She first bent forward over Tony's head to kiss the little girl and then continued, "Now, go on upstairs with Ida, my child, we'll be eating soon. Your mama and I want to talk, you see."

They were left alone.

"Now, my dear Tony, won't you stop crying? When God visits us with affliction, we must bear it with composure. Take up thy cross and bear it, the Bible says. But would you also like to go upstairs first, perhaps, and rest and refresh yourself a bit, and then come back down here to me? Our good Jungmann has readied your room for you. Thank you for the telegram. It really did alarm us, you know." She stopped, because tremulous, stifled sounds were coming from the folds of her skirt.

"He's a depraved man, a depraved man, depraved."

Frau Permaneder could not get beyond that drastic word—it was as if it possessed her completely. And all the while she pressed her face deeper into her mother's lap, even clenched her fist against the chair.

"Do you mean your husband, perhaps, my child?" the old woman asked after a pause. "Such an idea ought never to enter my head, I know, but you've left me no choice but to think that is whom you mean, Tony. Has Permaneder done something to hurt you? Have you reason to complain of his behavior?"

"Babbit!" Frau Permaneder blurted the word out. "Babbit!"

"Babbit?" Elisabeth repeated perplexed. Then she leaned back and let her pale eyes drift off to the world beyond the window. She now knew what the problem was. There was a long pause, interrupted now and then by Tony's gradually ebbing sobs.

"Tony," Elisabeth said after a while, "it's clear that he has indeed caused you great grief, that you have good reason to complain. But did you have to be so impetuous about it? Was it necessary to make a trip all the way from Munich, with little Erika—which to people less sensible than we might almost appear to mean that you never intend to return to your husband again?"

"But I don't intend to—never!" Frau Permaneder cried and, jerking her head back, she stared fiercely into her mother's face with tear-stained eyes, before suddenly dropping her head back into the folds of Elisabeth's skirt.

Madame Buddenbrook ignored this outburst. "All the same," she began again, raising her voice and slowly shaking her head from side to side, "all the same, now that you're here, that's fine, too. You'll be able to unburden your heart and tell me everything, and then we shall see how, with love and forbearance and prudence, the wrong can be set right again."

"Never!" Tony repeated. "Never!" But then she told her story, and although not every word was intelligible, because she spoke into the soft folds of her mother's skirt and would erupt now and then in furious cries of pure outrage, it was clear nevertheless that the facts in the case were as follows:

Around midnight between the 24th and 25th of the current month, Madame Permaneder, who had gone to bed rather late after having suffered all day from a nervous stomach, was awakened from a light sleep. The reason for this was a persistent noise on the staircase up front, a mysterious noise, as if there were a halfhearted attempt to stifle it—but one could clearly make out creaking stairs, a kind of cough or giggle, smothered words of protest, and very strange growls and moans. There could not be a moment's doubt as to the nature of this noise. In her drowsy state, Frau Permaneder had no sooner discerned this noise than she immediately understood what it was; and she felt the blood leave her cheeks and rush to her heart—which contracted, but continued to pump in anxious, heavy throbs. As if stunned or paralyzed, she lay there on her pillows for one long, ghastly minute; but then, when the scandalous noise did not stop, she picked up her lamp in her trembling hands, left her bed in horrified, grim desperation, put on her slippers, flung open the door, and, still carrying her lamp, hurried to the top of the stairs—the familiar Jacob's ladder that led straight up from the front door to the second floor. And there, on the upper steps of Jacob's ladder, she saw before her in the flesh the same scene that, to her increasing horror, her mind's eye had been forced to imagine as she lay in her bedroom listening to those unambiguous sounds. It was a brawl, an unseemly and indecent wrestling match, between Babette the cook and Herr Permaneder. The girl still had her key ring and candle in hand—she must have been taking care of some late chore in the house—and she twisted and turned to defend herself against the master of the house, who was holding her in a tight embrace and kept trying to press his walrus face to hers, occasionally succeeding in the attempt, with the result that his hat kept slipping farther down the back of his head. At the sight of Antonie, Babette blurted out, "Jesus, Mary, and Joseph," and Herr Permaneder echoed, "Jesus, Mary, and Joseph," and let her go. And, cleverly taking advantage of the moment, the girl vanished without a trace, while Herr Permaneder stood there with drooping arms, drooping head, and drooping mustache, facing his wife and stuttering something absolutely idiotic, like "Ain't that a hoot, what a pain in th' ol'!" But when he raised his eyes again, she was no longer there. He found her in the bedroom, half sitting, half lying on her bed, sobbing in despair, and repeating just two words over and over—"The shame!" He stood there leaning limply against the door frame; then he nudged one shoulder forward as if he were trying to give her a little cheerful poke in the ribs, and he said, "Now, cut that out. Hush, hush up, now, Tony gal. It's just that it was Franzl Ramsauer's name day, see, and we all got a little soused." But the strong odor of alcohol pervading the room now only whipped her frenzy to a peak. She had stopped sobbing, was no longer frail and weak, and, in a fit of exploding temper and wild despair, she poured out all her disgust, all her loathing, flung the contempt she felt for him in his face. Herr Permaneder did not just stand there. He felt his head grow hot—he had drunk not just a mug or two too many in honor of his friend Franz Ramsauer, but "bubbly" as well—and he answered her, answered in savage words. The quarrel that ensured was far more dreadful than the one marking Herr Permaneder's retirement. Frau Antonie gathered up some clothes with the intention of spending the night in the sitting room. But then, just as she was leaving, he called her a name, a name that she would never repeat, that would never pass her lips, a name . . . a name . . .

These were the main facts of the tale that Madame Permaneder divulged to the folds of her mother's skirt. But as to that "name," the "name" that had frozen within her very core since that awful night—no, she could not get over that, no, by God, she swore she would not repeat it, although her mother certainly did not press her to do so, but merely moved her head in slow, barely noticeable, thoughtful nods as she gazed down on Tony's beautiful ash-blond hair.

"Yes, yes," she said, "these are sad things you've told me, Tony. And I understand only too well, my poor little girl—for, after all, I'm not just your mother, but, like you, a grown woman. I can see now that your pain is quite justified and how completely, in the weakness of the moment, your husband forgot the respect he owes you."

"In the weakness of the moment!" Tony cried. She jumped up, took two steps back, and feverishly dried her eyes. "In the weakness of the moment, Mama? What he forgot was the respect he owes me and our family name—he never understood that from the very beginning. A man who takes his wife's dowry and simply retires. A man without any ambition, any drive, any goal in life. A man who has a gooey mixture of malt and hops in his veins instead of blood—yes, I truly believe he does. And then to sink to such a vulgarity as this with Babbit, and, when confronted with his own depravity, he replies by calling me a name . . . a name . . ."

She had found her way back to the name again, the name she would not repeat. Suddenly, however, she took a step forward and, in a much calmer, gentler tone of voice, she asked with interest, "How sweet—where did you get that, Mama?" She was pointing with her chin at a little basket of woven reeds, set in a small stand and trimmed with velvet bows. Madame Buddenbrook had been using it to hold her needlework for some time now.

"I bought it," the old woman answered. "I needed one."

"How elegant," Tony said, tilting her head to inspect it. Madame Buddenbrook's eyes rested on it now, too, but without seeing it—she was lost in thought.

"But now, my dear Tony," she said at last, once again extending both hands to her daughter, "however things may stand, here you are, and you know that you are welcome, so very welcome. We can talk all this over when you have calmed down. Go take off your things, make yourself at home in your room. Ida, my dear?" she called into the dining room, raising her voice. "Please set places for Madame Permaneder and Erika."

10

TONY HAD RETIRED to her room immediately after dinner, because at some point in the meal her mother had confirmed the fact that Thomas knew she had arrived—and she did not seem especially eager to meet with him.

It was six o'clock when the consul came upstairs. He went first to the landscape room, where he had a long talk with his mother.

"And how is she?" he asked. "How did she act?"

"Oh, Tom, I'm afraid she's adamant. Good heavens, she's so upset. And there was that name—if only I knew what the name was that he called her."

"I'll go up to her."

"Do that, Tom. But knock softly, don't startle her. And keep calm, do you hear me? Her nerves are quite jangled. She hardly ate a thing. It's her stomach, you know. Speak calmly to her."

As was his habit, he climbed the stairs to the third floor quickly, taking two steps at a time, and he twirled his mustache thoughtfully as he walked down the hall. But even as he knocked, his face cleared, because he had decided to handle the situation with humor as long as possible.

He opened the door when he heard a soft, anguished "Come in," and found Frau Permaneder, still completely dressed, lying atop the down quilt that covered her bed; the bed-curtains had been pulled back, and there was a bottle of digestive tonic on the nightstand beside her. She turned slightly toward him, propping her head in her hand, and gazed at him with a pouting little smile. He bowed very low, extending both hands in a slow, solemn gesture.

"Gracious lady, to what do we owe the honor of a visit from the capital of Bavaria?"

"Give me a kiss, Tom," she said, sitting up to offer him her cheek and then sinking down again. "Hello, my boy. You've not changed a bit, I see, since we were last together in Munich."

"Well, you can hardly judge that with the blinds down, my dear. And besides, I'm not about to let you steal the march on me when it comes to compliments, because it is only proper that I first remark"—and, still holding her hand in his, he pulled a chair over and sat down next to her—"as I have so often, that, except for Klothilde, you are . . ."

"Shame on you, Tom. How is Thilda doing?"

"Fine, of course. Madame Krauseminz takes good care of her and sees that she doesn't starve. Which of course does not prevent Thilda from doing an excellent job of gobbling down everything here on Thursdays as if she were eating for the week ahead."

She laughed harder than she had for a long time, but suddenly broke off with a sigh and asked, "And how is business going?"

"Yes, well, we manage. We have reason to be satisfied."

"Oh, thank God that at least everything *here* is as it should be. Oh, I'm not at all in the mood for amusing chitchat."

"What a shame. Because one should keep one's sense of humor, *quand même*."

"No, there's none left, Tom. You know all?"

" 'You know all,' " he repeated, letting go of her hand and pushing his chair back a little. "Good God in heaven, do you know how that sounds? 'All'! What all lies hidden in that 'all'? 'My pain, my love, I did inter them in that all'—right? No, now listen to me. . . ."

She said nothing, but merely let her eyes sweep over him in a profoundly amazed and profoundly offended glance.

"Yes, I expected to see that face," he said. "You would not be here if it were not for that face. But permit me, my dear Tony, to take this matter all too lightly, just as you are taking it all too seriously. That way we shall complement one another perfectly."

"Too seriously, Thomas, too seriously?"

"Yes. Good Lord, let's not make a tragedy of this. Let's speak a bit more modestly, rather than this 'All is over' and 'Your unhappy Antonie.' Don't misunderstand me, Tony. You know very well that no one could be happier than I that you've come. I have been hoping for a long time now that you would come for a visit, without your husband, so that we could just be together again *en famille*. But that you've come *now*, and like *this*—pardon me, but that's pure stupidity, my child. No—let me finish. Permaneder has behaved quite badly, true enough, and I'll make it clear to him that I think so, you can be sure of that."

"I've already made it clear to him how he behaved, Thomas," she interrupted, sitting up and laying a hand across her breast, "more than clear, let me tell you. If only as a matter of tact, any further discussion with my husband is fully inappropriate." And then she let herself fall back and gazed sternly and resolutely at the ceiling.

He bent forward, as if burdened by the weight of her words, and he smiled as he gazed at his own knees. "Well, then, I *won't* send him a nasty letter, just as you wish. It is your affair, after all, and it's quite sufficient if you haul him over the coals—that's your job as a wife. But by the light of day, one can't deny that there are mitigating circumstances. A friend was celebrating his name day, he comes home a little mellow and is guilty of a misdemeanor, a little unseemly escapade."

"Thomas," she said, "I don't understand you. I don't understand the tone you're taking—you, a man of principles. You didn't see him, the way he was grabbing at her, and how drunk he was."

"I can imagine he looked rather comical. But that's the point, Tony. You're not seeing the comic side of this—and your bad digestion is to blame for that, of course. You caught your husband at a weak moment, you saw him making a fool of himself. But that's no reason to be so dreadfully outraged; it should amuse you just a little, serve as a way to bring you closer together as man and wife. Let me be clear on this—of course you couldn't approve of his conduct, couldn't just smile and pass over it in silence, heaven forbid. You left, as a demonstration of your displeasure, perhaps a bit too spirited an action, perhaps a little too punitive—I certainly would not like to see him right now, sitting there woebegone—but a just action, all the same. My request is simply that you be somewhat less outraged by these things and regard them from a more politic point of view. This is just between us. I'm merely suggesting that in any marriage it is certainly not unimportant which side has the moral advantage. Do you understand me, Tony? Your husband has left himself open, there can be no doubt of that. He has compromised himself, made a fool of himself—a fool, because his crime is so harmless, something one needn't take so seriously. To be brief, his dignity is no longer unimpeachable, and you now have a definite moral advantage over him. And, assuming you know how to use it, your future happiness is assured. You'll see, if after, shall we say, two weeks—yes, I insist on having you to ourselves for at *least* that long!—if you then return to Munich, you will see."

"I'm not going back to Munich, Thomas."

"Beg your pardon?" he asked, screwing up his face and laying a hand to his ear as he leaned forward.

She was lying on her back, her head pressed firmly into the pillows, so that her chin was thrust forward with a kind of severity. "Never!" she said, letting out a long, noisy breath and then clearing her throat—slowly and significantly. It was like a dry cough and was beginning to become a habit with her—apparently it had something to do with her stomach problems. A pause followed.

"Tony," he said suddenly and stood up, rapping his hand firmly on the arm of the Empire chair, "you are not to make a scandal!"

From the corner of her eye, she could see that he was pale and that the muscles at his temples were twitching. She could not stay in this position. She made her move, and, in order to hide just how afraid of him she was, she turned loud and angry. She bounced up, letting her feet drop over the edge of the bed, and now she started in—with flushed cheeks, scowling brows, and quick, abrupt motions of her head and hands.

"Scandal, Thomas? You tell me not to make a scandal, after I have been covered with shame, after he simply spat in my face? Is that worthy of a brother? Yes, it's a perfectly justifiable question, if you please. Consideration and tact are fine things, heaven knows. But there are limits in this life, Tom—and I know as much about life as you—limits, when the fear of scandal verges on cowardice. And it amazes me that I should have to tell you that, especially since I am just a silly goose. Yes, that's what I am, and I can understand quite well if Permaneder never loved me. I am an ugly old woman—that may well be—and Babbit is prettier, that much is sure. But that does not relieve him of the respect that he owes my family and my upbringing and my feelings. You did not see it, Tom, you did not see the manner in which he forgot all such respect, and anyone who did not see it knows nothing about it, because there is no way to describe how disgusting he was in that condition. And you did not hear the name that he called me, your sister, as I was gathering my things to leave so that I could spend the night on the sofa in the sitting room. Oh yes, but I had to hear that name come from his mouth, a name . . . a name! In short, Tom, it was that name, in fact if you must know, that caused me, *forced* me, to spend the whole night packing and to wake Erika at the crack of dawn and to leave. Because I could not stay anywhere near a man who might utter such things at any time. And I repeat, I will not return to such a man—I would perish, I would no longer have any regard for myself, would have no basis to go on living."

"Will you please be good enough to tell me what that damn name was? Yes or no?"

"Never, Thomas. These lips shall never repeat it. I know full well what I owe you and myself within these walls."

"Then there's no talking to you."

"That may be; and I would certainly prefer that we speak of it no more."

"What do you want to do? Get a divorce?"

"That's exactly what I want, Tom. I am firmly resolved to do it. It is the course of action that I owe to myself and my child and to you all."

"Well, that's just plain nonsense," he said coolly, turning on his heel and walking away as if that settled matters for good and all. "It takes two for a divorce, my child. And that Permaneder would willingly agree to it without further ado—the idea is simply too funny for words."

"Oh, let me worry about that," she said—he had not intimidated her. "You think he will contest it, simply because of my seventeen thousand thalers *courant*. Well, Grünlich didn't want a divorce, either, but he was forced to. There are ways—and I shall go to Dr. Gieseke, who is a friend of Christian's, and he will stand by me. I know what you're going to say: that was a different situation back then—and that's true. The issue then was the 'incapacity of the husband to support his family,' right! So you see—I do know a thing or two about these matters, whereas you simply act as if this were the first time in my life that I ever got divorced. But it makes no difference, Tom. Perhaps it won't work, perhaps it is impossible—that may well be; you could be right. But it changes nothing. It changes nothing about my decision. Then let him keep his pin money—there are nobler things in life. But he will never see me again!"

And then she cleared her throat. She had left the bed and was sitting in an easy chair, one elbow set firmly on its arm, her chin buried so deep in her hand that four bent fingers clutched at her lower lip. And, turning to one side now, she stared out the window with fierce, reddened eyes.

The consul paced back and forth in the room, sighed, shook his head, gave a shrug. Finally he stopped directly in front of her, his hands clenched together. "You have the mind of a child, Tony," he said despondently, pleading with her. "Every word you've said is childish. I beg you, won't you please, for just one second, agree to look at the matter like an adult? Don't you see that you are carrying on as if something serious and awful had happened to you, as if your husband had cruelly betrayed you, holding you up to shame before all the world? Just consider for a moment—nothing happened at all! Not one human soul knows anything about that absurd scene on your staircase on Kaufinger Strasse. You will not prejudice your dignity, or ours, one iota if you return to Permaneder, perfectly calm and cool, and at most with your nose set slightly in the air. On the contrary—you will prejudice our dignity if you *don't* do it, because that would turn a mere bagatelle into a true scandal."

She hastily let go of her chin and looked him squarely in the eye. "Hold your tongue, Thomas. It's my turn now. Listen to me. So you think the only shame and scandal in life is what people gossip about, do you? Oh no. The secret scandals that gnaw at us and eat away at our self-respect are far worse. Are we Buddenbrooks the kind of people who want to be 'tip-top' on the outside, as they say here, while choking down our humiliation within our four walls? You do amaze me, Tom. Just picture your father and how he would react, and then judge as he would have. No, no, everything must be clean and out in the open. You can show the world your books at the end of every day and say, 'There you are!' And it dare not be different with any of us. I know how God made me. I am not afraid in the least. Let Julie Möllendorpf walk right past me and not say a word. And let Pfiffi Buddenbrook sit here every Thursday jiggling with joy at my misfortune, let her say, 'Well, how sad. That's the second time now, but *of course* it was the husband's fault both times.' But I am far above all that Thomas, far, far above it. I know that I have done what I thought was right. But to swallow insults and allow myself to be reviled in a drunken, illiterate dialect out of fear of Julie Möllendorpf and Pfiffi Buddenbrook, to live with such a man and in such a city, where I have to put up with that kind of language and with scenes like the one I saw on the stairs, out of fear of what they might say, to learn to deny my family and my upbringing and everything in me just so that I may *appear* to be happy and content—that is what *I* call a loss of dignity, that is what *I* call scandalous, let me tell you."

She broke off, buried her chin in her hand again, and stared fiercely in the direction of the windowpane. Tom was standing in front of her, his weight on one leg and his hands in his pockets; he was lost in thought, and his eyes gazed down at her without seeing her. Shaking his head slowly back and forth, he said, "Tony, you can't get away with that with me. I was fairly sure all along, but what you said there at the end betrayed you. It isn't your husband at all. It's the place. It wasn't that foolishness on the staircase at all. It's the whole situation in general. You haven't been able to adjust. Admit it."

"You're right, Thomas!" she shouted. She even jumped to her feet, stretched out her arm, and pointed directly into his face. Her own face was flushed. She held this warlike pose, with one hand, gesticulating with the other, and she made a speech—a stirring, relentless speech, seething with passion. The consul watched her in bewilderment. No sooner would she take time to catch her breath than new words were gushing and surging out of her. Yes, she was able to put it all in words, all the disgust stored up over the past few years—a little disordered and confused, but she found the words. It was an explosion, an eruption of honest despair, and it burst from her like some elemental force that brooked no opposition, for which there was no rebuttal.

"You're right, Thomas! Go ahead and say it again. Oh, I'll say it to you straight out—I am not a silly goose anymore and I know what I know about life. I no longer freeze when I learn that life isn't always so neat and proper. I've known people like Teary Trieschke and I was married to Grünlich and I know about our *suitiers* in town here. I'm no innocent from the country, let me tell you, and, believe me, taken just for itself and out of context, this affair with Babbit would not have chased me off. But the point is, Thomas, that I've had it up to here—and it didn't take much, the cup was already full, had been full for a long time, a very long time. It took little or nothing to do it—and then came this: the realization that I couldn't depend on Permaneder even in that regard. That was all I needed. It pulled the plug on the keg. And all of a sudden I was ready to follow through on my decision to get out of Munich for good—and it had been ripening for a long, long time, Tom. Because I can't live down south, by God and all His heavenly hosts, I can't. You have no idea *how* unhappy I've been, you can't know, because I didn't let on when you came to visit. No, because I know something about tact, I know better than to burden others with my complaints, to wear my heart on my sleeve. I've always tended to close things up inside me. But I suffered, Tom, everything in me suffered—my whole personality, so to speak. Like a plant, to use a metaphor, like a flower that has been transplanted to some foreign soil—though you may think the comparison inappropriate, because I'm an ugly old woman. But you couldn't have put me in more foreign soil, I'd just as soon end up in Turkey. Oh, we northerners should never leave here. We should stay beside our little bay and earn an honest living. There was a time when you used to mock me for my partiality for the nobility; yes, and in the past few years I've often thought about what someone—a very clever man, in fact—told me a long time ago. 'Your sympathies are with the nobility,' he said, 'and do you want me to tell you why? Because you're an aristocrat yourself. Your father is a great sovereign, and you are a princess, separated by an abyss from all us others, who don't belong to your circle of ruling families.' Yes, Tom, we feel that we are aristocrats, and we're aware of that distance, and we should never try to live where people know nothing about us and don't understand our worth, because it will only bring humiliation and they will think that we are ridiculously arrogant. Yes, they all thought I was ridiculously arrogant. No one ever said it, but I felt it every single hour, and I suffered because of it. Oh, a place where they eat their cake with a knife, where even princes can't get their don'ts and doesn'ts straight, and where they think a gentleman is courting a woman if he picks up her fan for her—it's easy to be thought arrogant in a place like that, Tom. Adjust to that? No, not to people who have no dignity, morals, ambition, elegance, or discipline, not to impolite, unkempt, slovenly people, people who are lazy and frivolous, sluggish and superficial all at the same time. I cannot adjust to people like that and I never will, as surely as I am your sister. Eva Ewers knew how—fine. But an Ewers is not a Buddenbrook, and, then, she has a husband who is good for something in life. And what was it like for me? Think back, Tom, to the very beginning, think back. I come from here, from this house. And that means something—it means people work hard and have goals. And I go down there with Permaneder, who takes my dowry and retires. Oh, it was genuine, quite in character—that was the one good thing about it. And then? I was going to have a baby. And I was so delighted. It would have made up for everything. And what happened? She died. She was dead. That wasn't Permaneder's fault, heaven knows. He did what he could, didn't even go to his tavern for two or three nights—God forbid. But it was all part of the same thing, Tom. It didn't make me any happier, as you can well imagine. I bore it all and didn't grumble. I went on, alone and misunderstood and with everyone calling me arrogant, but I said to myself, 'For better or for worse, till death do you part. He's a little plump and lazy and he's disappointed your hopes in him; but he means well and his heart is pure.' And then this happened, and I had to see him in that one disgusting moment. And I realized that he understands me so well, respects me so much more than the others that he can call me a name, a name that one of your warehouse workers wouldn't even call a dog. And I realized that nothing was keeping me there, and that it would be a disgrace to stay. And as I was riding up Holsten Strasse from the train station, Nielsen the grain hauler passed by and tipped his stovepipe hat, and I greeted him back, not arrogantly at all, but the way Father used to greet people—like this, with my hand. And now I'm here. And you can harness a team of two dozen draft horses, Tom, but you'll not get me back to Munich. And tomorrow I'm going to see Gieseke!"

This was the speech that Tony made, and when she was done she sank back wearily in her chair, buried her chin in her hand, and stared at the windowpane.

The consul stood in front of her—appalled, dazed, close to shock—and said nothing. Then he drew a long breath, raised his arms shoulder-high, and let them drop to his sides again. "Yes, well, then, there's nothing I can do," he said softly, turning on his heel and walking toward the door.

She watched him go, her face set in the same long-suffering pout with which she had greeted him. "Tom?" she asked. "Are you angry with me?"

He held the oval doorknob in one hand and gestured a weary protest with the other. "Oh no—not at all."

She reached her hand out to him and laid her head on her shoulder. "Come here, Tom. Your sister hasn't had it very good in life. Everything happens to her. And at this moment there doesn't seem to be anyone on her side."

He came back and took her hand—but with a kind of limp indifference, standing next to her and without looking at her.

Suddenly her upper lip began to quiver. "You'll have to do it all by yourself now," she said. "Christian is probably not going to amount to much, and I'm finished. I'm ruined. I won't accomplish anything more. Yes, I'll have to live off your charity, a useless old woman. I never would have thought that I could fail so miserably at being some help to you, Tom. And now you must see to it all alone that we Buddenbrooks hold our ground. God be with you."

Two tears—two large, clear, childish tears—rolled down her cheeks, where little wrinkles in her skin could be seen now.

11

TONY LOST NO TIME—she took matters in hand. In hopes that she would calm down, cool off, and rethink all this, the consul demanded only one thing of her for now: that she lie low and that neither she nor Erika leave the house. Everything might still turn out for the best. The town did not need to know anything as yet. The Thursday "family day" was canceled.

But the day after Frau Permaneder's homecoming, a letter arrived for attorney-at-law Andreas Gieseke, summoning him to Meng Strasse. She received him alone, in the middle room along the corridor on the second floor, where a fire had been lit and where there was a massive table on which she had arranged, for some reason or other, an inkwell, pens, and a stack of white foolscap taken from the office downstairs. They sat down in two armchairs.

"Dr. Gieseke," she said, crossing her arms, laying her head back, and staring at the ceiling, "you are a man who knows life well, both in a personal and a professional sense. I feel I can speak openly to you." And then she revealed to him the whole story of Babbit and what had occurred in the bedroom. Dr. Gieseke regretted to say that neither the distressing incident on the stairs, nor the insult to which she had undoubtedly been subjected—but about which she refused to go into greater detail—offered sufficient grounds for divorce.

"Fine," she said. "Thank you very much."

Then she had him review for her the current legal grounds for divorce and followed with an open mind and definite interest a lengthy supplemental exposition on the law concerning dowries, after which she cordially but sedately dismissed Dr. Gieseke for now.

She went down to the ground floor and demanded to see Thomas in his private office.

"Thomas," she said, "please write that man at once—I do not gladly speak his name. As to the status of my money, I have been informed in detail about that. He should state his position, one way or the other. But he shall not see me again. If he agrees to a legal divorce, fine—we shall demand a rendering of accounts and the restoration of my *dot*. Even if he refuses, we need not be dismayed, because you should know, Tom, that although Permaneder's claim to my *dot* makes it his property in the eyes of the law—that much I will grant you—I nevertheless have certain substantive rights as well, thank God."

The consul paced back and forth, his hands behind his back, his shoulders jerking nervously—the face she had made as she uttered the word *dot* had been so unutterably smug. He did not have time for this. He was buried under work. She should show a little patience, and think this over—another fifty times, if you please. His most immediate task was a trip to Hamburg—he would be leaving tomorrow, in fact, for a conference, for a disagreeable discussion with Christian, who had written that he needed financial help, a temporary loan, which Elisabeth would have to subtract from money set aside for his inheritance. His business was in dreadful shape, and although he was constantly complaining of his ailments, he was apparently amusing himself royally in restaurants, at the circus, and at the theater, and, to judge by debts that he had been able to pile up on the basis of his family's good name and that were just now coming to light he was living far beyond his means. It was well known on Meng Strasse, in the Club, and all over town that the person responsible for all this was a woman by the name of Aline Puvogel, who lived alone with her two pretty children. Christian Buddenbrook was not the only merchant in Hamburg who maintained intimate and costly relations with this personage.

In short, apart from Tony's wish for a divorce, there were a good many other unpleasant matters—the trip to Hamburg being the most urgent. In any case, it was likely that they would be hearing from Permaneder soon enough.

The consul left on his trip, and returned in an angry, depressed mood. And since there had been no news from Munich, he felt he had no choice but to take the first step. He wrote—a cool, businesslike, and slightly supercilious letter. He noted that it could not be denied that in her married life with Herr Permaneder Antonie had met with a series of grave disappointments. Without his going into detail, it was clear that she had not found the happiness she had hoped from her marriage. Any reasonable man would see that her wish to dissolve the union was justified. Her decision not to return to Munich appeared, unfortunately, to be irrevocable. And then followed the question as to how Permaneder intended to act in light of these facts.

Days of tense waiting followed, and then came Herr Permaneder's reply, an answer that no one—not Andreas Gieseke, or Elisabeth, or Thomas, not even Antonie herself—had expected. In simple terms, he agreed to the divorce.

He wrote that he sincerely regretted what had happened, but that he respected Antonie's wishes, realizing as he did that he and she "don't rightly belong together." If he had been a source of sorrow for her in the past few years, he hoped that she would try to forget and forgive. Since he would probably never see her and Erika again, he wished her and the child every possible happiness in the future—signed Alois Permaneder. In a postscript he expressly offered to make immediate restitution of her dowry. He could live without worry on his own income. He would need no extra time, since no business transactions were necessary. The house was paid for, and money was available upon demand.

Tony was almost a little ashamed and for the first time felt inclined to see something laudable in Herr Permaneder's lack of passion when it came to money matters.

And now Dr. Gieseke had a new task. He took over the correspondence with the husband in regard to grounds for divorce, and "mutual irreconcilable incompatibility" was agreed on. The suit was filed—Tony's second suit of divorce—and in the early phases she followed it with high seriousness, great eagerness, and considerable knowledge of the law. She spoke about it wherever she went, much to the consul's annoyance on several occasions. In her present state, she was quite incapable of sharing his distress. She was caught up in terms like "proceeds," "acquisitions," "accesions," "dotal rights," and "tangible properties," which she used constantly with both dignity and fluency, laying her head back and raising her shoulders slightly. In Dr. Gieseke's brief of argument there was one paragraph that made the most profound impression on her; it dealt with certain "contingent assets" residing in the dotal property, which were to be regarded as a part of the *dot* and restored upon the dissolution of the marriage. She told all the world about these "assets," which of course did not exist; she told Ida Jungmann, Uncle Justus, poor Klothilde, and the Ladies Buddenbrook from Breite Strasse, who, by the way, when they learned of these events had stared down into their laps, where their hands lay folded, and froze in ramrod astonishment that this satisfaction, too, had been granted to them; she told Therese Weichbrodt, whose lessons Erika Grünlich once again had the pleasure of attending, and even good Madame Kethelsen, who for more than one reason understood not the least part of it.

Then came the day when the divorce was granted by law and finalized, and Tony took care of the last essential formality—asking Thomas for the family papers and entering the new fact in her own hand. And now her task was to accustom herself to her new situation.

She did so with courage. With unruffled dignity she ignored the splendidly scornful barbs of the Ladies Buddenbrook; her eyes took on an unutterable chill whenever she met the Hagenströms and Möllendorpfs, staring over their heads; and she abstained entirely from the social whirl, which in any case had not been part of her parents' home for years, but took place now at her brother's home. She had her closest relatives—her mother, Thomas, and Gerda; she had Ida Jungmann and Sesame Weichbrodt, who was like a second mother to her; she had Erika, to whose *elegant* upbringing she devoted great care and in whose future, perhaps, she set her last secret hopes. This was her life. And time passed.

Later on, in some inexplicable way, various members of the family learned what the "name" was, the name that Herr Permaneder had so imprudently let slip. And what had he said? "Go to hell, *you filthy sow, you slut!*"

And so Tony Buddenbrook's second marriage came to an end.

PART SEVEN

1

A CHRISTENING—a christening on Breite Strasse.

All the good things that Madame Permaneder envisioned when she was expecting are ready and waiting. Without the least rattle that could disturb the ceremony in the salon, the maid is finishing off the steamy hot chocolate with whipped cream, gingerly pouring it into a great many cups crowded onto the huge round tea tray with gilded, shell-shaped handles. Meanwhile Anton the butler is slicing the towering layer cake and Mamselle Jungmann is arranging the candies and fresh flowers in silver dessert bowls; and, mustering everything one last time, she lays her head on her shoulder and spreads both pinkies as far as she can.

Once the ladies and gentlemen have made themselves comfortable in the sitting room and the salon, it will not be long before all these splendid things will be passed around, and one hopes there will be enough, since the whole family has gathered, though not the extended family, because through the Oeverdiecks there is a distant relationship to the Kistenmakers, and through them to the Möllendorpfs and so on. The line has to be drawn somewhere. The Oeverdiecks, however, are represented—by the octogenarian Dr. Kaspar Oeverdieck, the town's mayor.

He arrived in his carriage and climbed the stairs supported by his cane and Thomas Buddenbrook's arm. His presence enhances the dignity of the celebration. And there is no doubt—it is an occasion worthy of every dignity.

For in the salon is a table decorated with flowers to serve as an altar and, behind it, a young clergyman in black vestments with a starched snow-white ruff like a millstone around his neck; and he speaks, while a tall, strapping, well-nourished female, dressed in rich reds and golds, holds in her muscular arms a tiny something almost lost under all the lace and satin bows—an heir. A firstborn son, a Buddenbrook! Can anyone understand what that means?

Can anyone understand the hushed thrill with which the news, at first only a whispered hint, was borne from Breite to Meng Strasse? Or the silent elation that Frau Permaneder felt when she first heard it and embraced her mother, her brother, and—more gingerly—her sister-in-law? And now spring has come, the spring of 1861, and he is here and is about to receive the sacrament of holy baptism—the heir on whom so many hopes are pinned, about whom they have spoken for so long; after years of waiting and longing, of praying to God and hounding Dr. Grabow, he is here. And he looks so totally unimposing.

His tiny hands play with the gold braid on his nurse's bodice, and his head, covered by a pale blue lace-trimmed bonnet, lies turned slightly to one side on the pillow; his eyes pay no attention to the pastor, but peer instead out into the room full of relatives—blinking, inspecting, almost precocious eyes, with very long lashes and irises whose lustrous, vague golden brown hovers between the pale blue of his father's and the brown of his mother's, depending on the light. But the corners are set deep on both sides of the nose, are tucked in bluish shadows, lending his little face—hardly a face at all yet—a peculiar look of premature age hardly suitable for a four-week-old baby. But God will see to it that this bodes nothing unfortunate, because his mother, who is certainly in good health, has the same trait. But no matter—he is alive, and he is a boy, which was the real cause for joy just four short weeks ago.

He is alive—but it might have turned out differently. The consul will never forget how four weeks ago good Dr. Grabow, finally able to take leave of mother and child, shook his hand and said, "You have reason to be very grateful, my friend, it was a close call." The consul did not dare to ask how close a call it was. He simply puts aside the horrible thought that this tiny creature, for which he yearned in vain for so long, came into the world in almost eerie silence and very nearly met the same fate as Antonie's second daughter. But he is well aware that four weeks ago both mother and child survived a precarious hour, and in his happiness he bends down tenderly to Gerda, who is seated next to Elisabeth Buddenbrook and leans back now in her easy chair, her patent-leather shoes crossed on a velvet cushion in front of her.

How pale she still is, and how exotically beautiful her pallor is in contrast to her heavy chestnut hair and mysterious eyes, which rest now on the preacher in a kind of half-veiled mockery. He is the Reverend Andreas Pringsheim, *pastor marianus*, who, although still very young, assumed the pastorate of St. Mary's after old Kölling died unexpectedly. He holds his hands clasped fervently just below his upraised chin. He has short, curly blond hair and a bony, smooth-shaven face with an almost theatrical expression ranging from fanatical solemnity to radiant transfiguration. He comes from Franconia, where for several years he tended a little Lutheran flock in the midst of so many Catholics, and under the strain of producing a pure diction filled with pathos, he speaks a dialect peculiarly his own, a unique blend of long and dark vowels, which he often accents abruptly and flavors with an "r" rolled against his teeth.

He praises God with either a softly swelling or a suddenly loud voice, and the family listens: Frau Permaneder, wrapped in an earnest dignity that hides her delight and pride; Erika Grünlich, almost fifteen years old now, a robust young girl with a long braid coiled atop her head and her father's pink complexion; Christian, who arrived only this morning from Hamburg and whose deep-set eyes rove from one side of the room to the other. Pastor Tiburtius and his wife have not let the long trip from Riga discourage them from being present at the ceremony: Sievert Tiburtius, who has laid the two strands of his long, scraggly beard over both shoulders and whose little gray eyes now and then unexpectedly grow larger and larger, sticking out until they almost pop; and Clara, who stares straight ahead, with dark, solemn, severe eyes, occasionally putting her hand to her brow, because there is pain in there. They have, moreover, brought the Buddenbrooks a splendid present: a huge, stuffed brown bear, standing on its hind legs, its jaws gaping wide; one of the pastor's relatives shot it somewhere in Russia, and it now stands in the vestibule downstairs, a bowl for calling cards between its paws.

The Krögers' son Jürgen, the postal official from Rostock, is home on a visit—a quiet man, dressed very simply. No one knows where Jakob is at present, except his weak-willed mother, née Oeverdieck, who is secretly selling off the family silver in order to send money to her disinherited son. The Ladies Buddenbrook are on hand, too, and their delight on this joyous family occasion is profound; this, however, does not prevent Pfiffi from remarking that the child looks rather sickly, an observation which her mother, née Stüwing, and her sisters, Friederike and Henriette, unfortunately feel duty-bound to endorse. Poor Klothilde—gray, gaunt, patient, and hungry—is moved both by Pastor Pringsheim's words and by the anticipation of layer cake and chocolate. Those attending who are not members of the family are Herr Friedrich Wilhelm Marcus and Sesame Weichbrodt.

Now the pastor turns to the two godparents and instructs them as to their duties. Justus Kröger is one of them. Consul Buddenbrook refused to ask him at first. "Let's not tempt the old man to commit some folly," he said. "Every day there are the most dreadful scenes between him and his wife on account of his son. What little property he has left is melting away, and his worries are so great that he has started to be careless about how he dresses. And guess what will happen if we ask him to be a godparent. He'll give the child an entire table service of pure gold and won't even let us thank him for it." But when Uncle Justus heard that someone else was to be the godparent—Stephan Kistenmaker, the consul's friend, was mentioned—he was so hurt that they included him after all. And to Thomas Buddenbrook's relief, the gold beaker he gave the child was not inordinately massive.

And the second godparent? It is this dignified old gentleman with snow-white hair, who is sitting in the most comfortable armchair, bent down over his cane and wearing a high neckband and a soft, black cloth coat with the tip of a red handkerchief peeking, as always, from its back pocket—it is Mayor Oeverdieck. What a coup, what a triumph! A great many people cannot understand how it was accomplished—good God, they were hardly related. The Buddenbrooks must have dragged the old man in by the hair. And, indeed, it was the result of a plot, a little scheme contrived by

Madame Permaneder and the consul. Actually, it was only a joke at first, born out of the joy that both mother and child were safe and well. "It's a boy, Tony! He should have the mayor for his godfather," the consul shouted; but Tony picked up on the idea and developed it in earnest, and after due consideration Tom agreed to make the attempt. And so they hid behind Uncle Justus, who sent his wife to see her sister-in-law, who was the wife of Oeverdieck the lumber merchant, whose job it was to soften up her aged father-in-law. And then Thomas Buddenbrook did his part and paid a reverential visit to the head of state.

And now, while the nurse raises the baby's bonnet, the pastor carefully dips his fingers in the silver basin—lined with gold—that has been set in front of him, and he sprinkles two or three drops of water on the sparse hair of this little Buddenbrook, while slowly and expressively speaking the baptismal names: *Justus, Johann, Kaspar*. This is followed by a short prayer, and the relatives file past, each congratulating the silent, indifferent creature with a kiss on the brow. Therese Weichbrodt is the last, and the nurse has to hold the baby down to her somewhat; but then Sesame gives him *two* kisses. Each pops softly, and in between she says, "You good chawld."

It takes three minutes for them to group themselves in the salon and sitting room, and now the sweets are passed. Even Pastor Pringsheim sits there sipping at the layer of cool whipped cream above the hot chocolate; he is still dressed in his ruff and long robe, his broad, shiny black boots sticking out from under the hem, and he chats away with that same transfigured face, but in an easy conversational tone that is much more effective than his homily. Every gesture makes the explicit point: You see, I can put aside my priesthood and be a quite harmless and merry child of the world. He is an urbane, obliging man. When he speaks with old Madame Buddenbrook he is slightly unctuous; with Thomas and Gerda he is a man-of-the-world with polished gestures; with Frau Permaneder he takes a cheerful, hearty, roguish tone. Now and then, whenever he remembers to do so, he folds his hands in his lap, lays his head back, scowls, and makes a long face. When he laughs, he draws air in between his clenched teeth in a series of jerking hisses.

Suddenly there is a stir in the hallway, they can hear the servants laughing; and now at the doorway there appears a curious gentleman, who has come to offer his own congratulations. It is Grobleben—Grobleben, from the end of whose scrawny nose, no matter what the time of year, there always hangs a longish droplet that never seems to fall. Grobleben is a worker in one of the consul's warehouses, and he is allowed to earn a little extra on the side by polishing his employer's boots. He appears on Breite Strasse early every morning, picks up the shoes outside the door, and cleans them downstairs in the entrance hall. He appears at all family celebrations, however, dressed in his Sunday best, in order to present some flowers and to make a speech in his whining, sniveling voice—and all the while, the droplet dangles at the end of his nose. For this he then receives a small gift of money. But he doesn't do it *for that!*

He has donned a black coat—one of the consul's old ones—but still has on his greasy high-top boots and has wound a blue woolen scarf around his neck. In one of his gaunt red hands he holds a large bouquet of roses slightly past their prime—now and then a petal drifts slowly to the carpet. His small, inflamed eyes blink in all directions but apparently without seeing much of anything. He stays in the doorway, holds the bouquet out in front of him, and begins his speech at once, while old Madame Buddenbrook nods encouragement at every word and occasionally prompts him a little. The consul watches him with one pale eyebrow raised, and several other members of the family—Frau Permaneder, for instance—cover their mouths with handkerchiefs.

"I'm jist a poor man, ladies 'nd gents, but I got a tender heart, and the joy 'nd happiness what touches my master, Consul Buddenbrook, who's alliz been good to me, why, that touches me, too, so I'm here to heartily 'gratulate Herr Buddenbrook 'nd his good wife 'nd the whole 'spectable fam'ly, 'nd to wish this here child a long, healthy life, 'cause they well deserve it, afore God and man they do, 'nd there ain't many men like Herr Buddenbrook, no, sir, 'cause he's a fine gen'leman 'nd the good Lord 'll see to it he's rewarded. . . ."

"Fine, Grobleben! That was a right fine speech! Many thanks, too, Grobleben. And now what did you plan to do with those roses?"

But Grobleben is not finished yet; he pushes his whiny voice up a notch until it drowns the consul out. ". . . 'nd the good Lord'll see to it he's rewarded, I say, him 'nd his whole fam'ly, when that day comes when we're all astandin' afore His throne, for the day's acomin' when the grave'll take us all, rich 'nd poor alike, 'cause that's as His holy will 'nd counsel wants it, 'nd the one he gits an old crate, and t'other he gits a fine polished coffin made o' precious wood, but we'll come to rot, we'll all come to rot, to rot . . . to rot!"

"Now, now, Grobleben. We're here for a christenin', and you're already at the rottin'."

" 'nd here's some flowers for you, too," Grobleben concludes.

"Thank you, Grobleben. You shouldn't have. Why, they must have cost you a fortune. And I haven't heard a speech like that in ages. So, here you are, and you have a right enjoyable day yourself." And the consul puts a hand on his shoulder and gives him a thaler.

"Here, my good man," old Madame Buddenbrook says. "Do you love your Saviour?"

"Love 'im with all my heart, ma'am, that's the gospel truth." And Grobleben accepts her thaler as well, and a third from Madame Permaneder; and then, after much shuffling of his feet, he departs, so lost in thought that he takes his roses with him—at least those that are not lying on the carpet by now.

And now the mayor makes his move to leave, too—the consul escorts him down to his carriage. This is the sign for the other guests to say their goodbyes as well, because Gerda Buddenbrook needs her rest. The rooms quickly grow quiet. Old Madame Buddenbrook, Tony, Erika, and Mamselle Jungmann are the last to leave.

"Yes, Ida," the consul says, "I've been thinking about it, and Mother has agreed. You've helped raise us all, but once little Johann is a bit older—he still has his nurse right now, and will probably need a day nurse for a while after that—would you like to move in here with us?"

"Yes, Consul Buddenbrook, I would. That's if your wife is agreed."

But Gerda is content with this idea as well, and so the suggestion becomes a settled plan.

As they are leaving, however, and still standing in the doorway, Frau Permaneder turns around once more. She goes back inside to her brother, kisses him on both cheeks, and says, "What a beautiful day, Tom. I'm so happy, happier than I've been for years. We Buddenbrooks aren't on our last legs yet. And anybody who thinks we are is making a very big mistake, thank God. And now that little Johann is here—it's so wonderful that we have another Johann again—I feel as if a whole new era is beginning."

2

CLUTCHING HIS FASHIONABLE gray hat and yellow walking stick with the bust of a nun on the knob, Christian Buddenbrook, owner of the firm H. C. F. Burmeester & Co., Hamburg, entered the sitting room, where his brother was sitting reading with Gerda. It was nine-thirty on the same evening as the baptism.

"Good evening," Christian said. "Thomas, I need to speak with you at once. Excuse us, Gerda. It is urgent, Thomas."

They crossed to the dark dining room, where the consul lit one of the gas lamps on the wall and observed his brother. He had a bad feeling about this. Apart from their greeting that morning, he had not yet had an opportunity to speak with Christian; but he had watched him carefully during the festivities and noticed that he was unusually serious and uneasy, that in the course of Pastor Pringsheim's homily he had inexplicably left the salon for several minutes. Thomas had not written Christian a single line since that day in Hamburg when he had personally delivered ten thousand marks *courant* to him, an advance on his inheritance to cover debts. "Just keep it up," the consul had said, "and you'll soon have emptied your piggy bank. For my part, I only hope that you will cross my path as little as possible in the future. You have put my friendship to a hard test over these past few years." Why was he here now? Something very urgent must have driven him to it.

"Well?" the consul asked.

"I can't go on," Christian replied and sat down facing sideways on one of the high-backed chairs set around the dining table; he held his hat and walking stick between his knees.

"Might I ask what you can't go on with, and what brings you here to me?" the consul said; he remained standing.

"I can't go on," Christian repeated, shaking his head back and forth with dreadful seriousness and letting his little, round, deep-set eyes wander about the room. He was now thirty-three years old, but he looked much older. His reddish-blond hair was so sparse now that almost all the skin on his skull was visible. The bones protruded above his sunken cheeks, and his naked, fleshless, gaunt nose jutted out between them in one huge hook.

"If only it were just this," he continued, running his hand along his left side without touching his body. "It isn't a pain, it's an ache, you know, a constant, vague ache. Dr. Drögemüller in Hamburg told me that all the nerves on this side are too short. Just imagine, all the nerves on my left side are too short. It's so strange—sometimes I'm certain it is going to go into spasms or some sort of paralysis, permanent paralysis. You have no idea—I never get a good night's sleep. I start up in bed, because my heart isn't beating and that simply terrifies me. And it doesn't happen just once, but ten times before I finally fall asleep. I don't know whether you know the feeling. Let me try to describe it precisely. It's as if . . ."

"Spare me," the consul said icily. "I don't presume you've come here to tell me that?"

"No, Thomas, if only it were *that*; but it's not just *that*. It's my business. I can't go on."

"You're in trouble again?" The consul didn't bristle, didn't even raise his voice. He asked the question quite calmly, observing his brother's profile with a cold, weary eye.

"No, Thomas. To tell the truth—it doesn't matter really—I never got out of trouble, even with the ten thousand a while back, as you well know. It only kept me from having to close up shop. The thing is—right after that I lost more money, in coffee. And then there was that bankruptcy in Antwerp. That's the truth. After that, I didn't really do much of anything, just lay low. But a man has to live on something, and now there are my IOUs and other debts. Five thousand thalers. Oh, you have no idea what bad shape I'm in. And to top it off, there's this ache that . . ."

"So, you lay low!" the consul shouted, beside himself now. He had lost his self-control after all. "You just left the wagon there in the mud and sought to amuse yourself elsewhere. Do you think I'm blind, that I don't know what kind of life you lead, in the theater and at the circus and in your clubs, you and your trashy women?"

"You mean Aline, don't you? Yes, your tastes don't run in that direction, and perhaps it's my misfortune that mine do, far too much. Because you're right, it does cost me a lot of money and will continue to do so, because I have to tell you something—this is just between us brothers—her third child, the little girl, the one born about six months ago, she's mine."

"You ass."

"Don't say that, Thomas. Do be just, even if you are angry, be just to her and to . . . Why shouldn't it be mine? And as for Aline, she is certainly not trashy. I won't allow you to call her that. She is quite particular about whom she lives with, and she broke off with Consul Holm just for me, and he has more money than I do, that's how decent a woman she is. No, you have no idea, Thomas, what a splendid creature she is. She's so healthy . . . so *healthy.*" Christian repeated the word, holding up his hand to his face, with the back facing out and his fingers cramped, just as he used to do when telling about "That's Maria" and the "depravities" of London. "You should see her teeth when she laughs. I've never seen teeth like that in all the world, not in Valparaiso and not in London. I'll never forget the evening I met her. I was at Uhlich's, in the oyster bar. She was going with Consul Holm at the time; but I told a story or two and was nice to her. And so, when we ended up together later on—ah yes, Thomas. That's quite a different feeling from the one you get making a good business deal. But, then, you don't like to talk about such things, I can see it from your face—and it's all over now, in any case. I'll say my goodbyes to her, although I will stay in contact, because of the child. I'll pay off everything in Hamburg, all my debts, you know, and then close up shop. I can't go on. I've spoken with Mother, and she's willing to advance me another five thousand thalers, so that I can put my affairs in order, and I'm sure you'll agree to that, too, because it's certainly better if we just say that Christian Buddenbrook is liquidating his business and going abroad, rather than that he's bankrupt. You must admit

I'm right there. I'm going back to London, Thomas—I'll take a position in London. The independent life isn't for me at all, I can see that more and more now—all that responsibility. When you're an employee you can just go home each evening without a care. And I enjoyed my time in London, too. Do you have any objection?"

During the whole quarrel, the consul had stood with his back to his brother, his hands in his pockets, drawing little figures in the carpet with one foot.

"Fine, then, go to London," he said curtly. And without turning even so much as halfway toward Christian again, he left him behind and strode back to the sitting room.

But Christian followed him. He walked over to Gerda, who was reading to herself now, and extended his hand to her. "Good night, Gerda. Yes, Gerda, I'll be going off to London again soon. It's so strange the way a man gets tossed about in life. And so back again into the great unknown, you know, off to the big city, where adventure meets you at every step and there's so much to experience. It's curious—do you know the feeling? It sits right here, sort of in your stomach—really quite curious."

3

JAMES MÖLLENDORPF, the oldest of the merchant senators, died a grotesque and ghastly death. Diabetic and senile in his last years, he let his instincts of self-preservation desert him to the point where he succumbed more and more to his passion for cakes and pastries. Dr. Grabow, the Möllendorpf family physician, had protested with all possible energy, and the worried family had employed gentle force to cut off the old man's supply of sweets. But what did the senator do? In his deteriorated mental state, he rented a room, a chamber, little more than a hole on some disreputable street—on Kleine Gröpel Grube, on Engelswisch or An der Mauer—and then slunk into his hideaway to eat his pastries. And it was there that they found his lifeless body, his mouth full of half-chewed cake, crumbs scattered over his coat and the grubby table. A fatal stroke had put an end to his slow deterioration.

The family kept the gruesome details of his death secret as best they could; but the story spread quickly through town and became the chief topic of conversation on the exchange, at the Club, at the Harmony, in offices, at town-council meetings, and at parties and balls. For the incident had occurred in February—February of 1862—and the social season was still in full swing. Even the women who gathered for Madame Buddenbrook's Jerusalem Evenings would start to talk about Senator Möllendorpf's death whenever Lea Gerhardt took a break in her reading; in fact, the little Sunday-school pupils whispered about it as they reverentially crossed the Buddenbrooks' vast entrance hall; and Herr Stuht in Glockengiesser Strasse had an extended discussion about it with his wife, who moved in the highest social circles.

But people's interest could not long remain concentrated on past events. With the very first rumors about the death of the old gentleman, a very important question had simultaneously arisen, and once he was resting under the earth, that question alone aroused general excitement: who would be his successor in the senate?

What suspense, what subterranean activity. A stranger, come to have a look at the town's medieval sights and the charming environs, notices nothing—but what bustle, what agitation beneath the surface. And what a clash of opinions—solid, sound opinions without a trace of unwholesome skepticism. With much rumbling and blustering, convictions are tested and slowly, very slowly, move toward consensus. Passions are aroused. Ambition and vanity burrow in silence. Hopes long in their coffins awaken, stand up tall, and are disappointed. Henning Kurz, the old merchant from Becker Grube, who always gets three or four votes at every election, will once again sit at home on election day, trembling and awaiting the call. But he will not be elected this time, either; he will go on strolling down the street, tapping his walking stick, his face full of self-satisfaction and respectability. And he will carry to his grave his secret mortification that he was never elected senator.

When James Möllendorpf's death was discussed at the Buddenbrook family dinner on Thursday, Frau Permaneder first expressed her regrets several times, but then she began to let the tip of her tongue play along her upper lip and cast her brother a sly look—which caused the Ladies Buddenbrook to exchange indescribably knowing glances, and then, simultaneously, as if on command, they closed their eyes and mouths firmly for one long second. The consul acknowledged his sister's artful smile for a moment, but now changed the topic of conversation. He knew that people in town were openly talking about the same thought that Tony was blissfully turning over in her mind.

Names were suggested and rejected. Others emerged to be considered. Henning Kurz from Becker Grube was too old—it was high time for some fresh new energies. Consul Huneus the lumber merchant, whose millions would certainly have weighed in his favor, was constitutionally excluded because his brother was already a member of the senate. Consul Eduard Kistenmaker the wine merchant and Consul Hermann Hagenström held their own on the list. But from the very beginning, one name was constantly mentioned: Thomas Buddenbrook. And the closer election day drew near, the clearer it became that he and Hermann Hagenström had the best chances.

No doubt of it—Hermann Hagenström had his supporters and admirers. His devotion to civic affairs, the stunning speed at which the firm of Strunck & Hagenström had prospered and grown, the luxurious life the consul led, his grand home, and the *pâté de foie gras* he ate for breakfast—it all could not help making an impression. This large, rather stout man with a reddish, short-cropped beard and somewhat flat nose that hung down over his upper lip; this man who had a grandfather that no one, not even he, had ever met, and a father who had come close to social ostracism because of his marriage to a wealthy but suspect woman; this man whose own marriage had nevertheless connected him with both the Huneuses and the Möllendorpfs, thereby placing his name on the list of five or six ruling families and making himself their equal—this man was undeniably an intriguing and respected figure in town. But the real novelty, the distinctive trait that made him so attractive and conspicuous a personage and singled him out for a leading position in the eyes of many people, was his liberal and tolerant nature. The easy, flamboyant way he earned and spent his money was very different from the dogged, patient labor based on strict traditional principles that characterized his fellow merchants. This man stood on his own feet, unencumbered by the chains of custom and reverence for the past—he was a stranger to anything old-fashioned. He did not live in one of the old patrician mansions that wasted absurd amounts of space with white enameled galleries above immense paved entrance halls. His new house on Sand Strasse—the southern extension of Breite Strasse—was free of old architectural strictures; it had a simple painted façade and cleverly utilized its space; the furnishings were luxurious, elegant, and comfortable. And then, just recently, he had thrown one of his grand evening parties and had invited a soprano from the municipal theater to sing after dinner for his guests—among them, his lawyer brother, so renowned for his wit and love of the arts; it was said he had paid the lady handsomely. He was not a man who would rise in the town council to endorse the appropriation of large sums for restoring and preserving the town's medieval monuments. But it was a fact that he had been the first, absolutely the first, in town to illuminate his residence and office with gas. No doubt of it—if any tradition governed Consul Hagenström's life, it was the totally open, progressive, tolerant, and unbiased outlook he had inherited from his father, old Hinrich Hagenström—and this formed the basis of the general admiration he enjoyed.

Thomas Buddenbrook's prestige was of a different sort. He was not just one man—people honored in him the unique and unforgettable contributions of his father, grandfather, and great-grandfather; quite apart from his own success in commercial and public affairs, he was the representative of a century of civic excellence. The most important factor, to be sure, was the easy, refined, and irresistibly charming way he had of embodying that history and turning it to his own account. What distinguished him, even among more learned fellow citizens, was that he was a man of exceptional refinement and culture, which both disconcerted people and inspired their respect.

That Thursday at the Buddenbrooks, with the consul present, there was only brief, almost indifferent mention made of the forthcoming election, and even at those remarks old Madame Buddenbrook would discreetly avert her pale eyes. Now and then, however, Frau Permaneder was unable to refrain from displaying a little of her amazing knowledge of the constitution, whose articles about the election of senators she had studied as exhaustively as she had the laws of divorce on past occasions. She spoke about electoral chambers, electors, and ballots, weighing all conceivable eventualities and reciting verbatim and without a hitch the solemn oath the electors had to take; she pointed out that the constitution demanded "free and frank discussion," in each of the electoral chambers, of every man whose name was on the list of candidates, and expressed her keen desire to be allowed to participate in the "free and frank discussion" of Hermann Hagenström's qualifications. And in the next moment she bent forward and began to count the prune pits on her brother's dessert plate. "Tinker—tailor—soldier—sailor——senator!" she said, using the tip of her knife to flip the missing pit from her own little plate. After dinner, however, she could contain herself no longer, and tugged the consul by the sleeve over to the window seat.

"O Lord, Tom! Suppose you do get elected, and our coat-of-arms is hung up in the town hall's Chamber of War—I think I'd expire for joy, just keel over dead, you wait and see."

"All right, Tony—and now a little more self-control and dignity are in order, please. You usually aren't at a loss for those, are you? Do you see me carrying on like Henning Kurz? Our name means something even without the 'Senator.' And I hope you'll remain among the living either way."

And the furor, the debate, the clash of opinions continued. Consul Peter Döhlmann, the *suitier*, whose business was now in total ruin and existed in name only, and who every morning at breakfast devoured a little more of his twenty-seven-year-old daughter's inheritance, did his part by attending two dinners, one given by Thomas Buddenbrook, the other by Hermann Hagenström, and each time he addressed his host in a loud, resounding voice as "Senator." Siegismund Gosch, however, old Gosch the broker, walked about as a roaring lion, offering to throttle forthwith anyone who was not of a mind to vote for Consul Buddenbrook.

"Consul Buddenbrook, gentlemen—ah, what a man! I stood at his father's side back in '48, as with a single word he tamed the rage of the unchained rabble. Were there justice upon this earth, it would have been his father—indeed, his father's father—who was elevated to the senate."

Ultimately, however, it was not so much Consul Buddenbrook himself and his personality that set Herr Gosch's passions afire, as it was the young Madame Buddenbrook, née Arnoldsen. Not that the broker had ever exchanged so much as one word with her. He did not belong to the circle of rich merchants, did not dine at their tables or visit back and forth with them. But, as was noted earlier, Gerda Buddenbrook had no sooner appeared in town than she was spotted by the gloomy broker, whose roving eye was ever on the lookout for something extraordinary. With unerring instinct, he realized at once that this was a presence, a vision, aptly suited to give some meaning to his unfulfilled life, and although she barely knew him by name, he made himself her slave, body and soul. And from that moment on, like a tiger circling its tamer, his thoughts had circled around this high-strung and highly reserved lady, to whom he had never been introduced; if he chanced to meet her on the street he would, to her great surprise, doff his Jesuit hat and strike the cunning, fawning pose of a tiger, while bestial savagery played across his face. This world of mediocre men offered him no hope of committing some gruesome, ruthless deed in honor of his lady—but had he been called to account for it, he would have wrapped his hunchbacked body in his cape and stared them all down with gloomy cold indifference. But their boring conventions would never allow him to raise her to an imperial throne by committing murder and other foul, bloody crimes. All he could do was cast his vote in the town hall for her husband in token of his fierce respect, and perhaps, one day, to dedicate to her his translation of Lope de Vega's complete works.

4

THE CONSTITUTION DEMANDS that any vacant seat in the senate must be filled within four weeks. Three weeks have passed since James Möllendorpf's demise, and now election day is here. It is late February and a thaw has set in.

It is one o'clock in the afternoon and people are thronged along Breite Strasse in front of the town hall—the town hall, with its tracework of glazed tiles, its tapering towers and turrets silhouetted against the whitish gray sky, its covered staircase supported by projecting columns, its arcades whose pointed arches reveal a view of the market square and its fountain. People stand there, never flagging, while the dirty slush melts away under their feet; they look at one another, they crane their necks to see what is happening up front. Because there, just behind those doors, is the council hall, where the electors, chosen from the senate and the town council, are now seated in a semicircle of fourteen armchairs, awaiting the nominations from the electoral chambers.

It has proved to be a protracted affair. It appears that debate in the three electoral chambers simply will not die down, that the battle is hard, and that the three chambers have still not nominated the same name to submit to the electors in the council hall—otherwise the mayor would have immediately declared him elected. How strange! No one understands where all these rumors are coming from, how they get started; but somehow they find their way from behind the doors and spread out into the street. Can it be that Herr Kaspersen, the elder of the two bailiffs, who has always called himself a "servant of the state," is signaling what he knows to someone outside, by clenching his teeth or turning his eyes away or screwing up one corner of his mouth? The latest rumor is that the nominations have been submitted to the electors in the council hall, and that each of the three electoral chambers has nominated someone else: Hagenström, Buddenbrook, Kistenmaker. They can only hope to God now that there will be an absolute majority when the electors cast their first secret ballot. The people who aren't wearing warm boots begin to shift and stomp their legs to warm their aching cold feet.

There are all kinds of people standing and waiting here. There are sailors with bare tattooed necks, their hands stuck in their wide, low trouser pockets; grain haulers with blouses and knee breeches of black glazed linen and faces expressing vast integrity; wagon drivers, who with whip in hand have climbed up on piles of grain sacks to wait out the election results; servant girls wearing scarves, aprons, heavy striped skirts, and little white caps perched at the backs of their heads and carrying large market baskets over their bare forearms; the women who sell fresh fish and vegetables, wearing their straw scoop-bonnets; even a few pretty farm girls with Dutch caps, short skirts, and long, pleated white sleeves puffing out from their brightly embroidered blouses. And mingling among them, the middle-class folk: shopkeepers from nearby, who have stepped out without a hat to exchange views; young, well-dressed merchants; sons, who are serving three- or four-year apprenticeships in offices run by their fathers or their fathers' friends; schoolboys with bookbags and backpacks.

A woman is standing behind two tobacco-chewing workers with stiff sailor's beards; she eagerly weaves her head from side to side, trying to get a view of the town hall between the shoulders of these two strapping lads. She is wearing a kind of long evening cloak trimmed in brown fur and holds it together from the inside with both hands; her face is completely hidden behind a heavy brown veil. She shuffles her galoshes restlessly in the slush.

"By God, looks like your Kurz ain't gonna make it again this time," one of the workers remarks to the other.

"Nope, 'nd it didn't take you to tell me that, you nitwit. The votin' now is between Hagenström, Kistenmaker, 'nd Buddenbrook."

"So it's jist a matter of which of them three's gonna git the most votes, that it?"

"Yup, 't's what they say."

"Y' know what? I 'spect it'll be Hagenström."

"Y' think so, do you, smarty-pants. What the hell d'you know?" Then he spits tobacco juice at his feet, because in this crowd there is no way he can shoot in a wide arc, hitches up his trousers by the belt with both hands, and goes on: "Hagenström, he's such a tub o'lard he can't even breathe through his nose right, that's how fat he is. Nope, if my Kurz can't git it this time, neither, then I'm for Buddenbrook. He's smart as a fox."

"Well, say what y'want, Hagenström's a lot richer."

"It don't depend on that. That don't make no never mind."

"And then your Buddenbrook's alliz so damn swank in his silk neckties and starch cuffs 'nd that snazzy little mustache. Y'ever see him walk? Hops along like a little dickeybird."

"But that don't make no nevermind, you blockhead."

" 'nd what about that sister of his, what's used up two husband a'reddy?"

The woman in the evening cloak shudders.

"Yup, that's a problem. But whadda we know about that sorta thing? 'nd that ain't no fault of the consul."

"No, it isn't, is it?" the veiled lady thinks to herself, clasping her hands together under her cloak. "Most certainly not, thank God."

" 'nd then," the man who's supporting Buddenbrook adds, "what with Mayor Oeverdieck bein' his son's godfather—now, that counts for sumpin', let me tell y'."

"It certainly does," the lady thinks. "Yes, thank God, that did us some good." She flinches. A new rumor emerging from somewhere has run in a zigzag all the way to her. The first secret vote has been inconclusive. Eduard Kistenmaker, who received the least number of votes, has been dropped from the next ballot. The battle between Hagenström and Buddenbrook goes on. One self-important citizen remarks that, if there is a tie, it will be necessary to choose five arbitrators, who will then decide by simple majority.

Suddenly a voice up near the door cries out, "They've elected Heine Seehas."

Heine Seehas is a well-known drunk who pushes a little wagon and sells steamed dumplings. Everyone laughs and stands on tiptoe to see who the wag is. Even the veiled lady breaks into a nervous laugh that causes her shoulders to jiggle. But at once she straightens up impatiently, pulling herself together as if to say, "Is this a time for making jokes?" And now she peers anxiously between the shoulders of the two workers to catch a glimpse of the town hall. But at the same moment her hands drop to her sides and her cloak falls opens, and she stands there now with drooping shoulders—crushed, devastated.

Hagenström! The news has come—no one knows from where; it is as if it has sprouted from the earth or fallen from heaven, and suddenly it is everywhere at once. There's no denying it. The decision has been made. Hagenström! Yes, yes, so he's the new senator. Well, there is no point in waiting around here any longer. The veiled lady should have known all along. Because life is like that. So she can just go on home now. She feels the tears welling up inside her.

This state of affairs lasts for a mere second—then the whole crowd lurches backward in a wave of shoving that moves from the front to the rear, so that everyone is leaning back against the person behind; and at the same time something bright red flashes just behind the door—the red coats of the two bailiffs, Kaspersen and Uhlefeldt, in full regalia: three-cornered hats, white riding breeches, wide yellow cuffs, and ceremonial swords. They walk side by side, making their way through the crowd, which pulls back as they pass.

They move like fate itself: earnest, silent, secretive, looking neither to the right nor to the left, their eyes lowered, and with inexorable resolve they set out in the direction they have been told to take as a result of the vote. And it is *not* toward Sand Strasse—instead they turn to the right down Breite Strasse.

The veiled lady cannot believe her eyes. But everyone around her sees it, too, and as people jostle to follow the bailiffs in the same direction, they say, "No, no, it's Buddenbrook, not Hagenström." And all sorts of gentlemen are pouring out the doors now, talking excitedly, and they turn to stride rapidly down Breite Strasse, each hoping to be the first to congratulate the new senator.

The lady pulls her evening cloak around her and runs off. She runs—as a lady is not supposed to run. Her veil blows back and her flushed face is visible; but that is unimportant now. And although one of her fur-lined galoshes keeps flapping open in this slush and slows her down dreadfully, she outruns them all. She is the first to reach the house on the corner of Becker Grube, and she rings the bell in the vestibule as if to raise a hue and cry, and shouts to the maid who opens the door, "They're coming, Kathrin, they're coming!" She takes the stairs and bursts into the living room, where her brother lays aside his newspaper—he is actually a little pale—and gestures almost as if to ward her off. She hugs him and repeats the news: "They're coming, Tom. They're coming! It's you, and Hermann Hagenström has lost."

THAT WAS ON a Friday. And the very next day Senator Buddenbrook stood in the council chamber, right in front of the chair formerly occupied by James Möllendorpf, and, in the presence of the assembled city fathers and a committee from the town council, he swore the following oath:

"I will conscientiously discharge the duties of my office, strive with all my power for the good of the state, faithfully obey the constitution of the same, honestly administer all public moneys, and in the performance of my office, including my obligations as an elector, will regard neither my own advantage nor that of relatives or friends. I will execute the laws of the state and do justice to all alike, be they rich or poor. I will also be discreet about any matter that demands my discretion, and especially keep secret all things that must be kept secret. So help me God."

5

OUR WISHES and our endeavors arise from certain needs of our nervous system that we find difficult to put into words. What people called Thomas Buddenbrook's "vanity"—the attention he devoted to how he looked, the luxurious fastidiousness with which he dressed—was in reality something fundamentally different. It was originally nothing more than the attempt by a man of action to be certain that from head to toe he displayed the impeccable correctness that sustains self-confidence. But the demands that he made of himself and that others made of his talents and energies kept growing. He was swamped with private and public duties. When the senate met to divide committee assignments among its members, taxation was designated as his primary responsibility. But his time was also taken up by railroads, customs, and other governmental affairs; and in a thousand meetings of administrative and supervisory commissions over which he now presided as a result of his election, it took all his tact, charm, and flexibility constantly to make allowances for the sensitivities of men much older than he, to appear to defer to their long years of experience, while in fact retaining power in his own hands. If the most remarkable visible change in the man was an increase of "vanity"—that is, the need to refresh and renew himself, to restore the vigor of morning by changing clothes several times a day—the underlying reality was that at age thirty-seven Thomas Buddenbrook was losing his edge, was wearing out much too quickly.

Whenever Dr. Grabow begged him to relax a little, he would answer, "Oh, my dear doctor, I haven't reached that point yet," by which he meant that he still had an untold amount of work to accomplish before—someday far in the future, perhaps—he would achieve a state that he could then lean back and enjoy as a whole man who has attained his goal. The truth was that he hardly believed in such a state himself—but it drove him on and would not leave him in peace. Even when he appeared to be relaxing—reading his newspapers after dinner, for instance—a thousand plans were simultaneously at work in his brain, while he slowly, even passionately twirled one long tip of his mustache and the veins on his pallid temples swelled and stood out. And he devoted the same deadly earnest to planning a business maneuver or outlining a speech as he did to contemplating a complete refurbishing of his supply of underwear—to do it at last in one fell swoop, so that at least in that regard everything would be in perfect order for a while.

And if such purchases and refurbishments gave him some temporary satisfaction and reassurance, he certainly could allow himself to spend the money in good conscience, because business was now flourishing as well as it had only in his grandfather's day. The firm grew in stature not only in the town but also beyond it, and within the community his own reputation grew as well. Everyone acknowledged, whether out of envy or admiration, his cleverness and his hard work—and all the while he was wrestling in vain to find comfort in order and routine, because, to his despair, he found himself forever falling behind his own active imagination.

It was not out of arrogance, then, that Senator Buddenbrook spent this summer of '63 walking about with his mind full of plans to build a grand new house. A happy man stays where he is. But he was so restless that he felt driven to it, and his fellow citizens would also have been right to attribute the project to his "vanity," because that played a role as well. A new house, a radical change in his outward life—that would mean packing, moving, refitting his life, casting aside everything old and superfluous, the detritus of years past. The idea made him feel clean, new, refreshed, inviolable, strong—and he must have needed such feelings, because he reached out eagerly to grab his idea, fixing his eye on one particular spot.

It was a rather large lot at the lower end of Fischer Grube. The house, gray with age and in disrepair, had recently been put up for sale after the death of its owner, an ancient spinster, who had lived alone, a remnant of some forgotten family. The senator wanted to build his house on that lot, and when he walked down to the docks he would often make a point of passing that way to examine it with a careful eye. The neighborhood spoke in its favor: all solid middle-class houses with gables, the most modest of which was directly across the street, a little place with a flower shop on the ground floor.

He put great energy into the project. He made a rough calculation of the costs, and although he came up with a provisional sum that was by no means small, he decided he could manage it without straining his resources. All the same, he would pale at the thought that the whole thing might turn out to be a pointless folly, and even admitted to himself that his present home was more than large enough for himself, his wife, his child, and the servants. But his half-conscious needs were stronger, and, in the hope of finding further justification for his plan in an outside endorsement, he first revealed it to his sister.

"Well, Tony, what do you think? The spiral staircase down to the bathroom is amusing, I grant. But when you come down to it, the house is just a box. Not much to make one's mark with, is it? And now that you've managed to make a senator of me—in other words, do I owe it to myself?"

Oh, good God, what didn't he owe to himself in Madame Permaneder's eyes. She was all earnest enthusiasm. She crossed her arms and paced the room with her shoulders raised slightly and her head laid back. "You're right, Tom. Heavens, how right you are. There's no possible objection, not when a man has an Arnoldsen for a wife, with an extra hundred thousand thalers. And I am proud, you know, that you've taken me into your confidence first. That's very sweet of you. But if you're going to do it, Tom, then it has to be *elegant*, I insist!"

"Well, yes, I share your view. I'm willing to spend some money on it. Voigt will design it, and I can't wait to have you look at the plans with me. Voigt has very good taste."

The second person whose consent Thomas needed was Gerda. She was full of praise for the idea. The confusion of the move would not be pleasant, but she was enthralled with the prospect of a large music room with good acoustics. And as for old Madame Buddenbrook, she was quite ready to view the new house as the logical consequence of all the other things that had brought such happiness and contentment to her life, and for which she thanked her God. Since the birth of an heir and the consul's election to senator, she was more open than ever about expressing her maternal pride; she had a way of saying "my son the senator" that the Ladies Buddenbrook from Breite Strasse found most annoying.

These aging spinsters found all too few distractions to help them over the sensational upswing that Thomas's life had taken. There was little satisfaction in mocking poor Klothilde on Thursdays, and as for Christian, he was simply another Jakob Kröger in their eyes. They knew that he had found a job in London with his former boss, Mr. Richardson, and that recently he had sent a telegram containing the absurd wish to make Fräulein Aline Puvogel his wife, which had met with the sternest rebuff from Madame Buddenbrook. His case, then, was closed. And so they found what compensation they could in the foibles of old Madame Buddenbrook and Frau Permaneder—by turning the conversation to hairdos, for instance; because Elisabeth was perfectly capable of saying, with the most gentle look on her face, that she wore "her" hair quite simply—when any person whom God had endowed with intelligence, and above all the Ladies Buddenbrook, would have to admit that for many years now it had been impossible to call that unchanging reddish blond swatch under the old woman's bonnet "her" hair. But it was even more rewarding to induce Cousin Tony to say something about those persons who had had such an odious influence on her life thus far. Teary Trieschke! Grünlich! Permaneder! The Hagenströms! When provoked, Tony would raise her shoulder slightly and release those names into the air like so many little trumpet blasts, much to the delight of Uncle Gotthold's daughters.

And of course they could not conceal—indeed, found it irresponsible to be silent about—the fact that little Johann was horribly slow learning to walk and talk. They were right about that, and it must be admitted that Hanno—this was Gerda Buddenbrook's nickname for him, which they all used—found it impossible to make intelligible words of the names Friederike, Henriette, and Pfiffi, even though he was able to pronounce the names of all the other members of the family with passable accuracy. And in terms of walking, at fifteen months he had not yet managed a single independent step. It was at about this time that the Ladies Buddenbrook declared, shaking their heads hopelessly, that the child would be mute and lame for the rest of his life.

They were later permitted to admit their error in making this gloomy prophecy; but no one could deny that Hanno was somewhat backward in his development. At a very early age he had had to weather several crises that kept those around him in constant fear. He had come into the world as a silent and less than robust baby, and soon after his christening a three-day attack of cramps and diarrhea had come close to stopping his little heart, which Dr. Grabow had worked so hard to start. But he lived, and the good doctor now minutely regimented his care and diet as a preventative measure against the discomforts of teething, which was about to begin. But no sooner had the first white tip broken through the gum than the seizures began, which kept on recurring and growing worse, terrifyingly worse. And once again the old doctor could only silently press the child's parents' hands in his own. Hanno lay there in complete exhaustion, and the deep circles of shadow around the eyes and the oblique stare indicated inflammation of the brain. They almost hoped this might be the end.

But Hanno regained some strength after all, and his eyes began to fasten on objects. Although he made slow progress in learning to walk and talk, there no longer seemed to be any immediate danger.

Hanno had slender limbs and was rather tall for his age. His light brown hair was very soft and began to grow uncommonly fast at about this same time; very soon it fell in gentle waves down onto the shoulders of his pleated, pinaforelike dress. Facial traits began to take definitive shape, and the family resemblances grew noticeable. From the very beginning, his hands had definitely been Buddenbrook hands: broad, a little short, but with delicate fingers; and his nose was definitely that of his father and great-grandfather, though it appeared the nostrils would flair somewhat more softly. The lower part of the face, however, was long and narrow and was neither

Buddenbrook nor Kröger, but most decidedly belonged to his mother's side of the family. As did the mouth, which even now, at this early stage, he tended to hold closed, so that the expression was somehow both melancholy and apprehensive, and gradually this came to be matched by the look in his peculiar golden-brown eyes with their bluish shadows.

He began to live—watched over by the reserved but affectionate eyes of his father, tended by his mother, who gave particular care to his clothing and surroundings, worshipped by his Aunt Antonie, showered with toy soldiers and tops by his grandmother and Uncle Justus. And when his pretty little buggy was brought out on the street, people watched him with interest and expectation. But as for his dignified nurse, Madame Decho, who had cared for him until now, the decision had been made that it would not be she who would move into the new house, but that Ida Jungmann would replace her and that Elisabeth would have to look for other help.

Senator Buddenbrook put his idea into action. He had no difficulty purchasing the lot on Fischer Grube, and Gosch the broker was fierce in his determination to take on the task of selling the old house on Breite Strasse at once. Herr Stephan Kistenmaker, whose own family was growing and who, along with his brother, had been doing very well in the claret business, immediately offered to buy it. Herr Voigt took charge of building the new house, and soon the whole family could gather each Thursday to unroll his neat plans and gaze upon the façade before it was ever built: a splendid brickwork front with limestone caryatides supporting a great bay window and a flat roof, which prompted Klothilde to remark in her amiable drawl that they could have their afternoon coffee and cake up there. Then there was the problem of the ground-floor rooms on Meng Strasse, which would soon stand empty, because the senator planned to move his offices to Fischer Grube as well; but that issue was soon solved nicely, for it turned out that the Municipal Fire Insurance Company was prepared to rent the space for their offices.

Autumn came, and the old gray walls collapsed into heaps of rubbish. And as winter set in and then lost its fury again, Thomas Buddenbrook's new house rose above the roomy cellars. There was no more exciting topic of conversation for the town. It would be tip-top, the handsomest residence far and wide. Was there any finer in Hamburg, maybe? But it must be damn expensive, too, and the old consul would definitely never have allowed himself such extravagances. The neighbors who lived in the solid, gabled houses propped themselves in their windows and watched the men at work on the scaffolds, took great delight in seeing the walls rise, and tried to guess the date for the roof-raising.

The day came and was celebrated with all due ceremony. An old master mason gave a speech up on the flat roof, and when he finished he flung a bottle of champagne over his shoulder, while above him flags fluttered and the mighty wreath of roses, evergreen branches, and bright ribbons swayed on its pole in the wind. They then moved on to a nearby inn, where all the workers were treated to beer, sandwiches, and cigars; and Senator Buddenbrook, his wife, and his little son—borne on Madame Decho's arm—moved among the rows of diners and gratefully acknowledged the cheers raised in his honor.

Once they were outside, Hanno was placed in his buggy and Thomas and Gerda walked across the street to let their eyes glide along the red façade with its white caryatides. Directly across from them was the little flower shop with a narrow door and a window decorated with a few meager pots of lilies arranged in a row on a display shelf of green glass; and there stood Iwersen, the owner, a blond giant of a man in a woolen jacket, and beside him his wife, a woman of much slighter build, with a dark, Mediterranean-looking face. She was holding a four- or five-year-old boy by one hand and with the other she slowly rocked back and forth a little buggy in which a still younger child lay sleeping—and she was obviously expecting again.

Iwersen made a deep and awkward bow, while his wife, who went on shoving the buggy back and forth, watched with black, long, narrow eyes, calmly and carefully observing the senator's wife as she approached on her husband's arm.

Thomas stopped to point up at the pole and wreath with his walking stick.

"You did a nice job with that, Iwersen."

" 'tain't me you should thank, Senator. That's my wife's handiwork."

"Oh," the senator said, raising his head with a little jerk, and with clear, friendly eyes gazed straight into Frau Iwersen's face for a second. And then, without saying another word, he took his leave with a polite wave of his hand.

6

ONE SUNDAY EVENING in early July—Senator Buddenbrook had moved into his new home about four weeks before—Frau Permaneder paid her brother a call. She crossed the cool, flagstone-paved hallway, which was decorated with reliefs in the style of Thorvaldsen and from which a door led to offices on the right; she rang the vestibule door, which could be opened from the kitchen simply by pressing a little rubber ball, and as she stood admiring the roomy entrance hall, where the Tiburtiuses' bear now stood at the foot of the main staircase, she was informed by Anton the butler that the senator was still at work.

"Fine," she said, "thank you, Anton. I'll just slip in to see him."

But she first moved to her right, on past the office door, to stand in the vast open stairwell, which on the second floor was framed by a continuation of the wrought-iron railing and on the third by a gallery of white-and-gold columns; it ended in a massive burnished chandelier suspended from the dizzying heights of the "skylight." "How elegant," Frau Permaneder said in a low, satisfied voice as she gazed up into the bright, spacious splendor, which for her signified the prominence and triumph of the Buddenbrooks. But then it occurred to her that her mission was a sad one, and she slowly turned to the office door.

Thomas was sitting all alone, writing a letter at his desk beside the window. He looked up, raising one pale eyebrow, and reached a hand out to his sister. "Evening, Tony. What's the good word?"

"Oh, nothing all that good, Tom. The stairwell is just too magnificent, you know. And here you are sitting in the dark, or close to it, writing a letter."

"Yes, an urgent letter. So nothing all that good? In that case, let's take a little stroll in the garden; it'll be more pleasant out there. Come on."

As they crossed the entrance hall, the vibrato of a violin adagio drifted down from the second floor.

"Listen," Frau Permaneder said, stopping for a moment. "Gerda's playing. How divine! Oh, heavens, that woman—she's like a fairy. And how is Hanno doing, Tom?"

"He'll be having his supper with our good Jungmann at the moment. It's too bad he's not making much progress at walking."

"That will come, Tom, that will come. And are you satisfied with Ida?"

"Oh, how could we not be satisfied?"

They moved along the flagstone-paved hallway toward the rear, passing the kitchen on their right, went through a glass door, and stepped down two steps into the pretty and fragrant flower garden.

"Well?" the senator asked.

It was warm and quiet. The air was heavy with sweet odors from the tidy, neatly outlined beds, and from the middle of tall purple irises the fountain sent a softly splashing jet into the darkening sky, where the first stars had begun to flicker. At the rear a flight of stairs flanked by two low obelisks led up to a raised gravel terrace with an open wooden pavilion, its awnings lowered to shade a few garden chairs. On the left the lot was separated from the neighbor's garden by a wall, but on the right it was bounded by the house next door, covered to the roofline with a wooden lattice, which in time would be home to climbing vines. There were a few currant and gooseberry bushes at one side of the stairs and along the pavilion terrace; but the only large tree was a gnarled walnut near the wall on the left.

"Well, the thing is," Frau Permaneder began hesitantly as brother and sister set out on their stroll along the gravel path around the first part of the garden, "Tiburtius has written and—"

"Clara?" Thomas asked. "Please, tell me straight out. Don't beat around the bush."

"Yes, Tom, she's bedridden, and it looks bad. Her doctor is afraid that it's tuberculosis—of the brain—it's hard for me even to say the words. Here, this is her husband's letter. There's another letter enclosed, addressed to Mother, which says the same thing. We're to give it to her after we've prepared her a little for the news. And then there's a second enclosure—it's for Mother, too, from Clara herself, written in pencil in a very shaky hand. And Tiburtius says that she told him that these would be the last lines she would ever write. Because the truly sad part is that she's not really trying to live at all. She's always longed to go to heaven," Frau Permaneder concluded, drying her eyes.

The senator walked beside her, saying nothing, his head lowered, his hands at his back.

"You're so silent, Tom. But you're right—what can one say? And at the same time that Christian is lying ill in Hamburg."

This was indeed the case. Christian's "ache" in his left side had recently grown so intense that it had turned into real pain, causing him to forget all his minor complaints. He had not known what else to do and had written his mother that he felt he must leave London and come home for her to nurse him; then he had simply quit his job and started on his way. But he had made it no farther than Hamburg and had taken to his bed; the doctor had diagnosed rheumatic fever and ordered Christian transferred from his hotel to a hospital, any further travel being impossible at present. And there he lay now, dictating very mournful letters to the nurse tending him.

"Yes," the senator replied softly, "it looks like one thing after another."

She put her arm around his shoulder for a moment. "But you mustn't let it get you down, Tom. You've no right to let that happen. You need all your courage—"

"Yes, by God, I certainly do need that."

"What is it, Tom? Tell me. You were so quiet all afternoon at our gathering last Thursday. Why, if I may ask?"

"Oh—business, my girl. There was a good-sized shipment of rye that I wasn't able to sell at much of a profit. Well, to be honest, a very large shipment that I had to sell at a loss."

"Oh, those things happen, Tom. That's today, and tomorrow

you'll make a profit again. To let yourself get discouraged over something like that—"

"Wrong, Tony," he said, shaking his head. "My mood has not sunk to below zero because of a business loss. It's just the other way around. I truly believe that, and that's why things are as they are."

"But why are you so low?" she asked in alarmed amazement. "I would think you would be happy, Tom. Clara is still alive, and that will turn out all right, with God's help. And as far as the rest goes? Here we are walking in your garden, and everything smells so sweet. There's your new house, a dream come true. Hermann Hagenström lives in a hut compared with it. And you've managed it all yourself."

"Yes, it's almost too beautiful, Tony. By which I mean that it's all too new yet. It still bothers me a little somehow, and that may be why this bad mood comes over me, nags at me, and ruins everything. I was so looking forward to all this, but, as always, anticipation was the best part, because good things always come too late, and then, when it's finished and ready, you can't really enjoy it the way you should."

"Not enjoy it, Tom? A young man like you!"

"We're only as young or old as we feel. And *when* something good we've longed for finally does come along, it lumbers in a little too late somehow, loaded down with petty, annoying, upsetting details, covered with all the grime of reality that we never really imagined, and that is so irritating—irritating."

"Yes, yes. But we're only as young or old as we *feel*, Tom."

"Yes, Tony. It may pass—just a little out of sorts, I'm sure. But I'm feeling older than I am these days. I have business worries, and yesterday, at a meeting of the Büchen Railroad Commission, Consul Hagenström simply rolled right over me, rebutted everything I said, practically had everyone smirking at me. I feel as if that sort of thing wouldn't have happened before. I feel as if something is slipping away, as if I no longer hold it as firmly in my grasp as before. What is success? A mysterious, indescribable power—a vigilance, a readiness, the awareness that simply by my presence I can exert pressure on the movements of life around me, the belief that life can be molded to my advantage. Happiness and success are inside us. We have to reach deep and hold tight. And the moment something begins to subside, to relax, to grow weary, then everything around us is turned loose, resists us, rebels, moves beyond our influence. And then it's just one thing after another, one setback after another, and you're finished. The last few days I've been thinking about a Turkish proverb I read somewhere: 'When the house is finished, death follows.' Now, it doesn't have to be death exactly. But retreat, decline, the beginning of the end. Do you remember, Tony," he went on, slipping his arm under his sister's and lowering his voice even more, "when Hanno was christened, how you said to me, 'It's as if a whole new era is beginning'? I can still hear it quite clearly, and it seemed to me then you were right, because then came the election for senator, and I was lucky, and this house rose up here out of the earth. But 'senator' and 'house' are superficialities, and I know something else that you weren't even thinking about that day, something I've learned from life and history. I know that the external, visible, tangible tokens and symbols of happiness and success first appear only after things have in reality gone into decline already. Such external signs need time to reach us, like the light of one of those stars up there, which when it shines most brightly may well have already gone out, for all we know."

He fell silent, and they walked for a while, saying nothing, the quiet broken only by the splash of the fountain and the breeze whispering in the crown of the walnut tree. Then Frau Permaneder gave a labored sigh that was close to a sob.

"How sad you sound, Tom. Sadder than I've ever heard you. But it's good you've let it out. You'll find it easier to banish all this from your mind now."

"Yes, Tony, I've got to do that, to try as best I can. And now give me the letters from Clara and the pastor. I'm sure you'll not mind if I take matters in hand myself and have a talk with Mother tomorrow morning. But if it is tuberculosis, we shall have to resign ourselves to the worst."

7

AND YOU DIDN'T EVEN ask me? Simply went right over my head?"

"I acted as I believed I had to act."

"You've acted out of total confusion and behaved quite unreasonably."

"Reason is not earth's highest good."

"Oh, spare me the platitudes. It is a matter of simple justice, which you have ignored in the most outrageous fashion."

"May I remind you, my son, that your tone of voice betrays a lack of the respect you owe me."

"And may I reply, my dear Mother, that I have never forgotten the respect I owe you, but that in matters touching the firm and the family I assume the position of my father as the head of that family and am not to be regarded in my capacity as a son."

"And I want you to be silent, Thomas!"

"No, I'll not be silent till you admit your reckless folly and weakness."

"I can dispose of my own property as I choose."

"Fairness and reason impose limits on your choices."

"I would never have thought you capable of wounding me like this."

"I would never have thought you capable of a direct slap in the face like this."

"Tom! Tom, please!" Frau Permaneder's distraught voice broke in. She was sitting at the window seat in the landscape room, wringing her hands and watching her brother pace the room in dreadful, furious strides, while her mother, almost unnerved by anger and hurt, sat on the sofa, one hand propped against a cushion, the other rapping the table when she wanted to emphasize a point. All three of them were in mourning for Clara, who was no longer of this earth, and all three were pale and simply beside themselves.

And what was going on here? Something horrible, ghastly, something that seemed absolutely monstrous and incredible even to those involved: a quarrel, a bitter argument between mother and son.

It was a sultry August afternoon. Only ten days after the senator had gently prepared his mother before handing over to her the letters from Sievert and Clara Tiburtius, it had been his sad duty to give the old woman the news of Clara's death. Then he had set out for the funeral in Riga, had returned with his brother-in-law, Tiburtius, who had spent several days with the family of his dear, departed wife and had even visited Christian in the hospital in Hamburg. And now, two days after the pastor had departed for home, Madame Buddenbrook had, with visible hesitation, made a certain disclosure to her son.

"One hundred twenty-seven thousand five hundred marks *courant*!" he shouted, shaking his clasped hands in front of his face. "Forget the dowry! Let him keep the eighty thousand, even though there are no children. But the inheritance. To promise him Clara's inheritance! And not ask me—simply go right over my head!"

"Thomas, for our dear Lord's sake, be fair to me, please. Could I have done anything else? Could I? She has been taken from us and is with God now, and from her deathbed she wrote, in pencil, with a trembling hand. 'Mother,' she wrote, 'we shall never see one another again here below, and these are the last words I shall ever write, I can feel that so clearly. And my last fleeting thoughts are of my husband. God has not blessed us with children, but what would have been *mine* had I outlived you, let it devolve on him when the day comes that you follow me to that *better* world, that he may enjoy something of it in this life. Mother, this is my last request, a dying woman's request. You will not deny it to me, I know.' And I did not deny it to her, Thomas. I sent her the telegram, and she departed from this world in peace." Madame Buddenbrook wept bitterly.

"And you don't say one word to me about it. It's all kept secret from me. You simply go right over my head," the senator said again.

"Yes, I *did* keep it secret, Thomas. Because I felt that I simply *had* to comply with this last request of my dying daughter. And I knew that you would try to stop me."

"Yes, by God, I certainly would have!"

"But you would have had no right, because three of my children are on my side!"

"Oh, it seems to me my opinion outweighs two women and a sickly fool."

"You speak of your brother and sisters as harshly as you speak to me."

"Clara was a pious but ignorant woman, Mother! And Tony is a child—who knew nothing about this until now, either, by the way. Otherwise she would have let it slip by now, don't you suppose? And Christian? Yes, he managed to get Christian's consent, your Tiburtius did. Who would have expected that of him? Don't you realize yet what sort of man he is, your ingenious pastor? A rogue, that's what he is. A fortune hunter!"

"Sons-in-law are always scoundrels," Frau Permaneder said in a low voice.

"A fortune hunter! And what does he do? He goes to Hamburg, sits down next to Christian's bed, and wins him over. 'Yes,' Christian says, 'yes, Tiburtius, God go with you. But have you any idea of the pain here in my left side?' Oh, it's a conspiracy between stupidity and wickedness!" Beside himself now, the senator leaned against the wrought-iron grate of the cold stove and pressed both clasped hands to his brow.

This paroxysm of fury was out of proportion to the real circumstances. No, it wasn't the 127,500 marks *courant* that had reduced him to a state in which no one had ever seen him before. It was, rather, that, given his general irritable mood, this was the last link in a chain of defeats and humiliations to which he had been subjected in his business and in civic affairs over the last few months. Nothing was going right. Nothing was turning out the way he wanted. Had things gone so far now that, when it came to the most crucial matters, people simply "went right over his head," here in the house of his forefathers? That a pastor from Riga could swindle him behind his back? He could have prevented it, but his influence had not even been put to the test. Events had taken their course without him. But it seemed to him that this sort of thing could not have happened in the past, that it would not have *dared* happen in the past. It was another shock to his faith in his own good fortune, his authority, his future. And it was nothing more than his own inner weakness and desperation that erupted here in this scene with his mother and sister.

Frau Permaneder stood up and hugged him. "Calm down, Tom," she said. "Control yourself. Is it really that bad? You'll make yourself ill. Tiburtius need not live all that long, and after his death, the money returns to us. And it can be changed, of course, if that's what you really want. Can't it be changed, Mama?"

Madame Buddenbrook answered only with sobs.

"No, oh no," the senator said, pulling himself together and waving his hand in a weak, dismissive gesture. "Let it stand as it is. Do you suppose I'm going to run off to the courts and sue my own mother, turning a private scandal into a public one? Let things take their course," he concluded and moved wearily toward the glass door, where he stopped.

"But just don't believe that everything is going all that well for us," he said in a subdued voice. "Tony lost eighty thousand marks *courant*. And Christian has wasted not just the fifty thousand advanced him from his inheritance, but another thirty thousand besides—and there will be more, because he's not earning anything and he'll need to go to Oeynhausen for treatment. And now not only is Clara's dowry gone forever, but someday her whole share of the estate will leave the family for an indefinite period as well. And business is not good; it's been dreadful, in fact, ever since I spent a hundred thousand on my new house. No, things are not going well for this family, not when there are grounds for scenes such as we've had here today. Believe me—believe this if nothing else—if Father were alive, if he were here with us today, he would fold his hands and commend us all to the mercy of God."

8

WARS AND RUMORS of war. Soldiers quartered in homes. Bustle in the streets. Prussian officers move across the parquet on the main floor of Senator Buddenbrook's new home, they kiss the hand of the lady of the house and frequent the Club with Christian, who has returned from Oeynhausen; and on Meng Strasse, Mamselle Rieke Severin, who is Madame Buddenbrook's new companion, helps the housemaid drag piles of mattresses out to the "Portal," the old summerhouse, which is now full of soldiers.

Confusion, commotion, and tension everywhere. Troops march out through the gates, new troops arrive, overrun the town, eat, sleep, fill the citizens' ears with the din of drum rolls, trumpet blasts, and shouted commands—then they march off again. Royal princes are extended a warm welcome. Wave after wave of soldiers come and go. Then silence and suspense.

In late autumn and winter the troops return victorious, are quartered in homes again, and then depart amid the cheers of relieved citizens. Peace. The brief peace of 1865—the future gestates in its womb.

And between two wars, little Johann, with his soft wavy hair and his pleated pinafores, quietly and innocently plays beside the fountain in his garden or up on the "balcony," created especially for him by the addition of a little row of columns on the third-floor landing—a four-year-old at play. His games have a deeper meaning and fascination that adults can no longer fathom and require nothing more than three pebbles, or a piece of wood with a dandelion helmet, perhaps; but above all they require only the pure, strong, passionate, chaste, still-untroubled fantasy of those happy years when life still hesitates to touch us, when neither duty nor guilt dares lay a hand upon us, when we are allowed to see, hear, laugh, wonder, and dream without the world's demanding anything in return, when the impatience of those whom we want so much to love has not yet begun to torment us for evidence, some early token, that we will diligently fulfill our duties. Ah, it will not be long, and all that will rain down upon us in overwhelming, raw power, will assault us, stretch us, cramp us, drill us, corrupt us.

Great things were happening while Hanno played. War broke out, victory was uncertain, and then was decided. Hanno Buddenbrook's hometown, having shrewdly sided with Prussia, could gaze with some satisfaction on rich Frankfurt, which was now made to pay for its faith in Austria and was no longer a free city.

But in July, shortly before the armistice, a large wholesale house in Frankfurt declared bankruptcy, and at one blow the firm of Johann Buddenbrook lost the round sum of twenty thousand thalers *courant*.

PART EIGHT

*(Dedicated to my brother Heinrich—
to the man and to the writer)*

1

HERR HUGO WEINSCHENK had been employed as director of the Municipal Fire Insurance Company for some time now, and whenever he crossed the large entrance hall to pass from the outer to the inner office—striding with a swinging self-assured gait, elbows nonchalantly bobbing at his sides, clenched fists held in front of him—he cut a striking figure; and, indeed, dressed in his buttoned-up frock coat and sporting a small black mustache shaped in manly fashion to frame the corners of his earnest mouth and reveal his drooping lower lip, he seemed the epitome of a busy, prosperous gentleman.

In contrast, twenty-year-old Erika Grünlich was now a tall, pretty young lady in full bloom, with a fresh complexion enhanced by good health and youthful energy. If chance happened to find her descending the staircase, or standing on the landing, just as Herr Weinschenk was passing by—and chance managed this fairly often—the director would tip his top hat, revealing his head of short black hair just beginning to gray at the temples, emphasize the swing in his stride very slightly, and greet the young woman with a surprised and admiring glance from boldly roving brown eyes. And Erika would run off, sit down on a window seat somewhere, and weep in helpless confusion for an hour or so.

Fräulein Grünlich had been raised very properly under Therese Weichbrodt's watchful eye, and her thoughts were not wide-ranging. She wept over Herr Weinschenk's top hat, over the way he lifted his eyebrows when he caught sight of her and quickly let them fall again, over his absolutely royal posture and his carefully balanced fists. Her mother, Frau Permaneder, already saw farther.

Her daughter's future had been a worry for years now, because, compared with other marriageable young ladies, Erika was definitely at a disadvantage. Not only did Frau Permaneder not go out in society—she lived at war with it. The assumption that, because she was twice divorced, people in the best circles regarded her as an inferior had become fixed in her mind somehow, and she saw disdain and spite where often there was probably nothing more than indifference. It was quite likely that Hermann Hagenström, a freethinking and loyal fellow, whom wealth had made cheerful and magnanimous, would have greeted her on the street if he had not felt it strictly forbidden by the way she laid her head back and looked right past him, avoiding his *pâté-de-foie-gras* face, which, to use her own strong language, she "hated like the plague." And so Erika had grown up outside her uncle's social circle, attending none of the senator's balls and having little opportunity to make the acquaintance of young gentlemen.

It was nevertheless Frau Antonie's most fervent wish—particularly since she had "gone out of business" herself, as she put it—that her daughter would fulfill the hopes that had gone so awry for her, that she would marry happily and advantageously, bringing honor to the family and erasing the memory of her mother's fate. Particularly for the sake of her older brother, who had displayed so little optimism of late, Tony longed for some proof that the family's luck had not run out, that they were not finished and done with. Her second dowry, the seventeen thousand thalers that Herr Permaneder had so generously returned, lay ready for Erika; and the moment Frau Antonie's sharp, experienced eye noted the first tender bonds forming between her daughter and the director, she began to importune heaven with prayers that Herr Weinschenk would pay a visit.

And he did. He appeared on the second floor, was received by the three women—grandmother, daughter, and grandchild—joined in ten minutes of small-talk, and promised to return sometime for coffee and more leisurely conversation.

And he did that as well, and they all got to know one another. The director had been born in Silesia, where his aging father still lived; his family apparently did not have to be taken into consideration, inasmuch as Hugo Weinschenk was a self-made man. His self-confidence was typical of such men—not something he was born to, but a little uncertain, a little exaggerated, a little mistrustful. His manners were not quite perfect, and his conversation was frankly clumsy. It was also true that his workaday frock coat had several shiny places, that his cuffs, fastened with the large jet buttons, were not quite fresh and clean, and that an accident had shriveled the nail on the middle finger of his left hand and turned it black. The effect, then, was rather unpleasant, but that did not prevent Hugo Weinschenk from being a hardworking, energetic, and respectable young man who earned twelve thousand marks *courant* a year—or from being, in Erika Grünlich's eyes, a handsome man.

Frau Permaneder quickly reviewed the situation and arrived at an assessment. She spoke openly to her mother and brother about it. It was clear that here was a meeting of interests that complemented one another. Like Erika, Herr Weinschenk had no social connections whatever; the two were meant for one another, were a match obviously made in heaven. If the director, who was nearing forty and whose hair was already flecked with gray, wished to establish a family, something quite appropriate to his position and means, the connection with Erika Grünlich would provide him an opening into one of the first families in town, securing him in his job and advancing his career. As to her daughter's welfare, Frau Permaneder felt confident in saying that at least there was no chance of Erika's meeting her own fate. Herr Weinschenk bore not the least resemblance to Herr Permaneder, and, in contrast to Bendix Grünlich, Hugo Weinschenk was a man with a steady job and a good salary, which by no means precluded a further career.

In short, there was a great deal of good will on both sides. More afternoon visits by Herr Weinschenk followed in rapid succession, and in January, 1867, with a few brief, manly, and straightforward words, he made bold to ask for Erika Grünlich's hand.

From then on he was part of the family. He began to be included on "children's day" and was courteously received by the bride's relatives. No doubt he sensed at once that he was out of place, but he disguised his feelings by striking an even bolder pose; and Madame Buddenbrook, Uncle Justus, and Senator Buddenbrook—though hardly the Ladies Buddenbrook from Breite Strasse—were prepared to be tolerant of this diligent wage-earner, who might lack social graces but was a hard worker.

And tolerance was needed. For instance, when the family was gathered around the dining-room table, someone would have to make a light, diverting comment to break the silence because the director was all too busy dallying with Erika's cheeks or arms, or because he had asked whether orange marmalade was some kind of pudding—he said "puddin'," with a perky stress on the first syllable—or because he ventured the opinion that *Romeo and Juliet* was a play by Schiller. He would offer such comments with self-assured vigor, while nonchalantly rubbing his hands and leaning back to one side against the arm of his chair.

He got along best with the senator, who knew how to steer the conversation safely to politics and business and thus avoid any accidents. His relations with Gerda Buddenbrook, however, drove him to despair. He was so put off by this lady's personality that he was incapable of finding a topic they both could talk about for even two minutes. He knew that she played the violin, and this fact had made a great impression on him; and so, whenever they met on Thursdays, he would confine himself to repeating his jocular question: "How's the fiddle?" After the third time, Gerda Buddenbrook refrained from any reply.

Christian, as was his habit, wrinkled his nose and watched his new relative, and the next day offered an exhaustive imitation of Hugo's actions and speech. Consul Johann Buddenbrook's younger son had recovered from his rheumatic fever in Oeynhausen, but a certain stiffness lingered in his limbs, and he was certainly not free of the periodic "ache" in his left side—where "all the nerves were too short"—or of any other of the ailments to which he felt himself disposed: difficulties in breathing and swallowing, irregular pulse, and a tendency to paralysis, or at least the fear of it. He hardly looked like a man in his late thirties. He was totally bald, with only a few thin, reddish hairs at his temples and across the back of his head; his small, round eyes, roving about restless and pensive, lay deeper than ever in their sockets. And his large, hooked nose was bonier than ever, jutting out even more prominently from between his gaunt, sallow cheeks and above his drooping reddish blond mustache. And his elegant trousers of durable English wool flapped around scrawny, bowed legs.

Upon returning to his mother's home, he moved into his old room off the corridor on the second floor, but spent more time at the Club than on Meng Strasse, because life was not made easy for him there. Rieke Severin, Ida Jungmann's successor, who now managed the servants and looked after the household, was a stout twenty-seven-year-old woman from the country with red coarse-veined cheeks and pouting lips; and her peasant's eye for hard facts told her that she needn't have much regard for this idle teller of tales, who was foolish one day and ill the next, and whom the senator, the real head of the family, passed over with a raised eyebrow—so she simply neglected his needs. "Well, now, Herr Buddenbrook," she would say, "I ain't got time for you!" And Christian would wrinkle his nose and stare at her as if to say, "Aren't you the least bit ashamed of yourself?" and go his stiff-kneed way.

"Do you suppose I ever have a candle?" he asked Tony. "Very seldom. Most of the time I find my way to bed with a match." Or, since his mother could give him only a little pocket money, he might declare, "Hard times. Yes, it was all very different in the old days. Why, just imagine—I often have to borrow five shillings for tooth powder."

"Christian!" Frau Permaneder cried. "How undignified! With a match? Five shillings? Please, don't speak about it at least." She was outraged, shocked, it was an insult to her most sacred feelings—but that changed nothing.

Christian borrowed those five shillings for tooth powder from his old friend Andreas Gieseke, attorney for both civil and criminal law. He was lucky to have such a friend, it served him in good stead, because just last winter, when old Kaspar Oeverdieck had passed away in his sleep and Dr. Langhals had become mayor, Andreas Gieseke, the *suitier* who knew how to maintain his dignity, had been elected senator. But that had not changed the way he conducted his life. People knew that, in addition to the spacious townhouse in which he had resided since his marriage to Fräulein Huneus, he also owned a little, cozily furnished, vine-covered cottage in the suburb of Sankt Gertrud—its sole occupant an extraordinarily pretty, relatively young lady of unknown origins. Above the door was an ornate gilt inscription, just one shining word—"Quisisana"—and the idyllic little cottage was known all over town by that name, which everyone pronounced with soft "z"s and very indistinct "a"s. But as Andreas's best friend, Christian Buddenbrook had gained entry to Quisisana, and there he met with the same sort of success that had been his in Hamburg with Aline Puvogel—and on various occasions in London, Valparaiso, and so many other spots on the globe. He had "told a story or two," he had been "nice to her," and now he visited the vine-covered cottage with the same regularity as Senator Gieseke himself. It is unclear whether this occurred with the knowledge and permission of the latter; it is certain, however, that Christian Buddenbrook found, at no expense whatever, the same homey diversions that Senator Gieseke spent a great deal of his wife's money to enjoy.

Shortly after Hugo Weinschenk's engagement to Erika Grünlich, he offered his future brother-in-law a position in his insurance office; and, indeed, Christian did spend two weeks in the service of the Municipal Fire Insurance Company. But then, unfortunately, the work caused a flair-up not only of the old ache in his left side, but also of several other of those ailments so difficult to diagnose. There was also the problem that the director was a very stern boss, and if Christian made a mistake he did not hesitate to tell his brother-in-law that he was as dense as a walrus—and Christian felt compelled to quit his job.

But, for her part, Madame Permaneder was in such a happy, radiant mood that she was given to brilliant insights—such as: "This earthly life does have its good sides now and then." And, indeed, she blossomed during these weeks filled with the invigorating bustle of a thousand things to plan, with worries about where the couple would live and the feverish task of putting together a trousseau—all of which so clearly brought to mind the days of her own first engagement that she could not help feeling younger and full of boundless optimism. Much of her earlier girlish charm and high spirits returned to her face and gestures. In fact, her boisterous merriment proved such a profanation of the atmosphere on one particular Jerusalem Evening that even Lea Gerhardt let her ancestor's book fall to her lap and looked about the room with the large, oblivious, and mistrustful eyes of the deaf.

Erika was not to be separated from her mother. With Hugo's consent—indeed, at his express wish—it was decided that Frau Antonie, at least for the time being, would live with the Weinschenks, assisting the inexperienced Erika in managing a household—and it was this arrangement that produced in Tony the most exquisite feeling, as if there had never been a Bendix Grünlich or an Alois Permaneder, as if all the failures, disappointments, and sufferings of life were melting away, and as if she could begin anew with fresh hope. It is true that she reminded Erika to thank God for granting her the man she loved to be her husband, whereas she, Tony, had been forced by reason and duty to sacrifice her first and deeply felt love; and it is true that it was Erika's name along with Hugo Weinschenk's that she entered in the family records, her hand trembling for joy—but it was she, Tony Buddenbrook, who was the real bride. It was she who once again examined portieres and carpets with an expert hand, who rummaged through furniture and decorating shops, who was allowed once again to find and rent an *elegant* apartment. It was she who would once again leave the roomy but very pious home of her parents and no longer be merely a divorced woman; it was she who would once more be able to lift her head high and begin a new life that would act as a focus of attention and further the prestige of the family. Yes—but was it all a dream? Dressing gowns suddenly appeared—two dressing gowns, one for her and one for Erika, made of soft, knitted fabric, with broad trains and a band of close-set velvet bows, from neck to hem!

But the weeks of Erika Grünlich's engagement were passing quickly and would soon be over. The young couple paid calls to only a few houses, because the director, being a serious, hardworking man with little experience in society, was of a mind to devote his leisure hours to more intimate, homey activities. There had been an engagement dinner in the great salon of the house on Fischer Grube—attended by Thomas, Gerda, the future bride and groom, Friederike, Henriette, and Pfiffi, and a few close friends of the senator—during the course of which there was some embarrassment over the way the director kept tapping at Erika's neck, much of which was bared by her rather low-cut gown. And now the wedding day drew near.

The columned hall was the setting for the wedding, just as on that day long ago when Frau Grünlich had worn the myrtle. Frau Stuht from Glockengiesser Strasse, the lady who moved in the best circles of society, was there to help the bride arrange the pleats of her satin dress and trim it with sprays of green. Senator Buddenbrook gave the bride away, and Christian's friend Senator Gieseke served as best man; two of Erika's former friends from boarding school were the bridesmaids; Herr Hugo Weinschenk looked imposing and manly and stepped on Erika's long trailing veil only once on the way to the improvised altar; Pastor Pringsheim, his hands clasped under his chin, presided over the ceremony with his unique air of transfigured solemnity; and everything was done as custom and dignity dictated. When the rings were exchanged and they both answered "Yes" in clear though slightly hoarse voices that echoed through the hushed hallway, Frau Permaneder wept audibly, overwhelmed by her past, present, and future—they were still the same innocent and open tears of her childhood. As always at such events, however, the Ladies Buddenbrook smiled rather sour smiles, although Pfiffi had attached a gold chain to her pince-nez in honor of the occasion. Mademoiselle Therese Weichbrodt, who with the years had shrunk to even shorter stature than before, was present as well. Sesame had pinned her oval brooch with the portrait of her mother at her thin neck, and she spoke with that exaggerated firmness meant to hide a deep rush of emotion: "Be heppy, you *good* chawld!"

Then, surrounded by white gods, who still stood out against the blue wallpaper in the same serene poses as always, a substantial and sedate banquet was held, toward the end of which the newlyweds vanished to begin the honeymoon that would take them through several major cities. The wedding was in the middle of April; and for the next two weeks Frau Permaneder, with the assistance of Jakobs the upholsterer, completed one of her masterpieces, adding the final elegant touches to the spacious second-floor apartment she had rented for them in a house halfway down Becker Grube and topping it all off with a rich display of flowers to welcome the newlyweds on their return.

And so began Tony Buddenbrook's third marriage—and that was indeed the appropriate term for it. The senator himself had called it by that name one Thursday when the Weinschenks happened to be absent, and even Frau Permaneder had been delighted by it. All the worries of the household were hers, in fact, but she claimed all the joy and pride as well; and one day, when she chanced to meet Julie Möllendorpf, née Hagenström, on the street, she gazed straight at her with such a triumphant and defiant look that Frau Möllendorpf had no choice but to greet her first. The pride and joy on her face and in her movements became a kind of grave solemnity whenever she led visiting relatives through her new home—making Erika Weinschenk look like another admiring guest in her own house.

Sweeping the train of her dressing gown behind her, her shoulders raised slightly, her head laid back, her basket of keys trimmed with velvet bows dangling from her arm—she was simply mad about velvet bows—Frau Antonie showed her visitors the furniture, the portieres, the translucent china, the dazzling silverware, and the large oil paintings that Herr Weinschenk had chosen, either still lifes of edibles or female nudes—both genres very much his taste; and her gestures seemed to say: "You see, I've accomplished all this for the third time in life. It is almost as elegant as it was with Grünlich, and certainly more elegant than with Permaneder."

Clad in black-and-gray-striped silk and giving off the discreet fragrance of patchouli, old Madame Buddenbrook came to visit; she let her pale eyes glide leisurely over everything and, without actually giving word to her admiration, showed that she approved and was quite satisfied. The senator came with his wife and child, and while he and Gerda silently shared their amusement at Tony's blissful hauteur, he had all he could do to prevent his sister from gorging her adored little Hanno with dried currants and port. The Ladies Buddenbrook came and remarked in unison that it was all so beautiful that, given their own modest maidenly needs, they wouldn't really want to live there. Poor Klothilde came—gray, patient, and gaunt—paid no attention to the teasing, and drank four cups of coffee, offering words of praise for everything in her usual amiable drawl. Now and then, when he found no one at the Club, Christian would drop by as well for a glass of Benedictine; he talked about his intention to act as the agent for a firm that sold champagne and cognac—he knew something about that and it would be easy, pleasant work, you were your own boss, you occasionally jotted down a few orders in your notebook, and, quick as a wink, you had made thirty thalers; he then immediately borrowed forty shillings from Frau Permaneder so that he could present a bouquet to the leading lady at the municipal theater, and by some association of ideas—God only knew what they were—found himself talking about "Maria" and the "depravities" of London, moved on to the story about the mangy dog that had been shipped in a box from Valparaiso to San Francisco, and, now that he was rolling, went on to tell a wealth of stories with such verve and wit that he could have entertained a whole crowded auditorium.

He waxed enthusiastic, he was speaking in tongues now. He told his stories in English, Spanish, Plattdeutsch, and Hamburg dialect; he described knifings in Chile and robberies in Whitechapel, hit upon the notion of rummaging through his collection of comic songs, and now recited some and sang others, mugging like a professional comedian and displaying an especially whimsical talent for hand gestures.

Awalkin' down the street,
Just lazin' through my day,
I chanced to spot a lass
Up ahead a way.
In Paris togs she was,
A bustle at the rear,
A hat so grand on top,
I said, "How do, my dear."
And 'cause she was so cute
I offered her my arm.
She turned and eyed me hard

And spurned my manly charm:
"Go home, my boy, and tend your farm."

And no sooner had he finished the song than he decided to tell about the Renz Circus and began by repeating the dialogue from the opening act of an English clown—did it so wittily that you would have thought you were sitting at ringside. First there was the usual hubbub behind the curtain, followed by "Open the door, will you!" and the rest of the brouhaha with the ringmaster, and then came a whole series of jokes, all of them told in a broad, whiny patois of English and German. There was the story of the man who swallowed a mouse in his sleep and decided to see a veterinarian, who suggested he swallow a cat. And the story about "my grandmother, and a right lively ol' girl she was," who encountered a thousand adventures on her way to the train station, only to arrive just in time to see the train pull out right in front of her nose—"and a right lively ol' girl she was"; and as he delivered his punch line, Christian broke off and triumphantly shouted, "Music, Mr. Director, if you please!"—and, almost as if awakening from a dream, he seemed quite surprised when the music didn't start.

Then, very suddenly, he fell silent—the expression on his face changed, his arms and legs went slack. His little, round, deep-set eyes began to wander restlessly in all directions, and he passed his hand down his left side—it was as if he were listening for something inside him, where strange things were happening. He drank another glass of liqueur, which restored his spirits a little; he tried telling another story, but then, looking rather depressed, he got up to leave.

Frau Permaneder, who found it uncommonly easy to laugh of late and who had enjoyed herself immensely, was still in a merry mood as she accompanied her brother to the door. "Adieu, my agent for champagne and cognac," she said. "Wandering minstrel mine! Come back soon, you old muttonhead!" She almost burst with laughter as he started on his way, and then she went back into her apartment.

But Christian Buddenbrook had paid no attention to her, had

not even heard her—he was deep in thought. "Well," he said to himself, "guess I'll head on over to Quisisana now for a bit." And, with his hat cocked slightly, and making good use of his cane with the nun's bust on the knob, he slowly, stiffly limped down the stairs—almost as if he were a cripple.

2

IT WAS A SPRING EVENING in 1868, and at about ten o'clock Frau Permaneder stopped by her brother's house on Fischer Grube and made her way to the second floor. Senator Buddenbrook was alone in the sitting room; he had drawn one of the chairs upholstered in olive rep up to the round table in the center of the room, just beneath the large gas lamp that hung from the ceiling. He was bent slightly over the table, reading the Berlin *Financial News*, which lay spread out before him; he was holding a cigarette in his left hand, between his index and middle fingers, and a gold pince-nez, which he had been using for some time now for reading, was perched on his nose. Hearing his sister's steps in the dining room, he removed the pince-nez and gazed anxiously into the darkness until Tony entered through the portieres and moved out into the light.

"Oh, it's you. Good evening. Back already from Pöppenrade? How is your old girlfriend doing?"

"Good evening, Tom. Armgard is quite well, thanks. You're here all by yourself?"

"Yes, I'm so glad you've come by. I had to eat my supper alone tonight, as solitary as the pope himself. That's not counting Fräulein Jungmann, of course, but she's no company, because she's constantly popping up to run out and check on Hanno. Gerda is at the Casino—for a violin concert by Tamayo. Christian stopped by for her."

"My word! as Mother would say. Yes, I've noticed, Tom, that of late Gerda and Christian are getting along quite well."

"So have I. Since he's moved back here, she's begun to take a liking to him. She sits and listens attentively whenever he is describing his ailments. Good heavens, he amuses her. Just recently she said to me, 'He's not a solid citizen, Tom. He's even less of a solid citizen than you.' "

"Solid citizen . . . solid citizen, Tom? Well, it seems to me that there's no more solid citizen on God's earth than you."

"Well, yes, but that's not quite how she meant it. Now, take off your things, my girl. You look splendid. So the country air did you some good?"

"It was magnificent," she said, and after removing her mantilla and the hood of her cloak tied with purple silk ribbons, she majestically took a seat in one of the easy chairs by the table. "I slept well, my stomach is better—everything much improved in just that short time. Milk still warm from the cow, and sausage and ham—why, you can't help thriving like the cattle and the crops. And the fresh honey, Tom—I've always said it was the best nourishment. It's a pure product of nature. You know what you're eating there. Yes, and it was really quite sweet of Armgard to remember me after all these years since we were friends at boarding school and invite me. And Herr von Maiboom was terribly polite as well. They simply begged me to stay on for another few weeks, but you know how difficult it is for Erika to handle things without me, and especially now, with little Elisabeth."

"Ah yes, how is the baby doing?"

"She's holding her own, Tom, thanks. She's really doing quite nicely for just four months, even though Friederike, Henriette, and Pfiffi claimed she couldn't live."

"And Weinschenk? How does he like being a father? I never see him except on Thursdays, really."

"Oh, he hasn't changed. You know what a straightforward, hardworking man he is, a perfect model of a husband in a certain sense—he has no use for taverns, always comes directly home from the office and spends his spare time with us. But the thing is, Tom—we can speak openly, I know—he demands that Erika always be in a good mood, constantly wants her to talk and make little jokes, because, when he comes home exhausted and out of sorts, he says that's when he needs a wife who can divert him by being bright and gay, who can amuse him and cheer him up. That's what wives are for, he says."

"Idiot," the senator muttered.

"Pardon? Well, the worst part about it is that Erika tends to be melancholy, Tom—she must get that from me. There are times when she's more quiet and serious and caught up in her own thoughts, and then he scolds her and flares up, says things that, to be honest, are not exactly considerate. It's only too apparent sometimes that he's not from the best of families, that unfortunately he did not enjoy what people call good breeding. Yes, to be frank—a few days before I left for Pöppenrade, he threw the lid of the soup tureen to the floor, smashed it to bits, because the soup was too salty."

"How charming!"

"No, quite the contrary. But let us not judge him by things like that. My Lord, we all have our faults, and he is such a competent, high-principled, hardworking man. No, no, we mustn't judge, Tom. A rough exterior, but good to the core—there are worse things in this earthly life. I've just returned from a situation that is much sadder, let me tell you. When we were all alone, Armgard wept bitter tears."

"You don't say! Herr von Maiboom?"

"Yes, Tom, that's really what I wanted to talk to you about. We're sitting here just chatting, but in fact I've come to see you this evening about a very serious and important matter."

"Well, what is Herr von Maiboom's problem?"

"Ralf von Maiboom is a charming man, Thomas, but he is Squire Sport, a regular harum-scarum. He gambles in Rostock, he gambles in Warnemünde, and he has more debts than there's sand on the shore. You'd never know it spending a few weeks at Pöppenrade. The manor is quite elegant, and everything looks prosperous all around, and there's no lack of milk and sausage and ham. On an estate like that you lose all sense of proportion for the real situation. In short, things have actually gone to rack and ruin, Tom, and that's what Armgard confessed to me with the most heartbreaking sobs."

"Sad, very sad."

"You can say that again. But the thing is that, as I came to realize, they did not invite me there out of totally unselfish motives."

"How do you mean?"

"That's what I wanted to talk to you about, Tom. Herr von Maiboom needs money, he needs a great deal of money very soon. He knew that his wife and I were old friends, and that I'm your sister, and since he was in such straits, he had his wife do his work for him, and in turn she has enlisted me—you see?"

The senator ran the fingertips of his right hand along the part in his hair and scowled slightly. "I think I see, yes," he said. "Your serious and important matter appears to come down to some sort of advance on the harvest at Pöppenrade, if I'm not mistaken. But I'm afraid that you, and your friends, have approached the wrong man. First, I've never done business with Herr von Maiboom before, and this would be a rather curious way to strike up a relationship. Second, although there have been occasions over the years when we—Great-grandfather, Grandfather, Father, and I—have provided advances to some of the landed gentry, we did so only if their character or other circumstances guaranteed us a certain security. But as you yourself described Herr von Maiboom's character and circumstances not two minutes ago, any such guarantees are out of the question in this case."

"You're wrong, Tom. I let you have your say, but you're wrong. This is not about an advance. Maiboom needs thirty-five thousand marks *courant*."

"I'll be damned!"

"Thirty-five thousand marks *courant*, due within less than two weeks. The knife is being held to his throat, and, to put it bluntly, he has to find some way to sell now, at once."

"The whole crop? Oh, the poor man!" And the senator shook his head and tapped his pince-nez on the table. "But it would be a very unusual arrangement for our kind of house," he said. "I've heard of such deals, but mainly in Hessia, where quite a few of the gentry have ended up in the hands of Jews. Who knows what sort of cutthroat will get his clutches on poor Herr von Maiboom."

"Jews? Cutthroats?" Frau Permaneder cried in considerable amazement. "But we're talking about you, Tom, about *you*!"

Suddenly Thomas Buddenbrook tossed his pince-nez on the table, sending it sliding some distance across his newspaper, and turned now with a jerk to face his sister head on. "About—me?" he said, mouthing the words soundlessly with his lips. And then aloud he said, "Go to bed, Tony. You're too tired."

"Yes, Tom, that's what Ida Jungmann always used to say to us whenever we were just starting to have some fun. But I assure you that I've never been more awake and alert than I am now, coming here by stealth of night to present Armgard's—and so, indirectly, Ralf von Maiboom's—proposal to you."

"Well, I'll attribute that proposal to your naïveté and Maiboom's hopeless situation."

"Hopeless, naïve? I don't understand you, Thomas, not in the least. You are offered the chance to do a good deed and at the same time to make the best business deal of your life, and . . ."

"Oh, my dear, you're talking utter nonsense!" the senator shouted and threw himself back impatiently in his chair. "Forgive me, but you and your innocence can be quite exasperating. You don't understand, do you, that you are suggesting I become involved in a highly unrespectable, shabby operation? You want me to fish in troubled waters? To brutally exploit a man? To take advantage of this landed gentleman, to fleece the poor, defenseless fellow? Force him to sell me a whole year's harvest at half the price it will be worth, so that I can make a profit that is nothing but usury?"

"Oh, so *that's* how you see it?" Frau Permaneder said, cowed somewhat into gathering her thoughts. But then she continued, as lively as before, "But, Tom, you really needn't see it that way. Force him? But he's coming to you. He needs the money, and he would like to arrange the matter in a friendly way, under the counter, so to speak, with no one the wiser. That's why he picked up on the old connection with us, and that's why I was invited."

"Put quite simply, then, he is mistaken about me and the character of my firm. I have a tradition behind me. We have never made a transaction like that in over a century, and I am not inclined to be the first to be involved in such maneuvers."

"Of course you have a tradition behind you, Tom, and I certainly respect it. To be sure, Father would never have got involved in something like this—heaven forbid. But who said he would? But, as stupid as I am, I know one thing: that you are a very different man from Father, and that when you took over the business you set quite a different breeze blowing, and that since then you have done many things he would never have done. That's because you are young and enterprising. But I'm afraid that of late you've let yourself be intimidated by one setback or another. And if you're not having the great success you had before, the reason is that you've been so cautious and conscientious and anxious that you let every chance for a coup slip through you fingers."

"Oh, please, my dear child, you're making me angry!" the senator said in a stern voice, squirming in his chair. "Let's speak of something else."

"Yes, you are angry, Thomas, I can see that well enough. You were from the start, and that's why I've kept on talking, just to prove to you that you have no reason to be offended. But if I were to ask myself why you're angry, I could only reply that ultimately it's because you're not so averse to the idea of getting involved in this. I may be a silly woman, but I've learned one thing about myself and others, and that is that one only gets upset and angry when one is not quite sure of one's own power to resist an idea and is tempted deep down inside to go along with it."

"That's nice," the senator said, biting the mouthpiece of his cigarette—and said no more.

"Nice? No, it's the most basic lesson that life has taught me. But never mind, Tom. I don't wish to press you. Can I convince you to enter into such a transaction? No, I lack the expertise for that. I'm just a silly goose. What a shame. Well, no matter. It simply interested me very much. On the one hand, I was shocked, of course, and felt sorry for Maiboom, but on the other, I was glad for you. I thought, Tom's been wandering about rather glumly for quite a while now. He used to complain, but he doesn't even complain anymore. He lost some money here and there, and these are hard times—just when *my* situation has improved again, thank God, and I'm feeling so happy. And then I thought: This would be something for him, a coup, a profitable deal. This will allow him to make up for many a setback and show people that good luck hasn't quite deserted the firm of Johann Buddenbrook yet. And if you had picked up on it, I would have been very proud to have been the middleman, because you know it's always been my dream, my fondest hope, to be of some use to the family name. But enough, that takes care of it, I suppose. Though what really annoys me is the thought that Maiboom is going to have to sell his entire crop in any case, Tom, and if he should look around town here for a buyer, he's sure to find one. He's sure to find one, and his name will be Hermann Hagenström—the scoundrel."

"Oh yes, I doubt if he would turn down the offer," the senator said with bitterness.

And Frau Permaneder replied with three shouts: "You see, you see, you see!"

Shaking his head, Thomas Buddenbrook suddenly began to laugh in exasperation and said, "It's foolish to sit here talking with such a display of high seriousness—at least on your part—about something so vague, about some will-o'-the-wisp. As far as I know, I haven't even asked what it is all about precisely, what Herr von Maiboom intends to sell. I know nothing about the Pöppenrade estate."

"Oh, but of course you would have to go see for yourself," she said eagerly. "It's just a stone's throw to Rostock, and no distance at all after that. What does he want to sell? Pöppenrade is a large estate. I know for a fact that it yields more than a thousand sacks of wheat. But nothing more than that, really. As far as rye, oats, or barley go? Five hundred sacks of each, perhaps? Or more, or less? I don't know. It's all growing splendidly, I can tell you that. But don't ask me for figures, Tom, I'm just a silly goose. You would have to go see it for yourself."

There was a long pause.

"Well, it's not worth wasting two words over," the senator said firmly and curtly, picking up his pince-nez and shoving it into his vest pocket; he buttoned his coat, stood up, and began to pace back and forth in quick, strong, easy strides purposely designed to show that any further serious thought about the matter was out of the question.

Then he stopped beside the table and, bending down toward his sister and lightly tapping the tabletop with a crooked index finger, said, "Let me tell you a little story, my dear Tony, one that will show you how I feel about this entire matter. I know your weakness for the nobility in general and the aristocrats of Mecklenburg in particular, and so I beg your indulgence if one of those gentlemen gets his fingers rapped in my story. You know, I'm sure, that among them there are one or two who do not have all that much regard for merchants, although merchants are as vital to them as vice versa. Men of that sort lay a bit too much emphasis on the producer's superior position—which to some extent is undeniable—vis-à-vis the wholesaler in commercial transactions; and, indeed, they regard the merchant with much the same eyes as they would a Jewish peddler to whom one gives one's worn-out clothing, even though one is quite aware that he has the better of the deal. I flatter myself that in general I have not left these gentlemen with the impression that I am an exploiter and their moral inferior; indeed, I've run across some who drive a much harder bargain than I. But it took just one little bold stroke, which I shall now tell you about, to bring me a bit closer on the social scale to one such fellow. It was Count Strelitz, whose estate was Gross-Poggendorf—you've heard of him before, I'm sure. I dealt with him for years, in fact. A very aristocratic sort, with a square monocle clamped in his eye—I could never figure out why he didn't cut himself—wore patent-leather boots and carried a riding crop with a gold handle. He had a habit of gazing down at me from some lofty height, his mouth half open, his eyes half closed. My first visit was very significant. We exchanged some introductory correspondence; I went to see him, and was ushered by his butler into his study, where I found him seated at his desk. He responds to my bow by raising himself halfway up in his chair, and finishes the last lines of a letter. He then turns to me, looking right on past me, and strikes up negotiations about his grain. I lean back against the table next to the sofa, cross my arms and legs, and find this all quite amusing. I stand there conversing with him for some five minutes. Five minutes more pass and I sit down on the table, with one leg dangling in the air. Our negotiations continue, and after fifteen minutes, with a truly gracious wave of his hand, he casually says, 'Won't you have a seat?'—'Beg your pardon?' I say. 'Oh, that's not necessary. I've been sitting all along.' "

"You didn't? You didn't?" Frau Permaneder shrieked with delight. She had immediately forgotten all that had passed between them and was completely caught up in the anecdote. "You'd been sitting all along! That's marvelous!"

"Well, yes; and I assure you that the count's behavior toward me changed from that moment on, that he offered me his hand whenever I came and invited me to sit, and that as a result we became something akin to friends. But why have I told you this? In order to ask you—would I have the heart, the self-assurance, indeed the right to teach Herr von Maiboom a similar lesson as well, if during our negotiations about a lump-sum payment for his harvest he should forget to offer me a chair?"

Frau Permaneder was silent. "Fine," she said at last and stood up. "You may be right, Tom, and, as I already said, I don't wish to press you. You surely know what you must do and what you must leave undone, and that's that. If only you'll believe that I mentioned this with the best intentions. So, then, that's agreed. Good night, Tom. Or no—wait—I have to give Hanno a kiss first and say hello to dear Ida. I'll look in on you again before I go."

And with that she left.

3

TONY CLIMBED the stairs to the third floor, and, ignoring the "balcony" on her right, she moved along the white-and-gold railing of the gallery and passed through an open door into a vestibule, from which a door on the left led to the senator's dressing room. She carefully turned the handle of the door directly ahead of her and entered.

It was an extraordinarily spacious room, its windows hidden behind the folds of heavy curtains patterned with large flowers. The walls were rather bare. Apart from a very large etching in a black frame that hung above Fräulein Jungmann's bed—a portrait of Giacomo Meyerbeer surrounded by characters from his operas—the only decorations were a few English prints pinned to the bright wallpaper, depictions of towheaded babies in red frocks. In the middle of the room Ida Jungmann was sitting at the large extension table, darning Hanno's stockings. The faithful Prussian was in her early fifties now, and although she had begun to turn gray at an early age, her hair was still not white, but more a kind of salt-and-pepper; she still held her large-boned, robust frame very erect, and her brown eyes were as fresh, clear, and unwearied as they had been when she was thirty.

"Good evening, Ida, you dear soul," Frau Permaneder said in a hushed but cheery voice—her brother's anecdote had put her in the best of moods. "How are you doing, you old so-and-so?"

"How's that, Tony my child—old so-and-so? You're here so late?"

"Yes, I was visiting with my brother—business matters that couldn't be put off. Unfortunately it didn't turn out as I'd hoped. Is he asleep?" she asked, pointing with her chin at the little bed that stood along the wall to her left, its green-upholstered headboard set close to the door leading to the master bedroom.

"Shhh," Ida said, "yes, he's asleep." And Frau Permaneder tiptoed to the bed, carefully pulled aside the curtains, and bent down to gaze at the face of her sleeping nephew.

Little Johann Buddenbrook was lying on his back, but his face, framed by long, light-brown hair, was turned toward the room; he was breathing softly but audibly into his pillow. One hand lay crossed on his chest, the other was extended beside him on the quilt, just the tips of his crooked fingers peeping out from under the very long, wide sleeves of his nightshirt—they twitched slightly now and then. His half-opened lips were moving faintly, too, as if trying to form words. From time to time an almost pained expression flickered across his whole face, beginning with a trembling of the chin, then of the mouth, followed by a vibration of his delicate nostrils, and ending in a twitch of the muscles of his brow. His long lashes could not hide the bluish shadows brooding in the corners of his eyes.

"He's dreaming," Frau Permaneder said, touched. Then she bent down over the child, gingerly kissed his cheeks warm with sleep, carefully rearranged the curtains, and stepped back to the table, where by the yellowish lamplight Ida was pulling a new stocking over her darning egg; she first examined the hole and then began to mend it.

"You're darning, Ida. It's strange, I can never picture you doing anything else."

"Yes, yes, Tony. The boy tears holes in everything these days, now that he's going to school."

"But he's still the same quiet, gentle child, isn't he?"

"Yes, yes. But all the same . . ."

"Does he like school?"

"No, no, Tony. He would much rather have stayed at home here with me. And I would have preferred that, too, my girl, seeing as how those gentlemen haven't known him since he was a baby and don't understand how to help him learn his lessons. He has trouble concentrating, and gets tired quickly."

"Poor thing. Have they paddled him?"

"Heavens, no! *My boshy kock hanna*—they wouldn't be that hardhearted. One look from the lad's eyes and . . ."

"What was his first day at school like? Did he cry?"

"Yes, he certainly did. But he cries so softly—never loud, just sort of to himself. And then he tried to hold tight to your brother's coat and kept pleading for him to stay behind."

"I see, so my brother took him, did he? Yes, that's a difficult moment in life, Ida, believe me. Why, I can remember it as if it were yesterday. I howled, let me tell you, howled like a mournful hound. It was terribly hard for me. And do you know why? Because I had things so good at home, just like Hanno. The children from all the finer houses were crying—I noticed that at once. But the others didn't care much at all. They just gaped at us and grinned. Good Lord, what's wrong with him, Ida?"

She broke off her chatter, didn't even complete her hand gesture, and turned round to the bed, where the cry had come from—a cry of fear, which was immediately repeated, but now it sounded more anguished, more terrified, and then came a third, a fourth, a fifth, one right after another. "Oh! Oh! Oh!"—a desperate, outraged cry tinged with horror—a protest against something horrible that he was watching or that was happening to him. And in the next instant little Johann stood up in bed and stammered something unintelligible; his odd, golden-brown eyes were wide open now, staring not at the real world all around, but at some totally different world inside him.

"It's nothing," Ida said, "Just *pavor nocturnus*. Oh, sometimes it's much worse." And she quite calmly put down her darning, moved in long, heavy strides over to Hanno, and laid him back down under his blanket, all the while speaking in a deep, calming voice.

"Oh, I see, yes, *pavor nocturnus*," Frau Permaneder repeated. "Will he wake up now?"

But Hanno showed no signs of waking, although his eyes were staring wide and his lips went on moving.

"What's that? Well, well, let's stop chattering away now. What did you say?" Ida asked, and Frau Permaneder came closer, too, trying to understand his troubled muttering and stammering.

"To my . . . garden . . . I will go," Hanno mumbled, "Onions and sweet peas to sow. . . ."

"He's reciting a poem," Ida Jungmann explained, shaking her head. "Now, now, that's enough, lad, go to sleep."

"There a little hunchback stands . . . Sneezing, waving little hands," Hanno said, and then he sighed. Suddenly his expression changed and he closed his eyes halfway. Tossing his head back and forth on his pillow, he went on now in a soft, plaintive voice:

The moon rides high,
The babe doth cry,
Twelve strikes the clock,
That God may help the poorer folk.

And with these words came a sob so deep that tears formed on his eyelashes and slowly rolled down his cheeks—and that woke him. He hugged Ida, looked around with eyes still wet with tears, contentedly murmured something about "Aunt Tony," shifted in his bed, and then quietly fell asleep.

"How strange," Frau Permaneder said as Ida sat back down at the table. "What sort of poems were those?"

"They're in his reader," Fräulein Jungmann replied, "and right underneath it says 'The Youth's Magic Horn.' They're very odd poems. He had to memorize them this week, and he's been talking a lot about the one with the little hunchback. Do you know it? It's really very awful. This little hunchbacked man is everywhere, he smashes pots, eats the broth, steals the wood, keeps the spinning wheel from turning, makes fun of people—and then, at the end, he asks to be included in people's prayers. Yes, the lad's been fascinated by it. He's been thinking about it all day and all night. 'Don't you see, Ida? He doesn't do it because he's wicked, not because he's wicked! He does it because he's sad, but that only makes him sadder. And if people pray for him, then he won't have to do it anymore.' And this evening, when his mama came in to say good night on her way to the concert, he asked her if he should pray for the little hunchback, too."

"And did he?"

"Not that I could hear, but probably to himself. And there's another poem, too, called 'The Nursery Clock,' and he wouldn't even recite that one, just cried and cried. He cries so easily, the lad does, and then can't stop crying for ever so long."

"But what is so sad about it?"

"How do I know? He can never get past the start—the same lines he was just sobbing over in his sleep just now. And he cried over another one, too, about a wagon driver who gets up from his straw bed at three in the morning."

Frau Permaneder was touched. She laughed, but then made a more serious face. "But I must tell you, Ida, it's not good. I really don't believe it's good for him to take everything to heart so. The wagon driver gets up at three—well, good heavens, that's what wagon drivers do. As far as I can see, the boy's view of the world is all too intense, he lets everything affect him. And that gnaws away at him, believe me. Someone should have a serious talk with Dr. Grabow. But that's the problem," she continued, crossing her arms, laying her head to one side and tapping the floor crossly with her foot. "Grabow's getting old, and, even apart from that, as kind-hearted as he is, as honest and sincere a man as he is—I really don't think much of his abilities as a doctor, Ida. And may God forgive me if I'm mistaken. Take Hanno's nervous sleep, for example, the way he starts up and is so frightened by his dreams. Grabow knows about it, but all he does is tell us what it is, by giving it a Latin name: *pavor nocturnus*. Good Lord, now, isn't that instructive! Yes, he's a sweet man, a good friend of the family—all that. But he's no great intellect. An important man has a different look about him. You can tell even when he's a young man that there's something to him. Grabow was around during the events of '48—he was a young man then himself. But do you suppose he ever got excited about what was happening—about freedom and justice and the overthrow of privileges and arbitrary power? He's a learned man, but I'm sure that the Confederation's outrageous laws dealing with the universities and the press left him completely cold. He never once did anything even the least bit wild, never once kicked the traces. He always makes that same long, sympathetic face, prescribes squab and French bread and, if it's really serious, perhaps a teaspoon of marshmallow tea. . . . Good night, Ida. No, no, I know there are other kinds of doctors than that. What a shame I won't see Gerda. . . . Yes, thanks, there's light in the hall. Good night."

As she passed the dining room, Frau Permaneder opened the door to call good night to her brother in the living room. She noticed that the lights were lit in all the rooms and that Thomas was pacing back and forth, his hands behind his back.

4

ONCE HE WAS ALONE, the senator had sat down at the table again and taken out his pince-nez, intending to resume reading his paper. But after two minutes his eyes drifted up from the newsprint, and, without changing the position of his body, he gazed straight ahead into the darkened salon for a long time, his eyes fixed on the portieres.

How almost unrecognizable his face became when he was alone. The muscles of his mouth and cheeks, usually so disciplined and obedient to his will, relaxed and slackened; the alert, prudent, kind, energetic look, which he had preserved for so long now only with great effort, fell away like a mask and reverted to a state of anguished weariness; his dull, somber eyes would fix on some object without seeing it, would redden and begin to water—and, lacking the courage to deceive even himself, he could hold fast to only one of the many heavy, confused, restless thoughts that filled his mind: that, at age forty-two, Thomas Buddenbrook was an exhausted man.

He took a deep breath, letting his hand glide slowly across his brow and eyes, automatically lit another cigarette, although he knew they were not good for him, and went on gazing into the darkness through the smoke. What a contrast between the slack anguish on his face and the elegant, almost martial care he gave to how it looked—to his perfumed mustache, drawn out to long, stiff points, to his fastidiously clean-shaven cheeks and chin, to the meticulous cut of his hair and the way he made sure that the first hint of baldness on the crown was well hidden, to the two long waves that fell back from his delicate temples, to the carefully combed narrow part, to the very cropped trim above the ears that he had adopted of late in place of his old full curls, so that people could not see that his hair was graying there. He was fully aware of the contrast himself, and he knew well that the contradiction between the elastic, supple energy of his movements and the weary pallor of his face could not escape the eyes of anyone passing him on the street.

Not that he was any less of an important and indispensable person outside these walls than he had been before. Friends told him that constantly, and the people who envied him could not deny that Dr. Langhals had explicitly underscored the judgment of Mayor Oeverdieck, his predecessor: Senator Buddenbrook was the mayor's right-hand man. Nevertheless, the firm of Johann Buddenbrook was no longer what it had once been—that, too, was such common knowledge that Herr Stuht on Glockengiesser Strasse could share it with his wife over bacon soup at lunch. And Thomas Buddenbrook could only groan in response.

He himself, however, was the chief source for this impression. He was a rich man, and none of the losses he had endured, not even the especially heavy ones of '66, could have seriously endangered the firm's existence. For, although he continued, of course, to play the gracious host, to give dinners with the requisite number of courses his guests had come to expect, the notion that his good luck and success itself had flown—a notion that was more an inner truth for him than one based on external facts—had so reduced him to a condition of despondent worry that he began to hold tight to his money as never before and to save in almost petty ways when it came to private expenditures. He cursed himself a hundred times for having built his extravagant new house, which, or so he felt, had brought him nothing but misfortune. There were no more summer trips, and their little garden in town had to take the place of a stay at the shore or in the mountains. At his express and repeated wish, the meals he shared with his wife and little Hanno were so simple they seemed almost a farce in contrast to the spacious, parqueted dining room with its stately high ceilings and splendid oak furniture. For some time now dessert had been served only on Sunday. He kept up his elegant external appearance; but Anton, their butler of so many years, was able to tell the kitchen staff that the senator changed his white shirt only every other day now—too-frequent washing ruined fine linen. Anton knew other things as well. He knew that he would be let go. Gerda protested—three servants were hardly enough to keep such a large house in good order. But it was to no avail. Anton, who for so many years had sat on the coach-box when Thomas Buddenbrook rode to the senate, was sent on his way—with an appropriate sum of money.

These measures were consistent with the dismal tempo at which his business had been moving. There was no trace now of the new and fresh spirit that Thomas Buddenbrook had once brought to the firm; and his partner, Herr Friedrich Wilhelm Marcus, whose invested capital was small and who therefore could never have exerted any significant influence, was by nature and temperament a man lacking in initiative. Over the years he had become increasingly pedantic, until now he was a perfect eccentric. He needed fifteen minutes—of mustache-stroking, throat-clearing, and sidelong, circumspect glances—just to trim his cigar and tuck the tip in his wallet. When evening fell and every corner of the office was brightly lit by gas lamps, he never failed to set a burning stearin candle on his desk. Every half-hour he would get up, go to the tap, and run water over his head. One morning he found an empty gunny sack that had accidentally been left under his desk, took it for a cat, and to the great amusement of the staff tried to shoo it away with loud curses. No, despite the senator's current lethargy, Marcus was not the man to intervene and help the firm along.

And so the senator sat staring with weary eyes into the darkness of the salon, and a familiar sense of shame and desperate impatience came over him as he pictured the fallen state of the firm of Johann Buddenbrook and all its insignificant, small-scale, pennywise transactions.

But was it not, perhaps, all for the good? Misfortune, too, he thought, has its season. Was it not wise, perhaps, to lie low as long as it held sway, not stirring, but waiting and gathering one's inner strength? Why had they approached him with this proposal just now, prematurely rousing him from sensible resignation, filling him with doubt and indecision? Had the time come? Was this his cue? Should he take heart, stand up tall, and deliver a blow? He had rejected the proposal with all the determination he could put into his voice. But even though Tony had left, was the whole thing really decided? It appeared not—for here he sat brooding. "One only responds to an idea with anger when one is not quite sure of one's own power to resist it." What a damn sly person little Tony was!

What had been his objections? He recalled that he had put it very forcefully and well. "Shabby operation—fishing in troubled waters—brutal exploitation—fleecing a poor, defenseless fellow—usury"—excellent! Except that he now asked himself whether this was an occasion for loud counterarguments. Consul Hermann Hagenström would not have tried to find them, or have used them. Was Thomas Buddenbrook a businessman, a man of dispassionate deeds, or a brooder haunted by scruples?

Oh yes, that was the question, had always been the right question, for as long as he could remember. Life was hard, and business, as it took its ruthless, unsentimental course, was the epitome of life in general. Did Thomas Buddenbrook stand with both feet firmly planted in that hard, practical life—as had his father before him? He had often enough had reason to doubt it. From adolescence on, he had often enough had to revise his own feelings when confronted by that life—dealing hard blows, taking hard blows, yet never feeling them to be hard, but perfectly natural. Would he never completely learn that lesson?

He remembered the impression that the catastrophe of '66 had made on him, and he called to mind the overwhelming, unspeakable emotional pain. He had lost a great deal of money—but that had not been what was so unbearable. For the first time in his life he had been forced to experience personally and completely just how cruel and brutal business can be, had watched as all his better, gentler, and kinder sentiments had slunk away before the raw, naked, absolute instinct of self-preservation, had seen his friends, his best friends, respond to his misfortune not with sympathy, not with compassion, but with suspicion—cold, dismissive suspicion. But had he not always known that? Was it his place to be astonished by it? And later, in better and stronger hours, how ashamed he had been of those sleepless nights of outrage and disgust, when he lay there feeling irreparably violated by the ugly and shameless cruelty of life.

How foolish all that had been. How ridiculous such feelings, such sensitivities had been. How could he have entertained them in the first place? And so, to ask the question once again: was he a practical man or a tenderhearted dreamer?

Oh, he had asked himself that question a thousand times, and responded in one way in his strong and optimistic moments, and in another when he was weary. But he was too perceptive and honest not to admit the truth—he was a mixture of both.

All his life he had presented himself to other people as a man of action; but to the extent that they were correct in that judgment, was not action—to use the adage from Goethe he loved to quote—a result of his own deliberate plan? He had his record of past achievements, but had that record not risen from an enthusiasm, an impetus, provided by his own powers of reflection? And if he was despondent now, if his energies seemed spent—though not, God grant, forever—was that not the logical consequence of this untenable condition, this unnatural and exhausting contradiction inside him? Would his father, his grandfather, his great-grandfather have bought the entire Pöppenrade harvest? That made no difference, no difference at all. But that they had been practical men—stronger, more open to life, more natural—whole, full men, that much was certain.

A great uneasiness came over him, a need for movement, space, and light. He pushed his chair back, crossed to the salon, and lit several gas jets on the chandelier above the center table. He stood there, slowly, compulsively twirling one tip of his long mustache and vacantly gazing at the luxurious room all around him. Together with the sitting room, it took up the whole front of the house, its furnishings were all gentle curves and light colors; but the large grand piano, Gerda's violin case atop it, the end tables stacked with her music, the carved music stand and the bas-relief above the door with cupids happily playing instruments revealed that it was essentially a music room. The bay at the window was filled with palm trees.

Senator Buddenbrook stood there motionless for two or three minutes. Then he pulled himself together, returned by way of the sitting room to the dining room, and lit the gas jets there, too. He moved toward the buffet and drank a glass of water to calm his heart—or perhaps just for something to do. Then, with his hands behind his back, he moved deeper into the house. The smoking room was wainscoted and had dark furniture. He automatically opened the cigar cabinet, but immediately closed it again and then lifted the lid of a small oak chest on the card table—inside were playing cards, scoring pads, and similar items. He let a few ivory game markers run through his fingers; they clattered into the chest, and he closed the lid again as he turned to leave.

A little den with a stained-glass window opened off the smoking room. It was empty except for a nest of light serving tables, a liqueur cabinet on top. From here one entered the grand hall with its vast parquet floor and four high windows, with wine-red curtains and a view to the garden; this room, too, ran the full width of the house. It was furnished with a few heavy, low sofas in the same red as the curtains and a number of high-backed chairs that stood stiffly along the walls. There was a fireplace with imitation coals and stripes of shiny reddish-gold paper that seemed to glow behind the screen. Two tall, massive Chinese vases were set on the marble mantel, above which hung a mirror.

Now the whole floor was illuminated by a few gas jets, as if a party had just ended and the last guest had departed. The senator strode the length of the grand hall, stood there at the window opposite the den, and stared out into the garden.

The moon stood high and looked small among the fluffy clouds; the fountain leapt upward into the silence beneath the overhanging branches of the walnut tree. Thomas looked across to the pavilion at the far end, to the little glistening white terrace with its two obelisks; he studied the gravel paths, which had been raked just recently, the formal flower beds, and the lawn. But this delicate, quiet symmetry did anything but calm him—it annoyed and offended him. He held the window catch tight in one hand, laid his brow against the pane, and let his thoughts take their agonizing course again.

Where was all this getting him? He remembered a remark that he had made to his sister just now, recalled that he had no sooner said it than he had been annoyed at himself—it was so totally irrelevant. He had been talking about Count Strelitz, about the landed aristocracy, and had very clearly and explicitly voiced his opinion that the producer's social position was undeniably superior to that of the wholesaler. Was that true? Oh, good God, it made not the least difference if it was true or not. But was it *his* place in life to express such an idea, to consider it, even to entertain it in the first place? Could he ever explain to his father, his grandfather, or any of his fellow merchants how he could play with such an idea, let alone put it into words? A man who stands firmly in his profession, unshaken by doubts, knows only one thing, understands only one thing, values only one thing—his profession.

He felt the blood suddenly rise to his head, felt himself blushing at a second memory, which lay much farther in the past. He saw himself walking with his brother, Christian, in the garden of the house on Meng Strasse, caught up in a quarrel, in one of their deeply regrettable, heated disputes. With his usual compromising indiscretion, Christian had made a careless remark for a great many people to hear—a remark that had shocked him, made him angry, absolutely furious, and for which he had called him to account. Actually, Christian had said, every businessman is basically a swindler. And now? Was that insipid, contemptible remark really all that different from the one he had just allowed himself to make to his sister? He had been outraged, had furiously protested. But what had sly little Tony said? The only person who gets upset and angry . . .

"No!" the senator suddenly said in a loud voice, jerking his head up and letting go of the window catch, literally pushing himself back. And then he said, just as loudly, "No more of this!" He cleared his throat now to shake the unpleasant effect of the sound of his own solitary voice, turned around, and began to pace rapidly back and forth through all the rooms, his head lowered, his hands behind his back.

"No more of this!" he repeated. "There must be an end to it. I am frittering away my time, sinking into a bog—I'm getting worse than Christian." Oh, how immensely grateful he felt that he was no longer caught up in uncertainty about himself. It lay in his own hands to correct the situation. By sheer force! He would see, he would see what sort of an offer was being made. The harvest, the entire harvest of Pöppenrade? "I'll do it!" he said in a passionate whisper, even shaking the extended forefinger of one hand. "I'll do it!"

It was most assuredly what people called a coup, wasn't it? It was an opportunity simply to take an investment of, say, forty thousand marks *courant* and—exaggerating just a bit—to double it, right? Yes, it was a cue, a signal, that he should rouse himself. The point was that this was a beginning, a first stroke, and the risks connected with it were a further refutation of all his moral scruples. If he succeeded, his fortunes were restored, and he would be daring again, would hold fast to good luck and power again, keep it clasped inside him with a strong, elastic grip.

No, this catch would slip through the fingers of Messrs. Strunk & Hagenström—unfortunately for them. There was another firm in town that had the upper hand, thanks to personal connections in this case. In fact, the personal element was the decisive factor here. It was not an ordinary business deal to be handled coolly and by following the usual rules. Tony's status as middleman in initiating it lent it, rather, the character of a private matter, which needed discretion and tact. Oh no, Hermann Hagenström would hardly be the man for that. Thomas had a businessman's sense for market conditions, and by God he would know how to use them later, too, when it came time to sell. And, on the other hand, he was doing this hard-pressed landed aristocrat a favor, one which, given Tony's friendship with Armgard von Maiboom, he alone was called to do. And so he would write—write before the evening was out—not on the firm's letterhead, but on his personal stationery, with only "Senator Buddenbrook" printed at the top—write with utmost tact and inquire whether a visit would be welcome within a day or two. A ticklish matter, all the same. The ground was rather slippery and he would have to move with a good deal of grace—which made it that much more suited to him.

And he hastened his strides now and began to breathe harder. He sat down for a second, leapt up, and started wandering through all the rooms again. He thought the whole matter through one more time, thought of Herr Marcus, of Hermann Hagenström, Christian, and Tony, saw the ripe, golden harvest of Pöppenrade waving in the wind, fantasized anew about how the fortunes of his firm would revive after this coup, angrily cast all scruples aside, shook his finger again, and said, "I'll do it!"

Frau Permaneder opened the dining-room door and called out, "Good night." He answered without realizing it. Gerda, who had said goodbye to Christian at the door, entered the room now, and her exotic, close-set brown eyes had taken on the enigmatic shimmer that music always seemed to leave behind. The senator stood there mechanically, asking mechanical questions about the Spanish virtuoso and how the concert had gone and assuring her that he was about to go to bed himself.

He did not go to bed, however. He began wandering the rooms again. He thought of the sacks of wheat, rye, oats, and barley that would fill the "Lion," the "Whale," the "Oak," and the "Linden," reflected on the offer he planned to make—and it would certainly not be an indelicate offer. Around midnight he went downstairs to the office, and by the light of Herr Marcus's stearin candle he wrote a letter to Herr von Maiboom of Pöppenrade in one draft, and as he reread it, his head pounding and feverish, it seemed to him the best, most tactful letter he had ever written.

This was on the night of May 27. The next day he adopted a light, humorous tone to tell his sister that he had looked at the matter from all sides and that he couldn't simply turn the man down flat and leave him to the mercy of the nearest cutthroat. On May 30, he departed for Rostock, from where he hired a carriage for a trip to the country.

For the next few days, he was in a splendid mood—there was freedom and a bounce in his step, kindness in his expression. He teased Klothilde, laughed heartily at Christian, joked with Tony; and on Sunday he spent a whole hour playing with Hanno on the third-floor "balcony," helping his son hoist tiny sacks of grain to the top of a little red-brick warehouse, all the while imitating the hollow, drawling shouts of the workers. And on June 3, he gave a speech in the assembly on the most boring topic in the world, some tax problem or other, and it was so excellent and witty that it met with agreement on all points and made a laughing-stock of his opponent, Consul Hagenström.

5

IT WOULD NOT have taken much, and the senator—out of negligence, or was it intentional?—would simply have passed over a fact that Frau Permaneder, the most faithful and enthusiastic caretaker of the family records, now proclaimed to all the world: those documents assigned July 7, *anno domini* 1768, as the date on which the firm had been founded. The hundredth anniversary would soon be upon them.

It almost seemed as if Thomas was offended when, in a trembling voice, Tony called his attention to the matter. His soaring mood had not lasted long. All too soon, he had grown quiet again, perhaps quieter than before. He would suddenly grow uneasy, get up from his work in the office, and walk in the garden alone; stopping every now and then as if something were blocking his path or holding him back, he would sigh and cover his eyes with his hand. He said nothing, spoke openly to no one—and to whom could he speak? For the first time in his life, Herr Marcus had lost his temper—a most amazing sight—when his partner mentioned in passing the deal he had made with Herr von Maiboom; Herr Marcus had declined to share in any profits and absolved himself of all responsibility. But one Thursday evening, when his sister, Frau Permaneder, had been saying goodbye to him out on the street and made some reference to the harvest, he had given himself away by simply squeezing her hand and adding, "Oh, Tony, I should have resold it right away." Then he dropped her hand, abruptly turned around to walk away, and left Frau Antonie standing there, shocked and dumbfounded. That sudden squeeze he had given her hand was very close to a burst of despair; those whispered words were filled with a fear that had been pent up inside him for a long time now. But when Tony tried to bring up the subject again at the next opportunity, he wrapped himself in even more intransigent silence, ashamed of having let his guard down in a display of momentary weakness and embittered by his inability to justify the whole enterprise even to himself.

And now he said stodgily and peevishly, "Oh, my dear, I wish we could ignore the whole thing."

"Ignore it, Tom? Impossible! Unthinkable! Do you think you can simply sweep it under the rug? Do you think the whole town can forget the importance of the day?"

"I'm not saying it can be done. I'm just saying I would prefer it if we could observe the day in some quiet fashion. It's a fine thing to celebrate the past when one is feeling good about the present and the future. It's pleasant to remember your forefathers when you know that you are of one mind with them and are sure that you have always acted as they would have had you act. If only the anniversary had come at a better time—but, to put it bluntly, I'm not in the mood to celebrate it."

"You mustn't talk like that, Tom. You don't mean that and you know perfectly well that it would be a shame, a dreadful shame, to let the hundredth anniversary of the firm of Johann Buddenbrook pass without a peep. You're just a little nervous right now, and I know why, too. Although there's really no reason for you to be that way. But once the day is here, you'll be as happy and excited as the rest of us."

She was right—the day could not be passed over in silence. It was not long before a notice appeared in the *Advertiser*, promising a lengthy recapitulation of the history of the distinguished old firm on the day of its anniversary—though its admirers in commercial circles hardly needed their attention called to the fact. Within the family, Uncle Justus was the first to mention the upcoming event one Thursday evening; but the moment the dessert dishes had been cleared, Frau Permaneder saw to it that the venerable leather writing case with the family documents was solemnly brought out; and, as a kind of foretaste to the celebration, she made sure that everyone became intimately reacquainted with all the facts known about the life of the first Johann Buddenbrook, the founder of the firm and

Hanno's great-great-grandfather. With pious fervor she read it all aloud: when he had a case of boils and when he had genuine pox, when he had fallen from the fourth story onto the drying-room floor and when he had been delirious with a high fever. She simply could not get enough. She followed the story back to the sixteenth century, to the oldest known Buddenbrook, the man who had been an alderman in Grabau, and to the merchant tailor in Rostock who "had done very well"—this was underlined—siring a remarkable number of children, some of whom had lived, some of whom had not. "What a splendid man!" she cried and began to read aloud from some of the old yellowed, tattered letters and festive poems.

NATURALLY, the first person to offer his congratulations on the morning of July 7 was Herr Wenzel.

"Yes, Senator Buddenbrook, one hundred years," he said, balancing the razor in his red hands and deftly stropping it. "And if I may say so, I've shaved this fine family for a good half of them, and a man learns a great deal when he's the first to speak to the head of the firm each morning. Your late father, the consul, was always most talkative early in the day, and he'd always ask me, 'Wenzel,' he'd ask, 'what do you say about rye? Should I sell or do you think the price will go back up?' "

"Yes, Wenzel, I cannot imagine the whole enterprise without you. As I've often told you before, there's something very fascinating about your profession. When you've finished your rounds each morning, you're wiser than any of us. Because you've had your razor to the throats of the owners of almost all the leading firms and know what sort of mood each is in. We can all only envy you for that—it's very interesting information."

"Some truth in that, Senator Buddenbrook. But as far as the senator's mood goes, if I may say so—the senator's looking a bit pale again this morning."

"Is that right? Yes, I've got a headache, and as far as I can see, it won't be going away all that quickly, because today is going to be something of a drain on me."

"Can well believe it, Senator. People are quite enthusiastic, quite enthusiastic. You need only glance out the window when I'm done,

Senator. Flags everywhere. And the *Wullenwever* and the *Friederike Oeverdieck* are moored down at the foot of Fischer Grabe, banners aflying."

"Well, then, better make it quick, Wenzel. I haven't any time to lose."

The senator did not reach for his office jacket today, but for a black cutaway coat that went well with his light-colored trousers and revealed his white piqué vest. He could expect visitors this morning. He cast a quick glance in the dresser mirror, gave the long tips of his mustache a last stroke with the curling iron, and turned to go with a sigh. The dance was about to begin—if only this day were behind him. Would he have a single moment alone, a single moment to let the muscles of his face relax? He would be receiving guests all day and be called upon to respond to the congratulations of a hundred people with tact and dignity, to find for each the polite, appropriate word with just the right nuances—respectful, serious, friendly, ironic, witty, considerate, sincere. This was to be followed by a banquet in the town-hall wine cellar, lasting from early afternoon until well into the evening.

He did not really have a headache. He was merely tired. The refreshment of sleep was no sooner past than he felt his old indefinite gloom weighing down on him again. Why had he lied? Might it not be because his conscience always bothered him for feeling so down? But why? Why? But he had no time to worry about that now.

As he entered the dining room, Gerda greeted him cheerfully. She, too, was already dressed for receiving guests. She was wearing a flowing plaid skirt, a white blouse, and a light silk short-waisted jacket of the same color as her rich chestnut hair. She smiled, showing her large, regular teeth—whiter even than her lovely face—and her eyes, those close-set, enigmatic brown eyes with bluish shadows, were smiling today as well.

"I've been up and about for hours—and you can tell by that alone how excited I am to wish you all the best."

"What do you know! A hundred years even make an impression on you, do they?"

"The profoundest impression! But it may be it's simply because everything is so festive. What a day! This, for example"—and she pointed toward the breakfast table crowned with flowers from the garden—"is Fräulein Jungmann's handiwork. And you are sadly mistaken if you think you can have your tea now. The most important members of the family are waiting in the salon, with a gift for the occasion, in which I've had a small part myself. Now, listen, Thomas, this is, of course, only the first of the stream of visitors that will be arriving today. I'll manage for a while, but around noon I'm going to beat a retreat, let me tell you. Although the barometer has fallen a little, the sky is still shamelessly blue, which looks wonderful with all the flags—and the whole town is full of flags—but it will be dreadfully hot. Now, come along. You'll have to wait for breakfast. You should have got up earlier. Now you'll have to deal with the first wave of emotion on an empty stomach."

Elisabeth Buddenbrook, Christian, Klothilde, Ida Jungmann, Frau Permaneder, and Hanno were gathered in the salon, and the latter two were supporting, not without some difficulty, the family's gift for the occasion, a large memorial plaque.

Deeply moved, Madame Buddenbrook embraced her eldest child. "My dear son, this is a beautiful day . . . a beautiful day," she repeated. "We must never cease to thank God with all our hearts, to praise Him for all His mercies . . . for all His mercies." She wept.

The senator felt himself go weak in her embrace. It was as if something deep within him had worked itself free and left him. His lips trembled. He felt an enervating urge to remain there in his mother's arms, at her breast, where the gentle scent of perfume lingered on the soft silk of her dress, to close his eyes and never to have to see or say anything more. He kissed her and pulled himself up erect to shake the hand of his brother, who returned the gesture with the same half-distracted, half-embarrassed look he always wore for festive occasions. Klothilde said something amiable in her drawling way. Fräulein Jungmann, however, confined herself to a very deep bow, while her hand played with the silver watch chain dangling at her flat chest.

"Come here, Tom," Frau Permaneder said, her voice shaking. "Hanno and I can't hold this much longer." She was supporting the plaque by herself now, because Hanno didn't have that much strength in his arms, and she looked so thrilled and was straining so hard that she might have been a martyr in ecstasy. Her eyes were moist, her cheeks flushed, and the tip of her tongue played along her upper lip, giving her a look that was part desperation, part mischief.

"Yes, and now you two," the senator said. "What's that you have there? Come on, let go, we'll prop it up here." He leaned the plaque against the wall next to the piano, and stood there before it, surrounded by his family.

Framed in heavy, carved walnut and covered with glass were the portraits of the four owners of the firm of Johann Buddenbrook, each with name and dates printed in gold leaf beneath it. The portrait of Johann Buddenbrook, the founder, had been done from an old oil painting—a tall, serious-looking old gentleman, his lips set tight, his eyes gazing out stern and strong-willed from above his jabot; there was the broad, jovial face of Jean Jacques Hoffstede's friend Johann Buddenbrook; there was Consul Johann Buddenbrook, with his wide, creased mouth and his large, strongly hooked nose, his chin tucked in his high collar, his intelligent eyes, which hinted at religious fervor, fixed on his audience; and finally there was Thomas Buddenbrook himself, at a somewhat younger age. A stylized golden ear of grain twined its way among the portraits, and at the bottom, likewise in gilt letters, the years 1768 and 1868 stood side by impressive side. And above it all, written in the tall Gothic script of a hand familiar to his descendants, was the motto: "My son, show zeal for each day's affairs of business, but only for such that make for a peaceful night's sleep."

His hands behind his back, the senator examined the plaque for a long time. "Yes, yes," he suddenly said in a slightly mocking tone, "a good night's sleep is a fine thing." Then, turning to his assembled relatives, he said seriously, if perhaps a little perfunctorily, "My heartfelt thanks to you all, my dear family. It's a very beautiful and thoughtful gift. What do you think—where should we hang it? In my office?"

"Yes, Tom, right above the desk in your office," Frau Permaneder replied and gave her brother a hug. Then she pulled him over to the bay window and pointed outside.

Bicolor flags floated from every building beneath the deep blue summer sky—all the way down Fischer Grube, from Breite Strasse to the docks, where the *Wullenwever* and the *Friederike Oeverdieck* lay under full flag in honor of their owner.

"The whole town is like that," Frau Permaneder said, and her voice trembled. "I've already been out for a walk, Tom. Even the Hagenströms have hung a flag. They had no choice—ha! I would have broken every window in the house."

He smiled and pulled her back into the room; they stood beside the table.

"And here are telegrams, Tom, only the first, personal ones, of course, from family members. The ones from business friends have been delivered to the office."

She opened a few of the cables: from relatives in Hamburg and Frankfurt, from Herr Arnoldsen and his family in Amsterdam, from Jürgen Kröger in Wismar. Frau Permaneder suddenly blushed. "In his own way, he's a good man," she said, and passed the telegram to her brother. It was signed: Permaneder.

"But it's getting late," the senator said, flipping open the cover on his pocket watch. "I would like some tea. Won't you all join me? The house is going to be as crowded as a chicken coop soon enough."

His wife, who had given a signal to Ida Jungmann, held him back. "Just a moment, Thomas. You know that Hanno has to go for his private lessons. He would like to recite a poem. Come here, Hanno. Now, just as if no one were here—but don't get too excited."

So that he would not fall behind the rest of his class, little Johann had to be tutored privately in arithmetic even during vacation—and July was certainly vacation. Somewhere in the suburb of Sankt Gertrud, in a hot little room that did not smell all that good, a man with a red beard and dirty fingernails was waiting for him, to drill him in those maddening multiplication tables. But first it was his duty to recite a poem for his father, the poem he had painfully learned by heart while sitting with Ida on his third-floor "balcony."

Dressed in his Danish sailor outfit, with white trim at the neck and a thick knotted sailor's tie fluffed at the wide linen collar, he leaned against the piano, crossing his thin legs, his head and upper body turned slightly to one side in a pose that was both shy and full of an unconscious grace. His long hair had finally been cut two or three weeks before—not only his classmates had been making fun of him, but his teachers as well. But there was still a full, wavy growth on top, which fell down over his temples and delicate brow. He kept his eyelids lowered, so that his long, brown lashes fell across the bluish shadows around his eyes, and he held his tight-closed lips a little askew.

He knew quite well what would happen. He would start to cry, and then he would be unable to finish his poem—a poem that tugged at his heart, just like the music on Sundays, when Herr Pfühl, the organist at St. Mary's would play the organ in that special, thrilling way. He would cry, just as he always did when someone demanded that he perform, drilled him, tested his abilities and cleverness, the way Papa loved to do. If only Mama had not said anything about getting excited. It was meant to encourage him, but it had been the wrong thing to say, he could feel it. There they stood, watching him. They were afraid for him and were waiting for him to cry—how was it possible *not* to cry? He raised his lashes and searched for Ida's eyes. She was playing with her watch chain and nodded to him now in her dour, goodhearted way. He was overcome with a tremendous urge to snuggle up against her, to have her lead him away, and then the only thing he would hear would be her deep, comforting voice saying, "Hush now, Hanno, my boy, you don't have to recite."

"Now, son, let's hear your poem," the senator said bluntly. He had sat down in an armchair beside the table and was waiting. He was not smiling at all—no more today than on any other occasion. Raising one eyebrow, he earnestly measured little Johann with scrutinizing, even cold, eyes.

Hanno stood up straight. He ran his hand over the smooth, polished surface of the piano, let his eyes glide shyly over the faces of all those present, and, encouraged a little by the gentleness shining in his grandmother's and Aunt Tony's eyes, he began in a low but slightly hard-edged voice: " 'The Shepherd's Sunday Song' . . . by Uhland."

"Oh, my dear boy, that's not the way," the senator cried. "Don't hang on to the piano—fold your hands in front of you and stand up tall. And speak right out. That's the first thing. Here, stand between the portieres. And now hold your head up, and let your arms hang quietly at your sides."

Hanno took a position on the threshold to the sitting room and let his arms hang down, but he lowered his eyelashes until the others could no longer see his eyes. More than likely, they were already swimming with tears.

"This is the Lord's own day," he said very softly.

Which only made his father's voice sound that much louder when he interrupted. "A recitation begins with a bow, son. And much louder. Now, start again, please—'The Shepherd's Sunday Song.' "

It was a cruel thing to do, and the senator knew that in doing it he had robbed the child of his last remnant of composure and self-control. But the lad shouldn't let that happen to him. He shouldn't let himself get confused. He had to learn to be strong and manly. " 'Shepherd's Sunday Song!' " he said again encouragingly—and remorselessly.

But it was all over for Hanno. His head had sunk to his chest, and he was clutching at the brocade of the portieres now, the bluish veins visible on his pale little right hand where it emerged from the tight-fitting, navy-blue cuff embroidered with an anchor. "In meadows wide alone I stand," he managed, and then it was most definitely over. He was swept away by the sad mood of the poem. He felt terribly, overwhelmingly sorry for himself; his voice gave out for good and he could not stop the tears from rolling from under his eyelashes. Suddenly he wanted so much for it to be night, one of those nights when he was lying in bed with a sore throat and a slight fever, and Ida would come to give him something to drink and lovingly lay a fresh compress across his brow. He leaned to one side and, laying his head down against his hand, still clutching the portieres, he sobbed.

"Well, this is no fun," the senator said in a gruff, annoyed voice and stood up. "What are you crying about? Although it's enough to make us all cry that you couldn't put forth the effort to please me a little on a day like today. Are you a little girl? What's to become of you if you keep on like this? Do you think you can still break into tears when you grow up and have to give a speech to people?"

Never, Hanno thought in despair, I'll never give a speech to anyone!

"Think it over till this afternoon," the senator concluded. And as Ida Jungmann knelt down beside her charge to dry his eyes, speaking to him in a voice half reproachful and half consoling, Thomas returned to the dining room.

While he hastily ate his breakfast, his mother, Tony, Klothilde, and Christian said their goodbyes. They were to have their noonday meal here with Gerda—plus the Krögers, the Weinschenks, and the Ladies Buddenbrook—whereas, for better or for worse, the senator would have to dine at the town-hall wine cellar, although he did not intend to stay there all that long and hoped to find his family still here when he returned home this evening.

Sitting alone at the flower-bedecked table, he drank scalding tea from his saucer, quickly ate an egg, and then stopped on the stairs to take a few puffs on a cigarette. When he reached the foot of the stairs, where the brown bear stood on its hind legs collecting calling cards, he ran into Grobleben, who had just come in from the garden and now entered the front hall, wearing his wool shawl—in the middle of summer—with one boot pulled over his left hand, a polishing brush in his right, and a long drop dangling from his nose.

"Well, sir, Senator Buddenbrook, one hundurd years . . . Now, the one he's poor, and t'other, he's rich, but . . ."

"That's fine, Grobleben, right you are." And the senator slipped a coin into the hand holding the brush, then strode across the entrance hall and through the reception room opening off it. As he entered the outer office, the cashier, a tall man with loyal eyes, greeted him with carefully prepared phrases expressing the best wishes of the entire office staff. The senator responded with two short words of thanks and sat down at his desk by the window. He had barely begun to scan the newspapers laid out for him and to open his mail when there was a knock at the door leading to the front hallway—and the first well-wishers arrived.

It was a delegation of warehouse workers—six bowlegged men,

all big as bears, their mouths turned down at the corners in token of their vast integrity, their hands fiddling with the caps they held before them. Spraying brown tobacco juice about the room and constantly hitching at his trousers, their spokesman went on about "hundurd years" and "many a hundurd years more" in a frantic voice. The senator promised them a considerable bonus for the coming week and sent them on their way.

Civil servants arrived to congratulate their boss in the name of all those who worked in the tax office. At the door, they ran into a delegation of sailors, led by two helmsmen from the *Wullenwever* and the *Friederike Oeverdieck*, the firm's two ships now lying moored at the docks. And then came representatives of the grain haulers, dressed in black shirts, breeches, and top hats. And individual citizens arrived as well. Herr Stuht, the master tailor from Glockengiesser Strasse, appeared in a black coat that he had pulled on over his woolen shirt. There were various neighbors as well—Iwersen, the owner of the flower shop, offered his congratulations. An old mailman, a true eccentric with a white beard, rings in both ears, and rheumy eyes—whom on his good days the senator made a point of greeting as Herr Postmaster—stuck his head in the door and called, "*That* ain't why I come by, Senator Buddenbrook, 'tain't it at all. I know people're sayin' ev'rybody what comes by gets a little sumpin', but *that* ain't why I'm here." All the same, he gratefully accepted the coin. There was no end to it. At ten-thirty, the housemaid came in to tell him that his wife was now receiving the first guest in the salon.

Thomas Buddenbrook left his office and hurried up the stairs. At the entrance to the salon he stopped at the mirror for half a minute to set his tie straight and to take a whiff of eau de cologne from his scented handkerchief. He looked pale—even though his whole body was perspiring, his hands and feet were cold. Receiving all those guests in his office had almost completely drained him. He took a deep breath and entered the sun-drenched room to greet Consul Huneus—whose wholesale lumber business had made him a millionaire five times over—his wife, their daughter, and her husband, Senator Andreas Gieseke. Like many of the town's first families, these ladies and gentlemen had interrupted their July vacation in Travemünde and returned to town for the express purpose of celebrating the Buddenbrook anniversary.

They had not been sitting for three minutes in their stylish easy chairs—all gentle curves and light colors—when Consul Oeverdieck, the son of the deceased mayor, and his wife, née Kistenmaker, arrived. And as Consul Huneus was on his way out, he was met by his brother, who was worth only four million but bore the title of senator.

The round dance had begun. The large white door, topped by the bas-relief of cupids playing instruments, seldom remained closed for more than a moment, so that there was an almost unbroken view of the stairwell flooded with light and of the stairway itself—an unending parade of guests moved up and down it. The salon was large enough, however, to accommodate little groups that formed for conversation, so that the number of arrivals was much greater than that of departures; and once the maid had given up trying to open and close the door and simply left it open, the guests spilled out into the parqueted corridor.

Male and female voices buzz and hum in conversation, hands are shaken, bows and witticisms are exchanged, and loud, easy laughter is swept up among the columns of the stairway and echoes off the ceiling and the large glass pane of the skylight. Senator Buddenbrook takes up a position, now at the top of the stairs, now at the bay window, to receive all their good wishes—some murmured in serious and formal tones, some blurted cordially and heartily. Mayor Langhals, an elegant stout gentleman with short gray whiskers, the weary gaze of a diplomat, and a clean-shaven chin that he hides in a white cravat, is received with deference on all sides. Consul Eduard Kistenmaker the wine merchant and his wife, née Möllendorpf, along with his brother and partner, Stephen, Senator Buddenbrook's most faithful supporter and friend, plus the latter's wife, the extraordinarily healthy daughter of a gentleman farmer, all arrive together. The widow of Senator Möllendorpf sits enthroned in the middle of the sofa—and now her children, Consul August Möllendorpf and his wife, Julie, née Hagenström, enter, offer the obligatory congratulations, and move through the crowd, greeting one and all. His flat nose drooping over his upper lip, Consul Hermann Hagenström has found support for his bulk on the banister and breathes rather heavily into his reddish beard as he chats with Senator Cremer, the chief of police, whose brown whiskers are flecked with gray and frame a smiling face that betrays a certain cunning. Dr. Moritz Hagenström the attorney is also in attendance, accompanied by his beautiful wife, the former Fräulein Puttfarken from Hamburg, and when he smiles some of his pointed gap-teeth show. Visible for a moment is old Dr. Grabow, who clasps Senator Buddenbrook's right hand in both his own, only to be displaced in the next moment by Voigt the architect. Pastor Pringsheim—in lay dress, his high office suggested only by the length of his frock coat—ascends the stairs with arms spread wide and a perfectly transfigured expression on his face. Even Friedrich Wilhelm Marcus is on hand. Those gentlemen who are official representatives of the senate, the assembly, or the Chamber of Commerce are all dressed in tails. Eleven-thirty—it is getting very hot. The lady of the house withdrew about fifteen minutes ago.

Suddenly they hear the sound of stomping and shuffling in the vestibule downstairs, as if a great many people are crowding into the entrance hall all at once; almost simultaneously a loud, booming voice fills the whole house. Everyone rushes to the landing, thronging the corridor and blocking the doors to the salon, the dining room, and the smoking room, and they all stare in amazement down to where a group of fifteen or twenty men with instruments are arranging themselves around a gentleman with a brown wig, a gray sailor's beard, and wide-toothed yellow dentures that flash as he shouts each command. What is happening? Consul Peter Döhlmann has marched in with the band from the municipal theater. He mounts the stairs in triumph, waving a stack of programs in his hand.

The band strikes up—and the acoustics are absolutely impossible; all the notes run together, one chord devours the next, making every melody absurd, and dominating everything is the loud growl and grunt of the big bass trumpet, blown by a fat man with a desperate look on his face. The concert offered in honor of the Buddenbrook anniversary begins with a chorale, "Now Thank We All Our God"; this is quickly followed by selections from Offenbach's *La Belle*

Hélène, and then comes a medley of folk songs. It is a rather extensive musical program.

What a clever idea! They compliment Consul Döhlmann, and no one is inclined to depart until the concert is over. People stand or sit in the salon and out in the corridor, listening and chatting.

Thomas Buddenbrook had joined Stephan Kistenmaker, Senator Gieseke, and Voigt the architect at the back of the stairwell, between the door opening onto the smoking room and the flight of stairs to the third floor. He stood leaning against the wall, contributing a comment to the conversation now and then, but for the most part gazing silently and vacantly out over the banister. The heat had increased and become even more oppressive; but rain was no longer out of the question, because, to judge from the shadows drifting across the skylight, the skies were clouding over. The shadows were moving so rapidly, in fact, one after another, that the almost constant flicker of light in the stairwell hurt his eyes. The bright gilt trim of the plasterwork, the luster of the chandelier, the gleam of the brass instruments below would vanish one moment, only to flash brilliantly the next. Only once did the shadows linger a little longer than usual, and then five, six, seven times, with short pauses in between, there could be heard a soft clatter as something hard struck the skylight—a little hail, no doubt of it. Then sunlight filled the house again from top to bottom.

There is a form of depression in which everything that would normally annoy us and arouse a healthy response of anger, weighs down upon us instead, eliciting only dull, gloomy silence. And so Thomas brooded over the way little Johann had behaved, brooded over his reaction to this whole celebration, and still more over emotions that, try as he would, he was incapable of feeling. Several times he attempted to pull himself together, to put on a cheerful expression, and to tell himself that this was a beautiful day, a day that should only elevate his mood and fill him with joy. But although the sound of the instruments, the confusion of voices, and the sight of all these people jangled on his nerves and merged with memories of the past and his father, calling up a faint wave of emotion, the predominant feeling was a sense that the whole affair was absurd and embarrassing—second-rate music distorted by bad acoustics, banal people engaging in banal conversation about stock prices and banquets. And the blend of sentiment and anger plunged him ever deeper into gloomy despair.

At a quarter after twelve, just as the program of the municipal-theater orchestra was drawing to a close, an event occurred that, although it in no way detracted from or interrupted the general festivities, required the head of the house to leave his guests for reasons of business for a few minutes. There was a pause in the music, and at the same moment up the main stairs came the youngest office apprentice, a short, hunchbacked fellow, who was so terribly embarrassed by all these fine ladies and gentlemen that he tucked his blushing face between his shoulders even farther than necessary and swung one unnaturally long, thin arm in an exaggerated attempt to lend himself a look of nonchalant self-assurance. In the other he held up a folded piece of paper—a telegram. As he ascended the stairs his eyes bounced shyly in all directions, looking for his boss, and when he at last discovered him at the far end of the staircase, he worked his way back through the obstructing crowd, muttering hasty apologies as he went.

His embarrassment was unnecessary, because no one noticed him. Without even seeing him, people went on chatting as they shifted slightly to make room for him to pass, and hardly anyone glanced up to see him bow and present the telegram to Senator Buddenbrook, who then stepped away from Kistenmaker, Gieseke, and Voigt to read it. Even today, although almost all the cables were merely congratulatory, every telegram received during business hours was to be delivered at once, no matter what the circumstances.

At the foot of the stairs to the third floor, the corridor made a little dogleg, passing then along the length of the grand hall to the servants' stairs, next to which was a side door leading back into the grand hall. Across from the stairs was the door to the shaft of the dumbwaiter that brought food up from the kitchen, and next to it, against the wall, stood a large table, which the housemaid used when she was polishing silver. The senator stopped here, turned his back on the hunchbacked apprentice, and broke open the telegram.

His eyes suddenly grew so wide that anyone watching him would have pulled back in alarm, and he sucked air in a quick, convulsive gasp so violent that his throat dried out instantly and he had to cough.

He managed to say, "That will do." But his voice was inaudible above the hum of conversation behind them. "That will do," he said again; only the first two words were actually spoken, the third was a whisper.

The senator did not move, did not turn around, did not give so much as a hint of moving back down the hall, and so the hunchbacked apprentice stood there uncertainly for a moment, hesitating, shifting his weight from one foot to the other. Then he made another of his bizarre deep bows and started down the servants' stairs.

Senator Buddenbrook stood there beside the table. He still held the unfolded telegram, his hands hanging limply in front of him. His upper body swayed back and forth as he struggled for air in short, labored breaths through his half-open mouth, and kept rocking his head back and forth, as if he had been struck some incomprehensible blow. "That little bit of hail . . . that little bit of hail," he kept repeating pointlessly. Then, however, his breathing grew deeper and more regular, and his body rocked more gently. His half-closed eyes clouded over now—he looked spent, almost broken. And, giving a heavy nod, he turned away.

He opened the door to the grand hall and entered. Slowly, with lowered head, he strode across the polished floor of the spacious room and sat down on one of the dark-red sofas by the window at the far end. It was quiet and cool here. You could hear the fountain splashing in the garden, a fly was buzzing against the windowpane, and only a dull murmur came from the front of the house.

He laid his exhausted head against the cushion and closed his eyes. "It's better this way, it's better this way," he muttered to himself; and then, with a sigh, he said it again, content and relieved: "It really is better this way."

He lay there for five minutes; his body relaxed, and a peaceful expression spread over his face. Then he sat up, folded the telegram, slipped it in his breast pocket, and stood up to return to his guests.

But at that same moment he sank back down onto the sofa,

groaning in disgust. The music, the music was starting up again—what an idiotic racket. It was supposed to be a galop, with drum and cymbals to accentuate the strong rhythm, but the other, muddled masses of sound were out of sync, either ahead or behind—a brassy, jangling, insufferable, naïve hullabaloo of growls, blasts, and twitters, and, above it all, the mad fitful tootles of the piccolo.

6

"OH, BACH! Sebastian Bach, dear madam!" cried Herr Edmund Pfühl, the organist of St. Mary's, pacing the salon in great excitement, while Gerda sat at the piano, smiling, her chin propped in one hand, and Hanno listened to it all from an armchair, one knee clasped in both hands. "Most assuredly, as you've said, it was he who gained the victory for harmony over counterpoint. He was the creator of modern harmony, most assuredly. But by what means? Need I tell you the means? By developing counterpoint even further—you know it as well as I. And what was the driving principle behind that development? Harmony? Oh no, certainly not. But counterpoint itself, madam. Counterpoint! And to what, I ask you, would mere experimentation with harmony have led? I must warn you—as long as I have a tongue to speak—I must warn you of mere experimentation with harmony."

He was passionate about such matters, and he gave his passion free rein, for he felt quite at home here in the salon. Every Wednesday afternoon, this large, square-built man, who carried his shoulders a little too high, would appear on the threshold in his coffee-brown swallowtail coat that fell below the hollows of his knees, and as he waited for his musical partner he would lovingly open the Bechstein grand piano, arrange the violin parts on the carved music stand, and play a brief, light, tasteful prelude, resting his head contentedly first on one shoulder, then the other.

A tangle of tight little curls, an amazing growth of fox-brown hair flecked with gray, made his head seem unusually large and massive, although he held it poised nicely above his turndown collar—at the end of a long neck with a very large Adam's apple. His unkempt, bushy mustache was the same color as his hair and stuck out farther than his stump of a nose. Little puffy bags of skin hung beneath his round brown eyes—which usually sparkled, but turned dreamy when he played, his gaze apparently resting somewhere beyond the point on which they were fixed. There was nothing impressive about his face; at least, it showed no obvious mark of a strong and alert intelligence. His eyelids were usually half lowered, and often, without parting his lips, he would involuntarily let his clean-shaven chin go limp, which gave his mouth the soft, deeply secretive, stupid, abandoned look of a man cradled in sweet slumber.

This softness of the external man, however, contrasted sharply with the rigor and dignity of his character. Edmund Pfühl was a widely admired organist, and his reputation as a scholar of counterpoint was not confined within the walls of his hometown. He had published a little book on the function of musical keys in sacred music, and it was recommended for use in private instruction by two or three conservatories; his fugues and variations on chorales were played here and there, wherever organs resounded to the glory of God. These compositions, as well as the voluntaries to which he treated the congregation of St. Mary's on Sunday, were impeccable, flawless—and filled with the inexorable, imposing dignity and moral logic of the "austere style." All earthly beauty was alien to them, for they left untouched the ordinary human emotions of the layman. What spoke out of them, what triumphed within them, was technique as an ascetic religion—virtuosity for its own sake, holy in and of itself. Edmund Pfühl had little use for music that pleases, and, to be frank, he spoke disdainfully of beautiful melodies. But, puzzling though it may seem, he was not a dry, petrified pedant. "Palestrina!" he would say—and his face would turn dogmatic and terrifying. But in the next moment as he deftly executed a series of archaistic phrases, his expression was all sheer frailty, ecstasy, and rapture, and his eyes would come to rest in some holy, distant place, as if he saw in his work the ultimate conclusion of all human enterprise. This was his musician's gaze, which looked vague and empty, but only because it was caught up in a logic that was deeper, purer, more unsullied and uncompromised than the logic that shapes the ideas and thoughts embodied in language.

His hands were large, soft, seemingly boneless, and heavily freckled—and when he greeted Gerda Buddenbrook as she drew back the portieres and entered the salon, his voice would be soft and hollow, almost as if something were stuck in his throat. "Your servant, madam," he would say.

Rising slightly from his seat at the piano and respectfully lowering his head to the hand she offered him, he brought his left hand down on the firm, clear chords of a fifth, whereupon Gerda picked up her Stradivarius and quickly tuned the strings with a practiced ear.

"The Bach G-minor Concerto, Herr Pfühl. It seems to me that the whole adagio is still rather unsatisfactory."

And the organist began to play. But on most occasions, no sooner would he strike the first few chords than the door to the corridor would slowly, cautiously open and little Johann would soundlessly steal his way across the carpet and take a seat in an armchair. There he would sit very quietly, one knee clasped in both hands, and listen: both to the music and to what was said.

"Well, Hanno, come to snitch a little music?" Gerda said when they came to a pause, letting her glance drift his way—her close-set, shadowy eyes now radiant and moist from the music.

Then he stood up and bowed silently, extending a hand to Herr Pfühl, who let his hand pass gently and lovingly across Hanno's hair, which lay in soft, graceful curls along his brow and at his temples.

"And now listen, my boy," he said, with mild but firm emphasis. All the while, the child was shyly watching the way the organist's Adam's apple rose whenever he spoke. But then he quickly and quietly returned to his chair, as if he could hardly wait for the music and conversation to continue.

They played a movement of Haydn, a few pages of Mozart, a Beethoven sonata. Then, while Gerda was searching for some music, her violin under her arm, the most startling thing happened: Herr Pfühl, Edmund Pfühl, the organist of St. Mary's, who had been playing a casual interlude, gradually drifted into a very strange style, while a kind of embarrassed joy lit his faraway gaze. And from under his fingers came a swelling, blossoming, interweaving melody, from which arose in elegant counterpoint—at first only sporadic, but then ever more clear and vigorous—a great, old-fashioned, wonderful, and grandiose march, which moved toward a climax, intertwining, modulating, and finally resolving as the violin entered *fortissimo*. The overture to *Meistersinger* marched past.

Gerda Buddenbrook was a passionate admirer of this new music. But it had aroused such savage, outraged opposition in Herr Pfühl that in the beginning she had doubted she would ever win him over to it.

On the day when she had first laid the piano arrangements from *Tristan and Isolde* on his music stand and begged him to play it for her, he had leapt to his feet after twenty-five measures and, exhibiting every sign of utmost disgust, begun to pace back and forth between the bay window and the piano.

"I won't play this, madam. I am your most obedient servant, but I will not play it. That is not music, please believe me—and I've always presumed I know a little something about music. It is pure chaos! It is demagoguery, blasphemy, and madness! It is a fragrant fog with thunderbolts. It is the end of all morality in the arts. I will not play it!" And with these words he had thrown himself back on his seat and, amid coughs and gulps, while his Adam's apple bobbed up and down, managed another twenty-five measures, only to slam the piano shut and shout, "Shame, shame! No, good God in heaven, this is going too far. Forgive me, madam, for speaking so candidly. You do me great honor, and have paid me for my services for many a year now—and I am a man of modest circumstances. But if you force me to play such wickedness, I shall resign from my post—I shall do without it. And think of the child, the child sitting there in his chair. He stole in here quietly to hear music—do you wish to poison his mind for good and all?"

But although he carried on most dreadfully—slowly, inch by inch, she won him over by practice and persuasion.

"Pfühl," she said, "be reasonable, just take it in calmly. His unusual use of harmony confuses you. You find Beethoven pure, clear, and natural in comparison. But remember how Beethoven disconcerted his contemporaries, whose ears were trained to the old ways. And Bach himself, good Lord, they accused him of being dissonant and muddy. You speak of morality—but what do you mean by morality in art? If I am not mistaken, it is the opposite of every sort of hedonism is it not? Well, fine, you find that here as well. Just as in Bach. But grander, more self-aware, more profound than in Bach. Believe me, Pfühl, this music is much less foreign to your inner nature than you think."

"Sleight-of-hand and sophistry—if you will beg my pardon," Herr Pfühl muttered. But she proved right—the music was ultimately less foreign to him than he first thought. Granted, he never quite reconciled himself to *Tristan*, although, after much pleading on Gerda's part, he did at last very skillfully adapt the "Liebestod" for violin and piano. He first found a word or two of approbation for certain passages in *Meistersinger*—and then a love for this new art began to stir within him. He would not admit his growing irresistible attachment, and it almost frightened him—he would grumble and deny it. But once the old masters had been given their due, his partner no longer had to coerce him into the more complicated hand positions and he would glide easily into the vital, subtle weaving of leitmotifs, though always with a look of embarrassment and something close to anger in his eyes. Once he had finished playing, however, a discussion might well follow about the relation of this new music to the old "austere style"; and one day Herr Pfühl declared that, although it was not a matter of personal concern, he would add an appendix to his book on church music and title it "The Use of Traditional Keys in the Sacred and Folk Music of Richard Wagner."

Hanno sat very still, his little hands folded on his knees, his mouth slightly askew—he had a habit of rubbing his tongue against a molar. With large, unblinking eyes he watched his mother and Herr Pfühl and listened to them play and talk. And so it was that, after taking only a few steps down the path of life, he came to regard music as something extraordinarily serious, important, and profound. He understood only a word or two of what was said, and the sounds themselves were usually beyond his childish comprehension. Nevertheless he kept coming back to sit there hour after hour, never stirring and never getting bored—and it was faith, love, and awe that brought him.

He was seven years old before he began to try arranging his hands on the keyboard in order to imitate certain combinations of sound that had impressed him. His mother smiled and watched, corrected finger positions he had invented out of silent eagerness, and showed him why he needed a certain note to change one chord into another. And his ear told him that what she said was right.

Gerda Buddenbrook allowed him do as he liked for a while, but at last she decided that he should be given piano lessons.

"I don't think he will ever be a soloist," she said to Herr Pfühl, "and actually I'm quite glad about that, because it has its drawbacks. By which I don't mean the soloist's dependence on accompaniment, although that can be distressing on occasion. And if I did not have you, Pfühl . . . But there is always the danger that one may get caught up in nothing but virtuosity of one kind or another. And I certainly could tell you a tale about that. To be frank, I must admit that it seems to me that music only really begins for the soloist when he has achieved a very high degree of skill. It requires intense concentration on the treble voice and the phrasing of the melodic line, whereas polyphony remains something only very vague and general, and in someone of mediocre talents that can mean the atrophy of any sense of harmony or the ability to retain harmonic structures, which is very difficult to correct later on. I love my violin and have come rather far with it, but I value the piano more. What I am saying is that, for me, familiarity with the piano—which in its ability to recapitulate the most complex and rich harmonies provides a unique means of musical reproduction—results in a clearer, more intimate and comprehensive relationship with music. Hear me out, Pfühl—I would like to enlist you to teach him. Please do me the favor. I know very well that there are two or three other people here in town—all of them women, I believe—who could instruct him, but they are mere piano teachers. You do understand, don't you? It has little or nothing to do with training someone on an instrument, but, rather, with his understanding music. I trust you. You take the matter more seriously. And you shall see—you'll have fine success with him. He has Buddenbrook hands—and Buddenbrooks can span ninths or tenths. But they've never considered it important," she concluded with a laugh. And Herr Pfühl declared himself willing to give Hanno lessons.

And from then on he also came on Monday afternoons, and Gerda would join them in the living room while he worked with little Johann. He did not go about it in the customary fashion, because he felt that the child's mute, eager passion required more of him than a few piano lessons. No sooner had they put the first elementary exercises behind them than he began to teach music theory and made it easily understood by demonstrating the basics of harmony as his pupil watched. And Hanno did understand—it was actually only a confirmation of what he had always known.

Herr Pfühl tried as much as possible to take into account the child's eagerness to make rapid progress. He gave much loving thought and care to how he might best lighten the leaden load of instruction that fettered the boy's fantasy and eager talents. He was not all that strict about demanding great dexterity in practicing scales, or at least he did not see it as the purpose of practice. Rather, what he was aiming for, and soon achieved, was a clear, comprehensive, and effective grasp of musical keys, a personal and insightful familiarity with their interrelationships and connections, from which within a short time would come a quick eye for possible combinations and an intuitive mastery of the keyboard that would encourage fantasy and improvisation. He showed a touching sensitivity for the intellectual needs of his little student, who had been spoiled by having heard so much and was trying to develop a serious style. He did not dampen the solemnity and profundity of the boy's mood by making him practice banal little songs. He let him play chorales where one chord led logically to the next and he never failed to point out the laws of that progression.

Gerda would sit on the other side of the portieres, reading a book or doing needlework, and follow the lessons.

"You have exceeded all my expectations," she said to Herr Pfühl on one occasion. "But are you not going too far? Is your method not a little too out of the ordinary? It is eminently creative, I grant. He is already making honest attempts at improvisation. But if he is not worthy of your method, if he is not talented enough for it, he will learn nothing at all."

"He is worthy of it," Herr Pfühl said with a nod. "I watch his eyes sometimes, and there is so much going on in them, but he keeps his mouth shut tight. And later in life, when his mouth is shut even tighter perhaps, he must have some way of speaking."

She gazed at him, at this square-built musician with a fox-brown wig, unkempt mustache, bags under his eyes, and large Adam's apple—and then she gave him her hand and said, "My best thanks, Pfühl. You mean well, and who knows what all you will accomplish with him."

Hanno's gratitude to his teacher was boundless, and he abandoned himself to his guidance. The same boy who brooded over arithmetic without any hope of ever understanding it, despite all his special tutoring at school, understood everything that Herr Pfühl said to him at the piano, understood it and made it his own—if you can be said to make your own what has always belonged to you. Edmund Pfühl, however, seemed to him like a tall angel dressed in a brown swallowtail coat, who took him in his arms each Monday afternoon to lead him from his everyday misery into the realm of sound, where everything was gentle, sweet, consoling, and serious.

Sometimes the lessons took place in Herr Pfühl's house, a roomy old gabled affair with all sorts of cool hallways and nooks, where the organist lived all by himself except for an ancient housekeeper. Sometimes little Johann Buddenbrook was allowed to join him up in the organ loft of St. Mary's for Sunday services, and that was something very different from sitting down in the nave with all the others. High above the congregation, high even above Pastor Pringsheim in his pulpit, the two of them sat amid the surge of massive waves of sound, which together they unleashed and commanded—because sometimes, much to his great happiness and pride, Hanno was permitted to help his teacher in setting the stops. But once the postlude to the choral anthem was over and Herr Pfühl had slowly removed all ten fingers from the keys to let the bass of the tonic chord echo softly and solemnly, there would be a meaningful, artful pause, and then Pastor Pringsheim would lift up his voice from beneath the canopy of the pulpit; and at that point, it was not unusual for Herr Pfühl to start mocking the sermon and to laugh at Pastor Pringsheim's stylized Franconian accent, his long and dark or sharply accented vowels, his sighs, and the abrupt shifts of darkness and transfiguration passing over his face. Then Hanno would laugh, too, in quiet, deep amusement; for, without even looking at one another or saying a word as they sat there high above it all, they were united in the opinion that his sermons were rather foolish babble and that the real worship service was something that the pastor and his congregation probably thought of as a mere adjunct for elevating the mood of devotion—and that something was music.

The low level of musical interest that Herr Pfühl knew existed below him in the nave, among the families of senators, consuls, and other solid citizens, was a source of constant sorrow, and that was the real reason he liked to have his young pupil beside him—at least he could call his attention to the extraordinary difficulty of the piece he had just played. He indulged himself in the most remarkable displays of technique. He had composed a "reverse imitation," a melody that could be read either forward or backward and formed the basis of a fugue that could be played in "crab form." When he finished, he laid his hands in his lap, a gloomy expression on his face. "Nobody cares," he said with a hopeless shake of his head. And then, while Pastor Pringsheim preached, he whispered to Hanno, "That was a *cancrizans*, a crab-form imitation, Johann. You're not yet familiar with it, but it reproduces every note of a theme from back to front. You'll learn strict analysis of an imitation in due time. But I'll never torture you with the crab form, or force you to learn it. But never believe anyone who would tell you that it's just a game of no musical value whatever. You'll discover that the crab form has been used by the greatest composers down through the centuries. Only lazy and mediocre composers spurn such exercises—out of arrogance. Whereas *humility* is in order. Remember that, Johann."

On his eighth birthday, April 15, 1869, Hanno joined his mother to play a duet for the assembled family—a little fantasia of his own, a simple motif, which, when it came to him, had seemed so curious that he developed it further. But of course Herr Pfühl, to whom he showed it, found several things to criticize.

"What a theatrical ending, Johann! It doesn't really fit the rest, does it? It's all quite correct at the start, but why did you decide suddenly to leave B major for a fourth-sixth chord, for this interval of a fourth with a diminished third—that's what I want to know?

Mere tricks. And you add a *tremolo* besides. You've picked that up somewhere. And where? I know only too well. You've been paying close attention when I have to play certain pieces for your good mother. Change the ending, child, and then it will be a tidy piece of work."

But it was the minor chord and the ending that Hanno cared most about; and his mother was so amused by them that they were kept. She picked up her violin and played the treble melody and then a variation on it, ending in a descant of thirty-second notes, while Hanno simply repeated his part. It sounded marvelous. Hanno was so happy that he kissed her. And that was how they played it on April 15.

Old Madame Buddenbrook, Frau Permaneder, Christian, Klothilde, Herr and Frau Kröger, Herr and Frau Weinschenk, the Ladies Buddenbrook from Breite Strasse, and Fräulein Weichbrodt had joined the senator and his wife for a four o'clock dinner in honor of Hanno's birthday. Now they were all seated in the salon. They listened with their eyes fixed on the child, who sat at the piano in his sailor suit, and on Gerda, looking so elegant and exotic, who first played a splendid cantilena on the G string and then, with impeccable virtuosity, unleashed a sparkling, bubbly flood of cadenzas. The silver trim on the handle of her bow flashed in the gaslight.

Pale with excitement, Hanno had been able to eat almost nothing at dinner; but now, forgetting everything around him and removed from the world, he surrendered himself totally to his composition—which, alas, would be over in two minutes. The nature of his little melodic fantasia was more harmonic than rhythmic, and there was a very strange contrast between the basic, rudimentary musical resources at the child's disposal and the momentous, passionate, and almost elegant way he emphasized and enhanced them. Hanno stressed each modulation with a tilt and bob of his head, and, shifting forward to the edge of his seat, he used the pedal to give each new chord emotional value. Indeed, if little Hanno achieved any effect at all—even if it was limited only to himself—it was less a matter of sentiment than of sensitivity. By retarding or heavily accenting some very simple harmonic maneuver, he gave it a higher, mysterious, precious meaning. Raising his eyebrows, rocking or lifting his upper body, he would suddenly introduce a faintly echoing tone-color to some new chord, harmonic device, or attack, lending it a surprising nervous energy. And now came the ending, Hanno's beloved finale, which was to add the final simple, sublime touch to the whole composition. Wrapped in the sparkling, bubbling runs of the violin, which rang out with gentle, bell-like purity, he struck the E-minor chord *tremolo pianissimo*. It grew, broadened, swelled slowly, very slowly, and once it was at *forte*, Hanno sounded the dissonant C sharp that would lead back to the original key; and while the Stradivarius surged and dashed sonorously around the same C sharp, he used all his strength to crescendo the dissonance to *fortissimo*. He refused to resolve the chord, withheld it from himself and his audience. What would the resolution be like, this ravishing and liberating submersion into B major? Incomparable joy, the delight of sweet rapture. Peace, bliss, heaven itself. Not yet, not yet—one moment more of delay, of unbearable tension that would make the release all the more precious. He wanted one last taste of this insistent, urgent longing, of this craving that filled his whole being, of this cramped and strained exertion of will, which at the same time refused all fulfillment and release—he knew that happiness lasts only a moment. Hanno's upper body slowly straightened up, his eyes grew large, his tightly closed lips quivered, he jerked back, drawing air in through his nose—and then that blessedness could be held back no longer. It came, swept over him, and he no longer fought it. His muscles relaxed; overwhelmed, he let his weary head sink back on his shoulders. His eyes closed, and a melancholy, almost pained smile of unutterable ecstasy played about his mouth. And while the violin whispered, wove, surged, and dashed around his *tremolo*, he shifted the pedal and added the base cadence that slid into B major, abruptly swelled to *fortissimo*; and then, with one brief burst, it broke off without a trace of echo.

It was impossible for the effect Hanno's playing had had on him to be transferred to his audience. Frau Permaneder, for example, had not the slightest idea what the whole show was about. But she had seen the child's smile, the way his upper body had moved, the blissful way the little, delicate head that she loved so much had sunk to one side—and the sight had touched the depths of her easily stirred soft heart.

"How the boy can play! How the child can play!" she cried, close to tears, and hurried over to fold him in her arms. "Gerda, Tom, he'll be a Mozart, a Meyerbeer, a . . ." And since a third name of equal consequence did not immediately occur to her, she resorted to smothering her nephew with kisses—while he sat there totally exhausted, his hands in his lap and a faraway look in his eyes.

"Enough, Tony, enough," the senator said softly. "I beg you, don't give the boy ideas."

7

IN HIS HEART, Thomas Buddenbrook was not pleased with little Johann and how he was developing.

The easily shocked philistines had shaken their heads, but he had brought Gerda Arnoldsen home as his bride, because he had felt strong and free enough to show that, in comparison with those around him, his tastes were more distinguished, but in no way compromised his competence as a solid citizen. But was this child, the heir for whom he had waited in vain so long and who bore many physical traits of his father's family—was this child to be so completely his mother's son? He had hoped Hanno would one day continue his own life's work with a more skillful and easy hand—and was the boy now to grow up at odds with the whole world in which he lived and would one day have to work, to be by his very nature a stranger to and estranged from his own father?

Until now Gerda's violin playing had been just another charming adjunct to her unique character, as much a part of her as those unusual eyes he so loved, as her heavy, chestnut hair, as her whole unique presence. But he was forced to watch as her passion for music—which he had always found rather odd—took possession of the child at such an early age. In some sense it had been part of Hanno from the very start, and Thomas regarded music as a hostile force that had come between him and his child—after all, he had hoped to make a genuine Buddenbrook of him, a strong and practical man with a powerful drive to master and take control of the world outside him. But in his present irritable mood, it seemed to him as if that hostile force was making him a stranger in his own house.

He was incapable of drawing nearer to the music that so preoccupied Gerda and that friend of hers, Herr Pfühl; and Gerda, who was always impatient and exclusive when it came to matters of art, made any approach even more difficult, sometimes in truly cruel ways.

He would never have believed that the essence of music could be so totally alien to his family as it increasingly appeared to be. His grandfather had piped a little on his flute, and he himself enjoyed listening to pretty melodies that had either an easy grace or a quiet melancholy about them, or that perhaps roused him with their cheerful vigor. But if he expressed his preference for anything of that sort, he could be certain that Gerda would shrug her shoulders and say with a sympathetic smile, "How is it possible, my dear? Something so totally lacking in musical value . . ."

He hated this "musical value," a term that he could associate with only one thing: chilly arrogance. And he felt compelled to rise up against it, even with Hanno sitting nearby. There had been more than one occasion when he had flared up and exclaimed, "Oh, my dear, your insistence on 'musical value' seems to me rather tasteless snobbery."

And she replied, "Thomas, let me say once and for all that you will never understand music as art, and, as intelligent as you are, you will never see it as anything more than a little after-dinner treat, dessert for your ears. When it comes to music, your normally fine sense for what is banal fails you entirely. And that is the criterion for understanding art. You can see just how foreign music is to you by the fact that your musical understanding does not at all correspond to your usual demands and tastes. What kind of music do you enjoy? Things that have a certain insipid optimism, which, if you found them in a book, would prompt you to cast it with amused anger or total outrage into the nearest corner. The quick gratification of every vaguely aroused wish—prompt, cordial satisfaction before the will has even been engaged. Is that how the world works—like a pretty melody? That's merely flimsy idealism."

He understood her, he understood what she said. But his emotions were unable to follow her—he could not comprehend why melodies that cheered him up or moved him were cheap and worthless, or why music that seemed harsh or chaotic should be of the highest musical value. He stood before a temple, and Gerda stood at the threshold adamantly barring his way. And then he watched in pain as she disappeared inside with his child.

He did not let them see the anguish he felt as he watched the apparent estrangement grow between him and his son, and he would have recoiled at even the appearance of currying his son's favor. He had little leisure time during the day to spend with the boy but sometimes at meals he would banter with him amiably, with just a hint of sternness.

"Well, my lad," he said, patting him a few times on the back of his head as he sat down beside him at the dining table, across from his wife, "how are things going? What have you been up to? Studying?—Oh, and playing the piano? That's fine. But not too much, or you won't have energy for anything else, and you'll be set back a year come Easter." Not a muscle in his face betrayed his anxiety as he waited to see how Hanno would react to his greeting, how he would respond; he betrayed nothing of the painful wrenching inside him when the boy simply glanced his way with shy, golden-brown, blue-shadowed eyes that avoided looking directly at him, and then bent down mutely over his plate.

It would have been monstrous to express alarm at the boy's childish awkwardness. But as they sat there together waiting for the plates to be changed for the next course, it was his duty to show some concern about the boy, to test him a little on facts, to rouse his sense for practical things. What was the population of the town? Which streets led up from the Trave into town? What were the names of the firm's warehouses? Speak up, now, loud and clear!—But Hanno was silent. Not because he wanted to defy his father, or hurt him. Under normal circumstances, the population, the streets, even the warehouses were matters of complete indifference to him, but the moment they were raised to the status of questions on a test, they filled him with reluctant despair. He could be in a perfectly fine mood, even be enjoying a little chat with his father—but as soon as the conversation took on the least hint of a little oral exam, his mood sank to zero and below and all his powers of resistance collapsed. His eyes lost their sparkle, his mouth took on a despondent pout, and all he could feel was a great pang of regret that Papa had been so careless, because he surely had to know that these tests always turned out badly and spoiled the meal for himself and everyone else. He gazed down at his plate, his eyes swimming with tears. Ida nudged him and whispered the names of the streets and warehouses. But that was pointless, absolutely pointless. She didn't understand. He knew the names well enough, or at least most of them, and it would have been so easy to oblige Papa and answer his questions, at least in part—if only he could, if only it weren't for this overwhelming sadness. A stern word from his father and a quick rap of a fork against the cutting board made him flinch. He glanced at his mother and Ida and tried to speak; but the first few syllables were choked with sobs—he just couldn't. "Enough!" the senator shouted angrily. "Don't say anything. I don't want to hear it. You don't have to answer. You can sit there brooding like a deaf-mute for the rest of your life for all I care!" And they finished their meal in silent rancor.

Whenever the senator voiced his objections to Hanno's passionate preoccupation with music, he would fix on these very points: the dreamy softness, the weeping, the total lack of vigor and energy.

Hanno's health had always been delicate. From early on, his teeth in particular had been a source of trouble and the cause of many painful episodes. The fever and convulsions that had come with his first teeth had almost cost him his life, and his gums still tended to become inflamed and form abscesses, which Mamselle Jungmann would lance with a needle when they were ready. And now that his second teeth were starting to come in, his sufferings increased. The pain was sometimes almost more than Hanno could bear, and there were nights when he did not sleep at all, but lay in his bed crying, groaning softly, limp with a fever whose only cause was the pain itself. His teeth, which were as beautiful and white as his mother's, were unusually soft and brittle; they came in all wrong, crowding each other. And because these complications had to be corrected, little Johann was forced early on to make the acquaintance of a terrible man: Herr Brecht, the dentist who lived on Mühlen Strasse.

The man's very name reminded Hanno of the horrible sound his jaw made when, after all the pulling, twisting, and prying, the roots of a tooth were wrenched out. The mere mention of that name would jolt his heart with the same fear he felt whenever he had to sit cowering in an armchair in Herr Brecht's waiting room; with faithful Ida Jungmann directly across from him, he would breathe in the acrid air of the office and leaf through illustrated magazines—until the dentist appeared at the door of the consulting room and said, in a voice equally horrifying and polite, "Next, please."

The waiting room had one strange, fascinating attraction: an imposing, brightly colored, evil-eyed parrot, which sat in the middle of a bronze cage placed in one corner of the room. For some inexplicable reason it was named Josephus. In the scolding voice of an old woman, it would say, "Take a seat. One moment, please." Given the circumstances, it sounded like horrible mockery, and yet Hanno Buddenbrook felt a strange attraction for the bird, a mixture of affection and horror. A parrot, a big, brightly colored parrot named Josephus—and it could talk! Perhaps it had escaped from a magic forest or from one of the Grimm's fairy tales that Ida read to him at home. And whenever Herr Brecht opened the door, Josephus would repeat his "Next, please!" so emphatically that, strangely enough, Hanno would find himself smiling as he entered the treatment room and then sat down in the large, eerie contraption of a chair near the window, and nearer the treadle.

As to Herr Brecht himself, he looked very much like Josephus; he had a beak just like the parrot's—a stiff, lopsided nose that hooked down over his salt-and-pepper mustache. The worst thing, the really horrible thing about him, however, was that he was nervous and unable to cope with the torment his profession demanded he inflict. "We must proceed to an extraction, Fräulein," he would say to Ida Jungmann—and then turn pale. And Hanno would sit there in a limp cold sweat, unable to protest, unable to run away—in a state no different from that of a felon facing execution—and with enormous eyes he would watch Herr Brecht approach, his forceps held against his sleeve, and he could see the little beads of sweat on the dentist's brow and that his mouth, too, was twisted in pain. And when the ghastly procedure was over—and Hanno would spit blood in the blue bowl at his side and then sit up pale and trembling, with tears in his eyes and his face contorted with pain—

Herr Brecht would have to sit down somewhere to dry his brow and drink a little water.

They assured little Johann that what this man did to him was for his own good and that it would prevent much greater pain later on. But when Hanno compared the pain that Herr Brecht caused him with any noticeable positive results, the former outweighed the latter to such an extent that he could only regard these visits to Mühlen Strasse as the most useless and terrible torture imaginable. To make room for the wisdom teeth that would come later, four molars—four new, beautiful, white, and perfectly healthy molars—had to be removed, a procedure that was stretched out over several weeks in order not to overtax the child. And what weeks they were! It was a protracted martyrdom, during which the dread of the next visit set in before he had even overcome the strain of the last—and it proved too much. After the final tooth was pulled, Hanno lay ill in bed for a week—out of pure exhaustion.

His dental problems affected not only his frame of mind but also the function of several vital organs. Because he had difficulty chewing, he had constant digestive problems, including several attacks of gastric fever; and his stomach pains were partly responsible for occasional dizzy spells, when his heart would beat too hard or too weakly and his pulse became irregular. And all the while his old disorder—the one that Dr. Grabow had diagnosed as *pavor nocturnus*—continued—indeed, grew worse. There was hardly a night when little Johann did not start up in bed at least once or twice, wringing his hands and crying for help or pleading for mercy, exhibiting all the signs of the most awful panic, as if he were being burned alive or strangled, as if something ghastly beyond all description were happening to him. And in the morning he would remember nothing at all. Dr. Grabow attempted to treat this affliction with a glass of blueberry juice before bed—but that did not help in the least.

The afflictions to which Hanno's body was subject, the pain he had to suffer, could not help making him serious and wise for his age, making him what people call precocious; and although his precociousness was never obtrusive—perhaps in some way it was suppressed by so much talent and good taste—every now and then it would surface as a kind of melancholy condescension. "How are you feeling, Hanno?" one of his relatives would ask—his grandmother or one of the Ladies Buddenbrook from Breite Strasse—and his only answer would be a little resigned smile and a shrug of his shoulders, so prettily outfitted in a blue sailor suit.

"Do you like school?"

"No," Hanno answered calmly and with a candor that said it was not worth lying about such matters, given life's more serious problems.

"No? Oh. But you do have to learn reading, writing, arithmetic . . ."

"And so forth," little Johann said.

No, he did not like the Old School, the former convent school with its cloisters and Gothic-vaulted classrooms. He was not doing well in his subjects. He was absent too often because of illness and was totally inattentive because his thoughts would linger over some harmonic relationship or some unraveled marvel in a piece of music that he had heard his mother and Herr Pfühl play. The lower grades were taught by assistant instructors and teachers-in-training, narrow-minded men who were negligent about their personal hygiene, and he both feared them and secretly held them in contempt as social inferiors. Herr Tietge, the mathematics teacher, a tiny old man in a greasy coat, had been on the faculty since the days of the late Marcellus Stengel and was impossibly cross-eyed, which he attempted to correct with glasses whose lenses were as round and thick as portholes on a ship. At least once an hour, Herr Tietge would remind little Johann what a diligent, clever student of mathematics his father had been. Herr Tietge's constant severe coughing spells meant that the floor around his lectern was covered with the mucus he coughed up.

On the whole, Hanno maintained a quite superficial and distant relationship with his classmates. He was pals with only one of them, had been from the very first day of school—and the bond held firm. His friend was named Kai, Count Kai Mölln—a boy from an aristocratic family, but whose appearance was totally unkempt.

He was about Hanno's height, but instead of a Danish sailor outfit he wore a dingy suit of indeterminate color, with a button missing here and there and a very large visible patch on the seat of his pants. Sticking out from the short sleeves, his hands were always a pale gray, as if impregnated with dust and dirt; but they were narrow and exceptionally fine hands, with long fingers and long, tapering fingernails. He had a head to match those hands—disheveled, uncombed, and none too clean, but endowed by nature with all the marks of a fine and noble pedigree. His reddish-blond hair was carelessly parted down the middle, and when he brushed it back from his alabaster forehead, his deep-set but keen bright blue eyes flashed. He had somewhat prominent cheekbones, and both his mouth with its short upper lip and his nose with its delicate nostrils and narrow, slightly aquiline curve were already distinctive and characteristic.

Before they ever began school together, Hanno Buddenbrook had caught a quick glimpse of this young count once or twice, when he and Ida Jungmann had gone for a walk that took them northward, out through the Burg Gate. Quite a distance out of town—not far from the first village, in fact—was a little farmstead, a tiny, almost worthless piece of property that didn't even have a name. If you stopped to look inside the gate, the first thing you noticed was a manure pile, then several chickens, a doghouse, and, finally, a wretched cottagelike building with a low-hanging red roof. This was the manor house, the residence of Kai's father, Count Eberhard Mölln.

He was an eccentric, whom people seldom saw—a recluse who had forsaken the world for this little farm, where he bred chickens and dogs and grew vegetables: a tall, bald man who wore top boots and a green frieze jacket and sported a huge grizzled beard worthy of a troll. He always had a riding crop in his hand, although he did not own a single horse, and there was a monocle clamped in one eye, under a bushy brow. Apart from him and his son, there was no longer a single Count Mölln to be found anywhere in the country. The various branches of this once rich, powerful, and proud family had withered, died, and rotted away, and little Kai had only one aunt who was still alive—and his father was not on speaking terms with her. She published novels, written under a bizarre pseudonym, in various family magazines. What people remembered about

Count Eberhard was that, shortly after he had moved onto the farm out beyond the Burg Gate, a sign appeared on the low front door warning salesmen, beggars, or anyone else making inquiries not to bother him; the sign read: "Here lives Count Mölln, all alone. He needs nothing, buys nothing, and has nothing to give away." The sign had stayed there some time, until it served its purpose and no one bothered him anymore. Then he had taken it down.

Little Kai was motherless—the countess had died giving birth to him, and some old woman kept house for them—and he had grown up like a wild animal among the chickens and dogs; the first time that Hanno Buddenbrook saw him, he watched shyly from a distance as Kai bounded about like a rabbit in a cabbage patch, roughhousing with puppies and frightening chickens with his somersaults.

He met him again in the classroom, and the little count's savage appearance continued to make him feel a bit nervous at first—but not for long. His sure instincts allowed him to see through the dissheveled exterior and to notice, instead, the white forehead, the narrow mouth, the wide, finely shaped, bright blue eyes that gazed out at the world in a kind of angry astonishment; and Hanno had been filled with a great sympathy for this one classmate, to the exclusion of all others. Nevertheless he was much too reticent to muster the courage for the first step, and without little Kai's rash initiative they would probably have remained strangers. In fact, the eager haste with which Kai struck up a friendship frightened Johann at first. But the little, unkempt fellow went about courting the diffident, elegantly dressed Hanno with such ardor and impetuous, aggressive manliness that there was no resisting him. Granted, he could not help Hanno with his lessons—given his untamed, free-ranging spirit, he felt the same loathing for multiplication tables as dreamy, distracted young Buddenbrook did. But he gave Hanno everything he had to give as presents: marbles, wooden tops, even his small, battered tin pistol—his finest possession. They spent recess hand in hand, and he talked about his home, about the puppies and chickens; and sometimes he was even allowed to join Hanno at lunchtime, although Ida Jungmann always stood waiting at the school gate with a package of sandwiches, ready to take her charge for their midday stroll. On one such occasion he learned that young

Buddenbrook was called Hanno at home, and he immediately adopted the nickname and never called him anything else from then on.

One day he had insisted that, instead of walking along the Mühlenwall, Hanno come with him to his father's farm to see some newborn guinea pigs, and Fräulein Jungmann had finally given in to their pleas. When they arrived at the count's estate, they first inspected the vegetables, dogs, chickens, and guinea pigs and then entered the house, where in a long, low room on the ground floor they found Count Eberhard eating and reading at a low rustic table; the perfect image of defiant loneliness, he gruffly asked them what they wanted.

Ida Jungmann could not be persuaded to repeat the visit; indeed, she insisted that, if they wanted to be together, it would be better for Kai to visit Hanno. And so, for the first time, the little count entered his friend's splendid home—and was frank in his admiration, but not the least bit shy. From then on he came more and more often, and only the deepest snows of winter could prevent him from hiking all the way back into town to spend a few hours with Hanno Buddenbrook each afternoon.

They sat together in the large playroom on the third floor and did their homework. There were long arithmetic problems that filled both sides of their slates, and when you were done with all the addition, subtraction, multiplication, and division, the answer had to be zero—and if it wasn't, there must be a mistake somewhere, and you had to search and search until you found the nasty little beast and erased it, and you could only hope that it wasn't too far back, because otherwise the whole thing had to be done over. Then they had German grammar to do, to learn the rules of comparison and to write the examples in tidy and even rows—things like: "Horn is transparent. Glass is more transparent. Air is most transparent." And then there were exercises to be studied in their spelling books, such as: "Eve received word that she must leave the garden and grieved that she had believed the serpent and deceived Adam." The point of this tricky exercise was that you would be tempted to misspell "received" and "deceived" with "ie," "believed" and "grieved" with "ei," and "leave" as "leve" and "Eve" as "Eave"—which in fact had been done in every case, and now the task was to correct them all. But when they were finished at last, they put their books away and sat down on the window seat to listen to Ida read.

This good soul read to them about Liza-Kate, about the boy who left home to learn fear, about Rumpelstiltskin, Rapunzel, and the Frog King—all in a deep, unhurried voice and with her eyes half closed. She knew these fairy tales almost by heart—she had read them all too many times over the years—and turned the pages automatically with a moistened index finger.

But now something remarkable happened. Little Kai increasingly showed an interest in developing his own talents, wanted to imitate the book and tell stories of his own; and that was all the more welcome because it was not long before they knew the printed fairy tales, and Ida needed a rest now and then, too. At first Kai's stories were short and simple; they soon grew bolder, however, and more complicated—and more interesting, because they were not pure fabrications but had some basis in reality, but a reality bathed in a strange and mysterious light. Hanno especially liked to listen to the story about an evil but extraordinarily powerful magician, who tormented everyone with his wicked spells and had changed a handsome and very clever prince named Josephus into a brightly colored bird that he held captive in a cage. But there was a boy in a faraway land, and he had been chosen to become a fearless hero and would grow up one day to lead an invincible army of dogs, chickens, and guinea pigs into battle against the magician, and with a single stroke of his sword he would rescue the whole world and the prince—and especially Hanno Buddenbrook—from the magician's evil power. And once the charm was broken and he was free, Josephus would return to his kingdom, become a king, and promote Hanno and Kai to high positions.

Now and then Senator Buddenbrook would pass the playroom and see the two friends there together—and he had no objections. It was easy to see that the two were a good influence on one another. Hanno had a calming effect on Kai, he tamed him, almost ennobled him; and Kai dearly loved his friend. He marveled at the whiteness of his hands, and, just to please Hanno, he even let Fräulein Jungmann take a brush and soap to his own. And the senator would have been only too happy to see Hanno acquire a little of the young count's vitality and ruggedness, because Senator Buddenbrook was well aware that the constant influence of women was not likely to stimulate and develop manliness in the boy.

The loyalty and self-sacrifice of good Ida Jungmann, who had served the Buddenbrooks for three decades now, could never be repaid in gold. She had devotedly tended and nursed the previous generation—but Hanno was the apple of her eye. She wrapped him up in all her tenderness and concern, she idolized him, and at times she carried to absurdity her naïve, unshakable belief that he had an absolute right to his privileged place in the world. When called upon to act in his behalf, she could be amazingly, sometimes embarrassingly brazen. If she happened to be out shopping with him at the pastry shop, for example, she would never forget to reach coolly into one of the bowls of sweets on the counter and hand him something, without even thinking of paying—the baker should take it as an honor, shouldn't he? And if a crowd was gathered at a display window, she would take her charge by the hand and then, in her friendly but very determined West Prussian dialect, ask people to make way for him. Indeed, in her eyes he was so special that she found hardly any other children worthy of close association. When it came to the little count, her initial mistrust was overcome by the boys' affection for one another—and his title had dazzled her a bit, too. If she happened to be sitting with Hanno on a bench beside the Mühlenwall, however, and other children with their governesses would sit down next to them, Fräulein Jungmann would get up almost at once and move on after making some excuse about being late or sitting in a draft. The explanations she offered little Johann for this behavior could only lead him to believe that all his contemporaries either were scrofulous or had what she called "evil humors"—and that he was the lone exception. This did not exactly enhance his already somewhat meager sense of confidence and ease in dealing with other people.

Senator Buddenbrook knew nothing about such details; but he saw that his son's development, whether as a result of nature or external influences, was not, as yet, headed in the direction he would have wished. If only he could take Hanno's education in hand himself, he could then mold his mind, every hour of every day. But he did not have the time, and he was painfully aware that his occasional attempts at it had failed miserably, making the father-son relationship that much colder and more distanced. He had an image in his mind's eye and longed to shape his son after it: the image of Hanno's great-grandfather as he remembered him from his own childhood—a clever, jovial, natural, witty, strong man. Couldn't Hanno grow up to be like that? Was that impossible? And if so, why? If he could have suppressed and banned the music at least—it was certainly not good for his health, absorbed all his mental energies, and made him ill-suited for the practical side of life. And that dreamy way he had about him—did it not sometimes border on simple-mindedness?

One afternoon Hanno had gone downstairs alone to the second floor almost an hour before dinner, which was always at four. He practiced the piano for a while and then just lounged around the living room. Half lying, half sitting on the chaise longue, he toyed with the knot in his sailor's tie. His eyes had wandered off to one side, not looking at anything in particular, when he happened to spot an open leather writing case on his mother's walnut desk—the family documents. He propped his elbows against the cushion behind him, his chin in one hand, and gazed at them for a while from a distance. It was obvious that Papa had been busy with them this morning, after second breakfast, and had left them there to work on them later. There were still some things in the case; other, loose pages had been pulled out, and a metal ruler served as a provisional paperweight. The large gilt-edged notebook lay open among the various papers.

Hanno slid casually from the couch and went over to the desk. The book was open to a place where the family tree of the Buddenbrooks had been plotted out with parentheses, rubrics, and clearly ordered dates, all of it recorded in the hands of his forebears and, most recently, of his own father. Kneeling with one leg on the desk chair and one hand pressed against the soft waves of his light brown hair, he examined the manuscript a little from the side, studying it with a faintly critical, rather contemptuously serious, and completely indifferent, eye; his free hand played with Mama's gold-and-ebony penholder. His gaze wandered among all those names of men and women, arranged side by side or beneath one another, some written in an old-fashioned hand with curlicues and long, sweeping flourishes, the ink fading and yellowish now, some boldly set down in thick strokes of black ink to which bits of gold-sand still clung. At the very end, recorded directly under his parents' names, in Papa's small, neat hand that hurried across the page, he read his own: Justus, *Johann*, Kaspar, born 15 April 1861. That he found amusing. He straightened up a little, nonchalantly picked up both the ruler and the pen, laid the ruler under his name, and scanned the whole genealogical hodgepodge once more; then, with a passive, dreamy look on his face, he set the gold pen to the page and, with great yet somehow thoughtless and mechanical care, he drew two neat, lovely horizontal lines across the bottom—the upper line a little less thick than the lower, the way he had been taught to do on each page of his arithmetic book. He laid his head critically to one side for a moment, and wandered off.

After dinner, the senator called for him. He scowled and asked him gruffly, "What is this? How did this get here? Did you do this?"

He had to stop and think a moment whether he had or not. But then, shyly and nervously, he said, "Yes."

"What for? What were you thinking of? Answer me! What made you be so malicious?" the senator shouted, slapping Hanno's cheek with a lightly rolled-up notebook.

Pulling away and holding his hand to his cheek, little Johann stammered, "I thought . . . I thought . . . there wouldn't be anything more."

8

OF LATE, when the family sat down to dinner each Thursday, surrounded by the statues of gods smiling calmly down from the wallpaper, there was a new and very serious topic of conversation, which elicited only cool, standoffish looks from the Ladies Buddenbrook from Breite Strasse—and the most excited looks and gestures from Frau Permaneder. With her head laid back and both arms stretched straight ahead or straight up, she spoke out of anger, resentment, out of genuine, deeply felt outrage. She would proceed from the specific case at hand to more general observations about humankind as a whole interspersed with dry, nervous coughs related to her digestive problems; she let out little trumpet blasts of disgust in the throaty voice she always used when she was angry. And it sounded like: "Teary Trieschke! Grünlich! Permaneder!" But the remarkable thing was that a new cry had been added, and she uttered it with indescribable scorn and venom. It sounded like: "The prosecutor!"

But the moment Director Hugo Weinschenk entered the dining room—still dressed in his frock coat and late as always, because he was buried under work—and strode to his chair with an unusually lively swing to his gait, his clenched fists balanced in front of him, his lower lip drooping impudently under his small mustache, the conversation would die, and a painful, stifling silence would hang over the table, until the senator would extricate them from their embarrassment by asking quite casually how the affair was proceeding—as if it were just another normal bit of business. And Hugo Weinschenk would reply that the affair was going quite well—famously, in fact, as was only to be expected—and then would blithely change the subject. He was much more cheerful of late and let his eyes roam about with a certain wild unflappability and frequently asked, though without receiving an answer, about how Gerda's fiddle was doing. He chatted away merrily about all sorts of things. The only problem was that, in his naïve candor and extraordinary high spirits, he did not pay sufficient attention to what he was saying, and every now and then would tell a story that was somewhat out of place. One of his anecdotes, for example, concerned a wet-nurse who suffered from such an awful case of flatulence that the child she was nursing took ill. And in a manner which he doubtless thought was humorous, he imitated the family physician, who had shouted, "Who is making this stink? Who is making this stink here?"—and he noticed too late, or perhaps not at all, that his wife was blushing terribly, that old Madame Buddenbrook, Thomas, and Gerda sat there like statues, that the Ladies Buddenbrook exchanged pointed glances, that even Rieke Severin, at the far end of the table, looked offended and simply gazed straight ahead, and that only old Consul Kröger managed to splutter softly.

And what was Hugo Weinschenk's problem? This earnest, industrious, but chipper man with a rough exterior and no social graces whatever, this man who devoted himself to his work with a dogged sense of duty—this man was alleged to have committed a serious offense, not just once, but repeatedly. Indeed, he was accused of, and had been indicted for, having on several occasions engaged in a business maneuver that was not just dubious but contemptible and criminal. And he would have to face trial—the outcome of which was uncertain. And what were the charges against him? There had been fires in various localities, large conflagrations, and each of them would have cost his insurance company, which had underwritten the policies in question, large sums of money. It was claimed, however, that Hugo Weinschenk, having immediately received confidential news of these calamities from his agents, had with fraudulent intent reinsured the policies with other insurance companies, thereby passing the losses on to them. And now the matter lay in the hands of the prosecutor, and the prosecutor was Dr. Moritz Hagenström.

"Thomas," old Madame Buddenbrook said to her son when they

were alone, "tell me, please . . . I don't understand. What am I to think of all this?"

And he replied, "Well, my dear Mother, what can I say? Unfortunately there is some doubt whether everything was as it should be. But, on the other hand, I think it unlikely that Weinschenk is guilty to the extent that certain people would have you believe. In business today there are certain practices, they call them 'usages.' And a usage, you see, is a maneuver that is not quite all that it should be, not quite in accordance with the letter of the law, and looks rather dishonest from the layman's point of view, but which by the tacit agreement of the business world is common enough. It's hard to draw the line between a usage and something much worse. But no matter. If Weinschenk has done something wrong, it is most probably nothing more dreadful than what many of his colleagues have done—and got away with. But that does not mean I think the trial will go in his favor. He might be acquitted in a large city, perhaps. But here, where everything comes down to cliques and personal motives—well, he should have thought of that when he chose his lawyer. We have no outstanding lawyers here in town, no eminent intellect whose oratorical skills are overwhelmingly convincing, who knows all the tricks of the trade and is well versed in even the most ticklish business practices. You see, all our lawyers hang together. They have lunch or dinner together. They have so many interests in common, sometimes even relatives. And they have to show some consideration for each other. In my opinion it would have been wiser if Weinschenk had chosen a local attorney. But what did he do? He felt it necessary—I repeat, felt it necessary, which makes one wonder about how easy he is in his own conscience—to enlist a lawyer from Berlin, Dr. Breslauer, a regular hell-raiser with a smooth tongue, a crafty virtuoso of the law with a reputation for having helped keep any number of shady bankrupts out of prison. And there's no doubt he will handle the matter with a shrewdness equal to his very high fee. But will it do any good? I can see it coming—our gallant local attorneys will refuse to be impressed by the gentleman, will fight him tooth and nail, and the court will have a much more open ear for Dr. Hagenström's argument. And the witnesses? As far as his own office staff goes, I don't think that they are especially devoted to him. What we who wish him well call his rough exterior—he calls it that himself, I believe—has not won him many friends. And so, in short, Mother, I fear the worst. If disaster strikes, it will be very hard on Erika. But I feel sorriest for Tony. You see, she's quite right when she says that Hagenström was only too happy to take the case on. It involves us all, and if it ends in disgrace, we shall all be affected, because Weinschenk is part of the family after all—he sits at our table. As far as I'm concerned, I can manage. I know how I shall have to conduct myself. Publicly, I shall stand quite aloof from the whole affair. I dare not even attend the trial—although I would be interested in watching Breslauer. But if I am to protect myself from the charge of trying to influence the outcome, I cannot show any concern whatever. But Tony? I don't even want to think about how sad a conviction would be for her. And when you listen to her loud protests against slander and envious intrigues, what you hear is fear—the fear that, after all the misfortunes she has had to bear, she may have to forfeit this last honorable position in her daughter's respectable household. Oh, just watch, her assertions about Weinschenk's innocence will grow louder and louder, the more she feels herself hemmed in by doubts. Although he may very well be innocent, absolutely innocent. We'll simply have to wait it out, Mother, and be very tactful when dealing with him and Tony and Erika. But I fear nothing good will come of this."

THIS WAS STILL the state of affairs as Christmas approached, and with a pounding heart Johann counted the days, tearing them off one by one from the Advent calender Ida had made for him, until the day of days would arrive—the page with a Christmas tree on it.

There were more and more signs of its coming. On the first day of Advent, a colorful, life-size picture of St. Nicholas was hung on the wall in Grandmama's dining room. One morning Hanno found his bedspread, the rug beside his bed, and his clothes strewn with softly crackling golden tinsel. Then, one afternoon a few days later, as they were sitting in the living room—Papa was stretched out on the chaise longue reading his paper and Hanno was reading the story about the Witch of Endor in Gerok's *Palm Fronds*—the maid announced that "an old man was at the door, asking about the little boy." It was the same every year, and it was always a surprise. The old man was asked to come in, and he shuffled into the room, dressed in a fur cap and a long fur coat turned inside out and covered with tinsel and snowflakes, with black smudges on his face and a huge white beard and unnaturally thick eyebrows, both dusted with sparkling confetti. And just as he did every year, he declared that this *sack*—on his left shoulder—was for good children who could say their prayers and contained apples and golden nuts, but that this *switch*—on his right shoulder—was for wicked children. It was St. Nicholas. Well, of course, not the real, absolutely genuine St. Nicholas, perhaps it was actually only Wenzel the barber, dressed in Papa's fur coat—but if there was such a thing as St. Nicholas, then *this* was it. And Hanno was thrilled, just as he was every year, and managed with only one or two almost involuntary, nervous sobs to say the Lord's Prayer, and was permitted to reach into the sack for good children—which, as always, the old man once again forgot to take with him as he left.

Vacation began, and even the moment when Papa read the report card—which had to be issued at Christmastime, too—passed without much difficulty. The doors to the grand salon were kept closed, guarding mysteries; marzipan and gingerbread appeared on the table. And it was Christmas out on the streets, too. Snow fell, it turned cold, and the sharp, clear air was full of the cheerful and melancholy melodies of black-mustached organ-grinders, Italians who had come to town dressed in velvet jackets for the holidays. Dazzling Christmas displays appeared in the shop windows. And the gay, colorful booths of the Christmas fair had been set up around the tall Gothic fountain on the market square. Wherever you went, you could smell the sweet fragrance of fir trees being sold for the holiday.

And then at last came the evening of December 23 and the opening of gifts in the grand salon at home on Fischer Grube, just for their little family; but that was only the beginning, a kind of dress rehearsal for Christmas Eve, which old Madame Buddenbrook still claimed as her own, when, late in the afternoon on the 24th, the whole clan gathered around the table in the landscape room—even

Therese Weichbrodt and Madame Kethelsen and Jürgen Kröger, who had come from Wismar.

Dressed in her heavy silk dress with black and gray stripes, wrapped in the gentle scent of patchouli, but with flushed cheeks and excited eyes, the old woman received her guests as they entered, one after another, and with each embrace her gold bracelets jingled softly. She was trembling with excitement and exceptionally silent this evening. "Good Lord, you're in a dither, Mother!" the senator said when he arrived with Gerda and Hanno. "Everything will be all right, it will all be just as cozy as always," he added.

But as she kissed all three of them, she whispered, "For Jesus's sake. And for my dear, departed Jean."

Indeed, the entire solemn ceremony instituted for the occasion by the late consul had to be carried out to the letter, and a sense of responsibility for seeing to it that the evening proceeded in a worthy fashion, drenched in an atmosphere of profound, serious, and fervent joy, drove the old woman restlessly here and there—from the columned hall, where the choirboys from St. Mary's had now assembled, to the dining room, where Rieke Severin was putting the final touches on the tree and the presents, then out to the corridor, where a few old people stood about looking shy and embarrassed—the "poor," who were also supposed to share in the distribution of gifts—and back to the landscape room, where she punished every extraneous word or noise with a mute sidelong glance. It was so still that they could hear a distant barrel organ—like the sound from a tinkling music box, it drifted in from some snowy street. And although there were a good twenty people standing or sitting about the room, the silence was deeper than in a church, and the mood—as the senator very carefully whispered to his Uncle Justus—was just a little reminiscent of a funeral.

Not that there was any real danger the mood would be broken by the noise of youthful high spirits. One look sufficed to reveal that almost all members of the assembled family were of an age when manifestations of conviviality have assumed time-honored forms. There was Senator Thomas Buddenbrook, whose alert, spirited, even humorous expression was contradicted by the pallor of his face; his wife, Gerda, leaning back in her armchair, immobile, her lovely white face turned upward, her close-set, blue-shadowed eyes glistening strangely under the spell of the flickering light of the chandelier's crystal prisms; his sister, Frau Permaneder; his cousin Jürgen Kröger, the quiet, neatly dressed civil servant; his cousins Friederike, Henriette, and Pfiffi, the first two looking skinnier and taller than ever, the latter shorter and plumper, but all three with faces set in one standard expression—a caustic, malevolent smile disparagingly directed at all persons and things, as if they had but one constant, skeptical question: "Really? Well, for the present, we choose to doubt it." And finally there was poor ash-gray Klothilde, whose thoughts were probably focused on dinner. They were all over forty—and the hostess, her brother Justus, his wife, and Therese Weichbrodt well over sixty. And both Gotthold's widow—old Madame Buddenbrook, née Stüwing—and the now totally deaf Madame Kethelsen were already in their seventies.

The only person in the bloom of youth was Erika Weinschenk—certainly she was younger than her husband, the insurance director with graying temples and a small gray mustache that framed the corners of his mouth, who was standing beside the sofa, his close-cropped head outlined against the idyllic tapestry landscape. But whenever her pale blue eyes—Herr Grünlich's eyes—drifted toward him, her full bosom would rise and fall noticeably as she sighed a deep, silent sigh. It was clear that she was hard-pressed by anxious and confused thoughts about usages, accounting, witnesses, prosecutors, defense lawyers, and judges—indeed, there was probably no one in that room whose mind was not preoccupied with such un-Christmas like thoughts. Frau Permaneder's son-in-law stood under indictment, and the entire family was aware that present among them was a man who had been charged with an offense against the law, against civic order and commercial rectitude, an offense that might very well result in shame and a prison sentence—and his presence gave the gathering an altogether strange and unnatural character. Christmas Eve at the Buddenbrooks' with an indicted man in their midst! Stern and majestic, Frau Permaneder leaned back in her armchair—and the smiles of the Ladies Buddenbrook from Breite Strasse became a shade more caustic.

And the children? The family's rather sparse progeny? Were

they, too, aware of the faintly eerie atmosphere caused by this new and unheard-of state of affairs? As far as little Elisabeth went, it was impossible to judge her mood. Dressed in a little frock so richly trimmed with satin bows that it obviously reflected Frau Permaneder's taste, the child was sitting on her nurse's lap, her thumbs tightly clenched in her tiny fists and her slightly bulging eyes fixed straight ahead; she sucked on her tongue and occasionally let out a squeak, and then the nurse would rock her a bit. Hanno, however, was quietly sitting on a footstool beside his mother, gazing up, like her, at a prism on the chandelier.

Christian was missing! Where was Christian? Only at the last moment did they notice his absence. There was something even more feverish now about the way Madame Buddenbrook's hand kept moving in a gesture peculiarly her own, from one corner of her mouth up to her coiffure, as if she were tucking back a stray hair. She quickly gave some instructions to Mamselle Severin, and the young woman made her way past the choirboys and the "poor" gathered in the columned hall and hurried down the corridor, where she knocked on Herr Buddenbrook's door.

Christian appeared almost at once. He entered the landscape room slowly on skinny, bowed legs—his rheumatism had left him with something of a limp—and rubbed a hand across his bald head. "Damn," he said, "I almost forgot!"

"You almost forgot?" his mother echoed, freezing in place.

"Yes, almost forgot that today is Christmas Eve. I was sitting there reading a book, a travel book about South America. Good God, what Christmases we had back then," he added, and was on the verge of launching into a story about a Christmas Eve he had spent in a fifth-rate music hall in London, when suddenly the ecclesiastical stillness in the room began to have its effect on him, too—he wrinkled his nose and tiptoed to his place.

"Rejoice greatly, daughter of Zion," the choirboys sang, and although they had just been cavorting so loudly out in the hall that the senator had stood at the door for a moment to instill some respect, they sang quite marvelously now. Their bright, pure treble, borne above the lower voices, soared in praise and rejoicing and lifted every heart, softened the smiles of the spinsters, inspired the old folks to look within and review their lives, and allowed those who still stood in the middle of life to forget their troubles for a while.

Hanno let go of his knee, which he had been holding fast until now. He looked very pale; he played with the fringe on his footstool and rubbed his tongue against one tooth, his mouth half open and an expression on his face as if he were freezing. Every now and then he had to take a deep breath, because the choir that filled the air with its bell-like a-cappella carol tugged hard at his heart—he was almost painfully happy. It was Christmas. The scent of fir found its way through the cracks of the high, white-enameled folding doors, which were still closed tight; and the sweet spicy odor called up in his mind a picture of the dining room and the wonders inside—an unbelievable, unearthly splendor for which he waited each year with a pounding heart. What would be in there for him? Everything that he had asked for, of course, because you always got that—unless they had talked you out of it beforehand, saying it was simply impossible. The first thing that would spring up before his eyes, and which would show him where he was to sit, would be his theater, the puppet theater that he wanted so badly and had put right at the top of the list he had given Grandmama, underlined several times—it had been all he could think of since he had seen *Fidelio*.

As a reward, as a kind of compensation, for a visit to Herr Brecht, Hanno had recently been taken to the theater for the first time—the municipal theater, where from the first tier, right beside his mother, he had breathlessly followed the music and action of *Fidelio.* And since then, overcome with a passion for the stage, he had dreamed of nothing but opera scenes, had barely been able to sleep. When he met people on the street who, like his Uncle Christian, were known to be regular theater goers—Consul Döhlmann or Gosch the broker, for instance—he felt indescribably jealous. How could anyone bear the happiness of attending the theater almost every evening? If only he could go just once a week, sit there in the hall before the performance, listen to the instruments tune up, and gaze for a while at the closed curtain. Because he loved everything about the theater: the smell of gas lamps, the seats, the musicians, even the curtain.

Would his puppet theater be a big one? Big and wide? What would the curtain be like? He would have to cut a little hole in it first thing, because the curtain at the municipal theater had a peephole. He wondered if Grandmama—or Mamselle Severin, because Grandmama could not shop for everything herself—had found the scenery he needed for *Fidelio*. Tomorrow morning he would shut himself up in a room somewhere and give a performance just for himself. And in his mind he could hear the figures singing—music was the link that had immediately made him feel so close to the theater.

"Shout for joy, Jerusalem!" the choirboys sang to end their program, and after a kind of interwoven fugue, the voices arrived in joyful, peaceful harmony at the last syllable. The echoes of the chord faded away, and deep silence lay over the columned hall and the landscape room. Under the weight of the long pause, all the members of the family gazed at their feet. Only Hugo Weinschenk's eyes roamed, bold and unperturbed, around the room. Frau Permaneder coughed an audible dry cough that she simply could not suppress. Madame Buddenbrook, however, slowly strode to the table and joined her family, taking a seat on the sofa, which no longer stood off to itself at some distance from the table, as in the old days. She adjusted the lamp and pulled the large Bible over to her—the gilt on its immense embossed cover faded with age. Then she set her glasses on her nose, undid the colossal book's two leather clasps, opened it to the bookmark, revealing a heavy, coarse, yellowed page of huge print, took a sip of sugar-water, and began to read the Christmas story.

She read the familiar old words slowly, stressing each in a clear, stirring voice, her joy rising above the pious hush—and all hearts were touched. "And on earth peace, good will toward men," she said. And no sooner did she fall silent than the columned hall was filled with harmonious voices singing "Silent night, holy night," and the family in the landscape room joined in. They went about it rather cautiously, because most of them were not musical, and now and then a deep voice would sound a note quite inappropriate to the ensemble. But that did not detract from the effect. Frau Permaneder's lips quivered as she sang, for the carol sounded sweetest and saddest to a woman whose heart had known a troubled life and who could cast an eye back over it now in this brief, peaceful, solemn hour. Madame Kethelsen wept silent, bitter tears, although she could hear almost nothing.

And now old Madame Buddenbrook stood up. She grasped the hands of her grandson, Johann, and her great-granddaughter, Elisabeth, and strode across the room. The older ladies and gentlemen closed ranks behind her, the younger ones followed and were joined in the columned hall by the servants and the "poor," and they all lifted their voices in "O, Tannenbaum"—and Uncle Christian made the children laugh by lifting his legs like a funny, marching marionette and singing the silly words "Oh, Tinny Boom." And, with every eye sparkling and a smile on every face, they marched through the wide-open folding doors into heaven.

The whole room was fragrant with lightly singed evergreen boughs and glowed and sparkled with the light of countless little flames; the sky-blue wallpaper with its white statues of gods made the large room look even brighter. Set between the dark red of the curtained windows stood the mighty Christmas tree, towering almost to the ceiling—a shining angel at the top, a sculptured manger scene at the base; it was decorated with silvery tinsel and white lilies and flooded by the soft light of the candle flames that flickered like distant stars. A row of smaller trees trimmed with candy and more burning wax candles had been arranged on the table, which extended from the window almost to the door, its whole length covered with a white linen cloth and laden with gifts. The gas jets along the walls were lit, and thick candles were burning on four candelabra, one set in each corner of the room. The larger presents that did not fit on the table had been placed in a long row on the floor. At either side of the door were smaller tables, likewise covered with white linen, each ornamented by a little tree with candles aflame and laden with presents—the gifts for the servants and the "poor."

Dazzled by the light and feeling out of place somehow in the familiar old room, they went on singing as they filed past the manger, where a waxen baby Jesus appeared to be making the sign of the cross; and then, after a quick glance at the various decorations, they took their places and fell silent.

Hanno was completely confused now. The moment he entered the room, he had spotted the theater that his eyes were seeking so feverishly—there on the table, a splendid theater, looking much larger and grander than he had even dared imagine. But Hanno had ended up in a different place, directly across from where he had stood the year before, and this so disconcerted him that he seriously doubted whether that marvelous theater was really meant for him. Something else bothered him, too—sitting on the floor, right below the stage, was a large, strange object, something that he had not asked for. A piece of furniture, a kind of wardrobe, perhaps? Was that for him?

"Come here, my child, and look at this," Madame Buddenbrook said, opening the lid. "I know how you love to play chorales. Herr Pfühl will give you whatever lessons are necessary. You have to pump with your feet the whole time, sometimes harder and sometimes not so hard. And you never lift your hands, but only change your finger positions *peu à peu*."

It was a harmonium, a pretty little harmonium of polished brown wood with metal handles on both sides, a brightly colored treadle bellows, and a graceful little revolving stool. Hanno played a chord—and a gentle organ tone was released, so that all the others in the room looked up from their own gifts. Hanno hugged his grandmother, who pressed him gently to her; then she let him go and began to receive the thanks of everyone else.

He turned to his theater. The harmonium was like an overpowering dream, but he had no time to explore it more closely just yet. There was such a surfeit of good things that you could only pass quickly from one to the next, trying first to get some picture of the whole, but without feeling real gratitude for any single item. Oh, look, there was a prompter's box, shaped like a seashell, and behind it was the red-and-gold curtain that rolled up majestically. The stage was set for the final act of *Fidelio*. The poor prisoners stood with their hands folded; Don Pizarro, with massive puffy sleeves, stood in the foreground, striking a terrifying pose; and striding hastily in from the rear came the minister, who was dressed all in black and would now set everything to rights. It was just like in the municipal theater—almost even more beautiful. The jubilant chorus of the finale echoed in Hanno's ears, and he sat down at his harmonium, intending to play the part of it that he remembered. But then he stood up again and reached for the book of Greek mythology that he had asked for—it was bound all in red, with a golden Pallas Athena on the cover. He first sampled some candy, marzipan, and gingerbread from his plate, then inspected the smaller items—writing utensils and notebooks—and forgot everything else when he saw the penholder, topped by a tiny glass sphere. It was like magic—if you held it up to your eye, you suddenly saw a whole Swiss landscape.

Mamselle Severin and the housemaid now moved about the room with refreshments, and Hanno found time to look about him as he sat dunking a cookie in his tea. Chatting and laughing, people stood beside the table or walked up and down alongside it, showing off their own gifts or admiring those of others. There were objects of every sort—made of porcelain, nickel, silver and gold, of wood, silk, and linen. On the table was a long row of gingerbread cakes, glazed and sprinkled with almonds, alternating with loaves of marzipan bread, so fresh they were still moist inside. The presents that Frau Permaneder had wrapped or decorated—a needlework bag, a doily to put under a potted plant, a hassock—were trimmed with large satin bows.

Now and then relatives came over to little Johann, and laying an arm on his shoulder and stroking his sailor-suit collar, they would examine his presents and admire them with the ironic exaggeration adults typically show for the treasures of children. Only Uncle Christian was free of this adult arrogance. He sauntered over to Hanno's chair—he wore a new diamond ring, a gift from his mother—and he was as delighted with the puppet theater as his nephew.

"By George, that's a dandy!" he said, raising and lowering the curtain; he took a step back to size up the scenery. He fell silent, looking strangely serious, as if troubled by something, and his eyes wandered about the room, "Did you ask for it?—I see, so you asked for this, did you?" he suddenly said. "Now, why was that? Where did you get that idea? Have you ever been to the theater?—Oh, you saw *Fidelio*, did you? Yes, they did it well. And now you want to stage it yourself, is that it? Put on your own operas? It impressed you that much, did it? Well, listen to me, boy, let me give you some advice. Don't spend your time thinking too much about such things—theater and all that. It won't get you anywhere—trust your uncle. I've always been too interested in the stage myself, and I've never amounted to much. I've made some big mistakes, let me tell you."

He lectured his nephew with sober insistence, while Hanno looked up at him in curiosity. But then, after a pause, during which his bony, gaunt face brightened again as he examined the theater, he suddenly brought one of the figures forward on the stage and, in a hollow, croaking vibrato, began to sing, "Oh, what horrible offenses!" And then he pushed the harmonium stool over in front of the stage, sat down, and began putting on an opera, singing and gesticulating, now waving his arms in imitation of the conductor, now playing the various roles. Several members of the family gathered behind him, laughing and shaking their heads in amusement. Hanno watched with genuine delight. After a while, however, to everyone's surprise, Christian suddenly stopped. He fell silent and a restless, earnest look passed over his face; he rubbed his hand across his bald head and then down his whole left side. He turned around now to his audience—his nose wrinkled up, his face drawn and anxious.

"You see, as usual I have to stop," he said. "The same old punishment. I can never have a little fun without paying for it. It's not a pain, really, it's an ache, a vague ache, because all these nerves here are too short. They're all simply too short."

But his relatives took his complaints no more seriously than his jokes and said little or nothing in reply. They casually drifted away again. Christian sat staring mutely at the theater for a while, blinking his eyes as if deep in thought. Then he got up again.

"Well, my boy, have fun with it," he said, stroking Hanno's hair. "But not too much. And don't neglect your schoolwork because of it, do you hear? I've made my share of mistakes. . . . But now I'm off to the Club. I'm going to the Club for a bit," he called to the other adults. "They're having a Christmas party, too. Until later." And he left, walking down the columned hall on stiff, bowed legs.

Since they had all eaten lunch earlier than usual today, they consumed large amounts of cookies and tea. But no sooner had they finished than a large crystal bowl filled with a yellow, grainy puree was passed around: almond crème, a mixture of eggs, ground almonds, and rosewater. It tasted quite wonderful, but one spoonful too much and you ended up with the most awful stomach ache. Nevertheless, even though Madame Buddenbrook begged them "to leave a little corner for dinner," they helped themselves freely. And Klothilde performed miracles. In grateful silence, she spooned up almond crème as if it were porridge. And now came little glasses of sabayon to refresh their palates—served with English plum cake. Gradually they drifted back into the landscape room and, setting their plates down, gathered in little groups around the table.

Hanno stayed behind in the dining room alone. Little Elisabeth had been taken home, but for the first time he was to be allowed to stay for Christmas dinner on Meng Strasse. The servants and the "poor" had departed with their gifts, and out in the columned hall Ida Jungmann was chatting with Rieke Severin—although, as a governess, Ida as usual preserved a proper social distance when talking with a domestic. The candles on the tall tree had burned down and gone out, leaving the manger in darkness; but a few candles were still burning on the trees on the table; now and then a sprig would crackle as it was singed by a nearby flame, adding to the fragrance that filled the room. The least breath of air brushing the trees made the tinsel shudder and tinkle in metallic whispers. It was still enough again now to hear the barrel organ's soft tones floating in from a distant street on the cold night air.

Hanno surrendered himself to the scents and sounds of Christmas. His head propped in one hand, he read his mythology book and, giving the day its due, mechanically snacked on candy, marzipan, almond crème, and plum cake. The heavy uneasiness of an overfilled stomach blended with the sweet excitement of the evening to create a sense of melancholy bliss. He read about Zeus's struggles to become ruler of the gods, and now and then he would listen for a moment to the conversation in the living room, an extended discussion about Aunt Klothilde's future.

Klothilde was by far the happiest person in the house that night. She accepted their congratulations and the general teasing with a smile that turned her ash gray face radiant. When she spoke her voice would break with sheer joy. She had been accepted by the Johannis Cloister. Working quietly behind the scenes on the board of directors, the senator had got her admitted, although certain gentlemen had muttered in private about nepotism. They were talking now about this meritorious institution, the equal of any home for aristocratic ladies in Mecklenburg, Dobbertin, or Ribnitz, which offered suitable care and a dignified old age for indigent spinsters from established families. Poor Klothilde was now assured a small but secure pension, which would increase with the passing years, and when, as an old woman, she had finally moved into the highest bracket, she would even be given a quiet, tidy apartment in the cloister.

Little Johann spent a few minutes with the adults, but soon returned to the dining room—it was not so bright now and its glories were not so bewildering and intimidating as before, lending it a whole new charm. He found a strange delight in roaming about as if this were a half-darkened stage after the curtain had fallen and he could peek behind the scenery—he took a closer look at the tall tree's lilies with their golden stamens, picked up the animal and human figurines of the crèche, located the candle that had illumined the transparent star above the stable of Bethlehem, and raised the long panel of white cloth to look at all the boxes and packing paper piled under the table.

Besides, the conversation in the landscape room was becoming less and less interesting. Gradually, ineluctably, it had turned to the one dreadful theme that had been on everyone's mind all evening, but about which they had all been silent until now, out of respect for the festivities—Herr Weinschenk's trial. Hugo Weinschenk gave a little survey of the matter, with a kind of wild cheerfulness in his expression and gestures. The trial was now in recess because of the holidays, but he reported in detail the testimony of various witnesses, was very lively in his censure of Dr. Philander, the presiding judge, whose biases were only too obvious, and with masterful scorn he criticized the mocking tone that the prosecutor, Dr. Hagenström, had thought appropriate when addressing him or witnesses in his defense. But Breslauer had very wittily weakened various pieces of incriminating evidence and had assured him in no uncertain terms that there was no reason at present even to think of a conviction. Now and then the senator would ask a polite question, and Frau Permaneder, who was sitting on the sofa with her shoulders raised high, would mutter occasionally, calling dreadful curses down on Moritz Hagenström. The others, however, said not a word. Their silence was so profound that Hugo Weinschenk gradually fell silent himself; and whereas in the next room time sped past for Hanno on angels' wings, a heavy, oppressive, anxious silence lay over the landscape room—and continued until Christian returned at half past eight from the Club's Christmas party for bachelors and *suitiers*.

A cold cigar butt was wedged between his lips, and his cheeks were flushed. He entered by way of the dining room and, stepping into the landscape room, said, "Well, children, the tree still looks gorgeous. Weinschenk, we really should have invited Breslauer to join us this evening—I'm sure he's never seen anything like it."

His mother cast him a silent, reproachful glance. But the candid, questioning look on his face was one of perfect incomprehension. At nine o'clock they sat down to dinner.

As always on Christmas Eve, the table had been set in the columned hall. Madame Buddenbrook said the traditional grace with great fervor: "Come, Lord Jesus, be our guest and bless what Thou hast given us." As always on Christmas Eve, she concluded with a little admonition, the primary thrust of which was that on this holy night they should remember all those who were not as fortunate as the Buddenbrook family. And once this was taken care of, they sat down with a good conscience to a lengthy meal, which began with carp in drawn butter and a vintage Rhenish wine.

The senator slipped a few of the fish scales into his wallet so that it would not lack for money throughout the coming year, but Christian remarked gloomily that that was never any help. Consul Kröger had long since dispensed with such precautionary measures.

He no longer had any reason to fear the fluctuations of the market—his ship had arrived safely in harbor, even if with only a shilling or two. The old gentleman sat as far away as possible from his wife, with whom he had spoken hardly a single word for years, because she persisted in secretly sending money to disinherited Jakob, who at present was in London, Paris, or America—only she knew for sure. They were on the second course, and the conversation had turned to absent members of the family; he scowled forbiddingly when he noticed the boy's weak-willed mother dry her eyes. They spoke of relatives in Frankfurt and Hamburg, even mentioned Pastor Tiburtius in Riga without ill-will; and the senator and his sister, Tony, privately raised their glasses in a toast to Herr Grünlich and Herr Permaneder, who in some sense were still part of the family.

The turkey, stuffed with chestnuts, raisins, and apples, was praised by all. Comparisons were made with birds of years past, and it was concluded that this was the largest in a long time. There were roast potatoes, plus two kinds of vegetables and two kinds of stewed fruit, the bowls heaped so full that each looked like a hearty filling main course, rather than a side dish. They drank vintage red wine from the house of Möllendorpf.

Little Johann sat between his parents and managed to force down a piece of white meat and some dressing. He certainly could not eat as much as Aunt Thilda, and he felt tired and a little queasy. But all the same, he was proud that he was allowed to dine with the adults, proud that one of those tasty buns strewn with poppyseed had been placed on *his* napkin, too, and that there were three wine glasses set at *his* place, whereas normally he drank from the little gold beaker that Uncle Kröger had given him at his christening. But then, when Uncle Justus began pouring some oily, yellow Greek wine in the smallest glasses and the iced meringues appeared—red, white, and brown—his appetite returned. He ate a red one, although it hurt his teeth something awful, and then half of a white, and had to sample at least a little of the brown one, filled with chocolate ice cream. He nibbled on a little waffle, too, and sipped at the sweet wine while he listened to Uncle Christian, who was talking now.

He told about the Christmas party at the Club, which had been very festive. "Good God," he said in the same tone of voice he used when speaking of Johnny Thunderstorm, "those fellows were drinking brandy smash like water!"

"How awful!" Madame Buddenbrook said curtly, lowering her eyes.

But he paid no attention. His eyes began to roam, and his thoughts and memories were so vivid that they flitted like shadows across his face. "Do any of you know," he asked, "what it's like when you've drunk too much brandy smash? I don't mean being drunk, but what it's like the next day. The aftereffects are curious and disgusting—yes, curious and disgusting at the same time."

"Reason enough for a precise description, I suppose," the senator said.

"*Assez*, Christian, we are not the least bit interested," Elisabeth Buddenbrook said.

But he paid no attention. One of his idiosyncrasies was that at such moments he was impervious to all objections. He was silent for a while, but then suddenly what he had to say appeared to have ripened, and he went on. "You go around feeling rotten," he said and turned a wrinkled-up nose to his brother. "Your head aches and your bowels are not in good shape—but, then, that's the case on other occasions as well. But you feel *dirty*"—and here Christian screwed up his face and rubbed his hands together—"you feel dirty, as if you needed a bath. You wash your hands, but that does no good, they still feel clammy and unclean, and your fingernails are oily somehow. You take a bath, but that doesn't help, your whole body feels sticky and grubby. There's something annoying about your whole body, it itches, you're disgusted with yourself. Do you know the feeling, Thomas, do you know it?"

"Yes, yes," the senator said with a dismissive wave of his hand. But, with an extraordinary tactlessness that had grown only worse over the years, Christian went right on—never stopping to think that the entire explanation was embarrassing everyone at the table, that it was totally out of place in such surroundings on such an evening—and described the wretched condition that resulted from overdoing the pleasures of brandy smash, until finally he decided that he had presented it in sufficient detail and gradually lapsed into silence.

Before the last course of butter and cheese was served, old Madame Buddenbrook used the opportunity for another little speech. Even though not everything had turned out over the years quite the way one, out of shortsightedness, might have wished, she said, nevertheless there still remained such manifold and obvious blessings that their hearts should be filled with gratitude. Indeed, the interplay of moments of happiness and affliction only proved that God had never lifted His hand from the family, but that He had guided, and would continue to guide, its fortunes according to His deep and wise plan, which one ought never make bold to fathom out of impatience. And now, with hopeful hearts, they ought to raise a toast in harmony to the family's health and to its future, to a future that would still continue long after its oldest members present this evening had gone to their rest in the coolness of the grave.—And so, then, a toast to the children, to whom this holiday truly belonged.

And since the Weinschenks' daughter was no longer present, it was little Johann who had to make the round of the table all alone, and while they all exchanged a general toast, he had to lift his glass with each, starting with his grandmother and ending with Mamselle Severin. When he came to his father, the senator touched his glass to his son's and gently raised the boy's chin to look into his eyes. But he did not find them, because Hanno had let his long, golden-brown lashes fall deep, deep—until they covered the delicate bluish shadows beneath his eyes.

Therese Weichbrodt, however, took his head in both hands, kissed him on each cheek with a soft popping sound, and said in a voice so sincere that God Himself would have found it irresistible, "Be heppy, you good chawld!"

An hour later, Hanno lay in his bed, which had recently been placed in a little room off the third-floor corridor, just to the left of the senator's dressing room. He was lying on his back, out of deference to his stomach, which was not on good terms with all the things it had been forced to take in over the course of the evening; but he looked up with bright eyes as good old Ida, already dressed in her nightgown, entered from her room with a water glass, which she swirled in little circles as she brought it to him. He quickly drank the bicarbonate, made a face, and fell back into his bed.

"I think I'm really going to have to throw up now, Ida."

"There, there, Hanno. Just lie still on your back. But you see now, don't you? Who kept trying to warn you with little signals? And who wouldn't listen? The little boy, that's who."

"Yes, well, maybe I'll be all right after all. When will my presents arrive, Ida?"

"In the morning, my boy."

"Have them brought up here. So I can have them right away!"

"All right, Hanno, but first you have to get a good night's sleep." And she kissed him, put out the light, and left.

He was alone, and as he lay there quietly enjoying the beneficial effects of the bicarbonate, he closed his eyes and saw again the dining room full of gifts, glowing in all its brilliance. Somewhere in the distance he could hear choirboys singing "Shout for joy, Jerusalem," and he saw his theater, his harmonium, and his mythology book—the whole glittering scene. His head buzzed with a gentle fever, and under the disquieting pressure of his upset stomach, his heartbeat was slow, strong, and irregular. He lay there for a long time feeling queasy, excited, weary, anxious, and happy, and could not fall asleep.

And tomorrow there would be a third Christmas party, when presents were opened at Therese Weichbrodt's—and he looked forward to it as a kind of little burlesque farce. Therese Weichbrodt had closed her boarding school for good the previous year, so that, although Madame Kethelsen continued to live upstairs, Therese had the whole ground floor of the little house on Mühlenbrink to herself. The infirmities caused by her deformed, fragile little body had grown worse in the last few years, and, with meek Christian resignation, Sesame Weichbrodt trusted that she would soon be called to her heavenly reward. Which was why, for several years now, she had assumed that every Christmas would be her last and tried to lend the festivities in her little, dreadfully overheated home all the luster that her diminished energies permitted. She did not have the means to buy much, and so each year she gave away another portion of her modest possessions and set under her tree whatever she could possibly do without: knickknacks, paperweights, pincushions, glass vases, and scraps of her library, old books with odd shapes and whimsical bindings—*The Secret Journal of a Student of Himself*, Hebel's *Alemannic Poems*, Krummacher's *Parables*. Hanno had already been given an edition of the *Pensées* by Blaise Pascal, which was so tiny that you could not read it without a magnifying glass.

There was "bishop's punch" in undrinkable quantities, and Sesame's plain gingerbread cake was terribly tasty. But every year Fräulein Weichbrodt went about her last Christmas party with such jittery devotion to the task that the evening never passed without some surprise, some mishap, some little catastrophe that made all her guests laugh, but only increased their hostess's mute fervor. A pitcher of bishop's punch would topple over and flood everything in sweet, spicy red liquid. Or, at the very moment they all solemnly entered the room to receive their gifts, the tree with all its trimming would totter and fall over its own wooden feet. As he fell asleep, Hanno watched last year's accident pass before his eyes. It was just before the presents were to be given out. Therese Weichbrodt had read the Christmas story from the Bible, so impressively that all her vowels were out of place, and then she stepped back from her guests to stand in the doorway and deliver her little speech. The tiny, hunchbacked woman stood there on the threshold, her hands crossed at her childlike chest, the green silk ribbons of her cap falling down over her frail shoulders—and above her head, just over the door, was a fir wreath with lighted candles that illumined the words "Glory to God in the highest!" And Sesame spoke of God's goodness, mentioned that this would be her last Christmas party, and concluded by reminding them that, in the apostle's words, they were to rejoice, and was so caught up in her emotions that her whole body trembled from tip to toe. "Rajoice!" she said, laying her head to one side and shaking it hard. "And again I say, rajoice!" And in the same moment, there was a puffing, spitting, crackling noise, and the whole banner burst into flames. Mademoiselle Weichbrodt gave a little shriek and, with one agile, picturesque bound that no one would have expected of her, she leapt out from under the descending rain of sparks.

Hanno remembered that bounding leap the old spinster had made, and it so amused and touched him that he pressed his head into his pillow and laughed for several minutes—a soft, high-strung, nervous giggle.

9

FRAU PERMANEDER was walking down Breite Strasse, and she was in a great hurry. There was something disjointed about the way she carried herself, and only the set of her head and shoulders hinted at the majestic dignity in which she normally wrapped herself in public. In her violent haste, she had, as it were, snatched up only a shred of it and taken flight, the way a defeated king, pressed and harassed by his enemies, gathers up the remnants of his army.

Oh, she did not look well. Her upper lip—the same slightly protruding, arched upper lip that had always helped to make her face so pretty—was quivering now, and she was so overwrought that her eyes, although large with fear, kept blinking as they stared straight ahead, almost as if they, too, were in a hurry. Wisps of her disheveled hair were visible under the hood of her cape, and her face had taken on the same dull yellow hue that it always did when her digestion took a turn for the worse.

Her digestion had certainly been in a bad state of late. The whole family had watched it grow worse on succeeding Thursdays. Like sailors trying to avoid the rocks, they steered the conversation away from Hugo Weinschenk's trial—and inevitably foundered on it. Frau Permaneder herself would make straight for it, and then she would ask, excitedly demanding an answer from God or anyone else, how prosecutor Moritz Hagenström could possibly sleep at night. She could not comprehend it, would never understand—and her agitation increased with every word. "Thank you, I'm not eating," she would say, and shove her food away; raising her shoulders and laying her head back, she would retreat to the lonely heights of her outrage. The only thing she would put in her stomach was beer—the cold Bavarian beer she had been accustomed to drink since the days of her Munich marriage—and each time she poured it down, the nerves of her empty stomach rebelled and took their revenge. Toward the end of the meal she would have to excuse herself, and with the assistance of Ida Jungmann or Rieke Severin, she would go down to the garden or the back courtyard and suffer the most dreadful fits of nausea. Her stomach would empty its contents and then go on cramping, and the spasms could last for long, torturous minutes. Unable to vomit anything more, she would continue to gag miserably for a long time.

It was three in the afternoon of a windy, rainy January day. When Frau Permaneder reached the corner of Fischer Grube, she turned and hurried down the steep slope to her brother's house. A quick knock—and she went straight from the hallway to her brother's office. Her eyes flew across the desks to where the senator was sitting at the window, and she gave such a bitter shake of her head that Thomas Buddenbrook immediately laid down his pen and came toward her.

"Well?" he asked, lifting one eyebrow.

"A moment of your time, Thomas. It's urgent. It can't wait."

He opened the upholstered door to his private office, closed it behind him once they were both inside, and gave his sister a questioning look.

"Tom," she said with a quavering voice, wringing her hands inside her fur muff, "you'll have to provide it, just a temporary advance—you simply must, I beg you—the money to pay for his bail. We don't have it. Where are we to get twenty-five thousand marks *courant*? You'll get it back, every penny—all too soon, I'm afraid. You see—it's finally happened. The trial is now at a point where Hagenström has demanded that he be arrested or that bail be set at twenty-five thousand marks *courant*. And Weinschenk gives you his word of honor, he won't so much as set a foot out of town."

"So it has really come to this," the senator said, shaking his head.

"Yes, they've managed to do it, those scoundrels, those miserable scoundrels!" And with a sob of helpless rage, Frau Permaneder sank down onto an armchair that was covered in oilcloth and stood right next to her. "And they will manage to do worse, Tom. They'll carry it to the bitter end."

"Tony," he said, sitting down sideways on his mahogany desk, one leg crossed over the other, and propping his head in his hand. "Be honest with me—do you still think he is innocent?"

She sobbed a few times and then softly replied in despair, "Oh no, Tom. How could I think that? After all the awful things I've had to experience in life. I wasn't really able to believe it from the beginning, although I truly did try. Life makes it so dreadfully difficult, you know, to believe in anyone's innocence. Oh no, I've been tormented for a long time now by doubts whether his conscience is resting easy. And even Erika herself—he's driving her crazy. She cried when she admitted it to me. He's driving her crazy with the way he carries on at home. Neither of us has said a word, of course. But that rough exterior of his has only got rougher. And all the while he gets harsher and harsher in his demands that Erika be cheerful and keep his mind off his worries. He smashes dishes if she's too serious. You have no idea what it's like when he comes home late at night and locks himself up with his papers. And if you knock on the door you can hear him jump to his feet and shout, 'Who's that? What do you want?' "

She fell silent, but then started in again, her voice rising now. "Even if he is guilty, even if he did commit the crime—he didn't do it to fill his own pocket, but for the insurance company. Good God in heaven, there are certain things that must be taken into consideration in this life, Tom. He married into our family, he's one of us now, after all. They can't simply lock one of us up in prison, good merciful heavens!"

He shrugged.

"And you just shrug your shoulders, Tom? So you're willing simply to accept it? You'll let these dregs, these impudent upstarts, get away with their final insult? We have to do something! We can't let him be convicted. You're the mayor's right hand—my God, can't the senate just pardon him on the spot? I'll tell you something—just before I came here to see you, I was seriously considering going to

Cremer and throwing myself on him, begging him to intervene, to get involved in this. He is the chief of police. . . ."

"Oh, dear girl, that's mere foolishness."

"Foolishness, Tom? And what about Erika? And the child?" she said, lifting her muff, her two imploring hands still stuck inside. Then she fell silent for a moment and let her arms drop; her mouth widened, her chin puckered up and began to quiver, and as two large tears welled up under her lowered eyelashes, she added very softly, "What about me?"

"Oh, Tony, *courage*," the senator said, and, touched and moved by her helplessness, he slid closer and stroked her hair, trying to console her. "It isn't over yet. He hasn't been convicted. It can all turn out all right. And I'll put up the bail first thing—of course, I wouldn't deny you that. And Breslauer is a shrewd man, you know. . . ."

She wept and shook her head. "No, Tom, it won't turn out all right—I don't believe that. They will convict him and put him in jail, and then Erika and the child and I will face hard times. Her dowry is gone—it went for her trousseau, for the furniture and paintings. And if we sell it, we'll hardly get a quarter of its value back. And we've always spent his salary. Weinschenk never saved anything. We'll have to move back in with Mother, if she'll have us—until he's set free again. And then it will almost be worse than ever. What will become of him and of us then? We can't simply go sit on the stones," she said, sobbing some more.

"On the stones?"

"Oh, it's just an expression—a figure of speech. Oh no, it won't turn out all right. Too many troubles have rained down on me. I don't know what I've done to deserve it, but I have no hope left. And now Erika will have to endure what I endured with Grünlich and Permaneder. And you can see how it is already—you can see for yourself at close hand how things are, how they will turn out, how everything is going to just burst over us. But can I help it, Tom? I beg you, can I help it?" she asked a second time, nodding disconsolately, her eyes wide and filled with tears. "Everything I've ever tried to do has gone wrong and ended in misfortune. But my intentions were always good, God knows they were! My most heartfelt wish has been to accomplish something in life and to bring a little honor to the family. And now this has fallen apart, too. This is how it had to end. It's all over."

And, leaning against the arm he had put around her shoulder to soothe her, she wept over the failure she had made of life, its last hope extinguished now.

One week later, Director Hugo Weinschenk was sentenced to three and a half years in prison and arrested on the spot.

The courtroom had been packed on the day when the lawyers had made their final statements. And Dr. Breslauer from Berlin had delivered a speech for the defense the like of which no one had ever heard before. Siegismund Gosch went around for weeks afterward sputtering with enthusiasm about its irony, its pathos, its touching emotion; and Christian Buddenbrook, who had also been present, sat down behind a table at the Club, stacked newspapers like legal documents in front of him, and in perfect imitation delivered the speech for the defense verbatim. And once he got home, he expressed his opinion that law was the finest of professions—yes, it would have been the profession for him. Even Dr. Hagenström, the prosecutor, who was a man of taste and wit, let it be known in private that Breslauer's speech had been an absolute pleasure to listen to. But the famous lawyer's talents had not prevented his local colleagues from clapping him on the shoulder and explaining good-naturedly that they weren't about to be taken in.

And then, once everything had been sold that had to be sold after Hugo Weinschenk's disappearance, the town began to forget him. But every Thursday, when the family gathered around the table, the Ladies Buddenbrook from Breite Strasse confessed that, from the moment they first saw him, they could tell from the man's eyes that he was not all he should be, that there were serious flaws in his character, and that he would come to no good end. Their consideration for others—which, as they now observed to their regret, it would have been better to disregard—had led them to keep this unfortunate knowledge to themselves.

PART NINE

(Dedicated to the courageous painter Paul Ehrenberg, in memory of our evenings of music and literature in Munich)

1

PRECEDED BY TWO GENTLEMEN—old Dr. Grabow and young Dr. Langhals, a member of the Langhals family who had been in practice for about a year now—Senator Buddenbrook stepped out of his mother's bedroom into the breakfast room and closed the door.

"May I see you for a moment, gentlemen, please," he said and led them downstairs, across the corridor, and through the columned hall to the landscape room, where a fire was already burning because of the raw, damp autumn weather. "I'm sure you can understand my anxiety. Please, sit down. Set my fears to rest, if that is at all possible."

"Great Scot, my dear Senator," Dr. Grabow replied, burying his chin in his necktie, leaning back comfortably, and tucking the brim of his hat against his stomach, holding it tight in both hands. Dr. Langhals was a square-built man with beautiful eyes, a pointed beard, and brown hair combed back so that it stood almost on end; the expression on his face suggested vanity. He had set his top hat on the carpet beside him and was examining his extraordinarily small hands, covered with black hair. "There is, of course," Dr. Grabow continued, "absolutely no reason for serious worry at present. I beg you—a patient with your worthy mother's relatively good powers of resistance. Upon my honor as an old adviser to this family, I know what such a constitution can do. Really quite amazing for her age, let me tell you."

"Yes, but that's the point, at her age . . ." the senator said uneasily and twirled one long tip of his mustache.

"I'm not saying, of course, that your good mother will be taking a stroll tomorrow morning," Dr. Grabow went on meekly. "And I'm sure that's not the impression the patient made on you, my dear Senator. One cannot deny that her catarrh has taken a nasty turn in the last twenty-four hours. I did not like those chills yesterday evening, and today there is in fact a little pain in one side and a shortness of breath. And a light fever now, too—oh, insignificant, but fever nonetheless. In brief, my dear Senator, one must probably reconcile oneself with the pesky fact that the lung has been affected."

"The lung is affected?" the senator asked, looking from doctor to doctor.

"Yes—pneumonia," Dr. Langhals said, with an earnest, correct bow.

"Just the least touch of infection in the right lung," the family physician replied, "which we must do our very best to localize."

"So there is some basis for real concern, then?" The senator sat very quietly and gazed unblinkingly at the old doctor.

"Concern? Oh, we must, as I've said, be concerned to localize the illness, to ease her cough and grapple with the fever. And quinine will be effective there. But one thing more, my dear Senator—we shan't let certain symptoms unnerve us, shall we? Should her difficulty in breathing increase a bit, or if there should perhaps be a little delirium overnight, or a bit of sputum tomorrow—by which I mean a reddish brown expectoration, with a trace of blood—that's all quite logical, simply part of the condition, perfectly normal. And so please prepare our dear Madame Permaneder for the possibility, since she is the one who with such selfless devotion has taken charge of nursing her. *A propos*—how is she feeling? I quite forgot to ask how her digestion has been these last few days."

"About as always. I don't know of any change. Any concern about her own health has become somewhat secondary, naturally."

"But of course. By the way, that brings me to another thought. Your sister needs her rest, particularly at night, and Mamselle Severin probably won't be able to handle everything by herself. How would it be if we engaged a nurse, my dear Senator? We have our good Gray Sisters, the Catholic nuns you have always been so kind as to support. The mother superior would be so happy to be of service."

"You think it necessary, then?"

"I offer it as a suggestion. It is so much more pleasant that way. The sisters are invaluable—so experienced and composed. They have a calming effect on their patients, particularly in cases of this sort, where unsettling symptoms are involved. And so, if I may repeat myself, we shall keep calm and cool, my dear Senator, shall we not? And for the rest, we shall see—we shall see. We'll drop by again this evening, of course."

"Most assuredly," Dr. Langhals said, picking up his top hat and standing up with his older colleague.

But the senator remained seated—he was not finished, he still had another question, another topic to broach. "Gentlemen," he said, "one word more—my brother Christian's nerves are not good, he doesn't handle these things well. Would you advise me to let him know about Mother's illness? Suggest, perhaps, that he return home?"

"Your brother, Christian, is not in town?"

"No, in Hamburg. Temporarily. On business, as far as I know."

Dr. Grabow cast his colleague a glance. Then, with a laugh, he shook the senator's hand and said, "We can leave him to attend to his business. Why frighten him unnecessarily? Should there be any change in her condition that would make his presence advisable—to quiet the patient, let us say, lift her spirits—well, there'll be plenty of time for that, plenty of time."

The gentlemen walked back through the columned hall and along the corridor, stopping for a while on the landing to talk about other things—politics, the shocks and upheavals of the war just ended.

"But there will be good times now, don't you think, Senator Buddenbrook? Money in the country and fresh confidence everywhere?"

And the senator concurred in part. He agreed that the outbreak of war had meant a great improvement in the export of Russian grain, mentioning that oats in particular had been imported on a grand scale for delivery to the army. But the profits had been distributed very unevenly.

The doctors left, and Senator Buddenbrook turned around to go back to his mother's sickroom. He thought about what Grabow had said—there had been so much that he had left unsaid. One felt as if he were avoiding saying anything definite. The only specific thing that had been said was "pneumonia"—and there was little comfort in the fact that Dr. Langhals had chosen the scientific term. Pneumonia at his mother's age—the fact that there were two doctors in attendance was in itself disquieting. Grabow had managed it all quite casually, almost without his noticing. He was thinking, Grabow had said, of retiring sooner or later, and since his intention was for young Langhals to take over his practice, he enjoyed bringing him along on cases now and then, by way of introduction.

The senator entered the half-darkened bedroom with energy in his step and a cheerful expression on his face. He was so used to hiding his cares and fatigue behind a look of lofty self-assurance that, as he opened the door, the mask slipped over his face almost by itself, with only the least act of will on his part.

The curtains of the four-poster were pulled back, and Frau Permaneder was sitting on the bed, holding her mother's hand. She lay propped up on her pillows, her head turned toward the door, and she searched the senator's face with her pale blue eyes. It was a sidelong glance, full of both composure and instinctive, tense urgency—almost as if she were lying in ambush for him. Apart from her pallor and a feverish red spot on each cheek, there was no trace of exhaustion or infirmity in her face. The old woman was quite alert, more alert than those around her—she was, after all, the party most directly concerned. She did not trust this illness, and was most definitely not inclined to lie back in her bed and idly let matters take their course.

"What did they say, Thomas?" she asked in such a brisk, decisive voice that she at once began to cough violently, and although she first tried to quell it by holding her lips tight, the cough burst from her and forced her to press a hand against her right side.

"They said," the senator replied, patting her hand until the coughing fit was over, "they said that our dear mother would be back on her feet again in a few days. But that you can't get up yet, as you well know, because this silly cough has affected your lungs a bit. It's not exactly an infection of the lung," he added when he noticed her eyes gazing at him with greater urgency, "although that wouldn't be all that terrible—there are much worse things. And so, your lungs are somewhat irritated—they both agree on that, and they're probably right. Where is Severin?"

"She's gone to the apothecary," Frau Permaneder said.

"You see, she's off running errands again, and you look as if you are going to fall asleep any moment, Tony. No, things can't go on like this. Even if it's only for a few days—we have to bring in a nurse, don't you both think so, too? Wait a moment—why don't I inquire whether the mother superior of the Gray Sisters has someone free at the moment?"

"Thomas," Elisabeth Buddenbrook said, more gingerly now, to avoid unleashing another coughing fit, "please believe me—you only offend people by constantly supporting the Catholics rather than assisting the Black Sisters of the Protestants. You've arranged things so that they have advantages the others do not. I assure you that only recently Pastor Pringsheim was complaining about it in no uncertain terms."

"Yes, but that will do him no good. I am convinced that the Gray Sisters are more loyal, more devoted, and more self-sacrificing than those nurses in black. Those Protestants are just not the thing. They all want to get married at the first opportunity. In short, they are more worldly and egotistic, more common. The Gray Sisters are more self-effacing—indeed, they stand much closer to heaven. And they are to be preferred now, precisely because they owe me a debt of gratitude. What would we have done without Sister Leandra when Hanno had seizures while he was teething? I only hope that she is available."

And Sister Leandra came. She quietly laid aside her little handbag, her cape, and her gray cap, which she wore over her white one, and went to work, full of gentle and friendly words, her rosary dangling from her belt and clicking softly as she moved about. Day and night, she looked after the sick old woman, who was spoiled and not always patient; and then, almost in embarrassment at the human frailty to which she herself was subject, she withdrew silently when her replacement arrived, went home for a bit of rest, and soon returned.

Elisabeth Buddenbrook demanded constant attention at her bedside. The worse her condition grew, the more she devoted all her thoughts, the whole of her interest, to her illness, which she regarded with fear and blatant, naïve hatred. Once a lady of the world, a woman with a quiet, natural, and enduring love of living well, of life itself, she had filled her last years with piety and acts of charity. And why? Was it more than just respect for her late husband, perhaps? Was it an unconscious desire to reconcile heaven to her robust vitality and, despite her tenacious attachment to life, to convince God to grant her a gentle death? But she could not die gently. Notwithstanding a good many painful experiences in life, her body was unbent and her eye was still clear. She loved good meals, loved to dress in fine, elegant clothes; she preferred not to notice or to gloss over any unpleasantness that might exist or happen around her, and complacently shared in the widespread prestige that her eldest son had secured. This illness, this inflammation of the lungs, had invaded her proud, upright body without her soul's having had any chance to prepare itself for illness's work of destruction—to prepare her by undermining life, by estranging her from it, or at least from the conditions under which she had received it, and by awakening in her the sweet longing for its end, for other conditions or for peace. No, old Madame Buddenbrook was well aware that, regardless of the Christian course her life had taken in the last years, she was not truly ready to die, and she was filled with terror that this could be her final illness, that at the last moment and all by itself, with ghastly speed and great physical torment, it could shatter her resistance and force her to surrender herself.

She prayed a great deal; but she spent even more of her conscious hours watching over her condition, feeling her pulse, measuring her fever, fighting off her cough. But her pulse was not good; her fever might go down, only to rise higher still, propelling her from chills into hectic delirium; her cough grew worse, and with each coughing fit there was more bloody mucus and a sharper pain deep inside; her shortness of breath alarmed her. And all because it was no longer just one lobe of her right lung, but her whole right lung that was infected; indeed, if the doctors were not badly mistaken, the left side showed distinct signs of a process that Dr. Langhals—while gazing at his fingernails—called "hepatization" and about which

Dr. Grabow preferred to say nothing whatever. The fever gnawed away at her unrelentingly. Her digestion began to fail. With stubborn slowness, her energies continued to wane.

She watched them wane; and whenever she felt up to it, she eagerly took the concentrated nourishment she was offered, was stricter than her nurses about the dosages and times of her medication, and was so caught up in it all that she spoke with hardly anyone but the doctors—or at least showed genuine interest only when conversing with them. Visitors had been allowed to see her at first—old friends, members of her Jerusalem Evenings, women from the best social circles, and pastors' wives—and she received them apathetically or with absent-minded cordiality and quickly sent them on their way. The members of her family were hurt by the indifference with which the old woman greeted them, displaying a kind of disregard for them that said: "You can't really help me." It was the same even with little Hanno, who was allowed in one afternoon when she was doing better—she gave him a quick pat on the cheek and then turned away. It was as if she wanted to tell them, "Children, you're all dear people, but I, I may very well be dying!" She received the two doctors, however, with lively interest and warmth and conferred with them at length.

One day the ancient Gerhardt twins appeared, the old ladies who were descendants of Paul Gerhardt. They arrived wearing mantillas and large platterlike hats and carrying bags of groceries for their visits among the poor—one could hardly prevent them from visiting their sick friend. They were left alone with her, and God knows what they said to her while they sat beside her bed. But when they departed, their faces and eyes were clearer, milder, and more blissfully enigmatic than before; and inside the room Elisabeth lay quite still, with their look in her eyes, their expression on her face. She was quite peaceful, more peaceful than ever before; her breath was gentle and slow, and she visibly grew weaker from moment to moment. Frau Permaneder, who muttered one of her strong words as she watched the Ladies Gerhardt leave, immediately sent for the doctors. But no sooner had the two gentlemen reached the door than Elisabeth underwent a startling change. She awoke, began to stir, almost sat up. The mere sight of these two physicians, who had been hastily informed of the state of affairs, brought her back to earth with a bound. She stretched out her hands, both hands, to them and said, "How glad I am to see you gentlemen. Things are going so well that before the day is out . . ."

But, in fact, the day had finally come when there was no denying that she had pneumonia in both lungs.

"Yes, my dear Senator," Dr. Grabow said, taking Thomas Buddenbrook's hands in his, "we could not prevent it, it is now on both sides, and that is always precarious—you know that as well as I. One must call a spade a spade. Whether the patient is twenty or seventy years old, it is in every case a matter that one must take seriously, and if you were to ask me again today whether you should write your brother, Christian, or perhaps send him a little telegram, I would not advise against it, I would hesitate to discourage you. How is he doing, by the by? An amusing man—I've always been fond of him. For God's sake, however, don't go drawing any exaggerated conclusions from what I've said, my dear Senator. It's not as if there were any immediate danger—oh, how foolish of me to even put it that way. But under the circumstances, you know, one must always keep an eye out for some totally unanticipated turn of events. We have been exceptionally pleased with your good mother as a patient, really. She assists us so bravely, she never lets us down. No, as a patient she is unrivaled, and that's not a mere compliment. And so let us hope, my dear Senator, let us hope. Let us always hope for the best."

But there comes a moment when the hope of relatives is somehow artificial and dishonest. Some major change occurs in the patient, some alternation in his or her demeanor quite alien to the person we have known in life. Certain odd words come from her mouth, for which we know no reply, which cut off any retreat, as it were, which are themselves a covenant with death. She may be the dearest person on earth, but after all that has happened we can no longer wish for her to rise and walk. And if she should, it would somehow be as horrifying as if she had crawled out of her coffin.

Ghastly signs that dissolution had begun were now apparent, but the bodily organs still functioned under the direction of a tenacious will. Weeks had passed now since Elisabeth Buddenbrook had taken to her bed with a catarrh, and several bedsores had developed that would not heal and looked truly odious. She no longer slept—at first because of pain, coughing fits, and shortness of breath, but later because she resisted sleep and fought to stay awake. She slipped into a fevered stupor for only a few minutes at a time, but even when fully conscious she would speak aloud to people long since dead. One afternoon, as twilight fell, she suddenly said in a loud, anxious, but passionate voice, "Yes, my dear Jean, I'm coming." There had been something so strikingly immediate about her reply that they almost believed they had heard the voice of the late consul calling her.

Christian came home from Hamburg, where he had been on business, or so he said; but he stayed in the sickroom for only a short time. Passing his hand across his brow, his eyes wandering about the room, he said, "This is awful. This is really awful. I can't stand it any longer."

Pastor Pringsheim appeared as well, and after casting a cold glance at Sister Leandra, he prayed at Elisabeth's bedside in a lovely modulated voice.

And then came a brief improvement: a flickering of life, a deceptive return of energy, an ebbing of the fever, a cessation of pain, a few clear and hopeful words that brought tears of joy to the eyes of those around her bed.

"Children, we aren't going to lose her—you'll see, we aren't going to lose her," Thomas Buddenbrook said. "She'll be with us at Christmas, and we won't let her get so excited this year."

But the next night, shortly after Gerda and her husband had gone to bed, Frau Permaneder sent word from Meng Strasse that their mother was struggling with death. A cold rain was falling, and with each gust of wind it rattled against the windowpanes.

Both doctors were already on hand when the senator and his wife entered the room, which was illumined by the light of two branched candlesticks on the table. Christian, too, had been roused from his bed upstairs and was sitting off to one side, his back turned to the four-poster, his head buried in his hands. They were waiting for the old woman's brother, Consul Justus Kröger, who had been sent for as well. Sobbing softly, Frau Permaneder and Erika Weinschenk stood at the foot of the bed. There was nothing for Sister Leandra and Mamselle Severin to do now, and they gazed forlornly into the dying woman's face.

Elisabeth Buddenbrook lay on her back, propped up on several pillows, and both her quivering hands—those beautiful hands with pale blue veins, which were so thin, so emaciated now—were in constant motion, hastily, impulsively stroking the quilt. Under a white nightcap, her head never stopped shifting from side to side, with the dreadful rhythm of a metronome. Her lips appeared to have collapsed inward, and her mouth kept opening and closing as she gasped for each tormented breath; her sunken eyes strayed about in search of help, resting now and then on one of those around her with an appalling look of envy—they were up and dressed, they could breathe, life was theirs, and yet all they could do was offer one last sacrifice of love: to fix their eyes on her and watch. The night wore on without any change in her condition.

"How long can it go on like this?" Thomas Buddenbrook asked softly and pulled Dr. Grabow to the back of the room. Dr. Langhals was just giving his patient an injection. Holding her handkerchief to her mouth, Frau Permaneder joined them.

"Quite difficult to say, my dear Senator," Dr. Grabow replied. "Your mother may find release in the next five minutes, or this may go on for hours yet. I cannot say. What we have here is choking catarrh, a form of edema."

"I know," Frau Permaneder said, nodding into her handkerchief as tears streamed down her cheeks. "It often happens with pneumonia. A kind of watery fluid has collected in the pockets of the lungs, and if it gets very bad, you can't breathe anymore. Yes, I know."

His hands folded in front of him, the senator looked across to the four-poster. "She must be suffering so terribly," he whispered.

"No!" Dr. Grabow said, just as softly, but with incredible authority, determination in every wrinkle of his long, mild face. "You are mistaken, my friend, you are mistaken. The conscious mind is very clouded. Those are primarily reflex motions that you see there. Please, believe me."

And Thomas replied, "I hope to God they are!" But any child could have seen from his mother's eyes that she was totally conscious and aware of everything.

They sat back down. Consul Kröger had arrived as well, and he sat at her bedside now with reddened eyes, bending down over his cane.

The dying woman's movements increased. Her whole body, from her crown to the sole of her feet, was apparently overcome by terrible restlessness, by unspeakable panic and agony, by an inescapable sense of abandonment and hopelessness without end. She tossed her head and wheezed, and her eyes—her poor pleading, lamenting, searching eyes—seemed to break under the strain, and then they would close; or they would grow so large that the little veins on the eyeball were distended and bloodshot. But oblivion would not come.

It was shortly after three in the morning—Christian stood up. "I cannot take this any longer," he said, and, supporting himself on pieces of furniture that stood between him and the door, he limped out of the room. Both Erika Weinschenk and Mamselle Severin, apparently lulled by the monotone groans of pain, had fallen asleep in their chairs, their faces rosy with the flush of slumber.

Around four, it grew worse. They propped the old woman up and wiped the sweat from her brow. It looked as if she would stop breathing altogether, and her panic increased. "Something to help me sleep," she managed to say. "Sleep." But the last thing they wanted to do was give her something to make her sleep.

Suddenly, just as she had done once before, she began to answer someone or something that the others could not hear. "Yes, Jean, it won't be long now!" And right afterward, "Yes, my dear Clara, I'm coming."

And then the struggle began anew. Was it a struggle with death? No, she was wrestling now with life to gain death. "I want to," she gasped, "but I can't. Something to help me sleep. Have mercy, gentlemen, give me something so I can sleep."

At the words "have mercy," Frau Permaneder sobbed loudly and Thomas groaned softly, clutching his head with one hand for a moment. But the doctors knew their duty. For the sake of the family, they were required under all circumstances to preserve this life as long as possible, and a narcotic would have meant the immediate loss of all resistance, the surrender of life. Doctors were not placed on this earth to bring death, but to preserve life at any price. And there were certain religious and moral reasons as well—they had heard all about them at the university, although they might not be able to recall them precisely at the moment. And so, instead, they stimulated her heart with various drugs and induced vomiting several times, which brought some momentary relief.

Five o'clock—the struggle could not get any worse than this. Sitting upright, her eyes wide open for battle, Madame Buddenbrook flailed her arms, as if grasping for support or hands that were reaching out to her, and constantly answered calls that came from all directions, which only she could hear, but which seemed to be growing ever more numerous and urgent. It was as if not only her dead husband and daughter were present now, but also her parents, her parents-in-law, and other relatives who had gone before. She called out names, and no one in the room could say precisely just which of her dead relatives she meant. "Yes," she cried, turning first in one direction and then another. "I'm coming—soon—just a moment—but—I can't—Gentlemen, something to help me sleep—"

At five-thirty, there was a moment of peace. And then, quite suddenly, a shudder passed over her aged, pain-racked face—the features twitched in a rush of horrified joy, trembled with deep, fearful tenderness. In the next second, she flung her arms wide, and then—so abruptly, so instantaneously that both what she had heard and her answer seemed almost simultaneous—she cried out in the most absolute obedience, with boundless, fearful, loving submission and surrender, "Here I am!" And passed on.

They had all pulled back in shock. What had happened? Whose call was it that had caused her to follow instantly?

Someone pulled the window curtains back and blew out the

candles. Meanwhile, with a gentle look on his face, Dr. Grabow closed the dead woman's eyes.

They stood there chilled by the pale light of the autumn dawn that now filled the room. Sister Leandra covered the mirror above the dresser with a cloth.

2

FRAU PERMANEDER could be seen at prayer through the open door of the room where her mother lay. She was alone; the skirts of her black dress were spread around her on the floor where she was kneeling near the bed, her head bowed, her hands tightly folded and resting on the seat of a chair beside her. She murmured her prayers. She heard her brother and sister-in-law enter the breakfast room, heard them stop in the middle of the room, instinctively waiting for her to end her devotions—but she did not let that hurry her. When she had finished, she gave her little dry cough, gathered her skirt with slow solemnity, got up, and, without a trace of confusion, walked toward her relatives, carrying herself with perfect dignity.

"Thomas," she said, with some harshness in her voice, "as far as Severin is concerned, it seems to me that our dear, departed mother was nursing an adder at her breast."

"What do you mean?"

"I'm perfectly furious with her. It's enough to make one lose one's temper and forget oneself. What gives that woman any right to make the pain of this day so much more bitter, and in such a vulgar way?"

"But what is the problem?"

"First of all, she's outrageously greedy. She goes to the wardrobe, takes out Mother's silk dresses, flings them over her arm, and starts to leave the room. 'Rieke,' I say, 'where are you going with those?'—'Madame promised me I could have them!'—'My dear Severin,' I say, and, with all due restraint, I remind her that her haste is rather unseemly. But do you suppose that does any good?

She picks up the silk dresses, plus a whole stack of underclothes, and leaves. I can't come to blows with her, can I? And it's not just her—it's the maids, too. Laundry baskets full of clothes and linens are being carried out of the house. The servants are dividing things up right under my nose, because Severin has the keys to all the cupboards. 'Fräulein Severin,' I say, 'I want the keys.' And what does she say to me? In the most common language she makes it quite clear that I have nothing to say to her, that I am not her employer, that I did not hire her, and that she is going to keep the keys until she leaves."

"Do you have the keys to the silver?—Good. Let the rest go. That sort of thing is unavoidable when a house is being broken up, particularly when things have been somewhat lax toward the end anyway. I don't want a lot of uproar now. The linens are old and worn. And we'll check over what is left in any case. Do you have the inventory? On the desk? Good. We'll have a look."

And they went into the bedroom, just to stand a while there together by the bed. Frau Antonie removed the white cloth from the dead woman's face. Madame Buddenbrook was already dressed in the silk dress in which she was to be laid out upstairs in the columned hall later that afternoon. It was now twenty-eight hours since she had drawn her last breath. Her false teeth had been removed, and her mouth and cheeks had fallen in, so that her chin jutted up, sharp and angular. They stood there gazing down at her, and all three of them had trouble recognizing their mother in that face, its eyes firmly, irrevocably closed now. But beneath the cap that the old woman always wore on Sunday was the same reddish-brown, evenly parted wig that had always been an object of ridicule among the Ladies Buddenbrook from Breite Strasse. Flowers had been strewn across the quilt.

"The most beautiful wreaths have come already," Frau Permaneder said softly. "From all the families—oh, simply from everyone. I had them all placed out in the corridor. You'll have to look at them later, Tom. They are so sad and beautiful, Gerda. Satin bows this big."

"How far along are they with the hall?"

"They're almost finished, Tom. Almost finished. Jakobs has

done it in the finest taste, as always. And the . . ." She swallowed hard. "The casket came just a while ago. But do take your things off now, my dears," she went on and carefully pulled the white cloth back in place. "It's cold in here, but there's a little heat in the breakfast room. Let me help you, Gerda—one must be careful with such a splendid cape. May I give you a kiss? You know that I love you, even if you have always despised me. I'll take off your hat for you, and, no, I won't spoil your hair. Your beautiful hair! Mother had hair like that when she was young. She was never as stunning as you, but there was a time—I was already a young girl—when she was a truly beautiful woman. And now—can it be true, what your old Grobleben always says, that we must all come to rot? As simple a man as he is.—Yes, Tom, those are the main inventory lists."

They had returned to the adjoining room, and as they took their seats at the round table, the senator picked up the papers with the lists of things to be divided among the closest heirs. Frau Permaneder never took her eyes off her brother's face, and she watched, visibly tense and excited. There was something on her mind, one great, inescapable question that occupied all her anxious thoughts and that would have to be dealt with before many hours had passed.

"I think," the senator began, "we should hold to the usual rule that all gifts go back to the giver, so that . . ."

His wife interrupted him. "Forgive me, Thomas, but it seems that . . . Christian—where is he?"

"Yes, good Lord, Christian!" Frau Permaneder cried. "We've forgotten him."

"Right," the senator said, putting the papers down. "Wasn't he called?"

And Frau Permaneder went over to the bell rope. At the same moment, however, Christian opened the door and entered. He stepped into the room rather hastily and was not very quiet about closing the door; he stood there now, scowling, and his little, round, deep-set eyes wandered from one to another without really looking at anyone, and under his bushy, reddish mustache his mouth worked uneasily, snapping open and closed. It appeared he was in a rather defiant and irritable mood.

"I heard that you were in here," he said gruffly. "If there are things to be discussed, you should have informed me."

"We were just calling you," the senator replied calmly. "Have a seat."

But his eyes were fixed on the white buttons on Christian's shirt. His own mourning clothes were impeccable. His shirtfront, set off at the collar with a wide, black bow tie, stood out in sharp contrast to his black cloth coat and was fastened with black buttons rather than the gold studs he usually wore.

Christian noticed the look, and as he pulled a chair over and sat down, he ran his hand along his chest and said, "I know, I'm wearing white buttons. I haven't got around to buying black ones yet—or, better, I've neglected to do it. There's been many a time over the last few years when I've had to borrow five shillings for tooth powder and find my way to bed with a match. I don't know if I'm the only one to blame for that. And black buttons are not the most important thing in the world. I have no great love of formalities. I've never set much store by appearances."

Gerda had been watching him as he spoke, and now laughed softly.

The senator remarked, "I don't think you should try to hold yourself to that claim for very long."

"You don't? Well, perhaps you know better, Thomas. But I'm telling you that such things are of no importance to me. I have seen quite a bit of the world, and I have lived among far too many different kinds of people, with far too many different customs, for me to— And I'm a grown man in any case," he suddenly shouted. "I am forty-three years old. I am my own master, and I'm certainly entitled to tell anyone not to meddle in my affairs."

"It seems you have something weighing on your mind, my friend," the senator said in amazement. "As for your buttons, if I'm not mistaken, I haven't mentioned a word about them. You may choose whatever mourning attire you like, but don't think that you can impress me with your cheap broad-mindedness."

"I have no intention of trying to impress you."

"Tom—Christian," Frau Permaneder said. "Let us not be irritable with one another, not today, not here, while in the very next room . . . Go on, Tom. So all gifts are to be returned? That's only fair."

And Thomas went on. He began with larger objects and made a list of those that he could use in his own house: the candelabra in the dining room, the carved chest that stood in the vestibule. Frau Permaneder paid extraordinarily close attention, and the moment any doubt arose as to the future owner of a given object, she would say in her inimitable fashion, "Well, I'd be willing to take it," and look as if the whole world should thank her for such self-sacrifice. She claimed by far the largest share of the furnishings for herself, her daughter, and her granddaughter.

Christian, who had received a few pieces of furniture—including an Empire clock, even the harmonium—seemed quite content. But when they got around to dividing the silver and linens and the various sets of china, to everyone's astonishment he displayed an eagerness that looked very much like greed.

"And me? What about me?" he asked. "I would ask that you please not forget me entirely."

"Who's forgetting you? I've already put you down—here, look—I've put you down for a whole tea service with a silver tray. But only we would have any real use for the Sunday service with the gold plate, and . . ."

"I'm willing to take the everyday china with the onion pattern," Frau Permaneder said.

"And me?" Christian cried. He rarely became indignant like this, but when he did, it did not suit him—his cheeks looked hollower than ever. "I want my share of the table service. How many forks and spoons am I getting? Almost none, it looks like."

"But, my dear fellow, what do you want with such things? You have no use for them at all. I don't understand—it's better for such things to be used by the family."

"And what if I only want them to remember Mother by?" Christian said stubbornly.

"My dear friend," the senator replied with some impatience, "I'm not in a mood for jokes. But, to judge by your comments, you want to remember Mother by displaying a soup tureen on your dresser—that is how it looks, isn't it? I beg you not to assume that we're trying to cheat you. And if you get a few less of these items, it will be made up for in some other way. It's the same with the linens."

"I don't want money. I want linens and china."

"But why, for heaven's sake?"

And now Christian gave them an answer—one that made Gerda Buddenbrook turn hastily toward him and study his face with an inscrutable look in her eye, that caused the senator promptly to remove his pince-nez and stare directly at him, that left Frau Permaneder with nothing to do but fold her hands. What he said was this: "Well, to put it bluntly, I'm thinking of getting married sooner or later."

He said these words rather softly and quickly, flicking his hand as if he were tossing his brother something across the table; then he leaned back to let his eyes roam about irresolutely, and the expression on his face was strangely preoccupied and peevish, almost resentful. A longish pause followed.

Finally the senator said, "I must say, Christian, that you're rather late about making such plans—always presuming, of course, that these are real and practicable plans, and not the sort of ill-considered ones that you once suggested to our dear, departed mother."

"My intentions have remained the same," Christian said, still without looking at any of them, the same expression on his face.

"That's quite out of the question. You were only waiting for Mother to die, so that you could . . ."

"I waited, out of consideration for her, yes. You're apparently inclined to think, Thomas, that you have a monopoly on the world's supply of tact and discretion."

"I don't think you have any justification for that remark. As far as that goes, I can merely marvel at the extent of the consideration you've shown. Mother has been dead only a day, and you're already defying her openly."

"Because the subject came up. And the main thing is that Mother will not be upset by my taking such a step—no more today than she would be a year from now. Good God, Thomas, Mother wasn't always absolutely right, merely right from her point of view, and I respected that—as long as she was alive. She was an old woman, a woman from a different time, with a different way of looking at things."

"Well, let it be noted that, as far as the subject at hand goes, I share that way of looking at things."

"I can't worry about that."

"Oh, but you *will* worry about it, my friend."

Christian stared at him. "No!" he cried. "I will not! And what if I tell you I can't worry about it? Surely I know what it is I must do. I am a grown man."

"Oh, the 'grown man' part of you is very much a physical matter. You have no idea what it is you must do."

"Oh yes, I do. First of all, I will act as an honorable man. You aren't even thinking of the actual state of affairs, Thomas. Tony and Gerda are sitting here now—so we can't discuss it in detail. But I have told you before that I have responsibilities. And there's the last child, little Gisela. . . ."

"I don't know anything about any little Gisela, and don't want to know. I am certain that you're being lied to. And in any case, the only responsibilities you have toward this individual you're talking about are legal ones, which you may continue to fulfill as you have thus far."

" 'Individual,' Thomas? 'Individual'? You're very mistaken about her. Aline is a . . ."

"Silence!" Senator Buddenbrook shouted in a thundering voice. The two brothers glared eye to eye now across the table. Thomas was pale and trembling with wrath; and Christian's mouth was wide open with outrage, making his cheeks more gaunt than ever, and his little, round, deep-set eyes were wide with anger, a fleck of red visible under each—even the eyelids had suddenly turned red. Gerda looked from one to the other with a rather ironic expression on her face.

Tony wrung her hands and pled with them: "Now, now, Tom—now, now, Christian. And Mother lying in the next room."

"Are you so lacking in all sense of shame," the senator continued, "that you can bring yourself—no, it doesn't even cost you any effort—to mention that name here, under such circumstances? Your lack of tact is almost abnormal, pathological."

"I do not understand why I shouldn't mention Aline's name!" Christian was so agitated that Gerda was watching him with growing interest. "And I mention it now, Thomas, as you can well hear, because I plan to marry her. I long for a home of my own, for peace and quiet. And I insist, do you hear—please note the word I use—I *insist* that you stay out of my affairs. I am a free man—I am my own master."

"You're a fool, that's what you are! You'll find out when the will is read just how much of your own master you are. Provision has been made—do you hear me?—provision has been made to prevent you from squandering Mother's estate the way you've already squandered thirty thousand marks *courant*. I have been made guardian of the rest of your inheritance, and you will never receive more than your monthly allowance from me—I swear to you."

"Well, who would know better than you who talked Mother into setting up such restrictions. But I am amazed that Mother did not entrust the job to someone who is closer to me and whose feelings are more brotherly than yours." Christian was completely beside himself now. He began to say things that he had never uttered before in his life. He was bent over the table, rapping it steadily with the tip of his crooked index finger, and stared up with red-rimmed eyes and a bristling mustache at his brother, Thomas—who sat pale and erect, gazing down at him with half-lowered eyelids.

"Your heart is so icy and full of malice and disdain," Christian went on, and his voice was somehow muffled and squawking at the same time. "As far back as I can remember, I have felt such icy contempt coming from you that I've always been frozen to the bone in your presence. Yes, it may be a strange way to put it—but if that's what I really felt? You rebuff me just by looking at me, and you almost never even do that. And what gives you the right to act that way? You're human, too. You have your weaknesses. You were always a better son to our parents, but if you really were closer to them than I, then you might have adopted a little of their Christian kindness. And if brotherly love is so totally alien to you, one should at least expect a trace of Christian charity from you. But there's so little love in you that you never once visited me—not once—when I was lying there in the hospital in Hamburg, struck down by rheumatic fever."

"I have more serious things to think about than your ailments. And in any case, my own health is . . ."

"No, Thomas, you're in splendid health! You would not be sitting here acting like this if it were not quite excellent in comparison with my own."

"I may be less healthy than you."

"You may be what? No, now that's going too far! Tony! Gerda! He says that he's less healthy than I. What? Perhaps it was *you* who came close to death in Hamburg from rheumatic fever. Perhaps it's *you* who has to endure torments, indescribable torments, all over your body after every little distraction. Perhaps it's *you* whose nerves are all too short on the left side. Specialists have assured me that it's the case with me. Perhaps *you* are the one who experiences things like coming into a room at dusk and seeing a man sitting on the sofa, nodding at you, when there's no one there at all."

"Christian!" Frau Permaneder cried in horror. "What are you saying? My Lord, what are you two arguing about, really? You act as if it's an honor for one to be in worse health than the other. If *that's* the issue, Gerda and I might have a word to say, too, unfortunately. And Mother lying in the next room!"

"You still don't see it, do you?" Thomas Buddenbrook shouted vehemently. "That all these discomforts are the end result, the harvest of your vices, your indolence, your constant self-observation. Work! Stop pampering and indulging your condition—stop talking about it. And if you are crazy—and let me make it clear that I don't think that's out of the question—I will be incapable of shedding one tear over it. Because it's your fault, your fault alone."

"No, you won't even shed a tear when I die."

"You're not going to die," the senator said scornfully.

"I'm not going to die? Fine, I won't die, then. Well, we'll see which of us dies first! Work?—If only I could. But, good God in heaven, what if I can't do steady work? I can't do the same thing over and over for a long time without getting ill. And if you've been able to do it, still can do it, then be glad you can, but don't sit in judgment—it's not a virtue on your part. God gives the strength to some, and not to others. But that's the way you are, Thomas," he went on, still bent over the table, rapping it with his finger even more fiercely now, his face twisted into a grimace. "You're self-righteous. Oh, but wait, that isn't what I wanted to say, that isn't what I want to reproach you for. I don't even know where to begin, and anything I might say would only be a thousandth part—no, a millionth part—of what I have in my heart against you. You've won yourself a place in life, a position of honor, and now you stand here, so cold and self-assured, and reject anything that might confuse you for even a moment and throw you off balance. Because the most important thing for you is balance. But it's not the most important thing, not before God! You're an egotist, that's what you are. I still can feel some love for you when you rant and rave and stamp your feet and thunder and put me down. But the worst thing is your silence, the worst thing is when you suddenly dry up after I've said something, you pull back, so elegant and unruffled, and refuse all responsibility, leaving the other fellow helpless in his shame. You're a man without sympathy, love, or humility. Oh!" he suddenly cried, throwing his hands behind his head and then shoving them forward, as if to ward off the whole world. "I've had it up to here with all your tact and discretion and balance, with your poise and dignity—I'm sick to death of it." And this last cry was so genuine, so heartfelt, and so emphatic in its disgust and weariness that it was indeed something of a crushing blow—and Thomas actually sank back a little and lowered his eyes for a while, speechless and spent.

"I have become what I am," Thomas said at last, with emotion in his voice, "because I did not want to become like you. If I have inwardly shrunk away from you, it was because I had to protect myself from you, because your nature and character are a danger to me. I am speaking the truth."

He was silent for a moment and then went on in a curter, firmer tone: "But we have wandered away from the subject at hand. You have made a little speech about my character, a somewhat rambling speech, but one that contains some kernel of truth, perhaps. The issue, however, is not me, but you. You are thinking of marrying, and I would like to convince you for good and all, if I can, that it is impossible to do so in the manner you plan. First, the interest that I will be able to pay you on your capital is hardly an encouraging sum."

"Aline has been able to put quite a bit aside herself."

The senator swallowed hard and controlled himself. "Hmm—'put aside.' It is your intention, then, to merge Mother's inheritance with this lady's savings?"

"Yes. I want to have a home and someone who will show some sympathy when I am ill. And we're well suited to each other. We've both made our blunders."

"So you also intend to adopt any children there may be—which is to say, legitimate them?"

"I do indeed."

"So that, after your death, your estate would go to those people?"

As he said it, Frau Permaneder laid a hand on his arm and whispered imploringly, "Thomas, Mother is lying in the next room!"

"Yes," Christian replied, "that's only proper."

"Well, you are *not* going to do any of it," the senator shouted and leapt to his feet. Christian stood up, too; he stepped behind his chair, gripped it with one hand, pressed his chin against his chest, and stared at his brother—half outraged, half apprehensive.

"You are not going to do it," Thomas Buddenbrook repeated, almost mad with rage—pale, trembling, his hands jerking. "As long as I walk this earth, I swear to you that it will not happen. Just watch out—be careful. More than enough money has been lost by misfortune, stupidity, and mischief, without your throwing a quarter of Mother's estate in the lap of this female and her bastards. Not when another quarter of it has already been wheedled out of her by Tiburtius. You have already disgraced this family enough, sir, without your forcing us to have a courtesan for a sister-in-law and giving her children our name. I forbid it, do you hear? I forbid it!" he shouted in a booming voice that made the room ring and sent Frau Permaneder sobbing to one corner of the sofa. "And don't you dare act against my will, I'm warning you. Up till now I have merely despised and ignored you. But if you challenge me, push things to extremes, we shall see who comes out the worst for it. I'm telling you—be careful. I shall be ruthless. I'll have you declared incompetent, I'll have you locked up, I'll destroy you! Do you understand me?"

"And I'm telling you—" Christian began, and then the whole thing degenerated into an out-and-out row, a shabby, useless, deplorable quarrel without any real point, with no purpose except to injure and draw blood with words. Christian returned to the topic of his brother's character and searched the distant past for traits and embarrassing anecdotes that were meant to prove Thomas's egotism—things Christian had never forgotten, but had carried around inside him, drenching them in his own bitterness. And the senator retorted with scorn and threats, in terms so exaggerated that he was sorry for them ten minutes later. Gerda had propped her head daintily in her hand and watched the two with inscrutable eyes and an ambiguous look on her face.

In her despair, Frau Permaneder kept repeating, "And Mother lying in the next room—and Mother lying in the next room."

Christian, who had been pacing the room during this last part of the exchange, finally retreated from the field of battle. He was wrought up, incensed—his mustache was disheveled, his eyes were red, his coat hung open, his hand dangled beside him trailing a handkerchief. "Fine, fine! We shall see!" he shouted and walked to the door—and slammed it behind him.

In the sudden silence, the senator stood tall and erect for a moment, staring at the door through which his brother had vanished. Then he sat down without saying anything, hastily gathered the papers together, and in a few dry words took care of what still had to be taken care of. Now he leaned back and ran the tips of his mustache through his fingers, lost in thought.

Frau Permaneder's heart was pounding with apprehension. The question, the great question, could not be put off any longer. She had to speak up—and he had to give her an answer. But was he in any kind of mood to respond with gentleness and family feeling?

"Oh—and Tom," she began, first gazing down into her lap and then making a shy attempt to read his face, "what about the furniture? Of course, you've given careful thought to everything that is to belong to us—I mean to Erika, her baby, and me—but is it all to stay here? With us? I mean—what about the house?" she asked, wringing her hands—but not so that anyone could see.

The senator did not answer at once, but was lost in gloomy introspection and continued to twirl his mustache. Then he gave a deep sigh and sat up straight. "The house?" he said. "It belongs to us all, of course, to you, to Christian, to me—and, strangely enough, to Pastor Tiburtius as well, as a part of Clara's share of the inheritance. It's not for me alone to decide—I'll need your consent. But obviously the thing to do is to sell as soon as possible," he concluded with a shrug. And yet a look skittered across his face as if he were terrified by his own words.

Frau Permaneder's head dropped, then sank; her hands, which she had been holding tightly pressed together, fell slack. "Our consent," she said after a pause—it sounded sad, even a little bitter. "Good Lord, Tom, you know very well that you'll do what you think is right, and that the rest of us won't be able to withhold our consent for long. But if we might say just one word, and plead with you . . ." She went on now almost in a monotone, and her upper lip began to quiver. "The house—Mother's house! Our parents' house! Where we have all been so happy. And we're supposed to sell it. . . ."

The senator shrugged his shoulders again. "Please believe me, my dear girl, when I say that I feel only too deeply any objection you can raise. But those are not arguments against it, only sentimentalities. There is no doubt what must be done. Here we have this large piece of real estate—and what are we to do with it? For years now, ever since Father's death, the back building has been falling apart. There's a family of feral cats living in the billiard room, and you can't step out into the room for fear of going through the floor. Yes, if only I hadn't built the house on Fischer Grube. But I did, and now what am I to do with it? Would you prefer I sell *it* instead? But just stop and think—to whom? I would lose half the money I put into it. Oh, Tony, we have enough real estate, we have more than enough—warehouses and two huge homes. The ratio between our real estate and our liquid capital is all out of balance. No, we must sell, sell!"

But Frau Permaneder was not listening. She sat there, bent down, withdrawn into herself, her moist eyes staring at nothing.

"Our house," she murmured. "I can remember the housewarming. We weren't any bigger than *this*. The whole family was there. And Uncle Hoffstede read a poem. It's still in the family papers. I know it by heart—'foam-born Venus.' And the landscape room. And the dining room. And now strangers . . ."

"Yes, Tony, that's just what the people who had to give up the house back then must have thought when Grandfather bought it. They had lost their money and had to move away, and they're all dead and gone now. There's a time for everything. Let us rejoice and thank God that we haven't yet come to the same pass as the Ratenkamps back then, and that we take our leave from the house under more favorable circumstances."

He was interrupted by a sob—a painfully drawn-out sob. Frau Permaneder was so caught up in her woe that she didn't even remember to dry the tears streaming down her cheeks. She sat bent over, almost drawn up into a crouch, and didn't even notice when a warm drop fell on her hands, lying limp in her lap. "Tom," she said with soft, touching determination, recovering her voice despite the tears that threatened to choke it, "you can't know how I feel at this moment, you can't know. Your sister's life has not been an easy one, life has dealt harshly with her. Everything imaginable has rained down on me—and I don't know what I've done to deserve it. But I have endured it all—the trouble with Grünlich and with Permaneder and with Weinschenk—and I never lost heart, Tom. Because, whenever God smashed my life into little pieces, I was never completely lost. I knew there was a place, a safe harbor, so to speak, where I could find a home and be taken in, where I could flee from all the calamities of life. And even now, when everything fell apart and they led Weinschenk off to prison—'Mother,' I said, 'can we move back in here with you?' 'Yes, children, come home.' When we were little and we'd play tag, there was always a home, a little marked-off spot that you could run to when you were in trouble and about to be caught, a place where no one could touch you and you could catch your breath in peace. Mother's house, this house was that little marked-off spot for me, Tom. And now, and now . . . to sell it . . ."

She leaned back, hid her face in her handkerchief, and wept bitterly.

Tom pulled one of her hands away and took it in his own. "I know, dear Tony, I know it all. But we'll be reasonable, just a little reasonable, won't we? Our dear mother is gone now—we can't call her back. What are we to do? It's madness to hold on to the house, it's just dead capital—and it's my job to know about such things, isn't it? Are we supposed to turn it into a tenement? You find it difficult to imagine strangers living here; but it will be better if you don't have to watch. You and your loved ones can rent a pretty little house or an apartment somewhere outside the town gates, for instance. Or would you rather live here together with a lot of renters? And you still have your family—Gerda and me and the Buddenbrooks from Breite Strasse and the Krögers, even Mademoiselle Weichbrodt, not to speak of Klothilde, although I'm not sure whether she still enjoys our company. She's grown very exclusive since she's become a member of the Johannis Cloister."

With a sigh that was half a laugh, she turned away and pressed her handkerchief more firmly to her eyes, like a pouting child when someone has tried to make it forget the hurt with a joke. But then she resolutely dried her eyes, sat up, and, as always when dignity and character were called for, laid her head back and simultaneously tried to press her chin against her chest.

"Yes, Tom," she said, and with blinking, tear-stained eyes she stared out the window now, serious and composed. "I will be sensible—I already am. You must forgive me—and you, too, Gerda—for crying like that. It just comes over me—it's a weakness. But they are only outward tears, believe me. You know very well that I'm a woman who has been steeled by life. Yes, Tom, I can see what you mean by dead capital, I'm intelligent enough for that. I can only repeat that you must do what you think is right. You will have to think and act for us all, because Gerda and I are just women, and Christian—well, God bless him. We cannot oppose you, because any objections we might raise aren't arguments, just sentimentalities, that's clear as day. Whom do you suppose you'll sell it to, Tom? Do you think the sale will move along quickly?"

"Ah, my dear, if only I knew. In any case, I have already had a few words today with Gosch, the old broker. He didn't seem averse to taking on the task."

"That would be good, very good. Siegismund Gosch has his weaknesses. Those translations from the Spanish that people talk about—I can't recall the poet's name—that's really quite odd, you must admit, Tom. But he was a friend of Father's and he's an honest man, absolutely honest. And everyone knows he has a good heart. He'll understand that this is no routine sale, no ordinary house. What are you thinking of asking, Tom? A hundred thousand marks *courant* would be the minimum, wouldn't it?"

"A hundred thousand marks *courant* is really the minimum," she said, her hand on the door, as her brother and his wife started down the stairs. Then, left alone, she stood quietly in the middle of the room, her folded hands hanging in front of her, but with palms facing downward, her perplexed eyes searching all around her. She kept shaking her head—a little cap of black lace sat prettily atop it—and then, under the burden of thoughts, she slowly let it sink farther and farther down onto one shoulder.

3

IT WAS LITTLE JOHANN'S DUTY to say goodbye to his grandmother's mortal remains—his father had ordered him to do it. He was afraid, but he hadn't objected, hadn't said a word, not a peep. The day after old Madame Buddenbrook had wrestled with death, the senator had been sitting at the table with his wife, and he had made some harsh comments—quite deliberately in the presence of his son, it seemed—about the way Uncle Christian had behaved, slinking away to bed just when his mother's suffering had been at its worst. "Those were just nerves, Thomas," Gerda had replied; but, with a glance at Hanno, which the boy did not fail to notice, he had responded in an almost stern voice that there could be no excuse for such behavior. His dear mother had suffered so much that it was almost shameful to sit there and feel none of her pain, let alone to be so cowardly as to avoid the comparatively minor distress that came from having to watch her struggles. Hanno concluded from this that he did not dare object to paying his respects at the open casket.

On the day of the funeral, he walked between his mother and father through the columned hall and into the dining room. It looked as unfamiliar as it did when they entered it each Christmas Eve. Straight ahead, set on a black pedestal, was the copy of Thorvaldsen's Christ that had always stood out in the corridor; it shimmered white now against a semicircle of alternating large, dark green potted plants and tall silver candlesticks. Fluttering in the draft, black crape hung from all the walls, covering both the sky-blue background and the smiling white gods, who had always looked down on their happy family gatherings around the table. Little Johann stood beside the bier in his sailor suit, a wide band of crape around his sleeve; surrounded by his relatives dressed in black, he was dazed by the perfume drifting up from the host of bouquets and wreaths and blending with another, stranger, and yet curiously familiar odor that was faintly noticeable now and then, whenever he took a deep breath. And he looked down at the inert figure that lay stretched out before him, so stern and solemn among all that white satin.

That was not Grandmama. That was her Sunday bonnet with the white silk ribbons, and the reddish-brown hair beneath it was hers, too. But that pointed nose, those lips that had collapsed inward, that protruding chin, those yellow, transparent hands, folded in prayer and yet looking so cold and stiff—those were not hers. This was a strange wax doll, and there was something gruesome about the way they had dressed it up for this ceremonial occasion. And he looked across to the landscape room, as if he expected his real grandmama to appear at any moment. But she didn't—she was dead. Death had come and exchanged her forever for this wax doll, with its tightly closed, forbidding, unapproachable lips and eyelids.

He stood there, his weight on his left leg, his right knee bent slightly with the foot balanced on the toe; one hand was holding the knot of his nautical tie against his chest, the other hung down limply. He tilted his head to one side, his light-brown hair falling in soft curls down over his temples; and his golden-brown eyes ringed with bluish shadows blinked as he gazed with brooding disgust at the face of the corpse. He breathed slowly, hesitantly, because with each breath he expected to smell that odor, that strange and yet so familiar odor, which the billowing fragrance of the flowers could not always disguise. And each time the odor surfaced and he smelled it, he scowled a little more and his lips trembled for just a second. Finally he sighed; but it sounded so much like a sob—though there were no tears—that Frau Permaneder bent down to him, kissed him, and led him away.

And after the senator and his wife, along with Frau Permaneder and Erika Weinschenk, had stood in the landscape room for several hours, to receive the town's condolences, Elisabeth Buddenbrook, née Kröger, was consigned to the earth. Relatives had come for the funeral from Frankfurt and Hamburg, and for the last time they partook of the hospitality of the house on Meng Strasse. The salon, the columned hall, the landscape room, and the corridor were crowded with mourners as Pastor Pringsheim from St. Mary's delivered the eulogy by the light of flickering candles; he stood erect and majestic at the head of the casket, and his clean-shaven face, its expression ranging from solemn fanaticism to mild transfiguration, was turned toward heaven—floating above his wide, pleated ruff and a pair of hands folded just under his chin.

In tones now swelling, now fading away, he praised the qualities of the dear departed—her elegance and humility, her cheerfulness and piety, her charity and gentleness. He mentioned the Jerusalem Evenings and her Sunday school; employing all his rhetorical brilliance, he reviewed the long, rich, and happy life upon earth of her who had now gone to her heavenly reward—even the word "end" had to have its adjective, and he concluded by speaking of her "peaceful end."

Frau Permaneder was well aware of what she owed herself and those assembled—that in this hour she carry herself with impressive dignity. Together with her daughter, Erika, and her granddaughter, Elisabeth, she had claimed the most conspicuous position, close to the pastor, right next to the wreaths at the head of the casket; Thomas, Gerda, Christian, Klothilde, and little Johann, as well as old Consul Kröger, who sat on a chair, had to content themselves with less prominent places, as if they were more distant relatives. She stood very erect, her shoulders raised slightly, her black-bordered batiste handkerchief between her folded hands; and so great was her pride in assuming the principal role assigned to her for these ceremonies that it sometimes pushed her grief aside until she forgot it completely. In the realization that the whole town would be observing her, she kept her own eyes lowered for the most part, but now and then she could not refrain from letting her gaze sweep across the crowd, where she also spotted Julie Möllendorpf, née Hagenström, and her husband. Yes, they all had been duty-bound to come: the Möllendorpfs, Kistenmakers, Langhalses, and Oeverdiecks. Before Tony Buddenbrook left her parents' house for good, they had no choice but to gather here, one and all, to extend their sympathetic respects—despite Grünlich, despite Permaneder, despite Hugo Weinschenk.

Pastor Pringsheim's eulogy probed the gaping wound that death had left; he quite intentionally evoked vivid memories of what each of them had lost; he knew how to squeeze tears from those who would never have shed them on their own and were all the more grateful for having been so moved. When he came to speak of the Jerusalem Evenings, the old women who had been friends of the deceased began to sob—except for Madame Kethelsen, who could hear nothing and stared straight ahead with the secretive look of the deaf, and the Gerhardt twins, the descendants of Paul Gerhardt, who stood holding hands in one corner; their eyes were clear and dry, for they were happy for their dead friend and would have envied her, if envy and jealousy had not been totally foreign to their nature.

As for Mademoiselle Weichbrodt, she kept blowing her nose in short, energetic bursts. The Ladies Buddenbrook from Breite Strasse did not weep, however—it was not their custom. Their faces, a little less caustic than usual at least, expressed a gentle satisfaction at death's impartiality.

Then, when Pastor Pringsheim's last amen had died away, the four pallbearers in black three-cornered hats came forward softly, but so rapidly that their black cloaks billowed behind them, and they took hold of the casket. They were four footmen—and everyone recognized their faces—who hired themselves out for every dinner in the best social circles, passing heavy platters and sneaking some of the Möllendorpfs' claret from the decanters out in the hallway. But they were also indispensable at every first- or second-class funeral and were very adept at their work. They knew that both tact and agility were necessary to help people over this moment, when the coffin was snatched up by strangers from the midst of the deceased's family, to be borne away for all eternity. In two or three hasty, soundless, powerful moves, the bier was on their shoulders, and before anyone had time to realize the shock of the moment, the flower-covered casket swayed through the room at a steady, deliberate pace and vanished into the columned hall.

The women circumspectly crowded forward to shake the hands of Frau Permaneder and her daughter, and with downcast eyes they mumbled what must be mumbled on such occasions; meanwhile the gentlemen moved toward the stairs and their waiting carriages.

And now came the long, slow drive in a long, black procession through the gray, damp streets—out through the Burg Gate, down the avenue lined with leafless trees quivering in the cold drizzle, and into the cemetery, where, to the sounds of a dirge coming from behind some half-bare shrubbery, they got out and walked down soggy paths, following the casket to the edge of the little woods. There stood the Buddenbrook family vault, with its towering marker, the names in Gothic script, a sandstone cross at the top. The vault's stone cover, ornamented with the chiseled family crest, lay next to the black grave, which was outlined by wet green.

A place had been prepared down below for the new arrival. Under the senator's supervision, the vault had been tidied up a bit and the remains of older Buddenbrooks pushed aside. The music died away, and, suspended on the ropes of the bearers, the coffin hovered above the brickwork depths. It slid down now with a low rumble. Pastor Pringsheim, who had pulled on his wrist-warmers, began to speak again. His trained voice rang out clear, supple, and pious in the cool, hushed autumn air and drifted across the open grave and the mourners' heads, some bowed, some tilted wistfully to one side. Finally he bent down over the vault, addressing the dead woman by her full name and blessing her with the sign of the cross. When he had fallen silent and all the gentlemen stood praying mutely, their black-gloved hands holding their top hats in front of their faces, the sun broke through a little. The rain had stopped, and now and then a bird released a delicate, questioning twitter that blended with the sporadic sound of dripping trees and shrubs.

And then everyone moved forward to shake hands once again with the dead woman's sons and brother.

His heavy, dark overcoat sprinkled with fine, silvery raindrops, Thomas Buddenbrook stood in the receiving line between his brother, Christian, and his Uncle Justus. Of late, he had begun to get a little stout—the only part of his carefully groomed exterior that betrayed the advance of years. The long, pointed tips of his mustache still extended beyond his cheeks, and they were fuller now—but pale and sallow, without blood or life. His slightly reddened eyes gazed with dull politeness into the face of each gentleman whose hand he held in his own for a brief moment.

4

EIGHT DAYS LATER, a small, smooth-shaven old man with snow-white hair combed forward at his brow and temples visited Senator Buddenbrook in his private office. The old man was sitting crouched in the leather armchair at one side of the desk, bent over the white handle of his cane, his jutting chin resting on his hands. His lips were pressed tight and turned down maliciously at the corners, and the gaze he directed at the senator was so nasty, piercing, and treacherous that it seemed incomprehensible why the latter would not prefer to avoid the company of such a man. But Thomas Buddenbrook was leaning back in his chair without any sign of uneasiness, and he spoke to this sneering, demonic apparition as if he were just an ordinary harmless citizen. The owner of the firm of Johann Buddenbrook and Siegismund Gosch the broker were discussing the asking price of the old house on Meng Strasse.

This took quite a long time, because Herr Gosch's offer of twenty-eight thousand thalers *courant* seemed too low to the senator, whereas the broker said that to ask even one silver penny more would be an act of pure madness—damned if it wouldn't. Thomas Buddenbrook spoke of the central location and the unusually large lot; but, contorting his lips and hissing in a savage, choked voice, Herr Gosch now gave him a little lecture, punctuated by horrible gesticulations, about the crushing risk he would be taking—an explanation so trenchant and vivid that it was almost a poem. Aha!—When, to whom, and for how much would he ever be able to resell the house? How often over the course of centuries did a cry go up for such a lot? Could his honored friend and patron promise him, perhaps, that the next morning a nabob would arrive on the train from Büchen whose express wish was to set up house in the Buddenbrook family home? He—Siegismund Gosch—would be stuck with it—would be stuck with it, leaving him a beaten man, a man ruined for life, never to rise again, his clock run out, his grave dug—dug deep. And this phrase so captured him that he added something about shuffling wraiths and clods of earth falling with a dull thud upon his coffin.

This did not satisfy the senator, however. He spoke of how easy it would be to divide the lot, emphasized the responsibility he had to his brother and sister, and insisted on a price of thirty thousand thalers *courant*, whereupon he was forced to listen—with some nervousness, but also with relish—to yet another well-turned rebuttal by Herr Gosch. The discussion lasted for about two hours, during which Herr Gosch had the opportunity to pull all the stops on the organ of his personality. He played the double role, as it were, of the hypocritical villain: "Herr Buddenbrook, my youthful patron, let us agree, then—eighty-four thousand marks *courant*. It is the offer of an old but honest man." He said this with a sweet voice, his head tilted to one side, a smile of devoted innocence replacing the grimace that had ravaged his face till now—and he reached out a hand to the senator, one large white hand with long, trembling fingers. But it was mere lies and treachery. A child could have seen through the dissembling mask and recognized the horrible grin of deepest villainy behind it.

At last Thomas Buddenbrook declared that he needed time to think and that he would have to consult with his brother and sister before accepting twenty-eight thousand thalers—which probably would not happen in any case. And for now he shifted the conversation to a neutral topic, inquiring about Herr Gosch's business and personal health.

Herr Gosch was not doing well; with a lovely, sweeping gesture he rebuffed any assumption that he should be counted among life's fortunate. Old age, with its infirmities, was drawing near, and, as noted, his grave had already been dug. He could hardly put a glass of grog to his lips of an evening without spilling half of it, his arm trembled so damnably. Curses were to no avail. The will no longer triumphed. But all the same—he had a full life behind him, and no poor life, either. He had observed the world with eyes wide open. Revolutions and wars had raged, their waves pounding his heart as well—so to speak. Aha! Damned if that was not a different epoch, when he had stood beside the senator's father, beside Consul Johann Buddenbrook, during that historic meeting of the town council, and defied the onslaught of the raging rabble. What a horror of horrors it had been. No, his life had not been poor, not even his interior life. Damn, but he had felt the surge of his own energy, and "as the energy, so the ideal," to quote Feuerbach. Even now, even now—his soul was not impoverished, his heart was still young, it had never ceased, would never cease to encompass great experiences, to hold its ideals fast in a warm and faithful embrace. And he would carry those ideals with him to the grave, indeed he would. But did ideals exist only to be reached and realized? Certainly not! Behold the stars—we aspired not for them, but for hope. For hope—not for its realization. The best of life was hope. *L'espérance toute trompeuse que'elle est, sert au moin à nous mener à fin de la vie par un chemin agréable*. Those were the words of La Rouchefoucauld—beautiful words, were they not? Yes, but his honored friend and patron had no need of such knowledge. Whom the waves of active life have borne upon their shoulders, good fortune playing round his brow, that man had no need of such thoughts. But he who dreamed in the dark deeps had great need of them.

"What a fortunate man you are," he suddenly said, laying his hand on the senator's knee and looking up at him with moist eyes. "Oh, but you are. To deny it would be a sin. You are fortunate. You hold fortune in your arms. You ventured forth and your strong arm was victorious—your strong hand," he corrected himself, because he could not bear the repetition of the word "arm." Then he fell silent and, without listening to a word of the senator's reply of resigned demurral, he went on gazing into his face in a kind of dark reverie. Suddenly he sat up straight.

"But enough chitchat," he said. "After all, we are here to talk business. Time is money—let us not waste it by hesitating. So hear me out—because it is *you*, do you understand? Because . . ." And it looked as if Herr Gosch were about to plunge anew into beautiful thoughts, but then he pulled himself together and, with one of his broad, sweeping, and enthusiastic gestures, he said, "Twenty-nine thousand thalers. Eighty-seven thousand marks *courant*, for your mother's house. Agreed?"

And Senator Buddenbrook accepted.

As was to be expected, Frau Permaneder found the offer ridiculously low. Had someone—out of regard for the memories that were bound up in the house for her—laid a million thalers on the table for it, she would have considered it a respectable basis for bargaining, nothing more. But before long she became used to the sum her brother had named—because all her thoughts and plans were occupied with her future.

Her heart was filled with joy at all the fine new pieces of furniture that had come her way, and although no one even gave a thought to chasing her out of her parents' home so soon, she eagerly went about finding and renting a new apartment for herself and her family. True, it would be hard to say goodbye—and the thought could bring tears to her eyes. But, on the other hand, the prospect of change and renewal had its charms. Would it not be almost like starting over again, for the fourth time? And so she inspected apartments, consulted with Jakobs the upholsterer, negotiated with shopkeepers about portieres and carpet runners. Her heart pounded faster—no doubt of it, the heart of this old woman steeled by life beat higher.

Weeks passed—four, five, six weeks. The first snow fell, winter had arrived, the stoves crackled—and the Buddenbrooks' thoughts turned to the sad topic of how they should celebrate Christmas. Then, suddenly, something happened, something quite dramatic, something so surprising there were no words for it. Events took a turn that would soon engage the interest of the whole town. Something happened—it burst upon them. And Frau Permaneder stopped in the middle of what she was doing—she froze.

"Thomas," she said, "have I gone crazy? Is Gosch stark raving mad? Can it be possible? It's simply too absurd, too unthinkable, too—" She could say no more and held both hands to her temples. But the senator simply shrugged.

"My dear child, nothing has been decided yet. But the idea, the possibility, has come up. And after thinking it over calmly, you'll find that there's nothing unthinkable about it. It's a bit startling, I grant. I took a step back myself when Gosch told me. But unthinkable? What's to prevent it?"

"I won't survive it," she said, sinking down on a chair, and sat there perfectly still.

And what was going on? A buyer had been found for the house, or at least someone had shown an interest and even expressed a desire to take a thorough look at the property up for sale, with a view to further negotiation as to price. And that person was Herr Hermann Hagenström, wholesale merchant and consul for the Kingdom of Portugal.

When the rumor first reached Frau Permaneder's ears, she was paralyzed, flabbergasted, incredulous, incapable of conceiving the notion in all its ramifications. But now, as the matter took on form and substance and a visit to Meng Strasse by Consul Hagenström had been arranged, with the consul standing, so to speak, just outside her door, she pulled herself together and went into action. She did not revolt, she did not rise up in mutiny. But she found words—hot, cutting words—and she swung them like flaming torches and battle-axes.

"It will not happen, Thomas! As long as I breathe, it will not happen. When you sell a dog, you make sure what sort of master it will be getting. But Mother's house—our house—the landscape room!"

"But I ask you, what is there to stand in the way?"

"What stands in the way? Good God in heaven, I'll tell you what stands in the way. Mountains stand in that fat man's way, Thomas—mountains! But he can't see them. He doesn't even care, doesn't even sense that they're there. What is he, a dumb beast? The Hagenströms have been our foes since time out of mind. Old Hinrich played underhanded tricks on Grandfather and Father, and if Hermann hasn't been able to do you any serious harm, if he hasn't been able to put a spoke in your wheels, it's because you haven't given him a chance. When we were children, I slapped him right out in public, and I had my reasons—and his gracious, lovely sister, Julie, almost scratched my eyes out for it. That was just kid stuff—fine.

But they have sneered and watched with pleasure every time we met with misfortune, and usually it was I who provided them their amusement. God has willed it to be so. You know best yourself about all the things Consul Hagenström has done to try to eclipse you in business, to do you harm—it's not for me to tell you about that. And to cap it all, when Erika married well, it grated on him until he finally managed to get rid of Hugo and throw him into prison—by putting his brother up to it, that skirt-chaser, that lawyer from hell. And now they have the nerve, with no scruples at all, to—"

"Now, listen to me, Tony. First, we really have nothing significant to say about the matter, because we have settled accounts with Gosch, and it is up to him to do business as he pleases. I will admit that there's a certain irony of fate in all this."

"An irony of fate? Yes, Tom, that's *your* way of putting it. But I call it a disgrace, a slap in the face, and that's precisely what it would be. Don't you realize what this means? Well, give it some thought, Thomas. It would mean that the Buddenbrooks are finished, over and done with—they're pulling up stakes, and the Hagenströms are taking their place, with trumpets and drums. Never, Thomas, never will I play a role in this farce. Never will I offer my hand to that abomination. Just let him come, just let him dare come to see the house. I will not receive him, believe me! I shall sit in my room with my daughter and my granddaughter, and I shall turn the key and forbid him to enter—I swear I shall."

"You will do what you think best, my dear, but first stop and think whether it might not be wise to preserve some social decorum. It would appear you believe that Consul Hagenström will be deeply hurt by your conduct, am I right? No, that's wide of the mark, my girl. He would be neither pleased nor offended by it, he would merely be surprised—and coolly indifferent. The point is that you presume he harbors the same feelings against you and us that you have for him—wrong, Tony. He doesn't hate you. Why should he hate you? He doesn't hate anyone. He sits there in the lap of success and happiness, full of good cheer and general benevolence—please believe me. I have assured you on more than one occasion that he would greet you on the street in the most cordial way if you could bring yourself, just once, not to stare off into the distance with such a haughty, warlike look. It amazes him, and for about two minutes he senses a kind of placid, rather wry amazement. You can't throw a man off balance whom no one ever gets the better of. And what do you accuse him of? Suppose he has eclipsed me in business and successfully opposed me now and then in public affairs—that's perfectly fine. Then he must be a superior businessman and a better politician than I. That is certainly no reason to break into that strange, scornful laughter of yours. But to come back to the house—our old home has hardly any real importance whatever for the family—that has gradually been transferred to my own house. I say that to console you, no matter what happens. On the other hand, it is clear what got Consul Hagenström thinking about buying it. They have risen in life, their family is growing, they are related to the Möllendorpfs by marriage and are the equal of anyone in money and prestige. But they lack some outward sign of it, which until now they have deliberately and judiciously done without—the consecration of history, legitimation, if you will. They appear to have developed an appetite for it now, and they can procure some part of it by moving into a house—this house. Just watch, the consul will preserve almost everything just as it is. He won't remodel, he will leave the *Dominus providebit* above the door. Although one ought to be fair and admit that he alone, and not the Lord, has provided the impetus behind the good fortunes of the firm of Strunck & Hagenström."

"Bravo, Tom! Oh, it does me good to hear you say something nasty about him. That's really all I want. Good Lord, if I had your brains, I would put him in his place—would I ever! But you just stand there."

"So, you see, my brains don't really help me much."

"But you just stand there, I tell you, and talk about this matter with such incredible composure, explaining to me why Hagenström does what he does. But you can say whatever you like, you have a heart beating in your breast just as I do, and I simply do not believe that it leaves you as untouched as you pretend. You have all kinds of answers for my complaints—but perhaps you're only trying to console yourself."

"Now you're getting flippant, Tony. What I 'do' is what counts—and you will please take note of that. All the rest is no one else's business."

"Tell me one thing, Tom, I beg you. Won't it be like a nightmare?"

"Exactly like a nightmare."

"Like something out of a delirious fever?"

"You could say that."

"An absurd, howling farce?"

"Enough, enough."

And Consul Hagenström came to Meng Strasse. He came in the company of Herr Gosch, who was slouched down like a conspirator, Jesuit hat in hand, peering in all directions at once and over the shoulder of the maid to whom he had given his calling card and who held the glass door open for him and the consul as they entered the landscape room.

Hermann Hagenström was the sort of imposing fellow familiar on the stock market of any great city; he was dressed in a thick, heavy fur coat that reached to his shoes and hung open to reveal a greenish yellow winter suit of durable English tweed. He was so extraordinarily fat that not only did he have a double-chin, but the whole lower half of his face was double as well, and his close-trimmed blond full beard could not hide the fact. When he frowned or raised his eyebrows in a certain way, thick folds appeared in the skin under his short-cropped hair. Drooping flatter than ever against his upper lip, his nose sucked air in and out of his mustache. Now and then his mouth had to lend its aid and would fall open for a copious draft of air—which was always accompanied by a soft smacking sound as his tongue gradually freed itself from his upper jaw and gullet.

Frau Permaneder flushed when she heard that old familiar sound. It called up visions of lemon buns, truffled sausage, and *pâté de foie gras*, which for one brief moment threatened to shake her stony dignity. Clad in an exquisite fitted black dress with flounces from hem to waist and a mourning bonnet perched prettily atop her combed-back hair, she was sitting on the sofa, her arms crossed, her shoulders slightly raised, and as the two gentlemen entered she made some cool, casual remark to her brother—the senator had not had the heart to leave her in the lurch at such a moment. But she remained seated, until after the senator had strode to the middle of the room to receive their guests, exchanging a friendly greeting with Gosch and a civil, correct one with the consul; she then stood up as well, managed a restrained bow intended for both of them at once, and, with her enthusiasm well in check, seconded her brother's polite request that they have a seat—all the while keeping her eyes almost half closed in aloof indifference.

They sat there for a few minutes, during which the consul and the broker spoke by turns. With a show of appalling false humility and malicious cunning that deceived no one, Herr Gosch kindly begged them to forgive the inconvenience, but Consul Hagenström had expressed a wish to tour the premises with a view to eventual purchase of the house. And then the consul repeated the same thing in different words, in a voice that once again reminded Frau Permaneder of slathered lemon buns. Yes, indeed, once the idea had occurred to him, it had ripened quickly to a wish that he hoped he might be able to realize for himself and his family, provided, of course, that Herr Gosch did not intend to make all too great a profit from the sale—ha ha. Well, he did not doubt that the matter could be settled to the satisfaction of all parties concerned.

His demeanor was open, detached, and urbane—all of which was not lost on Frau Permaneder, particularly since he courteously directed his comments almost exclusively to her. In a tone that approached apology, he even went into some detail about his reasons for wanting to buy the house. "Room—more room," he said. "You wouldn't believe it, Madame Permaneder, nor you, Senator Buddenbrook—but my house on Sand Strasse has grown utterly too small for us. Why, there are times when we can barely turn around in there. Not to mention trying to entertain—simply impossible. If just the family assembles—the Huneuses, the Möllendorpfs, my brother Moritz's family—we're utterly like sardines in a tin. And why live like that—don't you agree?"

He spoke as if he were slightly indignant, and both the look on his face and his gestures seemed to say: "Surely you can see that I don't have to put up with this—that would really be too stupid.

Nevertheless, I do have the resources, thank God, to remedy the situation."

"But I wanted to wait," he went on. "I wanted to wait until Zerline and Bob would be needing a house, so that I could give them mine and then look about for something larger for myself. You do know, don't you," he interrupted himself, "that my daughter Zerline and Bob, the eldest son of my brother the lawyer, have been engaged for years now. They can't put off the wedding all that much longer—two years at the most. They're young, but so much the better. But the upshot is—why should I wait for them and miss a fine opportunity like the one presented to me at the moment? There'd be no conceivable point in that, utterly none."

General concurrence from all quarters—and the conversation lingered for a while on the subject of the consul's family and the approaching marriage; since such advantageous matches between cousins were not uncommon in the town, no one took offense at the idea. They inquired about the young people's plans, which, even at this early stage, included the honeymoon. They were thinking of the Riviera, Nice and so on. Their hearts were set on it, and so why not, really? And the younger children were mentioned as well, and the consul spoke of them with gusto and delight, and yet casually and with shrugs of his shoulders. He himself had five children, and his brother, Moritz, four—sons and daughters. Yes, thank heavens, they were all flourishing. And why shouldn't they, really? After all, life was good to them. Which brought him back to the topic of his growing family and his small house. "Yes, but this place here is quite another matter," he said. "I couldn't help noticing as I was walking upstairs—the house is a pearl, a pearl, no question about it, assuming such a comparison is possible on such a scale—ha ha! Why, these tapestries alone—I must admit madam, that I have been admiring the tapestries all the while I've been talking. A charming room, utterly charming. When I think that you've had the privilege of living your life here all these years . . ."

"With several interruptions—yes," Frau Permaneder said in that peculiar throaty voice she knew how to use on occasion.

"Interruptions—yes," the consul repeated with an obliging smile. He cast a glance at Senator Buddenbrook and Herr Gosch, and since the two gentlemen were deep in conversation, he drew his chair closer to Frau Permaneder's spot on the sofa, and bent toward her until she could hear his nose puffing heavily very near her own. Too polite to pull back out of range of his breathing, she sat there as stiff and erect as possible and gazed down at him with lowered eyes. But he seemed not the least aware of the unpleasant, constrained situation he had put her in.

"Let me think, Madame Permaneder," he said, "it seems to me that we struck a deal once before, didn't we? Of course, back then it was only a matter of . . . now, what was it? Something good to eat, some sweets, wasn't it? And now we're talking about an entire house."

"I don't recall," Frau Permaneder said, stiffening her neck even more—his face was unbearably, shockingly close to her own.

"You don't recall?"

"No, to be quite honest, I don't recall anything about sweets. I vaguely remember something about lemon buns with greasy sausage—some sort of truly ghastly morning snack. I don't know whether it was mine or yours. We were mere children then. But as far as the house goes, that, of course, is entirely in Herr Gosch's hands."

She quickly threw her brother a look of gratitude, because he had seen her distress and now came to her rescue by inquiring whether the gentlemen would care to take a tour of the house. They promptly agreed, and they took their leave of Frau Permaneder for the present, saying that they hoped to have the pleasure of seeing her again before they departed. And then the senator escorted both guests out through the dining room.

He led them upstairs and down, showing them the rooms on the third floor and those that opened off the corridor on the second, as well as the layout of the ground floor, even the kitchen and the cellar. Their tour was during working hours, and they decided not to enter the offices and disturb the employees of the insurance company. They exchanged a few remarks about its new director, and when Consul Hagenström declared him to be an absolutely honest fellow for the second time, the senator fell silent.

They walked through the bare garden, which lay under a blanket of melting snow, took a quick look at the "Portal," then turned back to the front courtyard; taking the narrow, flagstone path to the left of the scullery; passing between walls on either side, they entered the back courtyard, where the oak tree stood, and approached the back building. But there was nothing to see there but the dilapidation of long neglect. Grass and moss grew in the cracks between the cobblestones of the courtyard; the stairs were in total disrepair, and they barely disturbed the family of feral cats in the billiard hall—given the unsafe floor, they could only open the door and peer in.

Consul Hagenström said little and was obviously busy with calculations and plans. "Well, well," he kept saying in a sort of cool protest—meaning that, should he become the owner, it could not, of course, be left in this state. He stood for a while on the hard clay floor and stared up at the empty granaries with the same look still on his face. "Well, well," he said again, and now he set in motion the thick, frayed pulley rope—its rusty iron hook, which had hung motionless for years in the middle of the room, swayed like a pendulum. Then he turned around and left.

"Yes, my deepest thanks for you troubles, Senator Buddenbrook; we seem to have seen it all," he remarked; but as they hastily found their way back to the main building, he hardly said another word, not even when the two guests returned to the landscape room and, without sitting down, took their leave of Frau Permaneder. Thomas Buddenbrook accompanied them down the stairs and across the entrance hall, where they said their goodbyes. But no sooner had Consul Hagenström stepped out into the street than he turned to his companion, the broker, and engaged him in what was obviously a very lively discussion.

The senator returned to the landscape room, where Frau Permaneder was sitting on the window seat, but without leaning back and with a very stern look on her face; she was knitting a black wool skirt for Elisabeth, her little granddaughter, and as she worked the large wooden needles she cast an occasional sidelong glance at the "window spy." Thomas paced back and forth for a while, saying nothing, his hands in his pockets.

"Yes, I've left everything in the broker's hands," he said at last.

"We'll have to wait and see what comes of it. I think he'll buy the whole thing, live up front here, and use the back lot for something else."

She did not look at him, did not change her stiff upright position, did not stop her knitting—on the contrary, there was a marked increase in the speed at which the needles whirred in her hands.

"Oh, of course, he'll buy it, the whole thing," she said—making use of the throaty voice again. "Why shouldn't he buy it, really. There's no point in not buying it, utterly none."

Raising her brows, she looked down now through her pince-nez—she had to use it for handiwork now, although she had no idea how to put it squarely in place—and fixed her eyes sternly on her needles, which flew and clattered softly at a bewildering tempo.

CHRISTMAS CAME, the first Christmas without old Madame Buddenbrook. They celebrated the evening of December 24 at the senator's home, but without the Ladies Buddenbrook from Breite Strasse and without the old Krögers. The traditional "children's day" had been disbanded, and so Thomas Buddenbrook was not disposed to inviting and giving presents to all those whom the old woman had gathered about her at Christmas. Only Frau Permaneder, Erika Weinschenk, little Elisabeth, Christian, Klothilde of Johannis Cloister, and Mademoiselle Weichbrodt had been asked—although Sesame insisted that they join her in her overheated little parlor on the 25th, for gifts and the usual minor mishaps.

The band of "poor," who had always gathered on Meng Strasse to receive shoes and woolens, was missing, and there were no carols by choirboys. They simply struck up "Silent night, holy night," all by themselves in the salon, after which Therese Weichbrodt read the Christmas story with very precise diction—taking Gerda's place, because she did not particularly enjoy that sort of thing. Then, while they sang the first verse of "O, Tannenbaum" in rather subdued voices, they moved through the rooms to the grand hall.

There was no particular reason for a happy celebration. Their faces were not exactly radiant with joy, and their conversation was not exactly spirited. And what did they talk about? There was not much good news in their world. They mentioned their late mother, talked about the sale of the house, about the sunny apartment that Frau Permaneder had rented in a bright, cheerful house beyond the Holsten Gate, facing the park on Linden Platz, and about what would happen when Hugo Weinschenk was set free again. Meanwhile little Johann played some piano pieces he had practiced with Herr Pfühl and accompanied his mother in a Mozart sonata—not without several mistakes but with a rich full sound. He was praised and kissed, but then Ida Jungmann had to put him to bed, because by evening he looked very pale and tired, the result of an intestinal infection he had barely got over.

Even Christian—who had not said another word about getting married since the argument in the breakfast room and whose relationship with his brother had been re-established on the same old basis that hardly did him credit—was quite untalkative and not inclined to make jokes. His eyes roaming about the room, he made a brief attempt to awaken their sympathy for the "ache" in his left side; he left early for the Club, returning only for dinner, which consisted of the traditional dishes. And with that, the Buddenbrooks had this Christmas behind them, and were almost glad that it was.

Their mother's household was broken up at the beginning of 1872. The maids departed, and Frau Permaneder thanked God that Mamselle Severin, who had been insufferable and constantly questioned her authority in the house, took her leave as well, along with the silk dresses and underwear. Then the furniture vans lined up along Meng Strasse and the house was emptied out. The large carved chest, the gold-plated candelabra, and the other items that now belonged to the senator and his wife were hauled off to Fischer Grube. Christian moved his things to a three-room bachelor apartment near the Club, and the little Permaneder-Weinschenk family formally took possession of their sunny apartment on Linden Platz—and it, too, could still lay claim to some elegance. It was a pretty little apartment, and above the door was a shiny copper plate that read in dainty script: "A. Permaneder-Buddenbrook, widow."

The house on Meng Strasse was hardly empty before an army of workers appeared and began to tear down the back building, filling the air with the dust of old mortar. The property had passed for good and all into the hands of Consul Hagenström. He had bought it; indeed, he had apparently set his heart on it, because he had immediately outbid an offer that Siegismund Gosch had received from a party in Bremen. And now, with the same ingenuity for which he had been admired for so many years, he began to improve his property. By early spring he and his family had moved into the main house, which he left just as it was, except for a few minor repairs here and there and several modern improvements that he had promptly ordered to bring the house up to date—all the old bell ropes, for instance, had been removed and the whole house was now fitted with a system of electric bells. The back building had vanished entirely, and in its place rose a new trim, airy structure with several large, high-ceilinged storage rooms and shops that fronted on Becker Grube.

Frau Permaneder had frequently sworn to her brother that no power on earth could ever bring her to cast so much as a glance at their old parental home. But it proved impossible for her to keep her word, because now and then her path inevitably led her either past the display windows of the shops in the back building, which had been leased almost immediately at very handsome rents, or past the venerable gabled façade itself, where now the name of Consul Hermann Hagenström stood just beneath the *Dominus providebit*. And then Frau Permaneder-Buddenbrook would simply begin to weep audibly there on the street in front of everyone. She laid her head back like a bird about to sing, pressed her handkerchief to her eyes, erupted in a series of little wails that mixed protest with lament, and abandoned herself to her tears, despite passersby or her daughter's admonitions.

These were the innocent and refreshing tears of her childhood, which had served her faithfully in all the storms and shipwrecks of life.

PART TEN

1

IN HIS HOURS OF GLOOM—and they were frequent—Thomas Buddenbrook would ask himself what sort of man he really was and what could still justify his seeing himself as something better than any of his simplehearted, plodding, and small-minded fellow citizens. The imaginative élan and cheerful idealism of youth were gone. To play at work, to work at play, to strive, to direct one's half-serious, half-whimsical ambition toward goals to which one ascribes only symbolic value—that requires a great deal of vigor, humor, and a breezy kind of courage for debonair, skeptical compromises and ingenious half-measures; but Thomas Buddenbrook felt indescribably weary and listless.

He had achieved whatever he would achieve, and he knew quite well that he had long ago passed the highpoint of his life—if, as he told himself, one could speak of a highpoint at all in such a mediocre and shabby life.

Purely in terms of business, it was generally acknowledged that his fortunes were greatly reduced and that the firm was on the decline. And yet, if one included his inheritance from his mother and his share from the sale of the house and lot on Meng Strasse, he was worth more than six hundred thousand marks *courant*. The firm's capital, however, had been lying fallow for years. It was the same small-scale, pennywise operation that the senator had complained of back in the days when he was considering buying the Pöppenrade harvest; in fact, matters had only grown worse after that setback. Ever since the town had joined the Customs Union, the general business climate had been robust and triumphantly optimistic—little retail shops were able to grow into prestigious wholesale operations within a very few years. But the firm of Johann Buddenbrook slept, unable to profit from the achievements of modern times, and when someone asked its owner how business was doing, he would answer with a tired, dismissive gesture, "Oh, not much pleasure in it these days." An energetic competitor, a close friend of the Hagenströms, was heard to say that Thomas Buddenbrook's only function on the market was purely decorative; and the joke, playing as it did off the senator's neatly groomed appearance, evoked the laughter and admiration of the locals, who regarded it as an unprecedented rhetorical achievement.

And just as the senator's former enthusiasm and effectiveness in serving the old firm had been lamed by misfortune and his own inner exhaustion, so, too, his aspirations in community affairs had been thwarted by the limits of external circumstance. Years ago now—indeed, perhaps on the very day he was first voted into the senate—he had accomplished whatever could be accomplished. There were the various offices and honorary posts to which he was appointed, but no new realms left to conquer. There was the present and its petty reality, but no future ahead, no field for ambitious plans. Granted, he had known how to expand the scope of his power in local politics better than others in the same position might have done, and it was difficult for his foes to deny that he was "the mayor's right hand." But Thomas Buddenbrook would never be mayor himself, because he was a merchant and not a professional man—he hadn't even completed high school, wasn't a lawyer, had never pursued any academic degree. Because he had occupied his leisure time with reading works of literature and history, he had always felt that, compared with those around him, he was superior in intelligence, common sense, personal development, and cultural refinement; and so he could not get over his annoyance that his lack of conventional qualifications made it impossible for him to achieve the highest position available in the little world into which he had been born. "We were so stupid," he told his friend and admirer Stephan Kistenmaker—although by "we" he really meant only himself—"to have run off to work in an office so soon, instead of finishing school." And Stephan Kistenmaker replied, "Yes, you're absolutely right. But how do you mean?"

Most of the time the senator worked alone, sitting behind his large mahogany desk in his private office—in part because no one could see him when he would close his eyes and brood, his head held in one hand, but primarily because he had been chased from his place at the window in the outer office by the nerve-racking pedantry of his partner, Herr Friedrich Wilhelm Marcus, by the way he was constantly rearranging his writing utensils or stroking his mustache. Over the years, old Herr Marcus's meticulous, fussy habits had gone beyond eccentricity—they were a mania. But what Thomas Buddenbrook had found so unbearable about such annoyances and affronts of late was the fact that, to his horror, he had begun to observe something similar in himself. Yes, even he, to whom all pettiness had once been so alien, had developed his own kind of pedantry, although it grew out of a different personality structure and emotional makeup.

He was empty inside, and he could see no exciting project or absorbing task into which he could throw himself with joy and satisfaction. But he had a need to keep busy, and his mind never stopped working. He was consumed by his own restless energy, which for him had always been something different from his father's natural and solid joy in work, something artificial, more like a nervous itch, practically a drug—like the pungent little Russian cigarettes he constantly smoked. That energy had never left him, he was less its master than ever; it had gained the upper hand, had become such a torment that he wasted his time with a host of trivialities. He was harried by five hundred pointless trifles, things having mainly to do with keeping up the house and his own appearance; he would become so fed up with them that he would procrastinate and then find that he could not keep them sorted out in his mind and was more disorganized than before—all because he wasted such a disproportionate amount of time worrying about them.

What people around town called his "vanity" had long ago increased to the point where he himself was ashamed of it and yet unable to cast off the habits that had developed around it. From the moment he awoke from a night of, if not uneasy, at least logy, unrefreshing sleep, put on his robe, and entered his dressing room where his old barber, Herr Wenzel, was waiting—at nine o'clock nowadays, and he used to rise much earlier—he needed a full hour and a half to finish dressing and feel resolute enough to begin the day by going downstairs for his morning tea. He was so fussy about dressing, and so inflexible and rigid about the sequence of its details—from the cold shower in the bathroom to the moment when he flicked the last speck of dust from his coat and ran the tips of his mustache through the curling iron one last time—that the daily repetition of all these countless little tasks and rituals almost drove him to despair. Nevertheless, he would have been unable to leave his dressing room if he knew he had left something undone or had done it a little too hastily, for fear of forfeiting that sense of freshness, calm, and wholeness—which he would lose in any case within an hour and would then have to patch and cobble as best he could.

He was as parsimonious as possible about anything that would not expose him to gossip—except for his own wardrobe, every bit of which he had made by a tailor in Hamburg; he spared no expense in replenishing it and keeping it in repair. A door, which looked as if it led to a separate room, opened instead on a spacious closet built into one wall of his dressing room; inside were long rows of wooden hangers, each on its own hook, and hanging from them were coats, smoking jackets, frock coats, and evening clothes for every season and social occasion, from informal to formal, plus several chairs with piles of carefully folded trousers. The top of his dresser, with a massive mirror towering above it, was covered with combs, brushes, hair tonics, and mustache waxes, and inside was his large supply of underclothes, which, because he changed them frequently, were constantly being laundered, worn out, and replenished.

He spent a great deal of time in this closet, not only in the morning, but also before every dinner, every session of the senate, every public meeting—in short, whenever it was necessary for him to appear before his fellow men, even before normal meals at home, when there was no one present except himself, his wife, little Johann, and Ida Jungmann. And when he went out in public, the fresh underwear against his body, the immaculate, discreet elegance of his suit, his carefully washed face, the scent of brilliantine in his mustache, and the dry, cool taste of his mouthwash—it all contributed to making him feel at ease and ready to meet the world, much like an actor who has prepared every brushstroke of his makeup before stepping out on stage. No doubt of it—Thomas Buddenbrook's existence was no different from that of an actor, but one whose whole life has become a single production, down to the smallest, most workaday detail—a production that, apart from a few brief hours each day, constantly engaged and devoured all his energies. He completely lacked any ardent interest that might have occupied his mind. His interior life was impoverished, had undergone a deterioration so severe that it was like the almost constant burden of some vague grief. And bound up with it all was an implacable sense of personal duty and the grim determination to present himself at his best, to conceal his frailties by any means possible, and to keep up appearances. It had all contributed to making his existence what it was: artificial, self-conscious, and forced—until every word, every gesture, the slightest deed in the presence of others had become a taxing and grueling part in a play.

As a result, there began to surface certain peculiarities and odd whims, which even he noticed, to his own amazement and revulsion. Unlike people who play no role and prefer to remain out of view and unnoticed, so that they can then observe others, he did not like to have the light at his back, because it made him aware that he was in the shadows, watching others move about in the bright illumination before him. He could feel detachment and security—and the blind intoxication of self-production that made success possible—only if he was half blinded by light in his eyes, which turned other people, his audience, into no more than a shadowy mass in front of him, to whom he could then present himself as a genial, sociable man, an energetic man of business, the dignified head of his firm, the public speaker. In fact, he had gradually discovered that it was precisely this sense of intoxication that was the most bearable part of anything he did. He would stand at the table, wineglass in hand, an amiable expression on his face, and offer a toast replete with polite gestures and cleverly turned phrases that achieved their effect and were greeted with approval and general mirth—and at such moments he managed to look like the Thomas Buddenbrook of old, despite his pallor. It was much more difficult, however, to maintain command of himself when he sat quietly, doing nothing. Then weariness and disgust would rise up inside him, clouding his eyes, robbing him of control over his proud posture and the muscles in his face. And then just one wish would possess him: to give way to dull despair, to steal away and lay his head on a cool pillow at home.

ONE EVENING, Frau Permaneder dined with her brother's family on Fischer Grube—but she came alone. Her daughter, who had also been invited, had visited her husband in prison that afternoon and, as was always the case afterward, had felt tired and out of sorts and so had remained at home.

At dinner Frau Antonie had mentioned Hugo Weinschenk and said that she had been told he was very depressed; they then had discussed how one might, with some hope of success, go about petitioning the senate to get him pardoned. The three relatives had then moved to the living room and were seated now at the round table directly under the large gas lamp. Gerda Buddenbrook and her sister-in-law were sitting opposite one another, both busy with their needlework. Gerda's lovely white face was bent down over her silk embroidery, and in the soft light her heavy hair seemed almost to glow like dark embers; Frau Permaneder, her pince-nez set impractically awry on her nose, was carefully attaching a large, beautiful red satin bow to a tiny yellow basket. It was to be a birthday present for a friend. The senator, however, was sitting to one side of the table in a big upholstered easy chair with a slanted back, reading his newspaper; his legs were crossed and now and then he would take a puff on his Russian cigarette and exhale the smoke in a pale gray stream across his mustache.

It was a warm Sunday evening in summer. The high window stood wide open, filling the room with mild, slightly humid air. From the table one could look out across the gray gables of the houses opposite and see stars twinkling among the slowly drifting clouds. There was still a light on in Iwersen's little flower shop. Farther up the quiet street, someone was playing a concertina, and playing it very badly—it was probably one of the grooms down at Dankwart's stables. Occasionally it would turn noisy outside. A group of sailors passed by arm in arm, singing and smoking, on their way back from some dubious harbor tavern and looking for one even more dubious for further celebration. Their rough voices and shuffling steps died away down one of the side streets.

The senator laid his newspaper on the table beside him, slipped his pince-nez into his vest pocket, and rubbed his hand across his brow and eyes.

"Feeble, very feeble, this *Advertiser* of ours," he said. "I always think of what Grandfather said about bland, insipid dishes—'It tastes like you've hung your tongue out the window.' You can read it in three boring minutes. There's simply nothing in it."

"Yes, heaven knows, you can say that again, Tom," Frau Permaneder said, dropping her handiwork and looking up at her brother over her spectacles. "But how could there be anything new there? I've always said, even when I was still a silly young thing: This local *Advertiser* is a pitiful rag, really. I read it, too, of course, because usually there's nothing else around. But that Consul Such-and-such, wholesaler of whatever, is planning to celebrate his silver anniversary is not exactly earthshaking news. One should read other papers, the Königsberg *News* or the Rhine *Gazette*. You'd find things there. . . ."

She broke off. While she had been talking, she had picked up the paper and opened it again, letting her eyes glide disparagingly across its columns. But now her gaze was fixed on one spot, a brief notice about four or five lines long. She silently reached for her pince-nez with her other hand, and as her mouth slowly opened wide, she read the notice—and then let out two cries of horror, pressing the palms of both hands to her cheeks and holding her elbows out wide from her body.

"Impossible! It's not possible! No, Gerda—Tom! How could you miss it? How dreadful! Poor Armgard—so that's how it all had to end."

Gerda had raised her eyes from her work and Thomas turned in alarm to his sister. And now, with violent emotion, her throaty voice quavering and stressing every word as if it portended doom, Frau Permaneder read the news item, which came from Rostock and reported that during the previous night Ralf von Maiboom, owner of the estate of Pöppenrade, had committed suicide by shooting himself with a revolver in the den of the manor house. "Pecuniary difficulties appear to have been the motive for the deed. Herr von Maiboom is survived by a wife and three children." When she finished, she let the newspaper sink to her lap and leaned back to gaze at her brother and sister-in-law with uncomprehending, mournful eyes.

Even while she was still reading, Thomas Buddenbrook had turned away, looking past her through the portieres into the darkened salon beyond. "With a revolver?" he asked, after they had sat in silence for a good two minutes. And then, after another pause, he slowly said in a mocking voice, "Yes, yes, there's a country squire for you."

Then he once again sank back into a brown study. The rapidity with which he twirled the tip of his mustache in his fingers stood in marked contrast to the vague, glassy, aimless look in his eyes.

He paid no attention to his sister's plaintive words or her conjectures as to what her friend Armgard would now do with her life, nor did he notice that, without actually turning her head his way, Gerda had fixed her eyes—those close-set brown eyes with bluish shadows at the corners—firmly on him, searching his face.

2

THOMAS BUDDENBROOK was incapable of gazing into little Johann's future with the same weary dejection that colored his expectations of the rest of his own life. What hindered him from doing so was an inherited and ingrained sense of family, which meant that he looked not only to the past with a reverent interest in its intimate history, but also to the future; his thoughts were influenced as well by the loving, expectant curiosity with which his friends and acquaintances in town, his sister, and even the Ladies Buddenbrook from Breite Strasse regarded his son. He found satisfaction in telling himself that, no matter how hopeless and thwarted he felt his own life to be, when it came to his son, he was capable of exhilarating dreams of a future full of competence and a natural love of hard, practical work—full of success, achievement, power, wealth, honor. Yes, by caring, fearing, and hoping, he could find genuine warmth in his otherwise chilled and artificial life.

And what if one day, as an old man in quiet retirement, he might be able to gaze out on a rebirth of the old days, when Hanno's grandfather was alive? Was that such an impossible hope? He had thought of music as his foe—but was music really such a serious problem? Granted, the boy's love of improvisation at the piano, with no notes in front of him, revealed a rather remarkable talent—but he had not made extraordinary progress in his normal piano lessons with Herr Pfühl. No doubt of it, the music was due to his mother's influence, and it was no wonder that her influence had predominated during Hanno's early childhood. But the time had now come for a father to exert his own influence on his son, to draw him more to his side and offer manly impressions to neutralize previous feminine influences. And the senator was determined not to let any such opportunity go unused.

Hanno was eleven now, and along with his little friend Count Mölln he had been promoted to the fourth grade, but by the skin of his teeth—it had taken two extra exams in arithmetic and geography. It was decided that he would now take modern, scientific classes, because, of course, he was to be a merchant and would take over the firm someday. In reply to his father's questions about whether he was excited about the idea of such a future profession, he always answered yes—a simple, somewhat shy yes, nothing more. The senator would always try to elicit a little livelier, fuller answer—but usually to no avail.

If Senator Buddenbrook had had two sons, he doubtless would have let the younger graduate in the classics and go on to university. But the firm needed an heir; and besides, he believed he was doing the lad a favor by sparing him the unnecessary agony of Greek. He was of the opinion that the modern curriculum was easier to master and that, given Hanno's difficulties in concentrating, his dreamy inattention, and his delicate health, which all too often meant that he had to miss school, the boy would be able to make faster and more creditable progress there. And if little Johann Buddenbrook was ever to accomplish what life had called him to do and the senator expected of him, they must above all give attention to strengthening and enhancing his less-than-robust constitution, first by taking necessary precautions, and second by a program for systematically toughening his mettle.

Out on the playground or even just on the street, Johann Buddenbrook always stuck out among his towheaded, steely-blue-eyed, Scandinavian-looking classmates—despite his Danish sailor outfit. He had brown hair, which was parted to the side now and brushed back from his pale forehead, although it was constantly falling back in soft curls down over his temples; his eyelashes were long and dark, and his eyes were still a strange golden brown. He had grown quite a bit of late, but his black-stockinged legs and his arms—hidden under his dark-blue, full, quilted sleeves—were as small and weak as a girl's. And like his mother, he still had those bluish shadows in the corners of his eyes—eyes that looked out on the world hesitantly and defensively, especially when he glanced off to one side. He held his mouth shut tight in that melancholy way of his, slightly distorting his lips while he pensively rubbed the tip of his tongue against a tooth—he still didn't trust those teeth—and from the expression on his face it looked as if he felt chilled.

According to Dr. Langhals, who had completely taken over Dr. Grabow's practice and was now the Buddenbrooks' family physician, there was a definite reason for Hanno's unsatisfactory health and pallor: the boy's body unfortunately did not produce a sufficient quantity of red corpuscles, so essential for good health. But there was a medication for remedying this defect, a quite marvelous medication, which Dr. Langhals prescribed in large doses: cod-liver oil—good yellow, oily, viscous cod-liver oil, which he was to take twice daily from a porcelain spoon. And under the senator's explicit instructions, Ida Jungmann, loving but strict as always, saw to it that the medication was dispensed punctually. At first Hanno would throw up after every spoonful—his stomach did not appear very adept at accommodating cod-liver oil—but he got used to it, and if right afterward you chewed a piece of rye bread while holding your breath, it helped ease the nausea a bit.

All his other illnesses were simply a consequence of his lack of red corpuscles—"secondary phenomena," Dr. Langhals called them, while inspecting his fingernails. It was necessary, however, ruthlessly to attack such secondary phenomena. The care of his teeth—the fillings and extractions, if those were needed—was in the hands of Herr Brecht on Mühlen Strasse, the owner of Josephus; but for the care and regulation of his digestion, there was castor oil—good thick, silvery, shiny castor oil, which was administered with a teaspoon and slid down your throat like a slimy newt. And wherever you went and whatever you did for the next three days, you could still smell, taste, and feel it in your throat. Oh, why were all these things so incredibly repulsive? Only once—Hanno had been so ill that as he lay in bed he could feel his heart pump with unusual irregularity—had Dr. Langhals ever prescribed anything different, and that with some misgiving—a medicine that little Johann had liked and that had done him a world of good: arsenic pills. Hanno often asked for them later, too; he felt something like a tender yearning for the sweet solace of those little pills. But he was not given any more of them.

Cod-liver oil and castor oil were fine things, but Dr. Langhals was in total agreement with the senator that they were not sufficient in themselves to make a sturdy, rugged young man of little Johann—he had to do his part as well. For example, there were the gymnastic games that were supervised by Herr Fritsche, the physical-education teacher, and held out on Castle Yard once a week all through the summer—and there the town's young males were given a chance to show and develop their courage, strength, agility, and reflexes. But, to his father's annoyance, Hanno reacted to these healthy exercises with aversion—silent, aloof, almost arrogant aversion. Why did he have so little contact with boys his own age, his classmates, with whom he would later have to live and work? Why was he forever huddled with that little unwashed Kai, who was a good lad but a somewhat dubious fellow nevertheless, and hardly a proper friend for the future? In one way or another, from the very beginning, a boy has to earn the trust and respect of those around him, of the other boys he grows up with, whose good opinion will prove important to him for the rest of his life. There were Consul Hagenström's two sons, ages fourteen and twelve, two fine stout lads, strong and high-spirited, who organized real boxing matches in the woods outside of town, who were the best gymnasts in school, swam like seals, smoked cigarettes, and were ready for any kind of mischief. They were feared, loved, and respected. Their cousins, on the other hand, the two sons of Dr. Moritz Hagenström the lawyer, were more delicate and gentle by nature, but they excelled in their studies and were model students—ambitious, respectful, quiet, and busy as bees, they almost quivered with alertness and were consumed with the idea of being the best in the class and bringing home a report card marked "Number One." And they did just that, which won them the respect of their dumber, lazier classmates. But what did those same boys—quite apart from the teachers—think of Hanno, who was a very average student and a weakling to boot, who timidly tried to avoid anything that demanded a little courage, strength, agility, or enthusiasm? And if Senator Buddenbrook would happen to pass the third-floor "balcony" on his way to his dressing room, he often heard sounds coming from the middle room of the three—Hanno's room, now that he was too old to sleep with Ida Jungmann—either the tones of the harmonium or Kai's hushed, mysterious voice telling a story.

Kai, too, avoided gymnastics, because he despised the discipline and rules that they demanded he observe. "No, Hanno," he said, "I'm not going out there. Are you? To hell with it. Anything that's really fun doesn't count for them." He had learned phrases like "to hell with it" from his father. But Hanno answered, "If there were just one day when Herr Fritsche didn't smell like sweat and beer, I might let someone talk me into it. So, let's forget it, Kai, and now you can tell a story. You aren't anywhere near the end of the one about the ring that you found in the swamp." "All right," Kai said, "but when I give you a nod, you have to play." And Kai went on with his story.

If he was to be believed, not long ago, on a hot humid night, he had been wandering in a strange, murky region and had slid to the bottom of a slippery and unbelievably deep ravine, where, by the pale flickering light of will-o'-the-wisps, he had discovered a black swampy pond with shiny silver bubbles that kept rising to the surface, making soft gurgling sounds. One bubble close to the bank, however, was ring-shaped and kept reappearing the moment it burst, and after many long and dangerous attempts he managed to catch it in his hand, and when it didn't burst, he found he could slip it on his finger as a smooth, solid ring. And, wisely placing his trust in the unusual powers of the ring to help him, he was able to climb back up the steep, slippery slope, and once he was at the top he discovered a black castle, wrapped in reddish fog and silent as death. It was guarded by fierce defenses, but he forced his way in and, with the help of the ring, was able to perform the most astounding feats and release the castle from its spell. Hanno would play a series of ravishing chords to accompany special moments in the story. And if the staging did not pose insuperable difficulties, the stories would be acted out in the puppet theater, with musical accompaniment. But Hanno went to the gymnastic games only if his father expressly, and sternly, demanded it, and then little Kai would go along.

It was no different when it came to ice-skating in winter or to swimming in summer down by the river, in the fenced-in area run by Herr Asmussen. "Bathing and swimming," Dr. Langhals had said. "The boy must go swimming." And the senator was in complete agreement. But the main reason that Hanno avoided, if at all possible, going swimming, or ice-skating, or joining in gymnastics, was the fact that Consul Hagenström's two sons, who participated in all such activities to great acclaim, had it in for him; and although they lived in his grandmother's house, they never missed a chance to humiliate and bully him with their greater strength. They pinched him and mocked him during gymnastics; they pushed him into piles of shoveled snow when he tried to skate; they came storming across the swimming pool toward him, making menacing noises. Hanno did not try to escape—that would have been pointless in any case. He stood there up to his waist in the rather muddy water, his skinny girl's arms at his sides, his mouth slightly askew, and while green clumps of so-called goose grass drifted past him, he scowled and watched grimly from one corner of his eye as they approached in long, foaming leaps, sure of their prey. Both the Hagenström boys had muscular arms, and they would clamp them around him and duck him, duck him so long that he swallowed a great deal of dirty water, and even after he came up, twisting and turning, he had to fight for his breath for quite a while. But once he did get a little revenge. One afternoon, just as the two Hagenströms were holding him under the water, one of them suddenly started screaming with rage and pain and lifted up his stout leg—large drops of blood were running down it. And suddenly Count Kai Mölln appeared at his side; somehow he had managed to find money to pay his way in, and quite unexpectedly he had come swimming by and bitten the Hagenström boy—a big bite, using all his teeth, right in the leg, like a mean little dog. His blue eyes flashed from under the wet, reddish blond hair that hung down in his face. But the little count paid for his deed, did he ever, and he climbed up out of the pool badly battered. All the same, Consul Hagenström's rugged son limped noticeably as he walked home.

Nourishing food and physical exercise of all kinds—those were the basis of Senator Buddenbrook's efforts at watching over his son.

But he was no less attentive in trying to influence the boy's mind and provide him with vivid experiences in the practical world for which he was destined.

He began gradually to introduce Hanno to this sphere of future activities. He took him along when he had business to attend to down by the harbor, had Hanno stand at his side when he talked with the dockworkers in a patois of Danish and Plattdeutsch or conferred with the warehouse managers in their little, dark office or gave an order to the men hoisting sacks of grain to the upper stories, all the while shouting to one another in a hollow singsong. For Thomas Buddenbrook himself, this piece of the world here on the harbor—among the ships, sheds, and warehouses, where things smelled of butter, fish, water, tar, and well-oiled iron—had been a favorite spot since he was a boy, the most interesting place he knew; and since Hanno did not express joy and approval on his own, the senator felt compelled to awaken those feelings in his son. What were the names of the steamers that sailed the route to Copenhagen? "The *Naiad* . . . the *Halmstadt* . . . the *Friederike Oeverdieck*." "Well, you know those—and that's something at least. You'll learn the others soon enough. Yes, many of those fellows hoisting sacks there have the same name as you do, my boy, because they were christened after your grandfather. And my name is fairly frequent among their children, and your mama's name, too. And so we give them a little gift every year. But now we'll walk on past this warehouse and we won't speak to the men, either; we have nothing to say to them—they work for one of our competitors."

"Do you want to come along, Hanno?" he said one day. "A new ship that belongs to our fleet is going to be launched this afternoon. I'll be christening it. Would you like to come?"

And Hanno pretended that he did. He went with his father and listened to his speech, watched him break a bottle of champagne against the bow; but there was a strange look in Hanno's eyes as he watched the ship glide down the incline—the whole length of it smeared with green soap—hit the water with a burst of spray, and then steam off, puffing smoke, for its first trial run.

On certain days of the year—on Palm Sunday, when there were confirmations, or on New Year's Day—Senator Buddenbrook would take the carriage for a round of obligatory social calls; and since his wife preferred to excuse herself on such occasions with a migraine or a simple case of nerves, he would invite Hanno to join him. And Hanno would say he wanted to go along. He climbed into the fly beside his father and then sat mutely at his side in various parlors, watching with quiet eyes the easy, tactful, and yet so varied and carefully measured way his father dealt with these people. He watched closely as they took their leave of Colonel Herr von Rinnlingen, the local commander, who assured the senator that he was very honored by such a visit and that it was much appreciated, and took note of the way his father amiably but somewhat apprehensively laid an arm around the colonel's shoulder for a moment; at another home a similar remark was received with a calm, serious look, and at a third with an ironically exaggerated returned compliment. All of this was done with a formal refinement of both word and gesture, which the senator obviously wanted his son to admire and hoped would have an educational effect as well.

But little Johann saw more than he was meant to see, and his eyes, those shy, golden brown eyes ringed with bluish shadows, observed things only too well. Not only did he see his father's poise and charm and their effect on everyone, but his strange, stinging, perceptive glance also saw how terribly difficult it was for his father to bring it off, how after each visit he grew more silent and pale, leaning back in one corner of the carriage, closing his eyes, now rimmed with red; as they crossed the threshold of the next house, Hanno watched in horror as a mask slipped down over that same face and a spring suddenly returned to the stride of that same weary body. First the entrance, then small-talk, fine manners, and persuasive charm—but what little Johann saw was not a naïve, natural, almost unconscious expression of shared practical concerns that could be used to one's advantage; instead of being an honest and simple interest in the affairs of others, all this appeared to be an end in itself—a self-conscious, artificial effort that substituted a dreadfully difficult and grueling virtuosity for poise and character. Hanno knew that they all expected him to appear in public someday, too, and to perform, to prepare each word and gesture, with everyone staring at him—and at the thought, he closed his eyes with a shudder of fear and aversion.

Oh, that was not the effect that Thomas Buddenbrook had hoped the influence of his personality would have on his son. His thoughts were focused, rather, on awakening in him an easy nonchalance, a kind of ruthlessness, and a simple sense for the practical things in life.

"Looks as if you're living well, my boy," he said whenever Hanno asked for seconds on dessert or half a cup of coffee after his meal. "You'll have to become a hardworking merchant and earn a lot of money. Do you want to do that?" And little Johann would answer, "Yes."

Now and then, when the family was gathered around the table and Aunt Antonie or Uncle Christian would fall back into their old habit of making fun of poor Aunt Klothilde and begin speaking with her in her own drawling, meek, amiable fashion, it sometimes happened that Hanno, feeling the effects of the heavy red wine reserved for special occasions, would adopt that tone of voice himself for a moment and make some teasing remark of his own to Aunt Klothilde. And then Thomas Buddenbrook would laugh—a loud, heartfelt, encouraging, almost grateful laugh, like a man surprised by some very amusing stroke of good luck; he would even egg Johann on and join in the teasing—when in fact, for years now, he had protested against taking that tone with their poor cousin. It was so cheap, so safe, to assert one's superiority over humble, dull, skinny, and eternally hungry Klothilde, and despite the general harmlessness of it all, the whole idea seemed rather mean-spirited. But he fought against that feeling, too, just as he had to fight desperately against his own scruples in the practical affairs of everyday life—when a situation would arise and once again he could not comprehend, simply could not get over, the fact that, although he understood the ramifications, was able to see through to the heart of the matter, he still had to use the situation for his own purposes without any sense of shame. But to use a situation without any sense of shame, he told himself, that is what it means to be fit for real life.

Ah, how glad, how happy, delighted, and hopeful he felt at any little sign Johann might display that he was fit for real life.

3

OVER THE YEARS, the Buddenbrooks had grown accustomed to not traveling any distance during the summer, and even the previous spring, when Gerda had expressed a wish to visit her father in Amsterdam and play a few duets with him again after so many years, her husband had been rather curt in giving his consent. Granted, Gerda, little Johann, and Fräulein Jungmann spent their entire summer vacation at the hotel in Travemünde every year, but that custom had endured primarily for the sake of Hanno's health.

Summer vacation at the shore! Could anyone, anywhere, know what happiness that was? After the sludgy, excruciating monotony of countless days in school—four long weeks of peaceful, carefree solitude, filled with the smell of seaweed and the murmur of the gentle surf. Four weeks, a period that was so immeasurably vast at the start that you couldn't believe it would ever end, and merely to mention the possibility would have been rude, even blasphemous. Johann could never understand how, at the end of the school term, any teacher could bring himself to say something like: "And we shall pick up here after summer vacation and then move on to this or that. . . ." After summer vacation! He actually seemed to be looking forward to it, that incomprehensible man in his shiny worsted suit. After summer vacation—even to think such a thing! When it was all so marvelously remote, lost in the gray distance far beyond those four weeks.

He had presented his report card the day before and survived that more or less, and then had come the ride in the carriage packed high with luggage. They were staying in one of the two Swiss-style lodges that were joined by a long, narrow central building and formed a straight line with the façades of the pastry shop and the pump room. And now he awoke on the very first morning! What had awakened him with a start was a vague sense of joy, which suddenly went to his head and gave his heart a tug. He opened his eyes and let his eager, elated gaze take in the old-fashioned furniture and the tidy little room. A second of drowsy, blissful confusion—and then he realized that he was in Travemünde, would be in Travemünde for four infinite weeks. He did not stir; he lay quietly on his back in the narrow, yellow frame bed, its sheets exceptionally thin and soft from long use; now and then he closed his eyes briefly and felt joy and excitement quiver in his chest as he took long, deep breaths.

The room lay bathed in yellowish daylight pouring in now through the striped blind, but all around him everything was still silent—Ida Jungmann and Mama were both still asleep. All he could hear was the even, sedate sound of a laborer raking the gravel down below in the garden, and the buzzing of a fly trapped between the blind and the window and keeping up a steady assault against the windowpane. As it darted about, you could watch its shadow tracing zigzag lines on the striped canvas. Silence—and the lonely sounds of a rake and a monotone buzz. And the gently animated calm suddenly filled little Johann with a delicious awareness of the quiet, well-tended, elegant seclusion of this resort, which he loved more than anything else. No, thank God, here were no shiny worsted suits, worn by earthly incarnations of grammar and ratios—not a one, because it was all rather expensive here.

In a burst of joy he sprang from his bed and ran to the window in his bare feet. He pulled up the blind, loosened the white-enameled hook, and opened the casement, watching the fly as it sped off across the gravel paths and rose beds of the garden. Facing the hotel buildings and set within a semicircle of boxwoods, the band shell stood quiet and empty. The Leuchtenfeld flats, which got their name from the lighthouse that rose up somewhere off to the right, stretched out far before him under the bright white sky, until the short grass, interspersed with patches of bare earth, gave way to taller shore vegetation and then to the sandy beach, where he could make out rows of little private wooden pavilions and wicker beach chairs facing the open sea. There it lay in the peaceful morning light, the sea—smooth and ruffled streaks of bottle-green and blue—and a steamer moved between rows of red barrels that marked the channel. It was on its way home from Copenhagen, and you didn't need to know whether it was the *Naiad* or the *Friederike Oeverdieck*. And in that moment of quiet bliss, Hanno Buddenbrook took another deep breath of the spicy air sent by the sea, and he greeted the sea tenderly with his eyes—a silent, grateful greeting full of love.

And now the day began, the first of those paltry twenty-eight days, which at first seemed like an eternity of bliss, but dwindled away so dreadfully fast once the first few were gone. They had breakfast on the balcony or under the tall chestnut tree over by the children's playground with its large swing—and Johann was enchanted by all of it: the scent that rose from the hastily laundered tablecloth as a waiter spread it out before them, the tissue-paper napkins, the unfamiliar bread, the fact that they ate their eggs from metal eggcups, and with everyday teaspoons instead of the bone-handled ones they used at home.

And the rest of the day was so free and had no real schedule, a wonderful lazy and coddled life of ease that passed serenely and without a care. It started with mornings on the beach, while the band played its early program up above them—just lying and resting at the foot of the wicker chair, playing quiet, dreamy games with the soft sand that didn't even get you dirty, letting your gaze drift easily and painlessly across the endless green and blue, from which came a gentle swishing sound bearing a strong, fresh, and aromatic breeze that wrapped itself around your ears and made you deliciously dizzy, a kind of muted numbness that silently, peacefully dissolved every constraint, so that you lost all sense of time and space. And then a swim, which was much more enjoyable here than at Herr Asmussen's—there wasn't any goose grass here, only pale green, crystal-clear water that foamed when you splashed it, and instead of slimy wooden planks there was gently rilled sand under your feet, and Consul Hagenström's boys were far, far away, in Norway or Tyrolia. The consul loved to take his family on long trips in the summer—and there was no reason he shouldn't, was there? A walk along the beach to warm up, out to Seagull Rock or the Temple of the Sea, and then you sat in your wicker chair and had a snack—until the time came for you to go back to the room and take a little nap before dinner. Dinner was fun, the resort blossomed with people—all the families who were friends of the Buddenbrooks, and others from Hamburg, even some from England and Russia; they filled the hotel's great dining hall, and a man dressed in black stood at a special little table and served the soup from a shiny silver tureen. There were four courses, each tastier, spicier, or at least somehow more festive than at home, and when you looked down the long table some people were drinking champagne. Sometimes single gentlemen came from town, men who didn't let their business keep them chained to their desks all week; they amused themselves and liked to watch the roulette wheel spin after dinner: Consul Peter Döhlmann, for instance, who always left his daughter at home and could tell such loud, outrageous stories in Plattdeutsch that the ladies from Hamburg laughed till their sides ached and begged for mercy; or Senator Cremer, the chief of police; or Uncle Christian and his old schoolchum Senator Gieseke, who also came without his family and paid all Christian Buddenbrook's bills. Later, while the adults drank their coffee and enjoyed the music from under the pastry-shop awnings, Hanno would sit on a chair at the base of the band-shell steps and listen—and could never get enough. And there were things to do in the late afternoon, too. There was a shooting gallery on the hotel grounds, and off to the right of the Swiss-style lodges were stalls with horses, donkeys, and cows, and you could drink the warm, foamy, fragrant milk as an evening snack. You could go for a walk, into the village, along Front Row; and from there you could take a boat across to Priwall, where you could find amber on the beach; or you could join in a game of croquet on the playground or sit on a bench under the trees up on the hill just behind the hotel—that was where the large dinner bell was—and have Ida Jungmann read aloud to you. But the best idea, always, was to go back to the beach and sit out at the end of the rampart in the twilight, your face to the open horizon, and wave a handkerchief to the ships gliding by and listen to the little waves splashing against the boulders. The whole world all around was filled with that mild and marvelous swishing sound, which spoke to little Johann in a kindly voice and persuaded him to close his eyes in contentment. But then Ida Jungmann said, "Come on, Hanno, we have to go. Time for supper. You'll catch your death if you fall asleep out here." And when he came back from the sea, his heartbeat was so calm, untroubled, and regular. After he had eaten and drunk his milk or malted beer up in the room, and his mother had left to join the other guests for supper out on the hotel's glassed-in veranda, he slipped between those old, thin sheets and, to the soft, strong pumping of his contented heart and the muted rhythms of the evening concert, sank into sleep, without fear or fever.

On Sunday, like a good many other gentlemen who were kept in town on business during the week, the senator joined his family and stayed until Monday morning. But although there was ice cream and champagne at dinner, although there were donkey rides and sailing parties on the open sea, little Johann was not very fond of Sundays. The peace and seclusion of the resort was disrupted. A lot of people from town, who didn't really belong here—"middle-class day-trippers" was Ida Jungmann's patronizing term—crowded the beach and the grounds, to swim, listen to music, and drink coffee; and Hanno would have preferred to shut himself up in his room and wait for all these intruders in their Sunday best to be washed away again. No, he was glad when Monday put everything back on the old track, and he no longer felt his father's eyes, absent six days of the week, studying him, scrutinizing him critically all day Sunday—and, oh, how he felt them resting on him.

Fourteen days had passed, and Hanno told himself and anyone else who would listen that there was still plenty of time left, as much time as the holidays at Michaelmas. But that was deceptive comfort, because his vacation had reached its peak and now it was all downhill, speeding toward its end, racing so awfully fast that he wanted to hold tight to each hour and not let it pass, to take in each breath of sea air more slowly so that not a second of joy would be wasted.

But time passed, in the relentless change of sunny and rainy days, of on-shore and off-shore winds, of still, brooding heat and noisy thunderstorms that could not move out over the water and seemed to go on and on. There were days when wind from the northeast would fill the bay with a blackish green flood tide that covered the beach with seaweed, mussels, and jellyfish and threatened the pavilions. The dark, tossing sea was dotted everywhere with foam. Great waves rolled toward the shore with inexorable, appalling, silent power, pitched forward majestically, the swells shining like dark green metal, and plunged raucously with a hiss, a crack, and a boom onto the sand. There were other days when the west wind blew the sea back, exposing vast areas of the daintily rilled sandy floor and leaving naked sandbanks everywhere; and rain fell in sheets, melting heaven, earth, and sea into one another, while gusts of wind picked up the rain and drove it against the windows until drops became streams that ran down the panes, making it impossible to see out. Then Hanno would usually spend the day at the upright piano in the lobby, and although it had been battered somewhat by all the waltzes and schottisches played at balls, and he couldn't play the same rich improvisations as at home on his grand piano, it had a muted, gurgling tone that allowed him to achieve some very amusing effects. And there were the other days, too—dreamy, blue, perfectly calm, and sweltering, when the blue flies buzzed in the sun above the Leuchtenfeld flats and the sea lay silent and inert like a mirror, without a hint of a breeze. And, with three days to go, Hanno told himself and everyone else that there was still plenty of time left, as much time as the holidays at Pentecost. His arithmetic was impeccable, but even he didn't believe it, and his heart had long since come to the conclusion that the man in the shiny worsted suit was right after all, that four weeks did come to an end, and that you picked up again where you had left off and moved on to this or that.

The carriage, packed high with luggage, halted in front of the hotel—the day had come. Hanno had said goodbye to the sea and the beach early that morning; he now said goodbye to the waiters, who accepted their tips, to the band shell, to the rose beds, and to summer itself. And then, while the hotel staff bowed to them, the carriage pulled away.

They moved down the tree-lined road that led to the village and past Front Row. Across from Hanno on the back seat sat Ida Jungmann, bright-eyed, white-haired, and raw-boned, but he tucked his head into one corner of the carriage and looked out the window, ignoring her. The morning sky was overcast with white clouds, the Trave broken by little waves scurrying before the wind. Now and then little drops pricked at the windowpane. At the entrance to Front Row people were sitting on their stoops and mending nets; barefoot children came running up, curious to have a peek into the carriage. *They* would be staying here.

Once the carriage had left the last houses behind, Hanno bent forward to have a final look at the lighthouse; then he leaned back and closed his eyes. "We'll be back next year, Hanno," Ida Jungmann said in a deep, consoling voice; but that bit of consolation was all he needed, and his chin began to quiver and tears welled up under his long eyelashes.

His face and hands were brown from the sea air, but if their intention in sending him to the shore was to make him stronger, fresher, more energetic and robust, then they had failed miserably—and he was fully aware of that disheartening fact. Four weeks of sheltered tranquillity and quiet worship of the sea had left him even softer, dreamier, more spoiled and sensitive than before, and even less capable of summoning his courage when faced with Herr Tietge's ratios. And he was sure that he would lose all heart when confronted with memorizing historical dates and grammatical rules, that in desperation he would nonchalantly toss his books aside and fall asleep in the hope of escaping his fears of the next morning's classes, the catastrophes, the Hagenström bullies, and the demands his father made of him.

But then this morning's ride lifted his spirits a little. The carriage followed the puddled ruts of the country road, and birds were chirping everywhere. He thought about Kai and seeing him again, and about Herr Pfühl and his music lessons, about his grand piano and harmonium. And anyway, tomorrow was Sunday, and the first day of school, the day after tomorrow, was always quite harmless. Ah, he could still feel a little sand from the beach in his high-buttoned shoes—he would ask Grobleben to leave it in there, forever. So let it start all over again: the men in their worsted suits, the Hagenströms, and all the rest. He had what he had. When it all came raining down on him, he would remember the sea and the hotel gardens, and just the brief thought of the sound that the little waves made in the still of the evening—coming from far away, from some remote distance wrapped in mysterious slumber to splash against the rampart—would comfort him, put him out of reach of all life's hardships.

Then came the ferry, then Israelsdorfer Allee, then Jerusalem Hill, Castle Yard. The carriage passed through the Burg Gate, on its right the towering walls of the prison, where Uncle Weinschenk was; it rolled down Burg Strasse and crossed the Koberg, left Breite Strasse behind, and, with brakes set, started down the steep slope of Fischer Grube. There was the red façade with its bay and the white caryatides; and as they walked out of the noon warmth of the street into the cool of the paved entrance, the senator came out to greet them from his office, his pen still in his hand.

Slowly, slowly, and hiding his tears, little Johann learned to miss the sea again, learned to be both afraid and unbearably bored, all the while keeping a lookout for the Hagenströms and finding solace in Kai, Herr Pfühl, and his music.

The moment they saw him, the Ladies Buddenbrook from Breite Strasse and Aunt Klothilde made sure to ask him how he felt about school now that vacation was over—adding a teasing wink that pretended to say that they had great understanding for his situation, but it was really only that strange arrogance of adults that treats everything important to children superficially and, if possible, as a joke.

Three or four days after Hanno returned to town, Dr. Langhals, the family physician, paid a call on Fischer Grube to determine the effect of Hanno's stay at the shore. After a lengthy conference with Gerda Buddenbrook, he had Hanno brought in to conduct a thorough examination of his *status praesens*, as Dr. Langhals called it, inspecting his own fingernails. Hanno stood there half undressed, and the doctor felt his inadequate muscles, listened to his chest and the beating of his heart, had him describe the state of all his bodily functions, and finally, taking out a syringe, pricked Hanno's thin arm and drew blood, which he would analyze later at home—and, once again, on the whole seemed less than satisfied.

"We've got nice and tanned," he said, giving Hanno a hug as he stood there before him, and then, placing a hand—a little hand with black hair—on Hanno's shoulder, he looked up at Gerda Buddenbrook and Fräulein Jungmann and said, "but we're still pulling much too long a face."

"He's homesick for the sea," Gerda Buddenbrook remarked.

"Oh, so that's it. So you like being at the shore, do you?" Dr. Langhals asked, searching little Johann's face with his conceited eyes. Hanno blushed. What did Dr. Langhals mean by the question? He obviously expected an answer. And a crazy, preposterous idea rose up inside him, a wild hope based in his fanciful belief that with God nothing was impossible, despite all the men in worsted suits in the world.

"Yes," he managed to say, his wide eyes fixed on the doctor. But Dr. Langhals had not meant anything in particular by his question.

"Well, the effects of the swimming and good sea air are bound to show themselves in due time," he said, first clapping little Johann on the shoulder and then shoving him away; with a nod to Madame Buddenbrook and Ida Jungmann—the arrogant, benevolent, and encouraging nod of a wise physician, on whose every word his patients hang—he got to his feet. The examination was over.

It was Aunt Tony who showed the most ready understanding for Hanno's yearning for the sea, which was like a wound that slowly scabbed over but would begin to sting and bleed again at the least touch of the rigors of everyday life. She obviously enjoyed listening to his descriptions of life in Travemünde and joined in enthusiastically whenever he wistfully sang its praises.

"Yes, Hanno," she said, "the true things in life will always be true, and Travemünde is a beautiful spot. Until they lower me into my grave, I will always have happy memories, you know, of the weeks I spent there one summer when I was just a silly young goose. I lived with a family that I liked so much, and they were fond of me, too, it seemed. I was a pretty young thing back then—I'm allowed to say that now that I'm an old lady—and almost always cheerful and lively. They were fine people, let me tell you, honest, goodhearted, and straight-thinking, and so clever and well read and enthusiastic—I've never met anyone like them in all my life. Yes, what a wonderfully exciting time I spent with them. I learned so much there, you see, views and opinions and facts that have stood me in good stead all my life, and if other things had not interfered, all sorts of things that just happened—the way they do in life—I could have profited from it even more, even though I was a silly young goose. Do you want to know how stupid I was back then? I wanted some of those pretty colored stars that jellyfish have inside them. So I wrapped a whole bunch of them in my handkerchief and took them home and laid them out neatly in the sun on the balcony, so they would dry up. That way, I thought, only the stars would be left. Right . . . and when I went back to look, there was just a big wet spot. And it smelled a little like rotting seaweed."

4

EARLY IN 1873, Hugo Weinschenk's petition for pardon was granted by the senate, and the former insurance director was released six months before his sentence was up.

If Frau Permaneder had been truthful, she would have admitted that she was not exactly elated by this event and that she would have preferred if everything had remained just as it was for good and all. She lived a peaceful life with her daughter and granddaughter there on Linden Platz; she was in constant contact with the house on Fischer Grube and with her former boarding-school friend Armgard von Maiboom, née Schilling, who had moved to town after her husband's death. She had long known that there was no suitable, dignified place for her outside the walls of her hometown; given her memories of Munich, her increasingly weak and nervous digestion, and her growing desire for peace and quiet, she felt no need whatever at her age to move to a big city in her now united Fatherland, let alone to some foreign country.

"My dear child," she said to her daughter, "I must ask you something, something very serious. You do love your husband with all your heart, don't you? You love him so much that you would take your child and follow him wherever he may choose to go now? He can't remain here, unfortunately."

And in response Frau Erika Weinschenk, née Grünlich, broke into tears that could have meant almost anything and provided a dutiful answer—just like the one Tony had provided her father under similar circumstances in her villa near Hamburg—giving rise to the assumption that a separation was imminent.

The day on which Frau Permaneder drove to the prison in a closed carriage to pick up her son-in-law was almost as dreadful as the day on which Hugo Weinschenk had been arrested. She brought him to their apartment on Linden Platz; after greeting his wife and child in a dazed, helpless sort of way, he retreated to the room made ready for him. And there he stayed, smoking cigars from morning till night, never daring to go out in public, usually not even joining his family for meals—a skittish, gray-haired man.

Life in prison had not affected Hugo Weinschenk's physical health—he had always been a man of rugged constitution. But he was in a very sad state nonetheless. The man had probably done nothing worse than what most of his colleagues blithely did every day; and if he had not been caught at it, he would doubtless have gone his way with head held high and a perfectly easy conscience. But disgrace in the eyes of his fellow citizens, a guilty verdict in a court of law, and three years in prison had left him a morally broken man. With heartfelt conviction, he had assured the court that the clever measures he had undertaken for the benefit of his insurance company had been to its advantage as well as his own, that it was no more than usage in the world of business—and expert witnesses had confirmed this. The lawyers, however, were gentlemen who, in his opinion, understood nothing about such matters, they lived in a different world; and, proceeding from a totally different perspective, they judged him guilty of fraud—a verdict backed up by the power of the state. All of which had so shattered his self-confidence that he now dared not look anyone in the eye. The spring in his step, the enterprising swing in his stride as he walked along in his frock coat, fists balanced in front of him, eyes roving, the enormous vigor with which he asked questions and told anecdotes from the heights of unschooled ignorance—it was all gone now. And his family shuddered at the despondency, cowardice, and lack of self-respect that had replaced it.

After eight to ten days spent doing nothing but smoking cigars, Hugo Weinschenk began to read newspapers and write letters. After another eight or ten days, he declared in a roundabout way that there appeared to be a new position open for him in London, that he would be going there to arrange matters—traveling alone for now, but once everything was in order he would send for his wife and child.

Erika rode with him in a closed carriage to the train station, and he departed, without ever once having seen any of his other in-laws.

Several days later a letter arrived from Hamburg addressed to his wife; in it he explained that he had decided not to have his wife and child join him—or so much as hear from him—until he could offer them a home worthy of them. And that was the last sign of life from Hugo Weinschenk. From that day on, nothing, absolutely nothing more was heard of him. Frau Permaneder, who was well versed in such matters and both energetic and circumspect, made several attempts to locate him, her intention being, as she explained with a grave look on her face, to provide proof of willful desertion as grounds for divorce. But Hugo was and remained a missing person. And so Erika Weinschenk and little Elisabeth continued to make their home with Erika's mother in the bright apartment on Linden Platz.

5

THE MARRIAGE of which little Johann was the issue had never lost its appeal as a topic of conversation among the town's citizens. Just as both spouses had something extravagant and enigmatic about them, so, too, the marriage itself was considered unusual and problematical. And so the difficult task of getting behind mere appearances and of probing the bedrock of the relationship that lay beneath the few external facts, might very well have its rewards. And, the less people knew about Gerda and Thomas Buddenbrook, the more they spoke about them in parlors, bedrooms, clubs, and casinos—even on the exchange.

How had these two found one another, and what kind of rapport did they have with one another? People could remember with what firm, sudden resolve Thomas Buddenbrook had gone about wooing her. "This woman or none," he had said, and it must have been more or less the same for Gerda, too, because, until she was twenty-seven, she had rebuffed every suitor in Amsterdam—and then suddenly had accepted this one. A marriage of love, people were forced to conclude, for although they admitted that Gerda's three hundred thousand had played a role, they knew it was merely secondary. But when it came to love, to what people understood as love, there had been very few indications of that in their marriage. Instead, from the very beginning, people had noticed only a kind of courtesy in the way they treated one another, a very correct and respectful courtesy quite uncommon between man and wife, which seemed to have its origins not in emotional distance and estrangement but, rather, in a most peculiar, silent, and profound mutual trust in and knowledge of one another, in never-failing consideration and tolerance. And the passing years had not changed that in the least. The only change that time had brought could be found in the difference in their ages, which, although it was quite small when measured in years, had began to show itself in obvious ways.

People looked at them and saw a rather stout man who was aging quickly and a young woman at his side. People thought that Thomas Buddenbrook looked, as they said, rather tumbledown. Indeed, although his vanity—which had become almost comical by now—kept him propped up, "tumbledown" was the only word for him. Whereas Gerda had scarcely changed at all in the last eighteen years. The nervous chill that radiated from her personality seemed somehow to have preserved her. Her chestnut hair had kept its color, her lovely white face its symmetry, her figure its slender, tall elegance. And, as always, bluish shadows lingered in the corners of her somewhat too small and somewhat too close-set brown eyes. People did not trust those eyes. They had a strange look about them, and something was written there that people were unable to decipher. This woman, who was by nature so cool, so private, so closed, reserved, and aloof, and who seemed to release a little warmth only for her music, aroused vague suspicions. People rummaged in their limited knowledge of human nature and found dusty clichés by which to measure Senator Buddenbrook's wife: still waters run deep, or butter wouldn't melt in her mouth. And because they wanted so much to get a little closer to the heart of the matter, to learn and understand even something of what made her tick, their limited imaginations led them to assume—how could it be otherwise?—that beautiful Gerda was cheating on her aging husband.

They kept their ears and eyes open, and it was not long before they were unanimous in the opinion that Gerda Buddenbrook had, to put it mildly, overstepped the bounds of propriety in her relation to Lieutenant von Throta.

René Maria von Throta, a Rhinelander by birth, was a second lieutenant in one of the infantry battalions stationed in the town. His red collar looked very handsome with his black hair, which he parted on the left and combed back from his white forehead in a high, thick wave. And although he was a tall and strong man, the general effect he made, by his gestures and the way he talked and the way he kept silent, was that of a most unmilitary man. He loved to stick one hand between the buttons of his half-open undress jacket or to sit with one cheek resting against the back of his hand; his bows lacked any hint of stiffness, one did not even hear his heels click together; and he draped his uniform on his unmuscular body as casually and capriciously as if it were a civilian suit. Even his youthful mustache, trimmed on a slant to the corners of his mouth, was so spare that it could never have been shaped to a handlebar or extended to points, and that only added to his less-than-martial appearance. The strangest thing about him, however, was his eyes: large, extraordinarily keen eyes, so black that they seemed to glow somewhere in bottomless depths, eyes that rested on everything and everyone with a shimmering, enraptured seriousness.

There was no doubt that he had enlisted reluctantly and without any love of the military, for despite his physical strength he was neither a good officer nor loved by his comrades-in-arms; and he shared few interests and pleasures with other young officers, who had just returned from a brief, victorious campaign. He was considered a disagreeable and extravagant eccentric, who went for long walks by himself, who did not love horses, hunting, gambling, or women, and whose sole interest was music. He played several instruments and could be seen at every opera or concert, sitting there, eyes aglow, in an unmilitary, relaxed pose that was rather theatrical at the same time. He despised clubs and casinos.

He paid his obligatory social calls, with mixed success, on the town's most important families; but he refused almost all their invitations and spent time really only with the Buddenbrooks—much too much time, so people said; much too much time, so the senator thought.

No one knew what Thomas Buddenbrook was thinking, no one was allowed to know—and that was what was so terribly difficult: keeping the rest of the world ignorant of his sorrow, his hate, his helplessness. People began to find him a little ridiculous; but perhaps they would have curbed such feelings and felt some sympathy for him if they had even dimly suspected how he fretted, how hard he tried not to be thought ridiculous, how he feared it—and he had seen it coming, looming ahead, long before they had ever thought of the possibility. Even his vanity, his much-derided "vanity," proceeded largely from this same worry. He had been the first to cast a mistrustful eye at the growing discrepancy between his own appearance and Gerda's strange flawless beauty, which the years had left untouched; and now that Herr von Throta had entered his house, he had to combat and hide his worries with what little energy he still had. If he was to avoid becoming a laughing-stock, he had to keep his worries from becoming known.

Gerda Buddenbrook and the young, eccentric officer had become acquainted, naturally, by way of music. Herr von Throta played the piano, violin, viola, cello, and flute—all exceedingly well—and often the senator did not realize a visit was impending until he saw Herr von Throta's aide, a cello case on his back, pass by the green windowsill outside his private office and vanish into the house. Then Thomas Buddenbrook would sit at his desk and wait until he saw the man himself, his wife's friend, enter the house, until he heard the harmonious strains swell in the salon above him—lilting, lamenting melodies or superhuman exultations raised heavenward like clasped hands. After wandering in confusion and vague ecstasy, the sounds would then sink back down, sobbing and fainting, into night and stillness. But no matter, let them surge and bluster, weep and exult, sparkle and embrace in supernatural pantomime. The worst thing, the truly tormenting part, was the silence afterward, which reigned above him in the salon for such a long, long time and was too profound and inert not to fill him with dread. There were no footsteps to shake the ceiling, not even a chair scraped as it moved; it was a sordid, insidious, hushed, secret silence. Then Thomas Buddenbrook would sit there so terrified that he sometimes moaned softly.

What was he afraid of? People had seen Herr von Throta enter his house again, and with their eyes, so to speak, he saw the scene they pictured to themselves: he was sitting downstairs by the window in his office, an aging, worn-out, peevish man, and upstairs his beautiful wife was making music with her lover—and not just music. Yes, that's how it looked to them, he knew it. And nevertheless he knew that "beau" was not really the word to describe Herr von Throta. Oh, he would almost have been happy if he could have called him that, thought of him as that, if he had been able to despise him as a shallow, empty-headed, and vulgar young man who was working off a normal dose of youthful energy with a little music in order to win ladies' hearts. He made every conceivable attempt to transform him into such a creature. For that sole purpose, he tried to awaken within himself his forefathers' old prejudices: the established and frugal merchant's intransigent mistrust of the frivolous, adventurous, and socially unreliable military caste. In his thoughts, even in conversation, he made a patronizing point of calling Herr von Throta "the lieutenant"; and yet he knew only too well that this was the least applicable term for describing the young man's character.

What was Thomas Buddenbrook afraid of? Nothing—nothing he could put a name to. Oh, if only he could have defended himself with simple, tangible, brutal facts. He envied those people out there for being able to picture the affair so naïvely. But as he sat there, his head in his hands, listening in agony, he knew all too well that "cheating" and "adultery" were not the right words for the melodious and abysmally silent events happening above him.

Sometimes he would look out to the gray gables and to the passersby or let his eyes rest on the centennial plaque hanging on the wall, the one with the portrait of his father, and he would think about his family's history and tell himself that this was how it all ended, that what was happening now was the final chapter. Yes, the final chapter—he was being held up to ridicule, and, to crown it all, his name and his family's private life were the subject of gossip and scorn. And yet the thought almost made him feel better, because it seemed simple, plausible, and sane, something thinkable, sayable, in comparison with his brooding over this ignominious riddle, this mysterious scandal overhead.

He could bear it no longer; he shoved his armchair back, left the office, and climbed the stairs. But where should he go now? To the salon, to greet Herr von Throta, nonchalantly and somewhat superciliously, to invite him to join them for dinner, and, as so often before, to be refused? That was what he found truly unbearable, the way the lieutenant avoided him completely, refusing almost every official invitation and preferring instead the easy and private company of his wife.

Should he wait? In the smoking room maybe? Wait until Herr Throta left and then go to Gerda and speak his mind, have it out with her? But you did not have anything out with Gerda or speak your mind to her. And what about, really? His union with her was based on mutual understanding, consideration, and silence. He did not need to make himself ridiculous in her eyes as well. By playing the jealous husband, he would be proclaiming the scandal, putting it into words—admitting that those people out there were right. Did he feel jealous? Of whom? Of what? Oh, jealousy was wide of the mark. Such a strong emotion meant that you could produce evidence—mistaken, perhaps foolish evidence, but at least something real, something liberating. Oh no, all he felt was a little fear, a little tormenting and nagging fear of the whole affair.

He went upstairs to his dressing room to wipe his brow with eau de cologne and then returned to the second floor, determined to break the silence in the salon at any price. But the moment he took hold of the white door's burnt-gold handle, a storm of music surged up again and he shrank back.

He descended the servants' stairs to the ground floor, crossed the entrance hall and the cold vestibule, and stepped out into the garden; he went back to the entrance hall with its stuffed bear and stood fidgeting on the main staircase landing with its basin of goldfish—but he could find no rest anywhere, just stood there listening, lurking in the shadows, full of shame and sadness, crushed and driven by his fear of both the secret and the public scandal.

One day, in much the same mood, he stood leaning over the third-floor gallery, peering down into the bright, open stairwell, where everything was silent, and little Johann came out of his room, down the steps of his "balcony," and along the corridor, on his way to see Ida Jungmann about something. He held close to the wall, his eyes lowered, a book under his arm, intending to pass by his father with just a soft word of hello.

But the senator spoke to him. "Well, Hanno, what are you up to?"

"Working, Papa. I'm on my way to see Ida, to read my translation to her."

"And how's it going? What's the homework?"

And as always, swallowing hard and with eyelashes lowered, Hanno replied quickly, obviously trying to give a correct, clear, and sharp-witted answer. "We have a translation of Cornelius Nepos, a bookkeeping entry to copy, French grammar, the rivers of North America, a German essay to correct. . . ."

He fell silent, sorry that he hadn't added a final "and" before letting his voice fall, since he didn't know what else to say now. It made his whole answer seem abrupt and tentative. "Nothing else," he said, as decisively as he could, but without looking up. His father, however, hadn't seemed to notice; he was distracted somehow, not really paying attention to anything Hanno said. He just held the boy's free hand in his, playing with it and letting his fingers run slowly along the delicate wrist.

And then, quite suddenly, Hanno heard something being said above him that had no connection at all with their conversation—in a soft, anxious, and almost imploring voice that he had never heard before. But it was his father's voice, and it said, "The lieutenant has been in there with Mama for two hours now, Hanno."

And at the sound of that voice, little Johann raised his golden-brown eyes and fixed them—larger, clearer, and more loving than ever before—on his father's face, with its reddened eyelids beneath pale brows and its white, slightly puffy cheeks behind the long tips of the stiff mustache. God knows how much he understood. But one thing was certain, and they both felt it, that at that moment, as their eyes met and held, the estrangement and coldness, the constraint and misunderstanding between them fell away; and Thomas Buddenbrook knew that he could depend on his son's trust and devotion whenever, as now, it was a matter of fear and suffering, and not, as usual, a matter of energy, competence, and bright-eyed vigor.

But Thomas disregarded what had happened, worked hard to disregard it. And so, in the period that followed, he was stricter than ever about drilling Hanno in the practical things that would be important in his future life and work; he examined his intellectual abilities, pressed him for decisive statements about his love of the occupation awaiting him, and burst into rage at every sign of resistance and languor. The fact was that Thomas Buddenbrook, at forty-eight, had begun to count his days more and more, to reckon with the approach of death.

His physical health had grown worse. He had little appetite and trouble sleeping; chills, which had always been a problem, now forced him to consult Dr. Langhals on several occasions. But he never managed to follow the doctor's medical advice. His strength of will, shaky now after years of fussy, harassed inactivity, was no longer up to the task. He had begun to sleep very late of a morning, although each evening he would angrily resolve to rise early and take the walk before his morning tea that the doctor had suggested. But he actually followed through only two or three times—and it was much the same with everything else. All of this meant a constant strain on his will, and it brought him neither success nor a sense of satisfaction—only gnawed away at his self-respect and left him feeling desperate. He was not about to try to give up the narcotic pleasure of his pungent little Russian cigarettes—he had smoked them in great quantities since his youth. He told Dr. Langhals straight out, right to his conceited face, "You see, doctor, it is your duty to forbid me my cigarettes, a very easy and very pleasant duty indeed. But obeying that prohibition is up to me—you must realize that. No, we shall work together on my health, but the roles have been unevenly divided, and I end up with much the larger share of work to do. Don't laugh—that's not a joke. A man is so dreadfully alone. And so I smoke. May I offer you one?" And he held out his Russian nielloed case.

All his energies were fading; the only thing that grew stronger was the conviction that all this could not last long and that his demise was near. The strangest premonitions would come to him. Several times at the dinner table, the sensation had come over him that he was not sitting there with his family, but had drifted off to some hazy distance and was looking back at them.

I am going to die, he told himself, and one day he called Hanno in to him and said, "I can pass on sooner than we might think, my son. And then you must take my place. I was called to do just that early in life, too. What you must understand is that it's your indifference that torments me. Have you firmly resolved the matter? . . . Yes—yes. That's no answer. It's always the same—no real answer. I ask whether you've resolved to do it, with courage and joy in your heart. Do you suppose you have enough money and won't need to work? You'll have nothing, you'll be poor as a church mouse, you'll have to make your own way, all by yourself. And if you want to live, to live well, you'll have to work, to work long and hard, harder than I have."

But that was not all; what distressed him was no longer simply the worry about his son's or his firm's future. Something else, a new worry, descended on him, took hold of him, and drove his weary thoughts before it. Because, as soon as he began to think of the end of life as something more than a distant, theoretical, and minor necessity and regarded it, instead, as imminent and tangible, as something for which one must make immediate preparations, he began to brood, to search himself, to examine how things stood between him and death and what he thought about matters beyond this earthly life. And at his very first attempt to do so, what he found was hopeless immaturity and a soul unprepared for death.

Dogmatic faith in a fanatical biblical Christianity, which his father had been able to couple with a very practical eye for business and which his mother had then adopted later as well, had always been alien to him. All his life he had approached these first and last things with his grandfather's worldly skepticism; but his needs were too profound and too metaphysical for him to find genuine satisfaction in old Johann Buddenbrook's comfortable superficialities, and he had looked to history to answer the questions of eternity and immortality. He had told himself that he had lived in his ancestors and would continue to live in his descendants. The idea had fitted well with his sense of family, his patrician self-confidence, and his reverence for history; and it had also supported his ambitions and strengthened him as he went about the tasks of life. But now, as he gazed into the piercing eye of approaching death, it was apparent that such a view fell away to nothing, was incapable of providing him even an hour of calm or anything like readiness for death.

Although Thomas Buddenbrook had toyed with Catholicism all

his life, he was nevertheless imbued with a passionate Protestant's sense of responsibility—earnest, profound, remorseless, to the point of self-flagellation. No, when it came to the ultimate and highest questions, there was no help from outside—no mediation, no absolution, no soothing consolation. Every man had to untangle the riddle on his own, had to work diligently at it, at hot speed, all by himself; before it was too late, he must either achieve some clear readiness for death, or die in despair. And Thomas Buddenbrook turned away in hopeless disappointment from his only son, in whom he had hoped to live on, strong and rejuvenated, and began in haste and fear to seek for truth—which had to exist somewhere for him.

It was the middle of the summer of 1874. Silver-white, rounded clouds drifted in the deep blue sky above the delicate symmetry of the garden. In the branches of the walnut tree, birds were singing, their chirps ending in questions. The fountain splashed in the center of a wreath of tall, lavender-colored irises, and the scent of lilac was mixed, unfortunately, with a syrupy odor floating in on the warm breeze from a nearby sugar factory. To the amazement of his staff, the senator frequently left his office now in the middle of working hours and strolled about his garden, his hands behind his back; he would rake gravel, fish the algae from the fountain, or prune a rosebush. His face, with one pale eyebrow slightly lifted, was earnest and alert as he went about these tasks; but his thoughts were far away, following their own dark, arduous path.

Sometimes he sat down up on the little terrace, inside the pavilion, under the shade of its covering grapevines, and, without seeing anything, he would look out across the garden to the red-brick rear wall of his house. The air was warm and sweet, and it seemed as if the peaceful sounds all around spoke gently to him, trying to lull him to sleep. And now and then, weary from staring at nothing, from loneliness and silence, he would close his eyes—only to pull himself up with a jerk and hastily banish such tranquillity. "I must think," he said to himself, almost out loud, "I must put it all in order before it is too late."

But one day, in this same pavilion, he sat in his little yellow cane rocking chair, and with growing interest he read for four hours from a book that had come his way more or less by chance. Pausing in the smoking room for a cigarette after second breakfast, he had found it tucked in a corner of the bookshelf, behind a row of sturdy tomes, and recalled that he had bought it casually on sale at a bookshop years ago—a rather thick volume, poorly bound and badly printed on thin, yellowed paper, just the second half of a famous metaphysical system. He had taken it with him to the garden, and now, deeply engrossed, he turned page after page.

He was filled with an unfamiliar sense of immense and grateful contentment. He felt the incomparable satisfaction of watching an enormously superior intellect grab hold of life, of cruel, mocking, powerful life, in order to subdue and condemn it. What he felt was the satisfaction of a sufferer who has always known only shame and the bite of conscience for hiding the suffering that cold, hard life brings, and who now, suddenly, from the hand of a great and wise man, receives elemental, formal justification for having felt such suffering in this world—in this best of all possible worlds, which by means of playful scorn was proved to be the worst of all possible worlds.

He did not understand it all; some principles and premises remained unclear, and, not being a practiced reader of philosophy, he found he was unable to follow certain arguments. But it was precisely the alteration of light and darkness, of dull incomprehension, vague presentiments, and sudden enlightenment, that kept his breathless attention; and hours passed without his ever looking up from the book or even changing position in his chair.

At first he had left many pages unread and swiftly plunged ahead, hurrying unconsciously to find the main point, searching for what was important to him, absorbing only a paragraph here or there that happened to engross him. But then he came across a long chapter that he read from the first word to the last, with his lips tightly closed, his eyebrows pursed, concentrating—his face registering a total, almost deathlike look of earnest concentration—oblivious to every trace of life stirring around him. This chapter was entitled: "Concerning Death and Its Relation to the Indestructibility of Our Essential Nature."

He had only a few more lines to read when, at four o'clock, the maid came across the garden and announced dinner. He nodded, read the remaining sentences, closed the book, and looked about him. He felt his whole being somehow immensely broadened and filled with heavy, dark intoxication. He was dazed, felt totally inebriated by something so indescribably new, alluring, and full of promise that it reminded him of the first time he had felt the hopes and yearnings of love. As he put the book away in the drawer of the garden table, his hands were cold and unsteady. His head felt hot, and a strange pressure, a disquieting tension had built up inside it, as if something were about to burst. He couldn't complete a single thought.

"What was that?" he asked himself as he went into the house and climbed the main staircase to join his family in the dining room. "What happened to me? What did I learn? What did it say to me—to me, Senator Thomas Buddenbrook, head of the firm of Johann Buddenbrook, dealers in wholesale grain? Was it written for me? Can I bear what it says? I don't know what it was. I only know that it's too much, too much for my poor average brain."

For the rest of the day, he felt overwhelmed by this heavy, dark, unthinking intoxication. And when evening came he found he could no longer keep his head from nodding and went to bed early. He slept for three hours—a deep, sleep, immeasurably deep, unlike any he had ever known. He awoke abruptly with a delicious start, like a man awakening alone in his bed with love stirring in his heart.

He knew he was alone in the bedroom. Gerda slept in Ida Jungmann's room now, because the old woman had moved to one of the three rooms on the third floor to be closer to Johann. Darkest night reigned—the curtains at the high windows had been pulled tight. He lay on his back in the deep silence of the slightly oppressive sultry night air, and stared up at the ceiling.

But look—suddenly the darkness seemed to split open before his eyes, as if the velvet wall of night parted to reveal immeasurable deeps, an endless vista of light. "*I'm going to live!*" Thomas Buddenbrook said half aloud and felt his chest jolted by sobs somewhere deep inside. "That's it—I'm going to live. *It* is going to live . . . and thinking that it and I are separate instead of one and the same—that is the illusion that death will set right. That's it, that's it! But why?" He asked the question—and night closed over him again. And he perceived, he knew, he understood not one whit of it now and let his head sink back into the pillow, blinded and exhausted by that smidgen of truth he had been permitted to see.

And he lay there quietly in fervent expectation, was even tempted to pray for truth to return and illumine him again. And it did come. Not daring to stir, he lay there with his hands folded—and was allowed to watch.

What was death? The answer to the question came to him now, but not in poor, pretentious words—instead, he felt it, possessed it somewhere within him. Death was a blessing, so great, so deep that we can fathom it only at those moments, like this one now, when we are reprieved from it. It was the return home from long, unspeakably painful wanderings, the correction of a great error, the loosening of tormenting chains, the removal of barriers—it set a horrible accident to rights again.

An end, a dissolution? Empty words, and whoever was terrified by them was a pitiable wretch. What would end, what would dissolve? His body, his personality and individuality—this cumbersome, intractable, defective, and contemptible barrier to becoming something *different and better.*

Was not every human being a mistake, a blunder? Did we not, at the very moment of birth, stumble into agonizing captivity? A prison, a prison with bars and chains everywhere! And, staring out hopelessly from between the bars of his individuality, a man sees only the surrounding walls of external circumstance, until death comes and calls him home to freedom.

Individuality! Oh, what a man is, can, and has seems to him so poor, gray, inadequate, and boring. But what a man is not, cannot, and does not have—he gazes at all that with longing envy—envy that turns to love, because he fears it will turn to hate.

I bear within me the seed, the rudiments, the possibility of life's capacities and endeavors. Where might I be, if I were not here? Who, what, how could I be, if I were not me, if this outward appearance that is me did not encase me, separating my consciousness from that of others who are not me? An organism—a blind, rash, pitiful eruption of the insistent assertion of the will. Far better, really, if that will were to drift free in a night without time or space, than to languish in a prison cell lit only by the flickering, uncertain flame of the intellect.

And I hoped to live on in my son? In another personality, even weaker, more fearful, more wavering than my own? What childish, misguided nonsense! What good does a son do me? I don't need a son. And where will I be once I am dead? It's so dazzlingly clear, so overwhelmingly simple. I will be a part of all those who say, who have ever said, or will say "I": and, most especially, *a part of those who say it more forcibly, joyfully, powerfully.*

A boy is growing up somewhere in the world, and he is well equipped and well formed, capable of developing his talents, tall and straight and untroubled, pure and fierce and vigorous—just to look at him increases the joy of the joyful and drives the unhappy to despair. That boy is my son. *He is me*—or will be soon, soon, as soon as death frees me from this wretched delusion that I am not both him and me.

Have I hated life—this pure, fierce, and vital thing called life? What folly, what a misconception! I have only hated myself, because I could not bear life. But I love you all, I love you all, you happy joyous ones, and I shall soon cease to be excluded from you by this narrow cell; soon the part of me that loves you, my love for you, will be freed and be with you, become a part of you, be with and in you all.

He wept; he pressed his face into the pillow and wept. An intoxicating joy ran through him, lifted him up, and it was incomparably sweeter than the world's sweetest pain. This was it, this was the drunken darkness that had filled him since the afternoon, this was what had stirred in his heart in the middle of the night, awakening him, quickening like first love within him. And in being granted this understanding and realization—not in words and sequential thoughts, but in the sudden bliss of internal illumination—he was already free, was truly liberated from all natural and artificial bonds and barriers. The walls of his hometown, inside of which he had willingly, consciously locked himself, broke open now and he could gaze out into the world, the whole world, pieces of which he had seen in his youth, but which death now promised to give him whole and complete. The deceptive perceptions of space and time, and thus of history, his preoccupation with finding honorable historical continuity in his own descendants, the fear of some sort of ultimate, historical dissolution and disintegration—his mind let go of them all, and he was no longer hindered from understanding the constant flow of eternity. Nothing began and nothing ceased. There was only the endless present, and the energy within him, which loved life with such a painfully sweet, urgent, yearning love, and of which his own person was no more than an abortive expression—that energy would now know how to find access to the endless present.

"I am going to live," he whispered to his pillow. And he wept . . . and in the next moment he no longer knew why he wept. His brain stood still, his hard-won knowledge vanished, and suddenly there was nothing around him but darkness turned mute. "But it will come back," he assured himself. "Didn't I possess it?" And, sensing around him the irresistible shadows of sleep and numbness, he swore an oath never to let go of that immense joy, to gather all his energies, and to learn, to read, and to study, until he had made that view of the world—the source of all that he had felt—firmly and inalienably his own.

Except that it was not to be, and the next morning, when he awakened feeling slightly embarrassed by the intellectual extravagances of the night, he had an inkling of how impossible it would be to carry out his fine intentions.

He got up late and had to leave at once for a debate in the assembly. The public, political, and business affairs of life out in the gabled, narrow streets of this medium-size commercial town took hold again of his mind and energies. Still fully intending to read further from that wonderful book, he nevertheless began to ask himself whether his experiences of the previous night were truly something for him and of lasting value and whether, if death were to arrive, they would stand up to the practical test. His middle-class instincts were roused now—and his vanity as well: the fear of being seen as eccentric and ridiculous. Would such ideas really look good on him? Were they proper ideas for him, Senator Thomas Buddenbrook, head of the firm of Johann Buddenbrook?

He never managed to give the book another glance, despite the treasures buried inside—let alone to buy the other volumes of that magnum opus. The nervous pedantry that had taken control of him over the years devoured each new day. Harried by five hundred pointless, workaday trifles—just tending to them and keeping them all in order was a torment—he found himself too weak-willed to arrange his time reasonably and productively. And about two weeks after that remarkable afternoon, he had arrived at the point where he abandoned the whole idea and told the maid to fetch a book that for some reason was lying in the drawer of the garden table and put it back in the bookcase.

And so Thomas Buddenbrook, who had stretched his hands out imploringly for high and final truths, sank back now into the ideas, images, and customary beliefs in which he had been drilled as a child. He went about his day trying to remember the personal God, the Father of humankind, who had sent a part of Himself to earth so that He could suffer and bleed for us, who on the Last Day would call men to judgment and at whose feet the just would enter into eternity in recompense for their trials in this vale of woe—the whole rather vague and rather absurd story, which did not require that you understood it, but only obediently believed its abiding, childlike tenets, which would be there close at hand whenever the ultimate fear came over you.—Really?

Oh, he could find no peace in that, either. This man with his gnawing worries about the honor of his house, about his wife, his son, his good name, his family, this exhausted man, who with only the most painful, meticulous effort kept his body held erect and elegant—this same man tormented himself for several days with the question of how it actually worked: did the soul ascend to heaven immediately after death, or did eternal bliss first begin with the resurrection of the flesh? And where did the soul go until then? Had anyone ever said anything about it at school or in church? How could they justify leaving people in such uncertainty? And he was close to paying Pastor Pringsheim a visit and asking him for advice and consolation, until at the last moment he decided against it for fear of looking ridiculous.

Finally he gave up and left it all to God. But since he was so dissatisfied with his attempt to give some order to matters eternal, he decided at least he ought conscientiously to arrange his earthly affairs, in particular to take care of something he had long been planning to do.

As they were sitting in the living room one day, where they took their after-dinner coffee, little Johann heard his father tell his mother that he was expecting Dr. So-and-so, a lawyer, so that he could make his will—he really could not keep putting it off any longer. Later that afternoon, Hanno practiced his piano in the salon for an hour. Just as he was leaving and crossing the corridor, he met his father and a gentleman in a long black coat coming up the stairs.

"Hanno," the senator said curtly.

And little Johann stopped in his tracks, swallowed hard, and hastily answered softly, "Yes, Papa."

"I have some important work to do with this gentleman," his father continued. "Would you please stand just outside the door, here"—and he pointed to the smoking-room door—"and make sure that no one disturbs us? Do you hear? Absolutely no one."

"Yes, Papa," little Johann said and took his place outside the door after the two men closed it behind them.

He stood there, one hand holding the knot of his sailor's tie against his chest, his tongue scouring a tooth that he did not trust, and listened to the earnest, subdued voices coming from the room. His head was tilted to one side, and his light brown hair fell in curls over his temples; from beneath scowling eyebrows, he looked off to one side, frequently blinking his golden-brown eyes ringed with bluish shadows; and his face wore almost the same brooding, disgruntled expression it had worn the day he had stood beside his grandmother's casket and breathed in the fragrance of the flowers and that other, strange, and yet oddly familiar odor.

Ida Jungmann came by and said, "Hanno, my boy, where have you been? Why are you standing around here?"

The hunchbacked apprentice came up from the office, a telegram in hand, and asked for the senator.

And both times, little Johann stuck out his arm, so that his blue sailor sleeve with the embroidered anchors was a horizontal bar across the door. Both times, he shook his head and after a moment of silence said softly but firmly, "No one is allowed in. Papa is making his will."

6

AUTUMN CAME. And, rolling his beautiful eyes like a woman, Dr. Langhals said, "It's your nerves, Senator Buddenbrook—your nerves are the whole problem. And now and then your circulation leaves a little something to be desired. Might I make a suggestion? You should relax a little for the rest of the year. Those few Sundays in summer at the shore haven't been much help, of course. It's the end of September, and Travemünde is still operating. It hasn't emptied out entirely yet. You should go there, Senator, and sit on the beach for a while. Two or three weeks can set a great many things to rights."

And Thomas Buddenbrook said amen to that. But when he shared his decision with his family, Christian offered to accompany him.

"I'm coming along, Thomas," he said flatly. "I'm sure you have no objection." And although the senator actually had a great many, he once again said amen.

The fact was that Christian was now master of his own time more than ever; because of his precarious health, he had felt it necessary to give up his last commercial venture as an agent for champagne and cognac. The phantom gentleman who had sat on his sofa in the twilight and nodded to him had, fortunately, not returned. But that periodic "ache" in his left side had grown even worse, if that was possible—along with a great many other infirmities that Christian kept under careful observation and would describe with a wrinkled-up nose wherever he went. As in the past, the muscles that helped him swallow frequently did not work, and he would often sit there with his mouth full and let his little, round, deep-set eyes roam about. As in the past, he often suffered from the vague but unconquerable fear of a sudden paralysis of his tongue, throat, and extremities—even of his intellectual powers. Nothing, of course, ever became paralyzed. But was not the fear of such an event almost worse than the thing itself? He reported at length how one day he had been making tea and had held the lighted match over the open bottle of methylated alcohol instead of under the burner and had come close to sending not only himself to a ghastly death, but also the rest of the residents in his building—and perhaps a few in neighboring buildings as well. That was going too far. Making use of exhaustive and graphic detail in an effort to be understood, he was able to describe, however, a horrible anomaly which he had noticed of late, the nature of which was that on certain days—depending on the weather and his mood—he could not look at an open window without being overcome, for no reason whatever, by the urge to leap out of it—a savage instinct, a kind of mad and desperate foolhardiness that he found almost impossible to suppress. One Sunday, at dinner with his family on Fischer Grube, he described how it had taken all the moral energies at his disposal for him to creep on all fours to the open window and close it. General shrieks—and no one was willing to listen to any more.

He voiced these and similar symptoms with a certain horrified satisfaction. What he did not see—never noticed, because it was quite unconscious and therefore grew constantly worse—was the lack of tact that had come to characterize him with the passing years. It was bad enough that the anecdotes he told to his assembled family ought, at best, to have been restricted to the Club. But there were unmistakable signs that his sense of personal modesty was beginning to break down as well. For the purpose of showing his sister-in-law, Gerda, with whom he stood on friendly terms, the durable weave in his English socks and, by the way, just how skinny he had grown, he simply went ahead, with her sitting right there, and pulled his wide trouser leg clear up over his knee. "You see how skinny I am. Isn't that odd? I find it peculiar," he said gloomily, pointing with his wrinkled-up nose at his bony, badly bowed leg and scrawny knee, which made a woebegone knob in his white underwear.

He had, as noted, given up his commercial ventures; but he attempted to fill the hours of the day when he was not at the Club with various activities. And he loved to make a point of noting that, despite all his disabilities, he had never ceased to work entirely. He was constantly improving his knowledge of languages; recently, purely for scientific purposes and without any practical effect, he had attempted to learn Chinese—had worked very diligently at it for two weeks. At present he was busy "supplementing" an English-German dictionary that he considered inadequate. But since he needed a little change of scenery in any case, and because surely it was desirable for the senator to have some company, that particular task was not sufficient to keep him in town.

The two brothers drove to the shore along a road that was one vast puddle; and while rain drummed on the carriage top, they spoke scarcely a word. Christian's eyes wandered aimlessly, as if he were listening to something suspicious; Thomas sat muffled in his coat, shivering and gazing wearily ahead with red-rimmed eyes; the long, stiff tips of his mustache stuck out beyond his pallid cheeks. It was afternoon when they pulled up to the hotel gardens, their carriage wheels crunching in the soaked gravel. Old Siegismund Gosch the broker was sitting out on the glass veranda, drinking his rum grog. He stood up, hissing something between his teeth; and while their baggage was carried up to their rooms, the brothers sat down to join him in a warm drink.

Herr Gosch had stayed behind as a guest of the hotel, along with a few others—an English family, a Dutch maiden lady, and a bachelor from Hamburg—who were all presumably taking a nap before dinner, because the only sound breaking the deathly quiet was the splatter of rain. Let them sleep. Herr Gosch did not sleep during the day—he was glad if he could enjoy a few hours of oblivion at night. He was not doing well. He needed the curative sea air because of the trembling, the trembling in his limbs. Hell! He could barely hold on to his glass of grog, and—even worse, damn it—he could hardly write anymore, which meant that his translation of Lope de Vega's collected dramas was proceeding at a pitifully slow pace. He was very depressed, and even his blasphemies had no real joy in them. "Blast it all!" he said; this seemed to have become a favorite expression, because he repeated it constantly, and often in no particular context.

And the senator? How was he doing? How long were the gentlemen planning to stay?

Oh, Dr. Langhals had sent him for his nerves, Thomas Buddenbrook replied. He had obeyed his instructions, of course, despite the abominable weather—what didn't a man do out of fear of his physician. Actually, he was feeling rather miserable. So they would stay until he was better.

"Yes, and I'm feeling wretched myself," Christian said enviously, miffed that Thomas spoke only about himself; and he was just about to launch into descriptions of the man nodding on the sofa, the bottle of methylated alcohol, and the open window, when his brother stood up to go claim his room.

The rain did not let up. It made a muddle of the grounds and danced and bounded across the sea, which shuddered before the southwest wind and drew back from the beach. Everything was cloaked in gray. The steamers passed like phantoms and ghost ships and vanished toward the murky horizon.

Their only contact with other guests was at meals. The senator donned his mackintosh and galoshes and took long walks with Gosch the broker; Christian sat in the pastry shop with the girl who tended the counter and served him brandy smashes.

On two or three afternoons, when it looked as if the sun would break through, a few acquaintances from town appeared at dinner looking for a little amusement away from their families: Senator Gieseke, Christian's old schoolchum, and Consul Peter Döhlmann, who did not look well, either, and had been purging himself with far too much Hunyadi-Janos water. And then the gentlemen would sit in their overcoats under the pastry-shop awnings, facing the bandstand—although there was no longer any music—and drink their coffee and digest their five-course dinner as they chatted and gazed out at the autumnal gardens.

They talked about events in town: the recent flooding, which had spilled into a great many cellars and required people to use boats to get around in the low-lying streets; a major fire in the sheds down by the harbor; a senate election. Alfred Lauritzen, from the firm of

Stürmann & Lauritzen, wholesale and retail grocers, had been elected a few weeks before, and Senator Buddenbrook did not approve. He sat huddled in his caped coat, smoking cigarettes and joining in the conversation only to comment on this particular topic. He had not voted for Herr Lauritzen, he said, most definitely not. Lauritzen was an honest man and a splendid merchant, no question of that; but he was merely middle-class, solidly middle-class—why, his father had fished the pickled herring from the vat himself and wrapped them up in paper before handing them to cooks and housemaids. And so now they had the owner of a grocery shop in the senate. His, Thomas Buddenbrook's, grandfather had fallen out with his eldest son because the boy had "married a shop"—that's how things were in those days. "But standards are being lowered—yes, the general social *niveau* of the senate is on its way down. The senate is becoming democratized, my good Gieseke, and that is not good. Commercial competence isn't quite enough. In my opinion, we should not give up demanding a little more than that. The idea of Alfred Lauritzen with his big feet and boatswain's face sitting in the senate chambers offends me. I don't know why, but it offends something in me. It's a matter of decorum, it's simply in bad taste."

But Senator Gieseke was somewhat nettled. After all, he, too, was only the son of a fire chief. No, no—the only crown is the crown of merit. That was what it meant to be a republican. "And by the way, you shouldn't smoke so many cigarettes, Buddenbrook. What good do you get from the sea air?"

"Yes, I'm going to quit," Thomas Buddenbrook said, tossing the mouthpiece away and closing his eyes.

And while the rain inevitably picked up again and obscured the view, the conversation dragged sluggishly on. They got around to the latest scandal: some checks had been forged, and now Kassbaum, a wholesale merchant with P. Philipp Kassbaum & Co., was sitting behind bars. They were not outraged at all; Herr Kassbaum had simply made a foolish mistake—they laughed and shrugged their shoulders. Senator Gieseke told them that Kassbaum hadn't lost his sense of humor. He had no sooner arrived at his new residence than he had demanded a shaving mirror, since there was none in the cell.

"I'll not be here for years, but for years on end," he had remarked. Like Christian Buddenbrook and Andreas Gieseke, he had been a student of the late Marcellus Stengel.

Without any change of expression, the gentlemen laughed again through their noses. Siegismund Gosch ordered a grog with rum, but in a tone of voice that seemed to say, "What's the point in such a wretched life?" Consul Döhlmann was working hard on a bottle of aquavit, and Christian was back to brandy smashes, which Senator Gieseke had ordered for them both. It was not long before Thomas Buddenbrook lit another cigarette.

And the conversation returned again and again to business, how business was going for each of them, but the tone was languid, dismissive, skeptical, and nonchalant, their mood lethargic and indifferent after all the food and drink and rain. Even this theme failed to rouse anyone.

"Oh, there's not much pleasure in it," Thomas Buddenbrook said with a heavy sigh, laying his head back against his chair in disgust.

"Well, what about you, Döhlmann?" Senator Gieseke inquired with a yawn. "You've been busy almost exclusively with aquavit, I see."

"Where there's no smoke, there's no fire," the consul said. "I peek into the office every few days. Short hair is soon combed."

"And Strunck & Hagenström have all the important business in any case," Gosch remarked gloomily, his elbows spread wide on the table and his wicked old gray head propped in one hand.

"It's hard to outstink a pile of manure," Consul Döhlmann said with such studied vulgarity that his joyless cynicism only made them all the more gloomy. "Well, what about you, Buddenbrook—you doing anything these days?"

"No," Christian replied, "I can't work anymore." And, purely on the basis of his assessment of the general mood and a curious urge to make it worse, he pulled his hat down over his brow and suddenly proceeded to talk about his office in Valparaiso and Johnny Thunderstorm. "Ha, in *this* heat—good God! Work? No, sir, as you can see, sir." And then they had all blown cigarette smoke in the boss's face. "Good God!" And his face and gestures were absolutely perfect at expressing saucy defiance and good-hearted, lazy indolence. His brother did not stir.

After making an attempt to raise his grog to his mouth, Herr Gosch set it back on the table with a hiss and banged his unruly arm with a clenched fist; then he grabbed the glass again and brought it to his thin lips, spilling a good deal of it and downing the rest in one angry gulp.

"Oh, you and your shakes, Gosch," Döhlmann said. "You should just let yourself go the way I do. This damn Hunyadi-Janos water. I'm in such bad shape that I'll be at death's door if I don't drink a liter each day—and after I drink it, I really do feel like I'm at death's door. Do you know what it's like never to be able to pass your dinner—I mean once you've got it in your stomach?" And he treated them to several disgusting details, to all of which Christian Buddenbrook listened with gruesome interest and a wrinkled-up nose, and then countered with a brief, compelling description of his "ache."

It was raining harder than ever. It fell in thick sheets, and the sound filled the silence of the hotel gardens with an incessant, desolate, hopeless murmur.

"Yes, life is rotten," Senator Gieseke said—he had had a lot to drink.

"I've had enough of it," Christian said.

"Blast it all!" Herr Gosch said.

"Look, here comes Fika Dahlbeck," Senator Gieseke said.

She owned the cow barns, and as she passed by now with a pail of milk, she gave the gentlemen a smile. She was close to forty, plump, and sassy.

Senator Gieseke watched her with lascivious eyes. "What a chest!" he said. And this provided an opening for Consul Döhlmann to tell a very obscene joke—but once again the only response was brief, dismissive snorts of laughter.

Then the waiter standing nearby was called over.

"I've finished with this bottle, Schröder," Döhlmann said. "We might just as well pay up. We'll have to sooner or later. What about you, Christian? Ah, but of course Gieseke will be paying for yours."

Senator Buddenbrook came to life. He had been sitting there wrapped in his caped coat, his hands in his lap, a cigarette in one corner of his mouth, taking little or no part. But now he suddenly sat up and said gruffly, "Don't you have any money on you, Christian? Permit *me*, then, to lend you a little."

They opened their umbrellas and stepped out from under the awnings for a little stroll.

Now and then Frau Permaneder came to visit her brother. They would walk out to Seagull Rock or the Temple of the Sea together, which for some unknown reason always put Tony Buddenbrook in an excited and vaguely rebellious mood. She would repeatedly assert the freedom and equality of all men, dismissing class hierarchy out of hand, castigating privilege and the abuse of power, and expressly demanding that the only crown be the crown of merit. And then she would begin to talk about her life. And she could do that very well—much to her brother's amusement. During the course of her earthly sojourn, this fortunate creature had never once felt the need to swallow a defeat and overcome it in silence. Not one of life's insults or compliments had ever left her at a loss for words. No matter what she had received, every joy and every sorrow, she had given it back in a flood of banal and childishly self-important words, which she found perfectly adequate for what she needed to express. Her digestion was not as sound as it should be, but her heart was light and free—more than she even knew herself. Nothing left unsaid gnawed at her; no unspoken emotions weighed her down. And so she did not have to carry her past around with her. She knew that her troubled life had dealt her hard blows, but they had not left her weary or depressed in the least—ultimately she did not even believe any of it. But since they were publicly acknowledged facts, she used them—by boasting of them and speaking about them with a terribly serious face. She would slip into curses and in righteous outrage name the names of the people who had been detrimental to her life—and thus to the Buddenbrook family as a whole. With the passing of time, their number had become quite imposing. "Teary

Trieschke!" she cried, "Grünlich! Permaneder! Tiburtius! Weinschenk! Hagenström! The prosecutor! Severin! What scoundrels, Thomas. God will punish them one day, I firmly believe that!"

They climbed to the Temple of the Sea, arriving just as dusk was falling. Autumn had settled in now. And they stood in one of the little niches that faced the sea and gave off the same woody smell as the changing cabins at the pier. Its rough plank walls were full of carved inscriptions, initials, hearts, and poems. Standing side by side, they gazed down the wet green slope and across the narrow, rocky band of beach to the troubled, tossing sea.

"Broad the waves," Thomas Buddenbrook said, "ah, see them surging, watch them breaking, ever surging, ever breaking, on they come in endless rows, bleak and pointless, filled with woes. And yet there's something calming and comforting about them, too—like all things simple and necessary. I've learned to love the sea more and more—perhaps I preferred mountains at one time only because they were so much farther away. I wouldn't want to go there now. I think I would feel afraid and embarrassed. They're too arbitrary, too irregular, too diverse—I'm sure I'd feel overwhelmed. What sort of people prefer the monotony of the sea, do you suppose? It seems to me it's those who have gazed too long and too deeply into the complexity at the heart of things and so have no choice but to demand one thing from external reality: simplicity. It has little to do with boldly scrambling about in the mountains, as opposed to lying calmly beside the sea. But I know the look in the eyes of people who revere the one or the other. Happy, confident, defiant eyes full of enterprise, resolve, and courage scan from peak to peak; but when people dreamily watch the wide sea and the waves rolling in with mystical and numbing inevitability, there is something veiled, forlorn, and knowing about their eyes, as if at some point in life they have looked deep into gloomy chaos. Health or sickness—that is the difference. A man climbs jauntily up into the wonderful variety of jagged, towering, fissured forms to test his vital energies, because he has never had to spend them. But a man chooses to rest beside the wide simplicity of external things, because he is weary from the chaos within."

Frau Permaneder fell silent, feeling intimidated and uncomfortable, the way harmless people usually do when something fine and serious is said in the course of an ordinary conversation. "It's best not to say such things out loud," she thought, fixing her eyes firmly on the distance in order not to meet his gaze. And as a way of apologizing silently for feeling embarrassed for him, she drew his arm through hers.

7

WINTER HAD COME, Christmas was past—it was January of the year 1875. The snow on the sidewalks had become a firmly trodden mass of slush mixed with sand and ashes, and the high piles of it lining both sides of the streets were steadily turning grayer, growing more pockmarked and porous. There was thaw in the air. The cobblestones were wet and dirty, water dripped from the gray roofs—and above them the sky was a flawless pale blue. Millions of atoms of light seemed to flicker and dance like crystals in the azure air.

The center of town was lively and crowded—it was Saturday, market day. The butchers had set up their stalls under the pointed arches of the town-hall arcades, and they weighed their wares with bloody hands. The stalls of the fish market, however, had been grouped around the fountain out in the market square itself. And there plump women sat, burying their hands in fur muffs half smooth from wear and warming their feet at charcoal burners; they guarded their cold, wet prisoners and called out in broad accents, inviting the strolling cooks and housewives to buy. There was no danger of being cheated. You could be sure that you were buying fresh fish—almost all these fat, muscular fish were still alive. Some of them had it good. They swam about in the rather cramped quarters of buckets, true, but they seemed to be in fine spirits and enduring no hardships. Others lay there in agony on planks with ghastly goggly eyes and laboring gills, clinging to life and desperately flapping their tails until someone grabbed them and a sharp, bloody knife cut their throats with a loud crunch. Long, fat eels twisted about and contorted themselves into fantastic shapes. Deep vats teemed with blackish masses of Baltic shrimp. Sometimes a sturdy flounder would contract in a spasm of mad terror and flip off its plank, landing among the offal on the slippery cobblestones, so that its owner would have to run after it and scold it severely before returning it to the line of duty.

Around noon, there was a good deal of traffic on Breite Strasse. Schoolchildren with satchels on their backs came down the street, filling the air with laughter and chatter and throwing slushy snowballs at each other. Young commercial apprentices from good families, wearing Danish seaman's caps or clad elegantly in the latest English style and carrying portfolios, passed by with considerable dignity, proud of having escaped secondary school at last. Stolid, gray-bearded, and highly respectable citizens strode along tapping their walking sticks and turning staunchly National Liberal faces toward the glazed-tile façade of the town hall, before whose portal a double guard was posted—the senate was in session. Dressed in greatcoats and with weapons on their shoulders, two sentries paced the designated distance, striding resolutely through the filthy slush under their feet. They met at the middle of the main door, looked at one another, exchanged a verbal salute, and marched off again in opposite directions. Sometimes an officer would pass by in a greatcoat with an upturned collar, both hands in his pockets, hot on the heels of some sweet young shopgirl, but quite aware, too, of the admiring glances of the other young ladies from good families; and then each sentry would stand in front of his guardhouse, inspect himself from top to bottom, and present arms. It would be a good while yet before they would have to salute the senators as they left the building—the session was only forty-five minutes old. They would probably be relieved before then.

But then, suddenly one of the two sentries heard a short, discreet hissing sound from inside the building, and at almost the same moment he saw the flash of a red coat—bailiff Uhlefeldt, with his three-cornered hat and ceremonial sword, emerged, bustling with high officiousness, uttered a soft "Attention!," and hastily withdrew again, as approaching footsteps echoed across the tile floor inside.

The sentries came to attention—heels clicked, necks stiffened, chests expanded. They set their rifles at their sides, and then, with a few quick, snappy motions, they presented arms. A man of just barely average height strode between them in some haste; he tipped his hat slightly and raised one pale eyebrow—the tips of his long mustache extended out beyond his pallid cheeks. Senator Thomas Buddenbrook had left today's senate session long before adjournment.

He turned to the right, which meant he was not heading home. Correct, impeccably neat, and elegant, he walked along Breite Strasse with his characteristic, slightly skipping gait and was constantly forced to greet people as he went. He was wearing white kid gloves and carried his cane with its silver crook under his left arm. Bits of his white dress tie were visible under the thick lapels of his fur coat. He was carefully groomed as always, but he looked exhausted. As he passed, various people noticed that tears would suddenly well up in his eyes and that his lips were set tight, but in an odd, cautious, skewed sort of way. Sometimes he would swallow hard, as if his mouth were full of liquid, and they could tell from the muscles of his cheeks and temples that he was holding his jaw clenched tight.

"What's this, Buddenbrook, the senate's in session and you're playing hooky? Now, that's something new," said someone he had not seen coming, just as he reached the corner of Mühlen Strasse. And standing suddenly before him was Stephan Kistenmaker, his friend and admirer, who adopted Thomas's opinions in all matters of public interest as his own. His graying beard was cut round and full; he had terribly bushy eyebrows and a long, spongy nose. Several years before, he had retired with a tidy sum in his pocket and had left the wine business in the hands of his brother, Eduard. He now lived the life of a private gentleman, but was a little ashamed of the fact; and so he constantly pretended to have more to do than he could possibly keep up with. "I'm wearing out," he would say and stroke his hand across his graying hair, which he kept nicely waved with a curling iron. "But what's a man put on this earth for if not to wear out?" He would stand around on the floor of the exchange for hours on end, looking very important—although he had not the least business there. He was a member of a great many insignificant boards; recently he had got himself appointed director of the municipal swimming pool. He was a diligent juror, broker, trustee, estate executor—and he wiped the sweat from his brow.

"The senate's in session, Buddenbrook," he repeated, "and you're out taking a walk?"

"Oh, it's you," the senator said in a low voice, reluctantly moving his lips. "I'm in such terrible pain that I can't see much of anything for minutes on end."

"Pain? What sort of pain?"

"A toothache. I've had it since yesterday. I didn't sleep a wink last night. I haven't been to the dentist yet, because I had some business to take care of this morning and I didn't want to miss the session, either. But I couldn't stand it any longer. I'm on my way to see Brecht."

"Where exactly is the pain?"

"Here on the lower left. A molar. It's decayed, of course. It's unbearable. Adieu, Kistenmaker—you can understand that I'm in a hurry."

"Well, do you suppose I'm *not*? An awful lot to do. Adieu. And get well, by the way. Let him pull it. Get it out right now—that's always the best way."

Thomas Buddenbrook walked on, his jaw clenched tight—although that only made matters worse. It was a savage, searing, piercing pain, an ugly agony that had spread from the diseased molar to the whole lower left side of his jaw. The throbbing infection felt like little red-hot hammers; tears came to his eyes and his face was flushed with fever. The lack of sleep had been a terrible strain on his nerves. It had taken all he could do to pull himself together just now and keep his voice from breaking as he spoke.

On Mühlen Strasse, he entered a house painted a yellowish ocher and climbed to the second floor, where a brass plate on the door announced "Brecht, Dentist." He did not even see the maid who opened the door for him. The hallway was warm and smelled of steak and cauliflower. Suddenly he inhaled the acrid odor of the waiting room into which he was now ushered. "Take a seat. One moment, please!" an old woman screeched. It was Josephus, who was sitting at the back of his shiny cage, head tilted, staring at him with little, nasty, spiteful eyes.

The senator sat down at a round table and tried to enjoy the humor in a book of jokes and stories, but then shoved it away again in disgust; he pressed the cooling silver handle of his cane against his cheek, closed his burning eyes, and moaned. It was quiet all around him, except for the cracking, grinding sound Josephus made biting at the bars of his cage. Even when he wasn't busy, Herr Brecht thought it incumbent upon him to let his patients wait a little.

Thomas Buddenbrook quickly stood up and poured a glass of water from a carafe set out on a side table—it tasted and smelled of chloroform. Then he opened the door to the hallway and called out in an exasperated voice: if Herr Brecht had nothing more urgent to do, would he please be kind enough to hurry—he was in pain.

And, almost immediately, the dentist's salt-and-pepper mustache hooked nosed, and high bald forehead appeared in the door to the consulting room. "Next, please," he said. And Josephus screamed "Next, please." The senator accepted their invitation without smiling. "A bad case," Herr Brecht thought to himself and turned pale.

They both walked quickly across the bright room to the large, adjustable chair with head cushion and green plush armrests. It was placed directly in front of one of the two windows. As he eased himself into it, Thomas Buddenbrook briefly explained his problem, laid his head back, and closed his eyes.

Herr Brecht adjusted some screws on the chair and then set about examining the tooth with a little steel rod and a tiny mirror. His hand smelled of almond-scented soap, his breath smelled of steak and cauliflower.

"We must proceed to an extraction," he said after a bit, turning even paler.

"Then let us proceed," the senator said, closing his eyelids tighter still.

A pause followed. Herr Brecht set out some things on a low cabinet and assembled his instruments. Then he approached his patient once again.

"I'll paint it a little," he said. He began at once to put this decision into action, daubing the gum freely with a pungent liquid. And then, in a low voice, he implored Herr Buddenbrook to sit still and open his mouth wide—and went to work.

Thomas Buddenbrook grasped the velvet armrests firmly with both hands. He barely felt the forceps take hold of the tooth, but then he heard a crunching sound in his mouth and felt a growing pressure inside his head, felt the maddening pain intensify—and he knew that everything was going as it should.

"Thank God," he thought, "it will all take its course now. This will get worse and worse and rage out of control until I can't bear it anymore, and then comes the real catastrophe and an insane, screaming, inhuman pain will rip my entire brain to shreds. And then it will be over. I just have to hold on."

It took three or four seconds. Herr Brecht quivered with the exertion, and Thomas Buddenbrook could feel the tremor pass through his whole body; he was pulled up out of his chair a little and heard a soft squeak coming from somewhere deep in the dentist's throat. Suddenly there was a violent jerk, a jolt—it felt as if his neck had been broken—and one short loud crack. He quickly opened his eyes. The pressure was gone, but his whole head throbbed, and hot pain raged in his inflamed and maltreated jaw; and he felt quite clearly that this had not been what was intended, that this was not the solution to his problem, but simply a premature catastrophe that had only made matters worse.

Herr Brecht had stepped back. Looking like death itself, he leaned against his instrument cabinet and said, "The crown—I thought so."

Thomas Buddenbrook spat a little blood into the blue bowl beside him—his gum was gashed. Then he asked, half unconscious now, "What did you think? What about the crown?"

"The crown has broken off, Senator Buddenbrook. I was afraid it would. The tooth is in extraordinarily bad condition. But it was my duty to risk the try."

"And now what?"

"Leave it all to me, senator."

"What has to be done?"

"We have to extract the roots. By prying them out with a lever. There are four of them."

"Four? Which means that you'll have to pry and pull four times?"

"Unfortunately."

"Well, I've had enough for today," the senator said and thought about getting up, but then stayed seated all the same and laid his head back. "My dear sir, you mustn't demand the impossible from me," he continued. "I'm not all that steady on my feet as it is. I've had it for now, at any rate. Would you please be kind enough to open the window there for a moment?"

Herr Brecht did as he was asked, and then responded, "It would be perfectly fine with me, Senator Buddenbrook, if you came by any time tomorrow or the day after. We can put off the operation until then. I must admit that I myself am . . . Well, if you'll permit me, I'll rinse it out and paint it a little with something to help ease the pain for now."

He performed his rinsing and painting, and the senator got up to leave. Pale as death, Herr Brecht accompanied him to the door and gave a little compassionate shrug that cost him the last bit of energy he still had.

"One moment, please!" Josephus squawked as they crossed the waiting room, and he went on screeching the same words as Thomas Buddenbrook descended the stairs.

Pry the roots out with a lever—yes, yes, well, that was tomorrow. And now? Just go home and rest, try to sleep a bit. The pain in the nerves themselves had been numbed for now; there was only a dark, heavy burning sensation in his mouth. So go on home.—And he walked slowly along the street, mechanically returning the greetings people extended to him, but with a vague, bemused look in his eyes, as if he were preoccupied with how wretched he actually felt.

He reached Fischer Grube and started down the sidewalk on the left. He had gone about twenty steps when he suddenly felt nauseated. "I'd better stop in that tavern over there and have a brandy," he thought and stepped out into the street. But when he was just about in the middle, something happened. It was exactly as if someone had taken hold of his brain and with incredible force started swinging it in wide concentric circles that grew smaller and smaller, so that it picked up speed, frightening speed, as it whirled around and around, until at last it crashed with tremendous, brutal, merciless force against the stone-hard center of the circle. He turned halfway around, and then, raising his arms, he fell forward onto the wet pavement.

Since the street sloped steeply downhill, his head lay a good deal lower than his feet. He had fallen face-down, and a puddle of blood immediately began to form around his head. His hat rolled off down the street a little way. His fur coat was splattered with muck and slush. His outstretched hands in their white kid gloves had come to rest in a puddle.

There he lay, and he went on lying there until some people happened by and turned him over on his back.

8

GATHERING THE FRONT of her skirt in one hand and pressing her large brown muff to her cheek with the other, Frau Permaneder climbed the main staircase. She lunged and stumbled up the stairs more than she climbed them—the hood of her cloak sat wildly askew, her cheeks were flushed, and little beads of sweat had formed on her slightly protruding upper lip. Although she met no one, she never stopped talking as she sped up the stairs, and now and then, as she suddenly lurched ahead, her whispers would erupt in audible words that betrayed her fears. "It's nothing," she said. "It doesn't mean anything. The Lord can't want this—He knows what He's doing. I firmly believe *that*. It's nothing serious. Oh, dear God, I'll pray every day." Fear had her babbling pure nonsense as she took the stairs to the third floor and rushed down the hall.

The door to the antechamber was wide open and her sister-in-law came toward her. Gerda Buddenbrook's beautiful white face was twisted with horror and revulsion, and her close-set brown eyes ringed with bluish shadows blinked back tears of anger, bewilderment, and disgust. When she saw Frau Permaneder, she beckoned to her with outstretched arms; they embraced and Gerda buried her head on Tony's shoulder.

"Gerda, Gerda, what is it?" Frau Permaneder cried. "What's happened? What does it all mean? They told me he fell—and he's unconscious? How is he? The Lord can't want the worst to happen. Tell me, for pity's sake, tell me."

She received no immediate reply, but she could feel Gerda's whole body swell with a shudder. She managed to catch something of what the voice was whispering at her shoulder.

"You can't believe how he looked when they brought him in. No one has ever seen even a speck of dust on him, he never allowed that, his whole life long. What vile, insulting mockery for it to end like *this*."

They heard muffled sounds—the door to the dressing room was standing open now. In the doorway stood Ida Jungmann in a white apron, a basin in her hand. Her eyes were red. When she saw Frau Permaneder, she stepped back to make way for her and lowered her head. Her chin was pursed and trembling.

The long flowered curtains stirred in the draft as Tony entered the bedroom, followed by her sister-in-law. The odors of carbolic acid, ether, and other medicines wafted toward them. Thomas Buddenbrook lay in the broad mahogany bed under a red quilt; his clothes had been removed and he was dressed in an embroidered nightshirt. His glazed, half-open eyes were rolled back, and his lips moved in a silent babble under his mustache. Now and then gurgling sounds came from his throat. Young Dr. Langhals bent down over him, removed a bloody bandage from his face, and dipped a fresh one in a basin sitting on the nightstand. Then he listened to his patient's chest and felt his pulse. Little Johann was sitting on the laundry basket at the foot of the bed, playing with the knot of his sailor's tie and listening with a bemused expression to the sounds his father made behind him. Thomas's muddy clothes lay draped over a chair off to one side.

Crouched beside the bed, Frau Permaneder stared at her brother's face and took his hand—it was cold and heavy. She began to comprehend that, whether the Lord knew what He was doing or not, He evidently wanted "the worst."

"Tom!" she wailed. "Don't you know me? How do you feel? Do you want to leave us? You won't leave us, will you? Oh, it *can't* be!"

There was no response that could have been taken for an answer. She looked up imploringly at Dr. Langhals. He stood there with his beautiful eyes cast down, and his whole manner said, not without a certain smugness, that all this was God's will.

Ida Jungmann came back in to help in any way she could. Old Dr. Grabow appeared in person. He made a long, kind face, shook hands with everyone, regarded the patient, shook his head, and proceeded to do exactly what Dr. Langhals had done. The news had spread like wildfire through the whole town. The bell in the vestibule below kept ringing and ringing, and even from up here in the bedroom they could hear people asking how the senator was. His condition was unchanged, unchanged—they were all given the same answer.

Both doctors were of the opinion that in any case a nurse should be brought in for the night. They sent for Sister Leandra, and she came. There was no trace of surprise or horror on her face as she entered the room. As always, she quietly put aside her leather handbag, cap, and cape and went to work in her gentle, friendly way.

Little Johann sat on the laundry basket hour after hour, watching it all, listening to each gurgling sound. Actually, he should have left for his private mathematics lesson, but he realized that this was an event before which the men in worsted suits would have to fall silent. He thought briefly of his homework, too, and dismissed it with contempt. Whenever Frau Permaneder came over and pressed him to her, he would shed tears; most of the time, however, he simply sat there staring straight ahead, blinking now and then, but with dry eyes and a revolted, preoccupied look on his face. He was breathing cautiously, as if he expected to smell that odor, that strange and yet so oddly familiar odor.

Around four o'clock, Frau Permaneder came to a decision. She led Dr. Langhals into the next room, crossed her arms, and laid her head back, trying at the same time to press her chin against her chest.

"Doctor," she said, "there is one thing in your power to do, and I beg you now to do it. Tell me the unvarnished truth. I am a woman who has been steeled by life. I have learned how to bear the truth, believe me. Will my brother live until tomorrow or not? You may speak frankly."

And Dr. Langhals turned his beautiful eyes away, inspected his fingernails, and remarked how impossible it was for a frail human to answer the question whether Frau Permaneder's brother would survive the night or be called to his reward within the next few minutes.

"Then I know what I must do," she said. She left the room and sent for Pastor Pringsheim.

And he appeared, in a long robe but without his clerical ruff, threw Sister Leandra a cold glance, and sat down in the chair that someone had pulled over to the bed. He asked the patient to recognize him and give ear to his words; but, seeing that this request had borne no fruit, he now turned directly to God, addressing Him in his stylized Franconian dialect and modulating his voice, now darkening the vowels, now accenting them abruptly, while fanatical solemnity and radiant transfiguration played across his face. And whenever he rolled his "r" in his peculiar oily, urbane fashion, Johann had the vivid impression that Pastor Pringsheim had just finished his coffee and buttered rolls.

He said that neither he nor the others here assembled any longer importuned for this dear and precious life, for they saw that it was the Lord's holy will to take it unto Him. They prayed only for the mercy of a gentle passing. And then, after reciting, with striking expressiveness, two prayers appropriate to the occasion, he stood up. He pressed Gerda Buddenbrook's hand, then Frau Permaneder's, held little Johann's head between both hands, and, quivering with sorrow and sincerity, gazed at the boy's lowered eyelashes for a good minute; he greeted Fräulein Jungmann, let his eyes pass coldly over Sister Leandra one last time, and departed.

Dr. Langhals had gone home for a while, but when he returned he found everything as before. He held a brief discussion with the nurse and then took his leave. Dr. Grabow looked in again as well, attended to what could be attended to with a kindly face, and left. Thomas Buddenbrook's eyes were still glazed, and he continued to move his lips and make gurgling sounds. Dusk fell. The soft red glow of winter twilight shone through the window and fell on the muddy clothes draped over a chair in one corner of the room.

At five o'clock, Frau Permaneder impetuously let her feelings get the better of her. She was sitting on the bed opposite her sister-in-law, and suddenly, putting her throaty voice to use, she folded her hands and began to speak the words of a hymn—very loudly. "Bring now, O Lord," she said—and they all sat there rigid, listening—"an ending, to all his pain and woe; Thy strength and mercy sending, the grace of death bestow. . . ." But she was praying with such heartfelt intensity and was so caught up in each word she spoke that she did not stop to think that she did not even know the whole verse—by the third line she was hopelessly stuck. She recited it, and then, with her voice still raised, she broke off and substituted a dignified pose for the final lines. Cringing with embarrassment, everyone in the room waited for her to finish. Johann cleared his throat so loudly that it sounded like a groan. And then the only sound to break the silence was Thomas Buddenbrook's agonized gurgling.

It came as a relief when the maid announced that she had brought up something to eat. But as they sat in Gerda's bedroom and began to spoon their soup, Sister Leandra appeared at the door and beckoned them with a friendly gesture.

The senator was dying. He sobbed softly two or three times, then fell silent, and his lips stopped moving. That was the only observable change—his eyes had been dead all along.

Dr. Langhals arrived within a few minutes; he put his black stethoscope to the corpse's chest, listened for a while, and, having completed his conscientious examination, said, "Yes, it's over."

Sister Leandra carefully closed the dead man's eyes with the forefinger of her pale, gentle hand.

Then Frau Permaneder fell to her knees beside the bed, pressed her face into the quilt, and wept loudly; holding nothing back and surrendering herself completely to her emotions, she gave vent to one of those refreshing outbursts that she was fortunate enough always to have at the ready. When she stood up again, her face was wet with tears, but she was fortified, relieved, and at perfect peace with herself—and she immediately realized that death announcements would have to be prepared in great haste. An immense number of elegantly printed death announcements needed to be mailed right away.

Christian now appeared on the scene. What had happened was this: He had been at the Club when he heard the news of the senator's collapse, and he had left at once—but then, out of fear of the horrible sight that might await him, he had taken a long walk beyond the town gates, and no one had been able to find him. He had decided to come all the same, but as he stepped into the entrance hall, he learned that his brother had just died.

"It's not possible," he said and limped up the stairs while his eyes wandered in all directions.

There he stood beside the deathbed, between his sister and sister-in-law—stood there with his bald head, sunken cheeks, drooping mustache, and immense hooked nose. He stood there on bowed legs, bent in a kind of question mark, and his little, deep-set eyes gazed at his brother's face—and it was so silent, cold, dismissive, and impeccable, so totally beyond all human reproach. The corners of Thomas's mouth were drawn down, lending him an almost contemptuous look. The man who Christian had predicted would not weep for him when he died, now lay dead—had simply died without saying a word, had wrapped himself in elegant and unruffled silence, and, as so often before, with no sympathy for anyone else, had left them all helpless in their shame. He had always shown nothing but cold disdain for Christian's sufferings—his "ache," the nodding man, the methylated alcohol, the open window. Had that been fair of him, or contemptible? But the question melted away now, had become meaningless, because death, choosing sides as it always did in its willful and unpredictable fashion, had chosen and vindicated him, accepted him, taken him in, bestowed great dignity upon him, and imperiously made him the center of general if reticent interest. Whereas death had scorned Christian and would only continue to tease him with fifty little tricks and pranks that would command no one's respect. Never had Thomas Buddenbrook so impressed his brother as at this moment. Success is everything. Only death dignifies our sufferings in the eyes of others; death exalts even the most trifling of sufferings. "You've won—I give up," Christian thought, and with a quick, awkward motion he let himself down on one knee and kissed the cold hand lying on the quilt. Then he stepped back and began to pace the room, while his eyes wandered here and there.

Other visitors arrived—the old Krögers, the Ladies Buddenbrook from Breite Strasse, old Herr Marcus. Even poor Klothilde came, stood there gaunt and ash-gray beside the bed, and folded her hands in their worsted gloves; at last, with a face betraying no emotion, she said in her drawling, whining voice, "Tony, Gerda, you mustn't think I'm coldhearted just because I'm not crying. I have no tears left." And they all believed every word—she was so hopeless, dusty, and withered.

Finally they left the room to make way for an old woman, a disagreeable creature, who kept rubbing her toothless gums together and had come to help Sister Leandra wash and dress the body.

IT WAS LATE in the evening, but Gerda Buddenbrook, Frau Permaneder, Christian, and little Johann were still sitting in the living room, at the round table, hard at work by the light of the large overhead gas lamp. Their task was to prepare a list of people who would receive death announcements and to address the envelopes. Pens scratched. Now and then someone had an inspiration and added a new name to the list. Even Hanno had to help—time was short, and his handwriting was neat and legible.

It was quiet in the house and out on the street. Only seldom did they hear footsteps, which then echoed away. The gas lamp spluttered softly, someone muttered a name, paper rustled. Occasionally they would all look at one another and suddenly recall what had just happened.

Frau Permaneder scribbled away busily. But every five minutes, almost as if she were timing it, she would lay her pen down, press her hands together, bring them up to her mouth, and break into a lament. "I can't comprehend it," she cried—indicating that she had indeed gradually begun to comprehend what had really happened. "It's all over now!" she cried out quite unexpectedly in absolute despair, weeping loudly as she wrapped her arm around her sister-in-law's neck. And, with renewed strength, she then went back to work.

Christian was in much the same state as poor Klothilde. He had not shed a single tear and was a little ashamed of the fact. His sense of shame outweighed everything else he felt. His constant preoccupation with his own condition, with his physical and mental quirks, had left him exhausted and lethargic. Now and then he would sit up straight and rub his hand across his bald head and say in a choked voice, "Yes, it's terribly sad." He said this to himself, as a kind of stern reprimand, and forced his eyes to moisten a little.

Suddenly something happened that upset them all. Little Johann began to laugh. He had come across a name with a curious sound to it—it was just too irresistible. He repeated it with a snort, bent forward, began to shake, to gasp for air, and could no longer contain himself. At first they convinced themselves that he was crying; but that was not the case. The adults looked at him in bewildered incredulity. Then his mother sent him to bed.

9

A TOOTH—Senator Buddenbrook had died of a toothache, that was the word around town. But, confound it all, people didn't die of that! He had been in pain, Herr Brecht had broken off the crown, and afterward he had simply collapsed on the street. Had anyone ever heard the like?

But it made no difference now, that was *his* problem. The first thing that had to be done, however, was to send wreaths—large wreaths, expensive wreaths, wreaths that would do a person credit, that would be noted in newspaper articles and that showed they came from people with loyal hearts and substantial incomes. And they were sent, they poured in from all sides, from public organizations and families and individuals: laurel wreaths, wreaths of fragrant flowers, silver wreaths with black bows or bows in the town colors, with dedications printed in black or gold letters. And palm fronds, huge arrays of palm fronds.

All the flower shops were doing business on a grand scale, and Iwersen's, directly across from the Buddenbrook home, was doing as well as any. Frau Iwersen rang the vestibule bell several times a day and brought floral arrangements of various sorts—from Senator So-and-so, from this organization or that. On one such visit she asked if she might perhaps go upstairs for a moment and see the senator? Yes, she was told, she might, and, following Fräulein Jungmann, she climbed the main staircase, not saying a word, but letting her eyes glide softly over its polished opulence.

She climbed the stairs heavily—she was expecting, as usual. Over the years her looks had grown a bit more common, but her narrow black eyes and those Malaysian cheekbones were still attractive, and it was quite apparent that she must have been extraordinarily pretty at one time. She was admitted into the salon, where Thomas Buddenbrook had been laid out.

There, in the middle of the large and well-lighted room, from which the furniture had been removed, he lay clad in white silk, covered in white silk, bedded on the white silk pillows of his casket, and the strong, numbing potpourri of tuberoses, violets, and other flowers filled the room. At his head, at the center of a semicircle of branched silver candlesticks, stood Thovaldsen's Christ mounted on a pedestal hung with black crape. The floral arrangements—wreaths, baskets, and bouquets—had been placed along the walls, set out on the floor, or strewn over his silken coverlet; palm fronds rested against the bier, some of them hanging low over the dead man's feet. His face was abraded in places; the nose in particular looked badly bruised. But his hair had been trimmed just as he had always worn it in life, and Herr Wenzel had used a curling iron to set and curl his mustaches, so that they extended well beyond his white cheeks. His head was turned a little to one side and an ivory cross had been placed between his folded hands.

Frau Iwersen held back at the door, staring across the room to the bier. But then Frau Permaneder appeared—veiled in black and sniffling from much weeping. Pulling aside the portieres, she entered from the living room and gently bade Frau Iwersen to come nearer—and only then did she risk moving out a little farther across the parquet floor. She stood there with her hands folded across her protruding stomach, and her narrow black eyes took it all in: the flowers, the candlesticks, the bows, the white silk, and Thomas Buddenbrook's face. It would have been difficult to put a name to this pale pregnant woman's blurred expression. Finally she said, "Yes . . ."; gave one—just one—brief, suppressed sob, and turned to go.

Frau Permaneder loved these visits. She never left the house; with untiring devotion she supervised the demonstrations of respect that people felt they needed to show her brother's mortal remains. Again and again, she would read aloud in her throaty voice the newspaper articles that paid tribute to his accomplishments—just as they had on the occasion of the firm's centennial, except that now they also lamented the loss of such an important man. She sat in the living room to receive all the visitors who came to pay their condolences, after Gerda had greeted them in the salon—and there was no end of visitors, legions of them. She conferred with various people about arrangements for the funeral. She arranged the scenes of farewell. She invited the office personnel upstairs to say a final goodbye to their boss. And the warehouse workers had to come as well. Shuffling their big feet across the parquet floor, they filed in with the corners of their mouths turned down, expressing vast integrity, and exuding the odors of brandy, chewing tobacco, and physical labor. They stared at the ostentatious funerary display, at first in amazement and then with increasing boredom; they fidgeted with their caps in their hands, until one of them found the courage to depart, and then the whole troop shuffled out behind him. Frau Permaneder was enchanted. She claimed she had seen several of them with tears trickling down into their bristly beards. This was simply not true. It had not happened. But what did it matter, if she chose to see it that way, if it made her happy?

The day of the burial drew near. The metal casket was hermetically sealed and covered with flowers, the candles were lit, and the house filled up with people. Pastor Pringsheim stood at the head of the casket, erect and majestic, his expressive head resting on his wide ruff as if it were a plate.

A well-trained butler, something between a waiter and a majordomo, had been hired to oversee the ceremonies. Top hat in hand, he ran down the staircase on soft soles, and in a piercing whisper he called out across the entrance hall filled to overflowing with uniformed civil servants from the tax office and grain haulers in blouses, knee breeches, and top hats: "The rooms are full, but there's still a little space left along the corridor."

Then everything was silent. Pastor Pringsheim began to speak, and his elegant voice filled the whole house with sonorous, well-modulated tones. He stood there beside the figure of Christ, wringing his hands before his face or spreading them wide in blessing, while down below, in front of the house, the hearse drawn by four horses waited under the winter sky, and, behind it, a long row of carriages that reached all the way down the street to the river. Facing the door were two rows of soldiers, rifles resting at their sides; Lieutenant von Throta stood at the head of the company, his drawn sword held in his arm, his glowing eyes fixed on the bay window upstairs. A great many people craning their necks filled the street below or watched from windows all around.

Finally there was a stir in the vestibule, the lieutenant's shouted command rang out, the soldiers presented arms with a loud crack, Herr von Throta lowered his sword; the casket appeared. Borne by four men in black coats and three-cornered hats, it swayed gently out the front door. A gust of wind carried the scent of flowers across the curious crowd, ruffled the black plumes atop the hearse, tossed the manes of all the horses in the long line stretching down to the river, and tugged at the black ribbons fixed to the hats of the coachman and his grooms. A few straggling snowflakes descended from heaven in great, slow arcs.

The horses of the funeral coach were shrouded in black, with only their restless eyes visible. They slowly began to move, led by the four black grooms; the military closed in behind them, and now the rest of the coaches pulled up, one after another. Christian Buddenbrook climbed into the first with the pastor. Little Johann followed in the next, together with his well-fed relatives from Hamburg. And now, as the flags flying at half-mast on all the buildings flapped in the wind, Thomas Buddenbrook's funeral procession wound its slow, long, sad, solemn way through the streets. The civil servants and grain haulers marched on foot.

Followed by a host of mourners, the casket moved down the paths of the cemetery, past crosses, statues, chapels, and bare weeping willows, and approached the Buddenbrook family vault, where the guard of honor stood waiting and presented arms anew. From behind some shrubs came the muted, heavy rhythms of a dirge.

Once again the large stone cover with the chiseled family crest had been pushed aside, and once again the town's gentry gathered at the edge of the leafless woods and looked down into the brickwork abyss into which Thomas Buddenbrook was now lowered to join his parents. There they stood, these gentlemen of accomplishment and wealth, their heads lowered or held mournfully to one side—the legislators among them identifiable by their white gloves and neckties. And behind them stood the throng of civil servants, grain haulers, office-workers, and warehouse hands.

The music ceased; Pastor Pringsheim spoke. And as his benediction died away in the cool air, they all lined up for a final handshake with the deceased's brother and son.

It was a tedious formality. Christian Buddenbrook received all expressions of sympathy with the same half-distracted, half-embarrassed look he adopted on all solemn occasions. Dressed in his thick pea-jacket with gold buttons, little Johann stood beside him, his eyes ringed with bluish shadows and fixed on the ground; he never looked directly at anyone, but kept his head held on a slant, braced against the wind, a wry, hurt look on his face.

PART ELEVEN

(Dedicated to my friend Otto Grautoff)

1

SOMETIMES WE HAPPEN to recall someone, think of her, and wonder how she is doing, and suddenly we remember that she is no longer to be found strolling about the streets, that her voice is no longer part of the general chorus, that she has simply vanished from the arena of life and now lies beneath the earth somewhere out beyond the town gates.

Madame Buddenbrook, née Stüwing, Uncle Gotthold's widow, was dead. Death had likewise placed its seal of reconciliation and transfiguration upon the brow of this woman, who had once been the cause of heated argument within the family. But as her three daughters, Friederike, Henriette, and Pfiffi, received their relatives' condolences, they felt perfectly justified in drawing long, indignant faces, as if to say: "You see, your persecution has finally sent her to her grave." Although their mother had lived to a ripe old age.

Madame Kethelsen had gone to her rest as well. Having spent her last years tormented by gout, she had passed on gently, simply, firm in her childish faith and envied by her educated sister, who still had to do battle with rationalist doubts now and then, and who, although she had grown ever more hunchbacked and tiny, was bound to this sinful earth by a rugged constitution.

Consul Peter Döhlmann had been called home, too. He had consumed his entire fortune at the breakfast table. Finally succumbing to Hunyadi-Janos water, he had left his daughter an annuity of two hundred marks a year and relied on general respect for the name Döhlmann to ensure that she would be admitted into the Johannis Cloister.

Justus Kröger had also gone to his reward. That was unfortunate, because now no one could prevent his weak-willed wife from selling the last of the family silver in order to send money to degenerate Jakob, who was still leading a dissolute life out in the world somewhere.

As for Christian Buddenbrook one would have searched in vain for him around town—he no longer dwelt within its walls. Less than a year after the death of his brother, the senator, he had moved to Hamburg, and there, before the eyes of God and man, he had married a lady with whom he had long been on close terms, one Fräulein Aline Puvogel. No one had been able to stop him. What sums he had not already spent of his mother's inheritance—half the interest from which had always found its way to Hamburg—were now administered by Herr Stephan Kistenmaker, who had been appointed to that office by his deceased friend's will. But in all other matters, Christian was now his own master. As soon as rumors of the marriage reached her, Frau Permaneder wrote a long and extraordinarily hostile letter to Aline Buddenbrook of Hamburg, beginning with the salutation, "Madame!" and declaring in deftly poisoned words that she, Frau Permaneder, had no intention of ever recognizing either the addressee or her children as members of the family.

Herr Kistenmaker was the executor of the will, the administrator of the Buddenbrook estate, and the guardian of little Johann—and he held all three offices with great dignity. They vested him with very important responsibilities and allowed him to move about the exchange with all the hallmarks of overwork, including rubbing his hand through his hair and assuring one and all that he was wearing out. Nor ought it to be forgotten that for his administrative efforts he drew a salary, paid quite punctually, of two percent of the estate's revenues. On the whole, however, he was not very successful at his tasks and very soon incurred the wrath of Gerda Buddenbrook.

The situation was this: everything was to be liquidated and the firm dissolved, within one year. That was the senator's testamentary wish. Frau Permaneder responded to this with violent emotion. "And Johann, little Johann? What about Hanno?" she asked. She was disappointed—indeed, deeply hurt—by the idea that her brother had passed over his son and sole heir, that he had not wished to keep the firm going for his sake. She spent many hours weeping over it, because it meant that the firm's venerable shield, a treasure handed down over four generations, would have to be disposed of, that its history would come to an end—even though there was a legitimate heir. But then she found comfort in telling herself that the end of the firm was not the same as the end of the family, that her nephew would simply have to begin a fresh, new enterprise that would allow him to follow his high calling—which was to carry on the name of his forebears in proud splendor and to bring the family to a second flowering. It was not for nothing that he looked so much like his great-grandfather.

And so, under the direction of Herr Kistenmaker and old Herr Marcus, the firm began to be liquidated—and things went from bad to worse. The prescribed period was very limited, but it had to be observed to the letter and time was growing short. Pending business contracts were sold off much too quickly and on disadvantageous terms. One hasty and unprofitable sale followed another. The warehouses and stored grain were sold off at a considerable loss. And what didn't fall to Herr Kistenmaker's excess of zeal was ruined by old Herr Marcus's procrastination. Word around town had it that the old man carefully warmed not just his overcoat and hat beside the stove before going out in winter, but his walking stick as well. And if an opportunity for selling at a profit did present itself, he was sure to let it slip past. In short, the losses piled up. Thomas Buddenbrook's estate had been valued on paper at 650,000 marks. Within a year after the reading of the will, it was clear that nothing even close to that sum could be reckoned with.

Vague, exaggerated rumors began to circulate about this unprofitable liquidation, and they were fed by reports that Gerda Buddenbrook was thinking of selling her grand home. There were marvelous stories about why she was forced to do so, about how the Buddenbrook fortune was dwindling away to nothing. And so, gradually, a general mood began to spread through the town, and its effects soon reached the widow Buddenbrook's household itself—at first much to her amazement and dismay, and then to her growing indignation. One day Frau Permaneder's sister-in-law greeted her with the news that several repairmen and suppliers of household goods had been pressing her, Gerda Buddenbrook, in the most improper fashion, to settle some large accounts—and Tony stood there frozen in place for a while before breaking into dreadful laughter. Gerda Buddenbrook was so furious that she even mentioned the half-formed notion of taking little Johann, leaving town, and moving back to live with her old father in Amsterdam, where they could play duets together. But this aroused such a storm of protest from Frau Permaneder that Gerda had to put the idea aside for the time being.

As might have been expected, Frau Permaneder also had her objections to the sale of the house her brother had built. She complained loudly of the awful impression such a sale would leave and that it would lead to yet another loss of family prestige. But she did have to admit that it would be impractical to continue to keep up the spacious and noble house, which had proved to be Thomas Buddenbrook's most expensive hobby, and that there was some justification in Gerda's desire to have a comfortable little villa with a pleasant yard somewhere beyond the town gates.

A grand day dawned for Herr Siegismund Gosch the broker. His old age was illumined by an event that even brought the trembling in his limbs to a halt for a few hours. For he was accorded entry to Gerda Buddenbrook's salon, was allowed to sit in an easy chair directly across from her and to negotiate with her, eye to eye, about the price of the house. With his snow-white hair brushed forward from all directions into his face, and his chin thrust forward in a ghastly pose, he stared up into her face and managed to look the perfect hunchback. His voice hissed, but his words were cool and businesslike, and nothing betrayed the agitation in his soul. Stretching out one hand and smiling slyly, he offered to buy the house and proposed 85,000 marks. It was a reasonable offer—the sale of the house would inevitably entail some loss. But Herr Kistenmaker's opinion would first have to be heard. Gerda Buddenbrook had to show Herr Gosch out without concluding the sale; but it turned out that Herr Kistenmaker was not of a mind to permit any interference in how he carried out his duties. He scorned Herr Gosch's offer, laughed at it, and swore that they could get much more. And he kept on swearing for so long that eventually he was forced to sell the house for 75,000 marks, to an aging bachelor, who after long travels had decided to settle down here in town.

Herr Kistenmaker took care of the purchase of the new house as well, a pleasant little villa on a chestnut-lined street just beyond the Burg Gate; he paid somewhat too much for it perhaps, but it was set among lovely orchards and flower gardens and was exactly what the widow Buddenbrook wanted. And so, in the autumn of 1876, Gerda Buddenbrook and her son moved to their new home, taking with them the servants and some of the old furnishings, although many things had to be left behind and became the property of the aging bachelor—much to Frau Permaneder's distress.

And as if these changes were not enough, Mamselle Jungmann, Ida Jungmann, who had served the Buddenbrook family for forty years, left now to return to her West Prussian homeland and spend the evening of her life with her relatives there. The truth was that she had been let go. She had raised one generation, and when they had outgrown her care, she had nursed and tended little Johann, read him Grimm's fairy tales, and told him the story of her uncle who had died of the hiccups. But little Johann was no longer little, he was fifteen years old now, and, despite his delicate health, she could no longer be of much help to him. And for years now, her relationship with his mother had been rather strained. She had never regarded this woman, who had entered the Buddenbrook household much later than she, as a full-fledged member of the family; indeed, in her later years, she had begun to assume the airs of an old family retainer with exaggerated ideas of authority. She took herself all too seriously, which frequently led to trouble whenever she encroached on areas outside her proper role in the household. The situation was untenable, there were ugly scenes, and although Frau Permaneder interceded for her with the same eloquence with which she had pled for two family homes and their furnishings, old Ida was dismissed.

She wept bitterly when the time came to say farewell to her little Johann. He embraced her: then, putting his hands behind his back and shifting his weight to one leg while balancing his other foot on the toe, he watched her depart; and his golden-brown eyes rimmed with bluish shadows had the same brooding, introspective look that they had taken on when he stood beside his grandmother's corpse, when his father died, when their grand old home was broken up—or on so many other occasions, which had less to do with life's external events. As he saw it, old Ida's departure was consistent with the other instances of decline, dissolution, and termination that he had witnessed. That sort of thing no longer astounded him—had never astounded him, strangely enough. Sometimes, when he would raise his head with its curly brown hair and flair his nostrils fastidiously, his lips slightly twisted as always, it looked as if he were cautiously sniffing the air and the atmosphere of life around him, expecting to catch a whiff of that odor, that strangely familiar odor, which the fragrance of all those flowers beside his grandmother's casket had not been able to overpower.

Whenever Frau Permaneder came to visit her sister-in-law, she would draw her nephew close to her and tell him about the Buddenbrooks' past and about their future, a future for which they would have only him, little Johann, to thank—and, of course, God in His mercy. The more disagreeable the present appeared, the more she felt the need to provide lengthy descriptions of what life had been like in her parents' and grandparents' home and of how Hanno's great-grandfather had driven all over the country in a coach-and-four. One day she had a very nasty attack of stomach cramps—right after Friederike, Henriette, and Pfiffi Buddenbrook had proclaimed in unison that the Hagenströms were the cream of society.

There was bad news about Christian. His marriage, it seemed, had not improved his health. His morbid fantasies and fixations had grown worse, and more frequent, and at the urging of his wife and a physician he had entered a sanatorium. He did not like it there and wrote plaintive letters to his family expressing a strong desire to leave the institution, where they apparently were very strict with him, and to live as a free man again. But they kept him there—and that really was the best thing for him. At any rate, it allowed his wife, quite apart from the material and social advantages that she derived from her marriage, to continue her former independent life without embarrassment or regard to others.

2

SOMETHING IN the alarm clock's innards clicked, and it began its gruesomely dutiful rattle. It was a hoarse, jittery sound, more a clatter than a ring, for it was old and battered from years of service. And it went on and on for a desperately long time—it had been wound up very tight.

Hanno Buddenbrook panicked. It was the same every morning—this ugly and yet familiar sound would erupt on the nightstand, right beside his ear, and his insides would cramp in rage, protest, and despair. To look at him, he appeared quite calm; without changing his position in bed, he merely opened his eyes suddenly, rousing himself from some shadowy morning dream.

The room, chilled by winter, lay in total darkness. He could not see anything, not even the hands on the clock. But he knew that it was six o'clock, because he had set his alarm for six the evening before. Yesterday—yesterday. He lay on his back, tense and nervous, trying to bring himself to strike a light and get out of bed, and gradually all of yesterday came back to him.

It had been a Sunday, and after several days of abuse at the hands of Herr Brecht he had been allowed to accompany his mother to the municipal theater for a performance of *Lohengrin*. For over a week his life had been filled with joyful anticipation of the event. The sad part was that, as always just before a festive occasion, so many disagreeable things stood in the way and spoiled the simple enjoyment of anticipation until the very last moment. But at last Saturday had come, another week of school was behind him, and the treadle machine had hummed its painful hum and drilled in his mouth for the last time. He had survived, and everything else could be shoved aside, including his homework, which he had quickly decided to put off until after Sunday evening. What had Monday meant then? Was it even probable that it would ever come? You can't believe in Monday when you're going to hear *Lohengrin* on Sunday evening. His plan was to get up early Monday morning and do his stupid homework then—and that was that. And he had walked about a free man, cherishing the joy in his heart, dreaming at his piano, forgetting all disagreeable things.

And then the joy had become reality. It had swept over him with ineffable enchantments, secret thrills and shudders, sudden fervent sobs, and a rapture of insatiable ecstasy. True, the orchestra's second-rate violins had faltered a little during the overture, and the boat, carrying a fat, conceited man with a reddish-blond beard, had entered by fits and starts. And his guardian, Herr Stephan Kistenmaker, who was sitting in the next box, had muttered something about how this sort of thing distracted boys from their duties. But the sweet, exalted splendor of what he had heard lifted him up and away from all that.

It had come to an end all the same. The lilting, shimmering delight had faded and died, and he had found himself back home, in his room, with a feverish head and the awareness that only a few hours of sleep here in his bed separated him from the dreary everyday world. And he had been overwhelmed by one of those fits of total despondency that he knew so well. He had once again felt how painful beauty truly is, how it plunged you into shame and yearning despair and at the same time gnawed away at your courage and fitness for daily life. He had felt it as a dreadful, gloomy mountain pressing down on him so heavily that once again he was forced to admit that something more than private grief must be weighing him down, that some burden must have oppressed his soul from the very beginning and would suffocate him one day.

Then he had set his alarm and fallen asleep—the deep, dead sleep of someone who never wants to wake up again. And now Monday was here, and it was six o'clock, and he had not done an hour's worth of homework.

He sat up and lit the candle on his nightstand. But his arms and shoulders were so terribly chilled by the icy cold that he quickly sank back down and pulled his blanket up over him.

The hands pointed to ten after six. Oh, it was pointless to get up now and work—there was too much to do, there was something to learn for almost every class, it wasn't worth trying to start now, and the time he had set for getting up had passed anyway. He had been sure yesterday that it would be his turn to be called on today in Latin and chemistry, but was that really so certain? Yes, it was likely, in fact quite probable. As far as Ovid went, the names that had been called on recently had begun with the last letters of the alphabet, and so presumably it would start all over again today with "A" and "B." But it was not absolutely certain, not beyond all doubt whatever. There were exceptions to every rule. Good God, chance could work wonders. And as he toyed with these deceptive and farfetched possibilities, his thoughts grew muddled and he fell asleep again.

His little room lay cold, bare, and silent in the flickering candlelight: an etching of the Sistine Madonna above the bed, an extension table set in the middle, one shelf crammed untidily with books, a sturdy-legged mahogany writing desk, his harmonium, and a small washstand. Jack Frost had painted the window with flowers—the blind had been left rolled up to let the first daylight in. And Hanno Buddenbrook slept, his cheek nestled in his pillow. He slept with parted lips and long eyelashes pressed tight, lending him the expression of someone fervently, achingly devoted to sleep. His curly, soft, light-brown hair fell down over his temples. And slowly the little flame on the nightstand lost its orange glow as the dim light of morning fell hard and dull on the frosted windowpane.

It was seven o'clock when he awoke with a start. The hour of grace was past. There was nothing for it now—he had to get up and accept what the day might bring. One brief hour until the start of school. Not much time at all—let alone to deal with homework. Nevertheless, he lay there—saddened, exasperated, and incensed at the brutal necessity of having to leave his warm bed in the raw half-light and venture out into a miserable, dangerous world filled with stern and spiteful people. "Oh, can't I have just two more little minutes?" he asked his pillow with lavish tenderness. And then, in a fit of defiance, he gave himself another five—he just wanted to close his eyes a little. But from time to time he opened them and gazed in despair at the minute hand inching forward in its stupid, ignorant, precise way.

At ten after seven, he tore himself from his bed and began to move about the room in great haste. He let the candle burn, because there was still not enough daylight. He breathed on the frosted window, and saw that the world lay under a thick blanket of fog.

He was freezing terribly. Now and then his whole body would shudder from the painful chill. The tips of his fingers stung and were so swollen that there was no point in trying to use his nail brush. When he washed his neck and arms, his numbed hand simply let the sponge drop to the floor. He stood there, helpless and stiff with cold, steaming like a sweating horse.

Panting and bleary-eyed, he was ready at last and grabbed his leather satchel from the table; gathering together what desperate wits he still had left, he packed the books he would need for the day's classes. He stood there, staring nervously at nothing and muttering anxiously, "Religion . . . Latin . . . chemistry . . .," then stuffed the battered, ink-stained paperbound books in his satchel.

Yes, little Johann was actually quite tall now. He was well past his fifteenth birthday and no longer wore Danish sailor outfits, but a tan suit and a blue tie with white polka dots. The long, thin watch chain he had inherited from his grandfather dangled across his vest, and on the fourth finger of his somewhat broad but delicately formed right hand was the old family signet ring with the green gemstone, which likewise belonged to him now. He pulled on his thick wool winter coat, donned his hat, grabbed his satchel, blew out the candle, stormed downstairs to the ground floor, and, passing the stuffed bear, turned right to enter the dining room.

Fräulein Clementine, his mother's new lady's maid, a skinny girl with a curl in the middle of her forehead, a pointed nose, and nearsighted eyes, was already up and setting out breakfast.

"How late is it now?" he asked between his teeth, although he knew precisely what time it was.

"A quarter till eight," she answered, her thin, red hand—it

looked gouty—pointing at the wall clock. "You'd better be getting on your way, Hanno." And at the same time she set a steaming cup in front of him and shoved the breadbasket, butter, salt, and eggcup his way.

He said nothing more, just grabbed a roll and, without sitting down, his hat still on his head and his satchel under one arm, began to drink his cocoa. The hot liquid made one molar hurt terribly, the one that Herr Brecht had been working on. He left half his cocoa and refused the egg; his mouth still wrenched with pain, he made some sort of sound that might have been a goodbye and ran out of the house.

It was ten minutes before eight as he crossed the front yard, left the little red-brick villa behind, and began to hurry down the wintry street. Ten, nine, eight minutes left. And it was a long way. And in this fog you could hardly tell where you were. With all the strength in his narrow chest, he drew the icy fog in and pushed it back out again, held his tongue against the tooth that still ached from the cocoa, and forced his legs to go at a mad pace. He was bathed in sweat and yet frozen to the bone. He felt a stitch in his side from this morning constitutional. What little breakfast he had eaten rebelled in his stomach, he felt nauseated, and his heart was just a quivering, wildly fluttering mass that took his breath away.

The Burg Gate, only the Burg Gate—and just four minutes left. As he panted along the street—drenched in cold sweat, sick at his stomach, his tooth hurting—he looked all around him to see if there might be any other students still under way. No, no, no one else was on the street. They were all in their proper places by now, and the bells began to strike the hour. They rang through the fog from all the steeples, and to celebrate the occasion, those of St. Mary's were even playing "Now thank we all our God." And playing it off key, Hanno noticed in his mad despair, without any sense of rhythm, and very badly out of tune. But that was the least of his problems, the least! Yes, he would be late, there was no question of that now. The school clock was a little slow, but he would be late all the same, that was certain. He stared people in the eye as they passed. They were on their way to their offices and shops, not in all that much of a hurry, nothing was threatening them. Some of them returned his envious, plaintive gaze, studied his disheveled appearance—and smiled. Those smiles drove him to distraction. What were they thinking? How could people with no worries possibly judge his situation? "Pure callousness," he wanted to shout at them. "I mean your smiles, gentlemen. Perhaps *you* would enjoy collapsing dead in front of the closed school gates."

He was still twenty paces from the long, red wall with its two wrought-iron gates that separated the front schoolyard from the street, when he heard the steady, shrill bell, the signal for the beginning of Monday-morning prayers. There was no energy left to run or even increase his stride, and so he simply let his body fall forward in the hope that his legs would manage somehow not to trip him up, but would keep going on their own, stumbling and wobbling as best they could—and he arrived at the outer gate just as the bell stopped ringing.

Herr Schlemiel, the janitor, a squat fellow with a workingman's scruffy beard and face, was just about to lock the gates. "Well—" he said, and let young Buddenbrook slip through. Maybe, maybe all was not lost. The idea now was to duck into the classroom, wait there quietly for the end of morning prayers, which were held in the gym, and then act as if everything were perfectly normal. And, gasping for air, exhausted, stiff, and sweaty, he dragged himself across the red-brick schoolyard and pushed his way inside through one of the swinging doors with its pretty panel of stained glass.

Everything about the institution was new, neat, and attractive. It had caught up with the times, and the gray, dilapidated walls of the former convent school, where the fathers of the present generation had pursued scientific learning, had been razed to make way for a splendid, new, airy edifice. It was all done in the old style—Gothic arches still sedately spanned corridors and arcades. But in terms of lighting and heating, of bright, spacious classrooms, cozy teachers' lounges, and well-equipped, efficient lecture halls and labs for chemistry, physics, and drawing, it represented the latest in modern comfort.

Hanno Buddenbrook wearily edged his way along one wall and looked around him. No, thank God, he saw no one. From a distant corridor he caught the echoing hubbub of students and teachers moving en masse toward the gym, where they would receive a little spiritual uplift for the week of work ahead. But here at the front of the building, everything was deathly silent, and even the wide linoleum-covered staircase was empty. He climbed it cautiously—on tiptoe, holding his breath, listening for any sound. His homeroom, for students in their sophomore year of the modern curriculum, was on the second floor, directly across from the stairs. The door was open. Standing on the last step now, he bent forward to look both ways down the corridor and its rows of classrooms, each with a porcelain plaque above the door; he took three quick, soundless strides forward and was in the room.

It was empty. The curtains at the three wide windows were still closed, and the gas lamps hanging from the ceiling were lit and sputtering softly in the hushed room. Green shades diffused the light across three rows of two-seated desks made of light-colored wood, and across from them stood the teacher's platform—looking dark, sturdy, and pedagogical—with a high blackboard behind it. Yellow wainscoting ran along the lower half of the walls; the upper half was bare plaster, decorated with a few maps. A second blackboard, set up on an easel, stood next to the platform.

Hanno walked over to his desk, more or less in the middle of the room, shoved his satchel in the drawer, and sank down on the hard seat; stretching his arms out over the slanted top, he laid his head down. He felt a shiver of ineffable relief run through him. This bare, hard room was ugly, despicable, and a whole morning full of a thousand ominous dangers lay leaden on his heart. But for the moment he was safe and sound, and all the rest could take its course. And the first hour, religion with Herr Ballerstedt, was a rather harmless affair. The vibrating ribbons of paper tied to the circular opening in the wall above him showed that warm air was streaming into the room, and the gas lamps were helping to heat it as well. Oh, he stretched now and slowly let his sweaty, stiff limbs relax and thaw out. He could feel a delightful, unwholesome warmth rising to his head, making his ears hum and dimming his eyes.

Suddenly he heard a sound behind him—he jerked up and whirled around to look. And there in the back row, a head and a pair of shoulders emerged—it was Kai, Count Mölln. Working his way up from behind his desk, the young gentleman scrambled to his feet, clapped his hands together softly to dust them off, and beamed as he strode now toward Hanno Buddenbrook.

"Oh, it's you, Hanno," he said. "And here I crept to the back, because when you came in I thought you were an organ of the pedagogic body."

His voice was obviously changing and cracked when he spoke, which was not the case yet for his friend. And, like Hanno, he had grown considerably. But otherwise he was still very much the same. His suit was still an indeterminate color, with a button missing here and there, and the seat of his pants consisted of a large patch. As always, his hands were none too clean, but they were still narrow and exceptionally well formed, with long, slender fingers and tapering fingernails. His reddish-blond hair was still carelessly parted down the middle and fell across a flawless, alabaster forehead, beneath which deep-set but keen, bright blue eyes flashed. The contrast between his very unkempt appearance and the noble pedigree in the delicate bone structure of his face with its slightly aquiline nose and slightly pursed upper lip was more striking than ever.

"Kai," Hanno said, skewing his mouth slightly and rubbing his hand in the neighborhood of his heart, "how could you scare me like that! What are you doing up here? Why were you hiding from me? Did you get here late, too?"

"Heaven forbid," Kai replied. "I've been here for quite a while. It's Monday morning, and I just couldn't wait to get back to this fine institution—a feeling I'm sure you know best, my friend. No, I just stayed up here for the fun of it. Our high and august principal commands the day and deems it not abduction to drive the people to their prayers. And so I made sure that I kept right behind him the whole time. And at every turn he made, wherever he looked, I was always right behind our old mystagogue, until he started out of the room and I stayed here. But what about you?" he asked sympathetically and sat down gently beside Hanno on the bench. "You had to run the whole way, didn't you? Poor fellow—you look frazzled. Your hair's so wet it's stuck to your forehead." And he took a ruler from the desk and with a serious face carefully unstuck little Johann's hair. "So you overslept, did you? Oh, what do you know—I seem to be sitting in Adolf Todtenhaupt's place today," he said, interrupting himself and looking all around, "in the consecrated seat at the head of the class. Well, it doesn't matter for now. So you overslept, did you?"

Hanno had laid his head down on his crossed arms again. "I went to the opera last night," he said, heaving a sigh.

"Oh, right, I'd forgotten about that. Was it beautiful?"

Kai received no answer to his question.

"You've got it good," he went on, ignoring his silence. "You need to keep that in mind, Hanno. I've never been in a theater once, you know, and there's not the least prospect I ever will, for years to come."

"If only there wasn't this hangover afterward," Hanno said gloomily.

"Yes, I know all about that problem." And Kai bent down to pick up his friend's hat and coat, which had fallen to the floor beside the bench, and quietly took them out to hang them in the corridor. "I take it you don't have the passage from the *Metamorphoses* down cold yet?" he asked as he came back in.

"No," Hanno said.

"And presumably haven't prepared for the test in geography?"

"I haven't worked on anything," Hanno said.

"No chemistry or English, either, then. All right! Well, that makes us bosom buddies, comrades-in-arms." Kai was obviously relieved. "We're in the same boat," he declared cheerfully. "I didn't do anything on Saturday, because the next day was Sunday, and nothing on Sunday for religious reasons. No, I'm kidding. Mainly because I had something better to do, of course," he said, suddenly turning serious and blushing a little. "Yes, things could get lively today, Hanno."

"If I get another demerit," Johann said, "I won't pass; and I'm sure to get one if I get called on in Latin class. It's the 'B's' turn next, Kai, and there's no way to prevent it."

"Let's wait and see. Aha! Caesar comes to mind: 'Though dangers have threatened me constantly from the rear, they need only see Caesar's face . . .' " But Kai was unable to finish his oration. He was in a rather gloomy mood himself. He went up to the platform, sat down, and with a scowl began to rock in the armchair. Hanno Buddenbrook's head still lay resting on his crossed arms. They sat like that for a while, opposite one another; neither spoke.

Suddenly a dull droning came from somewhere; within thirty seconds it had grown to a roar that rolled menacingly toward them.

"The people," Kai said fiercely. "Lord, my God, how quickly have they done with it. Not even ten minutes knocked off the hour."

He stepped down from the platform and moved to the door so that he could blend in with the others as they arrived. But, as for Hanno, he simply lifted his head for a moment, made a wry face, and went on sitting there.

And here they came, shuffling and stamping—a tumult of baritones and tenors, with soprano descants and cracking voices that leapt between the two. A great wave flooded up the steps and flowed out along the corridors, streaming into this room as well, which was suddenly filled with life, movement, and noise. Here they came, all the young men, Hanno and Kai's schoolmates, the sophomores in the modern curriculum, about twenty-five of them, sauntering in with their hands in their pants pockets or swinging their arms—they took their seats and opened their Bibles. There were open, honest faces and closed, guarded ones; some looked hale and hearty and others more delicate; tall, strong rascals, who planned soon to be merchants or go to sea and who couldn't care less about school; and little grinds, who were well ahead of their classmates, stars in any subject that required only memorization. Adolf Todtenhaupt, the head of the class, knew everything; he had never given a wrong answer in all his life. This was due partly to quiet, passionate hard work, and partly to the fact that his teachers avoided asking him anything he might not know. It would have pained and embarrassed them, would have shaken their belief in human perfectibility, to have met with silence from Adolf Todtenhaupt. He had a strange bumpy head and his blond hair was pasted to it like smooth, shiny glass; there were black rings around his gray eyes, and his long, brown hands stuck out from under coat sleeves that were too short but always brushed and spotless. He sat down beside Hanno Buddenbrook, smiled softly—and a little slyly—and said good morning to his neighbor, adopting the current slang by contracting the greeting to a sassy, casual monosyllable. Then, while everyone else around him went on chattering in low voices, he yawned and smiled and began to make entries in the attendance book, holding the pen absolutely correctly in his slender, extended fingers.

Two minutes later, the sound of footsteps was heard out in the hall, and all the front-benchers rose unhurriedly from their seats; a few boys toward the rear followed their example, but the others were not about to be distracted from what they were doing and hardly even noticed Herr Ballerstedt enter the room, hang his hat on the door, and step up on the platform.

He was a man in his forties, pleasantly stout, with a large bald head, a full reddish-blond, short-cropped beard, rosy cheeks, and an expression on his moist lips that was both unctuous and cozily sensual at the same time. He picked up his notebook and thumbed through it without saying a word. The order in his classroom left much to be desired, and so he raised his head, stretched an arm out over the lectern, and feebly waved a flaccid white fist up and down a few times, while his face slowly swelled and turned purple, making his beard look pale yellow; working his lips strenuously to no real purpose for a good thirty seconds, he finally managed nothing more than a forced moan of "Well . . ." He struggled a while longer to find some further reprimand, then at last turned back to his notebook, and imploded again in apparent satisfaction. This was typical of Herr Ballerstedt's classroom method.

At one time he had wanted to be a preacher, but, given his tendency to stutter and his fondness for the good things of this world, he had turned instead to pedagogy. He was a bachelor of some wealth—he wore a little diamond on one finger—and was thoroughly committed to good food and drink. He was the one teacher on the faculty who associated with his colleagues only on an official basis and spent most of his free time in the company of fashionable, unmarried men from the world of commerce—even with officers from the local garrison. He dined twice a day at the best restaurant in town and was a member of the Club. If he happened to meet any of his older students somewhere on the street at two or three in the morning, he would swell up, manage to blurt out "Good morning," and let things go at that, for all parties concerned. Hanno

Buddenbrook had nothing to fear from him and was almost never asked a question. Herr Ballerstedt had spent all too much time in the very human company of Uncle Christian to seek out any conflicts with his nephew in the classroom.

"Well . . ." he said once more, gazing around the class and making another gesture with his feebly balled fist and flashing his diamond; he looked at his notebook. "Perlemann. A synopsis, please."

Somewhere in the class, Perlemann stood up—but not that anyone noticed. He was one of the smallest boys, one of the grinds. "The synopsis," he said in a polite, low voice, thrusting his head forward with a nervous smile. "The book of Job is divided into three parts. First, Job's condition before he found himself chastised by the rod of the Lord—chapter one, verses one through six. Second, the rod itself and what happened as a result—chapter . . ."

"That's correct, Perlemann," Herr Ballerstedt interrupted him, touched by so much timid subservience, and jotted a good grade in his book. "Heinricy, continue."

Heinricy was one of the tall rascals who no longer cared about anything. He tucked the handy jackknife he had been playing with into his pocket, stood up noisily, pouted his lower lip, and cleared his throat with a rough, raw, manly growl. They were all unhappy that it was his turn now, in the wake of mild-mannered Perlemann. The students daydreamed and let their minds wander, lulled half asleep by the warm room and the soft hiss of the gas lamps. They were all still tired from Sunday; they had all crept from their warm beds on this cold foggy morning, with a sigh and chattering teeth. They would all have preferred it if little Perlemann had babbled away for the whole hour, whereas Heinricy was sure to pick a quarrel.

"I was absent the day this was assigned," he said with a rough edge to his voice.

Herr Ballerstedt swelled up, waved his limp fist, worked his lips, raised his eyebrows, and stared young Heinricy straight in the eye. His head had turned purple again and he was quivering, straining to control himself, until he finally managed to say, "Well . . ."—and the spell was broken, the battle won. "One can never expect you to do any work," he went on with easy eloquence now, "and you always have some excuse ready at hand, Heinricy. If you were sick and missed the last class, you certainly have had time in the past few days to find out what we have already covered. And if the first part is about Job's condition before the chastising rod and the second about the chastising rod, you surely could have counted on your fingers and concluded that the third part is about his condition *after* he has encountered said tribulation. But you don't apply yourself. It is not just that you are weak-willed—you never fail to excuse your weakness and justify it. But mark my word, as long as you continue in this, there can be no question of improvement—or of promotion. Be seated, Heinricy. Wasservogel, continue."

Thick-skinned and defiant, Heinricy sat down again with loud creaks and scrapes, muttered a wisecrack to his neighbor, and pulled out his handy jackknife again. Wasservogel stood up—a boy with inflamed eyes, a pug nose, cauliflower ears, and badly chewed fingernails. He completed the "synopsis" in his insipid nagging voice, and began to tell about Job, the man from the land of Uz and what had happened to him. He had placed an opened Old Testament against the back of the boy in front of him, and he read from it now with a look of total innocence and thoughtful concentration, then stared at a spot on the wall and provided a wretched modern German translation of what he had read, pausing frequently to give a squeaky cough. There was something absolutely repulsive about the boy, but Herr Ballerstedt praised him for his efforts. Wasservogel had it easy in life, because most of the teachers were quick to praise him for his achievements—just to prove to themselves and the other boys that they would never let his ugliness tempt them to be unjust.

Religion class dragged on. Various boys were called upon to show what they knew about Job, the man from the land of Uz; and Gottlieb Kassbaum, the son of the unfortunate wholesaler Herr Kassbaum, was given an excellent grade despite his family's shattered circumstances, because he was able to state definitely that Job's substance consisted of seven thousand sheep, three thousand camels, five hundred yoke of oxen, five hundred asses, and a very great household.

Then they were allowed to open their Bibles, most of which were already open, and they began to read. Whenever there was a verse that Herr Ballerstedt felt needed some explanation, he would swell up, say, "Well . . .," and, after completing the other customary preliminaries, deliver a little lecture on the point in question, interspersed with general comments on morals. No one listened to him. Peace and drowsiness reigned in the room. With the help of the steady flow of heat and the gas lamps, the temperature had risen considerably and the air was rather stale from twenty-five breathing, sweating bodies. The warmth, the soft hiss of the gas flames, the monotone voice of someone reading aloud—it all wrapped itself around their bored brains and lulled them into stupefied daydreams. Lying open before Kai Mölln was not only the Bible, but also Edgar Allan Poe's *Tales of the Grotesque and Arabesque*, and he read it, his head propped on one aristocratic but slightly dirty hand. Hanno Buddenbrook leaned back, sank down into his seat, and gazed with a slack mouth and hot, bleary eyes at the book of Job, its lines of print fusing into a black muddle. Sometimes he would recall the grail leitmotif or the "Wedding March," and then his eyelids would sink slowly and he could feel sobs welling up from deep inside. And he prayed in his heart that this innocuous and peaceful first class would never end.

But it did, of course—and as per schedule the shrill howls of the bell jangled and echoed through the corridors, wrenching twenty-five brains from cozy trances.

"Enough for today," Herr Ballerstedt said and had Todtenhaupt hand him the attendance book so that he could sign it as proof that he had fulfilled his duties.

Hanno Buddenbrook closed his Bible, yawned nervously, and stretched till his muscles twitched. As he let his arms fall and relax, he automatically took a quick, labored breath to steady the beat of his heart, which had wavered and stopped for a second. Now came Latin. He threw an imploring look Kai's way, but Kai was still immersed in reading his book and apparently had not even noticed that class was over. Hanno pulled his Ovid from his satchel, a paperbound book with a marbled cover, and opened it to the verses that were to be memorized for today. No, it was hopeless—a long, regular column of black lines, every fifth one numbered, and with little pencil marks scribbled everywhere, and the lines stared back at him, so obscure and unfamiliar that it was useless to try to learn a few of them. He could barely make out what they meant, let alone recite even a single one by heart. And he could not decipher one line of the passage that followed, which they were supposed to have translated for today.

"What does '*deciderant, patula Jovis arbore, glandes*' mean?" he asked in a forlorn voice, turning to Adolf Todtenhaupt, who was busy beside him with the attendance book. "It's all gibberish! They just want to trick us."

"What?" Todtenhaupt asked and went on writing. "The acorns of Jupiter's tree—that's the oak, yes. But I don't really know myself."

"Just prompt me a little, Todtenhaupt, if I get called on," Hanno begged, shoving the book away. He scowled at the star pupil's response, an inattentive, noncommittal nod, pushed himself along the bench, and stood up.

The situation had changed now. Herr Ballerstedt had left the room, and someone else was standing in his place on the platform—a frail, little, emaciated man with a scraggly, white beard and a scrawny, red neck sticking up out of a tight turndown collar. He was holding his top hat upside down in front of him, clutching it in one hand, which was covered with thick, white hair. His students called him "the spider," but his real name was Professor Hückopp. During the break between classes, he monitored the corridor and was also responsible for order in the classrooms. "Turn the gas lamps off! Open the curtains! Open the windows," he said, lending his little voice as much military authority as possible and gesturing energetically in the air with one arm, as if he were turning a crank. "Everyone downstairs, outside for some fresh air, ye gods and little fishes!"

The lamps were extinguished, the curtains flew apart, anemic daylight filled the room, and cold foggy air poured in through the wide windows. The sophomores shoved their way past Professor Hückopp toward the exit; only the top student was allowed to stay upstairs in the room.

Hanno and Kai met at the door, descended the gentle flight of stairs side by side, and moved across the tastefully designed vestibule. Neither spoke. Hanno looked absolutely miserable, and Kai was lost in thought. Once outside, they walked back and forth across the wet red bricks of the courtyard, which was crowded with boys of various ages milling noisily about.

A young gentleman with a blond goatee was in charge down here. He was the smart dresser of the faculty. His name was Dr. Goldener; he also ran a boarding house for boys from Holstein and Mecklenburg, the sons of rich landed gentry. Under the influence of the aristocratic young men placed under his care, he dressed in a manner quite unlike that of his colleagues. He sported colorful silk neckties, a dandified coat, pastel trousers with straps that fitted under the soles of his boots, and perfumed handkerchiefs with bright borders. As the son of a humble family, he seemed out of place in this sartorial splendor; his huge feet, for example, looked ridiculous in his buttoned boots with pointed toes. For some mysterious reason, he was vain about his pudgy, red hands, which he constantly rubbed together or held clasped in front of him so that he could admire them. He liked to carry his head tilted back to one side, and he was forever making a face—blinking his eyes, wrinkling up his nose, and letting his mouth hang half open, as if he were about to say, "And what, pray tell, is going on here now?" But he was far too elegant and distinguished not to ignore all the little trespasses that occurred out in the courtyard. He ignored it if a student or two happened to bring a book along to do some last-minute cramming; ignored it when the boys who boarded with him would slip the janitor, Herr Schlemiel, some money for him to fetch them pastries; ignored the little showdowns between two freshmen that often ended in a fight with a circle of boxing experts gathered around; and he ignored it if behind his back someone was led off to the pump by his classmates, to be doused as a punishment for expressing an opinion that was considered cowardly, dishonorable, or lacking in the appropriate esprit de corps.

The noisy crowd surrounding Kai and Hanno was a doughty but somewhat uncouth crew. Having grown up in the atmosphere of a bellicose, triumphant, and rejuvenated Fatherland, they had embraced the habits of crude virility. They spoke in a jargon that was both slipshod and dashing and was replete with terms from technology. High on their list of virtues were physical strength, gymnastic skill, and prowess at drinking and smoking; the most despicable vices were effeminacy and dandyism. Anyone who buttoned his top collar button could expect a visit to the pump. And anyone who dared be seen on the street with a walking stick could likewise expect painful indignities to be visited publicly upon him during the next gym class.

The things that Hanno and Kai talked about were strangely out of place here, but were drowned out in the babble of voices that filled the cold, damp air. The whole school had known about their friendship for years. The teachers tolerated it, but only grudgingly, because they suspected something foul and hostile behind it; and their classmates, unable to figure them out, had simply grown used to it and permitted it with a certain reluctant contempt, regarding the two of them as outlaws and eccentrics who were best left to themselves. Besides which, Kai, Count Mölln, enjoyed a certain respect, since they recognized a wildness and relentless insubordination about him. And as far as Hanno Buddenbrook was concerned, even burly Heinricy, who thrashed anyone and everyone, could not bring himself to lay a hand on him for dandyism or cowardice—out of a vague fear of his soft hair, his frail limbs, his shy, gloomy, cold eyes.

"I'm scared," Hanno told Kai, stopping beside one of the courtyard walls. Leaning back against it, he pulled his jacket tighter, shivered, and yawned. "It's driving me crazy, Kai, it makes my whole body hurt. And is Herr Mantelsack the man to inspire fear like that? You tell me! If only this wretched Ovid class were over and done with. If only my grade was already in his book, and I'd failed the class, and it would all be behind me. I'm not afraid of *failing*, I'm afraid of the whole brouhaha that goes with it."

Kai was lost in his own thoughts. "Roderick Usher is the most marvelous character ever invented," he said suddenly out of nowhere. "I was reading it all during class. If only I could write a story as good as that someday."

The fact was that Kai was trying his hand at writing. That was what he had meant earlier that morning when he said that he had better things than homework to do, and Hanno had understood him well enough. His love of telling stories, so evident when he was a small boy, had continued to grow, and he was trying to become a writer. He had recently finished a piece, a fairy tale, a mad, fantastic tale of adventure, in which everything was bathed in an eerie light; it was set deep within the earth's most sacred workshops, where ores and mysterious embers glowed, but at the same time within the human soul, so that in some strange way the primal forces of nature and of man's soul were blended, altered, transformed, and refined—and all of it in a fervent, suggestive, and slightly extravagant language filled with delicate, passionate yearning.

Hanno knew the story well and loved it very much; but he was not in the mood to talk about Kai's or Edgar Poe's stories. He yawned again and then sighed, and simultaneously hummed a theme that he had composed recently at the piano. It was a habit with him. He would often sigh like that, releasing a long, deep breath that he had instinctively drawn to restore a more vigorous beat to his faltering heart, and he had got into the habit of turning the exhaled air into a musical theme, some little melody of his own or someone else's invention.

"Behold, the Lord God cometh," Kai said. "He is walking in his garden."

"Some garden," Hanno said and began to laugh. It was a nervous laugh, and he could not stop; he put his handkerchief to his mouth and peered across to the man whom Kai had called the "Lord God."

It was Director Wulicke, the principal, who now appeared in the courtyard—an extraordinarily tall man with a black slouch hat, a short, full beard, a potbelly, trousers that were much too short, and sleeves with funnel-shaped cuffs that were always very dirty. He strode rapidly across the red bricks of the courtyard—with such anger written on his face that it looked as if he were in pain—and pointed with an outstretched arm to the pump. Water was running! A group of students ran ahead of him, falling over each other in their haste to remedy the situation and turn off the tap. But then they, too, just stood there for a while, looking distraught and staring first at the pump and then the director, who had turned now to speak in a deep, hollow, excited voice to a red-faced Dr. Goldener, who had rushed over to him. What he had to say was shot through with unarticulated mumblings and snarls.

Director Wulicke was a terrible man. He was the successor of the jovial and warmhearted old gentleman who had been in charge when Hanno's father and uncle had been students here, and who had died early in 1871. At the time Dr. Wulicke was called to the position, he had been a professor at a Prussian secondary school. And with his advent a new spirit entered the Old School. Where previously classical learning had been considered a joyful end in itself and was pursued with a calm, leisurely, cheerful idealism, now the concepts of authority, duty, power, service, and career were held in highest honor; and in every official speech he delivered, Director Wulicke would unfurl the ominous banner of "the categorical imperative of our philosopher Kant." The school had become a state within the state, where the Prussian notion of rigorous service held such sway that not only the teachers but also the students thought of themselves as civil servants, interested only in advancing their careers and therefore always concerned to be well regarded by those in power. Soon after the new director's arrival, renovation and modernization of the old institution had begun—according to the very latest hygienic and aesthetic criteria—and been very successfully completed. It remained an open question, however, whether the school had not been a more sympathetic and generous institution in the old days—when a little less modern comfort and a little more kindness, sentiment, serenity, benevolence, and good cheer had held sway in its rooms.

As to Director Wulicke's personality, he was dreadful—as enigmatic, duplicitous, willful, and jealous as the God of the Old Testament. His smile was as terrible as his anger. The vast authority he held in his hands made him appallingly moody and unpredictable. He was perfectly capable of telling a joke and then turning in horrible anger on anyone who laughed. None of his trembling underlings knew how to behave in his presence. They had no choice but to lie in the dust and adore him—and hope that their almost frantic abasement might prevent his snatching them up in his wrath and crushing them in the mills of his great justice.

Kai Mölln and Hanno Buddenbrook used Kai's nickname for

him only between themselves and were careful never to let their schoolmates overhear it—out of an aversion to that fixed, cold look of incomprehension that they knew so well. No, these two boys had nothing whatever in common with their fellow students, who were content with simple revenge or obstinacy. That was not their way. They despised the usual nicknames given the teachers, because these were based on a humor that left them cold, didn't even make them smile. It was so cheap, so prosaic, so unfunny to call skinny Professor Hückopp "the spider," or Ballerstedt "the cockatoo"—poor compensation for their own compulsory service to the state. No, Kai Mölln could be a little more cutting than that! He had introduced the practice, just for himself and Hanno, of calling teachers by their proper last names, but with the addition of the word "Herr": "Herr Ballerstedt," "Herr Mantelsack," "Herr Hückopp"—and it added, as it were, the right ironic, dismissive coolness of tone, a mocking, quirky condescension. They spoke of the "pedagogic body" and could amuse themselves during an entire break between classes by picturing a kind of huge, fantastic, repulsive monster. And they usually spoke of "the institution," in a tone that implied it was much like the one in which Hanno's Uncle Christian resided.

Kai's mood was vastly improved by the sight of the Lord God, who continued to terrorize everyone for a while, turning faces ashen as he snarled horribly and pointed in various directions at the litter of sandwich papers tossed aside here and there around the brick courtyard. Kai pulled Hanno with him to the gate, through which teachers for the second period were now passing; and he began to make low bows before these pale, red-eyed, shabby teachers-in-training as they made their way to the back courtyard and their classes of fifth and sixth-grade boys. His bows were exaggerated, and he let his arms hang down as he looked up at these poor fellows with adoring eyes. Herr Tietge, the ancient mathematics teacher, appeared—a jaundiced, crookbacked old man, who held a few books in trembling hands at his back, spitting and squinting absent-mindedly in his absurd way; and Kai called out in an orotund voice, "Good morning, you old corpse." And his own clear, keen eyes gazed off in the air.

The bell rang out shrilly at the same moment, and at once the students began to stream toward the doors from all sides. But Hanno had not stopped laughing; he was still laughing so hard on the stairs that classmates in his and Kai's vicinity stared at him in cool amazement, were even a little repulsed by such foolishness.

A sudden hush came over the classroom, and everyone stood up in unison as Dr. Mantelsack entered. He was a full professor, and it was customary to show respect for a professor. He pulled the door to behind him and bent forward, craning his neck to see if everyone was standing; he hung his hat on its nail and stepped quickly toward the platform, making his head bob rapidly up and down. He now took up his position and glanced at the window while he stuck a forefinger, the one with a large signet ring, down inside his collar and rubbed. He was of average height, had thin, graying hair, a curly, Olympian beard, and myopic, bulging, sapphire-blue eyes that glistened behind his thick spectacles. He wore an open frock-coat of a soft, gray material, which he loved to smooth down around his waist with one short-fingered, wrinkled hand. Like all the teachers, except for the dapper Dr. Goldener, he wore trousers that were too short and revealed the shafts of a pair of uncommonly wide boots, polished shiny as marble.

Suddenly he turned his head away from the window, heaved a little friendly sigh, said, "Yes, yes," stared at his hushed pupils, and smiled affably at several of them. He was in a good mood, that was obvious. A tremor of relief passed through the room. So much depended—indeed, everything depended—on whether Dr. Mantelsack was in a good mood or not, for they all knew that he spontaneously succumbed to every mood without a trace of self-control. He was a man capable of the most imposing, boundless, and naive injustice, and his favor was as precious and fickle as fortune itself. He always had a few favorites, two or three, whom he called by their first names—and they lived in paradise. They could say almost anything they liked, and it was always the right answer. When class was over, Dr. Mantelsack would chat quite genially with them. But then came a day, after vacation perhaps, and one found oneself thrown down, dispatched, dismissed—God only knew why—and another boy would be addressed by his first name. When correcting the tests of these happy souls, he made light and dainty checkmarks next to the mistakes, so that their work still had a very tidy look even when it was filled with errors. But all the other papers were treated to angry, broad strokes of his pen, until they were swimming in red and looked shockingly sloppy. And since he did not count mistakes, but awarded censure and praise according to the quantity of red ink he had expended on any given test, his favorites always had a great advantage. He did not have the least compunction about using this method—he found it perfectly in order, never even suspected he was playing favorites. Anyone who might have had the unfortunate courage to protest would have forfeited all hope of ever being called by his first name. And no one was about to abandon that hope.

Still standing, Dr. Mantelsack now crossed his ankles and paged through his notebook. Hanno Buddenbrook sat bent forward, wringing his hands under his desk. The letter "B"—it was the "B"s' turn. His name would be called out and he would stand up and not know a single line—and there would be a scene, a loud and terrible catastrophe, no matter how good a mood the professor was in. The agonizing seconds dragged on. "Buddenbrook," he would say, "Buddenbrook."

"Edgar," Dr. Mantelsack said, closing his notebook but leaving his forefinger at the page; he sat down on his professional chair, as if everything were just as it should be.

What? What was this? Edgar—that was Lüders, fat Lüders, there, by the window, the letter "L", and it wasn't even close to being his turn. No—could it really be? Dr. Mantelsack was in such a good mood that he had simply singled out one of his favorites and paid no attention whatever to whose turn it actually was today.

Fat Lüders stood up. He had a bulldog face and brown, apathetic eyes. Although he had one of the best seats and could easily have read the passage from his book, he was too lazy even for that today. He felt secure in paradise and simply replied, "I had a headache yesterday and couldn't memorize."

"Oh, so you're leaving us in the lurch, are you, Edgar?" Dr. Mantelsack said sorrowfully. "You don't want to recite the verses about the Golden Age for me? What a frightful shame, my friend.

You had a headache, did you? It seems to me, however, that you should have told me about that before class, instead of waiting until I called on you. You had a headache not long ago, too, didn't you? You should do something about that, Edgar; otherwise there's always the danger that you'll find yourself falling behind. Timm, would you stand in for him, please."

Lüders sat back down. At that moment he was universally despised. It was quite obvious that the professor's mood had worsened considerably and that Lüders might very well be called by his last name tomorrow. Timm, who sat in one of the back rows, stood up. He was a blond lad with a rustic look about him, who wore a tan jacket and had short, fat fingers. He held his mouth open in an eager, silly way, so that it formed a kind of funnel, and he quickly shifted his open book into position while staring straight ahead. Then he lowered his eyes and began to read from it—but in a drawling, halting, monotone voice, like a child reciting its primer: "*Aurea prima sata est aetas . . .*"

It was clear that Dr. Mantelsack was calling on people in no regular order whatever and did not care at all who had not been examined for some time. It was no longer so appallingly probable that Hanno would be called on—that would require a stroke of dire misfortune today. He exchanged glances with Kai and began to unwind, letting his legs and arms relax.

Suddenly Timm was interrupted in his recitation. Whether because Dr. Mantelsack was having trouble understanding him or because he just wanted the exercise, he left his platform, strolled slowly among his pupils, and stood now, Ovid in hand, right next to Timm, who with one quick, imperceptible motion had moved his book out of sight—and was now completely helpless. His funnel-shaped mouth snapped at the air; he gazed at the professor with honest, blue, distraught eyes and managed not one syllable more.

"Well, now, Timm," Dr. Mantelsack said. "You've suddenly come to a halt, have you?"

And Timm grabbed his head, rolled his eyes, took a deep breath, and finally said with a lunatic smile, "I get all mixed up when you stand beside me, Professor Mantelsack."

And Professor Mantelsack smiled, too; his smile said that he felt flattered. He said, "Well, collect your thoughts now and continue." And with that he strolled back to his chair.

And Timm collected his thoughts. He pulled his book back in front of him, opened it, all the while visibly struggling to regain his composure by looking around the room; he now lowered his head and found his train of thought again.

"Satisfactory," the professor said when Timm had finished. "You've learned it well, no doubt about that. Except that you show very little regard for the rhythm, Timm. You seem to have some idea about the elisions, and yet you haven't actually spoken in hexameters. My impression is that you've learned the entire passage as if it were prose. But as I said, you've worked hard and have done your best—and he who always strives to do his best . . . You may be seated."

Timm sat down beaming with pride, and Dr. Mantelsack apparently jotted down "satisfactory" beside his name. The remarkable thing was that in that moment not only the teacher but Timm himself and all his classmates, too, were honestly convinced that Timm was truly a fine, hardworking student who had indeed earned a good grade. Even Hanno Buddenbrook was unable to resist this impression, although he sensed something deep inside rebelling against the idea. And now he listened attentively for the next name to be announced.

"Mumme," Dr. Mantelsack said. "Once more—*Aurea prima . . .* ?"

So it was Mumme. Thank God, because that meant Hanno was probably safe now. There was hardly any chance that the verse would have to be recited a third time, and it had been the "B"s' turn only recently to translate a new passage.

Mumme got up. He was a tall, pale fellow with trembling hands and unusually large, round glasses. He had bad eyes, was so nearsighted that when he stood up he could not read from the book on his desk. He had to learn, and he did. But because he hadn't expected to be called on today—and was so dreadfully untalented besides—he could not remember much of it and ground to a halt after the first few words. Dr. Mantelsack prompted him, prompted him a second time in a sharper tone; the third time he was downright indignant; and when Mumme got stuck for good, the professor erupted in fierce anger.

"That is totally unsatisfactory, Mumme. Sit down. What a sad figure you cut, let me assure you. You're an idiot—stupid *and* lazy is going a bit too far."

Mumme foundered and went under. He looked like calamity personified, and at that moment there was no one in the room who did not despise him. But once again Hanno Buddenbrook felt something rebel inside him, sensed a queasiness that made his throat contract. At the same time, however, he realized with terrible clarity what was happening now. With a flourish, Dr. Mantelsack made a mark fraught with doom next to Mumme's name and scowled as he paged through his notebook. It was only too clear—in his wrath, he had decided to go back to the regular order and was checking whose turn it actually was. And as Hanno sat there overwhelmed by this realization, he heard his name called—it was like a bad dream.

"Buddenbrook!" Dr. Mantelsack had said. "Buddenbrook." The sound still echoed in the air, and yet Hanno couldn't quite believe it. There was a buzzing in his ears now. He kept his seat.

"*Herr* Buddenbrook!" Doctor Mantelsack said, staring at him with bulging, sapphire-blue eyes that sparkled behind his thick glasses. "Would you please be so kind?"

Fine—so it was meant to be. It had to turn out like this. Very differently from what he had expected, but all was lost now. He was resigned to his fate. Would it end in a truly terrible outburst of rage? He stood up and was about to offer some inane, ridiculous excuse, to say he had "forgotten" to memorize the verses—when suddenly he noticed the boy ahead of him holding his book open for him.

The boy ahead of him was Hans Hermann Kilian, a small fellow with brown, greasy hair and broad shoulders. He wanted to be an officer and was so inspired by esprit de corps that he couldn't leave Johann Buddenbrook high and dry, even though he couldn't stand him. He even pointed a finger at the place to begin.

And Hanno stared at the book and began to read. With a faltering voice and pursed brows and lips he read about the Golden Age, which had arisen first, when of their own free will, with no compulsion, no law, men had kept faith and done the right. "There was no fear of punishment," he said in Latin, "no menacing words to be read on tablets of bronze; no suppliant throng to gaze in fear upon its judge's face. . . ." With an agonized, grim look on his own face, he purposely read badly and disjointedly, intentionally ignored elisions marked in pencil in Kilian's book, mangled the rhythm, groped for words, and made it look as if he were laboring to recall each one—expecting at any moment that the professor would find him out and pounce on him. The sweet, malicious joy of seeing the book open before him made his skin tingle; but he was totally disgusted with himself, too, and intentionally cheated as badly as possible, hoping that this would make his deception a little less sordid. Then he stopped, and silence reigned in the room—he did not dare look up. The silence was horrible; his lips turned white, he was sure Dr. Mantelsack had seen it all.

At last the professor sighed and said, "Oh, Buddenbrook, *si tacuisses*. You will excuse my use of the classical informal pronoun. Do you know what you have done? You have dragged beauty through the dust, you have behaved like a Vandal, a barbarian—you, a creature whom the muses have deserted, Buddenbrook, it's written on your face. If I were to ask myself whether you were coughing the whole time or reciting noble verses, I would be inclined to think it was the former. Timm has little developed sense of rhythm, but compared with you he is a genius, a rhapsodist. Be seated, unhappy man. You have studied, I grant. You have learned. I cannot give you a bad grade. You have made the best of your abilities. Although they tell me that you are musical and play the piano, is that right? How can that be? Well, enough, sit down, you've worked hard, it seems—that will do."

He jotted a "satisfactory" in his notebook, and Hanno Buddenbrook sat down. He felt now just as Timm the rhapsodist had felt before him. He could not help being sincerely moved by the praise implied in Dr. Mantelsack's words. In that moment he was truly of the opinion that he was a somewhat untalented but hardworking student, who had emerged from his trial with relative honor; and he clearly sensed that his classmates, including Hans Hermann Kilian, all held the same view. Something like nausea stirred in him again; but he was too exhausted to think about that. Pale and trembling, he closed his eyes and sank into lethargy.

Dr. Mantelsack, however, went on with the lesson. He moved now to the verse that they were supposed to have translated for today and called on Petersen. Petersen stood up, bright and cheerful and confident, striking a valiant pose, ready to fight the good fight. But he was doomed to perish today. The class could not come to an end without a catastrophe—one far worse than what had happened to poor myopic Mumme.

Petersen translated, casting a glance now and then at the right-hand page in his book, which had nothing to do with the passage. He did this very deftly. He acted as if something about it bothered him, and he passed his hand over it and blew at it as if there were a speck of dust or whatever that annoyed him and needed to be brushed away. And then something ghastly happened.

All of a sudden Dr. Mantelsack shifted his weight violently—and Petersen responded with an equally sudden violent motion. And in the same moment, virtually tumbling head over heels, the professor left his platform and headed directly toward Petersen with long, inexorable strides.

"You have a pony there in your book, a translation," he said, standing beside him now.

"A pony . . . no . . . I . . ." Petersen stammered. He was a handsome lad with a massive wave of blond hair that swept down over his forehead and extraordinarily beautiful blue eyes, which flickered now with fear.

"Do you have a pony in your book?"

"No, sir, no, Dr. Mantelsack. A pony? I most certainly do not have a pony. You are quite mistaken. You are wrong to entertain such suspicions." Petersen spoke in a way that none of the boys ever spoke. In his fear he carefully chose his words, hoping that this would rattle the professor. "I am not cheating," he said in his great distress. "I have always been honest, my whole life long."

But Dr. Mantelsack was all too certain of the painful truth. "Give me your book," he said icily.

Petersen clung to his book. He raised both hands in the air, and although he was half tongue-tied now, he continued to exclaim, "Please believe me, sir. There is nothing in my book, Dr. Mantelsack. I don't have a pony. I haven't cheated. I've always been honest."

"Give me the book," the professor repeated and stamped one foot.

Petersen went limp, his face turned gray.

"All right," he said, handing over the book, "here it is. Yes, there's a pony in it. You can see for yourself, there it is. But I wasn't using it," he suddenly shouted to the whole room.

Dr. Mantelsack, however, ignored this absurd lie, which was born of desperation alone. He pulled out the "pony," looked at it as if he had some putrid piece of garbage in his hand, slipped it into his pocket, and disdainfully tossed Petersen's Ovid back on his desk. "The class attendance book," he said in a hollow voice.

Adolf Todtenhaupt dutifully brought the class attendance book to him, and Petersen was given a demerit for attempted cheating, which would have devastating repercussions for a long time to come. It sealed his doom—he would be held back at Easter. "You are a discredit to this class," Dr. Mantelsack said and then returned to his professorial chair.

Petersen sat down, a ruined man. They all saw his neighbor edge away from him. And they all regarded him with a mixture of disgust, pity, and horror. He had fallen, and was now left alone, utterly abandoned—because he had been caught. They all shared one opinion about Petersen: he was truly "a discredit to the class." Without any resistance, they recognized and accepted this verdict, just as they had recognized and accepted Timm and Buddenbrook's success or poor Mumme's misfortune. And so did Petersen himself.

Of these twenty-five young men, those who had a rugged constitution, who were strong and fit for life as it really is, accepted the world as they found it at this moment and were not offended in the least. Things had taken their natural course and everything was as it should be. But there was another pair of eyes that stared ahead in gloomy thought—little Johann's studied Hans Hermann Kilian's broad back, and those golden-brown eyes ringed with bluish shadows were full of contempt, rebellion, and fear. Dr. Mantelsack, however, went on with the lesson. He asked for someone, anyone, Adolf Todtenhaupt if need be, to translate—he had lost all interest in trying to examine dubious scholars for today. And then it was the turn of another boy, who was poorly prepared and did not even know what "*patula Jovis arbore, glandes*" meant, and Buddenbrook was called upon to tell him. He said it softly and without looking up, because Dr. Mantelsack had asked him—and was given a nod of approval.

And once the students had been tested, they lost all interest in the class themselves. Dr. Mantelsack had one of his gifted pupils volunteer to continue the translation, but he paid no more attention to him than did the other twenty-four boys, who began to do the homework for their next class. It made no difference now. No more grades would be awarded here today, and there was no way of judging their conscientiousness in Latin now. And the class was almost over anyway. It was over; the bell rang. So this was how things had been destined to turn out for Hanno. He had even been given a nod of approval.

"Well," Kai said, as they moved along the Gothic corridor toward the chemistry hall with the rest of their classmates, "what do you say now, Hanno? 'They need only see Caesar's face.' You were incredibly lucky."

"I feel sick, Kai," little Johann said. "I can do without the luck, it makes me sick."

And Kai knew he would have felt exactly the same in Hanno's shoes.

The chemistry hall was a vaulted amphitheater with tiers of benches, a long lab table, and two display cabinets filled with vials. Their homeroom had been hot and close by the end of Latin class again, but here the air was saturated with the noxious stench of hydrogen sulfide. Kai flung open a window, then swiped Adolf Todtenhaupt's rewritten notes and hurriedly started to copy the section that had to be shown the teacher today. Hanno and several other students did the same. It took them the whole break between classes; then the bell rang and Dr. Marotzke appeared.

Kai and Hanno's nickname for him was "the deep professor."

He was a man of average height, a brunette with a very yellow complexion, two large bumps on his forehead, and a beard that was as bristly and greasy as his hair. He always looked unwashed and short of sleep, although that was probably a false impression. He taught natural sciences, but his specialty was mathematics, and he had the reputation of being an important thinker in the subject. He loved to talk about philosophical passages in the Bible, and sometimes, when he was in a whimsical good mood, he condescended to treat upperclassmen to strange exegeses on obscure verses. He was also an officer in the reserves—and served enthusiastically. Being both a civil servant and a military officer, he stood high on Director Wulicke's list. Of all the teachers, he demanded the most discipline; his critical eyes would pass down the rows of students, who had to stand at attention and provide sharp, curt answers to his questions. There was something a little revolting about this mixture of mysticism and military polish.

They pulled out the clean copies of their notes, and Dr. Marotzke walked around the room, tapping each notebook with his finger—although several pupils, who had not done the work, presented him with old notes or something from another class without his ever noticing.

Then the lesson began, and twenty-five young men now had occasion to prove the same zeal for boron, chlorine, and strontium that they had just shown for Ovid. Hans Hermann Kilian was praised for knowing that $BaSO_4$ or "heavy spar" was commonly used in counterfeiting. He was the star of the class in any case, since he wanted to be an officer. Hanno and Kai knew nothing, and they fared very badly in Dr. Marotzke's notebook.

But once the grades for quizzes and recitations had been meted out, the general interest in chemistry was as good as exhausted. Dr. Marotzke began to perform a couple of experiments, producing popping noises and colored vapors, but that was more or less just to fill up the hour. Finally he dictated the material to be learned for next time. Then the bell rang and their third class was behind them, too.

Everyone was glad of that—except Petersen, who had had a very bad morning—because now came an hour of fun that no one needed to fear and that promised nothing but high jinx and amusement. It was English with Modersohn, a young philologist who for several weeks now had been doing his practice teaching at the institution, or, as Kai, Count Mölln, liked to put it, was the understudy hoping to become the star. But there was little chance that he would be hired—his classes were much too exuberant.

Several boys remained behind in the chemistry hall and others went back up to their homeroom; but no one was forced to go down into the freezing courtyard, because Herr Modersohn was in charge of the corridor upstairs now and did not even dare try to send anyone outside. Besides, their task was now to prepare for his arrival in the room.

The noise level in the classroom did not diminish in the least when the bell rang for fourth period. They all talked and laughed in happy anticipation of the party. His head propped in his hands, Count Mölln went on reading about Roderick Usher, and Hanno sat quietly watching the show. Several boys made animal noises. A rooster crowed very loudly, and Wasservogel, at the back of the room, made sounds like a grunting pig, although you couldn't tell that the noise was coming from somewhere inside him. A large drawing adorned the blackboard, a cross-eyed face, the work of Timm the rhapsodist. And when Herr Modersohn entered, try as he might, he was unable to close the door, because a fat pine cone had been stuck in the crack—Adolf Todtenhaupt had to remove it.

Herr Modersohn was a small, ugly man who carried one shoulder hunched forward when he walked; his face was contorted in a peevish expression and framed by a very scraggly, black beard. He seemed in a constant state of embarrassment. He would blink his bright eyes, take a breath, and open his mouth as if he were about to speak—and then couldn't find the words he was looking for. He took three steps away from the door and stepped on a noisemaker, a noisemaker of such exceptional quality that it sounded as if he had landed on dynamite. He jerked back, wincing, smiled in his misery, and pretended nothing had happened. He stood beside the middle row of desks, propping the palm of one hand on the first desktop and assuming his customary skewed stance. But they knew that this was his favorite pose, and so someone had spilled ink on the spot, and Herr Modersohn's little, clumsy hand was now stained black. He pretended not to notice, put his wet, smeary hand behind his back, blinked, and said in a low, frail voice, "The order in this classroom leaves something to be desired."

Hanno Buddenbrook loved him in that moment and fixed his eyes on that helpless, contorted face. But Wasservogel's grunts were growing ever louder and more realistic. Suddenly a whole handful of peas pelted the window, bounced off it, and rattled across the floor.

"It's hailing," someone said in a loud, clear voice. And Herr Modersohn apparently believed this, because he immediately retreated to his platform and asked for the attendance book. He needed it not because he wanted to give anyone a demerit, but because, although he had taught the class five or six times now, he knew only a very few students and had to call out names at random from the written list.

"Feddermann," he said, "will you please recite the poem."

"Absent," a whole chorus of voices shouted at once. And all the while there sat Feddermann at his desk, big as life, flicking peas in all directions.

Herr Modersohn blinked and managed to find another name in his book. "Wasservogel," he said.

"Deceased!" Petersen called out in a fit of gallows humor. And, sliding their feet, grunting, crowing, and laughing derisively, they all confirmed that Wasservogel was dead.

Herr Modersohn blinked again, looked around, pulled a peevish face, and gazed back at his attendance book, running his little, clumsy hand down to the name he now decided to call. "Perlemann," he said, without much confidence.

"He's gone mad, unfortunately," Kai Mölln said in a clear, firm voice, and amid the growing pandemonium, Petersen's madness was likewise confirmed.

Herr Modersohn now stood up and called above the racket, "Buddenbrook, as punishment you will have an extra homework assignment. If you laugh once more, I will have to give you a demerit."

Then he sat down again.—And it was true, Buddenbrook had

laughed at Kai's joke, was seized by a fit of stifled, violent laughter that he could not control. It was a good joke, the humor of the "unfortunately" sent him into convulsions. But when Herr Modersohn barked at him, he calmed down and gazed in gloomy silence at the young teacher. At that moment he took in everything about the man: the few pathetic hairs of his beard that did not even cover the skin underneath; his bright, brown, hopeless eyes; the two sets of cuffs at the wrist of each little, clumsy hand, or so it seemed, because his shirtsleeves were as long and wide as the cuffs themselves; the whole wretched, forlorn figure. And he saw inside him, too. Hanno Buddenbrook was almost the only student whom Herr Modersohn knew by name, and he used that knowledge against him—constantly calling him to order, assigning him extra homework as punishment, and tyrannizing him in general. He only knew Buddenbrook's name because Hanno was so quiet that he stood out from the rest of the class; and he took advantage of Hanno's gentleness by exercising his authority over him, because he would not have dared do it with the loud, impudent boys. "People are so mean that they even make it impossible for you to pity them," Hanno thought. "I don't join the others in tormenting and bullying you, Herr Modersohn, because I think it's brutal, ugly, and cheap. And how do you repay me? But that's how it is, always will be, everywhere on earth," he thought, and felt fear and nausea rising up within him again. "And to think that I can see right through you with such revolting clarity."

Finally Herr Modersohn found a student who was neither dead nor mad and was willing to recite the poem in English. It was called "The Monkey," a childish bit of hokum that they demanded be memorized by young men whose main interest was to get on with the serious things in life, whether on the high seas or in the office.

> Monkey, little merry fellow,
> Thou art nature's punchinello. . . .

There were endless stanzas, and Kassbaum read them directly from his book—there was no need to stand on ceremony with Herr Modersohn. The noise had only grown worse. Every foot was in motion, scraping the dusty floor. The cock crowed, the pig grunted, peas flew. Twenty-five boys were drunk on anarchy. The undisciplined instincts of sixteen-and seventeen-year-olds were roused now. Pages with obscene drawings were held up for all to see and passed around, eliciting lewd laughter.

Suddenly everything was silent. The recitation faltered and broke off. Herr Modersohn himself sat up and listened. How charming—clear, bell-like, dainty tones floated up from the back of the room and filled the silence with a sweet, graceful, tender melody. Someone had brought a music box and it was playing "*Du, du liegst mir am Herzen*," in the middle of English class. But just as the delicate strains died away something truly dreadful happened—it burst over them like an unexpected, fierce storm, overwhelmed them, paralyzed them.

There had been no knock at the door, it was simply flung open wide, and something tall and monstrous entered, it growled and snarled, and with a single sidelong stride there it stood now right before their desks. It was the Lord God.

Herr Modersohn turned ash-gray and dragged his professorial chair down from the platform, all the while dusting it with his handkerchief. The students had leapt to their feet as one man. They pressed their arms to their sides, rocked forward on the balls of their feet, bowed their heads, and bit their tongues in a frenzy of servility. Deep silence reigned. Someone sighed from the strain of his exertions—and then everything was quiet again.

Director Wulicke reviewed the saluting ranks for a long time, and then he raised his arms with their funnel-shaped, dirty cuffs and lowered them again, fingers spread wide, like someone about to attack a piano keyboard. "Sit down," he said in his contrabass voice.

The students sank into their seats. Herr Modersohn's hands trembled as he pulled his chair over, and the director sat down beside the platform. "Please continue," he said; and it sounded as horrifying as if he had said, "We shall see now, and woe to anyone who . . ."

It was obvious what had happened. Herr Modersohn was supposed to demonstrate his teaching style, present a model lesson, and show what his sophomores had learned in six or seven hours under his instruction. This would decide Herr Modersohn's future, his very existence. He was a sad sight to behold as he stood there beside his platform, and now he called upon someone to recite "The Monkey." So far today it had been only the students who were tested and evaluated, but now the teacher would be examined right along with them. Oh, and things went badly for both parties. Director Wulicke's sudden appearance was a surprise attack, and except for two or three students, no one was prepared. Herr Modersohn could not possibly ask Adolf Todtenhaupt, who knew everything, to recite for a whole hour. And since they could not read "The Monkey" directly from their books with the director present, the recitation was a fiasco; and when they moved on to *Ivanhoe*, only young Count Mölln could translate a little of it, because he actually had some interest in the novel. The rest of them coughed and stammered and poked ineptly at the words. Hanno Buddenbrook was called on as well and could not get beyond the first line. Director Wulicke roared a sound that sounded like someone scraping violently at the deepest note on a contrabass. Herr Modersohn wrung his little, clumsy, ink-stained hands and kept wailing, "And it's always gone so well. It's always gone so well before."

He was still saying the same thing, half to his students and half to the director, when the bell rang. But the Lord God stood there erect and dreadful in front of his chair; he crossed his arms, nodded disdainfully, and glared out over the students' heads. And then he demanded the attendance book and slowly entered a demerit next to the names of all those whose performance had been unsatisfactory or worse—a good six or seven students in all. Herr Modersohn could not be given a demerit, but he was in worse shape than any of them. There he stood, a pale, broken, ruined man. Hanno Buddenbrook was among those who were given demerits. "I will destroy the careers of every one of you," Director Wulicke added. And then he vanished.

The bell rang; class was over. Of course it had to turn out like this. It always did. When your fear was at its height, things went well, or almost—as if to mock you. But when you suspected nothing awful would happen, then misfortune struck. It was definite now—Hanno would be held back at Easter. He stood up and walked out of the room with a weary look in his eyes; he rubbed his tongue against his bad molar.

Kai came over and put his arm around him, and they walked together down to the courtyard, surrounded by their classmates, who were excitedly discussing today's dramatic events. Kai looked anxiously and lovingly into Hanno's eyes and said, "Forgive me, Hanno, for translating just now instead of keeping quiet and getting a demerit, too. It's all so cruel."

"Didn't I answer what *patula Jovis arbore, glandes* means?" Hanno replied. "It's just how things are, Kai. It doesn't matter. Forget it."

"Yes, I suppose one must. But the Lord God wants to destroy your career. You will just have to submit to your fate, I suppose, Hanno, seeing as how it is his unsearchable will. 'Career'—what a lovely word! Herr Modersohn's career is shot now, too. He will never be a professor, the poor fellow. Yes, there are 'teaching assistants' and there are 'professors,' you see, but in our system there are no 'teachers.' This is a distinction not easily understood, because it is a matter for mature adults only, for those who have grown wise with years. One ought to be able to say that someone either is a teacher or he isn't. But I don't understand how one can skip the title entirely. You could, of course, present the issue to the Lord God or Herr Marotzke as a topic of discussion. And what would happen? They would take it as an insult and trample you underfoot for insubordination, because you have presented them with a much higher opinion of their profession than they could ever have themselves. Well, let them—come on, they're just thickheaded rhinoceroses."

They strolled across the courtyard, and Hanno listened with delight to Kai's banter, which was intended to help him forget his demerit.

"You see, here is a door, a courtyard door, it is open, beyond it lies the street. What would happen if we were to step out there and stroll up and down the sidewalk for a while? It's still recess; we have another six minutes, and we could be back in time. But the fact is: it's impossible. Do you understand? Here is the door, it is open, there are no bars, no barriers, nothing—just a threshold. And nevertheless it is impossible, the very idea of leaving for just one second is impossible. Well, let's disregard that and take another example. It would be quite absurd to say, if asked the time, that it is now about eleven-thirty. No, it is time for geography. That's reality. But now my question, for one and all, is: Is this life? With everything totally warped out of shape. Oh, good God, if only the institution would release us from its loving embrace."

"Right, and then what? No, forget it, Kai, it would be the same then, too. What would you do? We live a sheltered life here at least. Since my father died, Herr Stephan Kistenmaker and Pastor Pringsheim have taken on the job of asking me every day what I want to be. I don't know. I don't have an answer for them. I can't be anything. I'm afraid of the whole idea."

"Stop it. What kind of gloomy talk is that? What about your music?"

"What about my music, Kai? There's nothing there. Am I supposed to tour and play concerts? First, they would never let me, and second, I'll never be good enough for that. I can't do much of anything except improvise a little when I'm alone. And touring would probably be awful, too. It's different with you. You have more courage. You just walk around, laughing at the whole thing and challenging them with your ideas. You want to write, to tell people beautiful and strange stories—fine, that amounts to something. And you're sure to become famous, because you're so clever. And why is that? You're happier. Sometimes, during class, we look at each other for moment, like we did this morning when Herr Mantelsack gave Petersen a demerit for using a pony. We're thinking the same thing, but you just make a funny face and hold on to your pride. I can't do that. It wears me out. I just want to go to sleep and not have to deal with it. I want to die, Kai! No, I won't amount to anything. I can't even bring myself to want anything. I don't want to be famous. The idea scares me, as if it meant doing something wrong. I'll never amount to anything, you can be sure of that. I've heard that, during a confirmation class recently, Pastor Pringsheim said that they might as well give up on me, that I came from a degenerate family."

"Did he really say that?" Kai asked, paying close attention now.

"Yes. He means my Uncle Christian, locked up in an asylum in Hamburg. He's right, too. They should give up on me. I would be so grateful. I worry about so many things, and everything is so hard for me. For instance, I cut my finger or hurt myself some way—and it's a wound that heals for other people in a week, but it takes four weeks with me. It just won't heal, it gets infected, gets really ghastly, and gives me all kinds of trouble. The other day Herr Brecht told me that my teeth look horrible, that they're all deteriorating and wearing down, not to mention the ones he's already pulled. That's how things stand now. And what will I bite with when I'm thirty, or forty? I've lost all hope."

"Come on," Kai said and picked up the pace of their stroll. "And now tell me a little about your piano playing. I have an idea for a wonderful story, you know, absolutely wonderful. Maybe I'll start on it later, during drawing class. And are you going to play the piano this afternoon?"

Hanno was silent for a moment. A bleak, confused, feverish look came to his eyes. "Yes, I'll probably improvise a while," he said, "although I shouldn't. I should practice my études and sonatas and then stop. But I'll probably improvise. I can't seem not to, even though it makes everything worse."

"Worse?"

Hanno didn't reply.

"I know what you're thinking when you improvise," Kai said. And then neither of them spoke.

They were at a difficult age. Kai had turned beet-red and was staring at the ground, but without lowering his head. Hanno looked pale and very serious; he kept casting Kai enigmatic, sidelong glances.

Then Herr Schlemiel rang the bell, and they went back upstairs.

And now came geography and a test, a very important test about the province of Hesse-Nassau. A man with a red beard and a brown long-tailed coat came in. His face was pasty, and his hands had large pores and not a single hair. This was Dr. Mühsam, the witty professor. He suffered from occasional hemorrhaging of the lungs and always spoke in an ironic tone of voice, because he considered himself as clever as he was sickly. He had set up a kind of Heinrich

Heine museum at home, a collection of papers and memorabilia, all of it related in some way to that brash and frail poet. He now drew the borders of Hesse-Nassau on the blackboard and asked the gentlemen please to list in their bluebooks the province's important features, if any. He seemed to want to mock both his students and the province of Hesse-Nassau; but all the same, this was a very important test, and one they had all dreaded.

Hanno Buddenbrook knew nothing about Hesse-Nassau, or not much, or next to nothing. He tried to take a peek at Adolf Todtenhaupt's bluebook; but although he was supercilious, melancholic, and ironic, Heinrich Heine kept a restless eye on every movement. He noticed immediately and said, "Herr Buddenbrook, I am tempted to have you close your examination book, but I greatly fear that I would only be doing you a favor. Continue, please."

This remark contained two jokes. First, that Dr. Mühsam had addressed Hanno as "Herr" Buddenbrook, and second, the part about doing him a favor. Hanno Buddenbrook went on stewing over his examination book, but in the end he delivered only one, almost blank page. Then he left with Kai.

They had survived the day. Happy the lad who had made it through safely, whose conscience was not burdened by a demerit. He could now go sit in Herr Drägemüller's room and draw with a free and cheerful heart.

The art room was large and well lighted. Plaster casts of classical statuary were set out on a shelf that went clear around the room, and there was a large cupboard with all sorts of wooden blocks and dollhouse furniture that likewise served as models. Herr Drägemüller was a squat man with a full, rounded beard and a cheap, slick, brown wig that stuck out at the back of his neck, declaring itself an obvious fake. He owned two wigs, one with longer, one with shorter hair; whenever he had his beard trimmed, he would don the short-haired one. He was a man with several droll eccentricities. He called lead pencils "leads." And wherever he went he exuded the oily odor of spirits, and some boys said that he drank kerosene. His finest hours were when he was allowed to substitute in some other class besides drawing. Then he would lecture on Bismarck, and, gesturing in long, emphatic, corkscrew arcs that started at his nose and ended at his shoulder, he would speak of Social Democrats with hate and fear in his voice. "We must stick together," he would tell his students, grabbing one of them by the arm. "Socialism is at the gates!" There was something stilted and fussy about him. Exuding the strong odor of spirits, he would sit down beside a student, tap him on the forehead with his signet ring, blurt out a few words—like "Perspective!" "Light and shade!" "Use your lead!" "Socialism!" "Stick together!"—and then scurry away.

Kai worked on his new literary project the whole hour, and Hanno kept himself occupied by conducting an orchestral overture. Then class was over. They gathered their things from upstairs; the gates were opened and they were free to go home.

Carrying their books under their arms, Hanno and Kai walked in the same direction as far as the little, red-brick suburban villa. Young Count Mölln had to walk a good distance by himself after that, all the way to his father's manor house. And he wasn't even wearing an overcoat.

The morning's heavy fog had turned to snow, which fell in large, soft flakes and turned to slush on the ground. They parted at the gate to the Buddenbrooks' front yard; Hanno was already halfway across the yard when Kai came running back and laid an arm around his neck. "Don't get too down. Maybe you'd better not play," he said softly. Then his slender, disheveled figure vanished in a flurry of snow.

Hanno left his books in the bowl that the bear held out for him in the hallway and went into the living room to greet his mother. She was sitting on the chaise longue, reading a book in a yellow binding. As he strode across the carpet, she looked up at him with her blue, close-set eyes with bluish shadows that lingered at the corners. He stood in front of her now, and she took his head between her hands and kissed him on the forehead.

He went up to his room, where Fräulein Clementine had set out a little lunch for him; he washed and ate. When he was done he went to his writing desk and took out a pack of those little, pungent Russian cigarettes, to which he was no stranger now, either, and began to smoke. Then he sat down at his harmonium and played something challenging and austere, a fugue by Bach. At last he clasped his hands behind his head and looked out the window at the tumbling, silent snow. There was nothing else to look at—no elegant garden, no splashing fountain beneath his window. The view was cut off by the gray wall of the neighboring villa.

They ate dinner at four—just Gerda Buddenbrook, little Johann, and Fräulein Clementine, all by themselves. Afterward, Hanno went to the salon and got things ready for their music session; he sat at the piano and waited for his mother. They played a Beethoven sonata, opus 24. And in the adagio, the violin sang like an angel. All the same, Gerda was not satisfied; she took her instrument from under her chin, looked crossly at it, and said that it wasn't in tune. She decided to play no more and went upstairs to rest.

Hanno stayed behind in the salon. He walked over to the glass door leading to a narrow veranda and gazed out at the soggy front yard for a few minutes. But suddenly he stepped back and yanked the cream-colored curtains across the door, casting the room in a yellowish twilight. He walked hastily to the piano. He stood there for a while, his eyes fixed on nothing in particular—slowly they darkened, dimmed, misted over. He sat down and began to improvise.

He introduced a very simple theme, nothing really, a fragment of a nonexistent melody, a figure of a bar and a half; he first let it ring out in the bass, with a power one would not have expected of him, and it sounded like a chorus of trombones, imperiously announcing some fundamental principle, an opening onto what was yet to come—and with no clear indication of what it really meant. But when he repeated and harmonized it high in the treble, in tone colors like frosted silver, its essence was revealed to be a simple resolution, a yearning, painful descent from one key to another—a short-winded, paltry invention, which gained its strange, mysterious, momentous quality from the pretentious, resolute solemnity of its definition and presentation. And now followed agitated runs, a restless, syncopated coming and going, a searching and wandering, rent by shrieks, like a soul tormented by sounds that will not ebb into silence, but only repeat themselves in new harmonies, new questions and laments, new desires, demands, and promises. The syncopations grew more and more violent, helplessly jostled about by scurrying triplets. The intruding shrieks of fear, however, took form, closed ranks, became a melody—and then came the moment when they achieved mastery as a fervent, plaintive chorus of woodwinds raised in strong yet humble song. The prodding, faltering, straying, flagging uncertainty yielded and was conquered. In simple, determined rhythms, a contrite chorale resounded like a child's prayer. And ended in a churchly cadence. And now a *fermata*, and silence. But wait, suddenly, very softly, in tone colors like frosted silver, the first theme returned, that paltry invention, that silly or mysterious pattern, that sweet, painful descent from one key to another. And there arose a great rebellion and a wild, frantic commotion, dominated by fanfarelike accents, declarations of savage determination. What was happening? What was coming now? It rang out like bugles sounding the charge. And then its forces seemed to assemble, concentrate themselves; firmer rhythms joined together and a new theme established itself, an impudent improvisation, a kind of hunting song, daring and stormy—but not joyful. At its heart was a desperate defiance; its signal calls were also cries of fear, and again and again, under it all, were heard the wrenched, bizarre harmonies of the first theme, that enigmatic theme, so distraught, demented, and sweet. And now began an inexorable succession of episodes, whose meaning and nature were obscure, a picaresque adventure of sound, rhythm, and harmony, which Hanno himself did not control, but merely let take shape under his busy fingers, each episode a new experience that he had not heard coming. He sat bent down over the keys, his lips parted, a distant, rapt look in his eyes, and his brown hair fell down over his temples in soft curls. What was happening? What was he feeling? Was this his way of overcoming dreadful obstacles? Was he slaying dragons, scaling mountains, swimming great rivers, walking through fire? And, like shrill laughter or some inscrutable promise of blessing, that first theme wound its way through everything—a fragment, nothing really, a descent from one key to another. Yes, it roused itself again now to new violent exertions, pursued by mad octave runs that fell away screaming; and a slow, unyielding surge began its ascent, a chromatic struggle upward, full of wild, irresistible desire, abruptly interrupted by bursts of appalling, taunting *pianissimi*, as if the ground were slipping away underfoot and the long slide down into lust had begun. Suddenly it seemed as if one could hear, very soft and far away, the censure of those first chords of contrite, suppliant prayer; but then, immediately, a flood of ascending cacophony pounced on it, gathered into a solid mass that trundled forward, fell back, scrambled up again, subsided, ceaselessly struggling to reach the ineffable goal that had to come, had to come now, at this moment, at this terrifying pinnacle, while unbearable anguish panted on all sides. And it came, it could not be held back any longer, the convulsions of desire could not be prolonged; it came—like curtains ripping open, doors flinging wide, thorny hedges sundering, walls of flame collapsing. Resolution, dissolution, fulfillment, perfect contentment burst overhead—and in ravished exultation everything untangled into a beautiful chord that descended now with a sweet, yearning *ritardando* into another chord. It was the theme, the first theme again! And what happened now was a celebration, a triumph, an unrestrained orgy of that same theme, reveling in all conceivable nuances, spilling through every octave, weeping, fluttering in a *tremolando*, singing, rejoicing, sobbing, marching victorious and laden with all the bluster, tinkling chimes, and churning pomp of a great orchestra. It was the fanatical cult of nothing, of a fragment of melody, a brief bar and a half of childish, harmonic invention—and there was something brutal and doltish about it, and something ascetic and religious at the same time, something like faith and self-renunciation; but there was also something insatiable and depraved beyond measure in the way it was savored and exploited. It sucked hungrily at its last sweet drops with almost cynical despair, with a deliberate willing of bliss and doom, and it fell away in exhaustion, revulsion, and surfeit, until finally, finally, in the languor that followed, all its excesses trickled off in a long, soft arpeggio in the minor, modulated up one key, resolved to the major, hesitated, and died a wistful death.

Hanno sat very still for a moment, his chin on his chest, his hands in his lap. Then he stood up and closed the keyboard. He was very pale, his knees had gone weak, his eyes burned. He went into the adjoining room, stretched out on the chaise longue, and lay there for a long time without stirring a muscle.

Later that evening there was supper, followed by a game of chess with his mother, ending in a draw. But well after midnight, he was still sitting in his room by candlelight, at his harmonium and he played it, but only in his mind—noise was not allowed at this hour. Of course he fully intended to get up at half past five and do his most pressing homework.

This was one day in the life of little Johann.

3

TYPHOID RUNS the following course:

In the incubation period, a person feels depressed and moody, and this quickly grows worse, to the point of acute despondency. At the same time he is overcome by physical lassitude, which affects not only his muscles and tendons, but also the function of all internal organs, and most especially the stomach, which rebels and refuses to accept any food. There is a great desire for sleep, but, despite extreme weariness, such sleep is restless, shallow, and nervous and leaves the patient unrefreshed. He experiences headaches, and his mind feels numb, edgy, and dazed, with occasional spells of dizziness. A vague ache invades the limbs. Sporadic nosebleeds occur, for no apparent reason. This is the initial phase.

Then comes a chill that shakes the whole body and sets the teeth chattering—the signal for the onset of fever, which climbs to its height almost immediately. Small, lentil-sized red spots appear on the skin of the chest and stomach, which disappear under the pressure of a finger, but immediately return. The pulse races, up to a hundred beats a minute. This lasts for a week, with the body temperature hovering at about 104 degrees.

In the second week, the headache and pain in the limbs go away, but the dizziness increases significantly, with such a humming and buzzing in the ears that it can even render the patient deaf. The face assumes an idiotic expression. The mouth hangs open now, and the eyes are dim and apathetic. Consciousness is clouded; the patient wants only to sleep, but more often than not he sinks into a kind of leaden stupor without really sleeping. And then the room is filled with his babblings and loud, excited fantasies. Limp and helpless now, he becomes disgustingly incontinent. His gums, his teeth, and his tongue are covered with a blackish coating that turns his breath foul. The abdomen is distended and he lies motionless on his back. He sinks deeper into his bed and spreads his knees wide. His vital signs are rapid, shallow, and labored, both respiration and pulse, which can rise to one hundred twenty faint, fluttering beats a minute. The eyelids are half closed, and the cheeks are no longer flushed with fever as at the start, but have taken on a bluish color. The lentil-sized red spots on the chest and stomach have multiplied. The body temperature rises to 105 degrees.

In the third week, the debilitation is at its worst. The loud fits of delirium have ceased, and no one can say whether the patient's mind has sunk into the void of night or if it has become a stranger to his body and has turned away to wander in distant, deep, silent dreams, unmarked by visible signs or audible sounds. The body lies in total apathy. This is the moment of crisis.

In some individuals, special circumstances can make diagnosis more difficult. Let us assume, for example, that the symptoms of the incubation stage—moodiness, fatigue, lack of appetite, restless sleep, headaches—are usually present even when the patient, on whom his family pins all its hopes, is moving about in good health. And when such symptoms suddenly grow worse, they are hardly taken to be something out of the ordinary. What, then? A capable physician with a good medical education—a man like Dr. Langhals, for instance, handsome Dr. Langhals, with his little hands, thick with black hair—would nevertheless quickly be able to call the problem by its proper name; and the appearance of those nasty red spots on the chest and stomach will provide the conclusive evidence. He will have no doubt about what measures are to be taken, what medications administered. He will make sure that the patient's room is as large and well ventilated as possible and that its temperature does not exceed sixty-three degrees. He will insist on absolute cleanliness and attempt to prevent bedsores as long as possible—though in some cases it is not possible for long—by ordering that the patient's position be constantly shifted. He will arrange for the oral cavity to be cleansed frequently with moistened linen cloths; as for medication, he will prescribe a mixture of iodine, iodide of potassium, quinine, and an antipyretic; and above all, since the stomach and intestines are seriously affected, he will prescribe a light but very nourishing diet. He will fight the hectic fever with frequent baths, into which the patient is to be placed up to his neck every three hours, without exception, night and day, and during which cold water is to be slowly added at the foot of the tub. After each bath the patient is to be given a restorative, a stimulant such as cognac or even champagne.

All such therapies, however, are a matter of blind chance, employed more or less just in case they might have some effect, but with no certainty that there is any value, point, or purpose in them. For there is one thing that Dr. Langhals does not know, one question that he cannot answer, and so he gropes in the dark. Until the third week, until the decisive crisis, the question of either-or hovers in the air, and he cannot possibly tell whether in this case the disease he calls "typhus" is an inconsequential mishap, the result of an infection that might perhaps have been avoided and that can be combated with the resources of science—or if it is quite simply a mode of dissolution, the garment in which death has clad itself, though it could just as easily have chosen some other disguise, and for which there is no known remedy.

Typhoid runs the following course:

As he lies in remote, feverish dreams, lost in their heat, the patient is called back to life by an unmistakable, cheering voice. That clear, fresh voice reaches his spirit wandering along strange, hot paths and leads it back to cooling shade and peace. The patient listens to that bright, cheering voice, hears its slightly derisive admonishment to turn back, to return to the regions from which it calls, to places that the patient has left so far behind and has already forgotten. And then, if there wells up within him something like a sense of duties neglected, a sense of shame, of renewed energy, of courage, joy, and love, a feeling that he still belongs to that curious, colorful, and brutal hubbub that he has left behind—then, however far he may have strayed down that strange, hot path, he will turn back and live. But if he hears the voice of life and shies from it, fearful and reticent, if the memories awakened by its lusty challenge only make him shake his head and stretch out his hand to ward them off, if he flees farther down the path that opens before him now as a route of escape—no, it is clear, he will die.

4

IT IS NOT RIGHT, it is not right, Gerda!" old Fräulein Weichbrodt said in sad reproach, for probably the hundredth time. She had taken a place on the sofa this evening, joining Gerda Buddenbrook, Frau Permaneder, her daughter, Erika, poor Klothilde, and the three Ladies Buddenbrook from Breite Strasse, who all sat around the table in the center of the living room of her former student. The green ribbons of her bonnet were draped over her childlike shoulders, and she had to lift one of those shoulders very high whenever she wanted to make a gesture with her arm above the level of the tabletop; at age seventy-five, she was thinner than ever.

"It is not right, I tell you. It is not the right thing to do, Gerda," she repeated, her voice quavering with emotion. "Here I am with one foot in the grave, with so little time left to me, and you want to leave me—to leave us—to move away and leave us behind forever. If it were merely a trip, a visit to Amsterdam—but to leave us forever!" She shook her old birdlike head, and her clever brown eyes gazed at Gerda in distress. "It is true that you have lost a great deal. . . ."

"No, she has lost everything," Frau Permaneder said. "We cannot think only of ourselves. Gerda wishes to leave, and she will leave, there is nothing we can do. She came here with Thomas, twenty-one years ago now, and we have all loved her, although she probably always thought of us as something of a bother. Yes, we were a bother, Gerda, don't dispute it. But Thomas is gone now—everyone is gone now. And what are we to her? Nothing. It hurts a great deal—but go with God's blessing, Gerda, and with our thanks for not having left earlier, when Thomas died."

It was after supper on an evening in autumn. Well supplied with the blessings of Pastor Pringsheim, little Johann (Justus, Johann, Kaspar) had been lying at rest for six months now, out there at the edge of the little woods, under the sandstone cross and the family crest. Rain rustled in the almost leafless tress along the street in front of the house. Sometimes gusts of wind drove the rain against the windowpane. All eight ladies were dressed in black.

It was a little family gathering for the purpose of saying goodbye—goodbye to Gerda Buddenbrook, who was about to leave the town for good and return to Amsterdam, where, as once long ago, she would play duets with her father. No duties held her here now. Frau Permaneder had run out of objections to Gerda's decision. She had resigned herself to it, but deep inside she was profoundly unhappy. If the senator's widow had remained here in town, she would have retained her station and rank in society and kept her fortune here as well—and the family name would have retained a little of its prestige. But, be that as it may, Frau Antonie was determined to hold her head high, as long as she remained on this earth and there were eyes to see her. Her grandfather had driven all over the country in a coach-and-four.

Despite the troubled life she had led, despite her bad digestion, she did not look fifty. Her complexion had lost some of its glow and there was a hint of soft down on her cheek; there were even several hairs on her upper lip—Tony Buddenbrook's pretty upper lip. But there was not a single gray thread in the smoothly combed hair under her mourning cap.

Just as she had accepted all things in this world, poor Klothilde, her cousin, now accepted Gerda's departure with gentle calm. She had quietly eaten her supper, and had not been shy about heaping her plate, and now she sat there, ashen and skinny as always, adding a few drawling, amiable words.

Erika Weinschenk, who was thirty-one now, was likewise not a woman to get upset about her aunt's leaving. She had known heavier burdens, and had learned to bear them with resignation early on. Her tired, watery-blue eyes—Herr Grünlich's eyes—said that she had learned to submit to life's disappointments, and her composed, sometimes slightly whiny voice said as much as well.

As for the three Ladies Buddenbrook, Uncle Gotthold's daughters, their faces expressed annoyance and criticism, just as always. Friederike and Henriette, the two older girls, had grown bonier and gaunter with the years, whereas Pfiffi, the youngest at fifty-three, was much too short and fat.

Old Madame Kröger, Uncle Justus's widow, had been invited, too; but she was not feeling well, or perhaps had no suitable dress to wear—it was not certain which.

They spoke of Gerda's trip, about the train she was planning to take, and about the sale of the villa, along with the furniture, which Herr Gosch the broker was managing. Because Gerda was taking nothing with her. She was leaving just as she had come.

Then Frau Permaneder brought the conversation around to life; she regarded it from several important angles, expressing her views of the past and the future, although there was almost nothing to be said about the future now.

"Yes, when I'm dead, Erika can go away somewhere, too, for all I care," she said. "But I couldn't manage anywhere else, and as long as I'm still alive, we'll stay together here, we few who are still left. You'll all have to come to dinner once a week. And then we'll read from the family papers." And her hand brushed the writing case that lay before her. "Yes, Gerda, I gladly accept them. That's settled. Did you hear, Thilda? Although you could just as well invite us all to dinner, really, because you're no worse off than we are now. Yes, that's how it goes. One struggles and takes another running start and goes into battle again—and all the while you've just sat there and waited patiently. You really are a muttonhead, Thilda, if you'll pardon my saying so."

"Oh, now, Tony," Klothilde said with a smile.

"I'm sorry that I won't be able to say goodbye to Christian," Gerda said. And so they began to speak of Christian. There was little prospect of his ever leaving the institution where he was now confined, although he was not so bad that he could not have managed to live as a free man on his own. But his wife was only too pleased with the present state of affairs, or so Frau Permaneder claimed, and was in league with that doctor. And so, presumably, Christian would end his days in an institution.

Then there was a pause. Haltingly, tactfully, the conversation turned now to events just past, and when little Johann's name was finally mentioned, the room fell silent and the murmur of the rain outside grew louder.

The silence lay like a somber secret over Hanno's last illness, which must have been horrible beyond description. They did not look at one another as they spoke of it in hushed voices, hinting at it with guarded words. And then someone recalled the very last episode—when the patched and tattered little count had come to visit, almost forcing his way into the room where Hanno lay ill. Hanno had smiled when he heard his voice, even though he no longer recognized anyone, and Kai had kissed both his hands again and again.

"He kissed Hanno's hands?" the Ladies Buddenbrook asked.

"Yes, over and over."

They all thought about this for a while.

Suddenly Frau Permaneder broke into tears. "I loved him so," she sobbed. "You don't know how much I loved him, more than any of you—yes, forgive me, Gerda, and you're his mother. Oh, he was an angel."

"He *is* an angel now," Sesame corrected her.

"Hanno, little Hanno," Frau Permaneder went on, and the tears ran down those downy cheeks that had lost their glow. "Tom, Father, Grandfather, and all the others. Where have they all gone? We shall see them no more. Oh, how hard and sad it all is."

"We shall see them again," Friederike Buddenbrook said, folding her hands firmly in her lap; she lowered her eyes and thrust her nose in the air.

"Yes, that's what they say. Oh, there are times, Friederike, when that is no comfort. God strike me, but sometimes I doubt there is any justice, any goodness, I doubt it all. Life, you see, crushes things deep inside us, it shatters our faith. See them again—if only it were so."

But then Sesame Weichbrodt raised herself up to the table, as high as she could. She stood on her tiptoes, craned her neck, rapped on the tabletop—and her bonnet quivered on her head.

"*It is so!*" she said with all her strength and dared them with her eyes.

There she stood, victorious in the good fight that she had waged all her life against the onslaughts of reason. There she stood, hunchbacked and tiny, trembling with certainty—an inspired, scolding little prophet.

ABOUT THE TRANSLATOR

John E. Woods is the distinguished translator of many books, most notably Arno Schmidt's *Evening Edged in Gold,* for which he won both the American Book Award and the PEN Prize for translation; Patrick Süskind's *Perfume,* for which he again won the PEN Prize in 1987; Mr. Süskind's *The Pigeon*; Doris Dörrie's *Love, Pain, and the Whole Damn Thing* and *What Do You Want from Me?*; and Libuše Moníková's *The Façade.* Woods is also the translator of Thomas Mann's *Doctor Faustus* and *The Magic Mountain.*